ALSO BY JOHN RECHY

Fiction

City of Night
Numbers
This Day's Death
The Vampires
The Fourth Angel
Rushes
Bodies and Souls

Non-Fiction

The Sexual Outlaw: A Documentary

Plays

Momma As She Became—But Not As
She Was (One-Act)
Rushes
Tigers Wild

MARILYN'S DAUGHTER

A Novel

BY
JOHN RECHY

Carroll & Graf Publishers, Inc.
New York

First published in the United States by Carroll & Graf
Publishers, Inc. 1988

Carroll & Graf Publishers, Inc.
260 Fifth Avenue
New York, NY 10001

Library of Congress Cataloging-in-Publication Data

Rechy, John.
    Marilyn's daughter.

    1. Monroe, Marilyn, 1926–1962—Fiction.   I. Title.
PS3568.E28M3   1988   813'.54   86-11770
ISBN: 0-88184-272-9

Manufactured in the United States of America

Permission acknowledgements:

Don't be Cruel by Elvis Presley & Otis Blackwell copyright © 1956 by
Shalimar Music Corp. Copyright renewed and assigned to Elvis
Presley Music. All rights administered by Unichappell Music, Inc.
International copyright secured. All rights reserved. Used by
permission.

Heartbreak Hotel by Mae Boren Axton, Tommy Durden, Elvis Presley
copyright © 1956 by Tree Publishing Co., Inc. Copyright renewed. All
rights reserved. International copyright secured. Used by Permission
of the Publisher.

That Old Black Magic by Johnny Mercer and Harold Arlen. Copyright
© 1942 by Famous Music Corporation. Copyright renewed 1969 by
Famous Music Corporation.

For the memory of my mother
For Marilyn Monroe

And for Michael Earl Snyder

"Marilyn Monroe—a monument to the perfection of artifice."

—David Lange,
The Kennedys: Last of the Heroes

Part One
Texas

August 4, 1962

Dear Enid—
   Whatever happens now, please take care
of my daughter if she is alive.

Love!
Marilyn

N.J.R.I.R.

Spring! 1980

Normalyn, dear Normalyn!
   Marilyn Monroe is your real mother *and
she loved you and wanted you with all her heart!*

My love, too!
Enid

One

Normalyn crumpled the single sheet with the two hand-written entries and threw it down.

It fell on the soft carpet of Enid's bedroom, among scattered petals from the flower Mayor Wendell Hughes had given her earlier, plucked out of the one wreath on her mother's—on Enid's—grave. That single wreath, from the Mayor, asserted Enid's, and Normalyn's, isolated life in the secluded City of Gibson, a clutch of greenery within enclosing Texas deserts.

The newspaper that morning had noted the death of "one-time Hollywood starlet Enid Morgan." Normalyn had refused tears then, just as she had at the funeral—and did now in Enid's bedroom. Enid had wanted to take herself away from her, had swallowed with alcohol the pills that killed her—and so Normalyn would not cry. But her tears had stopped before that because crying had rendered her vulnerable to the woman who had loved her fiercely and then turned angry in the last years of her life.

Calmly, Normalyn tried to explain Enid's letter. Even out of death Enid was attempting to control her, as she had for the eighteen years of her life—but now with new intimations of dangers and mysteries, renewed assertions of love. That would keep her turbulently alive in Normalyn's memories. The proud woman had described herself as "cunning." "I always have a purpose. Remember that, Normalyn," she would emphasize.

Normalyn picked up the letter, smoothed it. The paper looked old—no, was just made to look old. She added to her explanation of Enid's strange motives. In one of her last pursuing moods of feared insanity—"the darkness, the blackness," she named it—Enid had written *both* parts of that letter, and so at the end extended her obsession to the point of sharing her own daughter with the woman with whom she claimed to have shared everything, the woman who haunted Enid's memories—Marilyn Monroe, evoked in a constant litany of reminiscences, at first only with love, then love brushed by anger.

Normalyn had stopped wondering whether Enid's intimate memories of the movie star were real or invented. Enid had traced them to childhood years: "Norma Jeane—that was her name before she became Marilyn Monroe—Norma Jeane and I ran away from the orphanage once." Enid had allowed a girl's laughter at a cherished adventure, before anger thrust out what eventually would become punctuation to her memories: "Marilyn Monroe was *created* over Norma Jeane!"

Normalyn studied Enid's room for new clues about the woman who had turned into a stranger. Now that the powerful presence was gone, she saw the dead room for the first time.

It was a starlet's bedroom!

The white furniture was gold-gilded, the bedspread silk brocade. Pale voile drapes sighed restlessly in a vagrant breeze. On a night table was a white figurine of a huddled angel with a chipped wing. Next to it was a small bouquet of faintly lavender, aging artificial flowers. There was a delicacy about everything here!

It was on the table with the flowers that Normalyn had found the letter, and a brown envelope she had not yet opened. Both had been propped against a glittery twin picture frame, each side of which contained a photograph Normalyn had not seen until today. One was of a dark-haired young woman with a vibrant natural beauty. The other was of an equally beautiful blonde woman, extravagantly made up, extravagantly created. Yes, the first was of Enid, so young and almost, almost smiling. And the other was of Marilyn Monroe. There was an odd resemblance between the seeming opposites.

Why did you stop loving me? Normalyn accused the dark-haired woman, the young Enid. *Did you?* She had never let herself believe that entirely, because Enid's maddest rages had always erupted into affirmations of love.

Looking away from the photographs, Normalyn allowed herself a glimpse of her own reflection in the gold-framed mirror over Enid's dresser. The woman's cherished gold-leafed makeup box, with sketchy outlines of pink rosebuds, remained there from her movie days: makeup always kept fresh, no longer used.

Normalyn removed her glasses. Enid had insisted she needed them, and they hid her from the world—from Gibson. She pushed her hair back—she had learned to comb it forward to conceal herself further. In the mirror misted gold, her skin was fair, her hair light brown, her eyes . . . not amber, like Enid's. They were gray, just gray. Today they looked blue. Normalyn touched her breasts. A fullness. No, ugly! She yanked her hand away. An enraged memory stirred, of a violent time by the dusty Rio Grande—three pairs of cowboy-booted feet, three shadows, three men standing over her.

Normalyn turned away from the lash of that despised time. . . . Had she seen in the mirror just now a hidden prettiness released by Enid's death? No. Enid had insisted, with quiet kindness the first times, then harsh assertion, that Normalyn was ordinary, plain—"and be glad!"—as if lack of beauty were kinder in the world.

Outside, the rising wind was ending an interlude of spring in the City of Gibson, spring swept away by dust and tumbleweeds. Enid hated those "goddamned Texas winds." "You think they're over with, and then they're back, burrowing under your skin to find where your damn soul went."

Grasped by that memory, Normalyn still refused to cry. *You killed yourself, Mother!* She had repeated that to herself many times since the recent morning when the sun had briefly warmed clinging wintry days and Enid did not come downstairs. Her door was locked. Normalyn had telephoned Mayor Hughes, who was there immediately, as always carrying one of his many elegant canes, to disguise a limp. He pried open the door. Choking tears, he summoned Dr. Phillips and Rosa. The Mayor instructed the maid, "Leave *everything* exactly where Enid left it; just tidy up." He remained in the room. "An *accidental* overdose of medication," he dictated to Dr. Phillips, who wrote the words dutifully in his report of death. No longer holding back his tears, Mayor Hughes said in wonder to Normalyn, "Just like her movie-star friend, that Monroe woman." Normalyn had not entered the room until today.

She read the letter again. The words Enid's signature claimed were desperately kind . . . no, they were attempting to seem so . . . no, they were mysteriously cruel. Normalyn studied the boldly inked letters: N.J.R.I.R . . . N.J.—Norma Jeane? She reread the saddened words—"if she is alive"—in the first note. What could have created doubt?

Placing the letter next to the frayed artificial lavender flowers, Normalyn tore open the brown envelope. She pulled out a birth certificate, newspaper clippings, a news-photograph.

On a fading sheet of ruled paper were penciled notes scrawled in a childish hand: "After the anger Norma Jeane and I laughed and played a game. Our secret! Neither one of us is a sad orphan now! An important day! The jacaranda trees are *so* beautiful, we call the petals when they fall to the ground 'lavender snow.' Next time *I* will be the movie star." After those words was another entry, in ink. The writing had matured: "*She* is the movie star!" There was one last entry: "Someday I will leave behind all the pain."

The birth certificate was Normalyn's:

Name of Child: Normalyn Morgan. *Date of birth*: June 1, 1962. *Place of Birth*: Private residence; Galveston, Texas. *Maiden Name of Mother*: Enid Morgan. *Name of Father*: Unknown. CERTIFIED: Wendell Hughes, Mayor, Gibson, Texas; August 11, 1962.

The printed and typed document had been revised with black ink to allow dual entries. A line had been drawn over the date of birth and another date written over it: "August 2, 1962." The place of birth had been ruled out with another line. Over it was written: "Los Angeles, California." *Name of Father*" remained "Unknown." Over the entry designating "*Maiden Name of Mother*: Enid Morgan," there was only the beginning of a drawn line—it did not even touch the typed name, as if the pen had been lifted suddenly, not able to continue. But above that name had been inked: "Marilyn Monroe."

Her eyes sweeping over words, Normalyn read the headlines of newsclippings: "MARILYN MONROE DEAD—August 5, 1962." "INQUEST POSSIBILITY LOOMS." "HUNT MARILYN'S MYSTERY FRIEND."

The news photograph revealed a woman wearing a scarf and dark sunglasses, trying to hide further from pursuing cameras by holding one hand shielding her face. The caption read: "One of the last photographs of Marilyn Monroe, in disguise, taken after reporters were tipped that she was in seclusion in—"

Normalyn stared at the longest clipping, and she realized only vaguely that her life was being pushed away by an unburied past. She saw urgent inked checkmarks emphasizing certain names, other names slashed with X's, some underlined, others ruled out, one signaled by a question mark, all on the aged newspaper clipping bearing the headline:

"MARILYN'S DEATH STUNS WORLD."

Two

Los Angeles Tribune   August 8, 1962

MARILYN'S DEATH STUNS WORLD

LOS ANGELES—The death of Marilyn Monroe on Sunday, August 5, sent shock waves across the world. The movie star died of an apparent overdose of sleeping pills in her home in the Los Angeles suburb of Brentwood. She was 36.

According to a highly reliable source who spoke on condition he not be identified, in her last year Monroe was "despondent over personal and professional problems." She was believed to have been in financial difficulty and had just been fired from her latest film. She had reportedly terminated "a very serious involvement with a very, very prominent man," according to the source, who said she had been in "semi-seclusion" even from close friends during her last months. "She became a very saddened, abandoned human being, just as she was in her childhood," he said.

While the official cause of death is still to be determined by the County Coroner's Office, reports indicate that the movie star took her own life late Saturday night or early Sunday morning after ingesting a lethal dose of Nembutal and Chloral Hydrate pills, obtained by prescription. The body was discovered by her psychiatrist, Dr. Ralph Greenson, summoned to her home by housekeeper Mary Allen, who became alarmed when the light to the star's locked bedroom remained on late into night. Dr. Greenson broke in through a window and found the star dead. She was holding the receiver of her white

7

private telephone. No clarification as to whom she was calling has been made.

Reaction from the famous and the unknown was swift and dramatic. Baseball star Joe DiMaggio, the actress's second husband, was not available to the press. Insiders report that the athlete was "stunned and cried uncontrollably." Playwright Arthur Miller, divorced from the star, was also unavailable for comment. Through a family spokesman, he was quoted as saying, "It had to happen. It was inevitable."

Her first husband, James Dougherty, a police deputy, could muster only, "I'm sorry." His present wife informed reporters that on hearing the news by telephone, Dougherty told her to "say a prayer for Norma Jeane." Norma Jeane Baker was the actress's name before she changed it to Marilyn Monroe. In 1950 Dougherty was assigned by the Los Angeles Police Department to hold off barricaded fans waiting for the entrance of his ex-wife, Monroe, into Grauman's Egyptian Theater during the premiere of her film *The Asphalt Jungle*.

Between sobs, acting coach Paula Strasberg said Marilyn had "a quality second to no actress in the world." Her daughter, actress Susan Strasberg, compared the star to a "butterfly," because "butterflies are very beautiful, give great pleasure, and have very short lifespans." Her remarks were in apparent reaction to earlier ones by cameraman Len Brakowitz, who called Monroe "an iron butterfly—frail but hard as nails. I still loved her, though," he added.

Gossip columnist Mildred Meadows acknowledged that she had "never been particularly fond of the blonde waif, but I came to admire her, for her spirit." Meadows called Monroe "the symbol of beauty in her time." It was Meadows who revealed the existence of Monroe's mother in a mental institution while the star and studio releases claimed the mother was dead. Meadows added, "With her suicide she may yet be able to pull down Hollywood and the other capital." She refused clarification. Industry figures infer her reference was to the expensive film Monroe had not yet completed for 20th Century-Fox. Its costly termination could affect studio executives and financial interests.

In Paris, Milton Greene, until recently a partner in Marilyn Monroe Productions, said his wife, Amy, "had a premonition that Marilyn was in serious trouble." Also in Paris, director Billy Wilder telephoned news services to "clarify" a remark attributed to him in an early story. "I said whatever I said, probably not all that kind," he admitted. "Then in the cab on the way to the hotel I saw the headlines. They never told me she was dead, those cruel S.O.B's." Monroe and Wilder were frequently at odds during filming of the star's hit comedy *Some Like It Hot*. Wilder has been quoted as saying, "The question is whether Marilyn is a person at all."

Praising her acting, director John Huston said he had feared while working with her that "it would be only a few short years before she died or went into an institution." The star's mother, Gladys Mortensen, has been in several psychiatric institutions as "mentally unstable."

Reporters attempting to reach Mrs. Mortensen where she is confined at Rock Haven Sanitarium were not allowed past the gates by sanitarium officials. When a reporter spotted the star's mother strolling on the lawn, he shouted the news of her famous daughter's death. According to witnesses, Mrs. Mortensen paused for only a moment and then walked on without comment.

Director Joshua Logan, who directed Miss Monroe in the hit *Bus Stop*, in which many claim the star became an actress, called Monroe "one of the most unappreciated people in the world." He emphasized that he meant both in her public and private lives.

Darryl Zanuck, president of 20th Century-Fox, who acknowledged "serious difficulties" with the actress, claimed "nobody discovered her, she earned her own way to stardom, and nothing could stop her." Sir Laurence Olivier, her costar in an unsuccessful endeavor, *The Prince and the Show Girl*, attributed her demise to the fact that "she was exploited beyond anyone's means."

Kay Gable, whose famous husband, Clark Gable, died of a heart attack soon after completing *The Misfits* with Monroe, said she "went to Mass and prayed for her." Monroe was known for keeping crews waiting on the set. Hally Towne, long-time makeup man at 20th Century-Fox, recalls that she would often be ready for filming and then smear the makeup off her face and demand he start again. "She stared at her reflection as if she could no longer see what she looked like," he remembered.

Dr. Greenson, her long-time psychiatrist, was grief-stricken and incoherent when approached by reporters. Actor Marlon Brando, with whom Monroe had been linked romantically, refused any statement. Patricia Newcomb, Monroe's publicist, shouted at news photographers when she reached the star's home after the death, "Keep shooting, vultures!"

Actor Peter Lawford, a close friend of the star and husband of President John Kennedy's sister Patricia, wandered along

the beach of his Santa Monica villa, according to neighbor
Antonia Fuchs, who claimed she was wakened late at night by
the sound of what she presumed was his helicopter. She recalled looking out to see the actor "outside and in a complete
state of shock . . . devastated, weeping."

A product of at least 10 foster homes, the illegitimately born
movie star gravitated toward strong, protective older women.
Reported to be the closest of these in latter years is Alberta
Holland, a prominent figure of power behind the scenes in
Hollywood. By several accounts, Holland, known as "counsel-
lor to the stars," was one of very few people who regularly saw
the star during her last months of semi-seclusion, when Monroe appeared only at brief intervals, often in disguise.

Rumors circulate that Holland has threatened "to rock the
film capital" with her account of the actress's "real death." In a
prepared statement in which she calls Monroe "the greatest
movie star—and one of the dearest," Holland labels her "a
victim." In her statement, she claims that "the truth will not
emerge for years, and only after more deaths." No further
explanation has been made. Holland's housekeeper, Juanita
Brogan, reports she has been instructed to say only that Holland was "fleeing incognito to Long Beach." Film sources
claim Holland has left the country "for reasons of her own."

Monroe's association with Holland and others of Hollywood's
politically "liberal" wing has been the subject of speculation
among Hollywood insiders. Holland became the object of scandal during the hearings by the House Committee on Un-
American Activities investigating alleged subversive associations
in the film capital. She named as "fellow travelers" "Washington, Jefferson, Lincoln, F.D.R." She was sentenced to a year in
prison for contempt of Congress. In a Tribune interview, Monroe had called her "one of the most courageous people I
know."

Dr. and Mrs. Benjamin Crouch, who handled legal aspects
of the movie star's relations with 20th Century-Fox Studios,
have refused further questioning, claiming they are "in shock
. . . we know nothing, we love her, we know nothing more."

Rumors of irregularities surrounding the reports of death,
including the time of death, supposed removal of private
documents and letters, and even the exact place of death,
continue to circulate. But Pulitzer Prize-winning writer David
Lange, former campaign adviser to President John F. Kennedy and an insider on the Hollywood and Washington, D.C.,
circuits, discounts the "rumors" as "expected." "There is noth-

ing mysterious about her death, only her life." He refused to elaborate.

Meanwhile the most famous body in the world lies unclaimed in the County Morgue. According to a spokesman, DiMaggio has taken steps to claim it upon his expected arrival in Los Angeles. The spokesman urged fans and friends to send donations in the star's name to the Children's Home Society in lieu of flowers. The actress had recently contributed $10,000 to that group of orphaned children.

Around the world, weeping fans hold vigils. Amanda Ullman, president of the National Marilyn Monroe Fan Club, claims the movie star's "sad early life" inspired her, while still in her teens, to keep her own illegitimate child instead of putting her up for adoption. Ullman sobbed, "There will never be another star like Marilyn. She was the greatest movie star of all time. We will always love her. I will teach my child to love her."

Even the first family of the country reacted to Monroe's death. President Kennedy, for whom the star sang "Happy Birthday" during a birthday salute at Madison Square Garden before 15,000 cheering Democrats, acknowledged "the great loss to motion pictures." After her rendition of "Happy Birthday," the President had remarked, "I can now retire from politics after having had 'Happy Birthday' sung to me in such a sweet, wholesome way."

In his home state of Texas for Youth Activities Week and the dedication of a commemorative plaque designating the school where he first taught as a grammar school teacher, Vice President Lyndon Johnson called the death of the actress "a shame, a rotten shame."

Attorney General Robert F. Kennedy, brother of the President, heard the news at a ranch south of San Francisco, where he was relaxing by playing touch football and horseback riding at the home of his host, John Bates. The Attorney General took time out from preparing his address for a meeting of the American Bar Association tonight to comment on the star as "a sweet, a dear woman, loved the whole world over." After his address and dinner with the Director of the C.I.A., Kennedy will vacation in an undisclosed location with his family.

In Hyannisport, Joseph Kennedy, father of the President, was informed of the movie star's death while he was performing convalescent exercises in his swimming pool and recovering from a recent stroke. Recalling that the actress had earlier sent the elder Kennedy a get-well telegram, the

John Rechy

only member of the family or staff who would comment on reaction there to Monroe's death was chauffeur James Abner. "A strange silence came over everybody who was there," Abner said.

Three

```
┌─────────────────────┐
│                     │
│  ENID MORGAN        │
│                     │
│  Died in Spring     │
│                     │
│  1980               │
│                     │
└─────────────────────┘
```

Normalyn read the inscription on the temporary marker, which would be replaced with a stone when it was ready. It, too, would contain the only words Enid wanted. She had paid for the plot, chosen the stone, announced, "I'll die in spring; I don't want snow covering my cold body." The soft earth about the marker was tentative, not ready to receive this new death.

Yesterday, in Enid's dusking bedroom—calmly—Normalyn had read once again every paper Enid had left her. The cryptic letters N.J.R.I.R. had been so assertively inked that they cut into the sheet. Standing in the room in order not to wrinkle Enid's bedspread, Normalyn went through the other newsclippings. The article about the "hunt" for "Marilyn's mystery friend" indicated only that a close friend, a woman, was being sought for information concerning the star's last days. Other articles repeated that reference and reported rumors of "high-level pressures" to halt an inquest into the death.

Normalyn inspected the markings on the newspaper account of reaction to the star's death. Next to Billy Wilder's name, there was a dismissive X. Mildred Meadows, a double slash, darkened over. Darryl Zanuck, a contemptuous expulsion. Peter Lawford, one solemn black line. Alberta Holland, a circle, the name underlined. Patricia Newcomb, all but obscured. Dr. and Mrs. Crouch, coiled tangles. David Lange, a dark question mark. On the margins, checkmarks signaled attention to certain names. The references to the Kennedy brothers were enclosed in a black-inked border—like an obituary.

Normalyn studied the dual entries on her revised birth certificate. During early years, Enid would convert an uneventful day into a sudden "birthday party," birthdays so erratic that Normalyn was not sure what the date of her birth was, nor where she had been born. Enid would dismiss any inquiries: "You're my little girl, that's all you have to know. You're born where your memories begin." Normalyn became sure that Enid obscured details of her birth because she was the illegitimate daughter of the despised man—"Stan!"—who had abandoned them long ago. And so it was as if she had been born in Enid's memories, and again, less powerfully, when she began accumulating memories of her own. But she had few. She remembered only Gibson and nearby cities—and, sometimes, a city near the shoreline, the sea, water, ocean.

Normalyn shifted her attention to the news picture of the disguised movie star, photographers circling her like predators determined on capture. The woman looked so despairing! Normalyn's eyes drifted to the night table, the twin frames of the two beautiful women. Placing the letter and the other papers in the brown envelope, Normalyn allowed herself to touch Enid's bed. Catching herself, she pretended to smooth the silk-brocade bedspread. She picked up a dark petal from the floor. She crushed it. Leaving the envelope on the table with the chipped angel, the lavender flowers, the two pictures, Normalyn closed the door of Enid's bedroom. Firmly. She decided: None of what Enid had thrust into her life would have any effect on her. None.

She went downstairs. She walked into her bedroom—pretty, in pastel hues, decorated by Enid so that Normalyn felt she herself was merely borrowing it. For moments, Normalyn knelt before the bottom drawer of her dresser, about to open it. Inside were books she had once cherished . . . might still. No! She had thrust them into the bottom drawer one terrible night and she would not return to them. When she finally fell asleep much later, Normalyn thought she heard Enid's soft sobbing in the house.

She woke into panic. Enid was dead! She counted her breathing, extending yesterday's tight control. She would return to the cemetery—to ensure the placement of the permanent stone. But she knew she would go there because Enid was there.

She extended beginning that journey, keeping it as a goal for this day's future. A day without Enid controlling it, a future without her? And tomorrow? There *would* be tomorrow.

In the startling morning-brightness of Enid's kitchen, Normalyn ate a forced breakfast. In the living room, she looked at the mosaic Enid had designed around the fireplace: "It's a peacock, can't you see?—just like Valentino had at Falcon's Lair—Doris Duke bought the house later." The living room was ordered, as it had always been during her lifetime— "everything in its place," Enid commanded nervously, hands fussing against disorder, even a stray wisp of her hair. Earlier in their lives, in spring and summer, she had filled patterned vases with fresh flowers from her garden. "Natural ones," she'd pointed out, "not artificial ones, except for the lavender bouquet," she asserted without explaining why she cherished it. One day, she'd stopped cutting the flowers, leaving blossoms in the vases until they darkened and pieces fell like dried blood.

Outside the house, Normalyn stood on its circular white steps and prepared for her journey to the cemetery. New spring leaves on trees had survived last night's raid by the wind. The only evidence of its rampage were abandoned tumbleweeds, those desolate tangles Normalyn detested. The day was warm, unstirring. Which route to the cemetery would expose her to fewer people, fewer words of commiseration masking the curiosity Enid aroused among "those damn Gibsonites"? Yes, they would have gone to her funeral, inquisitively, to be at the gravesite of "that woman who was in the movies," to scrutinize Mayor Hughes's reaction. But only the Mayor, Dr. Phillips, Rosa with her little boy, and the mumbling minister Mayor Hughes insisted on were there with Normalyn. With a sigh, the Mayor had agreed with her that Enid had lived apart; she would not have wanted anyone else there—"clucking their damn sympathies," Enid's voice said.

Normalyn would avoid the memorial plaza in the middle of Gibson's small business section. Enid hated the statue there, designated only as "A Texas Hero." It was noon, and in the plaza on its ornate benches would be familiar people Enid had kept apart from—and now so would she.

A window slammed. The divorced man next door was trying to get her attention again. An old man himself, he had just returned to live with his ancient mother and father. Normalyn saw his odd, tilted face staring at her from behind a screen.

Ahead, two small children played in the ghostly rainbow of a sprinkler. Dripping water from chubby bodies, they ran up to her. "Your crazy mother killed herself," the boy shot at Normalyn.

"Was she in the movies? How come you're not crying?" the girl whined.

Normalyn touched the shield of her glasses.

A woman rushed out of the house and gathered the fat children. "Now y'all hush and say sorry to poor Normalyn," she told them, not firmly.

"I'm not poor," Normalyn said. "My mother left me a fortune." What Enid might have left her, she had not even considered. She had never known the definite source of Enid's comfortable income. "An inheritance from blackmail! Those rich Texans who took me to Dallas didn't adopt me, they *bought* me." Enid would laugh darkly.

Normalyn began to walk away, stopped, turned. "You," she said precisely to the gaping woman and her children, "are silly morons."

That's what Enid would have said. Moving away, Normalyn tried to imitate the way Enid walked, hand raised gracefully at intervals as if to adjust her hair, her glamorous hat—and to brush away—like pesky gnats—the people who stared at her.

A youngman peeked out from behind the raised hood of his car. Once he had asked Normalyn out. She had run away. Emboldened by Enid's death, he swaggered toward her. "Sorry about your old lady," he drawled. "Is it true she was almost a movie star?—my mother says she never heard of her."

"How could she have? She doesn't know how to read." Normalyn crossed the street. A carload of young people drove by in a sports car. They waved at her. She did not wave back. One of the girls had done an imitation of her at school, walking rigidly, head lowered, fists clenched. Normalyn recrossed the street so anxiously that a car had to brake. Suddenly recognizing her, the driver shouted out irritated deepest sympathies. "I don't need them!" she yelled back.

Her frantic dodging had led her to the plaza! There it was, the despised memorial to "A Texas Hero," the statue of a mustachioed soldier, one hand planted on his heart, another on a rifle against his thigh. It was a greenish statue pocked with pigeon droppings. No one conjectured any more who the "hero" was, but nevertheless on patriotic holidays rigid old men of the Veterans of Foreign Wars solemnly placed a wreath on its stolid platform.

Boldly, Normalyn walked into the old square. She felt eyes. On this warm day several people sat on the coppery benches, eating lunch. Normalyn heard readied expressions of sorrow: "Sorry about your—"

"Liars!" she said. Then her defiance collapsed. Determined not to run from their stares, she stumbled. Her glasses fell. She picked them up, fighting terror.

When she reached the cemetery, she ran past tall iron-piked gates. Tense, breathless, she faced Enid's grave.

Behind her, she heard the crunch of footsteps in the otherwise deserted cemetery. She saw a tall lanky man moving swiftly toward her along stones, crosses, urns.

It was him!

Terrified, she flung herself on the moist dirt of Enid's grave.

2

She had flung herself on the sand of the Rio Grande like that one distant afternoon, a year ago, when she was seventeen. She had walked to the river, which, usually dry here, carves an indolent S about the greenness of Gibson. Much younger, when she had first started reading books, she had come here and imagined herself on a raft with Huckleberry Finn.

She sat dreamily on the sand reading the book she had checked out, again, from the public library, her favorite, *Wuthering Heights.* She was soon aware of evening shadows. She would have to run home to thwart Enid's anxiety, easily aroused by her absence beyond the time she was allotted to roam the library. Enid had threatened to lock the door, "as a lesson," if she was late again.

Normalyn heard the sound of tires scraping the graveled road near the river. She looked up to the embankment.

It was him!—tall, dark, the "gypsy cowboy." He had found her! She had seen him one day after school—exactly as if Heathcliff had stepped right out of *Wuthering Heights.* He had smiled at her that time, and then another day when he had driven past her in his white pickup. She stood up now in shy anticipation. They'd walk along the river, like Catherine and Heathcliff on the moors. She was about to smile in recognition when she saw he was not alone. He was flanked by two other "aggies"—his age, about twenty—"cowboys" from the nearby agricultural college in Langsdon.

The three rushed her.

She threw herself on the ground.

"You're the girl with the crazy mother," said one of the three. He was blond, skinny, with twisted features on a pocked face.

Short, nervous, dancing grotesquely about her, his hands on his groin, the second cowboy grabbed the book from her, thrust it away. "Always reading, huh? Never been fucked, huh? Bet you want it bad."

Normalyn turned desperately for help from the man she recognized. *It wasn't possible!—he* was leaning roughly over her, his long fingers pulling at her dress. His body pushed against hers.

The skinny cowboy grasped the dark man's shoulders. "Us first, spic," he laughed hoarsely. "This is *white* pussy."

"That's what y'all want, huh, Gonzales?" the other snickered.

He knelt so close to her that Normalyn felt his heated breath. She yelled out a hated apology: "Please don't! *I'm sorry!*"

Suddenly Gonzales stood up, adjusting his pants. He looked startled at the two men and then down at Normalyn as if in sudden new awareness.

The blond cowboy was tearing at Normalyn's dress. She flailed on the sand. His knees pushed her legs apart, a hand ripped at her underpants.

Gonzales shook his head. "Leave her alone," he said.

The blond man pushed between Normalyn's legs, to enter her clumsily. Normalyn scratched fiercely at him. The short cowboy pinioned her arms.

"*I said leave her alone!*" Gonzales ordered. He yanked the blond man off Normalyn. The blond man sprawled on the dirt, spitting dust. Normalyn kicked at the groin of the short man. Gonzales thrust his fist into the twisted face of the blond cowboy. The two grappled on the grainy strait of river. The short man waited. Normalyn heard the crunch of flesh over the yowling of rising wind. She ran under graying sheets of sky. She thought she heard a voice calling, "Wait, I won't hurt you! I swear it!"

An infinity later, Normalyn reached her house, shouting. The door was locked. She beat on it, beat on it. Enid flung the door open. In shame, Normalyn clutched her torn dress to cover her breasts. Her body trembled with her sobs.

"*Whore!* Like *her!* With *them!*" Enid shouted.

"I'm sorry!" Normalyn pleaded the despised words.

Enid held her, sheltering her, kissing her, crying with her. "I love you, I love you!"

3

In the cemetery now, the tall young man named Gonzales stopped a few feet away from Normalyn.

She stood up and faced him defiantly before Enid's grave.

He took off his cowboy hat. "Please don't run away," he said softly. "I *swear* I won't hurt you." He made a cross with his thumb and index finger and kissed it, swearing.

She brushed dirt off her body. Renewed wind pushed into the cemetery. She would not cry—not in fear or sadness! "Let me by!" she said firmly.

Gonzales squatted to show he would not advance. He lowered his head. "I want to apologize for that ugly afternoon. I've hated myself since then."

"Apologize! You son of a bitch! You started it!"

"I stopped it!" he reminded her—as he reminded himself over and over. "I *did.*"

"Because one of them called you a spic!" Normalyn shouted.

"No," he protested, "it was when you said 'I'm sorry'—that's when I saw how ugly it all was." But he wasn't entirely sure. He constantly had to reconstruct those simultaneous events to locate the sequence of his decision.

"Filthy liar!"

"I kicked their asses—fuckin' aggie cowboys!"

"You're one of them!" she said. He did look like the other agricultural students who came into Gibson, except that he was as dark as the Mexicans who worked in the outlying fields.

"Not any more," he rejected.

"I take it back. You *want* to be like them, but they reminded you you're not," she flung at him.

"I *wanted* to be," he said. That afternoon he and the two others had seen Normalyn heading for the river. He had bragged about how she had smiled at him, to impress these men he had just started running around with. The prodding began, the challenging into the ugly initiation to prove he was as mean as the two white aggies. "But I don't want to be like them any more," he reassured her now, sure of it himself. That night had been one of the darkest of his life, a night of harsh questioning, facing his denial of the Mexican part of him, even his Mexican name—and a night of hearing Normalyn's pleading, *Please don't! I'm sorry!*

Normalyn despised him, felt ugly. She pushed her hair closer to her face, to conceal herself.

He took a step toward her. "Please tell me how I can prove I'm not going to hurt you!"

"Keep away from me!"

He looked down at the ground. He said, "I've tried to talk to you before, and—"

She bent down and clutched the soft earth, to fling at him if he moved, just moved.

A figure appeared near the small chapel beyond rows of graves. An old man, he was limping toward them. "Gotta close the gates, dust storm's comin', gotta drive home, y'all gotta leave now," he said.

Repeating, "I *am* sorry, really sorry," to Normalyn, Ted Gonzales walked away. He felt dirty, futile. The old man waited for Normalyn to leave, too.

Under a sun turning gray in what would soon be another wind-swept sky, Normalyn felt inundated by loneliness and fear. Dust sliced across Enid's grave. Normalyn looked down at the newly scraped earth where Enid's body was buried. She would not cry!

4

Normalyn heard the cemetery gates clang shut behind her.

Clutching his hat away from the rising wind, Ted Gonzales waited a short distance away. He *had* to convince her he had changed. Standing there, just standing, she looked lost, scared. And afraid of him, he reminded himself. But he *had* stopped the assault, he clung to that for courage.

Normalyn did feel lost and scared as she faced the windy landscape. Familiar blocks of well-kept neighborhoods surrounding the old business section with the plaza at its center aroused a hundred altered memories.

She crossed the street to avoid Gonzales. She was safe in this neighborhood. Gleeful children fought the wind that had released them early from school to their parents. Normalyn moved into the street, against a traffic light. A tumbleweed clasped another, becoming one, scratching along the street. A car swerved to avoid it. The tumbleweed tangled under it. It freed itself in a clutch of dried splinters. Normalyn put her hands to her mouth to keep from screaming.

Ted led her to the sidewalk. She jerked away from his touch. He released her. A film of dust on her glasses blurred her vision, and she removed them. Wind shoved her hair back.

"You're so pretty—prettier!" Ted blurted, regretting words that would augment her fear.

She turned away from him, restoring her glasses. He was ridiculing her! Normalyn walked toward an open gas station. Parked there was the despised white truck she remembered. She turned her face in disgust.

Ted called out to her, "I left it here so it wouldn't frighten you, I swear it."

For a moment she believed him, didn't want to believe him—wanted to believe him!—because she felt so lonesome. He approached her slowly. For an instant she saw him as she had first seen him, so handsome—no, not quite, almost—with jagged features, an angular face, nose slightly crooked, light eyes, thick eyebrows. He did not look like what she thought of as "Mexican" except for the deep brown color of his skin, and he— Her disgust resurged. She hurried into the plaza. Near the memorial statue—the "hero" indomitable against attacking wind—she stopped. In the whipping wind, other people scurried past to their destinations. Exhausted, Normalyn sat on one of the benches.

Ted stood, not too near. If he rushed words, he might convince her he *had* changed: "I'm not studying agriculture any more, I'm in pre-law!" He had to shout to be heard over the howls of wind. "Because there's so much damn injustice in Texas—like making people ashamed of who they are, what they are." He had to hurry to present evidence of his changed self. "I'm Mexican, on my father's side—" He stopped himself from telling her his mother was Irish because that might compromise his words. "—and I used to be so ashamed of it that I never even learned Spanish!" Embarrassed by the abrupt confession yelled over the rampage of wind, and noticing that Normalyn was staring at the memorial, he blurted, "I hate that damn statue."

"I do, too," Normalyn said automatically. It was secretive, like Gibson. She let herself look at Ted Gonzales again. He sounded different, but that afternoon she had heard only his growled words. She stood up. "You're a damn bastard, that's all. And a coward!"

A coward. "Yes, I was," he said. "But now I—"

She ran for blocks. He did not follow. The white walls of her house—Enid's house—looked gray in the windstorm. A silenced voice would be there, still calling. She heard the roaring of a car engine over gasps of wind.

It was Ted Gonzales in his pickup. As he was about to drive back to Langsdon, his shame deepened. He had only increased her fear. He *had* to try again! He drove to her house, the way he had another time, imagined walking up, knocking, apologizing! Now he saw her through sheets of dust. Her steps slowed. She didn't *want* to go in alone. The only reason she had spoken even angry words to him was that she had no one. So damn sad! He shouted out the window, "I'll just park my pickup across the street so you won't feel so alone."

"I don't need you, bastard! If you try to come in, I'll shoot you—I've got a gun inside the house!" That was not true, but she wanted to convey the extent of her rage. She ran into the house, locked the door.

She held her breath. She looked at Enid's soft chairs, the muted haloes of her shaded lamps. She did not let herself see the "peacock" mosaic like Valentino's.

Enid's absence was everywhere, everywhere!

Something else was present, the letter that announced the birth of two restless ghosts. Lies! All made up! Normalyn told herself.

She stood alone in the quiet house left empty, and she asked the powerful presence, *Why do you want me to believe you're not my mother?*

Four

Only later, when Normalyn began trying to locate the point at which Enid's love turned to anger, did it seem to her that there had been traces of it from the very beginning, but, then, flashes of anger were quickly smothered by love.

Those early years of Normalyn's life had been full of joy. There were spontaneous trips in Enid's sporty M-G to "far-away cities" like San Antonio and El Paso. As they drove along the sweep of sun, sky, desert, Enid taught Normalyn "beautiful movie songs." At home, she invented games: "We'll play movie-scenes; I'll be Scarlett, then *you* be her! We'll do the scene where she swears never to be hungry again!" There were sudden "birthday celebrations": "Why, it's your birthday, Normalyn!" She would deny an earlier one. "This is the *real* one." Ice cream, presents, a dazzling ordered cake, hugs, kisses: "I love you, I love you, Normalyn!"

"And I love you, Mother." Normalyn would hug Enid.

"Do you, do you, my darling? Do you? Say it!"

"I love you, Mother!"

A trip to Dallas turned somber when Enid took her to Dealy Plaza. "This is where they killed him." At the site of John Kennedy's assassination, Enid's face clouded. She had held Normalyn's hand so tightly it hurt and the girl pulled away.

Sometimes Normalyn thought she located the anger even in her most distant memory, a first memory, which shaped only at times, only in fragments. It was a time when Enid took her, hardly a child, to meet "a woman who yearns to see you but must remain secret. *Shhh!*" On the dark beach where they

23

were to meet the woman, Enid said, "Look at the ocean, Normalyn, look into the darkness, very carefully, because you'll never see it all as clearly as now. Remember it—exactly." She disappeared just as a blonde woman, luminous even at night, took Normalyn's hand gently and kissed her. Closely, they walked along the darkened beach. At that point, Normalyn's memory of that time jumped ahead. She heard a *Click!* and saw the sudden flickering flame of Enid's cigarette lighter. She had followed, hiding. She yanked Normalyn away from the blonde woman. "You're mine!" Enid yelled against crashing waves, dissolving the memory.

A time later, at breakfast, Enid eased away the newspaper. Normalyn saw what she had just reacted to, an announcement that tonight a station would air a documentary of highlights from the lives of the legendary stars. A spectral glow about the extravagant body, one figure dominated the advertisement, obscuring images of Bogart, Lombard, Valentino, Harlow. Only at the last did Enid allow Normalyn to watch with her.

Silver satin dress like ice burning on sensual curves! Lips bleeding a rose of glossy lipstick!—the dazzling creation of Marilyn Monroe appeared on the screen. "She's beautiful!" Normalyn breathed—and recognized the woman on the shoreline. The narrator of the documentary announced the date of the movie star's death, August 5, 1962, the year of Normalyn's birth. Then it wasn't possible for Normalyn to have seen the movie star—unless Enid had altered the year of her birth also, as she had the date. No. None of what she thought she remembered of the dark beach had happened, Normalyn assured herself. All had been hallucination, part dream, shaped out of a glimpsed photograph and from pieces of Enid's recollections, all rearranged into one strange imagined meeting, a child's way of explaining Enid's constant assertion of closeness with the movie star.

At the end of the documentary segment, Enid made a prayerful fist with both her hands. "We were as close as two friends can get. We came to *feel* like each other. I loved her. She lost what she wanted most. Loss is a terrible thing. The world dies," she gave mysterious words to her sudden despair.

The next day Enid appeared on the stairs, made up glamorously, with a dark slanted hat, its veil specked with velvet dots, a dress that cut a triangle of white flesh into her firm breasts, one low strand of pearls. "Am *I* beautiful, too?" she asked Normalyn, who nodded yes, in awe. "They said I was a woman of mystery. I never smoked, just clicked my silver lighter for attention. Like *this!*" She clicked the flameless lighter until her hands were shaking and her face was wet with tears.

Assertions about Marilyn Monroe, about Norma Jeane, might dominate a whole day. Enid pushed away a book with the Technicolored face of the movie star on a glossy jacket. "More lies about her. She contributed to the lies herself. Why, some of what she said happened to her happened to me. She even tried to look like me—she wasn't a natural beauty." Enid pronounced all that with affection, the last without vanity, an observation. Later, accusation would taint the warmth: "She tried to conceal Norma Jeane, but Norma Jeane is strong." She spoke as if the subject of her remembrances were still alive. Then that book, like all the others, was discarded, kept away from Normalyn as if the life explored or the lies claimed—even the photographs of the gorgeous movie star—could affect the girl. Enid continued to remember, softly: "I was always there, through her troubles, even at the last, the most dangerous times, but it was too late."

Secluded in the handsome white-columned house in Gibson, Normalyn came to think of her own existence as a slow current winding through the flood of Enid's past, her "many lives—more than a cat's"—recalled as if she were willing them to her in place of a life of her own:

"I was born in the angels' city, all flowers, Technicolor, crushed dreams. I was baptized by that banshee Aimée Semple McPherson in her damn Temple of Divine Love." Enid was proud of that odd fact. "Now *there* was a star, that McPherson; she flew into her temple like an angel—sweet chariot attached to wires. Hypocrites, all of them, talking about good, doing ill—just look at the messy world." That was Normalyn's only lesson in religion, a fact she was grateful for whenever she heard snatches from the crazy rantings of preachers on the radio.

Enid's mother, Grace, also roamed through Enid's reminiscences, a figure now cruel, now loving, often courageous: "Why, at the MGM lab, Normalyn, Grace led the women who worked under her to safety when the building burned." Grace was in and out of mental institutions, like her own mother before her, a woman who had attempted to strangle Enid as a child. These stories frightened Normalyn even when Enid added admiration: "Grace kept walking out of those institutions, as if she was a *guest* there." Normalyn marveled at her grandmother's cruelty as she surrendered Enid to detested orphanages, temporary homes.

It was in one such orphanage, when they were both nine,

that Enid's close friendship began with Norma Jeane, at first in spirited competition, soon inseparable closeness. The longest interruption in this friendship—"stormy, cherished!"—occurred when Enid was "illegally adopted—*bought*—and carted to Dallas"—a fact she claimed had enabled her to "blackmail" the wealthy Texas couple into giving her total freedom at eighteen.

At times, Normalyn suspected embellishment—the stories might alter from one telling to another. Enid would dismiss all her questions with a testy "I told you, don't you remember?" Normalyn stopped wondering early about a father. She assumed he was "that bastard Stan." "He took off on his motorcycle to San Francisco when I was pregnant. But I paid him back—and back, and back!—the way I knew would hurt the son of a bitch most." Those dark words were followed by a sorrowful sigh, as if a memory of loss or pain had linked with that of revenge. There was another man evoked from her life, a man never named, a man remembered softly; he gentled her thoughts of betrayal and revenge: "He was an outlaw from life, like me. He loved me and couldn't love me."

That was from a time of near-stardom in Hollywood. Enid would speak about "glittery nights, premieres with an actor groomed for stardom, like me. There were Enid, Tony, Mitzi, Peter, *and* Monroe. We were 'the young crop.' " She severed her own laughter. "That was before I rejected it all, the corruption of it all."

Why Enid had come to Gibson, why she stayed, Normalyn did not know; but it seemed to her that Gibson enclosed them both in protection. From what?

In Gibson, Enid was a gorgeous figure of glamour. Thought "haughty," an "outlaw"—she used that word often—she welcomed her separation from the "Gibsonites," with one exception: Mayor Wendell Hughes—"a good man," she always added.

"The owner of Gibson and chunks of Texas," some called Mayor Hughes. The Texas Grand Hotel—where he lived in one whole wing; banks in Gibson, Langsdon, Dallas, Houston; acres of green land; concrete blocks and buildings on them—all of these were his, along with a strong voice in the politics of the State of Texas.

During his regular visits to Enid's graceful home, he entertained with stories of his powerful associations: "Why, without me that vulgar Lyndon wouldnuh been elected *any*thin'! D'you know that in his first big campaign he swore he'd have a map of Texas tattooed on his stomach if elected: 'The fatter I grow, the bigger the State of Texas gits,' he promised." Mayor

Hughes courted Enid's appreciated laughter. Then she would talk about her "starlet days, scarlet days": "Zanuck always glowering and conniving . . . Crawford whispering lies about Monroe to that evil columnist at Chasen's."

Sometimes Mayor Hughes would bring an expensive bottle of champagne—"from Dallas, of course!" Enid would say, "It's never too early for champagne!" Normalyn, then in her first grades of school, watched in delight the stately older man and the glamorous woman. Enid made sure she was always present during the Mayor's entire visits, even if that meant she must stay up past her bedtime. Then Mayor Hughes returned to his wife, Clarinda, who never came with him.

Normalyn liked Mayor Hughes. He was kind to her, always brought her a present. "Why, you're getting almost as pretty as your dear mother," he told her once. Enid marched over to Normalyn. She held her shoulders, to assert attention to her words: "Don't fill her with fantasies, Mayor Hughes, she'll believe you because you're a good man." She teased Normalyn's hair closer to her face. "She'll have to wear glasses soon—she's been squinting, she reads so much."

Normalyn was fitted with glasses. Enid adjusted them firmly when Normalyn said she hated them. "Don't be a vain little thing—you need them. Be grateful you're plain," Enid instructed. "And don't you dare cry."

Feeling increasingly unattractive, warned by Enid to "shelter" herself, Normalyn tried to make herself "invisible" at school. She moved very quietly, softly. Soon girls mimicked the way she walked. When boys whistled at her, she knew they were making fun of her. Considered "strange" now, she had no friends. Considering herself strange, she wanted none. She wrote secret poems and one-page stories, all titled *Life*.

"Invited courteously" by the principal to discuss the girl's inattention and poor grades, Enid stormed into his office, fox fur piece tossed over one shoulder. "My Normalyn is the smartest girl in your damn hick school," she informed him. "I don't doubt it, ma'am. I believe she just don't care to show it," the man said. Outside, Enid announced to a hall full of gaping children and teachers, "I hate injustice and ignorance, and they are rampant in this school!" Normalyn felt wonderful as she walked out; she even tried to imitate Enid's sexy gait and drew new whistles.

That night, Enid chastised: "You're so awkward. And dreamy, strange. Like her." By then, "her" had become "Monroe." "I'm sorry, Mother," Normalyn spoke the words that now came often, automatically. She had begun to feel that she was disap-

pointing Enid, who seemed to react to her as if she were two
people, the one she wanted her to be, the one she was.

Mayor Hughes brought Normalyn a book of myths!

"Why, Mayor Wendell Hughes," Enid chided flirtatiously, "I
didn't know a man of all your accomplishments was also a
literary man."

"Well, I am not," the Mayor did not hesitate to deny firmly.
"I simply asked one of the smart youngmen on my staff what
a bright young lady like Normalyn would enjoy and—"

"Norma Jeane gave presents on Thanksgiving." Enid's sigh
caressed a sudden memory. "She thought that was when you
thank *people*! She did that even when she was Monroe."

Normalyn loved the Mayor's present, marveled at Helen of
Troy, Ulysses, Icarus—who could just fly away!—and marveled at the angry gods who might be coaxed to intervene in
harsh destinies.

After school now, she was allowed by Enid to go to the
Public Library. She roamed the stacks, leafing through books,
putting away those that didn't interest her. She concentrated
on the Great Books section. There, she picked out *Huckleberry
Finn* because of the funny name.

I felt so lonesome I most wished I was dead. When Normalyn
read Huck confess that, she closed her eyes for a moment. *She*
felt dead sometimes, unborn. This would be her favorite book—
"forever," she swore. Huck so entranced her, made her laugh
aloud, that she decided to become like him—as a girl, of
course. They already had a lot in common. Huck was an
"outlaw" from society—like her! *That* was why she had no
friends. And he wanted to run away! Did she? She imagined
herself on a raft on the Rio Grande.

The library became her "real" world. She would sit in an
aisle of the library, on the floor, to read. It was there that she
discovered *Jane Eyre*. Jane was plain and didn't care!—brave
enough to go off and be on her own. Mrs. Rochester, locked
within her dark madness, frightened Normalyn. Pip in *Great
Expectations* annoyed her, but she was instantly fascinated by
proud Estella—and by Miss Havisham, hurt so cruelly that she
raised Estella to avenge her. Had Enid been hurt that deeply
by the despised Stan? Normalyn read more of Dickens, quickly
a favorite, and imagined asking him how it was possible that
his characters were realer than her life. Dickens was puzzled.

When she did not understand a character, she did not
hesitate to invent another in clarification. She conjured up a
fabulous messenger, a wise old man, to explain to Tom Jones
that he didn't *need* a father. Huckleberry Finn didn't want one.

And neither did she. None. Ever. Then she was able to finish reading *Tom Jones*, impressed that beautiful Sophia went off to London alone. But *this* Tom was just a grown Tom Sawyer.

On her fourteenth "birthday"—she wasn't sure it was the right day but she felt fourteen—Normalyn pleaded with Enid to let her make herself up. All the girls in school except her wore *some* makeup. "My mother let me make myself up one time, like a movie star," Enid remembered. "And I loved her forever for it," she seemed to barter, with a smile.

"And *I'll* love *you* forever," Normalyn swore.

Enid allowed Normalyn to use her special "movie makeup," kept in a pretty box in her bedroom. She waited downstairs to be surprised. When she saw Normalyn with darkened lashes, powdery rouge, gleamy lips, hair brushed into waves, her dress tucked tightly at her waist, Enid shouted, "You tried to look like *her* on purpose!"

Had she? Normalyn wondered. Guided by the face on the television screen, the shadowed one on the distant beach?

Enid wiped the girl's face into violent smears of paint. "Now go look in the mirror and tell me what the hell you see!" she commanded with a new fury. "And if you cry, I'll—!"

In the hallway mirror, Normalyn saw a sad face grotesquely distorted by makeup. "I'm ugly," she said to Enid.

Enid washed the streaked face. Then she traced the girl's features. The fingers paused tenderly on the tilt of her nose.

Normalyn lived increasingly in her imagination, nurtured by the books she read. To challenge her courage, she envisioned herself in situations of grave danger—to force herself to push away fear, prepare herself for when she had a life. Once she fantasized that in the dead of night—a windy, ominous night—she was coaxed—cunningly—to join a band of dangerous—but wondrous—people who had an abundance of life, daring experiences, not just memories. She matched *her* cunning against theirs.

These imaginary dangers allowed Normalyn to escape the one real danger of her life, the quiet danger of Enid's possessive love, entangling daily. She attempted to unknot it. When a boy asked her out, she forced herself to say yes. Nervous, she waited for him at the agreed time. Enid met him at the door. "You're at the wrong house." The bewildered boy faced Normalyn behind Enid. "Yes, ma'am," he said hurriedly.

"You shouldn't have, Mother," Normalyn managed to say.

"Don't dare cry over *that*!" Enid warned. "And don't ever let filth touch you."

It was an icy Texas night chilled by cold stars shivering at

the window. "Normalyn, you come get in bed with me, child—
wear your warmest gown, we'll sleep together. Every mother
sleeps with her daughter—it makes them closer. I slept with
mine." Normalyn huddled against her. "I have an inheritance,
Normalyn. Not the one from the rich Texans, this one's been
in my family very long. My grandmother passed it on to
Grace, and sometimes I think Grace tried to pass it on to me."
Normalyn felt Enid's body shiver. Then Enid named the inheritance: "The madness—the darkness, the blackness. Even
that I shared with Norma Jeane." She stopped. "We were both
so terrified to pass it on further!" She looked startled that she
had spoken that aloud. At the same moment, she had taken
her hand away from Normalyn's. She closed her eyes. "I love
the real blackness, the blackness of the ocean at night, its
natural beauty. 'The deep wet,' that's what Norma Jeane called
it." Enid held Normalyn's face, speaking words directly to her:
"When I die, that's where you'll find me, in the darkness at
the edge of the shoreline. Remember that."

With lunch, Enid had always cherished iced tea—with a
wedge of lemon, sometimes lime, a decorative sprig of mint;
"so civilized, even in winter," she said. Now her tea was replaced by a glass of wine, two, another at dinner. Soon she
drank more, earlier and later. "It softens the darkness—gray,
just gray." Increasingly moody, she took drives alone in the
daytime. After dinner she would face the television screen,
another glass of wine beside her. She would fidget with the
silver lighter retained from one of her "many lives," clicking it
absently. Sometimes she would call Normalyn out of her bedroom to watch the news, the documentary programs she favored. Tonight she had insisted Normalyn watch with her.

The announcer informed that they would be "going back in
time to that fatal day in June of 1968."

Normalyn saw: *A crowded ballroom, cheering people, a lanky
smiling man being reached for in adulation. Shots! The man fell.
Screams swept the hall. The announcer said, "And that is how it
happened, that June night in 1968 when presidential candidate Robert F. Kennedy was murdered in Los Angeles—"*

"Filthy!" Enid clicked off the television. She gulped the full
glass of wine. She held Normalyn close to her. "Nobody will
ever hurt you."

Soon the afternoon librarian—a sexy woman with astonishing auburn hair and knit dresses—Miss Stowe—began to suggest
books to Normalyn: "Have you read this one?"

Tess of the D'Urbervilles!—the beautiful woman driven to revenge. *The Mayor of Casterbridge!*—the drunken man selling his

wife and daughter. *The Scarlet Letter!*—proud Hester raising her child in solitude, blurring her origin, the child who forces her father to recognize her. *The Tales of Poe!*—the powerful pursuit of real and imagined ghosts. In all these books Normalyn looked for something that would illuminate her own life—make sense of it. In some, she thought she caught glimpses of Enid. It was possible to be "bought" by rich Texan parents, possible to be driven by great revenge, to be trapped by circumstances, controlled by ghosts.

Normalyn discovered *Wuthering Heights* on her own. She read it in one day, a Saturday. As evening approached, Miss Stowe, tiptoeing in order not to upset her deep concentration, relocated a lamp so she could read on. Catherine Earnshaw became Normalyn's favorite heroine, willing to reject even heaven if it kept her from living! . . . And there was Heathcliff.

Enid threatened to lock the door if she was late again: "I've been sick with worry!"

"I'm sorry."

That night, Normalyn imagined she was Catherine walking on the moors with Heathcliff. In the morning, it embarrassed her, pretending to be beautiful, passionate Catherine. Her embarrassment was assuaged later that day when she discovered in *The Concise Biography of Great English Novelists* that Emily Brontë was plain, lived an isolated life. And yet out of that isolation on the dank moors she was able to conjure up the wondrous Catherine and Heathcliff!

On a breezy day, almost spring, when she was sixteen, Normalyn "saw" Heathcliff! He was wearing a cowboy hat and boots and he was leaning against a white pickup truck across the school grounds. Dark, broody, so handsome in a jagged way. A "gypsy cowboy"!

School was out and Normalyn was hurrying away from the chatter of adolescent boys and girls with silly drawls, their giggles probably directed at her. Later, she would be shocked by what she did then. She took off her glasses and walked past the tall youngman. She suspected she might have smiled, because she had a feeling of warmth on her face. Did *he* touch his cowboy hat to tilt at her? She wasn't sure because she was already running away, clutching her glasses against her face all the way to the library.

A few days later she saw him again!

He was driving by in his white pickup. This time she was sure he smiled at her, but she didn't smile back because he was with two other "aggies"—"cowboys" from the nearby agricultural college—and she didn't want them to think she was smiling at them.

After that, she began wearing makeup she applied only after leaving the house. She rubbed it off carefully before she returned. Once she forgot. When she would not apologize, Enid ordered, "Wipe your face. And if you cry—"

"I don't intend to cry, Mother, you've warned me enough. And I don't intend to take off the makeup."

"Are you going to change, too, Normalyn?" There was no anger in her voice when Enid asked that. Her face darkened the way it did when she was about to be conquered by one of her moods of "blackness."

With a slightly sad smile, Miss Stowe told Normalyn, "I think you will like this book especially."

And Normalyn loved *Billy Budd.* She felt a sad closeness with him. She understood the enraged silence that led him to strike out at the demonic master-at-arms. For days, Billy Budd, doomed by his very innocence, haunted her.

Abruptly, Miss Stowe was replaced by a fat, menacing man with tiny rimless glasses. "I don't know anything about that woman," was all he said in answer to Normalyn's question. Grudgingly he handed her a note. It was from Miss Stowe! "I didn't have a chance to say goodbye," it said. "Thought you might like these." Under those words she had jotted the names of several books— with asterisks next to some. At the bottom the asterisks clarified: "Not ready for?" Below that was added: "And the plays of William Shakespeare, the greatest writer of all time."

Normalyn hurried to find the books with the asterisks. They were not on the shelves.

Soon after, a stark, locked glassed bookcase appeared behind the new librarian's desk. Normalyn asked him what it contained. "Books you shouldn't read and some you shouldn't have read," he snapped.

"Why are you so sulky, Normalyn?" Enid asked her that night. "You haven't even noticed there's lime for your iced tea." For herself, she had added a scotch to settle her nerves.

Normalyn told her about the forbidden books.

"Oh." Enid seemed uninterested. Later she said, "You can look at one of my movie books. Here."

Normalyn knew there would not be anything about Marilyn Monroe. She gasped. She saw a photograph of Hedy Lamarr.

"A natural beauty." Enid was leaning over her and the book. She smoothed her graying hair, touched her lips with a delicate finger.

Normalyn imagined later that she asked Hedy Lamarr what it was like to be so incredibly beautiful. "You get used to it," said Hedy Lamarr.

The next day Enid was waiting for Normalyn outside the high school. All the young people stared at the dramatic, glamorous woman. Normalyn was proud to be seen driving away with her. Facing the glowering librarian soon after, Enid asked Normalyn, "Which of those hidden books do you want?" Normalyn recited titles from the books with asterisks on the list Miss Stowe had bequeathed her.

"A minor can't have those." The librarian locked his arms before him.

"I am not a minor," Enid said. "Get the books you want, Normalyn." Normalyn finally decided on one, to give it full attention because not only had Miss Stowe placed an asterisk by it, she had underlined it. Enid announced to the entire library, "I saw good people in Hollywood destroyed for their decent beliefs by reactionaries like this bigot."

In a wistful mood that night over another scotch, Enid told Normalyn about "a cherished man" who was driven out of the movie studios for what he upheld. She stared away, then sighed.

In her room later, Normalyn encountered another world in *The Grapes of Wrath*. The book moved her, saddened her—and depressed her so much that she decided she would return it to the library without finishing it. But she resumed reading it the next day and wanted to protest for Ma Joad and Tom and Casy and— ... Was there still that much cruel injustice? She didn't want to believe it—and didn't welcome remembering that on their trips, now over, she and Enid had driven past weedy shacks to which Negroes and "illegal" Mexican laborers were banished. "An outrage," Enid had said, but did not connect it to Mayor Hughes—"a good man."

When Mayor Hughes came to visit, grand as ever, he walked into the house, flourishing a new cane. He hugged Normalyn, kissed her on the cheek, gave her a present—*The Arabian Nights*—"recommended by my reliable intellectual clerk." The Mayor would *never* take advantage of anyone; he was like Judge Thatcher, who befriended Huck, invested his money. But the "faces" of Ma Joad, others so full of outrage, haunted Normalyn.

Her next times at the library she followed Miss Stowe's P.S. and thrilled to the conspiracies of *Macbeth*, the romantic sacrifices of *Antony and Cleopatra*—she imagined Cleopatra would make a good friend because, although she would be intimidatingly beautiful and exotic, she came from another country, a strange world, and so knew what it was like to be an outlaw—like her. The elaborate plot to save Juliet by having her pretend to be dead! Normalyn did not believe two people could fall in love that powerfully as quickly as Romeo and Juliet did. She remembered when she first saw "the gypsy cowboy." Quickly, she thought of asking Shakespeare, "Is there any subject you haven't written about?" He answered honestly, "I don't think so."

"What will I do after I graduate?" Normalyn finally asked Enid a question she had been asking herself for some time.

Enid frowned over her fourth glass of wine. "What do you want to do?"

"Go to college."

"You can't go away."

"Why?"

"Because you'd be in danger."

Each day Normalyn returned from the library to the reality of Enid's moods, which now numbed whole days. Times of feared "darkness, blackness" lengthened—times of silence. Enid took pills to put her to sleep. "The damn demons won't rest any more." She added pills to wake her up. There would be eruptions within drunken slurs: "Why are you looking at me like that, Normalyn, accusing me with your sad eyes? I've done *everything* for you! What more can I do? Tell me, tell me!"

Then Normalyn was pulled into the brutal reality of the assault by the Rio Grande, the despised "gypsy cowboy" and the two other men over her—and Enid's accusation: "*Whore! Like her! With them!*" The incident was buried in silence. Normalyn felt that she would never forgive Enid, that she would never be able to smile again at anyone, nor at anything, that she would never again feel even a spark of joy.

She put away the makeup she had continued to use. She took the books she had begun to collect—to duplicate the ones she cherished reading at the library, where she had discovered them—and she put them into a drawer of her dresser. She would never be seduced into reading them again.

When she graduated, she did not wait for the ceremony to end. She clutched her diploma and walked away. Then she noticed that Enid was there, in the back of the old auditorium, hidden in the shadows, a somber presence now, gaunt, frail, but still wearing her glamorous hat. "Thank you for being here, Mother," she managed to say. Then she took Enid's unsteady hand and the two walked silently home.

That night, Enid stood in the living room of the two-story house in the cul-de-sac of the tree-lined street. Normalyn stared at the "peacock" mosaic around the unlit fireplace. Enid reached down and hugged her. Normalyn felt the woman's tears and she surrendered gratefully to the embrace. Enid's hug became a violent clasp. Normalyn tried to wrench from her. Then Enid thrust her away. She stared at Normalyn in angered surprise, as if at a stranger. She said softly, "You're my daughter and I love you."

Normalyn screamed at her, "No! You hate me, and I—" She could not finish.

Enid's hand lashed across Normalyn's face. Then she walked to the window and stared into the night. "It will soon be time," Enid said vaguely.

Increasingly there coursed into Enid's alcoholic recollections intimations of a "strange, great, terrible conspiracy" that involved her and Norma Jeane—"and Monroe—and powerful, powerful people." She would gasp blurred words of anguished guilt—"I tried, I *tried*!"—a somber statement, a question to ghosts, harsh hints of vast secrets from a past kept hidden: "I'm the only one who knows ... perhaps someone else. ... We were trapped by power that could crush us all! ... The Kennedys mustn't know! ... The truth disguised as a lie so it would be believed! ... I couldn't go to her funeral, it was too dangerous!" Her fingers touched her withered lips— *"Shhh"*—as if figures from the past might still overhear. Then the sighs and whispers of her old memories resumed.

Even in the early years, Normalyn had not been allowed to question. Now she did not want to know more about the intrusive new memories, because they conveyed grave present dangers—or prepared for further entrapment by Enid. "We have to stay protected. We can't leave Gibson. ... Mayor Hughes is a good man."

Deep in the night, Normalyn heard sobs seeping out of Enid's closed door. She went to her. The door was locked. After that when Normalyn heard the whispery sobs, she pressed her head into her pillow to silence them.

Enid saw only one other person, Mayor Wendell Hughes, who appeared regularly. He was increasingly solemn, especially one recent morning when he brought over what looked like a bank safe-deposit box. He hesitated for moments on his cane, as if he did not want to reach Enid's room.

"I want to tell you the truth, Normalyn." Enid appeared at the top of the stairs and called down to Normalyn that night.

In her bedroom suffused in dimming light, Enid sat in her

bed and faced Normalyn. Her graceful slenderness had turned into thinness. She did not eat, just drank. Gray hairs invaded the dark head. But in this amber-shadowed faintly glowing room the hints of her former beauty survived.

Enid touched the wounded angel, its bruised wing. Her hands flowed over the artificial lavender flowers. A ghostly smile received kind memories. Then only pieces of familiar recollections poured out: "All those orphanages I was in, Normalyn, never knowing how long, those angry adoptions. . . . Just like Norma Jeane. We invented a game in the home. Did I tell you?"

Normalyn nodded. She resisted touching the frail old woman. The trembling hands might push her away.

"Once my mother made me up to look so pretty, like I did you, Normalyn, remember?"

"When you smeared the makeup on my face?"

Enid's hands fluttered out, rejecting the harsh memory. "Oh, remember our trips, Normalyn, the songs, the movie games, the celebrations?"

"Yes."

"Yes, *Mother* . . . please," Enid coaxed softly.

"Yes, Mother." Normalyn allowed herself to respond to Enid's assertion of those happy times.

"Remember how I held you, protected you, cried with you?"

"The time I was attacked by three men? You called me a whore, Mother—and then you cried. You never asked me what happened."

"I was remembering something else!" Enid turned her face away. "Oh, did I tell you what Norma Jeane said when they brought her into the home? 'I don't belong in the orphanage, my parents are movie stars!' "

"You told me *you* said that."

"We both did. And I told you about the necklace? It was blue, like clean water, so beautiful. I loved it so. But I gave it back to him. I told you?"

No. Nor about "him." But Normalyn nodded.

"There was a man I loved, there was a man I hated." Enid touched her hair, wisps, as if she must put it in order, the way it had been when she was beautiful. She brushed her lips, lightly, as if to bring color to them. She resumed her recitation of memories: "I told you about when I was living with my aunt and Grace telephoned from the institution she had committed herself to?"

"Yes, Mother."

"Why, they wouldn't let her out unless family agreed to take her, and I said, Yes! She came and I was so happy for a time. She slept with me in the only bed available. She held me like I held you, Normalyn, and I was sure she loved me. But then she pushed me away and called the institution to take her back." The frail old woman thrust her hands out as if this memory required physical motion to be spoken. "I told you."

No, she had not told her the last part.

Enid's trembling hands fell to her lap. "Only later, Normalyn, did I understand she wasn't pushing me away. She was trying to separate me from *their* madness, *their* darkness." She said with deep sorrow, "Norma Jeane and I shared even that, the darkness." She looked up at Normalyn in sudden alertness. "We shared everything!" Then she sank into her bed as if finally the pills were granting her the blessing of peace.

2

Now, still standing within the silenced house left empty by Enid's death, Normalyn realized how very little she knew about the woman she had lived with for eighteen years; realized, as she tried to gather scattering memories, that although Enid had spoken often about her "many lives," she had told her only fragments, pieces of the mysterious life of an intimate stranger.

Five

The silence in Enid's house screamed!

Normalyn's hand choked her own cry as she stood in the house where, only nights before, Enid had taken pills and killed herself. It was the telephone that was ringing, pulling her out of Enid's past, into a life without her. She would not answer! But she had to stop the shrieking. She lifted the telephone. "Hello!"

"Normalyn! Why aren't you crying and your mother just died!" a man's voice shot at her.

"Because I'm not sad and I'm not afraid!" she yelled back at him—and even more defiantly at the cruel, empty house. She flung down the telephone. She had recognized the voice of the divorced old man next door. She was aware of the yowling wind enclosing the house in silence. The telephone rang again. She would run away from it—outside! She opened the door. The wind thrust dirt and shattered tumbleweeds at her.

In his pickup, Ted Gonzales saw her at the open door, lashed by dust. She was terrified to be alone! He ran out.

She saw him advancing out of ashen wind at the same time that she heard the telephone ringing again.

Ted halted before her on the steps. "Is something wrong!" he yelled over the wind.

The ringing died behind her.

Normalyn was about to push the door shut when the screaming of the telephone—of the house, of her own aloneness—resumed. She covered her ears.

Now at the door, Ted understood the source of her panic. "You want me to answer it?"

"Yes!" She backed away from him as he lifted the telephone.

The man's harsh questioning extended: "You're all alone, huh, Normalyn? Maybe if I—"

"She's *not* alone, you goddamn son of a bitch! You call again and I'll find out who the hell you are and I'll shut your fuckin' mouth for you! . . . Sorry about the bad words," he apologized aside to Normalyn. Then he hung up and faced her, hoping she would trust him now.

"You stay away! Remember I have a gun!"

He shook his head, knowing that for her he was just like the man who had telephoned just now—worse, much worse. He walked toward the door. "See," he said, "I've moved away. I'll leave . . . if you say so." He hoped, so much, she wouldn't.

"Yes, leave!" she said. But when the telephone shouted again, her hand reached out toward him automatically.

Over to the telephone in three gaits of long legs, Ted yelled into it, "You fucked-up bastard! I told you not to call her again. I warn you if— Oh, I'm *sorry*. . . . Yes, she is, sir." He covered the mouthpiece. Startled, he said to Normalyn. "It's Mayor Hughes."

Normalyn waited for Ted to put the telephone on the table before she took it. *Now* he would run away, because he'd be afraid she'd tell the Mayor—

But Ted didn't leave. *This* might assure his sincerity.

The Mayor's voice was concerned: "Honey, you all right? Someone botherin' you on the phone?"

Clasping control, Normalyn assured him—twice—that she was all right. Even now she could not speak about the horror by the river, and she did not want to arouse the Mayor's concern, nor be moved again by his desolate expressions of loss at Enid's death, not now when she had to remain calm.

"Well, I'm glad you're not alone. That fellow Gonzales sounded like he aimed to protect you. You know I'm aware of everything that goes on in Gibson, and someone called me, said you were sittin' in the plaza in this damn wind with that young fellow. Bright young man, maybe a little radical, hadn't known you knew him that well. . . . Now, honey, I want you to have lunch with me and Clarinda here at the hotel tomorrow. I'll have Lottie open the main dining room just for you, like I used to for you and Enid. We'll have us a long talk," he promised. "Some things I need to tell you."

About the letter! He would clarify everything! But now

Normalyn felt relief more than anything else because suddenly there was something to do tomorrow. Lunch! A goal!

The Mayor's voice was lowered, "I loved that mother of yours, honey. I will miss her with all my heart."

Normalyn's hands clenched the telephone. She looked up into the knotted darkness outside Enid's room. And inside, Enid was still commanding with the papers left behind.

"Now you call me if anyone bothers you again." The Mayor forced a more cheerful tone. "And, honey, you go ahead and bring that Gonzales fellow to lunch if you want to."

The extended invitation confused Normalyn. Did the Mayor want to avoid questions? Was he testing her own intention to ask?

Ted Gonzales was uncomfortable in the house of the dead woman. He had seen her walking along the streets, demanding attention, getting it. Yesterday his mother put down the morning paper and announced, "The movie star in Gibson is dead. Wonder how Wendell's taking it." Ted's mother often made references to a "secret relationship" between the Mayor and the "movie star in Gibson": "Of course, they're the only ones who think it's secret!" This morning she had added, "Now that odd daughter will be all alone." It was then that Ted decided he'd come into Gibson to find Normalyn. He drove the sixty miles from Langsdon, a "more sophisticated city" of almost fifty thousand.

When Normalyn put down the telephone, Ted was bold: "If it makes you feel safe, go ahead and get your gun, Normalyn. I promise you won't need it." It annoyed him to hear a trace of the Texas drawl he now disliked, tried to conquer. "Just please let me stay with you awhile." She looked so pretty! He was ashamed to think that at this tense time. At Langsdon College, there were a few very pretty "Latino" girls in the new liberal arts department. But Ted did not desire them. He was still attracted only to "Anglo" girls. That troubled him, because he was intent on shedding all the despised attitudes he had once wanted to adopt. Recently he had caught another harsh view of himself when an "Anglo" girl he went out with told him it made her feel "sleazy in a sexy way" to be with a "brown white man."

In Enid's house, night had thickened at the dusty windows. Normalyn stared at Ted. She was less frightened of him than of the house, the telephone, of being alone. She considered pretending to go get a gun, but that would only prove she had none. Tired, so tired. Still expecting the telephone to erupt with renewed terror, she leaned against the steps and faced

that she didn't want to be alone. For a moment she glimpsed
him as she had the very first time, across the schoolyard, "the
gypsy cowboy." But that person had existed only in her imagination and in the books she had loved and banished forever!

Ted had to seize these subdued moments to prove he was
someone else, present evidence he was no longer the man she
had seen at the river. He piled words nervously: "After what
happened that ugly time, I saw myself so damn clearly. I tried
to imagine what it would be like, to have someone come at you
like that." And he had tried. "But I couldn't, couldn't even
imagine it, that's how awful I knew it was." That had driven
him into a night of rage, which had ended when he smashed
his fist against the windshield of his pickup, to hurt *him*self.
He looked at the jagged scar on his hand, a reminder of that
time. "You know what it was like the night when I—?" He
stopped quickly. She had looked sharply at him.

"What it was like for *you*?"

Selfish! At this time *he* wanted *her* to understand what *he*
had felt when *she* had been the one cruelly hurt. His resolve
grew, to be with her now, when she was most alone. Would it
help to tell her how much he had wanted to ask her out when
he first saw her near her school, but he didn't know how she
felt about "Mexicans," even if he was half Irish? No, telling
her that might make it all worse now. Would it help to tell her
he had figured out that part of what had gone wrong that
ugly day was goddamned big Texas with its confusions of
power and violence everywhere? No, then it would seem that
he was evading blaming himself. He did seriously consider
telling her his Mexican father had come back soon after that
hated afternoon after years away in Dallas—a separation his
mother acknowledged only sometimes when she called her
husband "that damn Mexican I married." Now Ted had discovered he *liked* his father and his father liked him, maybe a
lot, and that the Gonzales family was— . . . Could he tell her
any of this? Not now. Maybe some time. And he would even
acknowledge that there had been desire, violent desire. There
was *still* desire, but not violent, never again, he knew. "If
you—"

Suddenly harsh lights flashed in through the wide living-
room window of Enid's house. Engine gunned loudly over the
diminishing wind, a car was aiming its headlights inside. Feeling trapped in their glare, which steadied for long seconds,
Normalyn pushed her body against the wall. The car sped
away.

"Just some driver lost in the windstorm," Ted tried to assuage. Even that had frightened her.

Was it just a car in the windstorm? Yes! That was all! She wouldn't allow Enid's letter and those strange papers to distort everything by seeming to verify new intimations of danger. "I'm *not* scared!" she said aloud firmly. She drew the drapes across the window. To warm away the sudden chill of fear, she walked to the artificial fireplace, lit it, and leaned over its clean blue flames.

Tinted by the golden glow, she looked even prettier, Ted saw. "It's a beautiful fireplace," he said. "Is it a peacock?"

Normalyn touched Enid's precious peacock mosaic. "Yes. It's like Valentino's, at Falcon's Lair," she spoke Enid's words aloud. And with them, suddenly, came one single memory, not of trips or songs or birthday cakes, but of Enid's delight in her creation as she placed the colored tiles in her exact design, to fashion something beautiful of her own; and it was that one memory that released Normalyn's tears, tears forced back for days, for years; and she asked aloud now the questions withheld from that deadly morning: *"Why did you stop loving me, Mother? Why did you kill yourself?"*

Jesus Christ! Her mother had committed suicide. Ted wanted to hold the shivering girl—the girl he had tried to rape—wanted to soothe the hurt pouring out at last. But he dared not risk touching her. He left his scarred hand extended for her to take if she wanted. If she could.

Normalyn looked at him, startled: She had spoken those intimate words to this man she hated. Guilt overwhelmed her instantly, and she had to explain away her judgment: "I disappointed her; I was always so ugly and she was so beautiful."

Then that was why, that afternoon, she had screamed "I'm sorry!" at him and the others attacking *her*—because her mother had already made her feel ugly, guilty for just living. Would he have gone through with it if the others had not called him a "spic"? *Had* he heard and been moved by *her* words, first? He had to believe that.

She removed her glasses, wiping away her tears, determined to force back her control.

Ted saw now that she was even prettier than he had seen, much prettier—almost as if the ghost of a very beautiful woman hovered, waiting to take over. He said, "Don't let your mother hurt you any more, and if—"

Her anger stopped more words: "What the hell do you know about her? Don't think I trust you! Now get out or I'll—"

He said firmly, "I'm going to stay out here on the couch. I *know* you don't want to be alone. You can lock your door, even keep your gun beside you."

No, she didn't want to be alone. "I'll goddamn use the gun, I swear." She toughened her voice.

He nodded, yes. But he knew she had no gun. He said, "I feel filthy for having hurt you."

He seemed about to cry! She saw, again, the "gypsy cowboy" she had once envisioned walking with her along the moors, the river. *The river where he had tried to rape her!* The image shattered. But the fear of aloneness remained. "I *will* keep my gun at my side," she asserted before she walked away.

Allowing him to stay only because there was no one else in the whole goddamn world, Ted knew.

In her room, Normalyn made loud sounds to convey she was locking the door, barricading it, looking for her "gun." She knew she was no longer in danger from him, but she would never forgive him, nor allow him to believe she would. He had contributed to the isolation Enid had sealed. She leaned against the door and closed her eyes. Suddenly she was aware of a sense of turbulent darkness. She opened her eyes quickly. Tomorrow through Mayor Hughes she would discover the truth—the lies—of Enid's letter.

Six

She woke to sun spilling into her bedroom. She pushed away an instant sense of fear. She reached for a robe and walked into her bathroom. Its door framed a full-length mirror she usually ignored. If she looked quickly, closing her eyes first, might she see again the vagrant prettiness she thought she'd glimpsed yesterday? She brushed her hair, letting it fall in natural waves. She made herself up with the cosmetics abandoned from the night of Enid's accusation. Before she could face herself fully in the mirror, her hands flew to her face, rubbing off the makeup that had outraged Enid.

In her room, she put on her glasses, but she left her hair the way she had brushed it. She rejected a dark dress that mourned; she chose a light one, a shade of blue. Then she restored some makeup, lightly.

In the living room, Ted's long body, fully clothed except for his boots, tossed awake on the couch. Sleep still nudging, he touched himself urgently to make sure he was dressed. Quickly, he put on his boots, reached for his cowboy hat, put it on, took it off.

Normalyn was about to laugh. But when he stood up, she felt a stab of renewed fear—quickly calmed when he looked at her so anxiously. She hurried to the kitchen. She made coffee, as she did on other mornings, several cups for Enid, to help the pills alert her. Normalyn placed an extra cup and saucer near the brewing coffee. Then she took away the saucer so the cup wouldn't look inviting. She sat down at the table with her own coffee.

44

Ted stood at the door, cautiously, to gauge her reaction. She did not look at him. He smelled the coffee, noticed the bare cup. With enormous formality, he asked, "May I?" She nodded. He filled his cup. He stood near the table, indicating a chair. "May I?" She hardly nodded. He stopped himself from reaching for the sugar. "May I?"

They drank the coffee in silence. Normalyn did not feel threatened by him, but she still would not face him. When he finished his coffee, he thanked her—"very much"—for it. He was exhibiting grand Texas manners, for her, Normalyn knew, but that didn't mean anything. Even the meanest people in the state had them.

Sitting awkwardly in the judging silence, Ted longed to ask Normalyn to have lunch with him. He'd been paid Friday at his job unloading at the Langsdon Trucking Company Warehouse. That provided part of his college tuition, the rest came from a scholarship. He prepared his invitation—but when he spoke it, it sounded odd: "Will you eat with me today?"

"I'm having lunch with Mayor Hughes," Normalyn informed him coolly.

"May I drive you there?" he offered in minor substitution.

"Not in that damn white pickup!" she reacted in anger—and remembered how for a time she had looked for the truck eagerly, expecting to see him.

"I'll walk you there if you want."

She only shrugged. She had let herself glance at him to determine whom she would see. The "gypsy cowboy"? No, never again, he *never* existed! The despised man by the river? She saw the man who had remained with her last night because he knew she was afraid.

Ted felt optimism. She was relenting toward him—if slowly. Later, he might be able to tell her how pretty she looked.

Outside the house, Normalyn saw lime-green buds sprouting on trees like tiny flowers. In a few days all the trees would be full of green life. "Tomorrow," she said aloud.

"Tomorrow what?" Ted asked her.

"Nothing." She had only tested the word. It meant a future, a possible future. Then she felt it, a smile on her face, a foreign sensation, warm.

"You smiled!" Ted said aloud.

"I did not!" Normalyn walked briskly along the street, avoiding the parked pickup.

She *had* smiled, Ted knew, a smile that had turned sad, as if she did not know exactly how to form it. If only he could bring it back, the way it must have existed before he'd contrib-

uted to banishing it. He felt glad to be walking along the
streets of Gibson with her.

They were inviting stares. That did not displease Normalyn.
When she'd gone out with Enid, she was sure it was only Enid
people looked at. This time they would be looking at her—she
didn't care why. They walked into the memorial plaza.

Ted shook his head in wonder at the "Texas Hero." "No
one knows who he is but everyone's so damn sure he's a war
hero—you notice how those old men take off their hats and
put them over their hearts when they walk by?" He firmed his
own hat on his head and blurted aloud what he had long
thought: "He looks to me like he's about to expose himself
under that old coat. Maybe he'll do it when those Daughters of
the Republic have their patriotic ceremony there."

Normalyn walked quickly ahead of him.

Because of what he had said! Stupid! He felt dirty! "I'm
sorry!" he yelled out to her.

But Normalyn had rushed away to disguise the fact that she
had to cover her mouth to keep from roaring with laughter at
his reference to the Daughters—whom Enid called "mummified clucks." She ran across the street, toward the flowered
patio of the Texas Grand Hotel.

2

The Texas Grand was a handsome old building of mixed
architecture, part Southern, part Spanish, with arches and
crenolated balconies.

Normalyn entered the elegant lobby. Ted followed her. She
pretended not to notice him.

White stairs swept into the two main wings—an entire one
of which was the Mayor's "quarters." A magnificent old chandelier floated over the stairs. A season's dust had settled on it
like mist. The hotel's atmosphere of displaced time extended
to the few "permanent guests" who sat in the lobby—an old
couple, a man alone, a woman in perpetual mourning, others, all
like ghosts from another country. Occasionally, tasteful tourists sought out the Texas Grand Hotel and found it "charming." It was Mayor Wendell Hughes who, at great expense,
kept the grand old hotel open.

"Well, darlin' child, it's *good* to see you, honey!" With one of
his expensive canes, Mayor Hughes was descending the stairs,
carefully, always concealing his limp. He was a portly man,
with a full head of proud white hair; he wore a good-looking

brown suit, purchased, like all his others, "at the only damn store worth talkin' about, Neiman-Marcus, bless 'em." He held Normalyn's hands warmly in shared loss. "And Ted Gonzales— ha'rya?" The Mayor often deepened his drawl, when he wanted to assert his allegiance to its origin. He extended his hand to Ted. "Hear your father's back from Dallas." The Mayor prided himself on knowing everyone. "Ha'n't seen your folks since y'all moved out to Langsdon. And your mother, Lorraine? Glad you could join us today—will you?"

Normalyn did not object to the reiterated invitation; Mayor Hughes seemed to want another presence. To control what might be asked? There was at least one subject she would bring up no matter who was there—her birth certificate.

Ted accepted the Mayor's hand. This warm, gracious, elegant old man did not act or look like the tyrant Ted had discovered him to be since his own awareness of himself and giant Texas—the old man ruled his portion of Texas by enforcing a serenity that concealed any injustice. In his social studies class in Langsdon, Ted had invited glares and approval when he referred to the Mayor as "an old dinosaur." "Thank you for inviting me, sir." He was not "sirring" an Anglo, just addressing an old man.

"Why, Normalyn, how pretty you look, honey." Mayor Hughes touched her cheek fondly, the flush of rouge.

Normalyn turned her head, embarrassed. He had not called her pretty since the day Enid had objected. She touched the shield of her glasses.

"But why shouldn't you be pretty? After all, Enid was a beautiful woman, and she *was* your mother." The Mayor's eyes seemed to scrutinize Normalyn for a reaction.

She caught his look. She *would* determine how much he knew.

Suddenly they were assaulted by the heavy odor of rose perfume.

On waves of it, Clarinda Hughes had floated down the stairs. She was a reedy woman with unreally blackened hair and eyebrows, fiercely red lips on a face so heavily powdered it looked calcimined. Her rose-scented perfume was meant to conceal the miasma of her alcohol. To disguise the origin of the scent, she pinned a felt rose on her shriveled chest. With readied dislike, she stared at Normalyn, the first time she and Enid's daughter had been this close. "What did you do to yourself, you look *painted*!"

Normalyn's hands started to rise, to remove the makeup. Instead, they dropped to her sides, fists. Enid had detested

the woman— "a worthless, unfeeling creature." "But *yours*,"
Normalyn said sweetly to Clarinda, "*your* makeup is so subtle
you'd hardly suspect you used any."

The Mayor disguised a brief smile.

"Ma'am!" Ted bowed slightly before Clarinda, to force the
old woman's clawing stare away from Normalyn.

Clarinda frowned at him. "You're Lorraine's boy. She married that Spanish man." She allowed a faint judgment on the
darkened line of her lips.

"My father is *Mexican*," Ted corrected.

Normalyn saw him stretching his full height, asserting his
new pride. For the longest time yet, she had not seen the
menacing man from the river.

"Well, now!" the Mayor summoned attention. "Let's have
our lunch! I opened muh main dinin' room just for this
orderly gathering."

3

Only a small portion of the dining room of the Texas Grand
Hotel was regularly kept open for the mothy presences who
still ate there. Today, deep-wine panels sprinkled with golden
fleurs-de-lis had been folded away. In the center of the main
dining room formed by rising arches, only one table, in the
middle, was elaborately set. About it, bare tables awaited vanished guests. Almost umber from seasons of desert sun, drapes
flanked tall windows screened by ashen lace. Spring sun filtered into the room in tiny bouquets of light.

Ted winced when he saw two Mexican men quietly arranging the elaborate table. Not too long ago, he would have
attempted to sever any association, retreating behind his
"half-Irishness."

"Mayor Wendell Hughes!" The ponderous presence of Lottie,
the Mayor's black cook, welcomed at the table. "And two
young folks." She pulled out the Mayor's chair. Clarinda glowered at her. She glowered back. The Mayor pulled Clarinda's
chair. Ted rushed to attend to Normalyn's: "Allow *me*."

Lottie beamed over the full table.

The Mayor pretended to whisper—to Lottie's chuckling delight: "If Lottie evuh left us, this whole beautiful hotel would
vanish!"

"Yes!" Ted said pointedly.

With strict control, Lottie oversaw the serving of lunch by
the two Mexican men. "I've told you, the salad fork is *first*!"

she scolded. In certain parts of Texas lunch persists as an ample, full meal, and this one was: golden chicken, pearly potatoes, emerald peas. And a beaded crystal pitcher of iced tea.

"Iced tea with lime wedges—for *you*, honey," Mayor Hughes confided to Normalyn, "just the way Enid favored hers."

"Tell her to bring *my* tea, Wendell." Clarinda would not speak to Lottie.

"You promised this morning," the Mayor reminded his wife. "You agreed, not until dinner," he said quietly.

"I said have her bring mine!" The woman's voice prepared to declare public battle.

The Mayor nodded yes to Lottie. Disappearing, she reappeared in moments with another glass, which she wafted over the table, to be identified; the commanding odor of whiskey sprang out. "Her *tea*." She gave it to the Mayor to give to Clarinda. *She* would not communicate with the white woman.

Bowing his head, the Mayor pronounced grace: "It's a damn blessin' to live in the State of Texas and the serene City of Gibson, God bless us all." He punctuated his "Amen" by flourishing his fancy napkin onto his lap. His monogram— "W.H."— was embroidered in swirly script.

"Now y'all enjoy my lunch!" Lottie added her own grace, before departing to tend to a promised "surprise."

Normalyn welcomed the delicious food. She had not eaten fully since Enid's death.

Leaning over, the Mayor pretended to conspire: "Known young Gonzales a long time, honey?"

Ted smiled at Normalyn, but when she said, hardly audibly, "Yes," and edged away, he knew the troubled past had stirred.

The Mayor's words to Ted sounded as friendly as they were abrupt: "I hear you been doin' some kinda 'research' on the workuhs out in muh fields."

"Yes, sir—for a school paper. I call it 'American Gothic.'" The title pleased Ted.

"Ummm." Mayor Hughes pondered it.

"I drove out to one of the big farms in the area to try to talk to some of the migrant workers about conditions—and a crazy man drove me away at gunpoint." Ted welcomed this opportunity to present more evidence of his changed consciousness. "I didn't know it was *your* farm, sir."

"All of Gibson and its environs are mine—in a mannuh of speakin'." The Mayor lengthened his drawl.

Normalyn looked at the Mayor, this kind man whom she cherished. For unwelcome moments she had remembered the book she had read, from the ones marked with an asterisk on Miss Stowe's list of long ago. No, she could not associate him with that kind of injustice.

"Well, I guess bein' inquisitive is part of being young." The Mayor dismissed the subject of Ted's "research" now that he had established he knew about it.

"Lost, damned, *and* accursed! That's what young people are today," Clarinda said. The stench of liquor battled the rose perfume.

Conspicuously ignoring her, Normalyn spoke her prepared words casually: "Mayor Hughes, I'd like to ask you a favor."

"Anything, honey, you know that." The Mayor's spread hands offered limitless bounty.

"A copy of my birth certificate."

The Mayor put down his fork, with puffy peas he had been about to bring to his mouth. He cleared his throat. "I'm sure you have one, honey." He did not look at her. "I certified it myself, here in Gibson. Enid never got around to it in Galveston." He gave intense attention to a morsel of crisp chicken.

"My mother did leave me a copy." Normalyn slowed her words, to capture the Mayor's slightest reaction. "But it's all marked up and faded."

A long silence hovered in the grand dining room.

"Of course I'll get you a new copy, honey," the Mayor said at last. "You can't go around feelin' you haven't been born!"

Not born! That was how Normalyn felt—abandoned out of a life that had ended.

The Mayor's voice was casual. "I myself don't put much store by official papers. Most of them don't mean a damn thing."

"Like work permits that turn illegal after the crops are picked!" Ted faced the Mayor.

The Mayor pulled his eyes from him. He said to Normalyn, "Honey, I bet you're thinkin' of takin' a trip out somewhere"— his voice lowered—"now that our beloved Enid has left us—"

"Amen," Clarinda toasted with mock solemnity. She sat back quickly like a conniving malicious child.

Normalyn ignored her challenge. She seemed much too eager to confront.

The Mayor resumed: "That why you want your birth certificate, honey?"

Leave Gibson? The thought did not startle Normalyn. It might have been there a long time. Was Mayor Hughes suggesting it, even inviting it? Was *he* trying to find out how much she knew about Enid's last acts?

"Modern cities are nests of corruption!" Clarinda spat. "Sodom and Gomorrah and Los Angeles."

"You may just be right about that, Clarinda," the Mayor agreed. "Why, honey," he directed at Normalyn, "that must've been why your blessed mother brought you here after she discovered our tiny piece of order—so you'd grow up in the clean State of Texas, away from all that depravity."

Was that the reason? Normalyn had expected clarity, but would this meeting provide only more questions? The Mayor's carefully arranged lunch obviated directness.

"John F. Kennedy was murdered in Dallas, *Texas*, sir, and *that* was depraved." Ted's measured words hardly controlled his anger.

Mayor Hughes locked an iron stare on him. "I knew Jack, youngman," he said. "Knew Lyndon, too."

"Vulgar school teachers, those Johnsons. I never received them," Clarinda sneered, touching her perfumed rose.

"I *liked* Jack," the Mayor told Ted. "A realistic man. Now *Robert*"—his voice turned harsh—"*he* didn't bend. He—" The Mayor stopped abruptly.

Normalyn had reacted in apprehension at the mention of the two murdered brothers. Enid's references to them at the last of her life—her rantings about "a terrible conspiracy"— had tinted the names for her with dangerous mystery. When Enid had taken her to Dealy Plaza, when they had watched the documentary on the murder of Robert Kennedy, Enid's reaction had been strong. Normalyn had never been certain whether that was in anger at them, or their violent deaths—or both. Had the Mayor severed his reference because he knew of Enid's vague assertions of association?

"Robert Kennedy is my hero," Ted announced staunchly, "*because* he didn't bend." In the past year of self-questioning, he had discovered the Kennedys through his history classes. He was sure that Robert Kennedy's commitment to justice had partly inspired his determination to become a good man himself. "He might have become the greatest President we ever had. And"—he added something no one had ever suggested but that he hoped was true—"I've been told that I resemble him." He looked down into his plate, not risking their scrutiny.

"Well, you do not!" Mayor Hughes dismissed.

Normalyn looked at Ted. Tall, yes, lanky. She remembered the smiling Senator she had seen on television, the crowded ballroom. Ted looked more like— She rejected the unexpected romantic image, fading.

The Mayor cleared his throat. "Now, Normalyn, I asked you

here for the obvious pleashuh of your company, but also to
discuss some important matters. Nothin' complicated." He banished secrecy by extending his look to the others there. "I am,
of course, the executor of your dear mother's estate. She was
real careful in her instructions. Said she left careful ones for
you, too." His eyes on her added emphasis.

Normalyn was startled. Careful instructions? She had left
her only mysteries.

"She left you enough to live on," the Mayor continued, "for
a period of . . . discovery. For whatever you may want to
explore."

A short period of discovery . . . whatever you want to explore. Was he speaking Enid's instructions? Normalyn wondered. He seemed to be imparting messages to her while not
allowing questions.

"Enid had some money, lived well—good Texas family
adopted her, though she never saw them that way." With a
soft laugh of indulgence, the Mayor glided over memories.
"Why, they sent her to that private school where she learned
the liberal ways that turned her against them! Enid had a way
all her own." His look drifted to the lobby as if he expected
the woman who had entered his memory to enter the hotel.
His tone became official: "The house is in your name, paid
for—"

"Bought for her by someone else!" Clarinda snorted.

"You don't know that." The Mayor clasped Clarinda's hand.
"This lunch will be orderly!"

Ted looked in fascination at this powerful man. That was
how he established "serenity" in Gibson, by demand.

Clarinda pulled her hand away. "Enid was a *strange* woman!"
She added in outrage, "And she never even asked to join the
Daughters."

"But she referred to them often—" Normalyn said seriously.

Clarinda waited in lofty anticipation.

"—as mummified clucks," Normalyn finished.

Ted laughed aloud, the Mayor hid his smile.

In substitute reaction, Clarinda located her empty glass defiantly before the Mayor. "Tell that woman to fill it again,
Wendell."

Mayor Hughes nodded to Lottie, who waited for his signal.

Clarinda pursued: "Enid was—"

"You hush and let Enid rest in peace now," the Mayor
ordered his wife.

"Why should she rest?" Clarinda struck the table. Her rose

snapped from its pin. "*She* wasn't peaceful. *She* didn't bring peace to *me*."

"Ma'am!" Ted began to protest for Normalyn.

Clarinda released coarse laughter into the resurrected dining room. "Your mother invaded Gibson, Normalyn. *And* our lives! She came all the way from Hol-lee-wood." She mocked each syllable. "All alone with her veiled hats and that lighter she never lit, demanding attention."

"And she got it." The Mayor allowed his own memory into the burst of his wife's anger. "Right here in the lobby of this grand old hotel, Enid snapped her silver cigarette lighter only once, and everyone knew she was here."

Then this is where Enid had first appeared in Gibson. Normalyn tried to evoke the beautiful woman pictured in the twin frame. That is how the Mayor had seen her, flaunting her "natural beauty," flicking away her veil to reveal a perfect complexion.

"Stood in that lobby"— Clarinda stabbed her finger in that direction—"and brazen as brass she announced to everyone that she expected a *long*-distance call from some man with the vulgar name of Stan—as if anyone cared!"

Stan. The object of Enid's passionate vengeance, whatever shape that had taken. The man who was probably her father. Normalyn listened attentively.

"And then she disappeared." Clarinda aimed the words at her husband: "Left *you*!"

"But she came back, just as I knew she would, and she stayed until she died." The Mayor looked at the surrounding tables as if noticing they were vacant.

"She came back with *you*, Normalyn." Clarinda hissed her vague accusation. "That's why she went away—to have *you*. She was so vain she didn't want anyone to see her pregnant."

The Mayor said solemnly, "And no one ever did."

Seven

No one saw Enid pregnant. Normalyn allowed disturbing words into her mind.

Clarinda crushed her perfumed rose. "*I* puffed up, with all the damn children Wendell wanted—"

"And never got," Mayor Hughes reminded quietly.

Clarinda flung away the crushed rose.

Mayor Hughes's voice remained calm. "Stop this display, Clarinda. It is *rude*." He slipped the glass of liquor from her.

She yanked it back. "Tell this girl why I drink, Wendell!"

Mayor Hughes continued to eat, careful bites of food.

Clarinda answered her own demand: "Because everyone knew that you and Enid—"

"That's not true," Normalyn protested Clarinda's words, and the Mayor's unexpected silence. She had always been present during the Mayor's welcome visits. "Is it, Mayor Hughes?"

Then Normalyn did not know the rumors his mother claimed "everyone knew." Ted saw how confidently she waited for the Mayor's answer.

The Mayor brought a tiny forkful of salad to his mouth. He wiped his lips with the edge of his linen towel.

"Is it, Wendell? Is it, is it?" Clarinda parroted.

The Mayor laid down his fork, his knife, arranged them just as they had been set. "I loved Enid from the moment she stepped into that lobby, so aware of her commanding beauty." He spoke so softly he seemed to breathe the words into the graceful room. "Is that what you want to hear, Clarinda?"

54

"Bastard!" The woman's tiny hands flailed at him. "You and how many others were there?" She tried to drink from her emptied glass. "She was a damn whore!"

"My mother was not a whore!" Normalyn defended against the word that slapped at her from the past, when Enid had thrust it at her.

"There were no others." Mayor Hughes studied his engraved initials on his napkin. "For her, there was only one man, and I regret to say it was not me."

Stan? or the unnamed man, Normalyn wondered.

"You *let* me believe!" Clarinda accused her husband from years back. "You let *everyone* believe—!" She tried to adjust to a more wounding truth.

"It was as close as I could come to her, to make the whole damn town believe that we were closer, that we were . . . lovers," he uttered the cherished word. "Oh, I loved her that much. But she didn't love me. She was only gracious enough, kind enough, to allow the rumors. And she gave me a sense of joy I had lost, of being alive, of sharing in her 'many lives.' "

More lives than a cat's! Enid's voice lilted in Normalyn's mind as it probably had for the Mayor.

"Enid gave me what you banished with your meanness and your rotten alcohol, and you did that before she came here, Clarinda," the Mayor said to the woman beside him. "You pushed me away long before that—and killed our unborn children every time. You didn't want my love until it was all gone, and then you wanted only to own it." The Mayor's words were drained of anger. Not even that would unite them after this day.

"Liar." The woman searched for her discarded rose.

"Oh, don't bother fussin' with your goddamn fake rose, Clarinda," the Mayor said. "*Nothing* can disguise the rancid stench of your damn booze."

Clarinda pushed her glass before him. The Mayor ignored it.

Hadn't he seen Enid, too, becoming an alcoholic? Had he understood why? Or had he loved her that much? Had he ever known the angered woman Enid became, the one *she* knew? Normalyn wondered. No. Full of joy and life—that is how he remembered her, still saw her.

Clarinda shoved her glass more insistently before the Mayor. "Call her!"

"You call Lottie yourself," the Mayor said.

"I will not address that creature!" Clarinda refused.

"Then you will do without," the Mayor said.

Clarinda banged her glass on the table. "Lottie! *Lottie!*"

At the kitchen door, her arms crossed tightly, Lottie did not move until the Mayor nodded. Then she placed the bottle before Clarinda—"Here's her *liquor!*"—and left her to pour it.

But the Mayor did—poured it, slowly, carefully.

When he had finished, Clarinda hissed at him: "The thought of having your children disgusted me!"

The Mayor remained impassive, as if he had not heard, or had known all along what Clarinda had confessed.

Normalyn addressed Clarinda: "I'm glad Mayor Hughes loved my mother."

Mayor Hughes held her hands in both of his.

Ted looked at Normalyn with added admiration.

Her eyes closing, Clarinda crumbled in her chair.

The Mayor leaned toward Normalyn as if even now his whispered words might restore his cherished secret: "Honey, you always knew there was nothing to know. For Enid there was only . . . him. And you, honey. She loved you." His hands on hers warmed his words.

Normalyn looked down, to keep from shaking her head in denial.

"Always you and that one man. And that Monroe movie star she talked about all the time, that Norma Jeane." He seemed for long to ponder his own words, what his next ones would be. "Named you after her, honey," he said.

Norma Jeane. Marilyn. Normalyn. The fact, never consciously explored, entered Normalyn's mind with new impact.

That Monroe movie star. . . . The Mayor had spoken the famous name carefully. Ted saw Normalyn react to it the way she had to the reference to the Kennedys, as if in avoidance. Ted remembered his mother's once saying that "the Gibson movie star" was rumored to have been "a friend of that Monroe woman." She had said that after she had read—in a tabloid she tried to conceal but quoted constantly from—that "they" were uncovering "all kinds of evidence that Marilyn Monroe was involved with the Kennedys." But how did any of that connect to Normalyn?

"My mother spoke a lot about you, too, Mayor Hughes," Normalyn told him—and wished she could have said that Enid had loved him. And perhaps she had, just differently from how he had loved her. Normalyn had glimpsed another Enid through the Mayor's eyes, and that had purged some of her anger. "She always said you were a good man," she added.

Mayor Hughes smiled. "Enid." He spoke the name as if that were the only eulogy required for the woman he remembered. He opened his hands, palms up, releasing memories held captive until today. "And now finally she's free of her 'blackness.' And you're free, too, honey," he said.

Free? The thought astonished Normalyn. It meant she had choices! She said experimentally, testing herself, testing Mayor Hughes, "I may go to Galveston, to find out more . . . about myself."

Oh, *would* she go away? Ted wondered.

"You won't find much there that you don't know already, honey," the Mayor told her. "Go where Enid began—to her 'city of lost angels—' "

Guiding her? Whether so or not, he was speaking his words carefully, Normalyn was sure.

"And I believe she knew someone there . . . someone mentioned kindly . . . someone important . . . talked about her, a lot, at the last," the Mayor added slow words, as if he might yet retract them. "Oh, yes, a Miss— . . . Yes, Miss Alberta—" His firmed look assured Normalyn's attention.

Alberta. Miss Alberta. . . . Normalyn tried to remember that name. The Mayor had spoken it precisely.

"Yes, go to her 'city of lost angels'—that's what she called it." He still cupped Normalyn's hands in his. "Go to her 'city of long beaches.' "

"You mean the City of Long Beach, near Los Angeles, sir?" Ted asked courteously—because the Mayor had paused as if to be corrected.

"Do I? Do I now?" The Mayor smiled. He said to Normalyn, "You do whatever you have to do now, honey. But walk softly," he seemed to warn. "Find out who you are." He pulled back. "Well, now, isn't that what *every* young person wants, to find out who they are?" The Mayor seemed to shake away a trance. "That's all I'll tell you, Normalyn, y'heah? Don't ask me more." He tightened his lips, sealing any more words.

To emphasize his loyalty to Enid's secrets and mysteries? Normalyn thought she had detected in the Mayor's voice the weariness of kept promises. That would explain his careful, vague words.

Now only the sounds of dishes being cleared controlled the enormous room. Lottie snapped peremptory orders at the two Mexican men, calling them "boys." Ted watched in confusion.

In the shifting sun, illumined motes of dust floated indifferently. Mayor Hughes stared about his dining room. Beside him, Clarinda did not move, as if the truth she had pursued

had defeated her. The Mayor passed his hand through a
diagonal of sunlight and stared at his fingers to see whether
they had collected dust. "I'm old now," he said aloud. "Steeped
too deep in the past."

Normalyn looked in surprise at the man she had known
throughout the years of her life. Was the sadness there only
now or had she never seen it before? His smile waned, the
flushed face looked desperate, the eyes were . . . lonesome.

"Why, honey," the Mayor sighed to Normalyn, "I just bet
your young friend here considers me an old dinosaur; heard
he even called me that out at that college he goes to, right,
Gonzales?"

"Yes, sir, I did." Ted wondered whether he should apologize, the man seemed so vulnerable now.

"And do you know who's going to render me extinct, honey?"
the Mayor asked Normalyn.

"Who, Mayor Hughes?" Normalyn asked, with kindness.

"Ted Gonzales, that's who." The Mayor smiled at Ted. Then
his face twisted, his voice resurged with strength. "Right, *boy*?"

"Yes!" This time Ted did not say "sir."

"But I warn you, youngman," the Mayor's voice gained
more force. "I'm not extinct yet, not by a damn long shot. I
still have lots and lots of power and I intend to hold on to it."
He folded his embroidered napkin, frowning at one jagged
edge that crushed his initials. He looked at Clarinda, slumped
in her chair. He stood up. "Well, now, wahn't that a sumptuous lunch Lottie fixed us up? That's why we all gathered here
together, in a civilized and orderly way."

Watching him standing, Lottie, carrying a hot pecan pie to
cut at their table, turned on her heels, knowing the lunch had
ended.

The Mayor walked past vacant tables and chairs and out of
the empty dining room.

2

Outside, it was a glorious afternoon under limitless blue.
Along the street, oleanders bloomed, pink, white, purple.

Her back to the Texas Grand Hotel, which seemed like a
surrendered relic now, Normalyn waited on the street. "And
now!" she said aloud.

"And now?" Ted turned her words into a worried question.
She looked so innocent, her cheeks flushed as if this short
journey to the Texas Grand Hotel had given her life.

She and Ted cut across the plaza, along tree-lined streets.

Before the house where Enid would no longer be, ever, Normalyn paused. Then she hurried toward it, almost urgently, to test its power. She felt excited and afraid.

At the top of the three steps outside the house, she turned to face Ted.

"Normalyn!" he said. "I hope you believe now that I would never hurt you, never. And that makes me want to tell you— . . . be able to tell you— . . . that I— . . . that I . . . like . . . you . . . a whole lot."

She saw the broody face which could become boyish in a moment, like now. She smiled. Then immediately she saw the face of the man who had thrown himself over her. She turned away. "You tried to rape me," she said.

He looked quickly at the scar on his fist. "That was someone else," he said. "Not me, *now*. Please look at *me*."

She did. The violent man was gone.

"Maybe I can change your memories," he said.

Could he? She sat down on the steps. He sat down beside her. She did not retreat from him.

"I'll even sing for you!" he said suddenly, determined to bring back her smile. He sang, hummed: " 'Memories, memories, of laughing eyes sweetened through the ages just like wine, sweet memories, memories'." Embarrassment conquered. "When I was a kid, I thought I was Elvis."

She felt a tenderness for this man, this other man, only him, the new Ted, the man she had met yesterday, only yesterday. She removed her glasses. She pushed her hair back, away from her face, welcoming a fresh breeze.

Ted saw her smiling, a beautiful new haunting smile. He touched her hand gently. She did not pull it away. He let his hand rest over hers, holding it.

She raised her head, looking up at the sweep of Texas sky, away.

Following her gaze, Ted said, "You're going away, aren't you, Normalyn?"

"Yes," she said.

3

Ted spent the rest of the day with her. He told her what he had considered telling her the first night he had stayed with her—about the night of guilt, angry remorse. He showed her the scar on his fist. "That—and so much else—is what changed me."

"I believe you," she said, and she did.

As evening approached, she insisted he return to Langsdon. She would no longer be afraid to be alone. She needed to test her resolve against the commanding house.

That night, the haunted voices were hushed, although, once, when she woke, she thought they were conspiring in whispers.

The next day Ted parked again before Normalyn's house. He had borrowed his mother's car so Normalyn would not see the white pickup of their ugly shared memory. She asked him to come with her to tell Mayor Hughes that she was leaving Gibson, that she was going to Los Angeles.

Sitting in the patio of his hotel in the warmth of a Texas spring day, Mayor Hughes sighed. He smiled a crushed smile. "Why, yes, of course, you must go, honey." He would make arrangements for her, himself, draw whatever money she needed, in traveler's checks from his own bank. He would give them to her on the day she left. If necessary, he would make further arrangements with a bank—when she was "settled." "But we'll wait and see about that, honey, won't we now?"

"I might just come out and see you *real* soon." Ted pushed his assertive words against the tone he detected in the Mayor's voice, a tone that prepared for final separation. Right there, Ted wrote down two telephone numbers where Normalyn could reach him—one where he worked, the other at home.

The next day, he drove Normalyn to the bus depot. She had decided to journey the whole distance to Los Angeles by bus, to be aware of the miles and miles she would travel away from Gibson.

In the lobby of the Texas Grand Hotel, where Enid had first appeared in Gibson, the Mayor gave Normalyn an envelope, with the traveler's checks. Then he gave her another envelope—"for later." Feeling apprehensive, Normalyn placed both in her purse, along with the ones Enid had left her, presences guiding her into another world, to other lives. Earlier, she had impulsively wrapped Enid's chipped angel in tissue and packed it in her suitcase, with Enid's makeup box.

"Sometimes I'd imagine that you were mine and Enid's," Mayor Hughes confessed to Normalyn.

She hugged him and kissed him. She wished she could have told him that she had imagined he was her father. But she hadn't, did not even want to think about a father.

Ted stared at the Mayor, so kind, so tyrannical.

When she walked back with Ted to the car, Normalyn knew that Mayor Wendell Hughes—"a good man" she would miss—was already moving into her past in Gibson, among ghosts.

At the station, while Ted checked her bags for her, she opened the second envelope the Mayor had given her. It was a copy of her birth certificate, without the markings Enid had added altering her identity. She felt relief, and breathed the cleansed air of this new season. And she missed Enid very much, so much.

They waited outside in the spring greenness until the bus was ready to depart. Then Ted's hands touched Normalyn's arms. He leaned toward her. She forced herself not to withdraw. Then it was easy not to. When his lips touched hers, she almost returned his kiss—but she heard the echo of a whisper of a turbulent windstorm persisting from the day of violence at the Rio Grande. She withdrew, slowly, trying to keep her hands from turning into fists.

He kissed her hurriedly before she boarded the bus. He called out, "So long, only so long. Remember!"

Normalyn looked out the window as the bus circled the plaza and its unknown "Texas Hero." She was leaving a cemetery of ghosts and memories. Ted Gonzales was the one real person alive for her. She glanced back and saw him standing where he had said "so long" just moments earlier. She pressed her palm against the window, extending his continuing reality in her life.

She looked ahead.

Gibson tumbled behind her, all the familiar sights of her life, the shops, the school, the library, the Texas Grand Hotel, and, in a sheltered cul-de-sac, the house, locked now, in which she had lived for the eighteen years of her life.

In the bus taking her to Enid's 'city of lost angels,' Normalyn thought of the woman, almost ghostly in her radiant blonde beauty, whose photograph remained next to Enid's in the dual frame left behind with the aging lavender flowers on the night table in the faintly glowing starlet's room.

Part Two
California

One

The ocean! "The deep wetness!" Enid had called it. No, it was "the deep wet"—and it was Norma Jeane who had called it that. Normalyn stood on the sand. Before her, the expanse of water fused with the horizon. She looked at her own shadow, so sharp on the sand. Yes, she was here! In California! In Los Angeles! On the beach! At the edge of the ocean, a new world! She had left Gibson!

In the bus she had collected gathering evidence of that fact as she traveled, looking out of different windows, rejecting sleep, wanting to see everything, grasp everything, new sights, new impressions, all hers, only hers: cities, towns, mountains, desert—people everywhere!—and miles and miles of highways between Gibson and the world!

Soon after the Greyhound bus had entered California, and in a small, hot—already hot—city with fat palmtrees everywhere, Normalyn transferred hurriedly to a bus whose designation indicated "BEACH." She would see the ocean first. When it appeared in the distance, she knew that as soon as the bus stopped, she would rush to its edge, claim her bags later. And she did that. She walked in as straight a line as she could from the terminal to the beach.

The sea breeze calmed whispering fears. On the sand, she bunched into herself, feeling her own warmth. She was exhilarated, wide awake, not tired at all. Although she did not remember having fallen asleep in the days of travel, she must have slept, oddly comfortably in the cramped seat—that's how alert she felt.

Under her bare feet now, the water was cool, the sand warm, a welcome dual sensation; she shifted her feet from

65

cool to warm. Did she remember *this* ocean, a house near
it—where Enid had released her to the blonde woman, and
then— . . . ?

Nearby, among scattered others still on the beach, a youngman
and a youngwoman in dancers' tights made slow ritualistic
movements as they faced the advancing mist. Outlining invisible shapes, their hands glided in a dance or a calm exercise.
They seemed to signal in welcome to the setting sun, the
coming night. Normalyn watched them in fascination. Later—
that thought thrilled her: *Later!*—later she would find a place—
. . . A chill crept into the warmth. A gauze of fog swept the
sand. She was all alone in a strange city! She walked away
from the beach.

The city was bathed in unclouded sunlight. She had not
expected that there would be so many sailors on its streets.
Tanned, in shorts, other young people whizzed by on bicycles.
On a strip of green park, Normalyn sat on one of several
benches. She closed her eyes, opened them suddenly to welcome a vision of the new city. Instead, she was terrified.

"Hi, doll, I bet you been looking for me."

"What?"

She faced a sailor. Light hair pushed from under his cocked
white cap. He was young, good-looking—and short.

"You look lost, doll," the sailor said.

"I am not lost!" Suddenly, she realized the enormity of even
routine matters, like picking up her bags— She jumped off
the bench. So many people. Where were they going? She
started to walk away. In which direction?

"My name's Jim, what's yours?" The sailor walked along
with her—a bouncing walk, on the balls of his feet.

She did not answer.

"Where you from, then?"

She answered because she wanted to hear her voice say it: "I
am from Gibson, Texas. I've left it!"

"No shit? I'm from Texarkana—that's in Texas *and* Arkansas!"

The streets were more crowded with sailors as evening neared;
they were everywhere, idling, moving.

"Why are you so scared?" Jim asked her.

"He bothering you, sweetheart?" an ugly, burly sailor asked
her.

"*You* are." Normalyn was much more menaced by *him.*

Jim linked his arm through hers, guiding her past the in-
truding sailor. "I saved you, babe," he whispered.

She pulled away. "Stop calling me those stupid names!" The
burly sailor lingered; so she did not move too far away from

Jim. She had expected the city to be much larger. It all looked different from what she had thought. Rectangular white chrome buildings faced the water beyond rows and rows of tall, slender palmtrees. A long bridge emerged out of clouds. She said to herself, "I thought it would be so much bigger."

Jim said in amazement, "You're the first person who ever thought the Pacific Ocean was small." He felt even shorter.

"Not the ocean," she said. "Los Angeles."

He laughed. "This isn't Los Angeles, doll, it's Long Beach!"

She felt humiliated, stupid, scared. In substitution, she struck at him: "Why do you walk so damn funny?"

"Because I'm fuckin' short. I walk on my damn toes to look taller," he flung back. Actually, he was a proud five feet and six and a half inches.

She was about to apologize, but he had embarrassed her, he was making her feel hopelessly lost. "I *know* this is Long Beach," she asserted. "I came here because I'm looking for . . ." Whom? ". . . someone!" To authenticate her ruse, she opened her purse, pretending to search for a noted name, a phone number. Her fingers touched the envelope that had brought her here—no, not *here*; she was in Long Beach! She shoved the envelope away, closed the purse with a snap. She tried to look perplexed: "I must have forgotten to bring the phone number." Her words sounded ridiculous even to her.

Jim knew she was lost—and frightened. Each time a sailor looked at her, she turned away. God, she was even putting on glasses, but she was squinting as if she couldn't see *with* them! She was strange, yes, but she was pretty, even without enough makeup, even with the glasses. She looked one way, acted another. "You could try looking in the telephone directory. There's one over there." He pointed to a red booth along the grassed partition.

She tossed an angry look at him. He was forcing her to prove she was not lost, pushing her into this ridiculous trap of having to convince him. This silly sailor was chipping away at the fragments of her confidence.

"Aw, cummon, admit it, you're lost."

His further words led her to the telephone booth. It had become essential to find a motive—any motive—for being *here*. She riffled through the pages of a fat directory. He stood beside her, peering over her shoulder. "You're looking under the Z's," he offered.

She yanked off her glasses. She had worn them only briefly during the last days and her vision was blurred with them. She forced an emphatic squint, to emphasize her dedication to finding a name. That she had made a ridiculous mistake menaced her increasingly. New fears joined old ones. She had embarked on a journey whose goal she was not entirely sure of—and even *that* had started wrong! Where would she look? For what? For whom! She ran her fingers down columns of gray print, names, gray names.

"Holland, Holland," she heard herself say aloud. Holland! The name she was pretending to seek had entered her mind from the news clipping Enid had left her. Alberta Holland! Yes, that was the name. The written markings beside it had given importance to the woman who had left facetious word that she was "fleeing incognito to Long Beach" after the death of Marilyn Monroe. She located further evidence that she had not made a stupid mistake. Mayor Hughes had guided her— ambiguously, yes—to Enid's "city of long beaches"—and he had mentioned *one* name then: Alberta! *That* was why she had taken the bus that had probably said "LONG BEACH," not just "BEACH," as she had thought. She felt powerfully triumphant now, vindicated. The very next moment she wasn't sure her rationale for being here was all that logical. But that didn't matter now because she had found a name to pretend to be looking for. "Alberta Holland," she said aloud, defiantly, to Jim. *"That's* who I'm looking for in Long Beach."

"She died years ago," Jim said easily. *"Everyone* knows that."

To keep alarm in abeyance—and it was suddenly as if she had really come here looking for Alberta Holland only to discover that she was dead—Normalyn sought the cleansing ocean. The horizon was almost lost behind gray clouds. She welcomed a ready object for her anger now—the sailor. "How the hell do you know so goddamn much?"

"In the first place, because I ain't stupid—and in the second, because I got an old friend here who knew her because she knows everything about old Hollywood. That's why the damn Dead Movie Stars are always trying to trick her into talking to them. But— "

"The dead what!" He was absurdly trying to scare her now— making her feel even more naive and—

Jim laughed. "The Dead Movie Stars—that's what they call themselves. It's like a secret club, but not too secret now that they're on the news; they say they discover all the secrets of the great old movie stars, even try to be like them. My old friend says they're just malicious weird kids who don't love the stars. That's why she won't talk to them." He added happily: "She told me about Alan Ladd—know who he was?—a movie star so short they had to dig a small trench for regular-size actresses to walk in so he'd look taller—and James Dean was no giant, either."

"As short as you?" Normalyn regretted that instantly—he wasn't *that* short, about her height—but he was bewildering her with his off-hand knowledgeability.

"Shorter!" he shot back. "And *you're* not all that tall." Being short made him brash with girls—and successful. He saw her looking about her, really confused. His voice lost its cockiness: "My old friend's just a batty old woman who takes walks along the beach sometimes; she's full of bullshit about movie stars, but it's good bullshit." He clarified what seemed an odd relationship. "Shit, it gets fuckin' lonesome out here in goddamn Long Beach." He added loyally, "Calling her batty don't mean I don't love her. I do. You wouldn't want to meet her, would you?"

She would return to the bus station! Claim her bags! Fly back on the next plane to—! Return to—! Go back to—! "Yes!" she said quickly to Jim.

"You mean it?" He looked at her in disbelief. But quickly he calculated: A visit with his old friend was always good for a long hour of exciting movie-star bullshit—and he could easily extend it into more. That would allow him time to try to convince this girl that the last bus to Los Angeles had left for the night, and then maybe, just maybe, she'd want to stay over. Maybe with him!

Swiftly he guided Normalyn along a block of scrambled colors—video arcades, surplus stores—sailors everywhere.

They turned into a side street. Normalyn prepared herself to run and scream if he so much as— Suddenly there was a gathering of stately Victorian houses, a change so abrupt that Normalyn looked back at the city, the clouding ocean, to reorient herself.

She and the sailor stood before a house that was aging gracefully, flowers and verdure allowed to grow freely in a garden.

Then Normalyn saw a tree to one side of the house, a tree with sparse feathery leaves and many tiny blossoms—tinted mist—on delicate limbs of mottled white. Some of the blossoms had fallen in careless filigree like—

Lavender snow.

The words, written in Enid's child's-scrawl in her sparse notes, entered Normalyn's mind at the sight of the haunting tree. Yes, and its delicate blossoms were the ones rendered artificially and kept beside the chipped angel on Enid's night table until she died.

Jim rang the bell of the house. "Have to know your name so I can introduce you."

"Normalyn." Even her name sounded as if it belonged to someone else, now that she had left Gibson.

"Damn!" Jim studied her. "Ever since I saw you, I been thinkin' who you resemble. My friend has pictures of her even before she became a big movie star. That's who you look like, yeah, you look like—"

Normalyn covered her ears. She saw Jim's lips begin to form a name, then stop abruptly in response to her sudden rejecting reaction.

Two

"Well, aren't you the pretty thing!" The old woman stood at
the ornate door, which needed oiling. Before Normalyn recoiled from the accusing word "pretty," she saw a woman in
her sixties, no, her seventies . . . older? Her hair was a network of red-dyed swirls. Her cheeks were shaded in an attempt to create highlights on her plump face. Thick glasses
enlarged giant artificial eyelashes. She was short, with an ample body. Yet she wore a flowing dress elegantly; it was the
color of a dark pearl. She scrutinized Normalyn. "Her hair
could stand a bit more curl," she commented aloud to herself,
then resumed addressing Normalyn: "And some more makeup,
dearheart." She puffed out from a small cigarillo, carefully
away from Normalyn; a few measured puffs only, before she
flicked off its ashes and put it out.

"Hi, doll!" Jim removed his cap and bowed in an exaggerated flourish before the old woman.

"Howya been, Jim? Glad ya brought someone to meet a fat
old woman."

She used a special tone with him, interjecting a gentle parody of his into her own, which was cultured despite its marked
casualness; that mutual tone affirmed their closeness, Normalyn
recognized and felt cold and alone standing at the door of a
stranger's house in Long Beach with the sun hardly smearing
the day.

"Come in, come in," the woman invited. She said to the
misting evening, "You're starting to get chilly early tonight,"

71

and then to them, "I was having a cup of chamomile tea. Now I can share it."

Normalyn nodded at the prospect. She only considered requesting iced tea. Any anticipation that she might learn something about Alberta Holland from this woman had vanished when she heard her vague mumblings. She suspected Jim had lied to her about this odd friend in order to bring her here. She was too tired to care.

"If you got a beer—" Jim started.

"Keep one for ya." The woman's dress sighed as she led them into the house. She carried her weight as effortlessly as a light balloon. "There aren't too many fat old women who have a good-looking sailor calling."

"If that's what you are—and I ain't agreein'—then you're the sexiest fat old woman God ever made." He parodied her with affection.

She chastised him with obvious pleasure: "Can't resist a pretty girl, can you?"

In the large living room there was a disordered tidiness. Solidly comfortable furniture nestled in no discernible order. Everything was clean. Like the garden, the interior of the house had been allowed to choose its own shape. On top of a grand piano graced with a colorful Spanish mantilla splotched with embroidered flowers, and on top of shelves crammed with books, and on tables, on walls were framed silver and black photographs of the great movie stars of a Hollywood gone.

And!—Normalyn stared at it in disbelief—there was an autographed picture of Jesus, smiling widely! The curious reality of this strange pleasant old woman and her house was exactly what Normalyn needed to provide respite from the assault created earlier by the questioning of this sailor, who was, she had seen in disguised glances, very cute.

Jim introduced her to the old woman: "I want you to meet my new friend. Her name is Normalyn. . . . Normalyn, I want you to meet my old friend, Miss Bertha."

Miss Bertha! Was Jim extending her ruse of earlier when she had told him she was looking for "Miss Alberta"? The old woman did not react in contradiction of the name. Besides, she had told him she was looking for "Alberta Holland." It was Mayor Hughes who had mentioned "Miss Alberta" as someone important at the last of Enid's life. Mayor Hughes *had* guided her here! Then was it possible that this woman could be—? No, Jim had asserted "everyone" knew Alberta Holland was dead and that his friend had known the powerful woman. . . . Her confusions earlier, her eagerness to find a reason for being in Long Beach instead of Los Angeles— *that* was why she was here with a sailor she had just met and in the home of a kind, slightly daffy old woman eager to be heard.

Miss Bertha's look behind the glasses had steadied on Normalyn. She separated the name: "Norma . . . lyn. What a beautiful name." Her pudgy hand, with one enormous green-stoned ring—certainly not an emerald—reached out to touch the youngwoman. Instead, she took a tiny step back. A frown prepared to cloud her forehead. A note of admonishment entered her voice: "Now, if you're one of those goddamned—!"

Jim understood: "I guarantee ya, she ain't a candidate for the Dead Movie Stars. She just came in from *Texas*—on the *bus!*"

If Normalyn had been less tired, she might have elbowed him for that.

Miss Bertha still considered, her arms crossed as if she were not entirely convinced. She sighed. "Can't blame a soul for being suspicious about that damn cult-club now that they're getting all that media attention promising to reveal scandal." Her dyed curls shook. "Nasty young people saying they're restoring glamour to Hollywood—not that it couldn't stand some." She said indignantly to Normalyn, "Dearheart, can you believe one of them burst in on me through that very window, kept shouting questions at me about the tragic death of Verna La Maye!"

"Verna La Maye was strangled with her own silk stocking!" Jim filled in for Normalyn about one of Miss Bertha's favorite stars. Then he apologized to the old woman, "I ain't gloatin', just tellin'."

"I know you aren't—ain't," Miss Bertha absolved him. She cleared a sofa for them. Jim sat close to Normalyn. Normalyn edged away.

Miss Bertha ambled over to a small table on which a carefully arranged silver tea service waited. She located herself before it on a soft chair, facing Normalyn and Jim; her tiny feet barely touched the rug. Three ordinary cats with streaks and spots waltzed about the woman's feet. Miss Bertha served Normalyn's tea, and her own, with grand propriety as cool ocean air lazed in through open windows.

Jim explained to Normalyn: "Those creepy Dead Movie Stars started a rumor that Miss Bertha is Alberta Holland— because she knows so much about her, and about all the movie stars."

"Just read it in all those books. Anyone can," Miss Bertha dismissed easily. She sipped, delighting in her tea. "*Now* I'll get something for you, sailor. She glided chubbily through the room, muttering softly in constant dialogue with herself, adjusting a vase here, blowing at dust where there was none. "Tidy up, tidy up!" she instructed herself. Here and there she repositioned a photograph for greater advantage. Her hand glided over gorgeous faces frozen in silvery black on the piano. "Hedy Lamarr, rare as a black orchid . . . Veronica Lake . . . Errol Flynn," she sighed the names. "Verna La Maye, Robert Taylor, Lana Turner, Norma Desmond, Tyrone Power." She addressed them as if they had gathered to hear her advice: "You mistook brief adulation for love, you thought you were invulnerable—so easily destroyed." She shook her head in dismay: "So long ago, another world."

She moved on as if she had only thought the words she had spoken. In the dining room, she paused. When Normalyn was looking at her, her attention drawn by the woman's stilled footfalls, Miss Bertha turned on a light under a large dramatic photograph on the wall. It illumined a silver form surrounded by black enclosed in a silver-chrome frame.

Normalyn had seen that picture before! No, it just reminded her of . . . a darkened shoreline, the blonde woman, a black horizon. The woman had lain on a darkness like that, before Enid reappeared. . . . Within this ordinary house, a strangeness stirred again for Normalyn. She felt Jim's eyes on her. "Why are you looking at me like that?"

"Cause I like lookin' at pretty women," Jim began to prop his invitation.

At those words—which still surprised her—Normalyn felt the familiar clash of reactions, which now included pleasure.

Miss Bertha returned with a frothing beer in a graceful champagne glass for Jim. She arranged her body, searching tiny comforts, on her chair. Tinkling teacups and spoons filled the silence.

Now why the hell wasn't Miss Bertha rattling out one of her movie-star stories? Jim needed time to make his own story hold, about no more buses to Los Angeles. This silence and Miss Bertha's stares would make Normalyn nervous; she was already fidgeting with her glasses, opening and closing her purse as if looking for something. "Normalyn came to Long Beach looking for Alberta Holland." Jim attempted to budge the peculiar moments.

"For Alberta Holland?" Miss Bertha propped the sculpted red mass of hair more firmly. "Why, whatever for, dearheart?"

She poured more tea into the dainty china cups. "That woman wouldn't have been found *dead* in Long Beach, for all her vaunted socialist beliefs!" She chuckled. "But then she *is* dead— died in Switzerland many years ago."

"Jim told me you knew her." Normalyn said that only to hear her deny it.

Miss Bertha said easily, "Everyone in old Hollywood knew about Holland. She was famous. Some said infamous. Yes, I admired Alberta Holland, long ago." Her voice was muted, as if she were about to confer with herself about that time. Instead, she said spiritedly to Normalyn, "Why sometimes, dearheart, I even pretend that I give advice to the great stars, just like she did, counseled the stars. But *I* save them from disaster, always."

Normalyn looked at her with new interest.

"Can't blame me if I make up a story or two now and again, dearheart," she answered Normalyn's look. "When you're old, there's not much left, except remembering—and imagining." She looked at the window, dark now. "Life is so short and a day is so long. Why, when you're old, every morning's like being born tired."

"You ain't old," Jim insisted.

"Did I say that aloud?" Miss Bertha questioned. "Oh, Lord, I meant to *think* it."

And *still* more silence! Normalyn would rush out in a min- ute, odd as she was and Miss Bertha acting stranger than ever. Jim encouraged: "Why don't you ask Miss Bertha for advice, Normalyn?" He immediately regretted his desperate plunge; Normalyn would think he was poking fun at her being lost in Long Beach, a risky subject. "Miss Bertha knows about a lot of things," he tried to amend, and it was true that Miss Bertha's rambling could make sudden sense.

"I don't need advice." Normalyn did not intend to be rude to this likable woman, just cool to Jim's suggestion.

Miss Bertha sniffed her delicate tea. "But she *does* look a little sad, a little scared," she commented to herself.

"You said that aloud," Jim said nervously.

"I did not!" Miss Bertha denied. A curl loosed itself over her forehead. She shifted a pin from the back to clutch the vagrant strand. "Jean Harlow had a hell of a time keeping *her* waves in place," she defended her hairdo. She addressed Normalyn: "Everyone needs advice, now and then, dearheart." For moments she discussed that in soft murmurs with herself. "Everyone from Socrates to Einstein!" she agreed emphatically with her own conclusion. "Why, *I* could have stood some good advice myself." A frown emphasized a troubled thought, a distant conflict. She cleared it away: "Going to have to go pee in a moment." She seemed startled. "Did I say that or just think it?"

"*Thought* it," Jim asserted.

"I suppose I'm getting batty." Miss Bertha laughed. Then her laughter stopped. Her words were precise: "I'm an old woman stumbling to death as gracefully as I am still able."

"You ain't old, I told you!" Jim insisted. Yet he was startled at how old she looked when she said that, sitting there, her memories all in pieces. Always alone except when he came by—not as often as he should—as if she were hiding from life. She hardly even took walks along the beach any more on warm days. "We all gotta die sometime," Jim muttered, to link with her solemn mood.

That yanked Miss Bertha out of her mood. "At your age, you never die."

"James Dean did, you told me," Jim said.

"But Alan Ladd lived on to grow an inch or two," she caught him. "And he found Veronica Lake, tiniest creature God ever made, hair longer than she was." The enlarged eyes stared at Normalyn and Jim. Her voice was bruised with sudden emotion: "Oh, isn't life a sadness?" Her round cheeks glazed with colored tears.

"Miss Bertha!" Normalyn reached out with concern.

"She's gonna cry again," Jim resigned himself. He had met her on the beach on a cloudy day. She was sitting in one of the last pockets of warmth, sobbing aloud. He asked her if he could help, and they became friends, a friendship sealed when she told him about Alan Ladd. Now he was used to her sudden bouts of crying.

In a deluge of tears, Miss Bertha lamented between incoherent sobs: ". . . the homeless sleeping on streets, children stooped in the fields, black people chained to concrete, the young prepared for war . . . poverty, hunger . . . injustice!" She mopped her face with a decorated handkerchief. "Was the world ever kinder or did the shit just gang up?" She retouched the makeup on her face. "There." The sobbing ended. She readjusted her body, with great attention. She pushed up with her elbows. "Now you two excuse me for a while. I love that chamomile tea, but it makes me pee up a storm." Two cats hopped into the relinquished warmth of her chair.

Jim let his hand slip over Normalyn's shoulder. To test the sudden warm sensation, she allowed it before she eased away.

Returning, Miss Bertha tousled Jim's wayward hair. Jim hugged her.

Normalyn turned away from their affection, close mother and son. Her eyes glided to the lighted photograph in the dining room. The silver smear was an extravagant body! Luminous flesh reclining on a dark background.

"That's Marilyn Monroe, dearheart; but of course you knew that." Miss Bertha was sitting down again. Fussy hands tested the careful pile of hair. "It's an original lithograph, numbered, real precious, my pride and joy." She added aloud, to herself, "And, sometimes, my deepest sorrow."

Normalyn turned away from the framed lithograph, avoiding stirred memories.

Miss Bertha lighted a fresh scented cigarillo. Sweet smoke wafted through the room. "I allow myself exactly three puffs," she explained, and snuffed it out. Then her eyes returned to the commanding portrait. "That's how she saw herself," Miss Bertha said, "enclosed by blackness, the darkness, the madness she said hopped from her grandmother to her mother. She thought it had already grabbed her and that it might claim the daughter she wanted most in the world. That's why Marilyn Monroe turned to me when she was pregnant—for advice, one misty afternoon."

2

Then she was Alberta Holland! "She came to you for advice?" Normalyn sipped her spice tea, not reacting, in control.

"I *imagine* she did," Miss Bertha said. "Lord, didn't I tell you that, dearheart—that I imagined the stars came to me for advice?"

"She did tell you that for a fact, Normalyn." Jim verified that Miss Bertha had spoken that aloud.

Just an old woman making up stories. Normalyn was glad she hadn't allowed herself to react in surprise at the woman's words.

"You know a lot about Marilyn Monroe, Miss Bertha." Jim invited a good story—and strategic time for his plans later.

"And it's a glorious story, a sad story," Miss Bertha responded. "Oh, there was a reason for all that sorrow. She had the craziest mother God ever made—Gladys. And her grandmother?—she tried to strangle Marilyn when she was just a child; the police carried the woman away screaming. Gladys was in and out of institutions, had bouts of *sanity,* led the women working under her at the RKO labs to safety when fire broke out. Dearheart"—she directed her story at Normalyn—"she would escape out of institutions to take Norma Jeane out of the orphanage for joyful and sad afternoons." Miss Bertha shook her head in wonder at such sorrow dotted with happiness. "Strangest woman God ever allowed; she telephoned Marilyn from an institution, begging her to get her out—and when she did, she called the asylum to take her back." Miss Bertha extended compassion: "Poor sad creature herself, abandoned pregnant by a man who fled to San Francisco on a motorcycle and never came back—"

That was Enid's life! Normalyn's cup of tea fell to the soft carpet, only spilling, not breaking. Instantly frantic, she dabbed with her hands at the floor. Jim sopped with his towel.

"Now, you two just sit down and leave the stain be. It'll just give the rug a bolder tone." Miss Bertha affirmed.

Normalyn was glad she had spilled the tea, perhaps on purpose. For moments that became the immediate source of her panic. It had stopped the assaulting recitation—but not this new question: *Who had borrowed from whom?* . . . Sitting on the sofa again, Normalyn let her eyes wander toward an open window. Across the withering light framed there, a branch of the tree she had noticed earlier dipped down, a few faint blossoms on the slender limb.

"It's a jacaranda tree." Miss Bertha traced Normalyn's gaze. "It blooms only briefly, the blossoms die in spring. Someone, long ago—a special woman who knew how fragile life can be—made perfect artificial flowers of them, lavender bouquets, to preserve what dies so soon in life. I have one I cherish, next to the lithograph of Marilyn."

Normalyn saw only the vaguest outline within subdued light, but her memory provided details from Enid's own cherished cluster of the same delicate flowers.

"Have you seen them in the daylight, dearheart?"

Normalyn shook her head. But she had.

"When their blossoms fall to the ground," Miss Bertha breathed, "it's just like lavender snow."

Sitting there so peacefully, this benign woman had recited details that Enid had told—through anger, laughter, pain—as her own. Now the woman was borrowing from words Enid had left her. "Where did you hear it called that?"

"Marilyn Monroe called it lavender snow." Miss Bertha looked about as if to locate the origin of her recollection in the many books about the room.

"She's a real fan," Jim said proudly.

"A *real* fan," Miss Bertha emphasized. Now her voice rose in passionate accusation as suddenly as her mellow sorrow had wafted through the room: "Not like those vulturous Dead Movie Stars—the same breed who called themselves fans and couldn't wait for Valentino to die so they could mourn before the cameras, the same who shouted at Norma Desmond's trial that she should have *stayed* dead, the same who went to see only if Judy could still perform—and she always did!—the same who sent Marlene into hiding so they couldn't gloat at her living ghost!" Her voice had gathered more anger: "And think what his fans still do to *him*!" She pointed to the picture of the smiling Jesus. "Still throwing stones at him and calling them prayers! . . . You're right, dearheart, it *is* autographed," she ended her enraged asseveration.

"It's an *actor*," Jim laughed. Surreptitiously he consulted his watch. Soon—

"I know it's an actor!" Normalyn felt foolish.

"I told the actor who played him that he was much handsomer than Jesus, and *that* gave him a big smile, and it got me an autographed Jesus." Then Miss Bertha assured herself aloud, "He *must* have smiled at least once."

"Are the others autographed? May I look?" Before Miss Bertha could answer, Normalyn walked to the photographs on the piano. She read inscriptions. *"To Bee. Thank you. Love. Ingrid." "For so much! Rita. XXX." "Never without you. Tyrone."* Under the picture of the smiling Jesus: *"You and me, babe. Spread the word! J.C." "To you! Harlow!"*

"I signed them all," Miss Bertha said.

"Did you *mean* to say that aloud, Miss Bertha?" Jim asked. She had never told him that.

Miss Bertha considered it. "Yes," she concluded tentatively.

Evening was clutched by shadows now. Miss Bertha roamed about, lighting soft lamps. The lithograph in the dining room swam in its separate darkness. Miss Bertha located herself comfortably in her soft chair again.

"How do you pretend to be Alberta Holland, when you imagine you gave advice to the movie stars?" Normalyn reached for more sugar for her freshened tea—calmly.

"I have to confess I cheat sometimes. I give advice that changes what really happened, when that was tragic or sad."

She *had* done that with him once, Jim remembered. In her version, Verna La Maye recovered to strangle her assailant.

"Guidance carries great responsibility, dearheart, not carelessly given," Miss Bertha said seriously. She shook her head. "They say that at the last Alberta Holland gave disastrous advice." She leaned conspiratorially toward Normalyn. "Would you like me to show you how I pretend I counseled the stars?" She was immediately enthusiastic. "I start by choosing a star. You want to choose?"

Normalyn shook her head, suddenly apprehensive.

"Then *I'll* choose. Let's see . . . I'll choose . . . Her eyes scanned the room. "*Her!*" Miss Bertha pointed to the lithograph in the adjoining room.

"Marilyn Monroe." Normalyn surprised herself when she spoke the name aloud. She could not remember ever before having pronounced it. It had belonged only to Enid until her death.

"We have to *see* her clearly first," Miss Bertha said. "She was . . ." She closed her eyes, as if the image that had entered her mind required special words, prepared with care: "Marilyn Monroe!" She held the name for seconds. "She carried magic as if it were something only in her hands, given *only* to her. She couldn't let go of it, and that might have turned into a curse. People always remember her in sequins—because she could glow even in shadows. Other stars needed special lights. Not Marilyn. She had her own radiance. No one had it like her before, no one will ever have it again." She opened her eyes. "That is how she *looked.* What she had inside was lots of hurt, from the years of her terrible childhood, drifting unwanted from home to home. Dearheart, she carried all that in her soul like an unhealed stab. Why, she couldn't take the painful knife out because she would bleed to death. That's what her beauty was always trying to soothe."

Normalyn looked like that, Jim thought, pretty *and* sad at the same time, especially as she had listened to Miss Bertha tell her about the movie star; she sat there so silently.

"Now we're ready to pretend!" Miss Bertha said, again spiritedly. "We'll imagine that Marilyn turned to me for advice, yes, on a hazy afternoon. Now *you* offer something, Normalyn." She waited, waited longer. When Normalyn did not speak, Miss Bertha sat back, hands crossed, lips closed firmly.

Enid's voice reminded Normalyn: "I was there at every crisis!"

"She was with a beautiful dark-haired woman, a natural beauty." Normalyn offered only that, to see how much the woman would pretend—and out of her own loyalty to Enid.

"Yes! I remember," Miss Bertha greeted eagerly. "How did you know, dearheart? Now we'll just say I met Marilyn at a charity—there were many of those—and let's say it was a benefit for unwanted children—there are many, many of those and she cared for them, she was one."

And so was Enid, Normalyn had to resist saying aloud; she was determined to provide nothing more to Miss Bertha's charade.

"Would you like to give a name to Marilyn's friend, dearheart?" Miss Bertha prodded. "We were going to pretend together," she reminded.

"*You* tell me." Normalyn did not disguise the testiness in her voice. She was ready to end this, annoyed she had invited it, pulled in only because she was tired, hungry, didn't want to have to decide anything yet.

"Why"—Miss Bertha held her hands as if she were preparing to reveal the answer to a difficult riddle—"at the charity with Marilyn was . . . Joan Crawford!" She seemed to delight in the elaborate introduction.

Normalyn was not sure why she breathed in relief—she had felt momentary alarm. But the old woman had merely doubled her imagined importance. Released from the attention she had been lulled into momentarily—Miss Bertha's curious reality—Normalyn could no longer avoid *real* decisions she would have to make: What would she do tonight? It was already tonight! Would her luggage have gone into Los Angeles? Would she have to stay in Long Beach overnight? Where! What would she do tomorrow? The next day! And—

Click!

Miss Bertha held a cigarette lighter. But there was no cigarillo in her mouth. *Click!* She snapped it again.

Enid's signal! *This woman was Alberta Holland!* Normalyn was sure at that moment. She was testing her, asserting she, Normalyn, was whom she had known she was when she first came in with Jim.

Click! *Click!* "When I *first* met Marilyn, she was with Crawford," Miss Bertha said slowly. "But when she came to me for crucial advice, she was with another woman, and they came because there was grave danger." *Click!*

She had intimated the turbulence Enid had evoked only at the last of her life! "The woman's name was Enid Morgan!" Normalyn responded to the eerie summons. Immediately, she felt trapped, angered.

"Oh, lord, can you believe I've been trying to light a damn cigarillo without putting it in my mouth? Thank heaven this old lighter doesn't work or I would've—" The flame flicked. She lit the cigarillo, took only three puffs. "Now, dearheart,"

Miss Bertha said, "let's do pretend, together, like we started to."

Normalyn refused to agree.

"Yeah!" Jim agreed for her. One of Miss Bertha's good stories would allow him just enough time for his own, about the buses.

"Well, then, Normalyn." Miss Bertha nestled into her chair. "I'll start, and then maybe you'll want to join along the way. Yes, *I'll* start, with a time long past . . . so well remembered . . . when I first saw her—"

Three

—in her own aura, a key light she was born with, Marilyn Monroe stood glowing in a white dress on a greenish lawn under an insignificant sun. Next to her was Joan Crawford; at the time she was assuming to be the younger star's experienced mentor.

Miss Bertha waited for a moment in the distance, so that she might later repaint in her mind the first time she had seen the blonde movie star in person. Then she walked up to her and introduced herself, only nodding at Crawford, whom she disliked but respected as an actress. Marilyn said politely, "And *I'm* Marilyn Monroe, Miss Bertha."

"Everyone knows who you are," Miss Bertha said.

"But *you're* really famous," Marilyn Monroe told her.

A part of the great star would remain awed child, Miss Bertha knew.

"Famous!" sneered Joan Crawford. "Infamous! A left winger. Maybe a communist." She did not bother to whisper.

"But they're for the people, aren't they?" Marilyn asked sincerely.

Miss Bertha could have hugged her. But she had already noticed Marilyn's guarded frailty, a certain caution as if she thought she could be hurt by everyone, anyone. For a second before she had time to prepare the extravagant smile, she winced when people approached her.

Joan stalked away, to talk to Hedda Hopper, who was showing off a hat with a little live bird in a cage. "Like Marie Antoinette," she kept saying. It was one of those affairs that everyone in Hollywood attends. On a veranda, Jane Russell waved at Miss Bertha and Marilyn, and blew them a kiss. With

83

extreme formality Marlon Brando was introducing everyone
to Movita, his new wife. John Derek at her side, Louella
Parsons sat like a toad on a peacock chair. Everyone ignored
Eve Harrington and her companion, Phoebe.

Miss Bertha and Marilyn chatted amicably.

"Did you really tell the Un-American Committee to go fuck?"
Marilyn asked that suddenly with delicious glee. She had used
her breathy tone, making the harsh word sound like lovemaking.

"Yes." Miss Bertha was flattered the young star knew so
much about her.

Marilyn leaned over to her. "Maybe you shouldn't have
wished them anything *that* good!"

Miss Bertha was impressed by her wit—and her keen intelligence. She told the young actress that.

"But don't tell anybody, not yet." Marilyn cautioned, indicating a knowledgability of the odd world of Hollywood a
beautiful woman had to move in. "Then I'll spring it on them
and catch them off guard." Suddenly, Marilyn Monroe tilted
her head, parted her lips, leaned slightly on one hip, inhaled,
then made the softest murmuring of sensual laughter—and
became the center of attention, as if she had turned a light on
inside herself. Everyone, everyone looked at her in awe. Miss
Bertha was not sure whether everyone gasped or whether it
was only she, hearing herself.

Miss Bertha gave Marilyn her card—and left the charity
event. She was not even aware that Lauren Bacall had just
kissed her on the cheek. She did not want anything to impinge
on her memory of the beautiful woman. She hoped that Marilyn would turn to her for advice soon because there were
rumors that "ruinous revelations" from the star's past were
about to be made by none other than the deadly columnist
Mildred Meadows—despised by Miss Bertha.

In the thirties, the forties, and into the sixties, counseling was
an established profession in Hollywood. Stars who didn't rush
off to their astrologers, fortune tellers, or spiritual guides turned
to Miss Bertha, respected by the intelligent in Hollywood. She
never pretended to be other than a counselor, in the tradition
of Socrates.

When she began in the business, a young woman herself,
she warned Harlow about her mother. Harlow did not listen.
Claiming God would heal her daughter from uremic poison,
the mother allowed her to die. Norma Desmond's attorney
turned to Miss Bertha to suggest how best to sway the jury in
favor of a verdict of justifiable homicide. Miss Bertha told
him, "Be respectful of her, treat her like a human being."

When Mildred Meadows—who was already emerging as arch-fiend for Miss Bertha—led the howls against "the adulterous Ingrid Bergman," Miss Bertha, whom the star went to consult one midnight, told her to face *them* down, expose *their* hypocri-sies: "Never flee!" But Ingrid was tired. She left the country in disgust.

In the fifties, there developed a terrible time in Hollywood. Political witch-hunts destroyed dedicated people, overnight. A reactionary madness swept the country, and with it came a tidal wave of false "morality." Terror, suspicion, secret inves-tigations, smashed lives, forced exile. Scandal magazines assas-sinated the stars monthly. Miss Bertha cried into morning with Liz Scott, slaughtered by false innuendoes. She accompanied Robert Mitchum when he turned himself in to jail.

Those turbulent times were peaking when the venomous Mildred Meadows began releasing a series of attacks on Mari-lyn Monroe. In her vile column she gasped that a few years earlier "the blonde waif" had posed for "pornographic pic-tures." Soon after, she announced, "with a mother's broken heart," that Marilyn's own mother, claimed to be dead, was alive in a state institution—"ignored, unloved, alone, shunned, a pauper while the 'blonde' starlet decorates herself in costly glitter."

Boldly, Miss Bertha turned for assistance to a trusted friend, "a trusted human being"—a Spanish woman of aristocracy who as a girl fought with the gypsies against the dictatorship of Franco. It was believed by some that she was the model for Maria in Hemingway's *For Whom the Bell Tolls*. If so, Miss Bertha claimed, the bullish author had taken giant liberties. The fact that Miss Bertha had sheltered this woman in exile became a factor against her when she was summoned before the House Committee on Un-American Activities. Following Miss Bertha's instructions—that there must be no bruiting of conspiracy—the Spanish woman pretended to run into Mari-lyn at a restaurant where the star ate in disguise. She gave her a note from Miss Bertha: "I have learned that the studios have decided to abandon you. Save yourself, admit everything, don't flee like Ingrid. Fight them!"

Marilyn met secretly with Miss Bertha. To survive the scan-dals, Marilyn would have to answer the accusations. Miss Ber-tha asked her all the expected harsh questions and they devised answers. She emphasized this: "Seem to flatter Mildred Mead-ows while slaughtering her."

Marilyn did. She admitted posing in the nude—for fifty dollars, because she was desperate for money. "How can anyone think of the body as pornographic?" she asked gathered reporters. "Do *you?*" She added, "I'm sure Mrs. Meadows doesn't think so either, since she is well known as a collector of classical statuary. . . ." She thanked Meadows graciously for giving her "the best news possible," that her mother was still alive. As a child, she explained, she had been placed in many homes by her beloved mother, separated from her for anxious years, to the point that she'd become confused as to who of all the women who became her guardians was her real mother. Now that Mildred Meadows had been so helpful, she would care for her mother—and she had already transferred her to an expensive private home, which she hoped Mrs. Meadows would visit "on one of her many excursions of charity." Amid sympathy and congratulations, Marilyn triumphed over the assaults. The studios re-embraced her. Mildred Meadows was hospitalized "for a brief rest."

Years later, Miss Bertha was having afternoon tea when the bell rang in her Brentwood home.

Marilyn Monroe stood at the door. Wearing a gray dress, dark glasses, a concealing scarf, she still ruled the spring afternoon. There was another woman with her. Yes, she was beautiful, too, in a natural way. She wore a dramatic hat that slashed a diagonal across her face; only her long reddened lips were stark. Miss Bertha let the two in quickly.

Marilyn sat nervously in the high-backed chair Miss Bertha offered her. The other woman stood by the window, looking out as if to scrutinize the street for intrusive presences.

From her earlier modeling days Marilyn had acquired a look that made her appear to be simultaneously a lost girl and a seductive woman. She had a sexual pout that was also a sad smile. Today she looked only like the lost child.

Miss Bertha offered the two women a cup of her spiced tea. Marilyn said yes, the other woman requested iced tea—odd, because it was a cool day. Marilyn sniffed the delicate scent of the tea. "This is lovely," she said.

Miss Bertha was amazed that she could say something so ordinary and make it sound as if she were caressing the words.

Then Marilyn went on to talk about fame: "How strange! People write things about me that never happened! . . . Yesterday, someone came right up to me and said, 'Who the hell do you think you are? Marilyn Monroe?' . . . And somebody who asked me to autograph a photograph of myself told me that's all I am now, a photograph! . . . Is the real me gone?" She looked sincerely bewildered.

Click! The woman with her snapped the lighter as if in

answer, a reminder. It was a gold lighter—no, silver, Miss Bertha noticed, momentarily confused only because it had caught a lost ray of sunlight and turned gold for that second. Oh, yes, this woman was very beautiful, too.

Miss Bertha knew Marilyn had been avoiding the reason for their visit, but she offered her observation on what the star had just told her about the strangeness of her fame: "That's because you're a legend, and legends are a hundred truths and a thousand fantasies."

"You're supposed to be *dead* before you're a legend," Marilyn said honestly.

"But some people are so astonishing they become legends before their very own eyes. That means you'll live forever," she tried to cheer the star.

"No!" Marilyn laughed—but she shuddered. "That's too long." She allowed only a breath of laughter. "And yet there's so much I'll never do."

"Like what, dearheart?"

"Oh, things, you know—like living in the White House," Marilyn said.

At the time, Miss Bertha thought that was just the extended daydream of an unwanted child. Yet she had said it softly, sadly.

Marilyn was looking toward the window. She said jubilantly, like an excited girl, "So many jacaranda trees on this street. When their petals fall, it's like—" With a smile, she waited for the other woman to finish.

"—like lavender snow," Enid smiled back.

The two beautiful women laughed, like schoolgirls involved in a private game, theirs only. It was an astonishing moment. A delicate shared memory had been able to pull them out of the darkening mood. The two were opposites—dark, blonde—but alike in an eerie way, in moments seeming to imitate each other.

Click! Enid flicked her lighter, flameless, ending the carefree interlude.

"Please help me, Miss Bertha, I'm pregnant," Marilyn pleaded suddenly.

"Do you want the child?" Miss Bertha had heard about several abortions.

"More than anything in my life. Finally. Yes!" Marilyn said.

"Then you must have your child." Miss Bertha did not hesitate.

Marilyn conveyed her terrible fears about childbirth. She had had miscarriages—yes, abortions—but she was willing now to do anything, stay in bed the whole length of that time, anything, anything! There was another powerful fear, though, of what she called "the darkness, the blackness"—the insanity that ran in her family. . . . Marilyn held out her hands, palms out, as if to show she already held the legacy.

At the same moment, Enid looked down into her own hands.

Miss Bertha counseled with conviction: "Have your child, dearheart. You want it too much to lose it. And the madness is too tired; it's gone through too many people, too many lives—it's exhausted. You'll be a wonderful mother because you've had too much pain to pass it on." She held Marilyn's hand, knowing she would not wince at the touch now. "Dearheart, leave your past behind; live in the present and for the future. Remember: You are now Marilyn Monroe, not an unwanted child anymore, not Norma Jeane—"

Click! Enid's lighter snapped, followed by a fusillade of angered clicks. At last the flame flicked. It cast a mesmerizing key light on Enid. After held moments, she spoke for the first time: *"Please* tell her," she urged Marilyn, with quiet kindness.

Rushing words, stuttering the way she did all her life during turmoil, Marilyn Monroe told Miss Bertha that there were more dangers than those of miscarriage, the possible legacy of madness. There were threats that included blackmail and—

As she heard the movie star's frantic words, Miss Bertha knew instantly that the birth of this child would involve horrifying clashes of great power. For the child to be born, there must be intrigue, deception, terrible dangers because of the man involved, the father.

Four

"None of that ever happened!" Normalyn stood up. Coldness pierced a rush of angered heat.

"But of course it didn't. We were imagining," Miss Bertha reminded her. She reached for a dead cigarillo and tried to force new life into it; she set it aside on the ashtray beside her. "We knew that from the start, dearheart."

Forcing instant composure at the woman's words, Normalyn sat back down and brought an empty cup of tea to her lips.

"Miss Bertha, you're not going to stop the story there, are you?" Jim asked anxiously.

"Yes—and I intended to all along," Miss Bertha asserted. Then she said to Normalyn, "Sometimes you have to rehearse with lies to prepare for truth."

"Uh, Miss Bertha." Jim tried to be tactful. "You said that aloud, and I ain't sure it makes sense."

"I know I said it aloud," Miss Bertha said.

Jim was right, what the woman had just said didn't make strict sense—almost, for a moment, then not. A message for her to interpret? What was entirely clear was that the old woman had tricked her into participation. Throughout, she had continued her testing, not speaking, crossing her arms, implying she would stop unless— And Normalyn had responded —naming Enid, locating her there, insisting on her beauty throughout, asserting she had asked for iced tea even on a cool day, that the lighter was silver, not gold. And in return what had she learned? Information contained in books, references to Mildred Meadows, ensnared within Enid's markings

89

in the clipping left to her. . . . Was that all? Normalyn was not
sure whether she hoped the answer to be yes or no.

"Well, even without what happened afterwards," Jim resigned himself, "that was one of your best stories, Miss Bertha.
It was like you were really there, seeing it happen, like in a
movie when people start remembering and then there they
are. I gotta admit at first I couldn't see the dark woman with
Marilyn—until Normalyn filled parts in, and then you just
went right on like *you'd* put her there all along, Miss Bertha,"
Jim congratulated. One part had chilled Jim, when Miss Bertha was talking about "the blackness" and Normalyn kept staring at the picture in the other room as if the darkness in it
were pulling her in.

But now, except for this damn silence, Normalyn seemed all
right, even though Miss Bertha kept studying her like an owl.
Jim glanced at his watch. He was seriously hungry. He'd take
Normalyn to a good coffee shop. Then she'd feel less bad
about missing the bus. He'd offer to rent a room for the night,
and— What if she didn't believe him? What if she said no!
Only now did he allow himself to consider that, because it
had all seemed so impossible at the beginning.

Suddenly Normalyn laughed, scaring the cats lounging about
Miss Bertha. The spell had broken. She was laughing at herself.
"So *that's* how you pretend, Miss Bertha."

"That's how, dearheart," Miss Bertha laughed with her.
"Lord, what a soul does to feel important."

Normalyn's laughter stopped. She had not wanted to offend
this sweet woman, just banish any lingering seriousness. Jim's
look was reproving her. Normalyn would have apologized
quickly except that Miss Bertha seemed just as eager as she to
laugh the seriousness away. *Why? Was she afraid? Of what?*
Those new questions occurred abruptly, just when she was
sure she was free of the story's spell.

Jim was not free of it either. The abrupt ending kept tug-
ging at him, so mysterious, with hints of great danger. "But,
Miss Bertha," he decided to try again, "*why* was there so much
danger?'

"Why?" Miss Bertha repeated vaguely. "Why?" She seemed
to transform the question into one of her own. She shook her
head as if to toss pursuing memories. She removed her glasses.
Her eyes had a new brightness. She raised her chin defiantly.
Then her words came in an outburst of rage, in a voice so
firm and strong that it was as if the placid woman had been
transformed into a powerful one charged by indignation: "It
was the goddamned evil times!" She seemed to address distant

figures: "I have opposed injustice in all its forms! So did my husband! I am no stranger to fascism, whether it calls itself patriotism, socialism, communism, or democracy! I *have* supported the just causes you decry! I said I would name fellow travelers, and so I will: Jefferson! Lincoln! Roosevelt!"

Relieved to recognize the story—startled by the transformation at first—Jim explained quickly to Normalyn, "That's what she told that damn Un-American Committee in Hollywood long ago. Go on, Miss Bertha!" The next was Jim's favorite part.

"And having named names, gentlemen of this committee," Miss Bertha continued in her renewed voice, "I will add a message of counsel to you fascists, you true un-Americans: *Fuck you!*"

Jim burst into delighted laughter, applauding.

Miss Bertha seemed suddenly startled by her recitation. She looked about her, as if to reorient herself. She looked at Jim and Normalyn as if not sure whether she had spoken or thought her passionate declamation. "Did I—?"

"Just thought it." A subdued Jim answered her concerned look.

Miss Bertha replaced her glasses. Her body softened, finding cozy edges of comfort in the large chair. She checked to see whether the architecture of her hair was surviving.

The words the old woman had spoken with such power were the words attributed to Alberta Holland in the clipping in Normalyn's purse—and Miss Bertha had referred to them earlier in her story. Normalyn leaned toward the woman, demanding her attention. "Enid Morgan died a few days ago," she said. Even now the words were drained of reality.

"Who was Enid?" Miss Bertha asked absently.

Jim was baffled: "Miss Bertha, Enid was the woman in your story."

Normalyn refused a sense of betrayal at the woman's words. She finished aloud, to herself now, "Enid was my mother."

"Was she, dearheart?" Miss Bertha sighed sadly. She bowed her head. "And that's why you're here from Texas."

"Your mother was that beautiful woman you put into Miss Bertha's story?" Jim understood. "Normalyn, did she really know Marilyn?"

"Yes," Miss Bertha answered. "Enid Morgan knew Marilyn very well." Her voice was weary. She closed her eyes.

The startling lithograph in the other room seemed alive to Normalyn now. "Are you Alberta Holland?" she asked quietly.

"Alberta Holland is dead; everyone knows that. She fled to

Switzerland, and died there, with a trusted friend. Why, her obituary is included in that book about her—it's somewhere here. It's where I read her words to that committee," Miss Bertha sighed.

"But you told me you said it." Jim was surprised; she had never denied *that*.

Miss Bertha's words drifted on: "Her obituary noted that she had courage at one time, stood up to the inquisitors, exhorted others never to flee. But when she made a tragic mistake, she ran away, and finally she did not speak out." She said to Normalyn, "So, dearheart, even if Alberta Holland were alive—and she isn't, everyone knows that—she would still be frightened to speak out." She adjusted the heavy lashes over one lid. Her voice was spirited again. "Now, when *I* pretend to counsel Marilyn, I tell her *not* to go to the Ambassador Hotel. That's where she got her first modeling assignment, where she started her journey"—the voice broke—"that ended in a lonesome locked room with a dead telephone connection." Behind her glasses, Miss Bertha's eyes blinked, closed for a moment. She faced Normalyn. "Are you, my dear, one of those candidates for those Dead Movie Stars—"

"No."

"—or are you really Norma . . . lyn?"

Normalyn nodded.

Miss Bertha raised her hand in an uncompleted gesture, perhaps a motioning to one of the cats, perhaps a blessing. Her hand rose toward her hair, stopped, abandoned the effort.

Then Jim realized how old Miss Bertha really was, how tired, nodding in her chair, eyes closed for lengthening seconds, trying not to fall asleep, her head leaning to one side. One day he would come over, ring the bell, and she would not answer. He gathered the two prowling cats and placed them on her lap.

He signaled Normalyn to leave, to leave softly.

Normalyn stood up, walking quietly away.

Miss Bertha nodded awake once more. She seemed to see Jim and Normalyn clearly again for moments. "Just remember, sailor, I'll always have a frosty beer for ya." Then out of a limbo of near-sleep, she sighed, "Come back when you're ready, dearheart . . . Normalyn."

A sweet woman, just a sweet old woman she was leaving behind now to move into her real journey of discovery, Normalyn thought with sadness and anticipation.

"Bye, Miss Bertha," Jim whispered.

Miss Bertha said to herself in sleepy wonder, "Why, it's

night already." Then she no longer resisted weariness. Tiny sounds of sleep emanated from her lips as her dyed curls released their firm hold, relinquishing the elaborate creation of her hair.

2

"She *lied!*" The moment Normalyn stepped out of Miss Bertha's unique reality—unreality!—she was enraged by what had occurred there—or what had not. She could not define either. What had she expected?

She and Jim stood on the sidewalk. A faded moon in a filmy sky gave Miss Bertha's garden a dark harmony.

"Lied about what?"

That further aggravated Normalyn. "About everything!" She tried to push away the lingering image of the placid sleeping form they had just left, so full of weariness. "And *you* tricked me into going there!"

So much for staying over. Jim led her away from the house a short distance. He faced her squarely: "I didn't get far in school because we was poor and I had to join the goddamn navy, but I told you before I ain't stupid. Miss Bertha told you right off she just imagines things. So don't talk like that about my friend. I love that crazy old woman—and don't *you* call her that," he warned quickly.

"And *I* told *you*—" She couldn't think of what to accuse him of. Her confusions were ganging up.

Mist hovered over buildings in the city as they walked into the electric streets, people everywhere, sailors, in and out of arcades with videos promising flesh and ecstasy.

"And don't think I don't know Alan Ladd wasn't short," Jim extended his loyalty. "She just told me that because she knew it would make me feel good, but I want you to know something: I *never* been self-conscious about being short."

"But Alan Ladd was short, everyone knows that." Normalyn knew.

"Damn," Jim said. And added, "You see!"

She felt close to him. He had disbelieved, the way *she* did about even possibly being "pretty," ever. "Besides," she said softly, "you're not really short." To resist the closeness she felt at his elated response, she walked ahead. Where? *This was her first night away from Gibson!* The nights on the bus had been shared with strangers. She was certain now that her suitcases would have gone on to Los Angeles. When she felt eyes on her, she waited for Jim to catch up with her.

Realizing that, he held her hand.

His touch felt warm, good.

The prepared bravado of his earlier imaginings evaporated; he said, "Normalyn, would you please consider staying over in Long Beach tonight?" He easily abandoned his story about the last bus out of Long Beach.

"With you," she said. She pressed his hand back. The pleasure she had tested grew. Fear stabbed. She slipped her hand away.

He looked at his own hand, abandoned.

I'm sorry, she wanted to say, but those were words of self-accusation from her past. Yes, if she was to allow life, she had to banish the fear that merely holding his hand had aroused. This youngman knew her within her brief present only, not in the long past that belonged entirely to Enid. He had been so kind with Miss Bertha. And she was attracted to him. Yes, she tested to herself. "Yes," she said. Just to hear the word aloud.

"Damn!" he congratulated this development. "Damn!"

"But without doing anything and in separate beds," she clarified. Like with Ted, that night of fear.

"What?" He looked baffled at this strange girl, really strange, and *so* goddamned innocent. She truly trusted him!—and that made him feel good, although maybe she trusted him only because she was so damn lost, in Long Beach and thinking it was Los Angeles!

"I mean it," she told him. "Only if you swear."

He couldn't believe it, but he was swearing—and he meant it! If she stayed over, that meant he could see her tomorrow, whatever *didn't* happen tonight; and then— "I swear," he said. "But you gotta promise to let me know if you change your mind." He had to be true to himself.

She drew back, ready to pull inside herself again.

"I promised," he reminded.

"Okay." Despondent with confusion, she looked up at the sky—murky.

Jim guided her along the street. "We'll get a room in that real good motel across the street, over there."

She looked at the oasis of palmtrees he had indicated, puddles of hidden pastel lights among units constructed like large colored plastic blocks about a pool.

"Is it all right?" Suddenly the motel looked awful.

"Yes," she said. From here, the small lobby shone with chrome.

"We'll register now and—"

"I'm hungry," she said, honestly.

"Okay, we'll get hamburgers first," he adjusted. "Come on!" Everything was *so* right he was becoming apprehensive.

She did not move. "You go ahead. I'll wait here."

He looked at her. She was so forlorn under the pale yellow street light. "I promised, Normalyn, and I mean it," he repeated. She was searching the street anxiously. He understood: "You intend to run away from me."

"Yes."

"You don't have to." He tried not to sound bitter. "I was going to lie earlier to you, tell you the buses stopped running at night and you'd *have* to stay over. But I didn't. So you don't have to lie to me."

Normalyn ran away in the direction of the beach—away from the memory of hands tearing at her dress as she spat out dirty sand.

Part Three
Los Angeles

One

A flood of morning light splashed Los Angeles. Early wind had banished the night's fog and swept away the smoggy haze.

In that light, even old buildings looked fresh. New buildings of chrome geometry—banks, corporations, hotels—floated on waves of reflected light. Everywhere, palmtrees pushed high into the sky.

Normalyn sat by the window of the bus and was dazzled. *Now* she was in Los Angeles, and Gibson was a million miles away!

Last night she had run to the beach, so terrified of pursuing memories that the darkness did not frighten her. She despised Ted Gonzales! She sat on the sand. Distant city lights shone mutedly on the water. Yes, on a shoreline like this Enid had led her to the blonde woman, who had lain in the dark, like Marilyn Monroe in the picture in Miss Bertha's dining room. The memory flowed away. She sat on the sand and cried.

She returned to the bus station, only to learn that the last bus out of Long Beach had left. On a bench, she tried to sleep, and told herself—knew, *had* to know—that tomorrow when Jim told Miss Bertha what had occurred, the old woman would explain— Everything!

In the morning she took the first bus into Los Angeles. Along the coastline white light swam on the water's surface.

In the bus depot in downtown Los Angeles, Normalyn felt disheveled but exhilarated. Dozens of people waited impatiently for their luggage. Poor people wandered among fresh-faced men and women. She would get her bags later. She wanted to be *in* the city.

99

She rushed outside of the beehive terminal. On the sidewalk, she looked down at her shadow. There it was, under the California sun!—*her* shadow, bold, present, hers. And she had seen it on the beach yesterday, too! She had acquired her own memories: of Miss Bertha, who would fade into a web of riddles and suddenly reappear, so clear; of Jim—she could return, but not yet, not yet retrace her steps— . . . And Ted? The new Ted? She resurrected him from the inundation of last night's anger.

Inside the terminal, she claimed her suitcases. She took out fresh clothes, cherishing the thought that she must look like a very experienced traveler. She left the bags in the rental boxes lining the walls, with timed keys.

In the slick restroom, an old rumpled woman slept on a pile of dirty rags, ignored by others at the washbasins. Normalyn recoiled. In Gibson, poverty was hidden—in the fields, in shanties.

Normalyn washed diligently. In a cubicle, she changed her clothes. Then before the row of mirrors, she brushed her hair. It had a new shine! With Enid's makeup box, she made herself up, lightly, without realizing that she was trying to hide what she was doing.

"You act as if you're not sure how you look," said a woman next to her, a reedy woman with a severe face that smiled with a frown.

I don't! Normalyn stared at herself.

"A little more blush. And remember, brush *up!*" the woman instructed. "Are you here to try to get into films?"

The old woman on rags roused herself from the floor. "Whore!" she yelled.

Normalyn reached up to her face, to wipe away the makeup.

"She was talking about herself," the reedy woman said to Normalyn. "Just pity her."

"Why should she?" demanded a heavy woman beside her.

"What!" the severe woman reacted.

"I said, why? Are you deaf or don't I talk clear?" She said to Normalyn, "Be careful who you listen to—lots of *locos,* lots of bad turns that look good. I oughta know." She shook her fleshy body.

"Awful!" said the lean woman.

"Why?" said the chubby one. "Cause you can't shake yours? Then rattle your damn bones!"

Normalyn fled.

She hired one of the men in uniform to wheel her bags outside. "How much am I supposed to tip you?" she asked.

When in earlier years she had taken trips with Enid, Enid had always charmed everyone, done everything right. Normalyn had not paid attention, certain no one would ever notice her.

"What are you trying to pull?" the man said suspiciously.

"I just asked—"

"What if I'da said ten dollars?" The man peered at her.

"I wouldn't have given you that much." She put one dollar into his outstretched hand. He abandoned her bags on the sidewalk.

In the warm sun, Normalyn tested her smile. She rehearsed a *wide* smile.

"Wha's happ'nin', baby?" a man winked at her.

She undid the smile and turned away. She motioned for a cab. As she waited, she saw her reflection, a glassy outline in a shiny window. At the same time, she heard—with terrified bewilderment—the words one youngman nearby spoke excitedly to another:

"That's Normalyn! She's Marilyn's daughter!"

"What?"

The two youngmen, one holding a smart tote bag over his shoulder, glanced at her, puzzled. They moved on.

Behind her, in the window of a theater-ticket agency, was a large poster:

Hollywood Four Star
Theater Club
Presents

A NIGHT OF LEGENDS

Starring
N O R M A - L Y N
"Marilyn's Daughter"
(Saturday P.M. Only)

Like an incandescent shadow over the length of the poster, the extravagantly curved black silhouette of a woman was outlined by a haze of silver. Only the lips—red—had been drawn on the face.

Normalyn turned away, for *any* protection from this startling moment. The cab driver was honking at her. She fled her own reflection superimposed on the other. The driver gathered her bags into the trunk.

"Where to?"

She didn't know! "The Ambassador Hotel." She remembered that name from—

As the car drove away, she concentrated attentively on the technicolored city, people, cars, buildings, an Art Deco shop like an imitation jewel, a glossy store with haughty tanned mannequins—and flowers, and trees, and palmtrees, palmtrees, more flowers! Still, her mind returned to the silver silhouette in the poster.

The cab stopped in the graceful but patched driveway of the sprawling hotel, new wings jutting from the old basic structure, embracing flowered lawns. Attendants hopped toward the car.

"Never can come here without thinking this is where they killed Bobby Kennedy," the driver said as if he had lost a friend there.

Was he mistaken? Normalyn remembered now where she had heard the name of this hotel. Miss Bertha had mentioned it. It was where Marilyn Monroe had received her first modeling assignment. But that had no further meaning for her. She had merely provided as her destination the only hotel she knew of. She paid the driver, tipped him, hoping it was the correct amount. He did not thank her.

A bellman carried her suitcases. Glass doors swooshed open before her. *This* hotel did not have the graceful drowsy grandeur of the Texas Grand Hotel. There was a drone of voices, men and women moving about busily to rooms, halls, dining rooms, elevators. Men with nametags on their lapels laughed loudly.

Inhaling, Normalyn prepared to walk the eternal distance to the desk. She would rehearse each movement before she committed herself to it. Unclench fists. Raise head. Too high!—she saw the ceiling. The first step, firm and— She could not walk! She pictured Enid's entrance into the Texas Grand Hotel, and she managed to reach the desk.

She gasped at the clerk, "I want a room overlooking the park!"

"The grounds," he corrected absently without looking up.

She regained control by counting her breaths. Three. Like Miss Bertha's puffs on her cigarillo.

"Your reservations are for—?" This time he almost glanced at her.

"Normalyn Morgan." She said that firmly, the way Enid would have announced, "Enid Morgan."

The clerk searched his reservations. "I'm sorry, I don't seem to have any—"

Please! Normalyn did not allow herself to speak that word. "I'm sure the reservations were made," she said in an emphatic tone, a slight drawl. "Mayor Wendell Hughes, from Texas, made them for me himself." She thought that up quickly.

He finally looked at her. Then he consulted his list again. "Here it is. And how long will you be with us, Miss Morgan?"

She wanted to thank him but wasn't sure whether he was being kind to her or mistaken. "I don't know," she answered her own question.

"I see. We'll have—"

She was sure he was going to ask her to pay in advance. She couldn't bear that. She'd beat him to it. She searched her purse, pulled out several books of traveler's checks. "I'll need to cash these—and I'll pay for the room in advance." She congratulated herself on this thwarting device.

"Advance payment won't be necessary, Miss Morgan. But I will need some identification to—" He looked at her in astonishment. "What is *this*?"

"My birth certificate."

Nearby, two other clerks stared at her in spreading astonishment. The man before her studied the document she had handed him. He tried to retain his indifference. "Do you have a credit card, Miss Morgan?"

"What the hell's better than a birth certificate?" volunteered one of the jubilant older men with nametags. Others with him agreed.

The clerk surrendered to the unknown. "Very well."

In the elevator Normalyn was safe—but not for long. She had to turn away from the scrutiny of other passengers. She put on her glasses, her vision blurred, she stared down. A bellman led her along the carpeted hallway into an attractive room with a large bed. Fussing airily, he waited, waited.

To be paid! "Please tell me how much to give you!"

"Ten bucks'll do it," the man told her. "More if you want." There was a derisive smile on his pinched face.

"Don't look at me like that!" she snapped. She had not even had to prepare the words.

The knowing smile fled.

She gave him five dollars.

"Thank you, miss," the man muttered.

When he closed the door, Normalyn felt she had survived several wars to reach her hotel room.

From her suitcase, she brought out, carefully wrapped in its tissue, Enid's figurine of the chipped angel. She placed it on a

table. She did not touch the hurt wing. Exhausted from her
journey into this room, she sat on a chair. She looked at the
birth certificate still in her hand. Then she saw that the one
Mayor Hughes had given her was different from the one Enid
had altered with inked entries. Enid's had indicated an "Unknown" father. In this one, in a type that matched that of the
other entries, a name—"Stan Smith"—had been entered as
that of her father. Enid had *never* allowed Stan a last name,
and the Mayor would have known that. Normalyn was certain
that the deliberately ordinary last name Mayor Hughes had
chosen was a gift to her of a less tentative identity, without
separating her from Enid Morgan. Suddenly Normalyn missed
Mayor Hughes—"a good man."

Outside her window the silver morning was tarnishing into
a gray afternoon.

In the large shiny bathroom, Normalyn allowed herself to
look at her naked body reflected in the full-length mirror on
the door. Had her body changed? Were her slender hips and
legs really curved? Were her breasts *really* round, firm?

Quickly, she showered in hot purifying water.

In a light robe, she sat on the bed and picked up the
telephone. "The Hollywood Four Star Theater, please," she
said to the operator.

" 'Night of Legends' at nine sharp, one performance, dancing later," a man's indifferent voice informed her on the
telephone. Even while she wrote down the information,
Normalyn was not certain she wanted to find out who the
radiant silhouette on the poster belonged to, who the woman
was with *her* name—and claiming to be "Marilyn's daughter."

2

It was night! She had been so tired that as soon as she'd
reclined on the bed, she had fallen into locked sleep. She woke
up famished. Laughter erupted in small bursts in the hallway
outside. She tried to imitate it, to prepare to join it when she
entered the dining room and said, "A table—"

For one.

She called room service and ordered from a menu by the
telephone: an elaborate sandwich. "And iced tea. And hot
pecan pie." No? Then lemon meringue.

A Mexican man with a generous moustache brought her
dinner. He arranged it neatly on a small table he had wheeled
in. She went to her purse, to pay.

"No—you just sign," he said in an accented voice. He handed her the tab, showed her where.

"How much do I tip you?"

Glad to be consulted, he told her how to figure it out. "The same everywhere," he added. "If you like someone, add a little more."

She added more.

He stopped at the door. "Miss, you shouldn't let people know you're so innocent." He hurried out.

As she ate the sandwich with frilly decorations, she thought of the misty figure in the poster, the pose so *sure*.

She dressed quickly, in a pretty dress, a flowered print. Enid had always bought her attractive clothes, but she had used hardly any of them; doing so would have emphasized that she went nowhere.

She applied makeup from Enid's gold-leafed box, carefully now. She was still not entirely able to "see" herself without Enid. She touched the etched roses on the lid of the box.

Her goal would be the lobby! No, first the hallways, *then* the elevator.

She made it.

In the lobby, several youngwomen with effortless smiles mingled among the men brandishing their names on their lapels. Normalyn imitated the smile of one of the prettiest girls, who quickly frowned at her. Her smile began to itch as Normalyn wandered about the lobby, as if she were waiting for— Looking for—

"Are you a hostess?"

She faced a tall, elegant man different from the others, except that he, too, wore a nametag. His temples were brushed with gray. He was about forty, and good-looking. "No." She pretended to understand his question.

Lines crinkled about his dark eyes when he smiled at her. "Just visiting?"

"Yes. And then I'll find a job." She allowed an easy explanation.

"What are you looking for in the city?"

A few feet ahead—and hiding from the man's view—the waiter who had brought her food was miming an urgent message to her: He clasped one hand tightly over the other. Handcuffs!

Forgetting to remove the smile, which was now hurting, Normalyn drifted away from the tall man. He called after her. She continued to move away, casually, toward the waiter. "I think he's a cop, miss," the waiter said, "and I know you ain't no whore cause whores know how to tip!" He disappeared.

Why would the man assume she was a prostitute! Suddenly Normalyn wanted to run away, back to her room, to hide— No! She faced the man, still there, still looking at her, still smiling at her. She tried to remember his exact words to her: "What are you looking for in the city?" As she turned away from his insistent smile—and hers disappeared—his words changed meaning, contained other suspicions: *What are you searching for in the city?*

Two

N*I*G*H*T * O*F * L*E*G*E*N*D*S

Normalyn read the glittering marquee. Under a hazy half moon, she stood before a violet building—a series of stone arches illuminated orange and blue, each adorned with a shimmery star, all crowned by a dome vined with beads of tiny lights. This purple creation—an attempt to reproduce the front of the Beverly Theater, a Deco-Islamic Palace built in 1925 as the first movie house allowed in Beverly Hills—is only a facade. It was constructed over what was once an abandoned warehouse in West Los Angeles. Now it is a brash nightclub called the Hollywood Four Star Theater.

Behind it, tall palmtrees, just darker than the inky sky, barely swayed in a breathless night. . . . Normalyn felt steeped in Technicolor.

At the Ambassador Hotel earlier—rejecting the abrupt suspicion created by the ambiguous encounter with the stranger in the hotel lobby—he was a man trying to pick her up, only that—Normalyn decided she would go to the Hollywood Four Star Theater Club. The theater was on Wilshire and so was the hotel. When she had traveled eternal blocks, she asked a man where the address she had written was. "Miles away, in West Los Angeles. You lost, girl?" he inquired happily. She took a cab, wincing at each click of the meter.

Immediately after she arrived, she almost fled. Whistles of approval greeted her from men—there were only men—waiting to get in. They were youngish to slightly older, studiedly casually well dressed, brimming with dogged enthusiasm. A sign clarified: "Gentlemen allowed only after 8:30 P.M." Holding her breath, Normalyn made her way to the entrance. A burly man with an open shirt guarded vinyl doors. With incre-

107

dulity, he studied her birth certificate as demanded "proof of age." "Okay, hon . . . I guess—if you got *that*," he surrendered, baffled.

Velvet-paneled doors opened with a gasp. Normalyn saw only women inside, women of all ages and shapes sitting at many small tables. Like the men outside, the women exuded determination to have a great, grand time.

The inside of the club flaunted an assaulting cheap opulence. Sprinkles of lights winked everywhere. Gold-edged red drapes swept the floor on both sides of a sleek plastic stage, empty now.

Normalyn was startled to discover that the waiters were shirtless, with silly collars, cuffs, bow ties, tight pants. Serving their last drinks of the evening, they were being replaced by youngwomen in black body stockings so sheer their flesh shone through.

Normalyn looked at her feet and counted her steps as she was led by one of the shirtless waiters with streaks of blond hair to a table where two other women already sat. "Crowded tonight. Gotta share, hon," the waiter explained with an etched smile. *Everyone* said "hon" here.

One of the two women at the table was pudgy, with glasses attached to her dress with an elastic strand. The other was younger, about thirty-five wearing a dress held up only by spilling breasts. Normalyn was relieved to learn from their spirited evaluation of tonight's "male strippers" that the "ladies only" portion of the evening was over. *Now* gentlemen would be allowed.

And here they were! The gentlemen swaggered in with growls of laughter. They lurked about the ladies, laughed, courted, watched, laughed, stood in studied poses, laughed, sat, laughed, laughed.

Normalyn quickly rejected two offers of "company" from roaming men she was sure were mocking her with easy invitations. The two women at her table stabbed her with stares.

When a waitress with peeking buttocks asked her what she wanted to drink, Normalyn echoed what the woman with attached glasses had just ordered another of: "A Margarita, hold the salt." It came. She hated it. "I'll have iced tea instead." The waitress's smile crumbled: "You'll have to settle for mineral water, hon, and if you want a twist, you got it."

When Normalyn rejected another of the roving gentlemen, this one with an astonishing moustache, the woman with the fancy snap glasses hissed to the one with proud bosoms, "She's keeping the men away, Belinda."

"I know, Pam," Belinda agreed, with a hoist of her breasts. "Are you sure this isn't female mud wrestlers night for gentlemen? That's not a good night for ladies," Belinda said.

"I told you, it's Legends, with a new attraction each week— and a surprise tonight. Andy at the door told me," Pam said knowledgeably.

Very tan, a man stood over their table. He wore a sports jacket and an open shirt. A giant medallion with an astrological sign nestled on his dark-haired chest. He said to Normalyn, "I'm Buck. Want a hunk?"

"Leave me alone!" Why did her hands hurt? Looking down, Normalyn realized she had held them locked into fists since walking past the men outside.

Buck's brash front toppled: "What the *shit*—?"

"Hey!" Belinda winked. "*We* like hunks."

Pam snapped her glasses.

"Fuck off!" Buck told them.

Pam said to Normalyn, "Listen, sweetie, you are out of place."

"Why not scram?" Belinda suggested.

"I'm—" Normalyn was about to apologize. Instead, she pushed her unwanted Margarita at the woman who had ordered the same. "You want this?"

"The nerve," said Pam. Belinda took the drink.

"Clumsy damn jerk!" The words erupted nearby. A middle-aged woman with a hundred ringlets of hair sprang up from a table. A waiter stood with a tray and an overturned glass. "You spilled it on purpose!" the woman accused.

Normalyn had never seen a body as muscular as the waiter's— and it was oiled. He looked odd with the bow tie, cuffs, and collar the others wore easily. On him, the very frailty of those objects bound his enormous body.

"Retire him!" a woman in her fifties said. "He's too old anyhow."

Although he did not look "old" to Normalyn, he *was* older than the other waiters, and his extravagant muscularity set him further apart from them.

The waiter tilted the tray, spilling drinks on the screaming women at the table. Then he removed the bow tie, collar, cuffs and flung them on the table—stood defiantly unadorned before the women. One of the hefty men who oversaw the club intercepted him as he walked away. Near the edge of the stage, their angered voices tangled.

Then Normalyn saw:

A glittering form emerged from shadows beyond the wings and guided the muscular man away from the other's wrath.

There was a roll of drums! A slick middle-aged man in a white tuxedo appeared within whirling lights on the stage: "Rusty Hills, your emcee, ladies and gentlemen! Welcome to A Night of Legends!" Rusty Hills promised "another spectacular entertainment" in the club's Saturday Night series: "And, remember, each night will feature a new legend! See them all come alive on our stage!"

There was dramatic music. Lights dimmed. Mingling became subdued.

"Our first legend, returning for her third week is . . . the princess of . . . love." The last word was a throbbing amplified whisper. "Our beloved . . . *Judy!*"

Within drained light appeared a woman wearing a black top hat, a mock tuxedo cut high on her thighs, exposing sheer black tights. Squeezed clothes did not conceal her plump body as she sat with her legs crossed on a high stool and leaned back, miming the recorded voice of Judy Garland— which suddenly wrested all attention from her, silencing the audience:

> A foggy day in London town
> Had me low and had me down. . . .

The great voice held at the edge of despair, tilted over for a daring moment, and rose exultantly, conquering even this tawdry nightclub.

Normalyn closed her eyes, listening to the magical voice.

Suddenly there was laughter!

On the stage, the woman's movements had slowly become a brutal exaggeration of the star's. Her hands grasped, her body quivered as if electrified. She strutted, stumbled. The voice of Garland, triumphant and hurt, soared even over the laughter invited by the clowning performer.

This was the intention—ridicule! Normalyn realized as the audience continued to release yowls of readied laughter.

Shaking his head in pretended disbelief, Rusty Hills called after the performer as the voice of Garland faded; "We'll *never* let you die, Judy!" And now he announced to the ladies and gentlemen: "The King himself! Elvis!"

Over the recorded voice of the singer, prepared squeals greeted a man with darkened sideburns. In a fringed gold and white outfit, he imitated the singer's dynamic motions, one hand up, hips gyrating. Then lights blinked. When they steadied, the performer had grown fat with added padding. Exploding laughter could not drown the gospelly, soulful sensuality of Presley's voice:

> Don't be cruel
> To a heart that's true. . . .

The audience encouraged panting, orgasmic thrustings: "Ugh! *Ugh!*"

Not fans, vultures! Normalyn remembered Miss Bertha's judgment. Waiting to pay them back because they had been adored. There were those who continued to love them always, but not here. Normalyn closed her eyes to purify the living voice:

> They've been so long
>   on lonely street
> They never will go back. . . .

Dressed in clashing tatters, a woman followed him on stage. She staggered about with a bottle of whiskey. Over the derision, Janis Joplin's voice lilted over hurt and joy. . . . A man in black vinyl pants followed, his hands at his groin hinting with coy naughtiness that he might expose himself.

"*I'll* light *your* fire, baby!" screamed a hoarse woman.

Normalyn would have left long ago, disgusted by the ugly spectacle of invited cruelty. She would have been certain the woman depicted in the poster would be another parody, except that *she* had been billed as "Marilyn's daughter," not as Marilyn Monroe.

Rusty Hills subdued the laughter. "And now, for the first time, the Legend of Legends. Marilyn Mon—" His voice a whisper, he paused to retain the magic of the name: "Marilyn Monroe's daughter!"

As he disappeared, a backdrop of light created a white dawn. Whistles shot out in anticipation of ridicule. No one moved into the horizon of light. The restive audience waited. Silence pushed at gathered laughter. The stage remained empty until the audience had quieted.

Then a silhouette of curves appeared against the artificial dawn. The woman assumed the pose in the poster, one white-gloved hand on her thigh, the other held up, out, a glamorous victor without challenge.

The audience surrendered silence. Only then did the woman on stage move. A leg parted a slit in the dress, arousing sequins. The purred words commanded:

That old black magic that I know so well . . .

This voice was not taped. It was the performer's. The voice,
the movements suggested Marilyn Monroe's, without mocking.
Gleaming red lips shaped the movie star's sexual breaths, but
in between were moments of a bluesy bitter-sweetness that was
the performer's, only hers. Her movements released an added
energy, a rhythm of sensuality as the woman stalked the stage
with perfect legs.

Lovin' that old black magic called—

Head tossed back, the woman tasted the delicious word, kissed
it, finally sighed it:

—that old black magic called . . . love. . . .

She moved up three steps of a platform. There she stood in
the same pose as that in which she had appeared within the
white dawn.
   Bewildered, the audience waited to be released into laughter.
   The woman on stage did not move. Demanding—
   —demanding applause! Normalyn knew. There was scat-
tered clapping. Normalyn joined it.
   The reluctant applause held, only held—this audience had
not come to cheer.
   The woman did not move.
   Garish lights pounced on the stage.
   There were loud whispers, giggles, laughter!
   Still the woman did not move.
   "She's *black!*" Pam explained deliriously to Belinda why peo-
ple in front were laughing.
   Trapped in crashing lights, the woman on stage refused
to move.
   The announcer leaned toward the audience to share a secret—
and to release the gathering, still tentative laughter: "And!—
ladies and gentlemen!—our performer wasn't *always* a woman.
. . . A stitch here, a snip there." His hand touched his chest,
dropped to his groin.
   Pam announced triumphantly, "She's a black transsexual—
that's what he means!"
   The black woman on stage did not surrender her lavish
sexual pose even when the cruelest jeering of the evening
erupted in the Hollywood Four Star Theater.

Three

Normalyn pushed through men and women again tracking each other now that the Night of Legends was over.

The performer's courage, her resistance to the demanded humiliation, had moved Normalyn, stirred memories of times when at school *she* had been trapped in laughter, had forced herself to control the hurt—and had hurt even more, secretly.

She made her way to the stage exit. She faced the same hefty man who had confronted the muscular waiter earlier. "You can't come in here, it's the dressing area." His arms were a map of tattoos; gray hairs pushed over the top of his shirt. "If you wanna apply for waitress, you gotta see Mr. Stephen Holden on Tuesdays; tonight he's out there scouting for mud wrestlers—"

Behind him, some of the waitresses in sheer tights milled; a few of the shirtless waiters lingered along a corridor reeking of sweat and perfume. Normalyn shouted into the hall, "Norma-Lyn!" Strange, yelling out her own name . . .

She saw a door open nearby. Dressed now, the muscular man walked toward her. He and the tattooed man exchanged threatening looks.

"What the hell do you want with her?" the muscular man asked Normalyn. He looked to be in his early thirties, then immediately older, then again younger. A deep tan emphasized tiny scratchy wrinkles on his rugged, handsome face. Combed casually to conceal the fact, his light brown hair was beginning to thin. His grayish eyes looked sad.

"I just want to tell her she was beautiful," Normalyn answered. The reason she had come to the nightclub—to ask the

113

performer who she was, why she called herself "Norma-Lyn, Marilyn's daughter"—had been forgotten.

Brushing the burly man aside, the muscular man led her to a door on which a large crude star was drawn with red lipstick. The man opened the door into an improvised dressing room.

Still in the white gown—unzipped at the back—the black woman sat before a mirror surrounded by lights strung on a cord in imitation of those in a fancier dressing room. Her gloves and shoes were discarded on the floor. There was a white simulated fur piece draped over the edge of the mirror. The woman's hair was tightly bunched against her head. On a stand was the platinum blonde wig she had worn.

Seeing Normalyn's reflection in the mirror, the woman spun about. She was beautiful, her heavy-lashed eyes yellow-specked, her features finely sculpted, her skin like chocolate cream. "Who the fuck are you?" she demanded.

Anger shoved away Normalyn's sympathy. "And who the hell are *you?*" She shot back the question she had first come here to ask.

"Hear that, Kirk?" the black woman asked the muscular man. "Girl busts into *my* dressing room and asks who the hell *I* am!" She reached out to touch the man's massive arm, to separate him from anger. Yet she did so almost cautiously, as if the touch might hurt the powerful body—and the man's body had tensed for a second. Then he hugged the woman's bare shoulders in reassurance, and she leaned back against him eagerly.

"She wants to tell you something," Kirk said to the black woman—and nodded to Normalyn.

Annoyed at being prodded, Normalyn hurried her words: "Your performance was beautiful."

The black woman lowered her head. She said quietly, "Thank you." Then the head reared up. "That fuckin' *Mr.* Holden tricked me!" She slammed the table; makeup trembled. "He *knew* I was gonna do it straight. How the fuck did he know I'm a—?" She couldn't finish. "Hate that word. It's like I'm still in transit, and I am not!" She fluctuated from a "shanty" tone to one that was precise, correct. She shook out her hair, black, curly, lustrous. She was even more beautiful now. She touched the platinum wig. "Wouldn't make fun of *her,* I love that gorgeous Marilyn." She stood up.

She was shorter than she had appeared earlier, just slightly taller than Normalyn. She looked so young without her stage makeup, close to Normalyn's own age, but she radiated experience; and so Normalyn calculated she had to be twenty-four.

Normalyn tried to soften any hint of judgment. "Why did you call yourself Norma-Lyn, her daughter?"

"You mean I couldn't be—because I'm black, girl?"

Normalyn felt both enraged and intimidated at being called "girl." But she knew the black women was hurting—a lot—and the man wasn't helping her that much, just sitting there on a canvas chair, silently, as if helpless despite his powerful presence. But then he, too, had been bruised in that arena outside. "No, I just wondered why you weren't just Marilyn."

"*Mr.* Stephen Holden *insisted.*" She raised her voice to assure being heard outside the door. "Stevey Holden *and* his bullies—that Franky Rich and that Rusty Hills! *Grown men with boy names!*" she shouted. She spread quieter anger: "That fuckin' reporter on that tabloid's been running those stories about a daughter. It was supposed to be a gimmick *only* till I came on."

A reporter . . . writing about a daughter. Normalyn retained unexpected information.

The woman shook the dress loose at her back, preparing to slip out of it. "What you starin' at?"

"I didn't know I was." But Normalyn realized she had been. She had heard of transsexuals, but she had thought they would look like men in women's clothes. This woman was magnificent.

"Go ahead, look. See?" The black woman cupped her breasts. "Round. *Mine!*" She ran her hands down smooth hips. *"Real!* All that's gotta be there *is*, and all that shouldn't *ain't!*"

Normalyn was confused. The woman had begun by challenging her, but at the end she seemed to be addressing Kirk.

"You're beautiful, hon, beautiful," he said.

The woman closed her eyes, as if to hear the words again.

The muscular man was crying! No, he was just holding his hands to his nose, sniffing something, Normalyn saw.

The black woman let the dress slide down. Almost naked, the brown body was like velvet. Normalyn looked away in embarrassment from the unself-conscious extravagant near-nudity.

The woman looked at her mirrored image. "How did that fuckin' Holden know!"

Normalyn shook her head. She could not imagine that this woman had ever been other than a beautiful female.

"Duke told him," Kirk said. "I saw him out there."

"I'll kill the motherfucker!" The black woman reached for anything on the table—a glass with a fresh rose. She flung it on the floor. She bent to retrieve the flower from the broken glass. "You gave it to me, baby. Sweetest present, opening-night present." She looked up at Kirk.

"Because I love you," he said. The voice was wearied, sad. In the canvas chair, the enormous body looked surrendered.

She kissed the rose and brushed Kirk's lips with it. "I'm sorry you took that ugly job," she told him, as if she hurt more for him than for what had been done to her.

"Made a few bucks." He half-smiled.

Normalyn looked away. She felt awkward, extraneous. Yet walking out now would call attention to that, make her feel even more so. She tried to think of something to say. . . couldn't . . . coughed.

The black woman slipped into a creamy apricot dress. She seemed to see Normalyn clearly for the first time. "How old are you, hon?"

"I'm twenty-one," Normalyn lied. She inhaled. "My name is Normalyn."

The woman tossed shoes, gloves into her bag. She searched for a lost stocking. Suddenly she looked up at Normalyn. *"What?"*

"That's my name," Normalyn said. "Normalyn Morgan—and I'm from Gibson—in Texas. I just got here—I slept in Long Beach last night." She kept adding words because she felt on trial before this woman who knew so much about life.

"That your name, huh?" The woman's anger waited or gathered.

"Yes."

"We got the same name, huh?" The words were steely.

"Yours has a hyphen," Normalyn said.

The black woman threw her head back and laughed. "Mine has a fuckin' hyphen!"

Kirk smiled, aware only of a light moment.

"Let me tell you something!" the woman addressed Normalyn. "That ain't my *real* name. Just part of *Mr.* Stevey Holden's gimmick!" she yelled at the door. The voice became lofty: "I, myself, have never favored a rhyming name."

"It does *not* rhyme. I should know. *I* write poems!" Instantly, Normalyn wanted to disintegrate.

"Girl writes poems with goddamn hyphens!"

"Don't call me *girl*, you!—whatever your name is!" Normalyn would not hold her anger any longer. "And let *me* tell *you* something now: Just because you are a Negro—"

"A Negro!"

"—or colored"— Normalyn held on.

"Colored!"

"—or black or whatever the hell you call yourself"—Normalyn did not relinquish—"*that* does not make you high and mighty. I may be white, but I have feelings, too."

The black woman's mouth stayed open.

This time Kirk laughed aloud.

"Got your own way of lookin' at things, huh?" The black woman seemed to approve. She smiled. "Never quite seen it that way." Then she said abruptly, "You're really green, aren't you?" There was real surprise in the words.

"*I am not!*" Normalyn presented the only evidence she could think of to prove her sophistication: "I'm staying at the Ambassador Hotel. Alone!"

"Did you *hear*—!"

Kirk shook his head quickly, stopping the woman's new tirade.

Siding with *her*. Normalyn welcomed the unexpected.

"Stayin' at the 'bassador Hotel, huh?" The black woman cocked her head. She smiled sweetly at Normalyn. "Normalyn. That *is* a real pretty name you got, especially without the hyphen." She laughed a honeyed laughter.

Normalyn laughed with her, marveling that her laughter sounded natural.

"Well, I'll just have to go back to being plain old Troja—"

"Always loved the name, sweetheart," Kirk approved.

"Troja!" Normalyn reacted to the exotic name.

"Don't know mythology, huh?" Without looking into the mirror, Troja painted her lips with one oval motion of her lipstick. "Her face launched a thousand ships."

"You must mean Helen of Troy," Normalyn was glad to correct. But this beautiful woman looked more like the Cleopatra she had once conjured up.

"Yeah—her!" Troja snapped. "Without no fuckin' hyphen!"

Normalyn was confused by the renewed assault, which had been automatic after conciliatory moments. She walked to the door. Her hand on the knob, she said, "Troja, one moment you're talking about how mean people were to you, and the next you're passing your anger on to me, and I came here only to tell you—" Damned if she'd repeat the compliment now. She opened the door.

"I'm sure Troja's sorry," Kirk said quickly, touching Troja's arm, coaxing an apology.

"I *am* sorry. Really." Troja's words were caring. "You did just come to do me a kindness, and I've been turnin' on you."

Life was wondrous! She had made two new—and very difficult—friends of her own. She had conquered through candor and protest. Normalyn added this to the top of her victories since leaving Gibson. "I accept your apology." She did not want to give in too quickly, but risk determined otherwise.

"Oh, *big* heart," Troja started again. She stopped herself. "You're named after Marilyn, aren't you, hon?"

Normalyn said, "I think so."

"And you're pretty. Got such pretty hair, pretty eyes."

Normalyn still felt embarrassed by the word "pretty." "Thank you," she barely whispered.

Troja removed Normalyn's hand gently from the doorknob. Then she aimed her words into the corridor: "I have some business to tend to with *Mr.* Stephen Holden before I go on again. I ain't ridiculing Marilyn or myself!"

Kirk stopped her at the door. "I'll get him for you, sweet-heart. Let *him* come to you." He left the door open.

Troja pointed to the lipstick star on it. "Kirk drew it for me," she told Normalyn. "Those bitches were so cruel to him out there. Did you hear them? Called him . . . old. He can't face that."

"But he's a man—" Normalyn could not imagine men fearing growing older.

For the first time, Troja looked really exhausted. "It's worse for men who *do* care—because they ain't supposed to care." She said to herself, "Some wounded keep walking straight, others stop; Kirk's deciding." She stopped quickly, hearing Kirk. She ran her hands down her stockings. When Kirk walked in and she looked up, her face had shed its weariness, or disguised it.

Kirk was rubbing his fists. "He fired us both, Troja. But I got our money."

Troja tossed tear-drop glass earrings into her large bag. With her fingers she combed the platinum wig on its stand. Then she arranged both carefully in the bag. "Back to Duke," she said. She told Normalyn, "He's my manager." She couldn't laugh.

"You don't have to go back to that fucking pimp," Kirk said.

Troja seemed to wait for him to add more words.

There was harsh pounding on the door. "Mr. Stephen Holden says if you ain't out of here, he calls the cops."

"You open that door, Franky, and two more fists are waiting for you *and* Mr. Holden, motherfucker," Troja promised. Pulling the white fur piece from the mirror and wrapping it about her shoulders, she thrust her head back. "Y'all ready for our exit?"

Kirk took the bag from her.

The tattooed man stood there with Stephen Holden, a sleazy man holding an iced towel to his puffed nose. The towel had a tint of red. Alerted, some of the youngmen and youngwomen who worked in the club gathered.

With her hand, the black woman rubbed away the lipstick star on the door. She linked one arm through Kirk's—and the other one through Normalyn's.

Startled, Normalyn quickly welcomed this new closeness. In this moment of giant crisis, *she* was with them! Life! she thought. Real life. *My* life. And she held Troja's arm closer to hers.

"Goodbye," called a waitress. "Bye," said a shirtless waiter. Others echoed farewells, answered by Troja. "Good luck, Normalyn!" a pretty youngman called.

They were including her! Normalyn was profoundly moved. Kirk must have told them her name, the support she had brought them. She nodded—shyly—in acceptance. This moment of surging life required more. She stopped before the youngmen and women. "I really appreciate—" she started.

"They sayin' goodbye to *me!*" Troja whispered.

Normalyn wanted to vanish forever, but Troja's firmed arm through hers reassured her. As they passed the two menacing men, the black woman said, "Whoevuh you are, Ah have always depended on th' kindness of—" She hurled substituted words: "—on the shittiness of motherfuckers like you!"

In the chilly night, the three walked across tangled weeds toward an old 1968 Mustang, its convertible top patched with adhesive tape turning gray and curling at the ends. Kirk placed Troja's bag and the folding chair into the back seat.

Soon she would be standing alone on this weedy lot, miles away from the hotel, from Long Beach, from Gibson, from life, Normalyn knew.

"Well, get in, hon," Troja said.

Inviting her! Normalyn jumped into the car. Fellow outlaws! Kirk turned the ignition. Nothing.

Troja got out. She lifted the hood of the car. Her head ducked under. One hand explored the motor, the other held out the white fur piece, protected, away from the engine. "Start the fucker!" A wisp of simulated fur floated into the night. The motor turned.

Normalyn looked at Troja with admiration as she jumped back into the car. Normalyn moved over. Kirk's thigh touched hers. Normalyn slid away carefully.

Only when the car moved away from the Hollywood Four Star Theater Club did Normalyn realize she did not know where she was going with two strangers she had just met in a city she had just arrived into. She held her purse against her body, because she was cold in the patched car—and because she was suddenly afraid.

Four

"Huccome you pressin' that purse of yours like you think someone's gonna snatch it?" Troja said coolly.

That increased Normalyn's fear. They drove along a decaying strip of Sunset Boulevard, near Western, a gray spectrum of cheap bars, abandoned buildings smeared with the smoke of desultory fires, walls plastered with ripped posters; all-night coffee shops in dirty puddles of light; aging motels with exotic names: THE FLAMINGO, HOLLYWOOD PALACE, GOLDEN SANDS.

Troja leaned back in silence, Normalyn sat guardedly away from Kirk. The night had turned chillier in this car which welcomed every draft.

Along the street, women idled. Many wore tight dresses cut to the edge of their buttocks. In body stockings the color of flesh, some women appeared nude under yellow cones of light. A few had a surrendered prettiness, Normalyn saw. Men with them guided them to cruising cars. Here and there, ragged derelicts, men and women, slept on crumpled papers, in doorways, on the sidewalks.

Normalyn felt as if she were passing through a foreign world.

"Get off this damn street!" Troja actually spoke harshly to Kirk. "Don't wanna remember!"

Her world once? Normalyn wondered. Difficult to imagine this grand creature on those streets.

Kirk steered the car away from the darkly sexual arena and into a residential neighborhood of small stucco houses just holding on. On a desolate block, a church loomed, all crosses and ornate windows—old, forbidding. Over a glassy enclosure

121

announcing that week's sermons, Gothic letters proclaimed THE THRICE-BLESSED PENTECOSTAL CHURCH OF THE REDEEMER.

Within night mist, about fifty young people in their teens, early twenties milled excitedly before the large church. They all wore vague costumes. Some of the girls were in negligées posing as evening dresses. A few of the youngmen wore improvised tuxedos, swatches of bright cloth doubling as cummerbunds, scarves. Others brandished leather jackets and jeans rolled high at the cuffs. A girl wrapped herself in a gouged fur coat. They looked like extras in a low-budget movie intended to suggest elegance. Or like children made up for an impromptu masquerade.

Accompanied by a tough-looking youngman wearing a bloused shirt and cowboy boots, a youngwoman in a filmy gown and with a giant fake orchid in her reddened hair skimmed past the others. The buzzing increased. A few of those waiting in line almost bowed reverentially to her. With her escort brushing them aside, she disappeared into the basement of the Thrice-Blessed Church. The rest of the gathered moved in after them, leaving the night intact.

"Those sick Dead Movie Stars and their midnight auditions!" Troja said in tired disgust. "Gettin' all that publicity now."

That group again! Miss Bertha had thought *she* might be one of those trying to join. They dredged up scandals about the great movie stars they tried to imitate. Normalyn looked back at the darkened church. What secrets could those shabby children know?

In a residential block illumined by dull yellow lights, Kirk parked before a small square house set into a lawn patched with dying grass, vibrant weeds. A short palmtree, just one, squatted before the house. Normalyn's heart sank. The house tilted! A portion of a small porch had collapsed. She almost slipped when she stepped out of the car.

"Slide area without even being on a hill," Troja remarked, scrutinizing the house.

They entered turmoil. There were three rooms; a large one ducked to one side to form a kitchen area bordered by a barlike counter with unmatched stools. A scrambled bed in the main room faced a dormant television. A few pillows patched the floor. Its long wire a series of coils and knots, the telephone on the floor was off the cradle, making no sound, disconnected. In another room, clothes were tossed everywhere. A third room was crowded with unpacked boxes—and a tidily made-up bed. An attempt to hang drapes had been abandoned. Only a few panels flanked windows.

Pulling clothes out of her large bag, Troja threw them over bare lamps to soften the harsh spectacle. She said cheerfully, "That bed's *real* comfortable." She indicated the made-up bed surrounded by boxes in the next room. "I sleep in it myself sometimes, hon. Know why? Cause that room gets the best breeze, and a nice view of the garden. That's why it's the *guest* room. I'm sure you'll be real comfortable, hon."

"What!" Normalyn remained near the door.

"Sit down, hon. Make yourself at home. Wanna drink?" Troja invited nervously.

Normalyn shook her head. Then she saw this:

On the disheveled bed, Kirk was snorting white powder from what looked like the tip of a tiny knife. As he sat hunched, his huge muscles seemed to intrude on him, as if they carried a heavier weight that was not physical. He extended a packet of powder to Troja.

Troja shook her head with exaggerated emphasis. In attempted concealment, she made a gesture that rejected a further offer of it, to Normalyn. "Takin' so much." She softened the words to Kirk by adding, "sweetheart." She said to Normalyn, "Too bad it's past checkout at that expensive hotel you're wasting your money on; we'd drive you for your luggage, save you all that wasteful rent!"

They needed her money! That was *all*! They had been fired, and that powder Kirk had been snorting even at the nightclub cost a lot, Normalyn knew that. She felt angry, foolish, ridiculously gullible, eager to be included, have "friends," so awed by *anyone's* life! She moved closer to the door.

Quickly, Troja stood before it. "You ain't going?"

A statement? Was she actually blocking her? Not possible! Normalyn looked at Kirk; he had supported her earlier. No, it was clear to her now that the silent exchanges in the dressing room conveyed signals about what was occurring now.

"Yeah, stay, hon," Kirk said to Normalyn. There was no menace in his voice, but there was little emotion in anything he said. It was as if the powder he was fingering demanded his total commitment.

If she side-stepped Troja, would the door be locked? Where would she run in the night? More than the burgeoning fear, Normalyn felt a sense of deep, cutting betrayal. "I thought you were my friends," she said.

Troja moved to one side of the door. "Turnin' mean—too fuckin' tired." She seemed to judge herself. But she remained near the door, not totally committed to remorse. Then she sat down on the floor. She looked defeated by the ugly night.

Or was she acting—to keep her here with less effort? Normalyn did not want to believe they had really intended to force her to stay. They just wanted her to pay for the room tonight, not to rob her. She needed to believe that. Even so, her earlier, easily given trust was tarnished. She prepared to walk out, keeping her eyes on both of them. They did not move. Normalyn turned the knob. Yet— . . . Outside was darkness, streets that seethed with silent violence, kept quiet and in slow motion by the night.

The sudden braking of a car outside was so harsh Normalyn jumped back. Troja sat up. Even Kirk was fully alert.

The police! To save her? Arrest her? Normalyn backed farther into the house. The door opened. A skinny man walked in.

"Duke—" Troja said.

He was small, wiry, with bony nervous fingers that tapped constantly on any surface, or no surface, as he moved into the cluttered room. In his thirties, he had ashy-blond hair, a scratchy complexion. Colorless eyelashes and eyebrows made his dark, deep-set eyes look stark, frightening. "How'd your gig go, babe?" he asked Troja.

"*You* know. You were there." Troja kept her voice firm. But her eyes avoided his.

Normalyn was astonished that Kirk said nothing. Were he and Troja afraid of this man?

Duke flipped a packet of cellophane near Kirk, caught it again, and jerked it away. He said to Troja, "Don't worry about what happened. I already got a date for you."

"She doesn't want to go out any more," Kirk spoke softly.

"How you gonna pay for your heaven?" Duke asked him. "Wanna go out yourself, stud?" He held the packet before Kirk as if he might pull it back. Instead, he let it drop to the floor.

And still Kirk said nothing! Normalyn saw him reach for the packet.

Duke extended a piece of paper to Troja: "Call this number, babe. Remember, you're the black Marilyn. Wear the blonde wig."

"Not any more, no more ridicule." Troja said. She hid her hands behind her, hiding the trembling.

"That's how your fans *love* you," Duke's voice mocked. He glanced at Normalyn against the wall. He smiled an icy smile. "I got the impression you were running out just now. Need a ride?"

"I'm *living* here!" Normalyn felt suddenly protected in this house. And challenged by this whole situation!

Under pale lashes, the black eyes focused on her. Then Duke pointed a finger in imitation of a cocked gun, which he clicked once at Troja, once at Kirk. "Got you, babes!"

When he was gone—and he left a long, tense silence behind him—Normalyn said to Kirk, "Why did you let that skinny bastard get away with all that?" Her blunt question surprised her.

Troja stood before her. "That 'skinny bastard' killed the most powerful black pimp on the street, and *Duke's* still alive!" She looked away, said quietly, "He pulled me out of the streets."

"Into the fuckin' phone booths for your dates," Kirk reminded. Only the words conveyed anger, not the voice.

"Made me high-priced like you were!" Troja shot back. "That's how we came together, babe—two whores trickin' with a married couple." Shocked by her own anger, she pulled back: "And I have never regretted it," she told Kirk eagerly. She knelt near him. "Have you?"

"You know I haven't," he told her. He held her shoulders tenderly. Troja crushed the paper Duke had left. Kirk eased it away from her hand. He smoothed it out, placed it on a table. Then he undid the new packet of cocaine.

Normalyn turned away from them—so much puzzling life. She would leave now . . . The night contained a new fear—of Duke. Waiting outside? She looked into the room with the prepared bed, so incongruous among the disorder everywhere else. She was more frightened to leave than to remain here. Still, she had to be cunning. She would stay, but she would not fall asleep. As soon as it dawned—before long now—she would jump out the window. "I *will* stay tonight," she announced. "But I want you to know I don't have any money with me, just some change and dollar bills." And that was true, she could prove it. "But I have more at the hotel." *That* would protect her!

Troja studied her. "I been scared like that myself, a lot. Nobody's gonna hurt you here, hon. Promise. Now you go ahead and stay." She smiled a crooked smile at her. "There's something sweet about you," she said to Normalyn. Then she walked into the room where lavish dresses were strewn. Kirk began to undress.

They did not sleep together. Normalyn rushed into the room with the boxes. She closed the door, considering pushing boxes against it. But she would be "protected" by Troja's presence, her promise. She took off only her shoes and lay back exhausted on the bed, waiting for the dawn, waiting to jump out the window the moment it was light. She heard night sounds, sirens and—

She woke—startled that she had fallen asleep.

The door was open. Ted Gonzales stood there without a shirt. His muscles—! It was Kirk!

Normalyn huddled against the wall. It felt cold. "Please, no," she whispered.

The door closed, the figure disappeared.

"I'm sorry," Normalyn heard herself whisper—to herself, to life.

Five

Daylight spattered the room. Normalyn sat up. The room *did* have a view, not provided by the small barren yard that belonged to this house, but by a garden next door, a lovely smear of flowers. And beyond were the veily lavender clouds of jacaranda trees! The unfocused joy Normalyn felt stopped when she realized she had slept through her planned escape and remembered, in the next moment, that last night Kirk had stood at the door and—

She had dreamt it! Past fears had fused with new ones during the tired night. The luminous morning and welcome ordinary sounds from inside and outside the house banished the dream entirely as she smoothed her clothes, brushed her hair. Jump out the window now? That seemed silly after she had spent the night unbothered except by a nightmare from the past.

When she opened the door, she saw Troja and Kirk in the "kitchen area." The black woman was already fabulously made-up; she wore a negligée so sheer her flesh smudged it smoky brown. She was cracking eggs into a giant sizzling skillet. Shirtless, Kirk was drinking coffee. Neither looked menacing. Normalyn turned away from Kirk's exaggerated body, which alienated her.

The place looked even more disheveled in the daylight—clothes everywhere, a raid of colors. In an honored space of an otherwise cluttered table was a photograph of Troja the way she had appeared last night on stage. No, it *was* Marilyn Monroe, in the same, sensual, curved pose. Troja had imitated

127

it during the courageous last moments of her performance last night.

"No need bein' shy, hon. Sit down and have breakfast," Troja said.

She pronounced "hon" differently now. She gave it a slight inflection at the end, almost two syllables, making it special, her own, different from the way the people at the nightclub had said it, Normalyn noticed. "I'm not shy," was all she could say, and sat down stiffly at the counter.

Normalyn was very, very hungry. She welcomed the plate of scrambled eggs and the white buttered bread Troja set before her, along with a cup of coffee. But the eggs were dry, the coffee black, the bread almost stale. She was too famished to reject the food.

"Not many places give you the best room *and* breakfast."

Oh, oh. Normalyn just kept eating.

"Go ahead and ask her," Kirk goaded Troja.

Troja arranged a look of great concern on her face; her voice matched it: "Hon, you payin' a lot at that fancy hotel. Bet you don't even have a kitchen. Have to eat out. Ex*pen*-sive!" she emphasized. "Why don't you room here, for a modest—"

"You need money badly," Normalyn understood.

"And *you* need experienced company in the big damn city," Troja snapped.

She did. Normalyn would keep a decision in abeyance. She would let them drive her to the Ambassador Hotel—as Troja was insisting. There, she would decide whether to leave by a side exit and take a cab to— She'd decide then.

In the Mustang, they drove out of the splintered neighborhood; Oriental, Mexican, black, a few white children played along the blocks. Ahead, green hills sailed toward the sky.

They passed an elaborate building, a rotunda with arcs. Vines lazed on it, with red flowers. That was it! Enid had described it. "My mother was baptized there by Aimée Semple McPherson!" Normalyn blurted excitedly.

Troja peered at her over gigantic sunglasses that were almost black. "Your mamma was baptized in a synagogue?"

"It's not the Temple of Divine Love?"

"That's way across town, in Echo Park," Troja said.

Kirk offered, "That Aimée McPherson was a real star—and a con artist. Maybe that's what a star is!" He actually laughed.

"Marilyn was baptized there, too," Troja informed Normalyn. "By that same preacher woman, in 1926."

"How do you know that?"

"*Everyone* who knows about Marilyn knows *that*," Troja said. "You love Marilyn, too, huh, hon?" she encouraged.

Another piece of Enid's life, a cherished one, was being given over to the movie star. "My mother knew her." Normalyn looked away from Troja.

"Hon," Troja asked cautiously, "is your mamma—?"

"She'd dead," Normalyn said, grateful that the battered Mustang was driving up the curved road to the Ambassador Hotel so she would not have to hear any more of Troja's profuse commiseration.

Valets hesitated to approach the ragged car. Normalyn hopped out. She agreed she'd check out, and if they had to move the car beyond the driveway she'd wait in front for them. Troja advised her to complain about the rotten service and get some money back.

As Normalyn moved through the parting doors of the hotel, she saw a tall slender man ahead, staring at her. It was the man who had talked to her yesterday! He was waiting for her! She walked past his intense gaze. Immediately, she was sure it was not the same man.

2

Shocked by what she owed for one night and one meal at the hotel, Normalyn knew she *would* move out. Soon she would have to call Mayor Hughes. And Ted? The memory of last night's dream made her resolve not to call him. Why had she linked Kirk with him, so different? As she thought of all this and paid at the desk, keeping only fifty dollars in cash, Normalyn decided that she would run away from Troja and Kirk.

She led the bellman carrying her bags to a side entrance she had spotted earlier. She pictured Troja and Kirk waiting for her, waiting, waiting longer. Then Troja—no, Kirk—would say, "We frightened her, we didn't treat her as good as we should have." And Troja would say, "But we didn't mean to scare her. Yes, you're right, Kirk. We should have treated her much better. We've lost a true friend. She would have stood by us."

"Please take my luggage back to the front entrance," Normalyn redirected the impatient porter.

Outside, she waved at Kirk and Troja. As they drove away from the hotel, she said aloud, "I'm glad I left Gibson, Texas!"

Kirk reminisced: "I was in Dallas once. A woman married to

an oilman invited me. Used to call myself 'Chance' then." He smiled at a wayward fond memory. "Hadn't been in the hotel more than five minutes when two men busted in, kept calling me 'boy,' said if I wasn't out of Texas on the next plane, they'd kill me." He told the extraordinary story in an ordinary tone. "I knew they meant it. Shit, if they could kill John Kennedy and cover *that* up, they could sure as hell kill me, easy."

"I *know* they killed him in Texas!" Normalyn snapped.

They reached the angled house with the single palmtree.

"I have to unpack and bathe!" Normalyn stalked in ahead of Kirk, who carried her bags. In the rumpled room, she removed boxes from a table she hadn't known was there. She located it next to the bed. Then she took out Enid's chipped angel. She placed it there. She touched the hurt wing. She faced Troja, who stood at the door. "These boxes have to go *out*!"

"Well, damn if you hain't taken ovuh th' manse. Freein' the darkies, Lord bless!" Then Troja's precise words shot out: "What you so mad about your first day as a *guest* in this house?"

"A *paying* guest!" Normalyn did not know why Kirk's story continued to disturb her.

"You're getting a bargain," Troja told her.

"Doing you a big favor." Normalyn counted money out of her purse and gave it to Troja. "Two days' rent. If I leave earlier, you can keep the rest."

"Not enough!"

Normalyn added five dollars. "And I might as well tell you," she raised her voice for Kirk to hear, "that I cashed enough money only for today. I left the rest in the safe deposit box at the hotel—locked." She congratulated herself for her cunning way of dealing with cunning people; but her triumph was instantly dampened by Troja's reaction.

The black woman roared with laughter. Then in her shantiest tone she said, "You a mighty smart young miss for a fact!"

Normalyn was not entirely sure she would stay through the day. Why had she even come back?

Kirk had already snorted two pinches of the white powder— "for energy," he told Troja—and gone to work out with weights in a small back porch. The clanging of the weights angered Normalyn even more as she pushed the boxes in the room against the walls. Then she discovered: a lamp, a prettily framed mirror, and a large walk-in closet. In a conciliatory mood, Troja donated a rainbow-spectrumed scarf to the lamp;

and even Kirk, through working out, was moving the boxes out.

"Look!" Troja had uncovered a trophy among the clutter. On it, the carved male figure of a muscular man was oxidizing. His, from a distant contest, Kirk held it as if it were something very delicate. Then he dumped it back into an old box. Normalyn had seen the designation: "3rd Place. Mr. America. 1963."

Troja followed him into the other room. He snorted the white powder twice into each nostril. He turned on the television, loud. The station's ridiculous "rhymin' weatherman Clive Barnes," was predicting "cheerful skies for worried eyes." "Fucking asshole!" Kirk clicked him off. The focused anger ended the abrupt mood.

At dinner—frozen food trays, Normalyn saw despondently—Troja and Kirk discussed new jobs: Kirk "bartending"—but not in "those fucking cuffs, goddamned bow tie choking me" —and Troja "entertaining"—but not, she emphasized, to be ridiculed. Neither mentioned Duke, but Troja fingered the paper he had left. Normalyn welcomed that Kirk offered to go rent an "old movie" to watch on their VCR. "A love story or a horror story," Troja recommended.

Feeling awkward in this foreign house she found herself living in—how, exactly, had it happened?—Normalyn went to "arrange" her room further. She was still there when Kirk returned with a movie cassette and a tabloid newspaper he claimed Troja liked and she claimed he did. "That fuckin' reporter's at it again about Marilyn Monroe having a daughter," he told Troja. Normalyn listened attentively.

"That's what made that jerk Holden insist on that crazy billing," Troja accused. "That reporter can't stop writing about that."

Normalyn stood at the open door.

Troja sat on the bed with Kirk, scrutinizing the newspaper. His arm was about her, loosely. Her body seemed to melt at the touch, as if it were *she* who was embracing him.

Normalyn forced herself not to move, to stay away from the newspaper they were reading.

Kirk saw Normalyn. "I heard him on a talk show once," he told her. "He kept saying he's going to find out the truth about Marilyn, but he wouldn't say what truth he's looking for."

"Just lies," Troja dismissed. "Like people always claiming famous dead people are still alive.

"Yeah, they keep saying that about James Dean," Kirk agreed.

"Know huccome?" Troja pressed closer to him. "Cause only *real* people die. Stars aren't real, they're *created*," she said proudly.... "That's a mean picture of her." Troja looked away from the newspaper photograph toward the one she kept framed of the movie star. "So beautiful," she said. "She *fought* for her beauty—wasn't born with it like that."

Pretending to be looking for "something" in the room, Normalyn positioned herself so she could look at the newspaper. She saw the headline:

NEW CLAIM MARILYN HAD SECRET DAUGHTER.

She took the newspaper—"Let me see that." Did she only imagine Kirk's eyes clamped on her as he relinquished the tabloid?

She saw immediately what Troja had called "cruel." On the front page under the screaming headline was a large photograph of Marilyn Monroe taken after one of her "crises"— unidentified. The camera had cornered her against the angle of two white walls. Although grainy, the picture revealed a despondent woman, trapped.

"May I?" Normalyn did not look at them, but she was sure both Kirk and Troja were staring at her now. The story under the headline claimed only that a woman in a sanitarium —"according to attendants"—asserted that the star had given birth to a child, a secret kept hidden by "powerful figures." That cursory account seemed intended to prop the last paragraph: "Recent disclosures involving the star's alleged involvement with the Kennedy brothers are stirring new interest in circles of power." In an adjoining boxed story next to it, about the Dead Movie Stars and their "sudden celebrity," someone "who goes by the assumed name of Lady Star" was quoted as announcing that the cult group was exploring "a dramatic recent development" that might shed "new light on the secret lives of one of the two greatest female stars in history." Lady Star had tantalized by saying that "the development" concerned either Verna La Maye or Marilyn Monroe.

The writer of both stories was David Lange. *There is nothing mysterious about her death, only her life.* Normalyn remembered the words attributed to this man in Enid's newsclipping. Enid had drawn a dark black question mark over his name. Years later he was still exploring the movie star's life!

Normalyn indicated her indifference to the article by pushing the paper away—"just trash." She sat on the floor to watch the movie Kirk had inserted into the VCR. "Has he been writing these lies for long?" Normalyn yawned to underscore her lack of interest.

"Yeah—a long time—but he's been at it really strong recently for"—Kirk paused, figuring it out—"for about two weeks, yeah, more or less."

"Oh," Normalyn said.

Kirk pushed the "start" button for the movie. "It's *The Maltese Falcon,*" he told Normalyn. "A favorite of mine."

"Mine, too." Troja prepared to share it with him. "I love it when the fake bird they've all been looking for just gets plopped right down before them."

Normalyn tried to watch the movie, but her attention refused it. The power of Enid's letter! She marveled at it. Right now it had even made her feel that the article was somehow addressed to *her!* She *had* to find one central, clear lie in Enid's claimed life, a lie powerful enough to render the letter itself a lie—and to free her from its terrible power. Without knowing it, Troja had told her earlier where she must go to find that lie.

Six

The old man stooped over the organ as if he were very, very tired, but his fingers glided over the keys as if they possessed a separate energy, life, creating notes that were resonant with passionate reverence. The strains of Handel's mighty *Messiah,* the "Hallelujah Chorus," reverberated throughout the cavernous Temple of Divine Love in Echo Park.

It was here years ago that Aimée Semple McPherson, the queen of religious drama, decked herself in saintly robes of white and gold and ruled over thousands of the devout, cajoling and pleading with them, a star of evangelists, soon to fall in scandal from the constellation of great preachers. She had been kidnapped! She was held in a secret place! She escaped! Those were the conjectures that befell her saintliness when she disappeared at the peak of her following; and that is what she claimed when she reappeared, triumphant, this lusty voice of God. But another truth emerged: She had kept a weeks-long tryst with one of the strong workmen at her Temple of Divine Love. She crashed from her private heaven, and was replaced by a new hierarchy, whose reigning stars were Katharine Kuhlman, subdued, ghostly, veiled in soft gauzes, draped in hair that cascaded to white shoulders, and Sister Woman, equally subdued, even more powerful—some said deadly—insinuating her strong fragile presence on television screens, uttering whispered blessings and curses in equal tones from this same pulpit.

The Temple of Divine Love remains inviolate, its great dome illumined by lightning streaks of gold, its divine pulpit

held aloft by a nest of worshipful flowers, its white rotunda a
configuration of azure pools. Across the street is a green park
with a lake, where giant waterlilies float on their own enormous leaves, as if shaped by the musical radiance emanating
from the Temple of Divine Love, where now the old man bent
over its great organ, golden pipes creating an altar before
him. And the bellowing notes of the wondrous *Messiah* soared
high to the gold-veined ceiling, floated there, trembled violently and then flowed gloriously released under arcs and
corridors that branched into rooms in the intricate network of
the Temple of Divine Love, which was decorated everywhere
with pictures of Christ in flowing ceremonial robes, resurrected, resplendent with faith.

Normalyn and Troja were awed. They practiced reverential
looks; both had worn subdued dresses—Troja had added an
elegant hat. They walked toward the stooped man. Old, old,
his form, with a silver head of hair, was frail over the organ.
As the two neared him, his body seemed to be wearying even
more; but as it wearied, the music became ever more vibrant,
as if he were pouring into it the very last of his sacrificial
waning life.

Normalyn made a soft sound, and Troja echoed with a
subdued cough, to make him aware of their presences.

The old man turned. His eyes were watery gray but shiny.
His long frail fingers pulled away from the keys of the organ,
abandoning the pulsing echoes. The bent body adjusted itself
stiffly.

"What the fuck you bitches want?" he thrust at them in an
ugly gravelly voice.

"What a dirty old man you are!" Troja rose to the assault.

"What do you mean, a-walking in like that and scaring the
shit out of me?" the old man said.

"Don't you talk to us like that, you feeble bastard," Troja
shot back.

"Just don't you call me names, bitch!" he snarled.

"Motherfucker!" Troja chose an exact word.

2

Earlier this morning, at breakfast, Normalyn had announced,
"Today I have to go to the Temple of Divine Love." She had
firmed her decision by speaking it aloud.

"Hon," Troja asked cautiously, "you're not one of those, uh,
born-agains?"

"No, I just have to—" She had not prepared an excuse. "I just have to look up some records, locate some relatives," Normalyn made up.

"Hmmm. How you gonna get there?" Troja inquired.

"Walk," Normalyn said.

Kirk almost laughed. "It's miles away. We'll drive you."

"Yes!" Troja agreed to the outing.

At the last, Kirk had decided he had to work out and: "There's an old movie I want to see this morning. Do you good to get away," he said to Troja.

Troja had looked despondently at Normalyn—feeling stuck with her, Normalyn was sure. She'd have to assert that Troja wait outside for her.

3

Now in the Temple of Divine Love, the old man said, "Will you two ladies kindly tell me what you want?"

"That's much better . . . sir," Troja said through tightened lips.

"Considering it's the Lord's house," Normalyn contributed sarcasm.

"Lord's house, shit. *McPherson's* house," the old man barked. "Crazy to the end; took an overdose and died. Flew in to preach once, hooked on a wire contraption thinking she looked like an angel, but I say she looked like a damn loon. Fooled everyone till they caught her with her pants down."

"What a foul-mouthed old man," Troja said loftily.

"You got a mouth on you, too, girl," the old man said.

"Don't you call her girl!" Normalyn protested.

"Well, you *both* are, because if you want something from me, you'd better walk light." He looked slyly at them, a trace of a grin. "Now, what is it?"

"Some official records." Suddenly Normalyn was tense. Earlier, Troja had simply walked in with her because: "You actin' real strange, hon."

"Should've gone to Records, then," the old man growled, "instead of sneaking into this sanctum—closed to the public except for services."

"It was *open*," Troja prepared to snap back.

"Okay, what?" the old man asked Normalyn.

Normalyn breathed deeply before she spoke: "I'm trying to locate the record of a baptism, a girl's, baptized here in 1926 by Aimée Semple McPherson." She had managed all the words.

"Norma Jeane Baker! Became that big movie star!" the old man said knowledgeably. He recited: "Baptized in December, 1926, by McPherson herself. They *all* come around asking about *her*." He shook his head at the puzzlement of stardom. "Come to ask about her, see where she was baptized."

"Not her," Normalyn said. "Someone else." There was no doubt in her mind, none. Enid had seized even her origin from Norma Jeane. Everything was a lie!

"Come along, I'll take you where you should have gone. Hell, I'm tired of the fucking organ."

They followed him through hallways. Along them, men and women nodded reverentially to him. "Afternoon, Brother." "Afternoon, Sister."

He ushered them into a waiting room with pictures of a shiny-faced Jesus. "What name?" he demanded.

"Enid Morgan." Suddenly Normalyn felt very sad, sad for the woman who had died in her starlet's room. She spelled her name softly, "E-n-i-d."

"I know how to spell, dammit! Do I look stupid?" The man wrote down the name, and he disappeared into smaller rooms.

Normalyn waited quietly. She did not look at Troja, did not want to have to interpret her reaction.

The man returned. "No one by that name. Not that year, not before, not after. Somebody gave you wrong information, girl."

Normalyn was exultant! Released! "Enid lied, my mother lied!" she told Troja, who frowned. One simple step and it was over.

"That Enid Morton was your mother?" The old man, too, was baffled by Normalyn's reaction.

Normalyn felt jerked back into doubts. "Not Morton— *Morgan*."

"Why didn't you say that?" . . . When the old man returned this time, he held another piece of paper. "She *didn't* lie. Here it is." He read: "Enid Morgan. Baptized in 1926 by Sister Aimée Semple McPherson in the Temple of Divine Love. Mother's maiden name: Kathleen Morgan. Father: Edward Stern."

4

A dark-haired youngwoman, almost smiling, radiating a natural beauty captured by the camera in the photograph left for Normalyn on the dresser in Gibson, Texas—that proud woman had rejected her own father's name, had chosen her mother's instead; she had dismissed him *and* his name. . . . Instead of a lie, Normalyn had found a truth that connected Enid and the movie star from the beginning.

Normalyn stood with Troja outside the Temple of Divine Love. They faced the park where waterlilies crowded the lake. Smallish houses like villas, tangles of bougainvillea crawling over them, occupied the area.

Troja adjusted her hat to shade the glaring sun. "What *really* happened in there, hon?"

"Nothing!" Normalyn said tensely.

Troja reacted to the anger: "Guess you just plain crazy then."

The shadow of a pine tree dipped over and clouded Normalyn's sight. "Don't you *ever* say I'm crazy!" she yelled at Troja. She fought the sudden feeling of being swept into darkness.

Troja gauged the intense reaction to the careless words. "Come on, we'll take a drive," she assuaged. "Do Kirk good to miss me."

The darkness receded as the pine tree swayed and the sun fell on Normalyn's face.

The ocean shimmered in the near distance when Troja swerved off the freeway. On this white day, exposed tanned bodies roamed the patchwork streets of Venice. As they walked along the edge of the beach, Normalyn told Troja about Enid's suicide, told her about the overwhelming love, then islets of it in what became a sea of anger in the last years.

"Sad, so sad," Troja said into the long silence.

Ahead was a gathering of bodybuilders with oiled muscles. Troja said, "Kirk was better. Did a movie once, gladiator movie, in Italy. Never released." She faced Normalyn. "He loves me, a *lot*, the way no one else ever has."

They left the beach, driving past hidden mansions in Bel Air, exhibitionistic ones in Beverly Hills—into Hollywood Boulevard before it shatters into dismal remains. When they entered the shabby part of Sunset Boulevard, Normalyn saw the loitering women there even in the early day. Troja swerved away. "Showdown's comin' with Duke, just know it. I'll return to freelance datin' before I go back to him!" she said darkly to herself. Then moodily she told Normalyn about her old neighborhood, Watts, here in Los Angeles. She'd been there when years ago outraged black people burned buildings in protest. "And nothin's changed," she said. She told Normalyn about an old beautiful structure made out of wire, cement, fragments of colored broken glass: "Watts Towers. Used to go and sit there when I was a kid cause it was the only pretty thing around."

They traveled across the city to a cemetery Normalyn mistook for a park until she noticed gravestones along the roads. Swans floated in a lake among flowers. Naked statues were situated among stately trees, green hills. Troja and Normalyn sat in one of the many alcoves in Forest Lawn. In the confessional mood that had developed between them, Troja told Normalyn about her operations, how much they had cost, the hormone shots. "And then at last I was the *me* I wanted."

Normalyn understood. Still, she found it impossible to think of Troja as other than the imposing beautiful woman she saw.

"All worth it," Troja said. "And, hon, I can't say it was one thing that made me decide, but part of it was Marilyn, because *she* created herself."

The reference to the movie star returned Normalyn to the avoided reality of earlier at the Temple of Divine Love. What battle had she fought? Won or lost?

As they sat in the shade of calm trees, Troja told Normalyn this: She had met Kirk when they were both hired to "perform sex" for a couple—she as "the black Monroe," he as a muscleman. Kirk did not know she was a trans— . . . Troja could not speak the word even now. She revised: Kirk did not know about her "operations." And Troja did not suspect that the couple had been told about her by Duke. It was to be part of the "entertainment"—at the height of the "performance" to confront Kirk with the fact that he was making love to a— . . . When he heard the hated word, Kirk pulled away in revulsion. He stalked out. But he waited outside for her. She tried to run past him. He held her while she cried; and he kissed her and reassured her, told her how beautiful she was. They slept together that night. But nothing more happened, ever, and for Kirk it was no longer possible, not with anyone: "He couldn', just *couldn't* any more," Troja told Normalyn. That was two years ago, two years of Kirk's steady decline. And for Troja two years of "tryin' everything, hon," everything to break away from the "goddamned sex dates" and from Duke.

Normalyn told Troja about the ugly afternoon by the Rio Grande.

Troja held Normalyn's hand, sharing the day's sadness.

5

But the closeness was pulled apart that same night. Troja put down the just-reconnected telephone after arranging "a goddamned date."

Kirk had been snorting cocaine. Without looking at her, he said, "You don't have to go out."

"How can you keep telling her that when it's you and that expensive powder that's pushing her out?" Normalyn could not hold back her words. She remembered the poignant vehemence with which Troja had talked about despising her "sex dates."

"Shut your goddamn mouth, girl!" Troja ordered. "You don't know nothing!"

"What she said is true, Troja," Kirk said. "I'd go out myself, Normalyn, but I can't do anything any more. And I'm fuckin' scared."

Normalyn did not want to be swept into pity for him. She turned away.

"*I'm* responsible!" Troja said.

"That's not true," Kirk protested.

Troja embraced the enormous, surrendered shoulders. She looked up at Normalyn and whispered, "Stop starin' at me with your sad mopey eyes, girl! What the hell *you* know about feelin' hurt!"

The words struck Normalyn like a slap. She walked into her room, she shut the door. The closeness and sharing of just hours ago meant nothing. She was here *only* because they needed her money. Goddammit if she would cry!

Minutes later, Troja knocked. Normalyn did not answer. The door opened. "Mean of me to talk that way," Troja said.

Normalyn looked away.

Troja sat on the bed with her. "I *am* sorry for that."

Normalyn could only nod her acceptance, still too hurt by the stinging words, the severed trust—and Troja had voiced only a qualified apology. "Okay, dammit," she managed to say.

Troja walked to the door. She paused, long, uncertain moments. Then she said softly to Normalyn, "Hon, how come you wanted so much to find out your mother lied? What are you trying to discover about her, and about Marilyn?"

When Normalyn did not answer, Troja's smoky eyes continued to inquire.

Seven

Morning with its new reality—a bright mistiness—tempered yesterday's events. Normalyn dismissed what she had discovered at the Temple of Divine Love. It did not confirm the truth of the letter. And she had come to Los Angeles to find her *life*, a life which assumed a jagged pattern jutting into Troja's and Kirk's. Everything still was in abeyance, but she did not know what "everything" included.

She was aware of a sense of allowed drifting, a protected drifting in this turbulent city. The feeling recurred that she had "brought" Gibson with her, extended its isolation by becoming immersed in the lives of others. She felt like a spy.

Yet Troja's and Kirk's lives, too, seemed paused—Troja's only to match Kirk's slow surrender; the black woman's flame-specked eyes flashed at times as if rebelling against that constraint. Normalyn was sure they did not want to be alone with each other during a crisis she saw only manifestations of. Therefore, she *was* wanted.

And so was her money. Normalyn didn't fool herself about that.

"Got an inheritance?" Troja startled Normalyn by asking.

"I'm going to get a job soon," Normalyn said through clenched teeth. And she would, she thought at the moment. She would become a—

"Why? With all your money you left back in that safety box at the Ambassador hotel," Troja gibed, not entirely unseriously.

References to money recurred. Troja had tried to collect rent for a following day, insisting she couldn't remember

141

Normalyn paying in advance. Normalyn would gladly have loaned Troja money—given it to her if she needed it—but she did not want it used for Kirk's destructive purpose. Instead, Normalyn had already bought bags of groceries. That would help them—and improve the quality of what they ate.

Normalyn learned this: Troja was a mixture of beautiful warmth and snappy "high-and-mightiness"—a description Normalyn kept to herself. What she could not accept, would not accept, were Troja's unpredictable rages.

Not wanting to be overheard—she did not welcome her reasons for being here probed—Normalyn called Mayor Hughes from a telephone booth in a gas station nearby. The drawly voice of the Mayor jolted her into an awareness, welcome, that she *had* left Gibson. The Mayor was as warm as always— "concerned you hadn't called me, sweetheart"; eliciting reassurances about her well-being—"ya sure now, ya swear?" "Business matters" were "in order," he informed her. Then he told her that Ted Gonzales had "most courteously inquired" about her. "Shall I give him your telephone number, honey?" No! she thought. "Yes," she said. She explained that the number she gave him was only temporary, belonged to friends. "I miss you, too, Mayor Hughes," she said truthfully.

In those days, Troja went out on "auditions," some of which were probably "dates." Normalyn could hear her growly voice as she made arrangements, "freelancin'." Kirk did not look at Troja when she left, only when she returned. Although she did not wear it, Troja combed out her blonde wig often. One such time, Normalyn stared at it, wanting to locate a ghostly memory it had almost aroused, of fugitive warmth.

More and more, Kirk seemed to be abandoning interest in everything except the powder he breathed, the weights he lifted until sweat oiled his body, and the old movies he saw, sometimes one after the other, on television or on his VCR, as if they contained more reality than his own life. His one seeming contact with the present was the tabloids he bought, as if the pages smeared with rumor and innuendo extending into the past of Hollywood linked him to a time he cherished.

Among Troja's more admiring movie books, mostly of star photographs, were pulpy ones they would pull out impulsively, books with titles like *Scandal! Exposé! True Gossip!* They would sit flipping through stories they repeatedly denounced as "dirty lies," often offering versions of "the real truth," gleaned from their own peripheral participation in that life.

"I didn't know that about Hedy," Troja said today as Kirk roamed through a book titled *The Best of Confidential: The*

Greatest Scandals! "Makes me like Hedy even more!" she approved. "Look at *this,* hon," she called to Normalyn—and emphasized, "such awful lies!"

Normalyn did not want to reject her invitation to share. Kirk moved over for her to sit down, but she sat next to Troja. Whatever Troja had wanted Normalyn to see, Kirk had already turned to another page of exclamatory scandal.

AGE STALKS LIZ!

"Who doesn't it stalk?" Kirk said seriously.

TYRONE AND ERROL: THEIR SECRET LOVE!

"Think of the beautiful little girl *they* would have had . . . if they could have had children," Troja drooled, and was quickly saddened.

ASYLUM HELL OF FALLEN STAR!

"The real truth was that Frances's *mother* was the crazy one," Kirk said.

SINATRA'S MAFIA FAN CLUB!

"Ugh!" was Troja's remark.

ALAN LADD—!

Normalyn touched the picture of the handsome actor.
"You like him, hon?"
"Yes." But Normalyn had been thinking of Jim in Long Beach.

VERNA LA MAYE'S BURIED SECRET!

"Those little Dead shits on television are actually claiming they know who really killed her," Kirk said. He bypassed the next headline. "Sick trash."

STAR'S SEX-CRAZED MOM! EVE HARRINGTON'S GIRL! UPPERS, DOWNERS, AND JUDY! HOLLYWOOD PINKOS! KAREN STONE PAYS AND PAYS! THE KING WAS KINKY! AVA'S GAMBLE!

"Such lies!" Troja reasserted.

JAMES DEAN ALIVE AND INSANE!

"Everyone who dies young gets that," Kirk reminded. "I guess some people *should* die young."

Troja turned that page swiftly. She moved even closer to Kirk, as if to keep him close forever. "Can't bear to look at another," she said, but she did.

"Nelson Eddy did *that?*" she marveled at the next revelation.

NASH MCHUGH AND LORNA REHNQUIST: WHY?

Kirk knew "the real reason": "He had to marry her because he was open about his male lover; so the studio got rid of his lover by calling him a commie and saying he liked young boys. Nash was so damn scared he'd be ruined that he married a lez."

Kirk looked away, toward a memory of his own. "Nash was one of Wilson's boys. Fuckin' agent picked guys off the streets, beaches, promised he'd put 'em in movies, hardly any made it—but *he* made everyone. I met him, once," he said quietly. Then he closed the book, snagged on the earlier memory. He pushed them away, book and memory.

All those beloved figures turned on in those ugly books, and in the brutal parodies at the Hollywood Four Star! The fascination with their lives! Did scandal make them realer? Normalyn thought, Miss Bertha had been right: There were real fans, who loved the movie stars—the way Troja adored Marilyn Monroe. And there were avengers, too. Sometimes one became the other.

2

When Troja went out in the daytime, Normalyn did, too. She did not like being alone with Kirk, although she was no longer afraid of him. Normalyn was used to walking in Gibson. Now she walked in Los Angeles. She would avoid the library. She was *living!*

She explored the neighborhood of small aging houses. The sweet presence of jacaranda trees, blossoms disintegrating right before her, gave her a wistful pleasure. Their lacy leaves were mere decoration for the beautiful dying flowers. She gathered some filmy petals from the ground. Gently, she crushed them into tinier bits, releasing them. She heard the delighted laughter nearby of two schoolgirls watching her. For a moment she thought she heard an echo of two other girls laughing years ago, inventing games. But that was not *her* memory; it was from Miss Bertha's imagined account.

In DeLongpre Park, a small city park, children played games while scattered derelicts slept in shade. There was a fountain, filled with discarded wrappers, newspapers, wine bottles. Ignored in its center was a bronze bust of a handsome man. Next to it a statue of a nude male staring into the sky. Titled "Aspiration," the monument was erected to Rudolph Valentino in 1930, the marker informed, by "friends and admirers from every walk of life, in all parts of the world, in appreciation of the happiness brought to them by his cinema portrayals." Yes, some fans continued to love them! She walked over the debris and wiped dust off the bronze head.

Impulsively, she took a bus that said "HOLLYWOOD." A few blocks along its route, she saw a mural painted on the side of a wall, larger-than-life depictions in bold colors: Humphrey Bogart! Bette Davis! James Dean! And, again dominating even those dazzling stars, Marilyn Monroe. Normalyn got off the bus, walked. In Hollywood, almost every bench displayed an advertisement for the Hollywood Wax Museum—with a reproduction of Marilyn Monroe, white skirt swirling about her legs.

She was on Hollywood Boulevard! The street looked spent, its colors faded. People—men—looked at her. She put on her glasses; that banished some of the stares. Quickly, she took off the glasses, briefly welcoming the attention before she banished it again. Wanderers everywhere, tattered people throughout the city, young and old. And across the street—!

A girl dressed in a gown, with a huge cloth orchid stuck into her flaming hair, was signing autographs for two plump teenage girls. Wearing a bloused shirt and pants tucked into cowboy boots, a youngman with her added his autograph and posed cockily for a giggly girl with a camera. Another youngwoman, with a huge wave of hair covering one eye, pushed into the picture. With them four other young people in similarly odd clothing lingered on display before a shabbily fancy ice-cream parlor.

"It's Lady Star and Billy Jack with the Dead Movie Stars!" a youngman in shorts whispered to a girl with him as they rushed to get a closer look.

Normalyn walked away. The group—and evening advancing with mist—frightened her.

"Hon!" Troja welcomed her at the house. "Been worried about you. You just in time for dinner."

To Normalyn's pleasure, Troja had managed a delicious chicken with whipped potatoes. When Normalyn complimented the meal as Troja's "very best," she was frosted with the information that *Kirk* had cooked that evening—probably in an excess of false energy, Normalyn concluded. Kirk's fingers were drumming soundlessly on the counter.

"What you lookin' for?" Troja asked Normalyn.

"My purse." She had just realized she had left it on the counter when she went out.

"It's on your bed, where you left it," Troja told her.

She found it there. She opened it urgently, looking for the letter, the newsclippings. All were there—and the traveler's checks she had hidden in the lining. Still, the contents seemed to have been rummaged through.

Troja had followed her. "Found it where you left it?"

"Did you go through my purse?" Normalyn's words bolted out angrily.

"Of course not!" Troja turned away.

3

Normalyn's life—the drifting—resumed during cloudy days when the lingering jacaranda blossoms seemed most alive, desperately alive.

"There's another article about Marilyn," Kirk said one afternoon to Troja. He indicated the tabloid he read regularly.

"What does it say?" Normalyn asked. Not to ask would emphasize her discomfort about an ordinary statement, but she did not want to look at the paper.

"It's about all the women who've called the paper after that story about Marilyn having a daughter," Kirk said. "All of them probably trying to get into the movies. Everyone comes here to get into the goddamn movies. Why did *you* come to Los Angeles, Normalyn? Never have told us."

It was not an extraordinary question. It could have been asked of anyone. But it made Normalyn apprehensive.

"She came here to find herself or lose herself, like everyone else," Troja offered. She was now reading the newspaper with Kirk. "How old are you, hon?"

"You asked me before. I'm twenty-one," Normalyn upheld her made-up age. She looked away from them—to sever the subject of her age from the story in the tabloid.

"Imagine! Being *Marilyn's* daughter!" Troja said. "Can you imagine, hon?" she asked Normalyn.

Normalyn's hands were trembling. She went to her room. She made furious sounds by rearranging the sparse furniture.

Troja had understood Normalyn's signals. She came into her room.

"You *did* go through my purse." Normalyn hated those words.

"Yes."

"You read a letter."

Troja hesitated. "Saw one." She did not look at Normalyn. "I borrowed some money from you—*had* to."

For Kirk's cocaine, Normalyn knew, with anger and sadness.

"I'll pay you back," Troja promised. "You didn't have much." She tried to laugh.

"Did you intend to steal more from me?"

"No."

"Why not?" Normalyn held her eyes on Troja.

"Cause after I did, I kept remembering the real close day we had together."

Anger at Troja's stealing from her was almost replaced by the warmth she felt at the assertion of closeness. For this moment she believed her! What she didn't dare ask was whether Kirk had seen the letter.

Normalyn jumped when the telephone rang in the other room.

Troja rushed to answer it.

She was eager to break these moments, Normalyn was sure. She heard Troja's purry sounds on the telephone. . . . *"Kirk!"* Troja screamed suddenly.

Normalyn ran out of her room.

Kirk was staring into his suddenly bloodied hands.

Troja hurried into the bathroom, returned with a pill. Kirk swallowed it. She dabbed at the bleeding nose with a towel. She filled her accusation with concern. "All that coke! Bound to happen."

"I'm all right now," Kirk answered her stare. "You go ahead now, sweetheart. Go ahead."

It was over! Another ordinary extraordinary moment in Troja's and Kirk's lives was over. How quickly Troja had learned to adjust her life to Kirk's. In minutes, she was ready to go—in a swirly pale yellow dress. As she passed Normalyn, she said, desperately, "You get prettier every day, hon. Really!" She blew Kirk a sad kiss, and then she was gone.

Kirk said, "She's right, Normalyn. You are very pretty."

Normalyn retreated from him.

"You know there's nothing to be afraid of from me," Kirk

said. "You had to know it from that first night when I came to your room."

It *had* been him, not a nightmare about Ted!

"I wouldn't have done anything," Kirk said in a tired voice. "I just wanted to know if I could still even think of becoming aroused. You looked so pretty that night, Normalyn; I don't think you knew it. But I wouldn't have done anything if I had been able to. I would never hurt Troja. I hope you believe that. I just wanted to find out, for myself." He turned away.

Without fearing him, Normalyn still hated him in those moments. She was about to close the door of her bedroom when the words of an announcer pulled her attention to the newscast Kirk had turned on.

"—shifting now to reporter Tommy Basich outside the Chinese Theater."

A man with a mighty moustache appeared on the screen. "This is where a group of young cultists were arrested and detained briefly," he said, "when they attempted to force their way into a reputedly secret cellar where, Hollywood legend has it, cement blocks of prints belonging to movie stars banished from the foyer are kept." The camera panned to reveal that next to the man was the youngwoman with flaming red hair, the felt orchid in it. About her, other painted faces vied for the camera.

"Lady Star—that *is* what you call yourself?" The announcer addressed the youngwoman. "What were you and your fellow Dead Movie Stars, as you call yourselves, looking for in the cellar of this famous theater?"

"The block with the prints of the great Verna La Maye," Lady Star said. "They were removed after the scandals that followed her tragic *unsolved* murder." The announcer reminded his viewers that according to police "the scandalous murder *was* solved." Lady Star let a strap of her filmy dress fall off a skinny shoulder. She adjusted it with a flip of her hand. "Not *correctly.*"

Back in the studio, anchorwoman Mandy Lange-Jones announced an upcoming "in-depth" series of news segments that would "probe fan-adulation and focus on bizarre activities, including midnight auditions, of the group known as the Dead Movie Stars."

"Rhymin' weatherman Clive Barnes" was beginning to deliver his forecast: "A breeze from the East— . . ." when Kirk clicked him off, locating a black-and-white movie.

Normalyn looked about the room for the discarded tabloid Kirk and Troja had been reading. She picked it up from the floor and took it into her bedroom. Tidied now, the room looked almost unoccupied to her in the midst of the clutter of the rest of the house.

The article, written by someone named Helena Wallace, stated that there had been "heavy response" to David Lange's recent story concerning "growing speculation" that Marilyn Monroe had given birth to a daughter in the last days of her life, eighteen years ago. Women of all ages—"without any substantiation"—claimed "personal association." The article quoted writer David Lange: "A recent death may result in possible dramatic information in this matter."

In the warm day hinting of heat, Normalyn felt cold. She did not say a word to Kirk as she left the house.

She walked to the telephone booth at the gas station. She dialed the number she obtained from Information. "David Lange, please," she said to an operator at the newspaper. The moment she pronounced the man's name, it seemed to have been extracted from another life. "It's in reference to a story he wrote. . . . Yes, that one." She was transferred to someone else. "Helena Wallace," the woman answered . . . "About the Marilyn daughter story?" Yes. "Leave a number and Mr. Lange will call you back," the woman said . . . *if,*" she emphasized, "you identify the *distinct* nature of your call." Normalyn understood. She was being asked for "evidence" of some sort.

"I can't be reached by telephone, but I'll call back within an hour for him to leave a number where *I* can call him." Normalyn's own words fascinated her. "Tell Mr. Lange that Enid Morgan died recently, and that my name is"—she separated the name carefully—"Norma-lyn."

She went to a drugstore nearby. She bought a paperback edition of *Wuthering Heights.* She located one of her favorite parts, where the angels fling Catherine out of a passive heaven so she can live her passionate life on earth.

She returned to the telephone booth. This time she looked around, as if she might be watched. She dialed again. The operator quickly transferred her. Yes, Helena Wallace said, Mr. Lange had left a number for her to call him directly.

Normalyn dialed. She held her breath. She imagined the reporter's harsh, curt voice. . . .

"This is Normalyn Morgan."

The soft voice said, "May I see you . . . Miss Morgan?"

Normalyn took down the address he gave her, and she hung up without another word.

Eight

Then Troja's life took over violently.

Normalyn had just returned to the house, still holding in her hand the mysterious telephone number and address she had written on a torn piece of paper, when Troja walked in.

Her pale yellow dress was slashed. Kirk held her trembling body. He said words to a new presence at the door: "I'll kill you— "

Coldly blond, eyes like black stones, Duke stood there. "Tell him what happened," he said to Troja.

"It wasn't Duke, Kirk." Troja rushed her words in panic. "It was someone else, waiting for me. Tore my beautiful dress with a knife—tore and tore." She looked down in astonishment at the violated dress. She held a gashed portion of it in her hand. "Duke stopped him, Kirk—I swear it—and he drove me here!"

Normalyn had to look away from Troja, hurting for her, remembering another time.

"You find out who it was and I'll cut *him* up," Duke said.

Troja did not face Duke as Kirk continued to hold her.

"Lucky for you I hear everything," Duke said. "How you been freelancin' and shit. That's real dangerous. Drove there to tell you that when I heard—and just in time, too." His dark eyes bored on Kirk and Troja. "You need protection, babe. This just shows you how bad you need Duke."

Normalyn longed to see Kirk advance on the man, smash the pale scruffy face. But he didn't. And it was clear that the ugly skinny man was responsible, had planned to be there to

150

stop the attack—a vicious warning. They just didn't dare acknowledge that.

"I even got some good news for you both," Duke said with a twisted smile for Kirk and Troja. "Got something for *both* of you again. No hurry on that." He placed a paper by the blonde wig on the stand on the cleared table with the glorious photograph of Marilyn Monroe in the pose Troja had imitated. His eyes glided icily over Normalyn. He nodded. Then he smoothed the hair on the wig. "Too pretty not to wear it," he said to Troja.

Troja shook her head, just slightly.

With mocking delicacy, Duke left Kirk a packet of cocaine on his bed.

"Troja—" That was all Normalyn could say.

2

That ugly incident was not possible! Normalyn sat up in her bed, wide awake. She heard no sounds. Dressing, she opened the door. Troja was still asleep. Yes, it all *had* occurred. There was the piece of paper near the wig. Kirk lay awake, his massive arms behind his head, looking up at nothing.

Determined not to connect with Duke, Troja went out on a few "leads"—real auditions. She would return exposing her dark moods to Normalyn, keeping them from Kirk. What had made her desirable as an entertainer, the black impersonation of Marilyn Monroe, was what she now refused to do since the sacrificial assault at the Hollywood Four Star. She did "perform" occasionally, as a "backup"—"for singers I can sing rings around," she asserted. Normalyn suspected that she still went out on guarded "dates." There was no absence of cocaine for Kirk.

Once Troja returned very tired, rubbing her feet as if she had been walking and standing for long. Normalyn did not allow herself to believe that she had again joined the women on the streets, increasing her dangers.

Kirk went on an interview once, to a bar in a wealthy beach community called Marina del Rey. While he was gone, Troja read aloud—twice, for Normalyn to congratulate—the advertisement Kirk had found in one of the entertainment-trade newspapers she bought daily: "*Must* be muscular *and* good-looking," she read the job requirements, and added, "They could've put Kirk's name on the ad, fits him so right." But

Kirk returned to inform that the job had "already gone"—to a "kid" he had once trained at Gold's Gym.

Since that one day of revelation, Troja had not proposed another drive. She seemed to want only to protect Kirk. So Normalyn would walk or ride the bus throughout the city of complicated wonders, tired and luxurious streets, broken and lofty buildings—and flowers everywhere. As spring aged, her joy at seeing the frail, now fading jacarandas was tainted by sadness.

Normalyn thought constantly of David Lange. She always carried with her his telephone number and his address. Whenever she passed the telephone at the gas station, she paused. It still surprised her to remember that she had made that first call.

Sometimes Normalyn would apply slightly heavier makeup. She had bought her own, with Troja's suggestions on "the best." She would see in the mirror, always fleetingly, "that someone else" she had seen before. Once she reached the front door on her way out before she returned to wipe away the extra makeup.

At times, aware of someone looking at her with interest, she would allow herself a momentary pleasure before the feeling of being set up for ridicule conquered. Once at the corner, a good-looking youngman filling the gas tank of his car started a conversation with her. Normalyn was definitely attracted, too. As soon as she became aware of that, she rushed away. Still, she hardly ever put on her glasses. She knew now she had never needed them, as Enid had insisted.

When Troja's telephone would ring, Normalyn might wonder now and then whether it would be Ted Gonzales. She was not sure whether that would gladden her or anger her.

"We are becoming one strange family," Troja observed once as they sat watching a silly mystery called *The Thin Man*. The detective was a pitiful alcoholic and everyone in the movie thought that was hilarious. Normalyn remembered Enid's pain-etched face—and remembered it now with such sorrow that she decided to escape the memory and the movie by taking a short walk.

She passed the telephone booth. She took out the slip of paper. She dialed David Lange's private number. She knew she would hang up once she asserted what she now thought she had only imagined: that his voice had been concerned, gentle. When there was no answer, it became imperative that she reach him! She dialed again, demanding the telephone connect her. She focused sudden anger on the numbers themselves, punching digits, letting the phone ring, hanging up, dialing again immediately. She was about to hang up and dial yet another urgent time when she realized that the telephone had been answered, by the same soft voice she remembered. Her fingers almost crashed on the receiver.

"Normalyn? If it's you, please don't hang up."

He knew it was her!—had expected her!—perhaps had even kept from answering the telephone, *knowing* she would become determined, and then— She stopped herself from attributing such enormous knowledgeability to a man she did not know. She drained all surprise from her voice: "David Lange?" She spoke the name her mind had been repeating so often in the past days.

"Yes."

She could not think of what to say. He suggested that she might like to come to his office for a talk. If she preferred, he would of course meet her anywhere convenient for her. Then he said, "I believe our meeting would be to mutual advantage, Miss Morgan." She set the time, and the date—tomorrow.

Of course she wouldn't be there. As she walked away from the telephone, it was as if she had not called, so strange did it all seem.

In the morning she decided to verify its full reality.

Normalyn's words stumbled on each other as she told Troja and Kirk that *she* was going "on an interview."

"Secretary job?" Troja said absently as she added rouged highlights to her cheeks with a moistened finger. "And why, with all your money, hon?"

"What makes you assume it's a 'secretary job'?" Normalyn was annoyed. "And as for all my money—"

"Goin' out myself," Troja said. "I'll drop you off if you're goin' my way."

Trapped. Normalyn did not want *any*body to know where she was going—especially not *why*, since she wasn't sure herself. Not able to think up a reasonable address, she consulted the paper where she had written David Lange's. She read it aloud, altering the last two numbers.

"Good address," Kirk reacted. "Agents, producers, big shits. Best section of the strip."

"Then I *can* drive you," Troja decided, insisting that it was "sinful" to waste good money on a cab "when there are needy people everywhere."

"Why are you so damn mysterious, hon?" Troja couldn't keep herself from snapping when she dropped Normalyn off.

Normalyn waited until the Mustang had disappeared along

the street before she hurried to the correct address. It was a small handsome building, only two stories high. Perhaps once it had been a comfortable home. As she walked up carpeted steps, a sobbing woman running out almost collided with her. She was in her sixties, attempting to look much younger; her hair was bleached colorless, her face was a calcimined mask outlined with makeup.

Along a wide hallway were six doors. One was open. She stood before it, before a large elegant room of quiet light.

"Normalyn," David Lange said from behind his desk.

Normalyn walked in.

Nine

She stood inside an oaken office, only two steps into it, committing herself only that far, leaving the door open.

The man who had spoken to her stood up instantly from a graceful leather chair behind an antique desk.

He looks so kind . . . and sad, Normalyn thought.

"Please." The man indicated an upholstered chair facing his.

Only when she accepted did he sit down again. Normalyn knew immediately she was not in danger from this gentle, courteous, intense man.

"I'm David Lange, Miss Morgan. I'm delighted that you're here." He clasped his hands before his chin and looked at her intently. "This is my private office, away from the newspaper. It's where I write, think." He seemed to want to explain the incongruity between this room and the tabloid he wrote for.

He was in his late forties, only slightly heavy, dressed impeccably in a suit. Brown hair was just beginning to thin. He wore glasses over dark eyes.

It was his eyes Normalyn had looked at first. They transformed what might have been a somewhat ordinary man into an extraordinary presence: eyes that were powerful and direct and yet seemed pulled into a depth of sorrow, as if they might command and plead at the same time.

His office was illumined only by sunlight reflected from the Hollywood hills through a large window sheltered by shutters, drawn open now, made of thin strips of wood, real wood. A stilled light that would probably remain constant for the greater part of the day created the impression that there were no shadows, only the controlled consistency of static light, compressed into one brilliant pinpoint within the very center of a beautiful crystal sphere on his desk. There were only two other objects on the gracefully carved desk: a cylindrical wooden container with pencils, a pad of long paper on a brown board. Books, mostly uniformly bound sets, lined paneled walls.

Behind the desk was an incongruous modern painting—bleeding slashes of smeared colors. About it, forming a perfect rectangle, each framed identically, were four photographs of—

Marilyn Monroe, Normalyn recognized.

In the first one, was she still Norma Jeane?—pretty, young, smiling. In the next photograph she had become a star—no, a demi-star, wearing a V-cut dress that adored her body, her head flung back in exultation before the camera. . . . Normalyn's eyes skipped to the last photograph—a woman grown somewhat older, a woman of almost unreal beauty, wide eyes questioning. Sorrow and joy had interlocked to create a look that defined only her. Her lips parted slightly . . .

. . . as if undecided whether to laugh triumphantly or scream, Normalyn thought.

She allowed her eyes to return to the third photograph—of a woman with dark sunglasses, a hand about to guard her face from the eager focus of a pursuing camera. This face revealed a shielded despair. Grainy, a blown-up detail of a larger one, that photograph was . . .

. . . so much like the one Enid had left her—or it had been taken during the same crisis. Normalyn was almost sure.

"Do you know who she is, Miss Morgan?" David Lange asked.

"Marilyn Monroe," Normalyn answered. Her eyes sought again the captured woman of the third photograph.

"Of course. Everyone recognizes her." David Lange dismissed his own question. "There's a President of the United States by that name, but today 'Monroe' evokes only her. She was a great actress, who gave one single performance—as Marilyn Monroe. Toward the last of her life, she seemed to survive only for the camera, existing only in photographs," he said. "That is the source of my interest, Miss Morgan," he explained, "the reality of artifice." He swiveled about on the leather chair to face the reproductions and the painting. Then, turning, he stared at Normalyn.

When Normalyn looked now at the redefined arrangement of photographs about the violent painting, she saw a collage of shapes and forms finding order. Suddenly they were not incongruous in this room.

David Lange's expression had changed, as if he had wakened from a dream. "Do you smoke, Miss Morgan?"

Even his subdued voice startled her in this hushed room. "No. Thank you." He had called her 'Normalyn' only once since she had arrived, when she stood at the door, as if then he had spoken the name aloud to himself.

"I'm glad. I don't either," he said. "The air is contaminated enough, isn't it?" He smiled, but when he picked a grain of dust off his desk, he frowned.

Normalyn noticed a pack of cigarettes on a small table.

"One can't resist without temptation, Miss Morgan," he said.

It was as if he spoke softly so as not to disturb the order of this room. Yet the voice was emphatic. Normalyn would—

"Monroe was a whore who lucked out and made it to the top, the very top."

He said those startling words in the same modulated voice.

Normalyn stood up, walked to the open door, ready to leave angrily. She would be bewildered only later. Now she responded automatically only to the lash of the words.

The caring voice drew her back, gentle and bruised now, as if it had hurt him to speak those words: "Please wait, Miss Morgan. I'm sorry." He stood up while she remained standing at the door for confused moments. "I had to be deliberately cruel to elicit your reaction, your loyalty. Forgive me for that. I had to make sure you really care for her, feel for her."

He seemed to be asserting his own loyalty, too, demanding that she match it—and she had. His eyes were even more surprising in their depth and strength when he removed his glasses, to perceive her more clearly—or to emphasize the honesty of his explanation. He remained standing until she responded, bewildered and fascinated, to his invitation to please sit again while he clarified.

"The others who call in response to the stories about her— the few I've seen here—are all so eager to agree to anything, even *that*," he said with disgust. "No matter how cruel, or how untrue, ready to pretend anything merely to be connected to her. That woman running out when you arrived was only one. On the telephone, she sounded . . . different. That sad old woman, even now trying to look like her, get close to her; she claimed to be involved in Monroe's last turbulent days. She even cried, poor, sad creature, when she knew I disbelieved her—and of course I would."

That last story in the newspaper had indicated the response he was telling her about, but not his disgust at the pretense. Normalyn felt he was warning her and testing her. She did not know the object of his test. Well, she would test him back! "Why do you write those lies about her?" She remembered from Enid's clipping—and his presence had reminded her—that he was an honored man, had been a respected, prized journalist.

"That cheap newspaper is all I have left," he said calmly. "And this office, from more respected times. Is that why you've come here, Normalyn, to judge me?" he asked lightly.

Again he had used her first name.

"But I didn't write lies," he said quickly. "What I wrote about the woman in the sanitarium is true. What *she* says are lies. She's just a poor hallucinating woman craving importance."

Like Enid! Normalyn wanted to think that. But could she, after what she had discovered at the Temple of Divine Love?

David Lange breathed the name as if by itself it summoned cautioning mystery: "Enid Morgan."

Normalyn controlled a sense of disorientation when she heard him speak Enid's name.

"You left it when you called," he said. "She was—"

"—my mother!" Normalyn emphasized.

"And your father is—"

"Stan! Stanley Smith!" She asserted the name Mayor Hughes had donated to her identity. Immediately she regretted having answered at all. She knew that both times she had done so to thwart his possible conclusions because she was not prepared to hear the words *he* might speak.

"And now Enid is dead, and that's why you're here," he said.

She had implied that in her message to him on the telephone, she reminded herself, to dispel a feeling—unjustified by what had occurred—that he knew more about her, or about Enid, than she had told him. She had to balance this encounter, this uninvited interrogation. And she knew how, because she had rehearsed with Miss Bertha! She gained courage from that memory. "Did you know her?" she asked him, her eyes as steady on his as his were on hers.

His hands touched the crystal perfection of the sphere on his desk. He said in a distant voice, "I met her only once, the same night she met Robert Kennedy." He readjusted the pad on his desk, as if unwelcome change perceived only by him had rendered the wooden surface disturbingly askew.

He had answered about Marilyn Monroe; she had asked about Enid. A deliberate evasion? Normalyn had to startle him with unexpected words, the way he had startled her throughout these minutes. "There is no mystery about her death, only her life," she said words he had spoken years ago about the movie star.

"It's still true," he merely said, with a smile. "I follow every clue to that mystery, Miss Morgan, of the last days of her life." His elbows on his desk, his unflinching eyes continued to study Normalyn, as if he were outlining her features. "Have you come here to find the truth, too, Normalyn?"

To Los Angeles? This office? To him? She would not answer, not anything! Still she had to remain—just longer—to find out what *he* really knew, what *he* was pursuing and why. His soft, firm voice startled her.

"Just assume, please, that I *know*."

In the silence, Normalyn heard her own breathing; she heard even the sigh of a breeze—but it stirred nothing in this frozen room.

"Assume that I know people who have been silent for too long, eager to speak, afraid to speak—who will speak only at the exact time, to the exact person. Assume that . . . Normalyn . . . and then I can say this." He leaned toward her, asserting concern: "Be careful. Don't move too openly. Exposure could rob you of what you long for most."

Her life! He knew!

"For now," his soft voice cautioned, "stay on the fringes."

On the fringes of her own life! That's where she was existing! He understood that, too. Might he guide her out of the maze exposed by Enid's letter? . . .

Suddenly Normalyn had to assault this man's strangely commanding words. "I don't trust you," she said quickly.

David Lange did not react in surprise. "I couldn't expect you to, immediately." He smiled. "Perhaps I don't trust *you*." He placed his hands firmly on his desk. "So we've met. Now we may proceed in stages to trust each other, mustn't we?"

Normalyn would not answer. Looking away from him, she noticed that the light had not altered throughout this encounter.

"May we agree only on this, Miss Morgan? Of course you don't have to," David Lange said. "May we agree that we are both searching the same truth?"

Normalyn rose, to leave—to leave and never return.

David Lange stood quickly. He said, "When you're ready for the next step, we'll proceed."

Ten

When she stepped into the street, all that had occurred in the controlled twilight of David Lange's office seemed to have happened in a distant world that was his, not hers. Normalyn remembered a similar feeling when she had left Miss Bertha's house in Long Beach. Was it possible that this man and that kind old woman shared the same twilight? With Miss Bertha she had played a clever game. What remained out of the encounter with David Lange was that his pursuit of the movie star's life contained the seriousness of accumulated years. Why?

As she turned away from the small street and into the bright "strip" of Sunset Boulevard, Normalyn was besieged by questions. It had seemed in moments that *he* needed her. Why? What had he meant when he warned her that "exposure" would rob her of what she longed for most? She had gratefully assumed then that he knew she wanted her life, her own life; his words echoed now with other implications. And why—?

None of that mattered now, Normalyn knew when she boarded the bus, because she had accomplished all she had intended—to assuage her curiosity about him. It had been assuaged. He was a cunning fraud, attempting to get information from her for another of his made-up stories. She would never see David Lange again—ever—nor his strange dark eyes.

But they haunted her.

2

Troja was mending the ripped yellow dress. It lay like a frothy cloud on her lap. In what Normalyn had come to think of as "his corner," Kirk sat watching the glassy screen of his television. They seemed hardly to notice her when she walked in. "Where you been?" Troja finally asked absently when Normalyn stood right before her.

"Interview, remember?"

"Oh, yeah, that secretary job," Troja dismissed.

Earlier, that conclusion had annoyed Normalyn. Now it enraged her. "What the hell makes you think the only job I would want is a secretary's? *I* could be going out on auditions like you!" Immediately she knew Troja had grasped an unintended meaning, a reference to her dangerous "freelancin'."

"What you say—?" The flecks in Troja's eyes ignited.

Normalyn said, "*I'm* living on the fringes, too, remember?" She had wanted only to feel proud of her survival, link it with theirs, but she had only repeated David Lange's exhortation to her earlier. "We're the wounded who walk straight, remember?" Now she wanted to remind Troja that *she* had once said that about them, but instantly she knew Troja had said it about *Kirk,* in secret.

"Where'd you hear that?" Kirk said moodily.

Normalyn could not make up a quick answer.

Troja knew Kirk had detected her reference to him. She shoved her anger at Normalyn: "You don't live on no damn fringes. What wounds you got? You just a rich visitor!"

Thrust away even from exile! Normalyn went into her bedroom. From under her bed, she pulled out one of her suitcases, still partly packed for lack of room. She wrapped the chipped angel in the tissue she had brought with her from Texas. She placed it in the suitcase, protected it further with clothes.

Then Troja walked in, closed the door. She said, "Don't know what to *do.* Found this today, hidden under his bed. That's why I'm panicked, hon, crazy with worry." From the folds of her skirt, she brought out a hypodermic needle. "He's shootin' up. But it just started," she added hope, "just started."

When Troja left, Normalyn "unpacked" the chipped angel and pushed back the suitcase under her bed.

3

Now she wasn't even drifting. Drifting assumed movement
even if it was slow. She paid Troja rent, by the day, sometimes
committing herself to two days. Troja went out, returned
tired, edgy. Deciding it was possible to read *and* live, Normalyn
bought *The Turn of the Screw* and read it in her room in one
sitting. She was certain the governess imagined the intrigue of
ghosts. When she read it again, she became certain that ghosts
were pursuing the woman.

She did not even glance at the telephone booth when she
passed it on one of her excursions to sit in the park with the
bust of Rudolph Valentino. She did not even check to see
whether she had the telephone number with her—that's how
completely she had succeeded in banishing David Lange from
her life. Yes, she could even allow herself to wonder what he
would have suggested as "the next step." Soon she would stop
even conjecturing.

Kirk continued to withdraw into his corner. He would touch
his muscles now and then, as if to assert that they, and he,
were still alive, still growing. There had been no further reference to his "shooting up." Normalyn saw him only breathing
the cocaine, then checking his finger for any stain of blood.
Normalyn had become used to his sudden nosebleeds. Troja
would give him the Decadron that controlled them, then nes-
tle next to him, looking like a lost child begging for protection.

They all sat on the floor watching a rented movie on Kirk's
VCR: *The Big Sleep.* Her hands cupped at the sides of her eyes
to enclose herself in the isolation she felt, Normalyn sat on a
ratty pillow. Either her mind was not on the film, or it made
absolutely no sense. She decided: It *didn't* make sense.

She would have gone for a walk, but it was night and the
streets turned sinister in the dark, many even in the daytime.
She was about to go into her room to read when she became
aware that for perhaps minutes a car had been idling outside.
She walked to the door. It was a new car and it was paused
before their house. Just waiting for someone. . . . But the car
remained there, the motor gunned faster as if in signal.

*Like the car that had flooded her house in lights that night with Ted
Gonzales in Gibson!*

Normalyn took a few steps toward the car, to see the driver.
A man. Did he look at her or only in her direction? The man
at the Ambassador Hotel! No, she couldn't see him that well.
But he was—

Behind her, at the open door, Troja called urgently, "You come on inside, hon!" She, too, had reacted in fear to the idling car, which now made a U-turn, paused across the street again, its engine growling, and then drove away.

Stalking her? Stalking Troja? Normalyn walked back into the house. Troja was trembling.

4

Normalyn did go for a walk the next day. She plucked out of the morning a new clarity. The car that had frightened both her and Troja had been just a car, period. She refused to give any deeper meaning to the fact that Troja was combing out the blonde wig today; she dressed it often, cherishing its touch.

Normalyn decided to go to an area she had seen once, only through the bus window, a beautiful neighborhood called Hancock Park.

She walked along blocks of magnificent homes, which were stately, proud. In places, trees formed green leafy corridors sequined by sunlight. Gardeners smiled at her as she strolled, the only pedestrian on these rich streets, with her purse firmly strapped diagonally over her shoulder. She actually felt . . . pretty.

Now she might go to Melrose Avenue, to one of several trendy shops she had glimpsed. She might buy a new blouse! She walked to a bus stop. When the bus approached, she saw that it had inherited on its side a poster of Marilyn Monroe, a new advertisement for the famous wax museum. She looked at the glorious face so long that the bus driver called out impatiently: "Are you coming in or not? Make up your mind!"

5

Normalyn called David Lange and agreed to meet him again at his office. There were some questions she wanted to ask, she told him. But she was going there *only* to find out what he would propose as "the next step"—so that she could dismiss it. When she was ready to leave the house, she told Troja and Kirk she had "a call-back" about her job interview, and she ran out.

The moment she entered David Lange's office, it was as if there had been no interruption between their first meeting and this one. The light was exactly the same, steadied twilight. Only his suit was different, but as carefully tailored. He sat behind his antique desk and thanked Normalyn—"so much"—

for being there. He spoke in the soft voice she remembered. He focused the probing, deeply caring dark eyes on her.

She made her words sound as casual as she had rehearsed them in the cab: "I have two questions." If only his eyes didn't look at her with so much sadness, concern!

"Please ask them."

What do you want from me! She had not had to rehearse that question, but she did not ask it. "What do you think I want more than anything else?" His assumption that he knew had festered from that earlier time.

"Your life, of course."

He did know!

"And your next question, Miss Morgan?"

"There was only one." He had disarmed her.

He leaned forward, reasserting allegiance. "Perhaps since I've answered your questions—your question—we may explore the possibility of taking the next step I suggested."

"Before I decide if I want to take it"—Normalyn knew she had to resist—"I'll have to know, from you, where we're moving."

"Then I'll tell you more," he said easily. "Yes, we'll move step by step until we trust each other." He smiled, to blunt the words he had spoken. "Please listen to me carefully because this may not be entirely clear to you now—perhaps it is; I promise it will become so . . . Normalyn." He paused.

She had begun to listen for when he called her "Normalyn," and he did so with a slight inflection of his voice . . . as if it were a signal to her. Of importance? Of doubt?

"When something elaborate is planned with exact precision" —he pronounced each word slowly—"and one single aspect goes wrong, the whole shatters into fragments. The fragments scatter. Then if it is to be understood, the whole has to be pieced together."

Normalyn longed to ask for clarity, but he had indicated he would say only so much. Moreover, she knew certain questions might commit her to a knowledge she did not want to expose, questions that might also give him information.

"There's only one person left who can put the parts together." David Lange continued the precise words. "And only one who can find out."

The same person? Two? Was one of them herself? Someone he would make available? Normalyn did not want her questioning to be perceived in her reactions—and he was studying them, she was sure—so she stared down at the carpet, noticing an intricate configuration of patterns not apparent before, colors buried in smooth darkness. When she looked up from the darkened colors, she heard him say in a whisper poised over the silence:

"We need proof."

Proof! He was trying to trap her into telling him about Enid's letter. She touched the clasp on her purse. "I don't have any proof." Rejecting him, she no longer avoided his eyes. "I don't know what proof you're looking for, nor of what."

"I didn't say 'proof,' Miss Morgan. I said 'truth.' "

Had he? He had posed his whispered question so that if she did not respond—with reference to Enid's letter—he might withdraw its implications, as he was now doing. She was sure of it. Or *had* she heard the wrong word, barely spoken?

"You're trying to trap me, David." The words of challenge pushed away her confusions. He knew nothing, spoke only in generalities. Who wouldn't know that what a person wanted most was her life?

"There was a letter—" David Lange said, and stopped.

He did know! Normalyn heard her own breathing. She held her purse—Enid's letter—closer.

"A letter containing lies—"

Then she *could* receive from him the proof of the necessary lie she had not found at the Temple of Divine Love! A brighter reflection of light seemed to Normalyn to have seeped into the room, nudging vague shadows, contrasts. She could trust him.

"—or did the letter contain truth?" David Lange converted his statement into a question. "Do *you* know who wrote that letter, Miss Morgan?"

Oh, but there were two parts to the letter—*two* letters. The second—Enid's—added force to the first. Normalyn cautioned herself: Don't trust him, not yet, don't react, look away from his pained eyes. "Do *you* know, David?" She threw the question back at him.

"Will you speak to someone who has essential information about it?" he asked very quickly.

"Who?" She didn't care whom he would name. She would not go.

"Mildred Meadows," David Lange said.

Enraged X's—Normalyn remembered Enid's markings next to that name on the newsclipping in her purse.

"An exiled queen eager to reclaim her throne." David Lange's voice was toneless. "A recluse—but she'll see you."

Normalyn had to know just this much more, and only to hear what he would say: "Who would you tell her I am, to make sure she'd see me?"

David Lange stood up. He turned to the photographs on the wall.

At that moment they seemed to Normalyn to radiate out of the tangled disorder of the painting at their center.

David Lange faced Normalyn. He smiled. "I'll tell her that I believe we have found . . . our Normalyn."

Eleven

"There were three people who mattered in Hollywood: myself, Zanuck, and—some said—J. Edgar Hoover. Parsons and Hopper were clowns. *I* ruled until—" Mildred Meadows aimed an unspoken accusation at Normalyn, who stood where a butler had only moments earlier abandoned her before the woman.

Tiny, frail, Mildred Meadows was certainly a well-preserved eighty years old, dressed in a purple gown outlined with gold lace. Darkened-silver hair in meticulous waves framed a delicately featured handsome face, made up impeccably.

She sat in a velvet chair with ornate armrests; its carved gold legs clutched thick carpeting that rendered footsteps soundless in the enormous house of chandeliers, lush furniture, white statues, paintings of pastoral landscapes, walls decorated with a filigree of gold bunching at tall arched doorways and windows that parted past thick folds of drapes into a white-stoned veranda clawed by violent vines spilling like blood onto a lawn of green perfection stretching to the edge of trimmed shrubbery, which surrendered to looming trees sealing this enormous mansion in the rich seclusion of the Bel Air hills.

Having introduced herself at the top of the hierarchy of power, Mildred Meadows commanded Normalyn, "Sit *there,* my dear, I've been expecting you. David called."

Normalyn did not sit in the chair the old woman directed her to. She sat in a taller one next to it.

"Hmmm. Zanuck's chair," Mildred Meadows deliberated.

And so Normalyn *had* called David Lange, to "suggest" that she "might be willing" to be "put in touch" with Mildred Meadows. David called her back at the public telephone booth

167

at the gas station. "She expects you at—" . . . Normalyn had decided to take just one more step—and *just* to find out what they would *claim* to know about the letter. Telling Troja and Kirk only that she might be late—"another call-back?" Troja probed—Normalyn had taken a cab, gasping as the meter soared.

Now in the Bel Air mansion, Mildred Meadows raised a crystal goblet to her thin lips. "Sherry soothes calm nerves," she said. "What may I offer you, my dear?"

"Iced tea." Normalyn made her answer a challenge.

"Iced tea. . . ." Mildred's brittle lips almost relaxed into a smile, only the memory of a smile. "Did David coach you to ask—?" The lips abandoned the faint smile, and withdrew the question.

Coach her? No. Normalyn was not even sure what David Lange had actually told this woman about her.

Mildred Meadows tinkled a bell, tiny like her. The butler entered the room soundlessly. "Baroness?" he asked.

"Iced tea for the young lady, and a bit more sherry for me." He left, bowing.

The woman said to Normalyn, "One of my husbands, I forget which, was a baron."

The butler returned with iced tea on a silver tray for Normalyn, and an amber bottle of cut crystal; he poured sherry into Mildred Meadows's goblet. The slightest flutter of her hand—she wore only one ring, a pearl—instructed him to leave the decanter beside her. She aimed words at Normalyn: "You responded to David's article about Monroe. Why?"

"The reason he gave you."

"Why are you here?"

"The reason he told you."

"Charming!" Mildred complimented the banter.

In response, Normalyn clinked her iced tea at the old woman before she sipped from it.

"But then David's reasons are sometimes *too* lofty to grasp immediately, aren't they? All we can know for certain is that he pursues pure truths—no matter how vulgar the route, like that newspaper he writes for. His nettlesome conscience makes him grandly vindictive." She pretended a slight shudder; she touched her hair as if even that much reaction might unsettle the waves. "He waits for years for his revenge."

A warning? Were they antagonists or co-conspirators?

"You came for information," Mildred asserted.

"Perhaps."

"Well, you'll *get* information." The tiny woman hissed. "Do you know who tried to poison her husband but he got her first? Do you know who kidnapped a starlet and kept her on drugs until she had the role they both wanted? What actor married in a white gown, what actress married him in a tuxedo? What aristocrat turned out to be the daughter of the chauffeur she had an affair with?" At each question she leaned more closely toward Normalyn, as if advancing on her.

Miss Bertha would despise this woman! Normalyn evoked an ally. She had no idea who the various objects of Meadows' flaunted malice were. To emphasize the irrelevance to her of vicious gossip, she offered one single name, that of the movie star constantly resurrected in the news: "They were *all* Verna La Maye!"

"Oh, you are a clever thing, my dear," Mildred Meadows approved, with what might have been subdued laughter if she had allowed her features to relax slightly more. "But do you know"—her voice lowered to a whisper; she held the goblet motionless before her—"what star's secret pregnancy sent shock waves to the White House?" She took the tiniest sip of sherry, dramatic punctuation.

Normalyn backed away from this pursuit. *Don't, dearheart!* she imagined Miss Bertha advising.

"Do *you* know, baroness?"

"Let's say that I do," Mildred Meadows declared, "since circumstances seem to require ambiguities and riddles." She savored the situation and the sherry. "Of course, during our chat, you do get to ask questions, but only intelligent ones. That's how I'll know whether you deserve intelligent answers. Otherwise I'll terminate our visit, my dear, I promise."

Like David, Meadows wanted something from her; she was asserting the opposite too emphatically.

"And if *you* don't provide intelligent answers, then *I'll* stop asking, I promise . . . my dear." Normalyn astonished herself.

"Checkmate!" the older woman adjusted her lacy cuffs. "For now," she added. "I never liked chess—a feeble, slow substitute for life." She said suddenly, "I detest those filthy birds!"

Normalyn heard the chirping of birds outside.

Mildred Meadows said, "They dirty my garden; they fall dead on my lawn with their withered legs straight up, feathers matted. Repulsive. Ugly. I detest ugliness, my dear. I have never allowed it to touch me." Her coiffed hands pushed as if ugliness might lurk unseen. "My only daughter, my beloved Tarah—she chose her own name—my Tarah was *beautiful*." Mildred kissed the last word. "Alas, beauty does not guarantee more beauty. She had a child who was . . . ugly." She distanced that word from its contamination. "Both died in an automobile crash," she said. To stop emotion from seeping into her voice, she placed a finger to her lips and outlined the careful arc of her lipstick.

Birds chirped.

The slight form rose from her throne and walked to the tall windows. She made a hissing sound to scatter the birds. In the light of the window, she was so small it seemed that if she took one more step she would disintegrate into the moteless air. With a sudden yank, she parted the drapes farther, releasing a stream of bright light on which she floated back toward Normalyn. Her eyes captured the youngwoman in their fixed gaze.

Normalyn's hands rose instinctively, to conceal herself from the stare of this woman who cherished beauty. Instead, she pushed her hair back defiantly. She removed the glasses she had worn. She looked up directly at the woman.

"Yes!" Mildred Meadows approved.

She returned to her throne. "You must know certain things about me," she announced peremptorily.

Why? Normalyn wondered and almost asked, to jab at the woman's self-importance; but she knew she must allow a gradual flow into the territory she was here to explore.

Mildred Meadows had already proceeded to define the time of her reign: "My newspaper column was feared, read by millions—everyone! But it was also, at *special* times, an intimate letter from *me*—personal messages conveyed, warnings issued, secret information given—recognized only by those it was intended for. Like this: 'Friends and family are hoping Ingrid will return to the United States to avoid the hot Roman summer.' She ignored the warning, and I announced the news of the illegitimate pregnancy!" Mildred thrilled to the memory of exorbitant power. "I could destroy with a single exclamation mark. A classic: 'Leftish bachelor Mark Poe claims he doesn't want children but insiders insist that that is—emphatically! —not so.' The exclamation mark was the dagger." Mildred was charged with remembered excitement: "It frightened his lover away and into marrying a true patriot, the Rehnquist heiress. . . . Quotation marks were inspired," she exulted, and recited: " 'An amusing story circulating Hollywood is that Errol Flynn claims he has become increasingly fond of 'statutory.' Of course, he means 'statuary.' As a well-known collector, he should know better.' Yes, and when Ava—"

Lies, Miss Bertha whispered indignantly to Normalyn.

"The stories were untrue," Normalyn interrupted Mildred

Meadows' ugly recitation of names she remembered hearing only distantly. She *had* to assert her hostility to this woman.

"Untrue!" Mildred waved her hand slightly, as if a fly had dared to annoy her. "What mattered then was the destruction of all that threatened the studios, and therefore the country! That's why the loyal in Hollywood turned to *me*. The others went to"—her mouth masticated the name—"to that creature—that Alberta Holland! That horrid left-winger who dared to challenge the august committee of patriots investigating subversion and immorality in high places! She actually told them to—" The thin lips sealed in outrage.

Say it, dearheart, Miss Bertha encouraged.

"—to fuck off." Normalyn had to close her eyes and inhale before she could pronounce the words. She *had* to affront this destructive creature she was sure Enid had loathed.

"How do you know that?" Mildred pounced.

"I read it in her autobiography," Normalyn said. In her mind earlier, she had begun placing Miss Bertha in her soft comfortable chair to confront this woman on her rigid throne. Powerful antagonists! No—the image evaporated into the benign memory of Miss Bertha, gentle, playful, pretending she had given salvational advice; slumbering into dreams. Or *had* Miss Bertha deliberately "rehearsed" with her to prepare her for a situation like this one? That would have to mean that the old woman knew this would occur, and that would have to mean she was— . . . Normalyn decided to leave Miss Bertha where she had placed her, near her.

Mildred Meadows flinched at Normalyn's answer. "Autobiography! Ha! *I've* written mine *three* times." She breathed composure from her sherry. "Holland got what she deserved—prison for contempt," she triumphed.

Miss Bertha, in prison? That gentle soul would not have survived. Yet there had been those moments of enormous strength, anger. Normalyn tried to fit the kind woman she had met in Long Beach into the turbulent life of Alberta Holland. . . .

I was young then, Miss Bertha reminded.

"And she came out of prison even more radical," Mildred extended her judgment, "still protecting that exiled Spanish woman who had betrayed her own aristocratic class to join the—the"—she could hardly form the word—"the *gypsies!* . . . How fitting that Holland should die in exile—but not before she lived to create her greatest catastrophe—when Monroe turned to *her*."

Miss Bertha had evoked a similar time, and so had Enid. Normalyn listened attentively.

"Monroe always needed strong women to protect her, but she turned to neurotic ones—Natasha, Paula, Holland!" Mildred denounced them merely in pronouncing their names. She stopped abruptly. "Those were older women." Her voice lowered. "But there was another woman, her age, someone more important than all the rest, a woman who lived in Monroe's shadow, or perhaps Monroe lived in hers. Perhaps they shared that, a shadow. Alike opposites," she whispered.

Alike opposites! That's how Normalyn suddenly remembered the two women on the shoreline.

"The woman was always there, during all the crises, clicking a silver cigarette lighter, conveying to Monroe a secret message understood only by them, as if—" It seemed still to baffle her, after years and deaths. "—as if Monroe must never forget something, something essential. . . . *You* name that woman, my dear," Mildred's command was abrupt.

Testing her! To make sure *she* knew, ascertaining *she* was who she said she was! Yes, yes, Miss Bertha *had* rehearsed her for this. *You must tell her the name,* Miss Bertha instructed.

"Her name was Enid, Enid Morgan," Normalyn said. And so for her, in this moment, Enid was born into a real past, into the life of Marilyn Monroe. Normalyn sighed, greeting this new life of the woman she had known intimately and then not at all. To maintain her own reality of her, Normalyn said, "She was my mother; she died a few weeks ago in Texas. And she was beautiful, too—"

Mildred cautioned, "Tears will disturb your subtle makeup."

"I'm *not* crying," Normalyn denied. She would let the tears dry on her cheeks.

"Oh, yes, Enid was quite beautiful." Mildred cherished her own memory. "You know she was my ally."

"That's a lie," Normalyn protested. Enid would not join with this evil woman. The violent slashes punctuating her name in the newspaper column affirmed that.

Mildred sipped the soothing sherry, allowing the matter in abeyance. "And so Enid killed herself."

Normalyn did not react in surprise—David would have told her that. What did surprise her was that there had seemed to be a note of sadness in the woman's voice! *Faked,* she dismissed.

Mildred Meadows shook her head slightly, as much as her entrenched composure would permit. "In a locked room and with pills. Like Monroe," she concluded. "And she left you . . . what, my dear?"

They were approaching the subject of the letter, but she must not donate information.

Pretend you misunderstood, Miss Bertha counseled.

"She left me enough to get by on, for a time," Normalyn spoke the Mayor's words to her.

Mildred's lips tilted. "I see." She adjusted the lacy collar higher about her neck. She studied the single pearl on her finger. "Monroe! Her innocent smile bled with sensuality." Then she said with undisguised pride: "It was I, you know, who exposed her lies." Her words shot forth in triumph: "*I* revealed the nude pictures! *I* discovered her mother was in an institution, not dead!" She calmed her words by sniffing at the goblet.

"But she wouldn't *let* you destroy her." Normalyn remembered Miss Bertha's account of the movie star's victorious survivals.

"Ah, but *then* I learned of the existence of the letter!" Mildred sighed deliriously.

Normalyn folded her hands over her purse, the letter.

Don't be frightened of her, dearheart!

"That's when I had to enlist David." Mildred congratulated herself on cunning. "It was a challenge, yes—because he didn't believe the *first* letter. It was the second one that convinced him."

How could they have discovered the existence of the letter Enid had written to her, perhaps only minutes before her death, and left for her in the bedroom in Gibson? . . .

Miss Bertha clarified—

No, even she was silent now, as confused as Normalyn. Mildred's powerful words had staked a territory that could not be avoided.

"How the hell do you know about the letter Enid left me!"

"What letter did Enid leave you, my dear?" Mildred's eyes clasped Normalyn's.

Normalyn attempted to withdraw: "I— . . ." She could not think now. "What letter are you talking about?"

"Why, the letter given to J. Edgar Hoover accusing John and Robert Kennedy of immorality, and the subsequent letter naming Monroe as one of their women—the letter that began it all!" Mildred's greedy fingers conquered her goblet. "My dear, were you thinking of *other* letters? Which? Which!"

Normalyn controlled her panic. This woman was not talking about the letter she was carrying with her this very moment. That meant David Lange did not know about it either! He, too, knew only of those Mildred Meadows had just identified. But now Normalyn wasn't entirely sure of that, not sure. She tried hurriedly to reconstruct David's words. Their meaning altered. . . . She had told this cunning woman—almost told her, she reassured herself—she had *almost* told her about Enid's letter!

Deny it all, dearheart! Miss Bertha found her voice.

Inspired, Normalyn said easily, "And so, dear baroness, *I* have tested *you* back!"

"Oh, so you have, so you have," Mildred Meadows said. "And because you have, and so cleverly, my dear, now I *will* tell you everything you need to know."

"Need? For what?" Normalyn was aware that the certainty she had regained moments earlier was escaping her voice. She revised its tone: "Need for what purpose, my dear?"

"For your purpose, of course," Mildred glided over her words. Again a tiny smile lurked over the composed lips. "You've convinced me that you do deserve information." Mildred moistened her lips with sherry, careful to touch them only with the edge of the crystal. She poured a few more drops into the goblet. "This will sweeten my account," she said to Normalyn. This time her smile shaped, then swiftly fled. Mildred Meadows leaned sightly forward from her throne: "Now listen carefully, my dear, listen very carefully . . .

"Joan—"

Twelve

—Crawford paused to adjust her lipstick before knocking at
the door of Marilyn Monroe's small duplex. She would remark later to Mildred Meadows that had it not been for her
close attention to her lips—Mildred approved of special attention to beauty—she would not have heard the harsh voices of
two women emerge out of the house; her knocking would
have interrupted them.

Joan and Marilyn had become friends a few weeks earlier
when Joan, who was forty-seven but looked no more than
thirty-five when makeup and light were exact—and her great-
star's instincts *made* them so—learned that the twenty-five-year-
old starlet considered her one of her "idols." Joan telephoned
the thrilled starlet at the studio—"Is it really *you*? It is *really*
you?" Marilyn kept asking. Yes!—and Joan had invited her to
Sunday brunch.

Crawford was a smart woman whose beauty toughened as
she grew older, so imposing that she appeared much larger
than she was—actually petite. Star-instincts told her that Marilyn Monroe might become a contender for the crown Crawford
was certain *she* still wore, though battered in the wars. How
better to deal with a potential rival than to befriend her?

At brunch, Joan graciously guided Marilyn about her Art
Nouveau home; shiny black and white floors reflected shrill
windows. Remarking on Joan's kindness in adopting several
children, Marilyn won the star over by saying *she* wished she
had been "this lucky" during the many times she was in homes.
"M-m-my mother is dead, you know," she said sadly, in the
slight stutter she would never lose. Joan assured her, with a
squeeze of her hand, that if Marilyn had been up for adoption

175

she would have "chosen" her as a daughter "despite the closeness in our ages. We would, of course, have been more like sisters."

Overhearing them, a small girl with yellow curls lunged headlong down the stairs toward them. Marilyn veered, wrenching her ankle. The child glared at the two women.

Marilyn adored children. "Please don't be angry with her. I'm sure she didn't mean us harm," she said to Joan.

"I *did!*" hissed the angered child.

Joan suggested the girl go upstairs. Later, she promised, they would have dinner together: "Perhaps some of that rare roast beef you enjoyed last night." When the child ran off, Joan said, "I do so worry about what she'll do when I'm gone."

In the following days of their friendship, Joan gave Marilyn expert advice—who knew the pitfalls of Hollywood better than the great Crawford? She even offered the younger woman some of her own clothes, knowing that Marilyn was just getting by, but the clothes were too small for the lusher actress.

All this came to the attention of Mildred Meadows when Darryl Zanuck, chief of production at 20th Century-Fox, told her that he was terminating Monroe's contract. He had never championed her, or even helped her. He'd hired her only at the instigation of a retired executive who believed in her. Zanuck—who had discovered Rin Tin Tin and years later fired his own son from the studio—did not like to be proven wrong. An item in Mildred's column would offset any studio criticism, especially from the East, where the starlet's champion still claimed some power with the Board of Directors. At the same time, Meadows's loyal confidante—Crawford—was befriending the starlet. How to satisfy both loyalties?

Item: That great actress and sublime beauty, the ageless Joan Crawford, is giving that blonde waif—inexperienced starlet Marilyn Monroe—a lesson in true stardom with generous guidance. Will the waif be grateful? Studio chiefs have reason to wonder, too, about the difficult starlet.

There was yet another purpose for the item in Mildred's column, the most important one. Mildred was used to being courted by the most powerful in Hollywood, and lesser aspirants knew they had to petition dutifully for her attention, granted or not. Monroe had made no overture. The item was intended to correct that oversight.

It did not.

Marilyn's friendship with Crawford thrived. In her silver

limousine, Joan went to Marilyn's apartment to pick up the needful starlet, exiled by Zanuck, taken in uneasily by Columbia Studios. The two women were going on a picnic, a drive along the dramatic Malibu coastline. Joan had Chasen's prepare an extravagant lunch, with champagne. Hoping to arouse the childlike pleasure the starlet expressed at surprises, Crawford arrived early—and walked to the door herself. Before knocking, she stopped to freshen her lipstick—

—and heard the raised voices of two women!

Crawford had a superb memory. She learned the script of *Rain* in one day and of *Mildred Pierce* in two and a half. When she was humiliated into having to audition for the latter role, she won it easily by performing key scenes without glancing at the script. So she recounted—verbatim, she swore—to Mildred Meadows the strange exchange she overheard in those moments before she announced her presence.

"She'll never leave you!"

"She'll never leave *you! I've* left her."

"It's not possible, you know that. You can't."

"I already have. I don't want to play any more."

"You can *never* stop."

The angry altercation—and Crawford was not sure who had said what; the voices jumped on each other as if this dialogue had occurred before—ended in tense silence. Suddenly the two women burst into girlish laughter! Seconds later, a woman emerged from the back of the apartment house and drove away in a nearby car. Joan had been able to see her: pretty, very pretty, with dark hair; about Marilyn's age.

Joan knocked, deeply puzzled by what she had heard. A game?

Marilyn made no reference to the matter. The chauffeur drove them to a secluded cliff, a miraculous patch of grass shaded by a cluster of palmtrees. Below, the ocean swept the blue horizon. Marilyn became heady with the chilled champagne she was not used to—later she would acquire such a taste for it that she would adjust any time of day to allow for "champagne brunch!" Joan suggested they drive back to her home, where Marilyn might take a nap and then join her for dinner. Within the intimacy of the limousine, Marilyn told Joan how badly she wanted children—a daughter, more than anything else in the world.

"It's difficult being a mother," Joan said seriously, sadly. "Sometimes you can try and try and still fail."

"I know, but I'd be a good one. I know I would." But she

was afraid, Marilyn told Crawford, because "there's a history of insanity in my family. My own mother is in a state institution."

Joan held the actress's hand. But she was baffled. Previously, Marilyn had told her her mother was dead; studio releases emphasized it.

After dinner the two actresses sat on a puffy couch and drank champagne. Joan let her hand slide . . . slowly . . . along Monroe's leg. Marilyn pushed it away and stood up in panic. The blonde little girl stared at them from atop the swirl of steps.

Crawford shouted at Marilyn, "Why the fuck are you pretending to be shocked, you bleached slut! I heard you with that woman in your house today!"

Marilyn looked bewildered. "You assumed that she and I were—" She laughed. "You're so wrong. I almost wish *that's* what it was!" She moved unsteadily toward the door, then turned around. "And I wasn't shocked or offended, Joan. Just surprised."

Crawford swayed up the stairs, feeling old, defeated. Her blonde child stood before her like a tiny judge.

Joan Crawford recounted all this to Mildred, explaining how deeply hurt she was that her attempt to comfort the insecure actress had been misunderstood. All was being slimed further by her own maid and chauffeur, who claimed to have overheard the incident and were now offering an ugly exaggeration of it to *Confidential* Magazine, then terrifying Hollywood with ruinous "exposés."

Mildred had had occasion to give the magazine choice items about subversives. She had often bartered: two exposés of those considered expendable by the studios in exchange for one to be protected. . . . Mildred suggested that perhaps Joan might provide her "more background" on Monroe: "Something about her mother, some ambiguity about whether she's dead or not; there's gossip—" Detecting the star's reticence, confusion about "loyalty," Mildred pointed out that—"unfairly" —Joan's own career was teetering. Joan knew that; she knew that Hollywood furies were eager to announce her fall. Mildred reminded, "You're almost fifty; the fall of a queen is a sad spectacle. A damaging article about you now will destroy you, Crawford. *She* will survive it with admiration. And the article *will* appear unless—"

Crawford told Mildred that, yes, there was "ambiguity" about Marilyn's mother.

The article Joan feared did not appear. Another replaced it,

the first in a series about "leftish actor-turned-writer Mark
Poe" and his "strange fascination for a leading male heart-throb."

In an alcoholic haze, Crawford wrote Marilyn a note, apologizing for what she had told Mildred—without saying what,
because she could not remember: "It was extorted. I didn't mean
to harm you. I was hurt and scared, *you* understand *that!*" She
tore up the letter. "What the hell," she said aloud, "I'm *still* the
Great Joan Crawford!"

Mildred learned that from Joan's new maid, who pasted the
letter together. Mildred did not mention the matter to Crawford,
because she despised the sentimentality that had led the aging
movie star—*once so beautiful!*—to such terrifying excess. Besides, Mildred knew that even better encounters would occur
between Crawford and Monroe—and Mildred could use
Crawford's confidence.

Then Marilyn Monroe became a star!

A bit role as a kept girl-woman had sent sexual shivers down
the spines of her fans; she sighed her dialogue sensually as if
only to *one* listener. Everyone was certain he was the listener.
Despising what he had to do, but being a crafty businessman,
Zanuck accepted Marilyn back into the fold, although he made
it clear to studio president Spyros Skouras that he considered
her success an "inexplicable fluke."

Photoplay Magazine, the most prestigious fan publication, announced that its coveted Gold Medal for best new star of the
year would go to—

Marilyn Monroe!

To throttle lingering rumors, and to show she was forgiv-
ing, Joan Crawford decided she would be in attendance in the
Crystal Room of the Beverly Hills Hotel, a pink creation of
Mission Revival architecture, where the awards would be
presented.

The Great Crawford would do what Monroe was becoming
known for: *She* would be late—later than "the starlet." She
would seize attention away from "the upstart."

Joan Crawford wore a dark gown, cut diagonally to expose,
starkly, one bare shoulder, one bare arm. On inspiration, she
wound one strand of pearls up the naked arm. As she walked
into the Crystal Room, each move of her legs exposed flashes
of gorgeous flesh, and proved that the body of the Queen of
Hollywood had lost none of its commanding power. Let the
furies stew! Popping camera lights created a giant halo about
her. She was dazzling! A sensation! She had shown the three
hundred or more of the most famous in Hollywood—and the
photographers, and the world, and Marilyn Monroe, who

would be sulking in the shadows—that she, *Joan Crawford*, was the star of stars, the—

Excitement poured away from her and gathered in a new wave as Marilyn Monroe walked in.

"That fucking slut!" Joan said.

Sewn into a gold lamé dress cut into a V so low it dipped to the top of her navel and so wide it exposed the edges of her magnificent nipples—men claimed to have glimpsed a flash of dark pink (the same who claimed the dress had sequins, but it was stardust)—Marilyn Monroe's body moved, part by part, curve by curve. The dress cherished every motion and kissed and hugged her breasts, her hips. She walked in a blaze of blonde sensuality.

They gasped.

The conquering star blew kisses.

With a wry smile, Jane Russell stood and applauded, champion to champion, while Leslie Caron giggled nervously and touched her own lovely but less lush breasts—nervously—at the same moment that Tony Curtis said, "My God, my *God*!" —jostling Robert Wagner against Clifton Webb, just as Lauren Bacall said in her huskiest voice, "I'll be *damned!*"—which drew a severe frown from heiress Lorna Rehnquist, there with Lance Renat, the sports-car racing ladies' man, who said, "She makes *me* want to be a woman!"

"A vile circus!" screamed Crawford to a reporter who rushed to capture her reaction. She cupped her breasts. "Look—there's nothing wrong with my tits, but I don't go around throwing them in people's faces."

The press, from Los Angeles to Paris, reported the event with exclamation marks. In the *Village Voice,* Norman Mailer recorded the reaction as a "moment of existential synapse." Crawford's reaction appeared in the *Los Angeles Times,* the word "tits" merely implied.

Crawford denied the vulgar implications to Mildred Meadows, who carried the denial in her next column:

> That great star and lady, Joan Crawford, lamented to me that a respected industry function was turned into a shameful display at the *Photoplay* Award presentations. The star was genuinely saddened when she observed that 'Marilyn Monroe has yet to learn that actresses must be ladies.' And so the blonde waif has made Hollywood hang its collective head in shame! Will she make amends?

Mildred waited for an answer to her personal question. Still, Monroe did not respond.

Instead, in her babbling column, Louella Parsons quoted Monroe as having said, "I've always admired Joan Crawford for being such a wonderful mother—for taking unwanted children and giving them a fine home. Who better than I—and Mildred Meadows—know what that means to homeless little ones?"

And Mildred Meadows!

Monroe had dared to utter her name in print! There had to be more. Her careful wording had been coached by Alberta Holland.

And instigated by Enid Morgan!

Raking through Monroe's past to verify her strategy and locate her exact targets, Mildred was startled to discover that she had seen the movie star and Enid years before when, "on a dutiful mission of charity expected of everyone in Hollywood," she had visited a home for unwanted children. The two girls—*so* pretty—walked right up to the smoked windows of her limousine and peered in.

Out of that past interlude, Mildred Meadows extracted present significance. Then, Norma Jeane had looked pleadingly, with longing, into the car—and Enid's amber eyes had challenged.

It was now time for war. Mildred had offered "the starlet" salvation too many times—only because of her growing beauty. First she would use stored ammunition:

Item: What blonde star—excuse me, starlet—claims to be an orphan while her mother pines for her in an institution? Don't ask me. Ask Marilyn Monroe!

Mildred Meadows considered granting redemption. But Marilyn Monroe did not seek it.

*   *   *

In Mildred's mansion, shadows were beginning to veil the windows. The old woman leaned slightly sideways on her throne, as if the past events had subdued her in the present only for paused moments.

Pulled into the narrative of tiny vengeances threatening now to gather into enormous ones, Normalyn had not interrupted the flow of Mildred Meadows' aroused memories. But she had accumulated many questions, and longed for information about the two women involved in what seemed to be a game, then not a game at all. There had been uncomfortable times when she felt the old woman was giving her information— probably to extort more from *her* later. . . . And Normalyn had retained, for further exploration, blurred areas in the narrative, places Mildred had slipped over or obscured—places forced into her narrative, like the emphatic conclusion that Enid was involved in the wording of Marilyn's newspaper statement about Joan Crawford and in the affronting inclusion of Mildred's name. *How* had that involvement been inferred? The account of Mildred's having seen the two pretty girls through smoky glass windows was introduced vaguely— signaling future importance? . . . And Normalyn's heart had broken to imagine Enid, so proud, in an orphanage. But even then the amber eyes had defied! . . . Why had Mildred been there? Certainly not on the proclaimed mission of "charity." Normalyn was beginning to see this clearly: Whether they hated her or loved her, everyone wanted to own Marilyn Monroe! There had been flashy interludes in Mildred Meadows's account that had been included only to fascinate, to dazzle with the star's magical presence. Or would even those interludes become central later?

At this moment, Normalyn did not know exactly why she felt so sad. Even the iced tea had become only slightly flavored water, its sweetness gone, gone with its lemony tang.

Mildred took another sip of her sherry. Revived, she said excitedly, "And then I *made* Marilyn Monroe come to me— *here!* It happened when Spyros—"

Thirteen

—Skouras, president of 20th Century-Fox, generously tried to save Marilyn Monroe from herself.

She had managed on her own. At the very brink, she had turned Mildred's accusing revelation about her mother's still being alive into "the best news possible," which would enable her to care for Gladys "in the most luxurious private sanitarium available." She converted into loving publicity the supposed wake during which she explained the existence of nude photographs. As the strap of her dress slipped accidentally from her shoulder, she sighed sadly to the male reporters. "Is the naked body pornographic?" No, no! they agreed.

She married one of the country's beloved athlete heroes.

Still, she sought disasters, as if to prove she could survive them. In freezing weather and with a fever, she wore a tiny dress to entertain thirteen thousand screaming Marines in Korea; a thin-lipped officer with a pencil-darkened moustache forbade her to sing Gershwin's "Do It Again"— "too suggestive." She was filmed in New York on Lexington Avenue with her white skirt billowing over panties and radiant legs while a thousand fans hollered, "Higher!"

Mildred scolded: "Having affronted patriotic servicemen with her lewdness, she extended her display to the streets of New York. Her husband turned away in patriotic shame!"

Then it all ganged up on the movie star, just as Mildred Meadows had known it would. With no regard to finances—paid little by the studio—Monroe was overdrawn; she divorced the athlete; with no instincts for business, she formed her own shaky production company; psychologically frail from her childhood, she came to rely on tranquilizers; groggy from pills, she drank. She fled to New York to be a "real actress" and became associated with a studio known for its "left-wing roots." *Then!* She announced she would marry a playwright facing a citation for contempt of Congress by refusing to provide the House Committee on Un-American Activities the demanded names of "fellow travelers." Without powerful support, Monroe would be undone by her "leftish" association.

"Let the broad sink," Zanuck advised Skouras. But Zanuck was intending to resign from 20th Century-Fox and Skouras had a four-picture contract with Monroe's production company. She *must* be saved! Spyros turned to Mildred Meadows for help—"because you are the king of queens," he tried to flatter in his quaint mode of speaking. Mildred promised him she would "guide" the rebellious star back into the fold.

"I hope you are pretty right like as usual, Mildred," Skouras blessed.

Mildred prepared for a monumental "first." She would initiate a meeting with the actress who had not come to her. She would not invite, she would summon. She sent a note: "Monroe! I will expect you at my home—" She signified a date, informed that Skouras would be there—and, to ensure Monroe's presence, added a peremptory P.S.: "This concerns grave secret dangers to your prospective husband."

"She will not come, so high-stronged and mighty, that sexy child," said Spyros. Mildred edged him away from the tall leather chair reserved for Zanuck.

"She *will* come," Mildred said. "Because of *him*." Armed with a goblet of her best sherry, she would command.

Spyros jumped! Chimes had sounded, the butler was answering. Spyros peeked out the window. "Bad news. She has come with another cute woman!"

"A dark-haired woman," Mildred knew. "But of course!"

Then the two magnificent women were there, the blonde star and her dark-haired companion. Monroe wore an orange-swirled dress, as if burnished by friendly fire. Enid wore a hat with a veil so thin it seemed meant only to accentuate the highlights of her face, expose superb reddened lips.

Even years later Mildred would cherish that spectacle of beauty.

The three women greeted each other with brief words. Monroe could not keep her sensual, wistful smile from her face, even at this time of confrontation.

Spyros shook her hand vigorously. "Marilyn," he enthused, "the more beautiful you are, the older you get."

Enid withdrew from the man's extended hand. Casually, she

took a silver lighter out of her purse; it caught a pin of reflected light tossed by the figure of a silver swan mounted on a crystal ashtray.

Meadows was direct: "Marilyn Monroe!" she issued. "Spyros has tried to counsel you. So have concerned others. That writer you intend to marry is refusing to speak out to the patriots. If he does not, you will be besmirched by the association."

"And I have a contract on you with four movies," Spyros reminded. "So it is not a question of what is best for the country and the studios but for you and me and Mildred in this beautiful country. Just look at her garden!"

Enid brought a tinted cigarette to her lips. About to touch it with the silver lighter, she stopped in that attitude.

Marilyn crossed her legs; she wore no stockings.

Mildred said, "Monroe! You will be ruined in the eyes of a saddened America."

"Your note said you wanted to tell me about 'secret dangers,' " Marilyn reminded. "That's the only reason I came."

Mildred stood up angrily.

"My God, you are *so* small!" Marilyn gasped.

"Don't you be a rude cutie to darling Mildred!" Spyros protested.

Mildred launched a new plan. "The dear child isn't being rude, Spyros. She's just being honest. All children are honest." She stood before Marilyn. "My dear, oh, my dear, dear child, that man cannot love you if he persists in taking a position that will allow you to be destroyed. I know you seek only love from him, dear *child*! Ask him to testify. Give him the opportunity he wants, to prove his love. He wants you to ask" —inspiration did not fail her—"as a child asks of a loving father."

The dark-haired woman ground her unlit cigarette into the ashtray on which the silver swan was poised.

"I think th-th-that I—" Monroe began to stutter.

Mildred had won! She had converted the star into the needful orphan she knew Monroe had been.

Mildred had to move fast: "At this point only *expert* guidance will save you and him."

"Will you p-p-provide it?" Marilyn asked softly.

"Of course I will," Mildred said to her vanquished, beautiful trophy.

Click! Click! Click! Enid snapped the lighter.

The reflected sliver of light pricked Mildred's eyes.

Monroe stood up. "I am *not* a needful child, Mildred! And I sure as hell won't tell him to testify to fascist bastards!"

Spyros lost control: "We'll see you in court, blondie!" he screamed at Monroe. "You'll never be heard from again! We'll break you! We'll—"

"—destroy you," Mildred pronounced her sentence.

Enid said almost lightly to her, "Oh, you can't destroy Marilyn Monroe. There's only one person in the world who can do that." Smiling, she faced the star, as if reminding her. "We both know who that person is." She raised the thin veil from her face. "Don't we?"

*　　*　　*

Mildred Meadows studied Normalyn as if to relocate herself in the present, or to connect the past to now.

Normalyn retreated from the penetrating stare.

No, dearheart, face her!

Normalyn did.

Outside, lush vines were about to surrender their violence to twilight, colors fading. Normalyn heard a destitute breeze captured briefly in the garden. She despised this old woman and her tainted memories. Yet she was learning from them. Enid clicked her lighter for attention—yes, to assert her strong presence, as she had that night on the blackened beach. But between the two women, the clicking was a signal, a reminder. . . . Too, even within Meadows' spotted account, Normalyn was discovering another Enid, a young woman she was increasingly admiring—determined, brave.

"Did Enid mean only Monroe could destroy Monroe?" Mildred Meadows still pondered the distant words. "Or that only *she* could destroy her? Or was she referring to someone else, someone they both knew—the subject of the altercation Crawford overheard?"

Normalyn shook her head. Those were questions she, too, had stored.

Dotting her lips with sherry, Mildred breathed into the listening room: "And then I learned about—"

*　　*　　*

—the letter!

J. Edgar Hoover called Mildred. "Exciting news!" There were three people he trusted: his constant male companion in the Bureau; the wealthy Cardinal Spellman, whom he visited clandestinely for late-night candlelit suppers; and Mildred Meadows.

Mildred did not like the man, but he was a trove of destructive information. She invited him to dinner to hear full details of his "exciting news." Because he could be petulant about giving offered information if he became displeased, she had her cook prepare his favorite dinner: Hungarian goulash and lime pie flown in from the Florida Keys. She detested both dishes. So for her, the cook fixed a stroganoff, with a dash more than the usual paprika to approximate the color of the goulash, and a light lime-and-lemon mousse.

Tonight Edgar was acting especially coy. He could become annoyingly childish under Mildred's aura of authority. He had had a powerful mother who would reward him only after he had performed certain boyish flirtations for her.

"The news, Edgar!"

With elaborate pretense of having lost what he was looking for—he searched every pocket of his suit—Edgar finally handed Mildred a letter, an exact copy of a letter.

On plain paper, and unsigned, it was written in a distinctive, clear script and addressed to Jack Warner, production chief of Warner Brothers Studio, where shooting on a film version of John F. Kennedy's PT-boat incident during World War II was about to begin. In cool, precise language, the letter asserted that soon the President would be exposed—with authentication—as a man of "vast immorality, insatiable in his lust for women." It provided the initials—with further clues—of women involved, including some of the most famous stars in Hollywood. It identified places of assignations—the Carlyle Hotel, the Beverly Hills Hotel—designating secret entrances. The letter went on to sweep into the "wave of immorality" the rest of the Kennedys, including the patriarch. "The scandal will kill your studio," the letter warned. In its last paragraph it revealed its purpose: "For far too long the Kennedys have been a menace to the Republic of the United States. The scandal will stem the tide of Socialism they are allowing to flood our shores."

Mildred felt an icy excitement. "Jack Warner turned this over to you?" If Edgar turned coy, she would—

"Yes." Edgar heard the urgency in Mildred's voice.

"But letters like this turn up frequently in Hollywood," Mildred had to observe.

"No, not like *this* one!" Edgar told her his "personal" investigation into the matter indicated that the writer was an "ex-ambassador," a powerful man high in Beverly Hills society. There were verifying fingerprints. And—Edgar took two quick bites of the lime pie to underscore the gravity of the linking information—he himself had "documented evidence of the reckless sexual liaisons involving Mr. President."

Mildred read aloud this sentence in the letter: "For far too long the Kennedys have been a menace to the Republic of the United States." Slowly, she nodded. *Yes!* After John, Robert Kennedy would inherit the White House, and after him would come Edward—all much worse than that socialistic monster Franklin Delano Roosevelt, who turned out to be only *one!*

"I'll leave this with you"—Edgar nodded toward the letter—"if I can have the rest of the pie."

Edgar gave her an odd look then, one she had not seen before—yes, somewhat mischievous, the way he looked at his most despicably childish—but there had been a slight squint to his eyes, as if with the powerful letter he had given her he was finally making himself her equal!

No matter his fantasies, Mildred had more important matters to consider. When Edgar left, she sat in her grand living room and evaluated the matter. Her eyes scanned the letter again. Among the women indicated y initials, Marilyn Monroe was not present. Only instinct—and mere breaths of gossip—had led her to expect— . . . No, only to *hope* that she might be there.

Mildred Meadows knew that everyone who is intensely loved is intensely hated. The Kennedys were hated by opposing factions. But Mildred did not clutter her mind with political nuances. She knew that was important. She was not impressed by symbols, but she knew their power. The Kennedys had come to represent, as David Lange had so earnestly told her, "all that is socially responsible, socially just, socially moral." Precisely! A socialistic Camelot!

For her move, timing had to be exact. She watched and waited.

Monroe walked off the set of *Let's Make Love* and flew to New York to sing "Happy Birthday" to President Kennedy before fifteen thousand cheering Democrats at Madison Square Garden. In a sigh of a dress, she looked nude, splashed with sequins, glowing like the only firefly of winter. She turned the inane song into a whispered seduction. Then she sang new words to "Thanks for the Memory," a tribute to the president's having confronted the venerable steel corporations!

In a late-night call, Edgar told Mildred that Marilyn Monroe was one of "Kennedy's women"—smuggled in to him through a secret passageway in the Carlyle Hotel! . . . Another night, another call: Marilyn Monroe had been "passed on" to "the unassailable moralist. . . ." Edgar emphasized the gravity by withholding the name for seconds: "Mr. Attorney General Robert F. Kennedy!"

"Is it all true?" Mildred had to know.

"Still only rumors," Edgar admitted, "even about a pregnancy," he tantalized. "I'm sure *you* will find out."

More was needed!—a firm connection, and an ally of impeccable credentials for unbiased credibility beyond Hollywood, someone who would defuse any skepticism that might intrude. David Lange, Mildred chose.

In his early years as a journalist, Lange had worked briefly for Mildred—"out of necessity." He had rebelled, began to write about "true democracy," won literary prizes, became a champion of John F. Kennedy, worked with devotion to see him elected. Who is more avenging than a bloodied idealist?

Mildred Meadows challenged David Lange's "staunch morality" by showing him the letter Edgar had given her. "A clear fraud," he laughed. He emphasized his rejection by informing her that that very evening he was finally *"really* meeting" his "greater hero," Robert Kennedy, at dinner in the home of Peter Lawford. "Your precious letter contains only lies, Mildred."

David Lange walked out on Mildred. And Mildred waited.

Then another anonymous letter arrived. This one was addressed to Mildred Meadows! It named Marilyn Monroe as "one of the women in John Kennedy's stable." It stated that now the movie star was "much more than casually involved" with the President's brother, "Robert Kennedy, the Attorney General of the United States." It challenged boldly: "Ask Monroe."

When she showed him that letter, David Lange believed Mildred.

Now! Mildred would proceed to undo the Kennedys, save the country, and—most important of all—force Marilyn Monroe to seek her help. Mildred had decided: In deference to Monroe's beauty, she would give her an option: turn to her for guidance or be destroyed with the Kennedys.

In her purling limousine with smoked windows, Mildred Meadows was driven to the star's home in Brentwood, a small Spanish-style house, not at all extraordinary—Monroe never acquired the opulent wealth of far lesser stars. But the house, in a quiet cul-de-sac in Brentwood, had a garden, a swimming pool, greenery surrounding it all. The star was proud of it because it was, finally, something *she* owned.

Presidents, generals, and queens themselves declare war—

and so did Mildred Meadows. She rang the lighted doorbell on Monroe's door. Shadows suddenly appeared at windows quickly darkened. They were avoiding her! Pushing away a branch that had threatened to smear her makeup, Mildred positioned herself on the lawn. Poised, aware of good light and accenting shadows, she shouted exact words at the house: "Monroe! Unless you open that door in thirty seconds, I will destroy you and the two brothers!"

The door was opened by—

Mark Poe!

The leftist Mildred had exiled from Hollywood! Befriended by Monroe! Holland was extending her villainous influence! "What do you want?" the man said arrogantly, calling her a despicable name.

Another voice behind him said, "Why are you here, Mildred?"

It was Enid.

Inside the house and against a sheet of light at a back window, the unmistakable outline of Monroe appeared.

Mildred thrust her words in: "There is a letter about to be released expressing outrage over immorality involving the President and his brother!"

"That does not concern us, Mildred," Enid said.

She didn't know! "Ask Monroe whether that concerns her!" Mildred demanded.

Enid spun about in the direction of the star. "Does it?"

"Yes!"

"Liar!"

In these thrilling moments, Mildred knew Enid would be learning for the first time of Monroe's reckless association! She knew now where to direct her wedge. "They abused your beauty, Monroe," Mildred said in genuine outrage. "They passed you between them. You're nothing to either of them!"

"He loves m-m-me."

Mildred had conquered. She had made the star stutter. Now she had to keep Enid in abeyance with new information. She had to rely on time, the impetus of the charged situation *she* was in control of. "Are you pregnant, Monroe!" Mildred fired.

"It's none of your goddamn business," the movie star shot back.

"And so what if she's pregnant?" Enid said.

Then Enid knew that, but not what Mildred sought now to discover: "By *him!* By a Kennedy!"

"*Is* it him?" Enid shouted at the movie star.

Exact aim! Her goals accomplished! Mildred left careful words: "Only I can save you from this scandal now, Monroe. I will give you"—she consulted her diamond watch—"exactly twelve hours to decide whether you want to hear *my* conditions for your salvation!"

"You vile, evil—" Mark Poe tossed more vulgarities at her as Mildred walked back to her waiting limousine. She heard footsteps behind her. Enid. *She* would be an ally more powerful than any other. Mildred faced her, aware, even then, of Enid's unique beauty, which roused memories of— . . .

"Is it true?" Enid asked softly.

"Yes, the President and his brother have treated her like a—"

At the same time that Mildred said, "—whore," Enid said, "— an unwanted orphan, a weak orphan."

*   *   *

"And Enid became my ally," Mildred Meadows told Normalyn in the darkening mansion. "She came here, you know. She sat in that exact chair you're sitting in, my dear. She chose Zanuck's chair, like you. And she asked for iced tea, like you."

Normalyn felt locked in a past littered with questions. How far could she believe this woman? Certainly she would not accept that Enid had become her ally. She was glad to learn that Enid had chosen the same chair she now sat in—she touched it, tenderly—and that both had requested iced tea. Or was this cunning woman still probing at what she had evoked earlier, the odd possibility that David Lange had "coached" her in certain matters. There were times during Mildred's narrative when it had seemed to Normalyn that the old woman was compelled to tell everything.

As if to make sure that her *version is heard, dearheart, in case you might hear another.* Miss Bertha had nodded awake.

Mildred Meadows had extended her moments of suspense long enough. She continued: "Enid agreed, the very day after our encounter, when she came to me, that she would persuade Monroe, had already begun to, of the absolute correctness of my guidance. Enid agreed with me that the child must not be born. That was the only way to separate Monroe from the scandal. She would abort the child."

That had been this evil woman's demand. For such enormous revenge there had to be more reasons than she was allowing.

Listen, dearheart, it's difficult, but just listen for now, listen carefully, Miss Bertha counseled, wide awake again.

In the withering light, Mildred Meadows looked like a delicately decorated moth, faintly powdery, as if she might turn into dust; but her voice was firm: "Enid told me when and where the matter would occur. Of course, I was there to verify it—" Only for a moment did the voice fade. "And I kept my word." The voice was again in full control. "Just as I agreed to, I reported in my column that Marilyn Monroe had, again, 'miscarried' after a 'sweet attempted reconciliation' with the 'most loving of her husbands.' " She drank soberly from the goblet. "It was my last column."

Within a sense of relief and release from Enid's letter, Normalyn felt sorrow for the sad movie star who had been deprived of what she had wanted most: a child, a daughter—

"But did she *really* abort?" Suddenly Mildred Meadows made a clutching gesture with one hand, as if resisting her own fading within the diminishing light of the day.

Normalyn winced at the startling words that yanked away the reality she had been eager to accept from this monstrous woman.

The old woman's voice was as cool, as casual, as if she were inquiring about a minor event: "Did Monroe *really* lose the child . . . Normalyn?"

It was the first time Mildred Meadows had used her name, in an inflection not unlike David Lange's. Normalyn turned away from the woman and her sudden burning scrutiny.

Mildred Meadows stood up. "So, Normalyn, you have come to face me! Then *face* me!"

Normalyn stood up. Then that was what David Lange had told her. And what else? She stared evenly at the woman.

Tense seconds extended, extended.

"Oh, my dear, please, let's do sit down," said the subdued voice of Mildred Meadows. "'I *do* like a bit of drama, don't you? But one can't hold it too long, and not at the expense of comfort."

Weary, confused, so confused, wanting to flee, Normalyn was about to sit back down. But she remembered Enid's and the movie star's defiance of this woman, that first encounter, and she said, "I will *not* sit down—and I am leaving *now!*"

The tiny form of Mildred Meadows glided across the glacial room. "Tell me why I received . . . *these?* Do you know who sent them just days before David called that you were here?" Even now she was in complete control.

Normalyn looked at what Mildred Meadows had gathered from a white marble table.

A clutch of lavender flowers! Jacaranda blossoms!

With disdain, Mildred let them fall to the floor.

They were like those left behind in Enid's abandoned room in Gibson, like those in Miss Bertha's dining room next to the lithograph of Marilyn Monroe—except that *these* were real. No. Real ones would have disintegrated when they fell.

Normalyn knelt to study them more closely. These, too, were artificial, but they were new, only recently fashioned. Normalyn touched the frail petals. She saw that several of the blossoms—*and parts of all of them!*—looked decayed, ugly.

Fourteen

She was not running away from Mildred Meadows, whom she left standing over the fallen flowers—she was running away from questions, questions, questions in the past, the present, even in the future. *How* could Mildred Meadows claim to have witnessed the losing of a child and still be wondering whether one had been born? *Who* had sent the artificial jacaranda bouquet mottled with decay—and *why* since her arrival in Los Angeles? Would she have to return to David Lange now, for answers or more questions? When would her life begin! She had been roaming with ghosts for hours. No, *she* was the ghost; the restless people in the past were more alive!

She realized that she had only thought she was walking out of the house. She had just moved farther into its cavern of rooms, all furnished in icy opulence. Certain the butler was following her to force her to return and answer Meadows's questions, Normalyn ended up on a veranda conquered by vines. The butler *did* appear, only to guide her to the front entrance and inform her that "the baroness's limousine and chauffeur" were at her disposal for her "return home." Normalyn walked with rigid dignity past the old woman and said, "No, thank you *very* much."

Outside, she ran across the vast lawn and past the stiff chauffeur waiting by the open door of the limousine. It looked sinister, an abandoned prop from the past.

194

Beyond the gates of the mansion, which sank behind her among trees, Normalyn stared at her surroundings: one long, long curving street, houses in seclusion behind closed gates, no one walking anywhere—and evening shadows about to banish remnants of daylight. She ran back to Meadows's gate. Door still open, chauffeur at its side, the limousine expected her. She got in wordlessly—and rode away from the past in the despised gray car.

She jumped out across the street from her house. She didn't want to have to explain to Troja why she was returning in a limousine.

2

"Got the job? Worked late?" Troja leaned against Kirk on the floor. Kirk stared so raptly at the television that it seemed to Normalyn that he had begun to watch the glass itself, removing himself even from the life of the old movies. Retreating from *too* much life, while she—

"No." That was all Normalyn said in answer to Troja's question. They had hardly looked at her. Determined to assert her presence, her *existence,* to be noticed, Normalyn went to the refrigerator, noisily pulling out whatever she could find to eat, clanging dishes, dropping silverware, becoming angrier. "Goddamn, goddamn, god*damn!*"

"Huccome you so rattled? You gettin' your period real bad, hon?" Troja said that with concern.

For Normalyn, that did it. "Are *you?*" she shot back.

Troja stood beside her. "I don't *get* no periods. That's huccome I can't have no babies—never!"

Normalyn felt utterly defeated. She had inadvertently bruised a deep, hurting wound in Troja. . . . It was all useless! And she would never be able to think of Troja as other than a woman, and if Troja didn't see that, then she had the problem! To thwart the apology she heard herself about to form—pleadingly—Normalyn went into her room.

She noticed a paper on her pillow. A note in Troja's handwriting: "Hon—Ted Gonx—Gonz—Gons—" Several attempts to spell "Gonzales" had been ruled out, but the message was clear: Ted Gonzales had called.

3

The next day proceeded in frosty silence between Troja and Normalyn. Damned if Normalyn would apologize for something she hadn't done when it was *she* who had been insulted.

Troja answered the telephone. "Yeah, sugar." She tried to sound light, but her voice trembled. "Yeah. Gotcha. Yeah!" She was writing down an address. "And thanks, sugar. . . . Thanks loads." When she put down the telephone, her hands were shaking. "He didn't say nothin' about being the black Monroe," she said in relief.

Duke had re-entered her life. Normalyn looked at Kirk in accusation.

Kirk went to the porch to work out; Normalyn heard the barbells clanging fiercely.

In minutes, Troja was ready to go out on the date arranged just now by Duke.

Normalyn walked to De Longpre Park—away from Kirk and away from the possibility that the telephone would ring and it would be Ted Gonzales. Her reaction at the prospect was in limbo. Would she hear the voice of the man he had become or the man he had been?

Normalyn sat on a bench near the littered memorial to Valentino. New dust had turned it gray. *She would not think about David Lange nor Mildred Meadows!* A few people, mostly young, idled about. Some children played noisily.

A youngman with a bandanna tied across his forehead like a head band sat next to her. "Wanna feed the pigeons?"

Normalyn looked around. There were no pigeons.

He threw crumbs on the grass. "Just in case they come," he said. His eyes were shiny, dark, his shirtless torso thinned into etched sinews. He said, "I'm gonna audition to be Montgomery Clift. Know who he was?"

Normalyn slid away on the bench, preparing to get up.

"Famous movie star," the youngman answered himself. "He died in a wreck. Then the studios had this *other* guy take over as him, see? To cover why he looked different, they said Clift had to have plastic surgery because of the accident. I'm gonna tell that as my tragic secret at the next auditions for Dead Movie Stars; never know exactly when till they're set—secret. You seen the Dead Movie Stars on TV? They're gonna be on 'Life As It Is' tonight. You ever seen that?" He fed more crumbs to more invisible pigeons. "You think I look like Montgomery Clift before the accident?"

"Yes," Normalyn said, although she wasn't sure whom he was talking about. She walked away, slowly, unobtrusively, not wanting to hurt his feelings. When he didn't even seem to notice—he was now talking to a girl with frizzled pinkish hair—she felt annoyed. She walked to the dry littered fountain and wiped the dust off the proud bust of Valentino.

She saw it, a car stopping abruptly in a no-parking strip nearby. Knots of youngish people loitering in the park reacted to it—they sat up; some walked away with studied casualness. Two men emerged from the car. Both wore sunglasses.

Normalyn had the ugly sensation that they were looking for her! She'd run! . . . She controlled herself; she had no reason to be afraid, none. She sat on the edge of the fountain.

The two men strolled into the park, surveying it. They stopped before someone, asked a cursory question. Now they were talking to the girl with pinkish hair and the youngman who had been feeding absent pigeons. One of the two men inspected the youngman's bare arms. The other one, heavier, faced in Normalyn's direction. She swung her legs at the edge of the fountain, just for something to do.

"What's your name, miss?" They were standing before her, with open wallets, exhibiting identification as police.

Hoping her voice was steady, she answered, "Normalyn. Normalyn Morgan." She had nothing to be afraid of, *nothing*.

"Normalyn," the heavier man repeated. "That's a pretty name. You from Texas?"

"How do you know that?" Her voice lost its firmness.

"Cause you got a soft drawl. Lived there myself a while," said the heavier man. The other, silent, studied her from behind dark glasses. "Got some I.D., Normalyn?"

She fished in her purse, feeling for the newer birth certificate, not wanting to be seen hunting. Had she chosen the right one!

The man scrutinized it. "How come your name isn't Smith, like your father's?"

"That's none of your—" Anger flashed, with relief that she had shown him the right document.

"No need to be scared, Normalyn. Just checking up on the park," the heavy man told her. "Now you have a good day." But they remained facing her for long moments. Then the man who had not spoken said, "Watch you don't get into trouble, Normalyn."

She was the last person they spoke to on their vague tour.

"Routine check for drugs and shit, man," the girl with frizzled hair said to her. "Just hassle, hassle, hassle."

Normalyn left the suddenly strange park. It was then she realized with a clarity that stunned her that she had been carrying with her a letter and papers that if believed—! ... She would hide them in one of her suitcases. Were they safe there? She'd place them in a safety box! That seemed even chancier, indicative of secrecy.... Again, she was imbuing everything with imaginary dangers! She knew that, completely, when she looked back at the park, so placid again.

She passed the telephone at the gas station. She stopped. She *did* think of calling David Lange. He was counting on her calling him. But she would not. On her own, she had to find someone out of that same past but not connected to David Lange.

4

Troja was in good spirits. "Been waitin' for you, hon. Wanna do your hair, show you makeup, like I been promisin'."

Normalyn didn't remember that exact promise, and she did not welcome the prospect, but it would calm the *un*extraordinary incident she kept remembering from the park, and she could not reject such an extravagant offer from Troja. So she sat in the chair Troja indicated.

In his corner, Kirk was watching a movie—*Leave Her to Heaven*—about a woman who loves her husband so much that she kills herself to bind him to her in death rather than lose him. Every few minutes, station breaks tantalized with hints of coming catastrophes to be revealed on the news.

For a moment Normalyn had considered telling Troja and Kirk about what had occurred in the park. *That* would show them that she, too, lived dangerously. But she hadn't been in danger. She *hadn't*.

"Now, you trust me, hon," Troja said. Now and then consulting an open book next to her as a guide, she expertly used a brush, water from a basin, a blow-dryer. "Got such pretty hair and you don't even know it."

Normalyn heard snipping scissors. She saw a strand of her hair fall to the floor.

The movie ended—the dead woman's sister married the beloved man—and Kirk shifted to another station. A mousy sportscaster with the absurd name of Jacques "Jock" le Sourd was announcing breathlessly that— Kirk clicked him away.

"Can we watch 'Life As It Is'?" Normalyn called out.

"It comes on in a few minutes, after the news," Kirk informed her.

"Hold still!" Troja said when Normalyn tried to look at the book she was consulting. "We'll let your hair set awhile." Her fingers touched her creation lovingly. "A little makeup now."

Normalyn was becoming impatient, nervous. She would have ended it except that Troja was so clearly wanting to be giving, bountiful.

On the television screen, Clive Barnes, the "rhymin' weatherman," was tipsier than usual as he predicted "patchy clouds bring lessened crowds to the beach."

"Hold real still or you'll ruin the eye shadow!" Troja said as "Life As It Is" came on.

"Today we'll take you to the Trianon Château off Franklin Boulevard." Tommy Bassich was identifying his location. "The château was built by William Randolph Hearst for his mistress, Marion Davies. Now among its tenants in its many decaying rented rooms live the founders of a group known as the Dead Movie Stars—"

And there they were, the odd young people in strange clothes surrounding the skinny girl with reddened hair and a felt orchid in it.

Tommy Bassich was explaining: "These young people claim to represent the glamour—"

"—and tragedy," Lady Star reminded as the camera panned a crumbling old building, its elegance in shreds, courtyard leprous with weeds, steps eroding into dust. "Glamour and tragedy go together." Lady Star spoke in a huskied voice that now and then slipped into a squeak.

"Lady Star, would you introduce us to the members of your group?" Tommy Bassich was deeply serious.

Lady Star waved a languid hand toward the others, who firmed their borrowed poses of glamour: "Hedy Lamarr, Tyrone Power, Rita Hayworth, Veronica Lake, Errol Flynn, Betty Grable, Billy Jack—" A youngman wearing an open shirt and cowboy boots pushed into the frame. Lady Star subtly edged him away and continued: "—James Dean."

"Hedy Lamarr isn't dead," Tommy Bassich informed. "Neither is—"

"They're dead when you *think* they're dead," Lady Star stated.

With profound gravity, Tommy Bassich reminded Lady Star that in an earlier news segment she had claimed that "the people who were there" provided them with the "secret infor-

mation" they claimed to possess, about tragedies and scandals.
"For example?" Tommy was probing, probing in depth.

Lady Star breathed moments of suspense. "For example . . .
the orphan!"

Behind her, the others joined in her tittering.

Clearly wanting to avoid controversy about homeless children, Tommy Bassich explained to his viewers: "In the short,
outrageous existence of the Dead Movie Stars, there has never
been allowed a candidate for—"

"They're *petitioners* first," Lady Star corrected in a high pitch
of irritation.

"—for the two female stars they consider the epitome of
tragedy and glamour—Verna La Maye and Marilyn Monroe.
. . . You told me earlier, Lady Star—"

"—that we *may* be allowing petitioners for them very soon,"
Lady Star interjected like an excited little girl. Then her colored lips parted, allowing breathed words: "*If* they qualify."

Tommy Bassich spoke to his viewers, one to one: "The
secret midnight initiations called auditions have begun to attract dozens of young—"

"Dozens and *dozens,*" Lady Star interjected loftily, "and most
are rejected."

Kirk whistled. "They're gonna start getting some real sickos,"
he predicted.

"Oh, turn them off," Troja said.

Kirk did, just as Tommy Bassich was guiding his viewers
into the next segment of "Life As It Is": "The strange, exotic
world of Buddhist—"

"There!" Troja had just brushed out Normalyn's hair.

Standing, Normalyn saw the book Troja had used as her
guide, a book of photographs titled simply *Marilyn.* The book
was open to an early picture of the movie star. "Why the hell
did you do that?" Normalyn backed away from the photograph.

"She made you look awfully pretty," Kirk assured.

"Hon, you gonna act strange again?" Troja asked Normalyn.
"Why don't you just go look in the mirror and see—?"

"I don't want to!"

Troja abandoned her and went to sit on the bed with Kirk.
"Ungrateful," she muttered to Normalyn.

Normalyn found herself in the bathroom before the full-length mirror. Another face had appeared on hers, drawn
there by Troja. A familiar face she had seen in David Lange's
office, the young face of Norma Jeane. Staring at it, Normalyn
wondered what it had been like for Norma Jeane when she
first looked in her mirror and saw the face of Marilyn Monroe.

5

When Normalyn emerged from the bathroom, she had combed her hair and wiped off some of the makeup Troja had painted on her. At the last, she had left traces of the fascinating creation. On her way to her bedroom, she stopped, trying to force Troja to look at her, to know she still demanded an answer to her earlier question. When Troja refused to look at her, Normalyn went into her room and started making sounds as if she were packing again.

Troja understood her signals. She stood inside the room.

Normalyn closed the door behind her. "You *did* read the letter in my purse when you stole money from me." She wanted to make her words as harsh as possible.

"Yes."

This astonished Normalyn: She felt relieved! Someone else, finally, knew about the letter, and it was Troja, someone she could trust. . . . Then: "Does Kirk know, too?"

"What difference—!" Troja was about to react in anger to an implied doubt that focused on Kirk. "No," she said, "just me." Then she spoke words quickly: "You do resemble her, hon, you know; really—when she was young, your age."

Fifteen

Mark Poe!

Normalyn awoke with that name on her mind. He was the man Mildred had raged against, had exiled from the studios; and he had been present during Mildred's harsh declaration of war against the movie star when Enid had been there, too! That's whom she had to locate! How? She'd just have to figure it out.

That same morning, Normalyn still felt relieved that Troja had seen the letter. She needed an ally. She could trust Troja; she *could,* she insisted , . . but only slowly, she revised . . . and Kirk maybe not at all.

Facing the bust of Valentino in De Longpre Park, Normalyn determined where she would start her hunt for Mark Poe: in the library only a few blocks away.

A few minutes later, in the periodicals room of the Hollywood Library, Normalyn roamed through microfilmed issues of the newspaper that had, proudly and prominently, carried Mildred Meadows' spewings. She skimmed columns full of slaughtering innuendoes, deadly exclamations, and quotation marks twisting inference into accusation. Thank heaven, there were no Saturday or Sunday columns! Finally she located the item Mildred had gloated over, about "leftish bachelor Mark Poe," the deadly disclaimer that he did not "want children." But it contained no more than Mildred had bragged about, nothing to guide her further to him nor to anyone else.

Normalyn went back through the columns of pertinent years,

wanting periodically to abandon the search through this mire, wanting—

Rehnquist!

She recognized that name, a woman's. Mildred had implied some connection between her and Mark Poe. No, Normalyn remembered the name from somewhere else, and the reference here tied it to another name. She read the column written in 1960:

Hollywood Today
_____
    with *MILDRED MEADOWS*

NASH McHUGH AND LORNA REHNQUIST:

A Happy Ending?

HOLLYWOOD—The film capital is abuzz with unconfirmed reports that Nash McHugh, dashing star dreamt of by millions of American women, avoided honorable service in the Army of his country. Cloudy details refer to a "temporary nervous disorder" as the reason for his non-participation in the noble conflict to support democratic principles upheld by Hollywood.

A possible recurrence of the "nervous disorder" is feared—silently—by loyal high executives at 20th Century-Fox, where Nash is scheduled to star in the multi-million dollar epic *Captains at Sea.* Insiders suggest, however, that Nash may merely be reacting—"probably only temporarily" —to persisting reports that his "close friend"—a stage actor with leftish connections—has been exhibiting "a very strong desire" to "help" vagrant teenage boys and children.

Is that why relatives of this minor actor are fighting him in court proceedings for the family home in Palm Springs, to keep it from becoming a "boys' camp"?

The *good* news in Hollywood is that those closest to Nash insist his patriotism is intact, and he is straight as an arrow in his personal life, relaxing in his own home in Palm Springs, with house guest Lorna Rehnquist. Executives at 20th report that Nash "just can't wait" to marry the beauteous, popular socialite, whose father is—

"Sick, so goddamned sick!" Normalyn said aloud in the quiet library.

"*Shhh!*" The librarian's pen was poised to tap again—and with added firmness.

There was no doubt that the "leftish" actor not named in this warning column was Mark Poe. Mildred had boasted that she had "frightened" Mark Poe's lover into marriage to the "Rehnquist heiress." Normalyn remembered that now, but there was another association she could not recall. Well, she had located Mark Poe in Palm Springs! . . . Years ago. She *had* discovered an essential name connected to him! . . . Obviously an acquired movie name—and suddenly Mark Poe's sounded like one, too. But there had been a family home! . . . Contested and probably lost. Normalyn felt frustrated, depressed. But there was one more column she had to locate: Mildred's last.

Written on a Friday—and just as Mildred had told her—the column announced the "sad news" that Marilyn Monroe had once again "miscarried"—after a "sweet attempt at reconciliation" with "the most loving" of her husbands. And yet, the thought returned constantly to Normalyn, *years later the old woman still wondered whether the demanded abortion she claimed to have seen had actually occurred!*

The Monday edition of the newspaper featured a bold-faced boxed announcement on its front page:

> Popular Hollywood columnist Mildred Meadows announced today that she will no longer write her internationally syndicated column, "Hollywood Today," avidly read by millions of fans. It will be missed by them—and other fans, the newspapers who were proud to have brought it to the world.

When she left the Hollywood library, it did not help Normalyn's spirits that even the day could not make up its mind. There was an interval of sun, two of gloom. Everywhere, blossoms of jacaranda trees were scattering into only faintly colored dust on the streets; their branches were sparsely leafed while other trees became lush, green.

2

Choosing another telephone booth this time, Normalyn dialed Information.

No, the Palm Springs operator told her, there was no listing under the name of Mark Poe. No, *no one* by the name of Poe. Nash McHugh? Normalyn offered his name only to extend the connection. No, the operator informed her, there was no listing under that name either, nor under M-a-c-Hugh.

And so that was that.

Missing him, she called Mayor Hughes. He made her promise she was "fine, just fine" and that she would turn to him if she needed anything—"anything, honey." Afterward, she missed him more . . . and now the sky had turned entirely gray.

So that the day would not be a complete disaster, Normalyn went to a drugstore and bought three books: *Crime and Punishment* because it had been on Miss Stowe's list, with an asterisk; *A Portrait of the Artist as a Young Man* because she was sure it would apply to women as well; and *Gone with the Wind* because that was the only book Enid had ever mentioned. No, it was the romantic movie Enid had loved.

3

Kirk had been waiting for Normalyn to walk in.

"He's got a secret he wants you to share, hon," Troja said excitedly. "Don't know what, myself."

Kirk was unusually nervous, cracking his knuckles. "Ready?" He actually smiled happily. He made Troja and Normalyn sit down with him and face the television screen. Then from under his bed he brought out a film cassette. Before any image appeared on the screen, Kirk fast-forwarded to an exact place. Then he punched the "play" button. "Look!" His voice was alive.

In an arena, six hugely muscular youngmen in brief gladiator costumes are fighting six sinister men who brandish lethal iron-spiked balls on heavy chains. The handsomest and most muscular leads the other youngmen to victory. Now he is being awarded a laurel-leafed crown by an admiring emperor. The triumphant gladiator says: "For the glory of Rome, sire!" The gladiator—

—was Kirk, young, so much younger. Normalyn recognized in the glorious exultant youngman on the screen the fading reflection of the man watching him, his image now only a smear over the television screen.

"I made it in Italy," Kirk said. "*Son of Hercules* movie." The voice had survived. "Didn't even know they'd released it till I saw it at the video store." He prepared to replay the segment. Instead, he yanked it out. "Just shit they're putting out on cassettes now, that's all," his defeated voice said. He reached for a fresh packet of cocaine and snorted twice into each nostril.

Troja took the packet from him and snorted, too.

Normalyn retreated into her room, away from these moments between Troja and Kirk. In her bedroom—even its neatness bothered her today—she tried to read *A Portrait of the Artist as a Young Man,* but she broke into tears before she had finished the third page.

4

Kirk's book of exposés! That's where she had first heard about Lorna Rehnquist and Nash McHugh. And Kirk had said he'd met Nash once. Normalyn remembered that at dinner. Troja had just returned from an audition—or a "date." Normalyn preferred not to know.

Idly, Normalyn looked through Troja's movie books; she was making sure she wouldn't be questioned about what she was doing. She found the book she was looking for: *The Best of Confidential: The Greatest Scandals!* She sat on the floor, very, very casually, leaning on one elbow and browsing through the book. She located the story. She said aloud, "I wonder what became of Nash McHugh." She realized at that moment that Kirk would have no idea, that he had probably just been bragging when he'd claimed that earlier day to have met him, that—

"Nash? He stopped making movies after all the scandal," Kirk said.

"Nash McHugh sounds like a made-up name." She tried to make her words sound aloof, an unconcerned observation.

Ambushed, Normalyn was thankful that Kirk merely went on to tell her, "Yeah, that's a made-up name—like all of Wilson's boys, that agent. He named Tab, Guy, Kip, Nash—"

"What was his real name?" Normalyn held her breath and avoided Troja's pursuing stare.

"Robert Kunitz," Kirk remembered easily. "Made himself over in the same gym I worked out in. I went to a party at his house once, years ago, in Palm Springs; that's when *I* met Wilson." Immediately he was moody.

It was night, but Normalyn did not care. She walked to the telephone booth at the gas station. She was glad it was still open, people milling there. As soon as she called the Palm Springs Information number, she felt defeated. She had grasped at anything, anything. But when the operator answered, she automatically spoke the name she had rehearsed: "Robert Kunitz, please."

Normalyn closed her eyes wearily. It was only because she was too tired that she didn't hang up before the inevitable words could come again: *I'm sorry but—*

"Please hold the line for the number," the operator said.

Had she really located Robert Kunitz? But would he know where Mark Poe was? Would he even want to remember after the poison that had separated them? What if his wife answered? Still, Normalyn dialed, excited, terrified.

"The Elms," a youthful female voice answered.

"What?" Normalyn's finger almost pushed down the cradle of the telephone.

"The Elms Arts School," the voice repeated. "If it's about a scholarship, please call between—"

"No, it's a personal call, and it's very important. I'm trying to locate Nash McHugh—" The wrong name!

"You mean Mr. *Kunitz*." The girl almost laughed. "He's not here right now, but his associate is. Hold on."

A buzzing. An extension was lifted. "Mark Poe," the new voice answered.

Normalyn hung up. She started to run back to the house, stopped, turned around, walked three blocks to another booth. She waited until a car that had slowed had moved on. She dialed Palm Springs again. "We were disconnected," she told the girl who answered and connected her again.

"Hello!"

"Mr. Poe, I'm sorry I hung up." Normalyn rushed the only words she could think to speak. "I've been in Los Angeles only a few weeks—from Texas—" She stopped because she was out of breath and could not think what else to say to this man.

Moments elapsed. The man was silent.

Normalyn gasped more words. "Enid Morgan died, a short time ago." She closed her eyes, she saw Enid's gravestone. The despised winds would have ended; there would be new trees.

"Who are you?' the man said.

"I don't know any more! Please help me find out!" When she heard the sudden doubt she had finally spoken, she revised instantly: "I'm Enid Morgan's daughter. I have to see you."

"Let me have a number where I can reach you. I may call you back tomorrow," he said.

She gave him her telephone number, Troja's.

"And so Enid died in spring, just as she said she would," Mark Poe said, to himself, quietly.

There was a man who loved me and could not love me, Enid's voice said to Normalyn.

Sixteen

That very night—when Troja was back from a "date," so depressed and tired that she hugged and kissed Kirk and went wordlessly to bathe—the telephone rang. For her, Kirk told Normalyn.

It would be Ted Gonzales. She looked at the telephone lying on the kitchen counter for her to answer. Did she want to talk to him? She tried to picture him as he had lingered near the statue of the Unknown Texas Hero. *Then* she would be able to speak to him—yes, if she remembered him with his cowboy hat shading the saddened angular face—

"Hello—" Her greeting was tentative; the memory she had managed to evoke might yet rush into a harsh one and—

It was Mark Poe!

Yes, he told her, he would see her. Could she come to Palm Springs . . . "as early as Sunday—to talk, just to talk?"

2

"Where you going?"

"To Palm Springs." Normalyn hugged an overnight bag she had tried to conceal with her purse. The bus schedules to the resort city were so complicated she had decided to go prepared to spend the night in a hotel if necessary. If so, she would call Troja from there, to obviate the very questions that were now being asked.

"Gonna *walk?*" Troja reacted to Normalyn's secretiveness.

"No—I have an interview." Normalyn spoke the only words she could think of. "For a job—not a secretary's job, it's . . . it's—"

Until a few minutes before, they had all been watching *The Big Sleep* on Kirk's VCR. Normalyn had tried to follow it—and couldn't—until she would make her planned, unobtrusive exit.

"It's Sunday, hon." Troja frowned at Normalyn. "Not making sense, hon."

"As much sense as that damn movie makes." Normalyn transferred her irritation.

Kirk laughed. "It doesn't make sense, *that's* why I like it."

"Here," Normalyn said to Troja. "I'll pay you for three days' rent." She still paid by the day, sometimes two days. Now she wanted to assert she was not intending to move out—and to stop the questioning.

"*This* ain't what I'm concerned about," Troja said indignantly, but she took the money. She nodded Normalyn back into her room. "You're going there to look for that actor guy you were asking about, and it's about that letter, isn't it, hon? You acted real strange all last night. Don't have to make up stories."

Again, Normalyn was relieved.

She was even more relieved when Kirk suggested they might drive her there. While Normalyn had her "interview," he and Troja would "hang around a favorite city." Troja was ecstatic. But at the last moment, just as Normalyn had expected, Kirk lost his enthusiasm, deciding he had to work out, felt wired. He wouldn't listen to Troja's protests that she wouldn't go either. "It's good for you to stay away from the goddamn telephone, sweetheart." He couldn't even say Duke's name. When the two women were leaving, Kirk was lifting weights. Troja blew him a sad kiss.

"Love you," he said back.

3

When the Mustang pushed into the concrete and steel network of the freeways, Normalyn wondered what Troja would do while *she* spoke to Mark Poe.

Away from Kirk, Troja seemed instantly rejuvenated. Hearing her laughter, Normalyn realized it didn't usually sound happy, the way it did now.

"I read in a magazine that Marilyn dreamt once that she

went into a church—naked!—and everyone applauded! I love that story," Troja said. She asked seriously, "You coming to believe that letter, hon?"

"No." That's all Normalyn said.

The desert parted before a long corridor of palmtrees. Tanned men and women of all ages wandered the purified streets of Palm Springs, its polished shops, hotels, restaurants. "Had some high-priced dates here," Troja remembered with tarnished pride.

Up a gracious road with a magnificent Spanish villa. Bougainvillea splashed balconies and tiled paths. A pool glistened in a patio of shrubs bursting with flowers.

"Pick you up in approximately—?" Troja consulted her watch. "I'll call before I come over—"

"*Please* stay!" It was an impulse. She was not sure how much she wanted to discover here, and she could use Troja's presence to control that. They could leave at any time. Too, she had experienced with David Lange and Mildred—and with Miss Bertha!—an altered perception once she left their rarefied atmospheres. Troja's view might allow a steadied perspective about what would occur. She already knew about the letter. And Normalyn was suddenly afraid. "Please!" She did not mind the anxiety in her exhortation.

Troja parked the Mustang in the shadow of a huge tree piled high in layers of branches.

"Over here!" A good-looking athletic man moved down the tiled steps of the house toward them. He wore tan slacks and a light blue shirt.

Instantly Normalyn wanted to flee the whole situation. Too late! "Mr. Poe—" she managed to say.

"Oh, I'm not Mark. I'm his lover, Robert Kunitz."

"And I'm Normalyn Morgan, and this is my best friend, my very best friend"—Normalyn was extending her introduction because she did not know her "very best friend's" full name, just the made-up first name—"my best friend, Troja O'Hara." Normalyn looked in horror at Troja when she heard the name she had given her.

But Troja accepted it with a gracious smile.

"Troja O'Hara? A dazzling name!" Robert Kunitz complimented.

Troja recognized the man's features, redrawn with more lines by the years. "I've admired your films, Mr. Kunitz." She did not remember a single one.

"I'm surprised you remember, such awful trash." Robert laughed. He guided them down a path formed by the parting of flowers and shrubs. At the end of the walk stood another man.

He was taller, slender. He wore emphatic glasses, as if to underplay his exceptional lean attractiveness. "Mark Poe," he introduced himself.

"Normalyn Morgan and Troja O'Hara," Robert introduced.

Normalyn faced Mark Poe. How had he looked when Enid first met him? *Was* he the man she had talked about with regret?

Robert Kunitz broke the tense stasis by leading them to an alcove created by an umbrella of flowered vines. There was a white iron table, chairs with backs like white peacock tails, a bowl of Technicolored fruit.

Nearby, about ten energetic youngmen and women swam in the pool.

"A charming house," Troja said in a meticulous tone. "Spanish, with a touch of Moroccan, isn't it?" She tilted her summer hat, rejecting the stare of the rude sun.

So poised, so elegant! Normalyn felt slightly amazed—and even clumsier by contrast. She almost missed the chair Robert pulled out for her.

"It was my mother's home," Mark Poe said. "We've converted it into an arts school for talented young people. Robert teaches acting and drawing."

"And Mark teaches writing and directing." Robert held the other man's hand. "Mark's mother made all this possible—the house, a trust fund for scholarships." He glanced at the young people in the pool. "They study very hard, work very hard . . . and swim very hard on Sundays. After they're through here"— he sighed at the disconcerting prospect—"it's hello, damn world!"

This is what Mildred Meadows had tried to besmirch with lies. These men had triumphed over her. Normalyn thought that soon she might be able to relax with them.

"What may we offer you?" Robert Kunitz asked.

Troja brushed away a strand of bougainvillea that was flirting with her hat in a feathery breeze. "Ms. Morgan?" She grandly relinquished the decision to Normalyn.

Her irritation growing at the ostentatious display of poise, Normalyn needed to match Troja's sophistication. She blurted, "Champagne! It's *never* too late for champagne!"

Troja and Robert looked at her in surprise. Mark Poe removed his glasses, seeing her without barrier.

Pushing on although she was about to crash into embarrassment—and her elbow slipped from the armrest—Normalyn corrected, "Never too *early* for champagne—that's what I meant, of course." She had spoken words Enid had once addressed gaily to Mayor Hughes.

Mark Poe's look drifted away, as if he had been summoned by an echo.

"Well, I don't see why not champagne," Robert rescued Normalyn. "After all," he teased Mark, "we've never claimed to be *austere* socialists." He went to arrange for the champagne.

In the glaring silence that contained Mark's open stare at her, Normalyn was glad that a dark-haired youngman had extricated himself from the others in the pool and was idling nearby, pretending merely to be drying himself.

"I think Michael wants to meet you two," Robert remarked when he returned with an ice bucket, champagne. "He's one of Mark's best directing students. And he's barely twenty-one."

"Very talented, has challenging ideas," Mark said proudly. "I wish these were better times for creative minds."

Robert looked at Mark with a slightly sad smile. "Mark would have made a wonderful father." He said quickly, "May I motion Michael over for a moment?" He already had. "He's the oddest combination of shyness and boldness," he whispered.

The youngman had intent dark eyes, a taut body. "Michael Farrell," he introduced himself. "I hope you stay over."

Why should he ever be shy, as handsome as he was? Normalyn wondered. He had rushed his very direct invitation. *To whom? She* did that, rushed words, when she wasn't sure her breathing would survive her voice. She was amazed at how easily she had smiled at him. Immediately, she felt hideously plain, especially next to Troja, so glamorous! Normalyn turned away from the youngman.

He reacted instantly: "I have to go prepare for my classes tomorrow." He yanked back his earlier boldness: "I hope I'll see you later," he said before he walked away.

Troja kicked Normalyn under the table for not responding.

Robert poured the champagne into tall, slim glasses.

"Baccarat flutes. Charming!" Troja trilled. She held one up so that it captured just one sunbeam.

Trying to surpass her, Normalyn tilted her glass and gulped from its tingly contents. "It's lovely, oh, just lovely." The echo of her words made her blush.

Then they were all silent.

4

Mark placed his hands firmly on the table. "Miss Morgan, you're here for a purpose." The soft tone of his words tempered their bluntness. "Now you—we—seem to be avoiding it. Perhaps you decided that earlier, and that's why you brought your lovely friend with you."

"Y'all don't concern yourselves about *me,*" said Troja, turning shanty. "Got important business of my *own!*" She was about to get up, paused only to take another sip of champagne. "And if Normalyn decides to stay, you watch how you talk to her!"

Normalyn tamed Troja's reaction by holding her hand in reassurance. What Mark Poe had said was true, but what she said now was equally true in this tense moment. "I trust her, Mr. Poe." And she did—staunchly—for having defended her.

"Mark doesn't mean to be rude or suspicious." Robert seemed to be used to explaining a familiar misunderstanding. "He's just very forthright. That's why he never got along in Hollywood."

"Well, Normalyn is forthright, too," Troja encouraged her.

"I apologize for how I sounded. Robert is right: I didn't intend rudeness." Mark Poe closed his eyes briefly as if he were tired of explaining this. "We have nothing to hide. For us the scandals are over."

Robert sighed. "Yes!"

"I'm certain that's how you found us, Miss Morgan, by tracing the public scandals?" There was a note of bitterness in his words.

Normalyn nodded.

"But I do have memories I've protected. You've come to learn about those. I'm sorry to ask that you convince me that there's good reason why I should share them with you."

Robert explained Mark's new bluntness: "There was another youngwoman who came here not long ago, pretending to inquire about a scholarship. She really wanted to know intimate details about our pasts, and those of others—for that dreadful cult group."

The Dead Movie Stars! A youngwoman like that had invaded Miss Bertha's house, Normalyn remembered . . . Then, like the others, Mark, too, was testing her.

"You told me on the telephone that you wanted to find out who you are," Mark reminded Normalyn; his voice was not unkind.

"It's true. I want to find out— . . ." Normalyn couldn't ask.

"—what Enid was like." She couldn't ask what she had really come to find out. Spoken aloud, those words would commit her to doubts she refused about her origin.

"Oh, is that all?" Mark said with a tinge of irritation. "She was brave, loyal, determined. She said she was cunning, but she was also vulnerable, and she was very beautiful." His voice softened. "And she said she would die in spring . . . Now you know how I saw her." He terminated his peremptory recollection.

"Miss Morgan—Normalyn," Robert said quietly. "After you called Mark, *I* urged him to telephone you back. If you would only be . . . direct . . . about your intentions for coming here."

Now even Troja seemed to encourage that. She put her hand over Normalyn's as if to buffer all difficulty.

Then there was no need to play the games she had played with Mildred and David, the games Miss Bertha had rehearsed her for—no need of that because *she* had located these men. David Lange, with his powerful voice—echoing at unexpected times, mournful, commanding—had *not* guided her here . . . And Robert was her ally. Perhaps at the same time he wanted to discover something of his own within Mark's recollections. Normalyn shaped the necessary words: "I know that before Enid left this city—"

The angels' city, Normalyn, the city of lost angels, she heard Enid's voice.

"—there was much . . . intrigue involving—"

Say it, dearheart, say it, Miss Bertha spoke unexpectedly.

"—involving her and Marilyn Monroe, and Mildred Meadows." *And perhaps it involved me*—she could not say that. "Enid trusted you," she said with the certainty of this moment. "That's why I've turned to you, Mark." She paused, wondering whether she could continue now. "And to find out, *really*, what Enid was like then. And what Marilyn Monroe was like. The way *you* saw them." Finally she had extended the territory of her search for identity into the life of Marilyn Monroe.

Mark Poe sipped his champagne, slowly. He smiled at Normalyn—a slightly saddened smile that accepted the reasons she had given him for being here.

"Marilyn gave Mark a job when nobody else would hire him." Robert guided Mark's loyalty.

"It was Enid who hired me," Mark said.

"It was brave of *both* of them," Robert said, "because the vile Meadows had made him unemployable in Hollywood with her ugly lies."

Normalyn looked away now, for moments, from the past she was about to roam again. She was aware that at a garden table nearby Michael Farrell, dressed, was studying intently from a book. Other swimmers had scattered away. Michael flipped a page loudly, to alert her attention. When she looked, he smiled at her. Caught, she stared away. Would there be time enough for matters like *that*? Not just for exploring the lives of ghosts?

Instant rage poured out Mark's denunciation: "Meadows is the most amoral person I've ever known. Her great evil is propelled by tiny petulance. When her daughter died in a car crash with her child, Mildred wouldn't allow the child to be buried in the same cemetery—because, she said, the child was 'ugly'!"

"She's obsessed with beauty to the point of illness," Robert said. "She despised Marilyn because Marilyn was the symbol of beauty and dared to ignore her," he continued, goading Mark's memories, "and Marilyn survived all her attacks."

"Except ... perhaps ... one," Mark said to Normalyn. Then he said to Robert, "Why don't you tell us how you saw Marilyn, and then I'll join your narrative."

"Oh, she was so hurt." Robert remembered that as foremost about the movie star. "She transformed her pain into defiant sexuality."

"That can happen," Troja said, "but the pain just changes; sometimes that's all."

Mark Poe encouraged Robert: "But tell us how you *first* saw her." As he said that, his eyes were gentle on Normalyn.

There was a man who loved me— ... Normalyn thought she heard Enid's voice in this flowered alcove.

Robert Kunitz whispered to them all in mock secrecy, "You must promise first not to tell *this* part to anyone." He announced dramatically, "Before I became Nash McHugh, I ... was ... a chorus boy for Twentieth Century-Fox!"

Troja applauded the courageous confession.

"It was my first movie," Robert Kunitz said. "We were rehearsing the big musical number. And then there *she* was!" He paused, preparing with silent moments for her grand entrance into his thoughts. As if she had sprung to life before him, Robert said, "Yes, there *she* was! Marilyn—"

Seventeen

—Monroe walked on the set of the musical *There's No Business Like Show Business*. She was wearing everything white, everything glittering, everything revealing. Two hidden slits at the bottom of her dress added the surprise of more flesh in unexpected glimpses as she moved. The dress was so sheer her skin tinted it a lighter shade of gold than her naked legs.

Robert Kunitz, then only eighteen years old, was so awed to see her—in person—that he tripped on a circular stair. "You stupid fool!" The dance director screamed. "Get out and don't ever—!"

"But *I'm* not ready yet," Marilyn challenged the choreographer. She went to Robert, who was rubbing his ankle. "Did you hurt yourself?" she asked him. He couldn't answer, not because of pain but because Marilyn was so close to him. "I've stumbled a lot," she told him. "And I-I-I stutter wh-wh-when I'm n-n-nervous." She exaggerated her stutter, for him. "That's what makes my voice so . . . b-b-breathy. And do you know the reason I walk like I do, so sexy? Because," she whispered only to him, "I have weak ankles!"

Robert could still not bring himself to speak to her. Even though she was not yet the greatest movie star, she was a magical presence. "Do you know how to drive?" she asked him.

He was able to gasp, "Yes!"

"I have a car, but I don't drive very well. Will you go to the beach with me, after the scene?"

Of course she knew he was gay; most of the chorus boys were. She just felt he needed company, and so did she. "Yes," he repeated the only word he thought he would be able, ever, to say to her.

Even with a hurt ankle, he was able to dance.

They drove to Malibu. It was almost sundown on the beach. A giant orange sun floated on violet mist. Fishermen cast their nets into the hungry ocean, inspected the retrieved catch, and rejected fish too small to sell.

When Marilyn saw the discarded fish on the sand, she yelled at the fishermen: "Bastards, fucking cruel bastards!" The rejected fish thrashed on the shore. She gave a desperate cry and began throwing them back into the frothing water. "They're still alive!" she insisted. In panic, she bent down, digging into sand in order not to miss one. She was tossing everything into the water—fish, seaweed, shells.

Robert joined her, although he knew the fish were dead. "You saved them all," he assured her.

Marilyn linked her arm through his and said, "*We* saved them. Now they'll live out their full lives."

Robert drove her home in her car. At her apartment, she said, "Thank you very much."

The youngman did not mind walking home, because he didn't want to distance himself too quickly from Marilyn Monroe. He knew why he had instantly loved her. Like him, she had to keep her real self hidden, create herself constantly, hide her wounds, decorate them—in order to survive.

Robert was fired from the studio soon after by the choreographer, who became head of Musical Production. When Robert returned to claim his last check, he saw Marilyn alone outside a sound stage. He watched her from the distance. She knelt, throwing pieces of bread at a few pigeons. That was the last time he saw her in person.

On his way to apply for a clerk's job at Bullock's-Wilshire to tide him over a difficult time, Robert accepted a ride from powerful agent Henry Wilson. Made over into a deep-voiced movie hero, Nash drew thousands of letters and marriage proposals from women. Hollywood was even more closeted then than now; a whisper about homosexuality destroyed. Nash dated many Hollywood beauties.

Mark Poe—that was his real name—was a serious stage actor with solid theatrical training. His mother was Charlotte Poe, one of the few screen actresses who managed the transition from silent films to talking motion pictures. Disgusted with Hollywood mediocrity, she married and became one of the first women to retain her own last name. When she divorced the cool, aloof millionaire, Mark chose to adopt his mother's surname. Two daughters, Allana and Michele, ostentatiously opted for their wealthy father's name. Charlotte adored Mark and came to detest the other siblings because of their lack of wit and sensitivity, their courtship of banality. Mark left a promising stage career in New York and returned to Hollywood only because Charlotte had a stroke that left her partially paralyzed.

Nash and Mark met in a bar where male homosexuals and lesbians went, in camouflaged couples. Mark was defiantly alone. The two men became lovers.

The House Committee on Un-American Activities was rampaging through lives then, exposing "communists" and "perverts." Nash's studio learned that the name of Mark Poe had been introduced, in secret, as a "probable subversive and known deviate closely associated with a well-known male movie star." Encouraged by his mother, Mark "went public" about his liberal views and his sexuality. He knew Nash would stand by him.

The studio alerted Mildred Meadows to "dangerous matters." She initiated the slaughter of Mark Poe and announced contingent salvation for Nash McHugh.

Accompanied by a studio executive, Nash had lunch at Perino's—at Mildred Meadows's table. He told her he was as shocked as she to learn about "leftish and other ugly involvements" concerning his "acquaintance" Mark Poe. He thanked her for the "timely information." The studio executive then gave Mildred thrilling news: Reports that Nash had avoided patriotic service were unfounded, and he was about to marry the socialite daughter of a "prominent American patriot." In her next column, Mildred granted Nash McHugh absolution.

Nash assured Mark nothing would change between them. "You don't know who you are," Mark replied in disgust.

Charlotte Poe had another stroke, fatal. Married to partners in a right-wing law firm in Seattle, Allana Wallach and Michele Feingold, who had not spoken to their "radical" mother for years, contested the will, which left everything to Mark. Meadows's implications that Mark was "interested in boys" was introduced against him. Charlotte had foreseen the nasty battle. She had created a trust to be overseen by Mark to award scholarships to "talented students, of whatever color, religion, gender, sexual persuasion." She included a clause: "I make this bequest with full knowledge and approval of my beloved son Mark Poe's sexual orientation, and his dedication to and respect for young artists." Mark won.

He turned to writing. His first novel, *After Twilight*, was about the creative young drifting in Hollywood. Daring for its time because of one scene of homosexual desire, it sold well but infuriated reviewers who saw it—in the words of one irate critic—as "a disgusting guide to perversion." Its wit and lyrical literacy were ignored. The jacket photograph of the handsome actor-turned-writer did not help the book's critical reception.

Floundering, drinking, Nash divorced Lorna Rehnquist. His career waned. He haunted the places where he knew Mark went. At Musso & Frank's Restaurant on Hollywood Boulevard, he finally found him. "I'm *myself* now!—Robert Kunitz," he told Mark.

Nash—Robert—abandoned films and moved in with Mark. Through a period of financial adjustments, Robert tended to matters of a prospective school, still a dream, while Mark returned to New York, where his first play was about to open. In search of a new actress for the lead, he was invited to see a young woman perform at the Actors Studio.

There he met Marilyn Monroe and Enid Morgan.

Powerful Hollywood studio heads considered movie stars—especially females—children, deserving "salubrious" periodical scoldings, at times by ridicule. To keep Marilyn Monroe "humble," Zanuck, apprised of the fact that she was drawing more fan mail than any other star on the lot, initiated an investigation to make sure that *she* was not responsible for the staggering quantity of mail. She was not, but a smirking item about that in Meadows's column caused laughter.

In revolt from demeaning treatment, Marilyn Monroe announced she was moving to New York to "learn to be an actress."

Supposedly inspired by the teachings of Constantin Stanislavsky, Lee Strasberg taught "the method," a mixture of confrontation and analysis. Actors drew upon their personal experiences for dramatic motivation. Strasberg had his critics. Some claimed he took actors to the brink of psychological collapse, sometimes past. Laurence Olivier called his "method" "nonsense." Stella Adler insisted that he had misunderstood Stanislavsky. For the devoted he was a father-God figure.

Strasberg "accepted" Marilyn as a private pupil, then allowed her to become an "observer" at the Actors Studio, which he had founded, and let her perform in class exercises reserved for members. The high priest of "method" acting and his wife, Paula, welcomed Marilyn Monroe into their "artistic family." In return, Marilyn made the studio famous and lavished them with gifts.

After the actress he had come to see was through performing, Mark Poe was about to leave when Lee Strasberg appeared to begin his class exercises.

" 'Scuse me," a soft voice said courteously to Mark; a woman moved past him to a seat next to him. Although most of the actors in the studio were aggressively casual in their attire—to decorate their disgust for "glamour"—this woman seemed naturally ordinary, wearing a baggy sweater, jeans, hardly any makeup. A plain scarf concealed all but wisps of blondish hair. Mark noticed that she was clenching and unclenching her hands, panic at war with control.

Somewhat professorial in appearance, Strasberg explained that evening's exercise in "sense memory": "Describe *only* what you see, and then convey what you feel, without describing feelings. Recall an emotional experience but don't tell us *how* you feel. Communicate what comes to your senses, what sounds in the room are like, what it smells like, how we are dressed." There might be validity in the exercise if clearly explained, Mark thought, but Strasberg had been misty, lofty, inexact. But all that seemed to please his gathered acolytes, who nodded gravely.

"Perhaps Marilyn Monroe would like to participate—" Strasberg delighted in bringing the famous into his studio, so that he could show how unimpressed he was by them.

The unextraordinary woman next to Mark stood up, hesitantly. " 'Scuse me, please," she said again to Mark. Her hand accidentally brushed his. Her fingers were trembling, icy with fear. Mark thought, there's no possibility she'll be able to control her feelings on demand.

While everyone pretended not to know who Marilyn Monroe was, she sat on the floor, where the exercises were performed. She wrapped her hands in the sweater, warming them. Mark thought she looked like a resigned supplicant.

"Now," Strasberg led her, "let's hear your description of this room. And remember," he warned, "no *described* feelings."

Marilyn closed her eyes momentarily, as if rehearsing every word before she would expose it aloud. "The—back—of—the—room—is—dark—so dark that if we were alone—we would f-f-feel—"

"No feelings!" Strasberg reminded firmly, his back to her, facing the others. "Just locate the feelings *in* you!"

Marilyn tried to revise: "—so dark that if we were alone, we would be scared—"

"Oh, dear God, what do you think *scared* is, Marilyn? Scared is feeling!" He emphasized his determination to be patient by folding his arms before his chest.

Marilyn's hands clenched at her mouth.

Strasberg seemed pleased by the prayerful attitude. He guided: "In this room—"

With difficulty, terrified, Marilyn began slowly describing the room's approximate dimensions, the colors, its walls, the darkness in the back, bunched shadows— . . .

"Stop, stop," Strasberg ordered. "Those are just facts."

The movie star looked up at him, frightened. This time her fingers locked tightly before her.

The tolerant professor, Strasberg nodded at Marilyn and released her from his command: "Now go on and locate *your* feelings. Find the truth in *your* action—inside, not out—then reverse it. *Feel* the room."

While the other actors listened as if he were making exciting sense, Mark became alarmed. In his grand display, a perform-ance goaded now by the reaction of his disciples, some of whom closed their eyes, hands clasped to their foreheads as if to absorb such enormous profundities, Strasberg was pushing the movie star into a battle that was only too real for her—the constant attempt to control her feelings, or hide them, in order not to be hurt. Seeing her struggling to contain her trembling, Mark thought of a pinned butterfly making tiny fluttering moves to live out its brief life.

"Marilyn." Strasberg's was the voice of a strict, kind father. "I said you may continue."

"I'm sorry!" she gasped. "I'm really sorry!"

Strasberg laughed just slightly, more of a derisive cough. "Well, now wouldn't you say that being sorry is feeling?" He faced the members of the studio. "Wouldn't *you?*" There were moody responsive sounds. He addressed Marilyn quickly: "Now! Just describe! Locate a feeling first. Of course you can do that, can't you?"

Her eyes unable to pull away from them, Marilyn went on to describe the room's shadows. "So d-d-dark, so dark—"

"You're about to introduce feelings again, aren't you?" The director hinted he might become impatient. "Sights, sounds, sights, sensations. When you locate the feeling, follow it. Guide yourself inward, inside, probe, feel but don't *tell* what you feel; describe, describe, inside, Marilyn, inside yourself. Guide your-self into the darkness of the room if you want to!"

"The darkness— . . ." Marilyn whispered, as if now she understood.

"Good!" Strasberg finally approved. "Now go *into* it!"

While demanding she not describe feelings, he was pushing her into the secret core of them! Mark knew that method

actors were used to emotional carnage—and dramatic displays—
forced epiphanies, quiverings at the edge of "sudden truths,"
controlled or actual "breakdowns." Marilyn Monroe was not
acting. In the glare not of adoring cameras but of judging
eyes—and pushed by Strasberg's harsh commands—she was
rushing into dark depths. Mark would have left, appalled by
the foolish exercise—*feel, don't feel*—but it was also cruel, and
he wanted to lend support if it became possible.

Inspired by his effect, Strasberg leaned over Marilyn and
whispered loudly to her bowed head: "Inside, inside yourself,
your own darkness, *that's* where you'll find your motivations,
your truths!"

Marilyn's words spilled: "*My* darkness, *yes,* and it's theirs,
too—my grandmother's, my mother's. The room's all shadows
and in the darkest part I see . . . *her! I have to run away from
her!*"

Click!

A woman in the back of the room had just snapped a silver
cigarette lighter, flameless. She stood half in shadow, half in
light, split in two.

Strasberg squinted to locate the origin of the intrusion. The
dark-haired woman, a haughty beauty, advanced boldly. She
was dressed in subtle elegance, a pearl-gray dress. Even the
determinedly indifferent actors gasped. The woman said to
Strasberg, "You're a fool!" With an intensity of caring that
Mark would always remember, she guided Marilyn up from
the floor, restoring her, and said gently to the movie star,
"You can't run away from her. You must never be unkind to
her."

Charged with strength, Marilyn removed her scarf, loosing
her hair, and she abandoned the sacrificial platform.

When Mark saw the two women outside, he offered to call
them a cab. Enid looked at him as if in welcome recognition.
"Instead, would you please walk her home?" she asked Mark.
He understood they needed to separate after the strange
interlude. The sounds of Enid's footsteps faded, with her, into
the night.

Marilyn walked along the streets with Mark—as if she had
not yet seen him. Mark felt as if he were with someone else,
not Marilyn Monroe—as if another presence had overwhelmed
the great movie star. No one recognized her along the well-lit
streets.

Suddenly!

She tossed her head back, her fingers shaped her hair. With
no need of a mirror she painted her lips. She bunched the

loose sweater. It embraced lush breasts. Her movements molded the jeans to her curves. And *there* was Marilyn Monroe!

People gaped in recognition.

That is great acting, Mark knew, as he watched this masterpiece of artificial creation on display.

"I just felt like being Marilyn Monroe again!" she said.

They walked along the East River. The sound of their slowed footsteps seemed an intrusion on the nervous noises of the city. As if to shed the earlier experience, Marilyn Monroe said, "I should have done my kitten improvisation for Strasberg." Her laughter released tension. "Want to see it?" She became soft, a furry kitten. She formed her hands into tiny paws. She meowed, she purred. Suddenly she made the sound of an attacking cat. Her hands became claws ripping at the darkness ahead.

When they resumed walking, her body relaxed against his and she was warmly aware of him. He told her he was gay. "So what?" She cuddled closer. "I've had lots of affairs, just like gay men do. Sometimes that's all I want to do, is fuck. What the hell difference does it make who you fuck as long as it feels good?" The bravado was gone, she sighed. "As long as it takes away loneliness."

*　　*　　*

The movie star on the set of the musical, on the beach saving rejected fish— Normalyn welcomed Robert Kunitz's tender memories. He had been harsh only about himself, when he told of his betrayal of Mark, and then Troja had listened in understanding of love that endures betrayal. . . . Normalyn knew now that Mark had deliberately invited Robert's gentler memories before he provided his own darker recollections. . . . Normalyn was beginning to see two women at the center of her life, and now, emerging, retreating, re-emerging, a third presence, evoked at the end of the cruel acting exercise, the same figure in the angry overheard "game."

For respite from the engulfing past, Normalyn sought out Michael Farrell. He answered her smile and nodded.

"Then Enid telephoned me," Mark Poe resumed. "She knew no one else would hire me in Los Angeles, and Marilyn needed someone to be with her, because, Enid told me bluntly, Marilyn had just been through a frightening experience and must be protected. Marilyn—"

Eighteen

—Monroe committed herself to Payne Whitney Psychiatric Clinic at New York Hospital. A few days earlier, "in a waking dream," she had opened the window of her high-story apartment, and, eyes closed, fists tightened, she prepared to fling herself into the peaceful unconsciousness—"a warm blackness," she described it—that she was sure occurs before a body smashes on the ground and dies.

"I heard footsteps on the street outside; I *had* to go to the window to see who it was." That was the only explanation she could provide for finding herself there.

"But you know you were too high up to hear footsteps," her psychiatrist told her.

"But I did, dammit, and I did *see* her. She was wearing a kind of flowery dress—pretty, I guess."

"Perhaps you were somewhat groggy, Marilyn, and just thought you saw her." But the "dream" alarmed the psychiatrist, and she urged self-commitment: "Only for a rest."

There were other reasons for suggesting this "rest." Marilyn's third marriage had just ended, her finances were again tenuous, she was acutely aware of being about to turn thirty-five. And:

Leaving the Actors Studio a few nights earlier, she had read a headline on a tabloid in a shabby newsstand:

WIFE BLAMES GABLE DEATH ON MARILYN!

With chilled fingers she bought the paper and in the sullied light of the newsstand read that Clark Gable's widow was suggesting that "pressures created by Monroe's erratic behav-

224

ior" on her latest film, *The Misfits,* had contributed to the actor's fatal heart attack. For Marilyn, Gable was an adored hero, "who looks," she told everyone, "just like my *real* father." She had flung the newspaper at the New York wind. Its sheets flapped like angry birds.

The ugly headline on the tabloid—black on gray—continued to loom in her mind like a tombstone. Before the "waking dream" that led her to the window, she had been experiencing nights she described as "feeling like dark ice."

On a cold day—the East River was icy—she took a cab to the skyscraper that houses the clinic. Against a darkening sky, the white building promised surcease. She wrapped her fur coat about her body. She liked to blow softly on the fur to test its luscious texture. When she did so today, she saw only cold mist from her mouth. She stopped. In a window dulled by misting fog that rejected reflections, she had glimpsed the gauzy outline of a woman, a silver ghost.

She rushed away, in. She registered herself under an assumed name—Faye Miller. Reason for admittance to clinic? She wrote on the form she filled out slowly, lingering over the prospect of surcease: "study and treatment of illness of undetermined origin."

The attendant who registered her at the psychiatric clinic recognized the new patient despite her attempt at concealment. As soon as the movie star was led to her room, the nurse told everyone she could find:

"Marilyn Monroe is here!"

Stripped of her own clothes and her fur coat—she blew once more on the gray fur, which looked like frozen snow now—the star was given a loose, drab hospital gown. Immediately desperate—feeling they were going to make her disappear! —she tightened it to assert her curves. She attempted to moisten her lips, but her mouth was dry. She entered her new room.

It was almost bare—no door to the toilet, no telephone, no windows, only a thick glass pane on the door, which locked behind her with metallic finality. Her body wrenched as if to escape and leave only a shell of herself in here. She whispered through the glass pane, "Please open the door. I've changed my mind." She waited for salvation, even a substitute. She shouted: "If you let me out, I won't make trouble."

Along the hollow tunnels of corridors, they were moving toward her in starched white uniforms that made scratchy sounds—orderlies, nurses, doctors, surgeons.

Lie on the cot, the star told herself, and *this* "waking dream"

will end the way the other one did when you were about to
jump out of the window, remember? She saw a woman's
powdered face staring at her through the door-window. A
nurse! Another face peered in. A man—a doctor! He invited
another face. Then there was another. She heard buzzing
voices at the door:

"It *is* Marilyn Monroe!"

Panic battled sedatives. She was sure that maddened fans
had captured her. In the morning new faces pressed against
the glass.

She stood up.

"Is it really Marilyn Monroe?" someone asked.

"It can't be," Marilyn Monroe thought she heard her own
voice answer, "because Marilyn Monroe couldn't be captured
like this." So it must be—?

She tore off the hospital gown; the most famous body in the
world stood naked before hospital attendants. She screamed at
them: "If you want to look at me, look at *me! I'm Marilyn
Monroe!*"

She was still screaming when the door opened and someone
covered her with a sheet; she was still screaming when they
transferred her to a security ward on a grayer floor; she was
still screaming when another door bolted from outside. She
smashed the single chair against the concrete wall. "God*damn*
you! God-fucking-*damn* you!" she kept screaming.

She bribed an orderly to make a telephone call for her: "I'll
give you my autograph!" She signed a paper.

"What the hell!" He gave it back to her.

She could not decipher her own name. She signed the
paper again, concentrating on each letter: "M-a-r-i-l-y-n M-o-n-
r-o-e." She added, "Love!" She was not sure whether the
orderly would keep his word.

News of her commitment reached her second husband, the
athlete, who was then in Florida. He flew to New York, rushed to
the hospital, and on the fourth day of her captivity he got her
out. As she was being smuggled through a freezing basement
passageway, she held her comforting fur coat close to her
body. She saw ahead, through a window, the indifferent East
River, freezing over in jagged shapes. She was pale, still disturbed. New lines scratched at her face. Her ex-husband went
ahead to make sure that outside there were no—

Newsmen, photographers—dozens of them sprang at her,
dancing madly about her, shouting questions—*"Why—?"*—firing
accusations—*"Did you—?"*—shooting at her with cameras. She
retreated back, back, farther back. Her ex-husband struggled

to reach her. The reporters and photographers advanced—crouching, kneeling. She was cornered. "I'm Marilyn Monroe!" she whispered. Behind her, her hands touched cold walls, ice on ice.

It was after the actress told her what had occurred—a crisis she had not lived through with her—that Enid telephoned Mark about employment: "Simply to be with her, help her—someone strong like you." Mark told Enid of his exile, the bruising scandals. She knew all about that, she told him. She admired him and his "beautiful novel, very much"; she knew they could trust him, she told him. She also knew that his play had been postponed: "I'm sure that it was beautiful, too."

He assumed she knew the reason for its postponement. A principal backer had only belatedly learned about his "questionable background."

The day Mark arrived at Marilyn's Brentwood home, the door was open. She was dancing alone, barefoot. "It's so *good* to be a movie star again!" She hugged him. "Are you still gay, dammit?" she teased. "Yes," he assured her and hugged her back. "Just as well," she said, "because that way the neighbors won't start rumors besmirching my *new* virginity." In an interview that had only recently appeared she had claimed she was "always a virgin between marriages."

She was not happy. Her latest film was not a success, and in it she had given perhaps her best performance. She hated her new movie, *Something's Got to Give,* and learned that its director, George Cukor, gossiped behind her back. She had difficulty getting to the studio on time, then getting there at all. There was talk of an impending suspension. She stayed home more and more. She made many calls, received few. Enid had disappeared again, but she called often, long distance. Those were among the rare times that Marilyn still laughed during that darkening period.

When Marilyn was especially restless, Mark called Robert in Palm Springs to inform him he might be late, might stay over. She and Mark would talk until her pills "clicked on." She would sit on the higher of two steps that led to the back of the house, the rooms and a bathroom she now grandly called her "quarters." She would sit there, Mark thought, as if to remain as close as possible to the "peaceful pills" in her bedroom. So difficult to think of this lonely woman as "Marilyn Monroe!" . . . Those times, she and Mark exchanged stories, shared their detestation of Mildred Meadows. Marilyn's accounts of her life were often contradictory, but always unaltered were the memories of many unhappy foster homes, of being unwanted, of a "crazy grandmother who tried to strangle me when I was a child," and of a "crazier mother," who would appear now and then, she told him, "with a huge chunk of kindness only to take it with her when she left me again." She talked about her dread of "the darkness," the madness in her background, and her fear of "passing it on" if she ever had a child, which she wanted "more than anything in the world."

One such late night Marilyn sat on the stairs in a robe and pressed her knees together as if she were cold. She told him about the "waking dream" that had preceded her commitment, and about the real nightmare of being in the psychiatric clinic.

As she related the eerie experience, she seemed drawn into it again. She gathered her robe, and she was shivering. She looked lost, frightened. Mark held her hand, soothing.

Suddenly she stood up. She threw off the robe. It fell to her bare feet, and she was naked. "I'm Marilyn Monroe"—she repeated the words she had told him she'd screamed at the clinic.

Mark said what he thought she needed to hear: "Yes, you're the most famous and beautiful movie star alive, perhaps of all time."

"Then *you* have to want me. *Every* man wants me." There was no exultation in the voice, just devouring need.

She was not reacting out of desire for him, Mark knew. At that moment she craved the whole world's love to attempt to fill the deep pit carved by years of abandonment.

"Aren't *you* a fucking man?" she yelled at him.

Mark did not soothe her sudden sobbing this time.

*　　*　　*

"She had turned into someone else," Mark said in the alcove in Palm Springs.

The sunlight was still bright, but Normalyn sensed thickening shadows, a new darkness. Again, she had heard events Enid claimed as part of her life being attributed to the movie star's.

"What she said to Mark was cruel, but I know she didn't mean it," Robert said, loyal to both. "It's just that by then she was living on the edge, like we have, Mark. Just like we have."

"Yes," Mark agreed. "I even think that—"

*　　*　　*

—Marilyn forgot what happened.

Soon after, she was renewed. Mark thought she was at work again, perhaps in a role she longed for, Grushenka in *The Brothers Karamazov*. He knew that Somerset Maugham had written her, to tell her he thought she would be "wonderful" as Sadie Thompson in a television version of his play *Rain*, and that Jean-Paul Sartre had just recently called her "one of the greatest actresses alive" and expressed his desire that she appear in his screen version of *The Life of Freud*. But her new excitement had another origin.

Her private line would ring and she would purr soft words into it. She began to suggest Mark "take a day off; you deserve it for putting up with me." She became coyly secretive: "Even if I told you—and I'm not going to—you wouldn't believe who I'm seeing!" she teased.

He found her in the kitchen, which she had converted into a jungle of vegetables, a clutter of utensils. She gasped that she had to cook dinner "for a very close, very important man." Now she was in a panic because she wasn't a good cook. "I know!" She looked like a pretty child who has conceived of an enormously clever plot to confuse demanding adults. "I'll send out for food, but I'll put it all in the oven and that will make delicious smells in the house, just like in a restaurant." She chose two bottles of champagne to chill. She looked mischievously angelic. She asked him please to wait for the ordered food—"and then you'll rush off because he's very private." She went to get ready "early."

"Do I look like *me*?" She stood in the kitchen.

At first he was shocked. Her hair was just brushed through; she was wearing hardly any makeup. She looked her age, looked like a pretty woman—but not the beautiful movie star she was. He understood her question and was moved. "Yes," he answered, "you look exactly like you, and you're lovely." He meant it.

"That's how I want him to see *me*." She kissed Mark gratefully on the mouth. She confided the reason for the elaborate evening: "Everyone will know soon, because he's going to ask me to marry him."

Mark left, glad to return to Palm Springs early to discuss deferred plans about the school with Robert. In the flurry of arrangements for the subterfuge dinner, he had forgotten some pages of his new novel. He drove back. As he approached the house, he saw a lean, angular man with tousled brownish hair; he was hurrying into Marilyn's house from a nondescript car parked several houses away.

*   *   *

Mark returned the next morning to find Marilyn sitting alone in the kitchen, her head on the table as if she had fallen asleep off and on in that position. Plates of dried, abandoned food remained on a table. Two champagne bottles were empty. He helped her to the bedroom.

The door did not open the rest of that day.

Her moods blackened. She stayed in bed into late morning; she woke up sick. There was no reference to her new lover. One night she appeared, spectral and weary, fully dressed, and insisted Mark drive her to the market. It closed at ten, he reminded. She insisted.

The store was closed. She got out of the car. She hurried to a telephone booth. He remembered she had told him that she had been hearing "weird interference" on her own lines at home. Lighted within the transparent cubicle now, she looked like a radiant captive. She dialed once, again, again, another time. He saw her lips moving. She dialed yet another time. Again her lips moved.

When she returned to the car, looking pale even in the dim light, she said to him in surprise, "He changed his private telephone number. I had to leave a message for him at the switchboard." She looked startled. "I told the night operator at the Justice Department and at the White House to tell Robert Kennedy that Marilyn Monroe had called."

Nineteen

When Mark moved into the account of Marilyn's clandestine calls that eerie night, Normalyn severed the visual contact with which she had encouraged his narrative.

"I believe Normalyn has heard enough," Mark said quickly.

"Normalyn is very brave, Mr. Poe. Whatever she has to hear—" Troja assured.

What a powerful ally she had in Troja, Normalyn knew—and trusted her, no matter what would be spoken here. One second later she felt a nasty jab of suspicion about Troja's motives. She conquered *those* doubts the very next second.

A loud flip of a page! Michael Farrell continued to assert his presence nearby, although shadows were tinting the book he was straining to study while glancing at Normalyn.

"And then, please?" Now Normalyn asked Mark to continue into the territory she had tried to isolate from scrutiny.

"And then," Mark said, "Marilyn began to drink heavily; she was abusive, then silent—"

Like Enid. Normalyn linked the two women more tightly.

"Tormented," Robert again defended. "People forget that the end of her life was very sad. She was terribly isolated, and she thought she was through. All people remember now is the legendary woman, forgetting that the real one suffered a lot. All that love came later. Sad, isn't it? She didn't know that after her death she would be idolized. So sad."

"She was tormented, yes," Mark agreed, "so troubled that—"

*　　*　　*

—she slept only when sedatives claimed her, at whatever time of day that occurred. She waited for one call that refused

231

to come. She learned the studio was about to fire her, and still she would not turn up. She merely wandered about the house as if she were preparing to become a ghost.

In the mornings, she would trace with a finger the deepening scratchy lines about her eyes, touching them only delicately, as if she expected them to heal.

She stayed in her "quarters," within controlled, familiar boundaries. At times she would lie by the pool, which, for her, was the most powerful symbol that she was a movie star. Today, she reclined on a lawn chair under a shading umbrella. She wore a large hat, doubly hiding her fair skin from the sunlight. Suddenly she threw off the hat, pushed the umbrella away—it spun in a whorl of colors. Removing her sunglasses, she stared at the indifferent sun.

Demanding that *it* see her.

Mark went to her. "For a while everyone *seemed* to love me," she said, "and then—" She opened her empty hands.

Coming to work the next day, Mark saw her standing before the entrance of the house she had bought with so much pride as "finally something of my own." She was staring at the Latin motto inscribed over the door by previous owners. "I found out what that means," she told Mark. "It says, 'I am nearing the end of my journey.'"

Mark was elated that afternoon to see that Enid was back. She was adjusting her slanted hat in the hall mirror.

"Enid!" he welcomed.

She turned, lifted the veil. It was Marilyn! "You thought I was Enid," she said.

Mark tried to dismiss her strange pleasure in having confused him.

Then soon after, laughter, happy laughter emerged from Marilyn's "quarters." Mark recognized Enid's voice. He welcomed the joyous laughter, incongruous in the previously moody house. It was the laughter of schoolgirls sharing intrigue with each other. Only Enid could accomplish that instant transformation in Marilyn.

"Hello, Mark." A time later, as unobtrusively as she had entered the house, Enid entered his office. He had deliberately stayed late in order to see her. She greeted him with a curious shyness, quick intense glances withdrawn, reasserted, a smile about to form, deciding whether it would. His memory of her had not done justice to her charm, her beauty. She looked gorgeous in the sliced shadows of the room.

He said aloud, "You really do exist," because when he had

first seen her, the only time before now, she had disappeared so entirely yet haunted his memories.

She only smiled the wryly saddened smile he remembered, not unlike Marilyn's during this period of reclusion. "I read your novel again," she told me. "It takes so much courage to be who you are, always."

"Or foolish doggedness." He tried to laugh.

"No," she said. "It's courage."

He thanked her, touched. He cleared a chair for her. She seemed tired. Pensive. "She's been unhappier than I've ever known her to be," she indicated familiarity with Marilyn's earlier panic. "But she'll be fine now," she said with conviction.

"Because you're here." Mark wanted to express his appreciation.

"Oh, no," she denied, "not because of that." She confided, "Before you came, she had a very delicate operation so that she'll be able again to have children."

Mark Poe had heard, like all of Hollywood, of the miscarriages, the reported abortions.

"She was very depressed because she believed the operation hadn't been successful," Enid clarified. Then she smiled, a full smile that made her face radiant. "But it was and she's pregnant again, and she'll do *everything* to have this child."

Enid's pleasure in the discovery astonished Mark because he thought he knew, with reasonable certainty, that Marilyn's only contact during the recent period of retreat had been "the very important man." But he was married, a father, a figure of national importance many thought would be President. With a stab of apprehension and sadness, Mark remembered that one day in a rare playful mood Marilyn had pretended with him to be heading a receiving line, although it was *she* who was doing the curtsying, as she had done with such quiet dignity when she was introduced to the Queen of England. That day she would whisper with elegant restraint, "Mr. Ambassador— ... Senator— ...." As far as Mark knew, there had been no word from the Attorney General since Marilyn's late-night call to the White House, the Justice Department. Enid was much too sophisticated not to realize the potential for danger in the startling news she had conveyed with such tender happiness.

"Oh, don't look so concerned, Mark," Enid teased. "Of course there'll be a remarriage."

A remarriage! Then either he was wrong or Marilyn had told Enid she was pregnant by one of her ex-husbands, reconciled. Mark worried even more when Enid said:

"Still, there's something else troubling her. She says there's nothing, just the natural apprehensions. But she's determined this time. It may be her last chance. She wants this child more than anything else in the world." As if dismissing the slightest brush of a doubt, she told Mark, "She tells me *everything*, you know."

"Yes." But Mark wondered then.

"She's resting now," she told Mark. "She'll be fine, I know it! . . . *I know it!*" she seemed to swear.

To entice her into staying, Mark asked what he might offer her.

She astonished him as always. "And why not champagne?" she actually flirted! She made her voice husky. "It's never too early for champagne!" Then, shyly—a shyness incongruous in a woman of her beauty—she asked in a quiet voice for "iced tea."

But Mark opened a bottle of champagne.

She had thrilling wide lips, a line of scarlet. Her eyelashes were thick, dark, long. Mark was surprised to discover she was wearing no mascara. Her eyes tilted just slightly, as if once they had delighted in mischief. He felt guilty for thinking that this is what Marilyn Monroe might have looked like had she been born a natural beauty like Enid. At that moment it seemed to Mark that Marilyn had drawn on her own face an artificial version of Enid's. Enid's body was as beautiful as Marilyn's, her breasts as lush, but she wore more loosely flowing clothes. In a shock of sensuality, the sudden curve of a leg as she settled into the chair, the quick movement of an arm, asserted the fabulous outline. Early in his life, Mark had felt attracted to women, "admired" men—the demarcation between admiration and desire blurred. That night, he felt a stirring of desire for this fascinating woman.

"Do you have a life of your own?" he felt close enough to ask her. During his contacts with her, only two including this day's, she existed as an extension of the movie star's life, yet emphatically so as herself, as if in protecting Marilyn she was protecting at least a part of her own life, so close, in a mysterious way.

Enid was answering his unasked question as if it were something she herself often deliberated, or redefined: "She's what I would have been, could be, am— What I must not become, what she cannot become— What we both are—"

It was an exceptional "answer" because up to then, or so he remembered, she had spoken with exactitude, knowing precisely what she meant to convey. Yet now it was as if she herself was trying to understand it, perhaps had always been trying to understand it.

She was looking down into her lap; her voice was hardly audible. "We see in each other what will always be there, what has to be there." She looked up at him, smiling wryly. "But perhaps what binds us is that we met under the shadow of an angel's wing, an angel that had abandoned hope of flying again."

He did not question her. She had been speaking privately. Yet he knew that even in the vague words she had attempted to share something intimate with him, and he welcomed it.

She asked him about his battles, the scandals, and he told her—about the litigation, the struggles now to maintain the school. He told her about Robert. And, laughingly, about his "brief life in Hollywood," when "the benevolent Dr. and Mrs. Crouch, the genial Hollywood executioners," had been assigned to remake his life for "patriotic acceptability."

Enid reacted in mock terror to his mention of the obsessively cheerful man and woman of enormous power who made anything, *everything* possible that was deemed desirable for "the studios." Wrong political allegiances, sexual indiscretions, illegitimacy, insanity, addiction—redemption for any or all of these was certified with purified documents. . . . With sudden playfulness, Enid said to Mark, "Oh, would you like to hear the 'bio' of Enid Morgan, ex-starlet, just as I told it to 'the genial executioners'?"

"Yes!"

Enid leaned forward with her champagne glass. "My name is Enid Morgan, dear Dr. and Mrs. Crouch. I chose my mother's last name—like you, Mark," she added, then resumed her imaginary interview. "—because, Dr. and Mrs. Crouch, my father was a son-of-a-bitch who left my mother and me. And my mother, God bless her, was crazier than my grandmother, who tried to strangle me when I was a child—"

But that was Marilyn's life! Mark remembered, confused.

Enid had closed her eyes; her words softened: "I remember her being carried away screaming. . . ." She continued her interview, but her voice was not as firm as when she had begun: "I was in so many foster homes, Dr. and Mrs., that I can't remember them all—except one." She moved on quickly. "And then I was bought—yes, *bought,* for money—by vulgar rich Texas bastards who couldn't wait to adopt me. But I fixed them, dear Dr. and Mrs. I blackmailed them into sending me away to school. And then—" She looked into her hands, dormant on her lap. They sprang to life; she opened them in a releasing gesture: "—at age eighteen I was born! I no longer cared who my real father was, or even my mother. I chose to be *me!*"

She was looking at him; now he understood her earlier compliment to his "courage."

"Oh, and just a few more things, Dr. and Mrs. Crouch." She tried to force the levity she had abandoned. "For a time I lived with a petty crook who wasn't worthy of me and whom I am going to destroy, very cunningly, because I know what will hurt him the most. You must know that, Dr. and Mrs., so you will figure out how to turn *that* into a springtime romance!" She laughed, trying to temper seriousness. "And one thing more! Up to now I have remained a starlet, just a starlet because"—there was no mocking in her voice as she said— "because beyond everything, I refuse to change the life that made me what I am. All the pain is *my* pain and gives me strength." She smiled warmly at Mark. "That's a line from your novel, Mark; I've made it my own."

Mark reached out and touched her then, because it was suddenly as if she were about to become the earlier woman of mystery, as if she carried her own shadows within which to hide, disappear. And he did not want her to hide, or to vanish from his life. In only moments he had come to feel magically close to her, as if they shared a unique exile—a *beguiled* view of the world, not cynical as it was perceived. And of course she had known him longer than these interludes—she knew him from his novel, within which she had found intimate connections to herself. And he knew her—now—from the playful sorrowing biography of her life. He sat next to her and held her hand. She answered its signals. Her lips parted. He kissed her, a series of kisses each more eager. Their bodies pressed closely. Desire did not lessen, no, but their bodies eased away slowly, parted by the memory of someone else. They withdrew.

Standing, Enid said quickly, "You have someone you love, very much, and I have someone I hate—passionately! We must be true to both."

Enid opened the door so quickly that in Mark's mind it was as if she had walked out before he heard her say, "You see, I really don't exist."

*   *   *

"So possible, to love and destroy," Troja reinterpreted Enid's words just recounted.

That brief, that intense, those moments full of beautiful possibilities had continued to exist forever *because* they had never been tested. Yes, Mark Poe was the man Enid had spoken about, Normalyn welcomed, the man Enid kept within an enclosed memory of her own. . . . There were other discoveries Normalyn had made during Mark Poe's account, but she would rummage through them later—tomorrow, when she would be able to cope with their implications. Not now. But she could not banish all her questions. What enormous revenge had Enid been planning, with such determined cunning, on the man Normalyn was certain was Stan? . . . Normalyn was reconciling—sadly—the beautiful vibrant youngwoman Enid had been with the alcoholic woman uttering pained memories in her dimming room in Gibson, Texas.

As Mark had spoken about the close interlude between him and Enid, his hand had rested firmly on Robert's.

Mark continued: "Without warning—"

Twenty

—Mildred Meadows stepped out of her gray limousine in front of Marilyn Monroe's house. Tiny, erect, she marched into her staked battlefield. She rang the doorbell, she beat on it with miniscule fists. When there was still no response, she moved to one side of the house. Almost tripping, managing to regain control, she located herself dramatically on the lawn and shouted into the house:

"Monroe! If you don't open the door, I'll destroy you!"

Mark Poe had heard the limousine. Enid and Marilyn emerged from the star's "quarters." Laughing with genuine pleasure, Marilyn shouted back at Mildred loud enough to be heard out of a window, "Fuck you, you malicious bitch. You can't hurt me, you've tried often enough! Now get the hell away from here or I'll call the cops to arrest you for trespassing!" Mark and Enid roared with her at the inspired prospect.

"And I will destroy the two brothers!"

Marilyn's laughter stopped.

"What brothers?" Enid asked quickly.

"Shut her up!" Marilyn's agitation sprang.

Mark opened the door. "What the hell do you want, you tiny shit?"

Mildred winced, recognizing the man she thought she had banished. Through the open door, she thrust into the house a rampage of frightening words: There were two letters in her possession, and soon to be released, exposing the immorality of the two most powerful men in the country—the Kennedys—and naming—

238

In cool command at the door, Enid challenged Meadows: "That doesn't concern us."

"Ask Monroe if it concerns her," Mildred demanded. "I dare you! Ask her how they treated her, dismissed her, shared her like a plaything!"

A premature sadness crept into Enid's whispered words to Marilyn: "Is that why you've been so sad?"

"Yes!" Marilyn said.

Enid turned her face, a recoil from shock.

"But he r-r-really loves me," Marilyn stuttered.

Meadows grasped for these moments of vulnerability: "Are you pregnant?" She would verify by command.

"Yes!" Marilyn defied proudly.

"By *him*!"

"Don't answer her!" Enid demanded.

"I believe she's already told us!" Mildred said. She delivered her exultant ultimatum: "Only I can help you, Monroe, with the power of my column. I can choose what will become the truth about you in this." She spoke her words precisely to underscore their irrefutable logic. "And the only way that even I can save you is that there be no continued pregnancy."

Mark had not thought it possible to underestimate Mildred's evil—until now. Her demand was clear, deadly. Yet even at this moment her voice was capable of seeming to thaw in order to add a grotesque postscript to her cruel logic: "My dear, why should you even *consider* destroying your beauty for a *child*?" She consulted a tiny watch embedded in a pendant. "I must have your agreement by—" She set the time of her summons. "And then you will learn my full terms."

She walked back to the waiting limousine. Enid followed. Mark heard an exchange of words between her and Mildred. Then Enid turned toward the house and clicked her lighter, once.

Inside the house, Mark focused attention on the real danger: "She means it all, no matter how insane. She'll use those letters."

Marilyn Monroe laughed angrily, pushing away the horror.

Enid stopped her laughter: "You let the Kennedys treat you like a needful orphan!"

"And what about you, with that pimp you love?" Marilyn challenged.

"*Loved*," Enid corrected. "I'm making him pay and pay!" Then she pleaded, "Don't you see you were hurting her?"

"*You're* the one who hurts her. *You* won't leave her alone!" Marilyn accused.

"She loves you; she loves us," Enid said softly.

"I hate her!"

Enid slapped Marilyn. "Don't ever say that!"

Marilyn raised her hand to strike back. Instead, she said, "It's just a game, it's just a game, remember? Enid, remember?"

With urgent tenderness, Enid held Marilyn, calming her, assuring her she would have the child she longed for.

The next day, early, Marilyn and Enid went out together, a rare occurrence. They hurried into Enid's car. Mark assumed they had gone to verify Mildred's vile terms of blackmail. He was awed by the old woman's cold monstrosity. As always, magnified tiny reasons were motivating her enormous demands. She would offer Marilyn Monroe the terrible protection in order, finally, to control the star who had for years affronted her, control the ultimate symbol of beauty. Yes, Mildred Meadows cherished beauty to the point of illness.

Marilyn returned to the house alone, and stayed in her room. There were not even the sounds of urgent dialing. The house was stilled with a quiet tension, Marilyn at its center, like a captive of it. Days passed.

*   *   *

Again there had recurred the commanding unnamed presence, that figure who roamed so powerfully through the private "game." Mark had deliberately left that interlude unexplored, Normalyn knew; and she knew that the love between the two women was as strong as the rage, whatever its origin. That mixture created the closeness, which had survived death. . . . With a new glow, desert light illumined the garden in Palm Springs. Normalyn allowed her eyes to wander in search of Michael Farrell, no longer at the table near the pool, no longer outside.

"I suppose it was inevitable," Robert lamented, "that the two most powerful men in the country and the orphan who became the greatest movie star would link in an American Gothic tragedy."

"And the orphan would lose," Troja understood.

"I was sitting in the room I worked in," Mark said, "when I heard aggressive footsteps. I looked up, and I saw—"

*   *   *

Alberta Holland!

Her hair was so red it flared like flames even in shaded light. The moment he opened the door, Mark recognized her, a woman he respected—as had his mother—for her confrontation of the political inquisitors. Nodding in brief greeting to Mark, the sturdy form moved into the house and up the two steps that led to the back rooms, where, it seemed, Marilyn now lived.

So powerful was Holland's presence that only now did Mark realize another woman had arrived with her and was still standing politely at the door to be allowed in. "Please—" Mark invited.

"Thank you." The woman entered and smiled graciously at Mark.

Delicate, exquisite as a pretty bird, she must be Teresa de Pilar, Mark knew. How difficult to think of this small creature at the center of the vortex that had finally sucked Alberta Holland into prison because during the notorious hearings into "left-wing" political associations, the formidable red-haired woman had continued to "grant asylum" in her home to the Spanish exile who had confounded her aristocratic family by supporting the Popular Front against Franco.

"May I?"

When Mark nodded, the small woman followed Alberta's path.

A time later Alberta Holland emerged alone. "I'm glad to meet you, youngman. Your services have been exemplary, exemplary. They will no longer be needed, thank you." She pumped his hand and left. Mark was hurt by the brusqueness; he had heard her described as a woman "*driven* by her sense of justice."

"Forgive Alberta," said Teresa de Pilar. She had just emerged with Enid, who remained pensively at the top of the two steps. The Spanish woman had retained her charming smile. "When she sniffs injustice, she's blind to the amenities of life, but she's the kindest of human beings. I'll see that she writes you a note." She spoke with the slightest cultured accent.

She had a curious, endearing manner. As she spoke, she gestured delicately with her fingers, as if they were constantly fashioning something fragile . . . Still smiling, she looked back and nodded to Enid, in affirmation of allegiance.

Alone with Mark, Enid said, "I know you'll leave now. Thank you especially for that beautiful night when we were strong exiles."

Mark Poe would never forget that moment, cherished and sad, sad because it would be the last time he would see her.

"Enid, if ever we—" he started.

She put a finger to his lips, stopping words of regret. "Shhh," she said to him.

*   *   *

In the garden, cooling in the late afternoon, Mark paused for long moments in tribute to that memory of Enid.

Yes, he had loved her, too, Normalyn welcomed.

Mark's hand was still on Robert's. "I did receive a note from Alberta Holland, by messenger, that same day," Mark laughed. "It said, 'Thank you again for your services—A.H.' " But even that soft laughter seemed abandoned within a mood of solemnity that had settled over the alcove in Palm Springs.

"Is Alberta Holland dead?" Normalyn asked casually.

"She died in Switzerland," Mark said. "The Spanish lady was with her, loyal to the person who had been loyal to her."

Once again Normalyn had roamed through what she was now sure was the inception of the "great conspiracy" that had finally found expression in Enid's gasped words at the last of her life, out of withheld memories. With only minor variations, Mildred's account of her raid on Marilyn's house had survived Mark's version. "And then?" Normalyn asked Mark. He had taken her in his narrative to the point of crucial answers, at least essential clues.

"And then—" Mark said. He glanced at Troja, stopped his words.

Normalyn caught that—and so did Troja, who looked away with grand aloofness. Was Mark hesitating because of Troja? There had been times earlier when he had proceeded with caution, and Normalyn had encouraged, at times leaning toward Troja, once gently brushing a leaf from her shoulder to assert their closeness, her trust. Even when he had identified the man Marilyn Monroe had said she had called at the White House and the Justice Department, he had done so cautiously. At times his account had flowed easily out of commanding memories; and then he had paused, contemplative, before proceeding more slowly.

"And then"—he meted out careful words—"I *did* leave. And later I read in Mildred's column that Marilyn had miscarried during an attempted reconciliation with one of her ex-husbands," he hurried those words.

"Then her child did die," Normalyn said quickly.

"There is no way Meadows would have carried such an item unless she was convinced that her terrible demand had been fulfilled," Mark asserted. "And perhaps the item *was* accurate." He did not face Normalyn. "The man I saw entering her house the day of her sad dinner might have been one of her ex-husbands I mistook for— . . . I'm not sure." He said that to Troja—and still avoided looking at Normalyn.

Tempering his account. Normalyn thought Robert had assumed that, too. He sighed, played nervously with his empty glass.

Whatever had not been spoken, Normalyn was willing to allow Mark's conclusion, even though it did not reconcile with Mildred Meadows's own expressed doubts. Perhaps the old woman had deliberately lied to her for a hidden purpose.

"What would she have been like, if she had lived longer?" Normalyn asked. Those were not the words she had intended to speak; she had substituted others, suddenly.

"Marilyn would have been a grand lady. Can't you see her? Imagine! Glamorous! Indomitable! Always beautiful!" Robert was sure.

"Some people should never age, should remain young," Troja reminded quietly.

"But as a *mother*—?" Normalyn was able now to ask the words she had just withheld.

Robert said, "Oh, a woman that magnificent would have loved her child, especially a daughter—given her everything she had not had, made her beautiful like her, without the pain."

"Perhaps she might have kept her from becoming beautiful," Mark Poe said, as if speaking a thought aloud. "Did Enid speak to you about me?" he asked Normalyn.

"She loved you," Normalyn said.

"She told you that?" Mark's voice seemed young, eager.

"Yes," Normalyn asserted.

Mark's sigh added death to his memories of Enid. He smiled a bemused smile. He said only, "Enid."

Still bright, the desert had begun to gather shadows.

Robert said slowly, "If Enid . . . and you . . . if you both had chosen to— . . . Would *you* have—?"

Mark held both of Robert's hands in both of his.

Robert sighed, smiling, accepting the reassurance he had sought in the sheltered memories.

Mark said firmly to Normalyn, "And now you know what you came to discover—all that I know of it."

"Yes," Normalyn said. But there remained questions—no answers, but *clearer* questions.

Now the intimacy that had occurred among strangers was threatened by sudden awkwardness. Robert attempted to contain the anarchy of memories within this ordered present: He told them more about the school, the students, the creative pleasure and peace it all brought them.

Troja filled the next long silence: "We have a mutual friend, Mr. Kunitz . . . Robert. Kirk Thomas—he's my husband."

It was clear that Robert could not recall the name.

Troja had converted Kirk into her husband! . . . Normalyn longed to prod Robert into remembering him. "He was in many wonderful movies," Normalyn encouraged, remembering the exultant gladiator in the film clip Kirk had shown them.

"But he chose to leave films—like you, Robert; he, *too*, chose. He was also a famous bodybuilder, Mr. America," Troja added.

"Oh, but of course," Robert pretended to remember. "Who could ever forget Kirk Thomas? One of the very best!"

Normalyn wanted to hug him.

Again silence.

"There's a blessed peace at night in this old house so full of ghosts," Robert said. "I love to watch it change with the light of day."

"Please let us show it to you." Mark Poe stood up.

"May Michael Farrell join us?" Robert consulted the two women. "He's been so eager to be with you, and I think his earlier boldness has made him morbidly shy."

That pleased Normalyn, Michael's morbid shyness.

"Yes," Troja interpreted Normalyn's silence, correctly.

Robert went to find Michael—and did immediately because he was already advancing to join them.

2

The edge of the sky would reveal stars before long. In the clean air was the scent of mixed flowers.

The five walked toward the house, then into it along an arched corridor. They entered a grand Spanish dining room— "now a study room and library," Robert informed. There were books on shelves, on tables. About seven students sat reading, on the carpeted floor or on comfortable elegant chairs. "It's good for them to feel in touch with what was grand in the past—and some things were," Robert said.

Normalyn noticed among the students a very pretty girl smiling at Michael. Boldly, she led the way out of the room. They walked along mosaicked halls, into rooms that opened onto verandas laced with the flowers of slender vines.

"I'd like to show her—them—my classroom," Michael said. "Both of you," he said to Normalyn and Troja. "I mean, *all* of us."

Of course! He was attracted to Troja, Normalyn thought. Who wouldn't be? She felt plainer than before.

"You mean you'd like to show *Normalyn* your classroom." Troja understood Michael's invitation.

"Yes!"

Normalyn tried to drift away, unnoticed. Troja went after her, linking her arm through hers, returning her. Then in her grandest manner, Troja announced, "I'd like to look at the Renaissance pastorals we just passed."

Robert grasped her intention immediately, directing her and Mark back to the paintings. Mark smiled, understanding.

Normalyn stood abandoned. Michael took her hand and led her into a spacious room with oak beams, a Spanish chandelier, carved wooden chairs with bright upholstery. Pretending to want to look more closely at a small elevated area, like a stage, Normalyn eased away from Michael's hand still holding hers.

"We're all here on scholarships," Michael informed her. "Mark—Mr. Poe—is a great teacher. So is Robert, of course," he added somewhat dutifully.

To have teachers like that! Normalyn marveled—and remembered Miss Stowe in the Gibson Public Library.

Then they were surrounded by silence.

"What do you do in Los Angeles?" Michael broke the silence firmly.

She wanted to sound sophisticated, like Troja. "Oh," she answered, "I go to parties, to nightclubs. I go ice-skating—" *Where* had she heard *that*? She remembered—there had been a segment about ice-skating on "Life As It Is," but it hadn't been about Los Angeles. She hoped he hadn't heard her.

"Ice-skating?"

"Yes!" She snapped at him for her slip.

"It sounds great," he said with genuine enthusiasm. "I mean, all those great swirls and circles on the ice. It's very visual! I'd like to go with you!"

She looked at him, just slightly baffled. He had said that honestly. "And what do you do?" she was able to ask him.

"Study, mostly. I love directing!" he said enthusiastically. "I swim a lot, too," he laughed. "And I read a lot."

"So do I!" she told him, wondering whether she had sounded too enthusiastic. "I used to," she said, more to herself. "What were you reading earlier?"

"Stanislavsky's *An Actor Prepares.* It's better for directors than for actors, actually."

"I'm reading *A Portrait of the Artist as a Young Man,*" she told him.

Michael snapped his fingers with delight. "Damn, isn't that something! Mr. Poe told us just last week that everyone should read that. He tells us to read fiction—novels. You know why? Mark believes that 'realistic' art is a lie because it pretends to be telling the truth. But fiction announces that it's telling lies. So it's more honest!"

Normalyn felt excited, to be talking this way, so intelligently. And what he said—what Mark Poe said—made perfect sense.

"But I wasn't really reading earlier," he confessed. "I was just looking at you."

He moved closer to her.

She did not move back.

"God*damn,* would I love to kiss you!" he said.

She looked at him, so handsome, so intelligent. She waited.

His lips touched hers.

His kiss felt warm. She kissed him back—because he read and because— Suddenly she pulled away from the lovely sensation.

"I'm sorry." He retreated in embarrassment. "The reason I'm so aggressive is because otherwise I'd be shy."

"It's not you," she said, trying not to sound nervous. "It's just that desert wind always . . . scares me."

He listened. "The wind's not blowing now. Maybe you heard the air conditioner."

But Normalyn knew what she had heard—an echo aroused even by this wonderful kiss she had welcomed, an echo stirring memories of violence. Pretending to run her hand along the surface of a table, she moved to the door. "I *am* sorry," she said, meaning it.

"I come into Los Angeles sometimes. I'll call you!"

"I don't have a telephone yet."

"Is that true?" he asked her.

She wanted to extend the lie, so that she could tell him she'd call him when she did have a telephone. But the dark, serious eyes on her really wanted to know the truth. "No," she said, "it isn't true."

"I like you very much. Do *you* like me?" he asked bluntly.

"Yes. But I'm scared." With regret, she heard her own footsteps moving away from him.

3

Troja looked at her suspiciously when Normalyn returned alone.

"I'd like to show you my study," Mark said swiftly to Normalyn. "That's where I was when Robert convinced me to call you back." He seemed to want to emphasize the location of his decision.

Inside, Normalyn saw it immediately: a gathering of lavender blossoms in a decorated vase on Mark's desk. She moved close to them. They were untainted with decay, perfect in their artifice.

"They arrived in the mail, without any indication from whom," Mark told her. "Only a few days ago."

The artificial jacarandas—a signal to her? A least in part, had they goaded Mark to speak to her this afternoon? Normalyn grasped for a connection, any connection, to render these moments less disturbing. "Enid had some like those. She had them from a long time ago."

"Alberta Holland sent some to Marilyn; they arrived the day I was leaving. I took them to her in her room. She told me she loved them because—I remember her words because they moved me so much. . . . She said she loved them because—"

*   *   *

"—what dies so early in real life, can go on living like *this*." Marilyn touched the flowers, and she leaned over, to smell them, as if the perfect artifice would have been able to capture even the essence of their perfume.

*   *   *

"I think that she—and others—came to see those flowers as a symbol of herself," Mark Poe said to Normalyn.

Normalyn wondered now whether as she searched out the lives of the two women, someone else was searching with her.

When Robert invited them to dinner and Mark echoed the invitation, Troja declined immediately: "It would be lovely, but my husband is very demanding of my presence."

They would now go back, Normalyn thought, and then Troja would change again, giving up pieces of her life to Kirk.

Mark and Robert accompanied the two women to the car. "Good night, Normalyn and Troja; please do come back." Robert tried to hide a note of sadness.

As Normalyn was about to enter the car, Mark Poe drew her

gently aside. He walked her several steps away from the others. Near the shade of two imposing elm trees, he told her, "I did leave soon after, but I remained long enough to believe that there was a plot to allow Marilyn to have the child she wanted. Alberta Holland was involved. I believe Mildred Meadows was elaborately deceived. None of this could have occurred without Enid's participation. I believe, Normalyn, that Marilyn's child was born. Now I've told you everything, including what I believe."

He led her silently back to the car, to Robert, Troja. There, he kissed her, tenderly, on the cheek.

Normalyn hugged and kissed him back, and thought, *If only he had been my father!*

Twenty-One

"God-fuckin'-damn!"

Normalyn saw what had caused Troja to curse and brake. After miles of private silence, they had exited the freeway onto Sunset Boulevard, into the bruised part of Western.

Ahead, on the street itself, about sixty women were scattering from policemen mounted on fierce horses and motorcycles. All the women were heavily made up, dressed in tight skirts, tight pants; many were Mexicans, many black, some white. Corralled by the leering policemen and herded into one column, they were forced to move ahead of three squad cars driving slowly behind them with red lights whirling. In their sexual attire the women maintained tawdry dignity as the cops laughed, poked each other suggestively. At the sight of the ugly parade, spectators, mostly men, goaded the ugly roundup.

Normalyn stared in horror at the procession of trapped women.

"Fuckin' goddamn pigs!" Troja spat. "Marchin' them to be booked. I could've been there!"

Then she *had* returned to those desperate streets to avoid Duke's control. Normalyn wanted to hold her friend, but she seemed too vulnerable even to be touched.

Normalyn felt relief when they drove up to the familiar house, the palmtree, the inclined porch. Out of the car, they were aware of a stillness within the house.

Kirk lay on the floor in his briefs. The enormous muscles looked odd in awkward repose. Blood, umber, had dried on his face.

"Hon! Sweetheart! Hon!" Troja knelt over him, cuddling the enormous man.

Normalyn prayed, *Let him be alive.*

Kirk opened his eyes. Normalyn helped Troja gather him onto his bed. Kirk moaned. Troja covered him, wiped his face with her dress. Normalyn moistened a towel. She searched for any first-aid supplies, but all she could find were pills. Normalyn gave the towel to Troja.

"Shouldn't've left him alone, shouldn't've left him," she moaned, mopping his face, chest.

"Two guys . . . surprised fuck outta me . . . not hurt bad," Kirk assured himself.

"Oh, I know," said Troja, "cause, baby, you are the very strongest."

Normalyn's eyes scanned the house. Everything was in familiar disarray—except her room, which was intact. Whoever had come in had taken nothing. Placed in the middle of the living room was the blonde wig on the mannequin's head. Pinned to it was a note. Near it was a cellophane packet of white powder.

"Was it Duke?" Troja asked, hardly audibly.

"No," Kirk said.

But they had come at Duke's instructions, and Kirk and Troja knew it. Normalyn picked up the note—and pushed away the packet of cocaine. She read:

To the black Monroe and her boy—an extra thank you for no hard feelings!

There were the names of a man and a woman, a telephone number—all underlined twice and followed by several commanding exclamations marks—and a P.S.

Call them!—or send the *real* blonde, the *real* woman— with him!

Normalyn crumpled the note. Troja held her hand out, demanding it. She read it, held it in a fist.

Straining—"not hurt bad"—Kirk pinched some powder to his nose. "This'll help." He tried to smile.

Troja snorted once in each nostril, then again. Again!

"Troja, goddammit! Not you, too!" Normalyn shouted at her.

Troja's despair burst into rage. "What you say, girl?"

"Don't start on *me*, Troja," Normalyn said quietly. Only

earlier Troja had been so grand, so loving. In Kirk's world, she became someone else.

Troja snorted even more of the powder, flaunting the fact to Normalyn. She said tauntingly, "Want a taste, girl?"

Normalyn told herself not to respond. Troja was hurting deeply. In one moment she would take it all back. Yet she, too, was feeling the anguish of this day. She would not be baited by Troja. She turned away.

"Girl! When you gonna start *livin'* and stop *watchin'* and *listenin'!*" Troja tore into the closeness of the afternoon in Palm Springs. "When you gonna join the parade? When you gonna start hurtin' like the rest of us?"

Just earlier, Troja had soothed her, given her courage. "I do hurt, Troja, you know that so well. But does *that* stop it?" She pointed to the cellophane packet.

"Yeah, girl—and Kirk knows that!" At this moment she seemed to want to share even his defeat. "Want some?" Troja taunted Normalyn with the powder.

Normalyn snatched it from her. She managed clumsily to pinch some into her hand, the way she had seen them do. Defiantly she breathed it in, easily.

"Don't!" Troja said too late. "Dammit," she yelled, "don't you know it's killing Kirk?" She said quickly, "Didn't mean that."

"But it's true," Kirk said. He took the crumpled note from Troja's fist.

Troja protested its accusation: *"I am a real woman!"* She sat on the floor, near the blonde wig, and covered her face.

The wig on the floor seemed alive, commanding.

In that instant Normalyn felt yanked by the drug into a hurtling current. The intense rush abandoned her on the memory of the darkened shoreline with Enid and— . . . Perspiring, confused, Normalyn pulled herself out of the compressed, speeding moment. Why had it led her *there?*

Kirk was saying, "I'm sure they didn't intend to hurt me bad, and they didn't. It was just a warning." He smoothed out the paper with the names left by Duke. "Maybe we should do it," he said to Troja.

"Maybe," Troja said wearily.

2

"I am sorry, I am very, very sorry," Troja apologized to Normalyn in the morning, not even waiting for her to come out of her room for breakfast.

"Thank you," Normalyn said sincerely.

"And don't you never touch that cocaine shit again!" Troja admonished.

Normalyn considered extracting a similar promise back, but after the ugly night, that seemed chancey for now.

Before Normalyn left her room, she touched Enid's hurt angel. Enid had kept it in reminder of another—a statue, Normalyn had concluded—the angel Enid had told Mark Poe about at the time she conveyed her playful but sorrowing biography: the angel resigned never to fly again and under whose shadow she had first met the movie star.

Kirk and Troja were already having breakfast. Kirk had not been badly hurt. He'd even prepared for a workout later by bandaging the wrist he had twisted during last night's warning. What would they do now? Normalyn wondered sadly.

She waited until Kirk was working out. She paid Troja for a whole week's rent in advance, to show her she was not afraid to stay on—but she was!—and to help them at least that much for now—now when she was really needed.

Then she went out, with her copy of *A Portrait of the Artist as a Young Man,* to finish reading it if she ended up at DeLongpre Park. She had finally located the origin of her fascination with the memorial to Rudolph Valentino there. It reminded her of Enid's "peacock" fireplace, which was "just like *his* at Falcon's Lair!"

Normalyn did go to the park. There, on a bench and among the usual desultory gathering of afternoon idlers, she finished the novel by James Joyce—thrilled, thrilled by it, exhilarated by the ending, knowing that Stephen Dedalus is going to leave the city to explore the world!

Moved, she stood up.

Now what would she do?

Now where would *she* go?

3

She went to the public library and easily located the newspaper item:

Los Angeles Tribune   October 17, 1962

"STAR-COUNSELOR" HOLLAND
DEAD IN SWITZERLAND

SWITZERLAND—Alberta Holland, known in Hollywood as "Counselor to the Stars" and for her strongly worded refusal to testify before the House Un-American Activities Committee, is dead, according to her long-time secretary, Teresa de Pilar. Miss Holland, who left the United States without public announcement earlier this year, was 59 years old when she died in her home in Switzerland as a result of unidentified "physical complications."

In accordance with Miss Holland's wishes, she was cremated in private and with no commemorative ceremony planned, Miss de Pilar informed reporters.

Miss Holland won national exposure when she refused to furnish the names of other members of organizations reputed to have "extreme left-wing connections." The Committee investigating "subversive activities" in the film colony devoted special attention to Miss Holland's support of Popular Front groups during the Spanish Civil War. At the time, Miss Holland was accused of granting "personal asylum" to Miss de Pilar, reputedly exiled for insurgent activities by dictator Francisco Franco himself.

Cited for contempt of Congress, Miss Holland was sentenced to one year in prison. On her release, she wrote her memoirs and continued in her capacity as "counselor." In the short period of her life abroad, she became reclusive, shunning all publicity.

During her career as "counselor," Miss Holland was reputed to have advised, during crises, many of Hollywood's most famous stars, including Ingrid Bergman, Tyrone Power, Lana Turner, Zachary Scott, Vivien Leigh, Montgomery Clift, and Greta Garbo. Miss Holland was reportedly a close confidante of Marilyn Monroe.

Miss Holland left no known survivors, according to Miss de Pilar, who will remain in Europe, "as near to my native Spain as possible so that when the reign of the tyrant Franco is ended, I may return to my country, along with the paintings of Pablo Picasso."

It seemed clear to Normalyn that everything about the alleged death of Alberta Holland was ambiguous, all information attributed to only one person, the loyal woman she had protected in exile.

Normalyn located Alberta Holland's autobiography, *My Life*. The markedly restrained account documented her birth in Evansville, Indiana, into a wealthy family "crushed by the Depression"; her family-nourished "social consciousness," stirred further at the New School for Social Research in New York; her wistful but brief marriage to a professor of anthropology at Yale. Clearly protective of the movie stars she came to cherish and counsel, she was anecdotal about them, at times deliberately vague: "Tyrone Power had problems he turned to me about before he married the beautiful Annabella. Soon after, I received an angered note from Errol Flynn, then in Cannes."

The major part of the book derided—with acid humor— "the Un-Americans," the committee she had confronted with her famous "suggestion that they copulate themselves." The book contained nothing about Mildred Meadows—only one reference to "a tiny female dinosaur, a newspaper columnist of inexhaustible stupidity and meanness." A chapter called "Into the 60's" professed her "joy and belief" that the election of John F. Kennedy would usher the country into a period of "social renewal," to which, she added, "I dedicate myself profoundly."

About Marilyn Monroe—"a very special woman, a favorite human being, a star of great inner and outer beauty"—she wrote with clear affection of their meeting at a fund-raiser for orphaned children, of having once had "a cherished tea" with her, of finding her a "most extraordinary, caring, and talented person." The book was finished before the death of the movie star and ended with these words: "Having been jailed for my beliefs, I now hold them dearer. I hope, even as I begin my stumble toward death, always to speak out, never to flee from a struggle I consider to be just."

Normalyn studied the one photograph included of Alberta Holland "in her latter years," the time of the book. In her mind, she tried—then, squinting, managed!—to draw onto the formidable woman the smooth features of Miss Bertha.

When she left the library, Normalyn knew she must return to Long Beach—at *exactly* the right time, with information she was sure now Miss Bertha had required—

Come back when you're ready, dearheart, the dozing voice reminded.

She had some information now—from Mildred Meadows, from Mark Poe. From David Lange? Yes, but every time she tried to recall exactly what she had learned from him, it all blurred. Well, she *would* see him again, and this time *nothing* would thwart her directness. . . . Of course, when she finally returned to Long Beach, she would also see Jim.

Stopping at every public telephone along the way, Normalyn telephoned David Lange at the newspaper and at his private office until she reached him. He agreed immediately to see her.

4

A breathtaking corridor of palmtrees opened ahead into the Hollywood Hills. Normalyn paused to admire it. She *had* moved away from Gibson.

She delayed entering the building where David Lange would be expecting her. This time he would not budge her resolve to confront him directly. She would devise an unassailable strategy! Certainly he would ask her questions about her encounter with Mildred Meadows—that was at least in part why he had sent her there. She would have to answer—carefully, of course—in order then to question *him*—yes!—in keeping, she would remind him slyly, with their agreement to trust each other "step by step."

Enjoying a wonderful sudden breeze that rustled only the tops of the palmtrees, she refined her strategy. She could easily anticipate some of the questions he would definitely ask: "Did Mildred tell you who wrote those letters?" Sounding amused, she would answer, "I don't think the poor old soul really knows herself, David." *Then* would be her turn! She would ask— . . . What first? Yes! "David!" She would pronounce the name peremptorily, so he would understand her resolve: "David! Why did you turn away from the men you claimed to admire—the Kennedys—and to Mildred, who detested them?" . . . Perhaps she should be cautious with that question. She might not be ready for certain answers. She dismissed the question further because Mildred hadn't claimed David had joined her as an ally against the brothers, only that he came to believe her. No matter, there were many other questions. What was important was that she was prepared to get answers!

"Normalyn."

David Lange stood up immediately when she paused at the door of his dusky office. Leading her in, he held her arm so gently that she did not wince at the delicate touch.

She sat in the elegant chair before his desk, facing him. The crystal sphere like a large flawless marble, the pad of white paper on the brown leather backing, the cylindrical container, the books, the reflected light, the photographs—*Norma Jeane, the glittering almost-star, the fleeing woman, and finally the great movie star in her last and most beautiful glowing*—and the disturbing painting of shattered colors—everything was in its exact place, ensuring, again, a sense of unbroken, undefined continuity between each of her meetings with David Lange.

He said, "I worry that you'll continue to distrust me, that you won't come back, or that you'll become so desperate to know, quickly, that you'll turn to people who may harm you, create the situation that would devour your life."

She heard a sad accusation in his voice, as if she had violated his trust, creating the need to re-establish his loyalty to her. What was she here to challenge? . . . She was being lulled again by his emphatic expression of caring! She was here for a purpose, she reminded herself. She had prepared a clever strategy, to use his inevitable questions to her advantage. Feeling strong, confident, her resolve intact, she waited for his first question. And waited.

But he asked none.

"I assume you've decided to take the next step," he said.

She crossed her arms over her chest, demanding he ask his first question so that she could confound him with her strategy.

He tore a sheet of notepaper from the leather backing on his desk, with care, assuring the paper would sever neatly. As he handed it to her, he said, "He, too, has another piece of the truth we're trying to locate, Normalyn. I believe you'll recognize the name."

He was putting her in touch with someone else then, a "next" person. Normalyn prepared not to be surprised; she knew the note would contain the name of another of the people in Enid's newsclipping.

Stanley Smith!

The paper designated that name, a telephone number, a city—"Palm, California." She tried to battle clashing confusions so she could cope with these present moments. But she had been set adrift. A last name she had thought made up by Major Hughes was suddenly a real one, and the man who bore it threatened—so suddenly!—to become much more than a denounced figure in Enid's life—Stan, the object of her mysterious vengeance. That was the name Normalyn had given David that first time, when he had asked about her father. She held the paper tightly in both hands so he would not see them trembling.

"Why didn't you tell me you knew of him, where he was—when I told you he was my—?" Now that he had become much more than a remembered name, she did not want to call Stan her father.

David Lange leaned forward, on his elbows, his fingers pressed together under his chin as if he were pleading. "We were just moving to trust each other then, Normalyn, remember? Remember? Step by step?"

Step by step. That was what she had intended to use on him in her collapsed strategy.

"He's part of that same time of mystery, Normalyn. He, too, will speak only to the exact person."

Had Mildred determined that person was her—Normalyn? "Are you sure he'll talk to me, see me?" Another kind of apprehension had entered her voice.

"No, I'm not. I'm sorry. That's what *you'll* have to find out." David Lange still leaned toward her. "The step is yours to take. Or not . . . Normalyn."

5

Outside, Normalyn looked at the paper in her hand. It was real. The name on it was real, and the telephone number. With relief and fear, she knew she could now locate her father, and he would verify what she knew, had of course known all along—that she was Enid's daughter. That's *all* she wanted to know from this man, nothing more—and not to see him, ever!

She found a telephone booth in a recently abandoned lot off Sunset Boulevard. Not yet entirely demolished, the walls of a building remained, slabs of broken wood, dying plaster. She was too anxious to call, and too tired to move, even to locate another telephone. She merely looked away from the desolate lot, up, at the lofty fronds of indifferent palmtrees.

She asked the operator where Palm was. "Two, three hours out of Los Angeles, but it's still long-distance." For control, Normalyn counted the sounds her quarters and dimes made as she deposited them. She felt relief when the ringing extended. A woman answered . . . No, Stan wasn't home . . . Maybe back in an hour, half an hour. The woman seemed agitated. Who was calling? Normalyn told her she would call back.

Even more tired now, she sat on the curb of the street. She began rereading Joyce's story of Stephen Dedalus's flight into the world. . . . Slightly more than a half hour later, she dialed again.

"Hello—"

"Stanley Smith?" Normalyn hated pronouncing the name.

"Yeah. Who are you?" The man spoke in a strong voice.

"I'm Normalyn."

"I don't know you," came the firm voice. "Must have the wrong Smith. Happens."

"I'm Enid Morgan's daughter." Into the following silence, Normalyn sighed, "Enid died, just weeks ago . . . Stan."

The silence lengthened. Then the man's voice shot out in rage: "I can't grieve for Enid Morgan. For me she died when she took our son from me."

Normalyn held the telephone away from her, as if *it*, not the words, were assaulting her.

The man's voice said with quiet anger, "Our son is dead, and now Enid's dead, too. Let her goddamned vengeance be finished." Then his voice regained control. He said firmly, "Leave me alone, Normalyn. I am not your father!"

Even after Normalyn depressed the telephone hook to end the connection, even then she continued to clutch the receiver, to force out different words. Her hand tightened until she felt pain. She released the telephone. The receiver dangled life-lessly. . . . *Enid had had a child by Stan—a boy, and he had died.*

6

About to put on the blonde wig just as Normalyn walked in, Troja made a hurried attempt to hide it. All the way here, Normalyn had hoped she'd be able to talk to her, just talk to her! But now Troja's and Kirk's lives demanded immediacy.

Kirk was dressed in a good-looking sports jacket, shirt open low enough to reveal the sharp definition of his chest. Troja was wearing one of her fanciest chiffons, of mixed pastels. She had painted her lips bright red, lined her eyes heavily, drawn a black beauty mark on her brown cheek. Her own dark hair was pinned tightly to accommodate the wig.

They had decided to answer Duke's command. Normalyn thought they looked like a saddened bride and groom.

Kirk removed his jacket angrily. He sat on the bed. With the remote control, he snapped on the television. "Can't do it, can't do it, sweetheart. Troja, I'm too fuckin' *scared*."

Troja held the blonde wig at her side. "Is it because of *me?*" she asked him.

Normalyn read Troja's pained, angered eyes. She thought Kirk was afraid of going out with her because he would again have to come in sexual contact with *her*, a trans— . . . Or was Kirk afraid that age would judge *him*?

"No," Kirk said to Troja. "It's not because of you."

Troja pushed her fingers into her own hair, releasing the fine lustrous halo. "What the hell. Duke didn't really care if you want out or not, Kirk. It was just his extra special torture on me."

Kirk pulled Troja protectively against him.

Normalyn went into her room with the shreds of her own life. Carefully she reconstructed the words she and Stan had spoken on the telephone: The man she had spoken to had denied being her father—without her ever having asked him.

Twenty-Two

She left word at the newspaper that it was urgent she see David Lange today at his office. She designated the hour she would be there—*"exactly,"* she added for import.

If he was not at his office—she thought this as she entered the handsome building—at the time she had demanded, she would wait on the windowsill in the corridor until he *did* come.

He was already there. He ushered her in with concern. "Your message sounded frantic. Is anything wrong? I would have called you back instantly, but I have no number—"

Seated, she grasped the armrests on the tall chair. "The man you asked me to call—"

"I didn't ask you to call him, Normalyn."

Trying to intercept her accusation before it formed! She wouldn't allow it. "He denied being my father—without my even suggesting it!" She almost jumped ahead to her major challenge—*You told him what to say, David*—but she had to mount her accusation with gradual evidence.

His voice contained no impatience. "I'm sure you told him you're Enid Morgan's daughter. Certainly he assumed you know he was involved with her. If he thought you were here to make demands on him, Stanley Smith *would* deny he was your father."

Yes, the "son-of-a-bitch" Enid had come to despise and who had walked out on both of them *would* deny it—if he had made the assumption David claimed. It was possible. Suddenly—again!—what had seemed so mysterious last night was tempered with logical explanations. Still, she felt frustrated, angry. She would not pull back: "He didn't even ask how I got his telephone number." Her voice had lost its thrust.

260

"It wouldn't be difficult; his number's listed." David Lange spoke patiently, as if expecting her doubts to be aroused, willing to clarify them whenever necessary. He reminded, "I even told you I wasn't sure he'd speak to you. When we took our first step, I warned you there were some people involved who are afraid to talk, perhaps not because they believe they're in danger now, but because they may have to face harsh matters—about themselves." He glanced away from her. "Don't *you* believe he's your father, Normalyn?"

Don't tell him what the man said about a son! This may be a trap, dearheart. Not even Miss Bertha was entirely sure about David Lange. So Normalyn did not answer. She didn't *want* Stan to be her father; she just wanted the mystery of Enid's letter, of her identity, to lift.

"Do you truly want to find the truth—or only what you wish would be true?" David's voice was at its gentlest.

Normalyn felt struck by his words. She had been looking for only one "truth," the one she had grown with. Each time she thought she had found confirmation, there followed contradiction, ambiguity.

"Perhaps Stanley *isn't* your father," David said.

In rushing retrospect, it seemed to Normalyn that that's what he had wanted her to discover, when he had so easily given her Stanley's number. She felt vulnerable now, terribly alone.

"The next step, David," she said, words she had not come here to speak.

"The Dead Movie Stars—" he said distantly.

He couldn't be guiding her to *them*, those ragged children and their presumed knowledge? Oh, she had misunderstood him, she knew as he continued. Or, again, had he deliberately conveyed a split meaning? How quickly doubts could resurge!

"The Dead Movie Stars know what allows the great stars to go on living fully for others long after their actual deaths. Yes, those silly derided young people *do* understand that—that the stars they idolize lived fiercely, at the very edge. That very ferocity, that existing at the edge, made them tragic and reckless—but it gave them the glow of specialness, a glowing despair, a rage to live, even to die early to sustain it! Monroe had it!" His voice had gained excited admiration.

Normalyn waited for him to connect what he was telling her with "the next step." He would, she knew; she listened carefully.

"Even her funeral acknowledged the extravagance of her life." He shook his head as if assaulted by that clear memory. He spoke, quietly again, into the moteless light: "The day of her burial—"

—the gates of Westwood Memorial Park were locked, guards hired to keep out the curious. Just a few friends would come. Of her husbands, only the athlete turned up, with his son. The time of Marilyn Monroe's burial had been kept secret.

Television crews on steady vigil erected an elevated structure outside the walls for their cameras. Invading fans converted it into bleachers. They sat on the boards, eagerly waiting.

A large woman wrestled with a man for a choice post atop the scaffold. With her was her eight-year-old daughter, platinum-bleached hair sprayed to stay intact in a burnished halo. Her lips were drawn into a pout, the lids of her small eyes heavy with black liner, a beauty spot on one thin cheek. She wore a white dress, all flimsy pleats. When the cortège appeared below, the large woman held the sad doll-child up like a trophy and shouted:

"Here she is! The new Marilyn! Marilyn appeared to her in a vision just last night and told her to be here!" Cameras swirled. The woman ordered the sad child, "Pout, dammit, pout like I taught you, sexy, sexy—like Marilyn showed you in the vision. Go on, goddammit! *Whoosh!*" the fat woman commanded.

Assuming a grotesque leer, the little girl flung her white skirt up, the way Monroe did in the famous movie scene.

The crowed hooted approval.

At the star's crypt, a nondenominational minister read an adaptation from the Book of Psalms: "How fearfully and wonderfully she was made by her creator." "Over the Rainbow," a favorite of Monroe's, in Judy Garland's undying voice, was piped in. The brief ceremony was over. Hearing the ominous buzzing of looming fans, the few invited people hurried away.

Fans jumped over the wall, battling television reporters and cameramen into the cemetery. They pushed, trampled, fell on graves, rose, rushed the crypt. There they tore at floral arrangements, as if it were her body they had come to claim with angry adulation, fighting over plucked flowers.

The little girl with platinum hair made her way over the wall. On the grounds she huddled near the sheltering statue of an angel. Her scream rose in a wail as fans ran past her with their torn mementoes, along graves, to the gates.

Locked!

They were trapped in the cemetery!

In a mass they shoved at the gates, still fighting for the

remains of flowers. The gates would not give! They propped each other over walls. Some who managed to climb out, pushed others back. They fell cursing, then roaring with laughter. Security men opened the gates and the fans pushed out with their mangled flowers.

*   *   *

By moving in such detail through the violated mourning at the movie star's grave, David Lange had illuminated the extravagance of the movie star's life spilling over—resisting—the intended quiet of the burial. At times, he had seemed to be confirming her death, to himself. Vaguely frightened, Normalyn waited for the connection he was elaborately constructing toward "the next step" to be taken—and she might not take it, might not take it at all. She looked out the window. Distant houses were like tombstones in a cemetery. She remembered Enid's lament that she could not be at the star's funeral because there was "danger" in her presence. . . . David Lange's harsh words, spoken softly, startled Normalyn out of her revery:

"Monroe feared madness. She feared passing it on, the way she thought it had been passed on to her by her mother. Would her daughter share that darkness? Or would she find the strength to survive what had conquered *her* mother?"

A challenge! His eyes were so powerfully on her that Normalyn had to break their contact. She glanced at the commanding photographs on the wall. . . . Norma Jeane seemed to be inquiring about her life. The photograph of the fleeing woman looked different today—as if the woman depicted had not attempted to conceal herself. Now the startled face seemed deliberately exposed, daring. That impression changed back quickly: The woman was avoiding the hounding photographers.

David seemed to be waiting for an answer to his disturbing question! Normalyn did only this: She locked her arms across her chest.

The question left to echo powerfully, David Lange evoked more memories of the star's ending. He said in his softening voice, "When her famous daughter died—"

*   *   *

—reporters and television crews, learning she had not yet been told of the death, rushed to North Light Sanitarium to interview Marilyn Monroe's mother. Alerted, guards were situated to keep them out. Cameras watched the white and green grounds. They saw her! Accompanied by an attendant holding her arm, Marilyn's mother looked shrunken, tiny, this woman Monroe had loved and hated, who loved and hated her back.

A reporter next to David Lange shouted from the distance, "Marilyn Monroe is dead!"

Marilyn's mother did not interrupt her walk.

"Norma Jeane is dead!" David Lange called to her.

On the grounds of North Light Haven, the old woman jerked her hand away from the attendant's arm. Seized by terrible power, she stood erectly. Her rigid hands shot upward. She shouted into the white day, *"Norma Jeane!"*

Then she walked on.

*   *   *

In locating Marilyn Monroe's mother in the sanitarium, David Lange had evoked the lineage of "darkness" that haunted Marilyn Monroe. And Enid, Normalyn thought. He had asserted the authenticity of his knowledge, his presence there. And he had provided her with intimate information—that wafting suspicion recurred, just briefly. But how did that prop his connection to "the next step," which she wanted him only to define now because she knew she would not take it? Sensing that, would he leave her merely to infer it? Vaguely, she thought she already did.

"The next step?" He seemed this time to ponder it. "Perhaps we must wait until there's trust, real trust—"

He was withdrawing from her! She felt deeply abandoned. What would he require for that trust? Her showing him Enid's letter?

Don't ask him, dearheart! Don't say anything! He'll continue.

When Normalyn said nothing, hiding her sense of abandonment, he extended his words: "—and perhaps we *are* beginning to trust each other now."

"Yes," she tested. After all, *she* had turned to him first; he had responded to *her,* her needs. His disturbing questions were presented only for consideration, to underline certainties, clarify her doubts as she—they—moved . . . step by step. He knew her confusions intimately, her desire to live her life, and he had guided her with protective concern in her journey. And who else was there who cared this much? Certainly not Stan! She realized only now how wounded she had been by his rejection. He had carved a deeper isolation, banished her further from knowledge of her origin. "How can I find out who I am, David?"

No! Miss Bertha warned—too late.

Now David Lange spoke words so softly that Normalyn would not have been able to hear them if he had not also pronounced them precisely, slowly, one by one. "Find *them*, Enid *and* Monroe, who they really were—in order to learn how they shaped you. For you to know who you are, Normalyn, you will have to discover that, and—fully, fully—the artificial creation known as Marilyn Monroe." He addressed the photographs that depicted the evolution of a pretty youngwoman into the greatest movie star. "She defined herself by the daring with which she lived. Discover that."

He had included Enid and then focused on the movie star, as if, at least for now, he was sure she was more central. At first it seemed to Normalyn that his words were touched with admiration. Then they seemed to her to be spoken in awe. But when he uttered them again, slightly altered, a whisper—and by then he had turned back to face her, as if to connect her to the photographs while he stood behind his desk, one hand resting on each side of its surface, controlling symmetry—when he whispered his words again, they were spoken only, or so it seemed to Normalyn, as a reminder that *she* had no life because she was afraid to live. In that room of intact twilight, it seemed to her that his words were an exhortation, a judgment, a challenge—the next step:

"Dare, Normalyn. Dare to live. Dare to live fiercely. Like her."

Twenty-Three

Dare, Normalyn, dare to live, dare to live fiercely like them!

Normalyn was still hearing those words—exactly? altered?—
when she left David Lange's office, its dusky memories. This
time the reality of what had occurred there did not evaporate
entirely. Its judgment remained: She had no life *because* she
was afraid to live. For the first time, she had left David Lange's
office with no clear designation of what "the next step" would
be. She knew only that it would be hers to take ... *into the
lives of the two women,* David Lange had asserted, then veered
away, centering on the movie star. Because he believed *she*
was— ...?

There was another figure she increasingly felt she must
locate—the elusive presence that recurred in the "game" and
in the confrontations between the two women. Another woman.
Whoever was sending the artificial flowers reminding of the
last days of turmoil? An earlier child of one or another of
the two women?

Or was that figure "the orphan" the Dead Movie Stars
had claimed on television was among those they learned their
"secrets" from? The two women *had* met in an orphanage, and
near the shadow of a frightened angel. David had seemed at
one point to be about to guide her to that strange group of
young people dredging up scandals. If they had no information of their own, might they know who did? A girl among
them had been able to locate Miss Bertha, perhaps Mildred.
And Mark Poe.

2

The Mustang and the palmtree welcomed her when she returned home.

Sitting on a stool at the kitchen counter, Troja was drinking unusually early. She was dressed in her "date" clothes—she had already gone out this morning on another of her "freelance dates," defying Duke; the wig had not been removed from its block. Kirk lay in his bed, awake, his fingers drumming on nothing. It was as if the jolts of energy the cocaine produced were only enough to keep his body, just his body, charged against surrender. His eyes were closed.

Touching her lips with a silencing finger, Troja pointed to a hypodermic needle on the counter. "Started shootin' up again," she whispered. "Still hidin' it." She seemed to find some consolation in that.

Kirk sat up. He cracked his knuckles over and over.

Troja went to him. "Been waitin' for you to wake up." She pretended the restless body had been asleep. "You don't rest much, so I didn't wanna wake you. But you *promised!*" Her voice edged into urgency.

"Promised?" Kirk's breathing was rapid, gasps.

Troja's voice was in tightest control. "Yeah, hon, that we'd drive out to the ocean? Promised when I left real early." She said to herself, clenching her fists, "It kept me going through that fuckin' horror." She touched one eye, lightly bruised. "You *promised!*" Control snapped into accusation. She closed her eyes; she said sweetly, "Sea air and sand, hon, make you new." Her eyes pleaded with Normalyn to add her encouragement.

"Go on, hon, you, too. Go on!" Her hands clasped again.

"It *will* Kirk!" Normalyn encouraged. She felt a sudden lift! She would welcome the clear ocean air! A purified distance from all her questions and doubts! She would insist on buying food to eat at the beach, really delicious, *special* food for this cleansing occasion. She would surprise them with a bottle of . . . champagne!

"You can make it, babe! You *can!*" Troja said triumphantly when she saw Kirk gathering his jangled body to rise from his corner. "You can, baby!"

"I can," Kirk asserted.

They had to move quickly within this assertive current. Other times, at the last moment, Kirk had retreated.

Troja had enlisted Normalyn's help and Normalyn would

offer it. She wouldn't even take the time to change her clothes—
Kirk had already found a pair of favorite trunks! Normalyn
rushed to her room, to get a sweater for the usual cool evening. When she returned, Troja said, "No, hon, *me* and *Kirk*
gonna go."

But Troja had said—!

Normalyn knew, horrified, that she had misunderstood. She
felt ridiculous. "I *know* that," she told Troja, "but that doesn't
mean I can't put my sweater on if I'm cold!"

"Suit yourself," Troja said. She linked her arm through
Kirk's.

Normalyn put on her sweater. She felt even more ridiculous, because the day was hot. She would not cry. She heard
the goddamned Mustang start easily ... purring. She followed the sound of the motor until it faded into the vast,
lonely city. She sat on the floor. She refused to remove the
sweater. She reached for her purse, put on her glasses, removed them when everything blurred, threatening nausea.
She pushed her hair over her face and held it down with her
hands, concealing herself.

From here, her bedroom looked unlived in, as if her presence left no impression anywhere. She *had* to start living. *Dare!*
That's what David had understood, that's what he had meant.
Much more caring than a father—whom she didn't want—*did
not want!—never, never wanted!*—David Lange was trying to
guide her. The memory of his soft voice soothed her with its
concern.

Normalyn pulled the letter out of her purse, as if to *demand*
that it yield more answers.... She knew, again, that she
should hide it—somewhere—and she would, soon.... She
looked at the words, which still startled: "Marilyn Monroe is
your mother and she—" ... She read the declaration of love
that included both women, and that warmed her.... N.J.R.I.R.
Her eyes fixed on those initials that joined the two letters
otherwise separated in time by eighteen years! N.J.—Norma
Jeane. But now she wasn't even sure of *that.* She put the letter
away.

She continued to sit on the floor. *Dare!* ... She didn't know
how to begin!

She touched her face to make sure she had not cried,
touched her cheeks, smooth—her nose, tilted.... She would
let someone else teach her to live!

She went to the shelf where Troja kept her movie-star
books. She located the one Troja had used to make her up
that one time, the book titled only *Marilyn.* Leafing through it,

she stared at the famous calendar photograph, "Golden Dreams." The naked body lies on red velvet, exulting in its profligate sensuality.

With one finger, Normalyn outlined her own breasts, their own tilted firmness. She turned the pages of the book.

From photograph to photograph, arranged chronologically, a pretty girl became almost beautiful, beautiful, more beautiful. Soon the earlier woman had disappeared entirely. Another had taken over—unreally beautiful, as if she were only a photograph. In the last photographs, the earlier girl seemed to have returned to haunt the new creation, as if the older woman were about to free a captive soul. The painted narrowed eyes were touched by the wistful sadness within the urgent eagerness of the young woman.

Normalyn turned to the very last photograph. The movie star's lips were parted sexily. No, it was as if they were about to utter . . . what words? For an eerie moment Normalyn was sure she knew! The impression vanished.

Riffling through the book, she chose one of the earlier photographs, in which the two faces still showed through. She took the book into Troja's room and placed it on the dressing table before the rectangle of lights where Troja made herself up. She sat down, choosing among Troja's makeup. She would keep from looking at her full reflection in the mirror, concentrate only on each part of her face. Glancing now and then at the open book, she brushed her hair, which had lightened with the sun, and she tilted the edges, framing her face. She smoothed a soft wave over the right side. She applied light blush to her cheeks, a darker shade to her cheekbones. She tinted her eyelids barely blue, carefully smudged the edges. She smoothed mascara over her long lashes. With a tiny brush, she made them still longer, thicker, darker. She colored her lips, full, red, glossy, still fuller, redder. She was about to add a beauty spot with a black pencil on the same cheek as it appeared in the photograph; but she drew it on the opposite side.

In Troja's closet, she found the dress she was looking for, just back from the cleaner's. It was pale blue with two straps. Defiantly—Troja had life to spare—she slipped into it. She adjusted the dress to her own body, with pins, a belt.

Before the full-length mirror in the bathroom, she closed her eyes, tilted her head, moistened and parted her lips. She opened her eyes and saw the woman she had created.

Someone else! The impression of having erased herself was so powerful that she looked away, but not before she had glimpsed another unexpected resemblance—to Enid! No, *only* to the blonde woman on the darkened shoreline, the woman she had made herself up to look like—from the book and from fragments of memories. She forced her eyes back to her own reflection.

3

The specter of elegance barely floated over the three stories of the building William Randolph Hearst once gave Marion Davies. What had been a pampered lawn was seized by clawing weeds creeping up a ruined foundation. Chunks of plaster had crumbled, leaving gray scars on the walls of the château's two wings. Some windows were gouged, glass panes smashed or painted over, a few in bright colors in place of drapes, others replaced with wooden squares. The sounds of busy streets mocked the dying château.

When Normalyn stepped out of the cab she had taken to the approximate location identified in the television segment on the Dead Movie Stars, three other young people were waiting like supplicants before the courtyard—two skinny youngmen and one fat girl. Another youngwoman dashed crying out of the château.

A languid sun, only a hint in the sky, created no shadows.

Normalyn followed the anxious gaze of the three young people beside her—up, up to a window in the violated building.

"It's *her*!" gasped one of the boys.

Normalyn saw a youngwoman drape herself on the sill of the open window. In a ray of light, her satin gown gleamed electric blue. She had hair so orange it seemed capable of scorching the orchid stuck in it. Loftily, her hand rose in a measured gesture of acknowledgment.

"She saw me!" screamed the second youngman. He wore a pin-striped suit with hugely padded shoulders.

"She's calling *me*!" The youngman who had spotted the youngwoman at the window wore a leather jacket, scruffy engineer boots.

"*Clearly*, Lady Star is signaling to *me*!" The fat youngwoman with pinched red lips and a thousand yellow ringlets of hair tried to be haughty.

Normalyn knew that the powdery apparition at the window had focused her attention only on her.

Like a stuntman, a wiry youngman sprang out of one of several entrances to the building. He wore tall, glazed boots, shiny like linoleum, and a widely opened bloused shirt imitating satin. On his chest was a tattoo of a black tombstone, cracked. Out of the crack, a red flower bloomed.

"It's *Billy Jack!*" one of the youngmen gasped, dancing excitedly with the two others about the young Dead Movie Star. Normalyn did not move. Her eyes were still on the window, the figure there about to rule what would occur down here.

"Who are you petitioning to be?" Billy Jack barked at the three.

"Shelley Winters!"

"Rudolph Valentino!"

"Zachary Scott!"

"Hmmm." Billy Jack glanced back at the figure poised on the windowsill. With one finger, she sliced at her throat, twice, commanding execution. Then she spread out her hands, in an indifferent flutter.

Billy Jack said to the rotund girl, whose pouty face seemed constantly about to produce tears or sprinkles of giggles, "Don't you know that Lady Star *hates* Shelley Winters? She's not glamorous at all, and her *only* tragedy is that she can't shut up."

"I said Shirley Temple," the plump girl revised.

"Get outta here and don't come back." Billy Jack's wrath swept over to the skinny youngman picking nervously on a bad complexion: "*You* want to be *Valentino*? In a *leather* jacket and those fucked-up boots?"

"I m-m-meant James Dean," said the assaulted youngman.

"James Dean had a *red* jacket, and it wasn't leather," said Billy Jack, "and we already got a James Dean—and three pretenders waiting for him to crash and die, so you haven't got a fuckin' chance, man."

"Zachary Scott," the youngman who had received ambiguous indifference from the figure in the window reminded.

"You can try again, that's all." Billy Jack interpreted Lady Star's gesture. "I'll even give you a tip," he growled. "Curl your eyelashes some more."

"Thank *you!*" the youngman hardly breathed. "Give my love to Lady Star. Tell her I'll be back!" He walked jauntily away, separating himself from the banished fat girl and the skinny youngman.

In his bloused shirt and shiny boots, exhibiting the tattooed tombstone and rose, Billy Jack stared at Normalyn. "Wow," he said. Normalyn only stared back.

In the window of the château, Lady Star touched the flower in her hair and nodded.

"Cummon!" Billy Jack said to Normalyn. "Me and Lady Star been waiting for you!" Heavy eyebrows, darkened, loomed over colorless eyes. His inky black hair was slicked straight.

Disoriented by his words, Normalyn retreated. They were expecting her?

"Don't you recognize me?" Billy Jack struck a three-quarter profile. "I'm Billy Jack—on TV and other me-dee-ah!" He elongated the mighty word. "Me and Lady Star founded the Dead Movie Stars. The reason we use different names is so we can be whatever movie star we want, when we want. And Billy Jack is"— he glowered as if at himself—"just a name I chose." He discarded unspoken words. As if wired to an electric source, he could not stand still. He tangoed about, cocked his head, tried another expression—many vague people seeking to become one clear one. When she still was not impressed, Billy Jack warned, "I wouldn't be so confident about looking like *her*." He withheld the ineffable name. "We've never allowed anyone to get as far as being a *contender* for her." He still did not utter the awesome name. "And this time there's another real good petitioner for her," he added to his ominous warning.

He had easily assumed whom she had made herself up as, Normalyn thought with some satisfaction, some apprehension.

In the courtyard, debris gathered where there should have been flowers, perhaps waterlilies floating in the fountain. Now only sputters of yellow peeked out of weeds. Even the "Rooms and Apts For Rent" sign had aged.

Normalyn followed Billy Jack into the old château.

The wallpaper, which remained clinging but graying, had been painted over. Lightbulbs, bare, were mounted on ornate fixtures that might once have held candles. Leprous fragments of carpet still hinted of a former thickness crushed by unnoticing steps.

Normalyn went up the stairs with Billy Jack, into another corridor. The semidarkness was broken only by streaks of light where it managed to scurry in through a broken window.

Billy Jack stopped on a step, in a puddle of light created by one lonesome bulb, still glowing. "You think I look like Valentino? That's who I'm thinking of trying out—for a while."

Normalyn thought of the proud statue in the small park. She shook her head, no.

In a second, Billy Jack—who was about eighteen—turned for her into a boy dressed oddly, reacting against rejection. He slicked back his hair with saliva-moistened palms, regaining his shaken stature. "Cummon!"

He stopped before a door. "I got this fantasy," he confessed with sudden wistfulness, "that *she* really comes back and out of all the guys who said they loved her, she chooses *me*—just in time!"

He knocked on the door.

"*Just* in time. You know huccome? So you won't have to kill yourself again, Marilyn Monroe," he addressed Normalyn.

Twenty-Four

"Pass through!" commanded a deepened female voice behind the closed door.

Kill herself? Normalyn looked at the strange youngman who had said that, so easily. He was smiling as if he had made a joke.

"Shouldn't've called you Marilyn Monroe," he confided. "We don't allow petitioners the name of the Dead Movie Star until they pass real hard auditions." He opened the door.

The room was darkened except for a cone of light. Within it, the youngwoman in electric blue reclined now on an old chaise whose fabric had torn, creating eruptions of gray cotton.

Billy Jack twisted the fringed shade of a floor lamp. Light sprang on Normalyn.

Lady Star rose from the chaise and strided toward Normalyn. In her hair, the orchid, real today, had begun to wilt. "My Gawd!" Lady Star gasped at Normalyn. "You're *good!*"

Billy Jack stood proudly beside Normalyn as if he had discovered her.

Reedily slender, the youngwoman in the shiny gown was the same age as Billy Jack. The satin dress dipped at small but proud breasts. On her whitened face, her mouth gleamed orange-red. An improvised slit on the lower part of her gown allowed one thin leg to emerge.

Normalyn matched Lady Star's gaping stare, blink for blink.

The sparsely furnished room was cluttered with black-and-white movie-star photographs—on walls, propped on tables.

Lady Star whipped the edge of her gown; it made a slicing

274

sound. She moved back and stood by her chaise, one hand on its curved back. Like Billy Jack, she subdued her initial reaction of approval.

"So! You aspire to be a Dead Movie Star, darling! Well, you have to know at the onset—" She paused to verify the word to herself. "Outset?" She shrugged. "You must know how difficult the prospect of becoming a Dead Movie Star is, but we will take your petition under advisement." She tossed the last word as proudly as she tossed her reddened head. The hair did not move, the orchid fell. "Shit!" She was about to retrieve it, but she disdained: "Let the old wither and die," she pronounced. "A secret admirer has been sending fresh orchids." She plucked a slightly soiled felt orchid from a box on a table nearby; cheap jewelry spilled out, opaque glass.

Normalyn studied this extraordinary creature she had seen giving interviews on television.

"There was a reasonable petitioner for Lana Turner earlier today—down there." Lady Star's hand indicated the vast world outside her window.

Billy Jack said confidentially but with a slightly mischievous boyish grin, "Lady Star, Lana Turner isn't dead."

Lady Star slammed her hand against the back of the chaise. "How many times do I have to tell you *and* the world?—they're dead when you think they're dead—or when they grow old and awful." She flung out despised words.

"*Every*one knows Lana Turner isn't dead," Normalyn said. *And she's more beautiful than ever,* Miss Bertha verified. "And she's more beautiful than ever!" Normalyn said. Although she wasn't exactly sure who Lana Turner was, Normalyn bristled against the cruelty.

With a stabbing finger, Lady Star indicated a canvas chair for Normalyn to sit on; there were several about the room.

Normalyn chose another chair. She decided she would be deliberately subdued, quiet, mysterious. Like Enid.

"Now!" Lady Star got down to essentials. "This is how it works, darling: From among *many* would-be petitioners for Dead Movie Stars—" She waved her hand royally toward the window to indicate that they were even now gathering outside the château longing for an audience with her.

"There're four more already!" Billy Jack reported, looking out the window.

"From those many, many, we select, for preliminary interview, a few perhaps *likely* candidates. Like you," she tossed away. "And if—*if!*—" Her finger rose in admonitory emphasis. "—if, based on certain, uh . . ." She paused to rehearse the next word. "—devicements"—she shrugged—"if you survive as a would-be petitioner—and don't think it's easy," said a squeaky voice, "you may be allowed at our next auditions," resumed the throaty one.

"*Secret* auditions," Billy Jack added gravely.

"Yes, it is the only time we do not welcome outside attention," Lady Star added solemnly, and continued to explain the chain of elevation: "And *if* you sustain our interest through preliminary examination, you may, just may, be granted the status of . . . *pretender*! And if—*if*—and it gets harder and harder," she said with girlish breathlessness, again deepened, ". . . *if* you survive more scrutiny, you will enter the last and most difficult phase of auditions . . . as a *contender*! And *then*!"

"*Then!*" Billy Jack intoned.

"Then if—and this is the biggest if of all," said the excited voice, once again conquered by the deepened one, "if you pass rigorous attention—and we allow a range of creative approaches to convince us—you may, just may—just possibly may—be deemed worthy to become . . . a Dead Movie Star"—she closed her eyes— "for Marilyn Monroe!"

Petitioner! Pretender! Contender! Allowed . . . permitted . . . the words themselves made Normalyn wince. This was what those eager young people outside, and so many others, were willing to put up with to join this motley group? Normalyn forced an extended yawn, calling attention to it by pretending to disguise it.

Billy Jack whispered to Lady Star.

Lady Star glared at him. "She needs *us*!"

Normalyn controlled her suspicions. What *was* there to suspect? She stood up, stretching as if now doubly wearied.

Quickly Lady Star allowed, "Oh, I suppose, darling, that you do have a certain, oh, *shane-see-kwa—*"

"What?" Billy Jack stared at Normalyn to see what Lady Star had detected on her.

"It's French," she informed, "for I-don't-know-what."

Normalyn's hope that she might find something relevant here—perhaps some source of information—had disappeared. She would not stay any longer.

"We can help you . . . darling," Lady Star said.

Had her voice become sinister? "If I help you?" Normalyn challenged. She was sure that earlier Billy Jack had whispered a warning of restraint to Lady Star.

"Tit for tat!" Lady Star plucked twice at the darkened air.

Step by step. An echo of David Lange's words—

Billy Jack quickly answered a knock at the door. A man, slightly hefty, middle-aged, in an ordinary business suit, stood there; he carried a camera, paraphernalia. He looked at Normalyn.

Past him and through the still open door, Normalyn hurried out and down the corridor—the wrong way! Billy Jack caught up with her at a dead end. She felt trapped against the grimy wall. A cracked window allowed twisted light in. Through the broken pane, there was suddenly the incongruous scent of flowers.

"Huccome you ran away like that?" Billy Jack demanded.

"Because I don't want to be photographed—yet!" Normalyn added the qualification to placate his further suspicions.

"Okay," Billy Jack accepted after a few thoughtful moments. "You can stay in my room till he's gone." He led her into a small jutting corridor within lurking shadows. He opened a door with his key. Normalyn did not go in.

"I see him! He's got his camera!" Billy Jack coaxed her in.

Normalyn dashed into the room—and only then was sure no one else had been in the hallway. Billy Jack locked the door behind her.

Normalyn saw: a rumpled army cot, a small shower without curtains, boxes as furniture, scattered clothes, dozens of photographs of movie stars, movie posters. And there was a colored blowup of Marilyn Monroe. Normalyn gasped—it was her own reflection in a streaked, yellowing mirror!

Billy Jack aimed a spotlight, hooked to a wall, at a splintered mantel over a fireplace sealed with crossed boards. On the shelf was a framed photograph of the nude body of Marilyn Monroe on red velvet, "Golden Dreams." Next to it was another framed photograph, the same size.

"Go ahead and look at it," Billy Jack said.

In the second photograph, Billy Jack, naked, posed so that his body seemed to be reacting sexually to the one next to it.

"I told ya, my fantasy," Billy Jack said huskily. He opened his shirt on the tattoo of the cracked tombstone and flower. He turned the spotlight on Normalyn.

Her body fought new and remembered terror. She pressed against the wall, where the bold light had smashed and frozen. "I trusted you!" she yelled.

"Shouldn't've," he said. "You're fuckin' gullible." He advanced on her. "You trust too much—just like her. *She* believed lies, too!"

"I'll scream—" Normalyn's mouth was so dry she could hardly form words.

"In this fuckin' dump?" Billy Jack sneered. "People scream all the time. Scream, goddammit! I like that!" His wiry arms reached out for her.

She prepared to claw at him, kick—

He doubled over laughing, like a nasty child. "Fooled ya! I was just acting! Pretty damn good, huh? You really thought I was gonna rape you, huh? See—that's what you're going to have to do at auditions: be convincing, act out dramatic scenes from the secret lives of the movie stars—rape, murder, suicide— glamorous shit like that."

The reversal was so startling that Normalyn did not yet feel relief.

"Now I gotta go make sure I'm in the picture with Lady Star!"

When he left, Normalyn pulled at the door. Locked! There was one window, painted black, partly open. She looked out. Too far to jump! She saw the desolate garden below. She pushed against the flimsy door.

"Sorry about locking the door." Billy Jack was back. "Just do it automatically. Did it scare you? The photographer's gone."

"Move away from the door!" Normalyn used her most as-sertive voice.

"Aw, cummon," he said, "you don't have to be scared of me. I'm just helping you rehearse for auditions—because," he said, "we *want* you to be a contender."

"Why?" She could not rein her suspicions.

He shrugged. "Cause that's what makes auditions good," he said easily. He moved to one side, and, bowing, spread his hands to assert her safe exit.

In a tangoing step, he accompanied her along the corridor. Lady Star waited at the open door of her room. "It was a short sitting—but worthy, worthy. A feature in *L.A. Weekly*," she dismissed. "Oh, the mee-dee-ahs"—she trilled the word —"are crazy about us! . . . And, darling, if you don't have a place to stay, I *may* be able to importune on the manager for an occupancy—"

Billy Jack said, "There's *always* rooms in this dump. All you have to do is wait an hour for some old creep to die."

"I myself hope to die at midnight on my twenty-ninth birth-day," Lady Star sighed. She tossed over her shoulder at Normalyn, "Darling, now all you have to do to become a petitioner is to come up with a spectacular secret about *her*— something only *you* know. And of course you must already know one or you wouldn't be here!"

You're doing it again, Normalyn warned herself; you're

letting yourself suspect everything, everyone! But this persisted: Lady Star wanted something from her.

Lady Star fished a fake-pearl necklace from her improvised jewel box; she wound it experimentally about her arm. "Joan Crawford wore it once, like this." She showed Normalyn.

Normalyn had heard that from—

Like decorated shadows in the darkened room, several young people walked in: a youngwoman with blonde hair piled on her head in giant curls; another with ink-black hair framing a whitened face; one with an eye obliterated by a yellow wave; a red-jacketed youngman with pouty lips, squinty eyes, tousled hair; one with a thin strip of a moustache, and a red bandanna about his neck; and another with thickened, long, long eyelashes, darkened eyebrows.

Lady Star greeted them in her little-girl voice: "Hi, Betty Grable, Hedy Lamarr, Veronica Lake, James Dean, Errol Flynn, Tyrone Power . . . Where's Rita Hayworth?"

"Her *mother* found her!" gasped the tiniest, Veronica Lake.

Errol Flynn and Billy Jack elbowed each other playfully, jostling Betty Grable, whose hands flew in horror to make sure her structure of curls was intact. "Watch it, stupids," she warned.

Glaring at the antics, Hedy Lamarr said, "Lady Star, we were scouting the Boulevard for real talent to consider for petitioners, and I have become of the firm opinion that we are getting entirely too many suicide-petitioners."

Tyrone Power agreed. "We need more kidnappings."

"Rapes!" said Errol Flynn.

"Murders," Betty Grable offered.

Humped over on the floor, James Dean mumbled his secret: "*I* was murdered. People just think I crashed."

Pointedly—amid furtive glances—they all pretended not to see Normalyn, although Veronica Lake lifted her wave momentarily to stare at her.

Lady Star called for silence. "We will take under due advicement—"

Veronica Lake covered her ears at the word.

"—the matter of greater proportion in disallowing suicides. Thank you for bringing it to our attention, Miss Lamarr."

Hedy Lamarr rejected gratitude.

Lady Star walked over to Normalyn and touched her briefly. She paused to gather silence. "We have a *possible* candidate for . . . Marilyn Monroe!"

All eyes were on Normalyn.

At Lady Star's words, as if awakening out of a dream but

still wearing the clothes she had worn in it, Normalyn felt a sudden, clear astonishment that she was here. Had she really thought these odd young people would illuminate anything relevant to her? How stupid she had been, how desperate! She judged herself. How lonesome and eager. She walked to the door.

The Dead Movie Stars stared at her like abandoned children.

"Wait," Lady Starr said in her smallest voice.

"Don't go," Billy Jack said, as if she were leaving only him.

Normalyn's hand was on the doorknob.

Lady Star said, "You need our secrets."

"Yeah!" Billy Jack agreed.

Normalyn turned the doorknob. "You don't have any secrets." All they had were their drab, real lives, which they were trying to abandon while she was trying to *find* hers.

Firmly adjusting the orchid in her blazing waves of hair, Lady Star posed before her chaise. Her voice was husky, the deepest ever. "Do we have secrets?" she asked the Dead Movie Stars.

Veronica Lake said to Normalyn, "You know why I didn't marry the man who married Jacqueline Kennedy—Ar-is-to-tle O-nas-sis?" She gave import to each syllable of the name.

"You know how I made *fuckin'* sure I'd be acquitted of statutory rape?" Errol Flynn asked.

"You know why my husband really tried to buy up all the prints of my nude movie sequence?" Hedy Lamarr smoothed her inky hair.

Betty Grable held her curls in place. "Know the *real* reason Alice Faye despised me?"

Tyrone Power said to Normalyn. "You know why the studio wouldn't let me attend *any* of Errol Flynn's movies?"

Lady Star roused James Dean, bunched on the floor.

"Uh, yeah," he said to Normalyn. "Uh, you know why 'they' said I crashed?—who I was, uh, rushing to in my Porsche?"

"And do you know what Valentino *did* with Nazimova *and* Winifred Shaunessy?" Billy Jack leered.

"Well, *do* you, darling!" Lady Star demanded of Normalyn.

Normalyn opened the door.

Lady Star advanced on her. She fired words like rapid bullets: "Do you know what mysterious woman guided Mildred Meadows to the secret clinic where Marilyn Monroe was to lose the child Alberta Holland was determined to protect? Do you!"

Normalyn slammed the door closed. "That's a goddamned lie! Enid was *never* Mildred's ally. And how the hell do you know anything about Enid?"

Lady Star closed her eyes, carefully, so as not to upset her false eyelashes. "I think the orphan told us about her. No, Dr. and Mrs. Crouch did. Maybe Mildred. No, I believe we heard about her from the other petitioner, who's doing fabulous research!" Then Lady Star said triumphantly: "None of the above, darling! *You* just told us about Enid."

Twenty-Five

Normalyn did not respond, not even when the Dead Movie Stars burst into laughter at Lady Star's verbal pursuit of her. By speaking Enid's name, she might have sprung Lady Star's trap—Normalyn suspected Lady Star had known the name all along, had wanted only to enlist her by making her verbalize her knowledge of it. But Lady Star had provided possible connections to the fragmented truth she was gathering. *Someone* had told her about the events of the movie star's last crisis. Too, the other youngwoman in close pursuit of the movie star's life—the same who had accosted Miss Bertha and Mark Poe—might lead her to others. So Normalyn stayed.

Blue in her cone of light, Lady Star sat on her chaise, her command post, and announced to Normalyn, "Darling! You have, with alarcity—"

"—alacrity?" Veronica Lake pondered.

"—with *alacrity*"—Lady Star glided on—"you have proven yourself a worthy petitioner. You *do* know something or other about secrets. You have passed our first phase."

The other Dead Movie Stars buzzed agreement.

"And you may come with us tonight to the Silent Scream Club."

Normalyn caught Lady Star's knifing look admonishing the others not to protest the exceptional invitation. There was a reason for this further extension to her. Normalyn said, "I'm not sure I want to come with you." "The Silent Scream" sounded like an ugly place. Her fear—dammit!—had infiltrated her voice.

"Are you scared, darling?" Lady Star challenged.

Dare! "No ... I'll go with you," Normalyn decided, then added, to thwart any sense of victory Lady Star might attempt to snatch, "And I'll take into consideration your invitation to attend your next—what do you call those things?—auditions?"

"What the fuck!" Errol Flynn protested her mistreatment of enormous honor.

"The nerve!" said Hedy Lamarr.

"You know how *many* we reject—?" Tyrone Power was about to add his wrath.

Veronica Lake watched Lady Star slyly.

Lady Star's raised hand stopped the protests. Heavy-lashed eyes narrowed on Normalyn. "Done, darling!" she agreed. "Tit for tat!" she smoothed the folds of her skirt with grand insouciance.

Step by step. Normalyn frowned at the association. . . . Then *she* smoothed the folds of *her* dress. Of course she would *not* be a "petitioner." She was here to *live*—and to discover what "secrets" they *did* have. Besides, it would be good for Troja and Kirk to miss her.

2

"Here come the creepy Dead Movie Stars!" said a fuschia-haired girl next to a gaunt youngman decorated with plastic chains rouged to look rusted.

"Step aside so glamour may enter—*punks*!" Lady Star ordered.

Ahead, a narrow corridor smirched by light led into pockets of phosphorescent green and red within the swimmy darkness of a cavernous room, into which Lady Star, escorted by Billy Jack, led Betty Grable, Tyrone Power, Hedy Lamarr, Errol Flynn, James Dean, Veronica Lake, with one eye blinded by hair, and Rita Hayworth, who, having just escaped again from a capturing mother, looked about suspiciously.

Normalyn separated herself slightly from them. In the interim before meeting them at the château for this defying trek, she had gone to a movie. She was so used to Kirk's old ones that this one looked strange—a hateful attempted comedy with an unfunny actor named Eddie Murphy. Afterward, in a coffee shop dark enough to shield her from attention, she ate hungrily—and resisted the temptation to call Troja, who would have begun to worry about her. Good!

The Silent Scream was situated in the shabbiest heart of Hollywood, near Sunset, in the lower depths of an abandoned

porno theater. The whooshing of cars on the overpass of a
freeway sliced into heavy-metal sounds shoved from a small
elevation by an aggressive band of three youngmen and one
youngwoman, all in trashy clothes. Mounted on a wooden
crate, a television set—volume turned off, stations shifting
automatically—projected mute images of bright-toothed smiles,
freeway catastrophes, cloud formations, game winners and
losers, murder, war, terror.

Normalyn stared into the neon-splotched darkness, which
pulsed in gasps of dyed light to the shattered music, all within
a stench of alcohol and marijuana. Young people leaned against
walls, like slightly living props. Swirling dirty-orange lights
brushed the darkness with spectral fire. Sliced by cold lasers,
youngmen and women danced, twisting as if in pain, the
music a rejected antidote.

Two factions mixed here: those in studiedly vulgar attire—
girls in mesh, leopard stripes, youngmen in ripped shirts,
gruff metallic decorations; and those in attempted "glamorous" costumes from the near past of Hollywood—draped shirts
and skirts, cocked and veiled hats. The latter faction was here
to emulate and court favor from the founding Dead Movie
Stars. Crushed in this color-spattered catacomb, the groups
looked like indifferent survivors of separate apocalypses.

Normalyn forced herself to approach the currents of noise
and flashing images—the spillage of life! she told herself. A
youngman had walked along the corridor with her. Now he
was following her. He was slim, wearing battle fatigues streaked
in colors and tucked into combat boots, a sleeveless army shirt,
a bandanna across his forehead. He did not seem to belong
clearly to either faction here—an outsider like her. Normalyn
welcomed him, for now.

At the mouth of the huge room, a puny youngman with
olive-slicked hair and giant padded shoulders pushed through
the crowd to stop Lady Star in her tracks. "Lady Star!" he
shouted over the crashing din. "Can I have your autograph!"

"Of *course*, darling!" Lady Star tried to yell back while main-
taining her lowest voice.

Having captured her attention, the fan gasped, "Lady Star,
please let me audition again for the Dead Movie Stars. I've
gotten better, I swear to God, and I know a *real* tragic scandal
about Clark Gable."

"Out of my way!" A betrayed Lady Star shoved at the
youngman, but not before she had taken his offering of several tiny pills. She parted waves of massed bodies.

The sudden center of adulation—and of insults—the Dead

Movie Stars posed in a tight group within the vortex of bodies.
"They're scouting for *new* Dead Movie Stars!" said a thrilled
voice. Billy Jack passed a small vial of cocaine among them.
"It's bitchin' shit, a Robert Mitchum candidate donated it—we
might consider him at least for a while."

He held some powder to Normalyn's nose. She didn't want
it. The first time had aroused a speedy anxiety. "Go on!" She
sniffed, thinking she might be able to flow out of it quickly.
She felt the uncomfortable surge of eager energy without
goal—and then she was jolted into the throbs of the room.
Beside her, the youngman in combat clothes snorted from his
own tiny container. Normalyn rejected his further offer.

"You're the prettiest Dead Movie Star," the youngman with
the red bandanna said to her. He had to shout to be heard.

She could almost believe him! If she *was* someone else, then
she might be pretty. "Thank you!" She yelled words that were
incongruous at the Silent Scream.

So were his: "You're welcome."

He didn't fit here at all. Was he, like her, forcing himself to
experience— . . . ?

Rita Hayworth held a lit joint to Normalyn. "Don't look at it,
sweetie. *Puff*!" Normalyn did. If Troja and Kirk could see her!
She coughed so violently the youngman patted her on the
back. He eased the joint away from her and took a deep puff
before Rita Hayworth snatched it back. "Who are *you*?" she
derided. "John Wayne?"

Colors in the room had become slightly liquid. In recurring
moments of intensified awareness, Normalyn felt herself gentled on smooth waves. Extending out his hands to her as his
body swayed, the youngman coaxed Normalyn to dance; his
movements were slower, to a different rhythm, than those of
the others, who writhed to the anarchy of the music. But
Normalyn didn't know how to dance! The thought occurred
as an abrupt intrusion into her decision to do so. Enid had
taught her some ballet steps, but she considered herself clumsy.
Now her body glided naturally against the loud jagged rhythms,
but she remained in the periphery of tinted darkness. The
youngman moved deeper into the intersection of lasers, his
hands out toward her. "Come on, just follow me, trust me, I'll
guide you."

Normalyn's body froze. That exhortation sounded like a
command, and it seemed to have come not only from him but
from a recent memory. She tried suddenly to locate the origin
of this night. It was when Lady Star dared her to join them.
Trapped again in suspicions aroused by ordinary words! That

would keep her always on the edges, even here in this giant room. Moving cautiously at first, then more easily, Normalyn's body swayed, began to respond to two rhythms—one turbulent, this room's; the other smooth, hers.

Then she saw her, a youngwoman forcing her attention by standing very still near her, among twisting bodies. As fiery tongues of light swept over them, Normalyn saw the youngwoman's platinum-blonde hair, the reddened mouth, the beauty spot on her cheek, her body hugged tightly by a dress that forced the illusion of lushness. Nearby, Lady Star nodded at both of them in introduction. This youngwoman was the *other* "petitioner"! *That's* why Lady Star had insisted she come here, to create rivalry. Smiling just slightly, the youngwoman retreated into the churning room.

The youngman in combat clothes leaned over to Normalyn and said, "Cops are gonna bust this place very soon."

Normalyn reacted in surprise both to the announcement and to its easy tone. "Why?"

"Drugs, minors," the youngman enumerated. She'd warn the others! But he grabbed her hand. "Come on, I'll lead you out." She tried to pull away from his grasp. She shouted to Lady Star— *"Leave!"*—but her voice was swallowed into the cacaphony of sounds.

Swiftly he led her out through a half-hidden exit behind the platform, into a short underpass of the freeway. On its walls were painted huge figures in bright colors—Elizabeth Taylor, James Dean, Vivien Leigh, Clark Gable. Over them graffiti was splashed in black and red.

"I saved you," the man said to Normalyn. He removed the headband, pushed his hair free. He was older than he had attempted to look inside the darkened Silent Scream.

Normalyn looked beyond the mouth of the tunnel. Nothing was occurring to sustain his prediction of a raid. "You lied to me," she said.

"Oh, there'll be a raid all right," he told her.

Heated wind was rising in gusts, stirring debris in the tunnel. Palm fronds rustled, scratching against the dusty scrim of this strange night, a night that had begun *before* Lady Star's challenge at the château. Normalyn still searched its origin. Was it when she had made herself up in Troja's mirror, with Troja's makeup?

"How do you know what's going to happen?" Normalyn asked.

"One guess," he said.

"You're a policeman." Normalyn felt she was in danger, but

she did not know of what—as if the danger itself were deciding what shape to take.

"That means you're safe with me." He moved closer to her.

Dried palm leaves tossed on the sidewalk. Gray dust sliced the streets, the few passing cars. She tasted dirt. Wind pushed more heat into the tunnel. "Stay away from me," Normalyn said to the man.

"I saw you snort cocaine," he said.

"So did you!" she told him.

He shook his head in easy denial. "*You* did, just you," he asserted. He placed one hand on her shoulder. "Now what would your family think if they knew you'd been caught in a raid with drugs and—?"

Terror snapped again. Was he really a policeman? Would any car stop if she yelled? She could run, but she did not want to excite with a sudden movement. "I don't have a family," she said. "I don't have anyone." The last words were not spoken to him.

With one finger the man outlined the features of her face, tracing the makeup. "You don't have to be afraid," he said. "I never use force, it's always willing." His finger touched her lips.

She turned her face from his touch and spat out angrily, "If you knew who my father is!" she warned. Over the wind, which came in interrupted breaths, heavy with dead heat, she heard him say:

"Who is your father, Normalyn? I was sure you had a family."

"How the hell do you know my name?" She pulled back.

"Marilyn?" the man asked. "That's who you're trying to look like for the Dead Movie Stars. And you do—you know that—you really do."

Now she was sure he was reacting in excitement only to the reflection she had managed of the movie star. She had only imagined he had spoken her name.

"*Is* your father a powerful man?"

"Yes!"

"Who?"

"Mayor Wendell Hughes. He *owns* Gibson, Texas!" She would have said Mark Poe, but she had to convey official authority. This man wanted information about her—indirectly, disguising his intentions, his questions, scaring her into answering. . . . The two men in the park, the man in the hotel! Was she really being followed secretly?

"How old are you?"

"Twenty-one!"

"More like eighteen."

He knew! "You're playing an ugly game with me." She backed away, a foot, another, near the edge of the curb. "If you try to touch me or follow me, I'll run into the street."

"I'm not going to follow you." His icy smile remained.

She ran out of the tunnel, along the block, against gusts of wind and dirt, her feet tangling on a dead palm frond, which curved over. Its spiky edges scratched at her flesh. She ran until she reached a busy intersection. Breathless, she looked back. The man had not followed. She tried to explain away invisible dangers: He was probably a policeman, or using that as a ruse. He had been drawn to the specter of the woman she evoked. He knew she'd seen him snort cocaine, and he believed her when she said Mayor Hughes was her father. There was no further mystery!

Like painted shadows, women now strolled these blocks, lingering within the windy night. Single men in cars circled blocks swept by loose rubble. Normalyn felt as if she had walked into Troja's past—wearing Troja's clothes. Perhaps she would be here. Terrified, determined, she forced herself to move along the street. Troja would never again accuse her of not joining "the parade"! Yet she was safe among so many wanderers.

A car slid alongside her. It stopped, just ahead. The driver looked back, signaling. Normalyn crossed the street, away. Several extravagant women in a group eyed her.

"What you doin' on this street, gal?" said one of the women in a tight red skirt. "You *high*-class shit!"

A man with them offered to get her a "hot date."

Like a tarnished oasis, an all-night coffee shop floated in dirty light out of the misty night. Inside, Normalyn sat in one of several vacant booths.

"Sit at the counter. Booths are reserved for more than one," a harsh waitress, trying to look younger than her fifty years, said.

"But she's not alone." A middle-aged man, well-dressed, slipped into the booth and across from Normalyn. He looked fresh, as if he had just ventured into the tired night. He had dark hair brushed with gray. He smiled conspiratorially at her, against the waitress's dogged admonition. A Mexican busboy cursorily cleared the table. The angered waitress demanded their order. Normalyn asked for a sandwich. "Any kind."

"Tuna!" the woman wrote.

"No," Normalyn confronted the glaring woman. "Chicken— with only white meat. And iced tea with two wedges of lemon."

The man ordered coffee. "And perhaps some courtesy from you," he said to the waitress, like a man used to having it. The woman gaped at his audacity but said nothing.

Normalyn welcomed him only for now. She felt safe, yes, and she was tired, and he was kind. Oh, this night had begun when she looked through the book of photographs and saw the pretty girl changing into another person. No—when she stared into the mirror and saw someone else, not herself.

"Have you been long in the city?" the man asked her.

She had seen him before! He was the man at the Ambassador Hotel. No, the quiet man with the heavy one in the park. No, he was the man who had driven up beside her, just minutes earlier. Now she was sure of it. Then she wasn't sure whether she had ever seen him before.

On the smoke-smeared windows of this coffee shop, reflections of people drifted in dirty light. Outside, the female wanderers huddled from blades of dust, painted faces glancing steadily about the street.

The waitress brought a listless sandwich and two cups of coffee. "Anything else, *sir!*"

Normalyn was too weary to protest. She welcomed the warmth of the cup of coffee in her hands.

The man's eyes traced her outline, her features. "You look innocent and frightened under the marvelously brash makeup. Is that what you intended? What are you looking for?"

The strangeness of the night was seeping into this booth. Normalyn slid to its edge, preparing to leave. "I think that I—"

"Shhh," he silenced her quickly, a finger at his lips. "Forgive me." He extended his courteous manner. "It's just that unwanted words banish fantasy. They have to be exact words. Let me create you only in my imagination. Please, just answer what I ask—"

The heat from the coffee intensified on her hands. He was a man who wanted to buy a fantasy. Yet his words resonated with a further, inquiring meaning, camouflaged within a contradictory situation: *Answer what I ask—* . . . It did not disturb her that he might think she was a prostitute, because she was on Troja's street teeming with risky life. What she heard clearly, beyond implied questions, was the suggestion that she needed no identity of her own, no life, that she remain a reflection determined by others. *That* is what she would not be! Easily, she turned over the cup of coffee, letting the ugly dark liquid spill on him.

"Stupid bitch!" He jerked back.

She stood up. Her defiance receded at his accusing words. "I'm sorry!" She yelled the hated apology. But she didn't hear her own words. She heard the voice of the movie star, as she had been captured in the last photograph of the book she had looked through earlier, the lips parted, still and always ready to apologize for living! Yes, those were the words Normalyn had been ready to identify earlier, from her *own* constant apology for *wanting* to exist.

Normalyn ran out of the coffee shop. She had located the origin of this night. It had begun in David Lange's office, with his soft commands. With that realization, she felt she had awakened from another's dream. *She* had made only futile motions of living.

Normalyn's hands flew up to her face. She smeared the makeup into red and dark slashes, destroying the face she had recreated over her own.

Twenty-Six

"You dreamed it all, hon—and, hon, we were worried *sick* about you."

"Troja, it all happened! I lived it!" But she felt even more now that she had made only motions of living. "You asked me if I'd ever join the parade, remember?"

"You'd better not have!"

"I didn't, not exactly. But I *was* there."

"Well, we missed you a whole lot. Worried sick, weren't we, Kirk?"

"Yeah, Normalyn. You shouldn't've scared us like that by staying away so late."

"But *you* left me."

"We shouldn't've, Troja, just like you said. We shouldn't've left Normalyn like that."

"And I intended to buy special food, even a chilled bottle of champagne for *all* of us to have at the beach."

"Oh, hon, that makes me feel even worse, you being so generous and us going alone without you to the beach. Hate myself being so selfish. We missed you so much. And, uh, hon, you sure one of those awful Dead Movie Stars didn't, uh, slip you . . . something?"

"You've said I have no life of my own. Now you don't *want* to believe me!"

"Don't blame you being upset, hon. It's just that we missed you so damn much."

As she rode in the cab she had just located at a motel on Western Avenue, that is how Normalyn imagined Troja's and

291

Kirk's reaction when she returned. It was deep night, beginning of darkest morning. Moving away from the strange night,
Normalyn was sure she had been followed by the two men she
had encountered, and she was just as certain that they had no
connection with David Lange. What had occurred with them
did not fit *anything* she knew of David. As the night's events
furthered, she was able to attribute concealed motives only to
the man in the tunnel, and, finally, not even to him, when,
within waves of relief, she saw the beautiful, singular palmtree
ahead. Even in darkness, it appeared newly lush.

The Mustang was not there! They had gone out looking for
her! She paid the cab and ran into the house.

All was dark, silent. Kirk was not in his bed. She stubbed
her toe on the mannequin's head. The blonde wig had been
removed. Normalyn ran into Troja's darkened room.

Troja sat on the floor in darkness. Her knees were gathered
under her bowed head. Normalyn reached to turn on a lamp
decorated with colored scarves. At the last moment before she
would leave, Troja would often slide a scarf away and drape it
about her neck. With that incongruous memory, Normalyn
was trying to establish familiar order.

"Don't turn the damn light on!" Troja said.

Normalyn waited for more words, waited to hear Troja say
melodramatically, "Cause I'm a mess—wait till I make myself
up." But she didn't.

Beyond the window, gray filtered into the inky sky.

Normalyn touched the fragile scarves on the lamp.

"Worried sick—" Troja said.

She *had* missed her! And Kirk had gone out looking for her!
Naturally Troja would be subdued now that she was relieved
to see her back, maybe a little angered. Normalyn approached
Troja. "I'm all right," she said. She tried to coax the unfin-
ished expression of concern, to bask in it: "You said you
were worried sick—"

"Sick to my heart. He's gone."

Troja hadn't meant her! Normalyn turned away. She saw,
clear even in dim light, the blond wig flung on the floor. Her
mind bolted back to the night by the ocean, with Enid. It had
not been imagined! To force more of the suddenly strong
memory, she leaned over the blond disheveled hair—

"Leave that fuckin' thing there!" came Troja's growl.

Normalyn saw that Troja's face was bruised. "Kirk hit you!"
she said angrily. And the memory of a distant ocean night
drifted away.

"Girl!" Troja snapped ferociously."Kirk *never* hit me. We

never quarrel. You don't know nothin'!" her shanty voice seized control. But then her hand extended to Normalyn. Normalyn took it. Troja urged her to sit with her, near her. "Where you been, hon?"

Normalyn clasped her hand. Her heart was filled with wonder at life. Rejected, then needed! She said, "I've been— . . . living!"

"Yeah," Troja said, as if she hadn't heard. She looked at Normalyn. "I wore the wig, hon."

She was apologizing to her for wearing the wig that mocked the movie star. "It's all right," Normalyn said. She asked softly, trying to force an ordinary answer with her casual tone, "Where is Kirk?"

"Took the car. Said he was gonna kill Duke."

No—

"In all that time living together, I never knew he kept a gun," Troja accused herself. "Maybe if I'da *cleaned* the damn place now and then, I woulda found it!"

In that moment of bitter humor, Normalyn felt even closer to Troja. She looked out into the other room, to the bed where the defeated muscular form so often lay for hours.

Troja said urgently, "I should've listened, I should've believed him—when we lay on the sand, hon, when he took my hand and—"

*   *   *

—he kissed it. He had been quiet, as if listening to himself. "I've given you so much pain, Troja—and more each day." His finger on her lips stopped her denial. "If I wasn't such a fuckin' coward, I'd kill Duke to get him out of your life. Instead I keep him there with my drugs, I know that—and now you're taking them just to be close to me, I know that, too."

"We are close," she said. "*That* matters. And you're not a coward."

At that moment, a group of youngmen and women gathered on the strip of beach. Troja had chosen it because it was secluded. Kirk's eyes focused on the young bodies. He looked down at his own, in trunks. It was muscular, more than those of any of the youngmen who had suddenly appeared, but the sunlight on the white sand revealed scratchy lines on his fading tan.

He said, "I've missed the beach, been hiding from it, I guess. This is where I buried my youth."

That was the first time he had ever spoken about himself as aging. That terrified Troja.

"I have to face it."

"And then, baby?" Troja asked hopefully.

Kirk shrugged. "Live or die."

"Live," Troja said, and added, *"please."*

He kissed her. "I love you."

"I know," she said.

"When I first saw you, the time we were both whoring"—he tried to laugh, but it was bitter laughter—"I thought you were the most beautiful woman I had ever seen. I've told you that, but I'm not sure you believe me, because of what happened."

"When you found out I was a *made-up* woman!" Troja could not keep the accusation away, from the ugliest of times, when Kirk had pulled away from her in disgust.

Kirk stood up. He looked out at the ocean. Behind him, the laughter of the younger people echoed. Fog hovered on the shoreline. Birds that gather in flocks late afternoon on the beach had begun to swoop onto the sand as if something invisible were drawing them to acknowledge the advancing night.

Kirk faced Troja. He tried to laugh. "I've been faithful to you, hon; can't do it with anyone else either."

Not since then. She knew that.

He said, "I wish I could prove my love for you." He opened his hands, shrugged as if he were puzzling how.

"You do all the time," she told him.

The ocean breeze swept the sand. More birds gathered in the cold light.

*   *   *

In the silenced room tinged with purple light, Troja shut her ears. "Can't remember what else he said!"

"What *did* he say, Troja?" Normalyn wanted to help her face whatever she was avoiding.

"He said," Troja said dully, "that maybe the only way he could show his love for me was to . . . just go away."

Normalyn pulled away from the echo of those words. Troja seemed to hear them anew. . . . And when they returned home, they missed me! Normalyn felt instantly guilty for thinking that at this time. But she wanted to know it only so she could concentrate on the wonder of sharing another's life, so intimately, when there was trust.

"When we came back here," Troja remembered—

*   *   *

—Kirk called up the number Duke had left them, of the couple who wanted him and her. On the way back from the beach, Kirk had brought up the possibility, just a possibility—"try; expect nothing"—and then, in surprise, they both said, yes, testing the other, then meaning it—still afraid. Kirk made the arrangements with the couple. He smiled at Troja with certainty. She understood, so clearly: Those moments on the beach—facing things—had given him courage. He longed to reconstruct that beginning—the origin of their love *and* their alienation—and so to assert the love and conquer what had turned ugly.

Kirk dressed in casual clothes. He looked tanned, handsome. Troja made herself up. She pinned back her hair. She put on the blonde wig the couple demanded.

*   *   *

"And we made beautiful love!" Troja said exultantly to Normalyn.

Dawn seeped into the room.

Then how did it go wrong? Normalyn wondered, knowing that Troja's and Kirk's lives had been moving swiftly at the same time hers had—life in all its shifting currents; but now was Troja's time, to find strength by ordering the events of her long night, hers and Kirk's, its beginning.

"It happened in the house we went to, in Bel Air," Troja said—

*   *   *

—a house the couple had rented from a producer in Europe.

A woman of about forty and a man slightly older waited for them. They were dressed with austere formality, he in a dark suit, she in a tailored dress. He was slightly heavy, careful about his weight; she had anxious features, a blocky body; she made clawing gestures as she smoked. They were drinking, slightly drunk. They had bought cocaine through Duke and had waited for Kirk to show them "exactly how" to snort it.

All four moved into the bedroom, into hidden softened lights. An enormous bed was covered with satin sheets. There were plush chairs about the room.

"The black Monroe." The man's eyes raked Troja's; so did the woman's. The woman approached Kirk, who—Troja saw, with tenderness—automatically flexed his biceps.

The man said, "Specimens!"

"Yes!" the woman approved.

Troja's eyes were only on Kirk, Kirk's on her.

The couple breathed more white powder—clumsily, hungrily. Tiny grains spilled on their clothes. Holding tinkling glasses of liquor, they prowled about the two beautiful bodies.

Kirk's hands touched Troja's shoulders, and hers slid over his. Kirk's fingers eased the dress from the brown body, revealing golden breasts. The dress fell slowly to the floor. The glowing body was naked. Kirk's hands outlined the amber curves.

The woman gasped, "Ahhh!"

"He can't get hard," the man reminded himself with urgency.

Troja heard the ice in their glasses scrape. Duke had told them that! Afraid, she pulled Kirk to her, before this moment shattered; she held his tense body until it relaxed again. The difficult moment flowed away. Troja unbuttoned Kirk's shirt. He removed his clothes, his muscles naked. In the soft glow of this room the two bodies shone. He touched Troja's breasts lightly. She pulled back, in fear, the earlier memory invading. He guided her back to him.

Circling, the man and the woman stared, sighed.

The woman's voice hissed: "Made-up breasts. Artificial breasts!"

Kirk's movements stopped. Troja's eyes closed, to contain the rage. Duke had told them that, too. That was part of what was meant to entice the man and the woman. Now Kirk would withdraw, like the first time, in doubled disgust—

Kirk licked the perfect nipples. Then gently he removed the blonde wig and freed Troja's own hair with his fingers.

"No!" the man protested.

But it was now as if Kirk and Troja were alone. She felt his groin harden against her body.

"You're supposed to be impotent!" the woman rasped at Kirk—and hurled the words at the other man, too.

"You weren't supposed to get hard!" the man accused Kirk. His hands plucked at his own groin.

Rejecting the surrogate battle the man and woman had staged in substituted anger at themselves and each other, the two beautiful, created people pressed their bodies together. Their mouths touched, opened.

"Artificial! Made up!" the woman accused Troja; her hands explored her own concealed body.

"Made-up bodies. Unnatural!" the man said.

Kirk's mouth glided down Troja's breasts to her stomach. He held her hips. His lips slipped down. He kissed the soft opening between her legs. Troja leaned back on the bed, guiding Kirk over her. She parted her smooth legs. The two constructed beautiful bodies fused as he entered her.

After Kirk came inside her, he and Troja held each other. The man and the woman retreated with wounded gasps to prepare a new assault.

*　　*　　*

Sun was beginning to sweep into the apartment. A few feet away, the wig lay lifeless.

Troja sighed, wanting to linger longer over cherished moments. Normalyn had listened quietly, knowing this was life, just life. . . . Troja's fingers absently stroked Normalyn's hair. "Hair's so pretty hon," she said.

"I made myself up," Normalyn said, "like when you—" But she had wiped the makeup off entirely in the cab. "I wore your dress," she confessed guiltily.

"Noticed," Troja said. As if remembering the treasured closeness with Kirk, she pulled away slightly from Normalyn.

Normalyn pulled away, too, to reject her back.

Troja's further sigh acknowledged that the paused moments had to move on. "After that—"

*　　*　　*

—in a frenzy of frustration, their displaced revenge thwarted, the man and the woman hovered over Troja and Kirk, over naked flesh sheened with a film of perspiration.

His breathing chopped into gasps, the man still tried to arouse his cock. "The pimp told us you were impotent!" he accused.

"Frigid!" the woman yelled.

"You fucked a goddamn man!" he yelled at Kirk.

Troja knew she did not have to be apprehensive, not ever again. Kirk had made love to *her*. He had kissed all the parts on her body that had been created; he had asserted and acknowledged her unique creation, had found her beautiful.

"Can you feel anything—in *there*!" the woman shot at Troja.

"In your artificial cunt!" the man lashed.

Troja turned her head, as if slapped by the words. Kirk held her face, forcing her to look at him. She did. He kissed her lips, several times.

Suddenly he stood up. He smashed his fist into the man's face. The man fell against the woman, who staggered. On the floor, the man still tried to arouse his dead cock. The woman laughed with harsh desire. The man stood up. He breathed more cocaine from both his palms.

"We won't pay you!" the woman shouted to Troja and Kirk. "We didn't get what the pimp told us."

"An impotent aging muscleman disgusted by a black transsexual playing Monroe! A man *disgusting* the other!" The man substituted words for what he had been deprived of.

Duke had arranged this cruelty against her and Kirk, guaranteeing a recurrence of that first time. It had turned out otherwise, Troja knew in triumph.

"We won't pay you!" the woman kept taunting.

"Doesn't matter," Troja said. And she meant it.

"It does matter," Kirk said. "They wanted revenge, they have to pay; so does Duke."

The woman flung readied money on the floor.

"Pick it up," Kirk ordered the man.

"Help me," the man said to the woman. She shook her head. On his knees, the man gathered the money, excitedly.

Kirk counted it. "Just wanted to know how much Duke thought humiliation would be worth." He gave the money to Troja, who clenched it with the wig.

They dressed quickly and walked out of the enormous frigid house. They drove down the deserted roads of Bel Air. When they reached home, Kirk opened a fresh packet of cocaine and snorted twice into each nostril. He pretended that was all he had located, but Troja saw the gun. "No," she pleaded. "We got so much, hon."

"Yes," Kirk agreed. "That's why I have to make sure Duke'll leave you alone. . . . I love you, remember that."

"I love you," Troja said back to him. Only in her mind did she repeat, *Remember that.*

Twenty-Seven

"Remember that," Troja said now. As if she had allowed a banished meaning, she stood up suddenly. "So damn quiet in here! He always turned on the television, first thing." She rushed to the other room, turned on the television, as if by restoring the daily routine she would bring him back with it.

Yes, voices rendered the absence less harrowing. The television flickered in colors into Troja's room, distant sounds and images of the outside world that confirmed to Kirk, every morning, that he was still alive.

Normalyn looked at the lightening morning outside. Night had not taken away its sadness.

Troja sat back down on the floor and leaned her head on Normalyn's shoulder. "He just went out to scare the shit outta that pimp—to keep him away from us," Troja asserted. "That's all."

"That's all," Normalyn assured.

"Missed you a lot, hon," Troja said. "Where you been?"

Normalyn tried to control the overwhelming emotion she felt at that admission. "You *did* miss me!" she said.

"Of course. You're my friend," Troja said.

"And you're *my* friend," Normalyn said. "You really missed me?"

"Told you!" Troja retreated from the threatened flood of Normalyn's emotion.

Normalyn welcomed that tone only now; it assured Troja's spirit was intact.

"Where were you?" Troja asked. The television, on, was soothing, affirming the familiar.

"With the Dead Movie Stars—"

"Those creeps?"

"Yes—at the old château near Franklin. And I went to a weird place called the Silent Scream."

"Just trash there," Troja disapproved.

"They almost raided it." Normalyn added the note of danger, although she knew now that had been a lie. "I was there!" She could not restrain the exultant tone in her voice. She would seize these interludes for herself. Later she would tell Troja, and Kirk, everything. When Kirk returned. When they were eating. "I was almost bashed!"

"Bashed! Those pigs *hit* you?" Troja's voice shook with rage.

"No—I mean—uh . . . bashed?"

"Busted." Troja understood.

"Yes." Normalyn felt now that she had lived even less.

"Worried me—and Kirk—sick. Kirk said you and me got a special closeness between us, a real special friendship, hon."

"We do," Normalyn said, and missed Kirk so much.

"Why don't he call? Why don't he just drive up!"

"He's all right," Normalyn said, feeling tired.

"I know it," Troja said. "Just couldn't find that evil pimp, that's all. Maybe went for a drive."

"Nothing . . . is . . . going . . . to . . . happen," Normalyn said drowsily, seized by sudden weariness pushing her toward sleep.

Troja's body jerked. *"No!"* she screamed.

Normalyn sat up, awake instantly.

In the other room, before the television, Troja screamed again.

"No!"

From the television, which each morning had brought distant disasters, an announcer was uttering words that gathered into one remorseless meaning: "—shot and killed a known drug dealer and procurer, a possible murderer, known as 'Duke.'" On the television screen, a body sprawled askew against a wall was being covered with sheets. "He was killed by a man who was still inside the house when police arrived. According to police, the man then walked out of the house with his weapon in his hand and they fired. The man's revolver was empty, arousing speculation that the man drew fire to himself. He is reported to be a former Mr. America; his name is being withheld pending notification of next of kin."

On the screen, attendants moved with a stretcher toward an

ambulance. The outline of Kirk's muscles showed through the sheet turning red.

"No, no, no!" Troja refused.

"Troja!"

The bloody images were replaced quickly with those of a commercial; on a bicycle a boy—

Normalyn turned the set off, angrily banishing its horror.

Troja gasped. "He never was Mr. America, just came close, real close!" She sank to the floor, moaning. Normalyn tried to hold her, but Troja's hands struck out, fiercely, at death.

A cruel beautiful morning lightened the house.

Troja shouted, "He killed Duke, yeah. But he didn't let himself be killed! Fuckin' pigs killed him and made that up. He didn't let himself be killed, *he didn't!*"

But had he? Normalyn wondered. To remove from Troja's life two presences, one despised, the other deeply loved, both destructive—and so to let Troja live.

2

When the police and all the others were through with him, Troja claimed Kirk's body. An attorney who had once represented her after an arrest arranged it. There was no other "kin." His body was cremated at "the movie star cemetery," Forest Lawn. Normalyn offered Troja the necessary money, but Troja had enough—the money Kirk had insisted they be paid that beautiful then fatal night.

With the urn containing his ashes, they drove to the ocean at sunset, to the place where Kirk had said his youth was buried. Knowing she should, Normalyn stayed behind and watched as Troja walked to the edge of the beach and scattered Kirk's ashes. A breeze glided over the sand. *Good-bye, Kirk,* Normalyn said silently.

Troja said, "Good night."

They walked back to the car. "He was the only man who was ever kind to me, the only man who ever loved me, really loved me." Troja said to Normalyn. "And he did love me, a lot."

"Yes." Normalyn was sure now.

They drove back in silence.

When they approached the single desolate palmtree, Troja's face grew taut. In the few preceding days, they had come and gone, attending the details of death. Now they would enter the full emptiness of the house.

The place Kirk had occupied was vacant. Troja gasped at

the absence. She pulled at Kirk's belongings, gathering sheets, pillows, clothes. She held a shirt with short sleeves, one of Kirk's favorites, tight. Then she replaced all the objects about the area again, leaving a disheveled monument. Near the bed, she found a packet of white powder—and a syringe.

"Throw them away!" Normalyn coaxed.

Troja breathed in the powder, into one nostril, then the other. She breathed into each again. She tilted her head back, to get its full effect. She held the syringe.

"No, Troja," Normalyn said.

The drawn face stared at Normalyn.

"Please don't."

"What?"

"Please don't take any more of that," Normalyn said softly.

"What?" Troja snorted again. Her body jolted. She fumbled with the syringe as if to stab at her arm.

Normalyn saw her own hand thrust the needle away from Troja. It fell with a tiny sound.

Troja's look darkened. "What you do that for?"

"You don't need that stuff, it's . . . shit."

"Girl usin' dirty words, huh? Girl learnin' bad things."

"Troja, don't do that to me! And please"—Troja *had* to hear this—"please don't destroy yourself, too."

"Too?" Troja walked up to her. "Who the hell you think you are to judge him?"

"I wasn't, I'm trying to help *you*. I know you're saying all this because you're so hurt: so I won't listen."

"You *listen!*" Troja said. "You gonna help me?" she derided. "Don't need you! Don't want your sad mopey face around me. Judging, judging—just like you was judging him all the time. Wasn't you always judging him—accusing him of hurting me?"

Normalyn heard her own words, softly spoken but precise: "You told me he faced that, on the beach—his destruction . . . and yours."

Troja frowned. She reached out as if to touch Normalyn. Instead, she pulled back. "What did you just say . . . *real* woman?"

"You're a woman, too—you know that!" Normalyn said quickly.

Troja's eyes were maddened with sorrow. "If I was a *real* woman, I'd be carrying his baby right *here!*" she pounded her stomach with both hands. *"This* can't bear no child!" she reached for a bottle of bourbon on the counter. She gulped, a swallow, another. She held her head in her hands, as if to crush her thoughts. She said, "Get out, Normalyn, I have to be alone. Pack your things, leave. Don't wanna *see* you!"

"Do you mean it?" Normalyn asked.

"Yes!"

"Do you really mean it—not just because you're hurting?"

"Goddammit, yes, I mean it—yes, yes, *yes!*" Troja screamed. She rushed into Normalyn's room. "I'll pack for you!" She pulled at Normalyn's clothes, opening a suitcase, crushing clothes in. She grabbed the chipped angel from the table. She thrust it at Normalyn. "Take it!"

Normalyn reached for it. It slipped, fell to the floor, smashed. She knelt over it, attempting to gather the pieces. It would be impossible to restore the shattered figurine. Normalyn faced Troja. "God *damn* you!"

Troja grasped Normalyn fiercely. Normalyn's hands lashed at her with equal fury. They faced each other, for long moments.

"*Now* do you believe I don't want you here?" Troja said and walked out.

Normalyn closed her suitcase.

In the kitchen, Troja sat at the counter.

Normalyn called a cab. She bit her lip, to stifle tears. She glanced at the empty bed, Kirk's, and then at her own. She faced this: A part of Troja had always been raging at her because she had been born a woman; and the fact that Troja had not, had separated her, until the very last, from Kirk.

Normalyn waited at the door with her suitcases. She was sure Troja would turn and urge her to stay. Yes, she could hear the words: "Hon, hon! I didn't mean any of that. Hon—"

Troja's back remained to Normalyn.

Even when the cab drove up, Normalyn paused. The driver honked. She waited longer, outside, on the porch. But no words came from the woman inside the quiet house.

3

Normalyn took the cab to the château that William Randolph Hearst had given Marion Davies years, years ago. Kind evening shadows bestowed upon the building and its courtyard some of its surrendered grace.

In the cab, Normalyn had concluded that to uncover all that was available from the Dead Movie Stars, she would let them believe that she *might* want to join them. From the earlier time with them, this had survived: They knew *something* of the past she was searching through, though perhaps no more than they had already revealed—and they wanted her.

She was able easily to rent a room. To the manager's shock, she requested one "with a view," and to her own relief, the room was not entirely ugly. It had tall windows that opened into the courtyard. There was a small bed. A round table of shiny plastic tried unsuccessfully to pass for wood. An oval mirror looked gold-glazed but was only streaked. Normalyn opened a suitcase, to place Enid's angel on the table. She remembered it had smashed. She substituded Enid's makeup box.

She was tired and depressed as she unpacked only necessities. She told herself that she must keep moving now, into her own life, resolving the past. She tried unsuccessfully to force her thoughts away from Troja and Kirk. Finally, she lay on the bed and surrendered to exhaustion.

When she woke much later, it was into an immediate, stark awareness of all the horror of the past few days—the violence, the deaths, the separations. She longed to return to Troja and Kirk. But Kirk was dead! She was sure Troja hadn't meant for her to leave; they had trapped each other. She would call her! But what if she hung up? If only she had asked once more, to stay. Troja had been terrified, grieved. *And cruel!* Normalyn reminded herself.

She must keep moving! She went to the tiny bathroom and showered. She dressed quickly. Now from memory she would locate Lady Star's room along the maze of halls.

She knocked on a door that looked familiar. A shriveled old woman with a parrot on her shoulder opened it. The parrot shouted, "Get out of my life, get out of my life!" Normalyn backed away. As she tried to reorient herself to the gloomy corridors, she thought she heard furtive, darting footsteps. The Dead Movie Stars? Aware she was here? She knocked on another door—this one *really* looked familiar. An eye looked out of a peephole. The door opened.

"But *of course* you're back!" Framed by the door of her room, Lady Star posed in a feathery lounging chemise. She tossed a strap off one freckled shoulder.

Normalyn faced her in the once gold-gilded, now ashen corridor.

"Come in, darling, come in," Lady Star invited. "There's a vile draft."

There wasn't. The air was still and hot.

Lady Star retreated to her chaise under the dripping umbrella of light.

Normalyn sat on a chair to one side of the chaise so Lady
Star would not seem to be granting her an audience.

"As you can plainly see, darling, I am Carole Lombard
today." A tiny feather floated up from an airy boa Lady Star
tossed recklessly over a bare shoulder blade. "Carole gives me
a kind of mystery, an aura." She tortured waves of newly
colored hair stabbed by a felt orchid. "So! You've reconsidered
about auditions—of course!" she declared.

"I'm *exploring* the possibilities," Normalyn clarified, and reminded, "Tit for tat."

"Hmmm." The felt orchid drooped over Lady Star's eye.
"A fresh one is due any moment from the secret admirer,"
she explained. "If it's one minute late, I shall refuse it!" She
snapped her fingers. Another feather escaped her boa. She
snatched it expertly and thrust it back into place.

She trilled, "You should have been with us last night, darling. We paid a visit to the Crouches—Dr. and Mrs. What with
auditions coming up—real soon!" she confided, "we needed to
brush up on tragedy, scandal, secrets. That's how we test
candidates and those who make it to auditions." Leaning forward, she said with honest indignation, "You'd be amazed at
how many of them try to *make up* scandal!"

Dr. and Mrs. Crouch. Those names again, from the earlier
time here—and from Enid's newspaper clipping, from Mark
Poe's recollections. Lady Star was clearly tantalizing with her
close association with intimate knowledge.

Normalyn put derision into pretended familiarity: "That
man and his wife know the *truth?*"

"That man and his wife were hired by the studios to hide
the truth; so they must *know* it!" Lady Star was affronted.
"They even know who—"

A knock at the door. "Enter only if you're a Dead Movie
Star." Lady Star posed a bare leg, ready for any eventuality.

Slick, dark, ominous, Billy Jack wore a flashy suit with giant
shoulders, broad lapels, shirt open revealing the edge of the
flowering tombstone. Quickly disguising his relief at seeing
Normalyn, he went on to tell her he was "trying on" Johnny
Stompanatto. He pretended to stab himself, crumble with
agony. He brushed his suit. "You gonna audition, huh? We
knew it!"

Normalyn didn't answer. She would not even attend their
silly auditions, much less audition.

"Oh, she's just exploring possibilities," Lady Star echoed
Normalyn's words. "—unlike, darling," she addressed Normalyn,
"the petitioner you met at the Silent Scream, who's uncovering

remarkable things, we hear. . . . But I'm *sure*—" This was to Billy Jack—Johnny Stompanatto. "I'm sure *this* one has better secrets." She pointed a long finger at Normalyn.

Tantalizing, extorting, Normalyn was sure, remaining mysteriously quiet.

Another knock at the door. Billy Jack opened it.

A youngwoman with a veiled hat and a gray dress entered. She held a silver cigarette lighter in her hand. She seemed about to click it.

Normalyn stopped her with angered words: "Who the hell are you pretending to be?"

"It's just I!" Veronica Lake removed the veiled hat. She shook her hair loose, rearranged a lump of it over one eye.

Lady Star said to Normalyn, "Who did you think it was, darling?" Billy Jack and Veronica Lake laughed. "Oh, and by the way—we have a confirmation from . . . Sandra. She *will* attend auditions. . . . She's a surprise guest from the past."

Sandra. . . . The figure in the "game"? In the captive twilight of this fallen château, Normalyn felt weighted by the resurrected past.

"Are you sure you won't be part of auditions, darling?" Lady Star addressed Normalyn.

"I'll *attend*," Normalyn decided—and felt so damn sad, so alone, afraid, missing everyone.

Twenty-Eight

"Auditions!" Lady Star intoned. "Will now begin! For a few—!"

"Very goddamn few." Billy Jack asserted his tough say. He opened his shiny shirt to expose the authoritative tombstone cracked by a rose. Today he was again Billy Jack.

"—for a very few Dead Movie Stars . . . *darlings*!" Lady Star flung the endearment at the worried petitioners seated before her in the basement of the Thrice-Blessed Pentecostal Church of the Redeemer. With a real orchid in her newly reddened hair—she was once again Lady Star—she sat in a high-backed chair once used by a church minister awaiting the time of his sermon. Billy Jack sat on her right, Veronica Lake on her left; the rest of the founding Dead Movie Stars flanked them on either side, all behind a table draped with a lacy sheet of starry silver and propped on a small platform.

Before them in rows of folding chairs were about twenty-five youngmen and youngwomen, all preselected from among many more as "petitioners," and all dressed somewhat like the movie stars they longed to be. In the shadows beyond the ashen circle of light over the clearing containing the platform, other young people sat scattered on the floor: allowed "supporting players" who would perform only when—*if!*—a particular petitioner reached the ultimate stage of examination. There was in the large murky room a buzzing tension, the restiveness of outsiders confined to rules.

Front row center, Normalyn, in her own attire and makeup, faced Lady Star. She prepared to remind herself as often as

307

necessary—and that was now—that she was here only to find a possible guide into areas of truth. In the row behind her sat the girl Normalyn had encountered at the Silent Scream; her lips were painted red, red.

News of the date for midnight auditions had been conveyed only earlier today to the qualified. From a sheltered vantage, the Dead Movie Stars had earlier overseen the entrants, safeguarding against the uninvited. Alerted to irregularity, Lady Star would slice a finger across her throat, signaling to Otto, the enormous hulking caretaker of the Thrice Blessed Church, to bar a questionable presence. Otto provided the large basement for free in exchange for "hobnobbing among glamour" —Lady Star's words. Hairy hand planted passionately on his groin, he guarded the door and kept strict discipline during auditions.

Now in her tall chair and behind her silvery table, Lady Star introduced Billy Jack, Veronica Lake, Tyrone Power, Betty Grable, Errol Flynn, Hedy Lamarr, James Dean, and— "Where the hell is Rita Hayworth?"

"I think her mom's sick," Tyrone Power offered.

Lady Star went on to address the assemblage: "As we begin this memorable evening of discovery, keep in mind that glamour and tragedy go hand in hand. It is that that allows the great stars to glow *forever*." She explained the stages to Dead Movie Stardom. Each petitioner, darlings, would be evaluated quickly on appearance and at least the hint of a secret. Those deemed worthy of further exploration would become pretenders. The panel would be allowed any question at any stage. Five or more "nos" from the founders meant unappealable impeachment in the first two phases. "If you don't accept our just decision peacefully, our most competent paramilitarian—"

"Parliamentarian," Veronica Lake adjusted.

"—is ready—and *able*—to assist you out into the dark, *deserted* street," Lady Star warned. "Of course, we prefer that you remain as loyal fans." She swept on to explain, darlings, that those passing the first two rigorous phases would be designated contenders, then permitted to perform "scenes"—with supporting players, if desired—from the life of the great star under consideration. Seven "yesses"—out of a possible nine from the founders—"*if* Rita Hayworth gets here in time," she complained only to Billy Jack—would bestow the supreme accolade of Dead Movie Star.

Sighs of ambition rose pleadingly to the ceiling.

"Now previews!" Lady Star tantalized. "This evening we will have two thrilling firsts, auditions for two of the greatest

female movie stars ever! And we have with us a most distinguished special guest!" Lady Star motioned toward the back
now, to an older woman, in her fifties, who looked down into
her lap. Seeming out of place, she wore a dark blue dress. "We
may inspire her to address us in the course of this memorable
evening. Darlings! She was actually there when *it* happened,"
she added suspense.

Sandra? . . . At the same moment that Normalyn turned to
look at her, the older woman adjusted her glasses to peer at
her. There was a sudden flutter of the woman's hands, as if
she were deciding whether or not to signal.

Lady Star captured the exchange. "We *may* have other
surprises."

Normalyn did not flinch.

Lady Star intoned grandly, "Darlings! Some advice. Speak
distinctly. Don't be tongue-tied; don't wave your hands about
like *this*. Make gentle, flowing, gestures—*smooth*. Don't chew
the scenery, don't shout or split our ears, don't clown to get
some easy laughs, don't overdo your scenes. But don't be
timid, either. Allow the tragic lives you'll be exploring to be
your inspiration. And let this be your guide: We're here to
find the secret truths." She paused then added, ". . . darlings!"

Then she called the first mighty name.

"The petitioner for Judy Garland!"

Errol Flynn questioned the chubby girl: "When did you try
to kill yourself the first time, how old, why?"

"Fourteen, because I was lonesome," the plump girl answered.

"Wrong!" flung Errol Flynn. "Judy was twenty-eight; MGM
had just dumped her because she was getting fat."

The girl protested, "I really did try to kill myself when I was
fourteen. Look." She raised scarred wrists.

Lady Star meted out harsh judgment: "You are not tragic
nor glamorous, just fat and neurotic. We recommend you seek
help elsewhere for both maledictions."

"Maladies?" wondered Veronica Lake.

"Can I try out for Greta Garbo?" the petitioner pleaded.

"Petitioner for Marlon Brando!" Lady Star wiped the girl
aside.

The youngman, in ripped tank top, hardly shreds, had
bleached spiked hair, knotty muscles.

"Do we think Brando's, uh, dead?" James Dean consulted.

Lady Star knifed him with a look.

"Present evidence of worthiness!" Billy Jack barked at the
petitioner.

The petitioner for Marlon Brando told of a deprived childhood marked by one single joy: "—playing my harmonica by the river."

Betty Grable placed the matter on firmer ground: "Why did you really flee to Tahiti and become a mess?"

"Huh? Well, uh— . . . Huh?"

Marlon Brando grew old, and his soul remained beautiful, Miss Bertha whispered to Normalyn. *And Judy? What can these creatures do to Judy?*

"Gong!" James Dean led the banishment.

The petitioner walked up to him, drawing gasps. "I'll just have to make damn sure your car crashes, motherfucker, and then I'll fuckin' take *your* place."

"Try it now if you can get your finger out of your ass, shit-face," James Dean spoke clearly.

"Malcontents," Hedy Lamarr sighed.

Otto hauled out the threatening petitioner.

Lady Star spoke the next name with a tip of distaste; Billy Jack had been *adamant* about this inclusion: "The petitioner for Jayne Mansfield!"

Hair a spray of bleached waves, a tittering youngwoman in a clutching dress bent forward. Amid whistles from a contingent of "reformed bikers"—Veronica Lake identified them knowledgeably—Billy Jack sex-growled at the petitioner, "Prove those fuckers are real!"

Nipples of enormous breasts escaped. Billy Jack and Errol Flynn led applause. Tyrone Power yawned.

Lady Star blinked twice in disapproval.

Tyrone Power tested the petitioner: "What did you and Mr. Universe *do* in your pink bedroom every Friday night for three hours?"

"Posed stark naked in the mirror!"

Billy Jack and Errol Flynn led a burst of approving cheers from reformed bikers.

"That," Lady Star squelched, "is neither glamorous nor tragic, petitioner! Stars were *always* dressed in their glamour. Rejected." She relied on impetus.

"Rejected!" Veronica Lake touched small, proud breasts.

"Rejected," Betty Grable issued.

"Out!" lashed Hedy Lamarr. Then Lady Star, Veronica Lake, Betty Grable, and Hedy Lamarr glared at Tyrone Power, who, with an indifferent shrug, banished the petitioner.

The youngwoman cupped her breasts at the rejecters. "You're jealous of *these*!"

Betty Grable challenged her back.

A hefty male supporting player offered the rejected petitioner "private auditions" as Otto escorted her out eagerly.

With dignity and firmness, Lady Star subdued the crowd: "If this irrelevance continues—"

"—irreverence," Veronica Lake sighed.

"—if this continues, we will not hesitate to take drastic measures—like removing the culpits from the hall!"

"Culprits."

"The petitioner for Pola Negri!" Lady Star restored order.

A spectral figure in mourning glided forth.

"Tell us about you and Hitler!" Betty Grable was on her toes.

"I only prepared for Valentino's funeral," came the plaintive voice behind the shroud.

"Questions!" Lady Star unleashed the panel.

Billy Jack barraged: "Were you ashamed as a kid cause you were so damn skinny? Did your fuckin' old man whip you while you were naked and your sisters watched?"

"Did, uh, *yours*?" a baffled James Dean inquired of Billy Jack, who sat back in sudden moody silence.

To strengthen her diminishing resolve for remaining here, Normalyn glanced back at the older woman, who almost raised her hand as if in greeting.

The petitioner in mourning quivered. "I *do* have a secret. I'm the Madonna of Sorrows. I had a vision on Hollywood Boulevard just earlier. She told me to come here and tell you to erect a chapel in her name at—"

"I just knew we'd start getting the religious nuts, with all those suicides we've been taking." Hedy Lamarr softened her gorgeous hair.

Otto led the protesting figure out.

Rita Hayworth dashed into the basement, up the platform. "Sorry I'm late, guys. My mom's dying. Who's out?"

Billy Jack filled her in.

"The petitioner for Marlene Dietrich!"

"She's not dead," a male voice from among the supporting players reminded. "Neither is Brando."

Veronica Lake identified the intrusive voice as that of a "punker."

"And he's all *right*!" Betty Grable assured.

"They. Are. Dead. When. You. Think. They. Are." Lady Star engraved each word with acid. "Where the hell is Dietrich?"

"Here!" A tall body with a top hat, a tuxedo jacket, tight shorts, sleek stockings, spiked heels, and legs wide apart conquered an aisle.

"Who was Ferde?" Tyrone Power shot.

"He was my insane husband," the deep voice declared. Ambushed by ridiculing looks, the petitioner gambled for unimpeachability: "I read it in Mildred Meadows's column."

At the mention of Mildred Meadows, there was a long inhaled sigh, released as a gasp of rage into the ensuing silence. It came from the older woman.

"You're bluffing," Tyrone Power reprimanded. "We don't like that. Ferde was the owner of a French dyke bar."

Hedy Lamarr leaned toward the petitioner. "More to the point, Dietrich is not a man, and *you* are!"

If she focused on these mean distortions, she might shove back her urgent pain. In Normalyn's mind, Kirk was receding into a shadow, as if he had carried death all along. His muscles had not concealed his sorrow, in her new memory of him. At this moment, Troja was probably bunched in pain, alone, but if—

"The Divine Joan Crawford!" Lady Star called, and warned the square-lipped, square-shouldered petitioner, "Don't dare rant about what that awful daughter claims."

Removing shoulder padding, the petitioner adjusted to perceived antagonism. "I've changed my mind, I want to petition for Hedy Lamarr. She was filmed in the nude!"

"Some secret," sighed Rita Hayworth, fussing with long, orange fingernails.

"You've got your nerve!" Hedy Lamarr introduced herself to the petitioner.

The youngwoman remained as a fan.

"The petitioner for Valentino," Lady Star summoned.

A sinister youngman held a shiny black cylinder. "This is the dildo I gave Manuel Dante. He was murdered with it."

"Are you auditioning for Manuel Dante or Valentino?" Lady Star had already decided—neither. The others agreed.

The petitioner raised the dildo and his middle finger at the panel. He was shoved out by Otto for disrespect to the founders.

With dizzying swiftness, the petitioner for John Derek, aided by a dazzling overlay of added eyelashes, almost became the evening's first Dead Movie Star, with a secret so sensational no one even attempted to verify it. He created confusion when, heady with success, he offered to petition also for Shaun Calhoun.

Lady Star was aghast: "You cannot hope to be *two* Dead Movie Stars; that's schizofrantic."

"—phrenic," Veronica Lake clarified to herself.

"Yeah, well, just wait until you hear what I discovered about

Shaun Calhoun." The again-petitioner was cocky. "His *only* movie—in a *bit* part—drew over eighty thousand letters. He was murdered by Mae Barton, the cosmetic heiress; she bet Tony Mora, the big Vegas gambler, a hundred thousand dollars that she'd be the one to make Shaun break his promise to be faithful forever to his dead twin sister."

"Everyone knows that," Billy Jack reminded.

"But *was* he faithful?" Rita Hayworth was impatient to affirm the endurability of true love.

"No—because Tony Mora seduced him first. And *that's* why Mae Barton killed him. And I know even better stuff about John Smith, another of Wilson's boys. He—"

"You are disqualified as *everyone!*" Lady Star spoke for the panel. With unblemished poise, she moved on:

"The petitioner for Alan Ladd!"

Jim! Normalyn almost-hoped. No, the sailor who loved Miss Bertha would not fit in this arena of cruelty. When she saw him again—and she would—she would tell him how much handsomer and taller he was than this petitioner.

Betty Grable snapped her fingers at the good-looking dark youngman: "Why'd you finally O.D.?"

"Because my old man and my old lady wouldn't stay off my fuckin' back, man," the petitioner yelled. Voted out, he shouted at Veronica Lake, "Hey, Rosa! Remember me, babe? Pete Mendoza? From Valley High?"

In horror, Veronica Lake aimed emphatic words at the giggling panel and congregation: "I have *never* in my *entire* life seen this *awful* creature, much less at some place called Valley High!" She demanded, "Doesn't anyone have a decent scandal tonight?"

"I'm pregnant and on probation," offered a trembly girl.

Lady Star throttled the tiny tragedy by calling for: "The petitioner for Frances Farmer!"

Pretty, disheveled, she became an easy pretender. "My mother committed me to an asylum, where I was raped and—"

An older woman rushed down the hall.

"Mother!" the pretender exclaimed.

"Oh, oh," Rita Hayworth empathized.

The woman pulled the girl brusquely out of the dark hall. "You won't get out *this* time!"

"Was she a supporting player?" Errol Flynn wanted to know.

They waited for the girl and the woman to return. They didn't.

"The petitioner for Nash McHugh!" Lady Star pushed away
the disturbing moments.

"Nash McHugh was a spy for the goddamned commies,"
said the youngman, "and his lover molested little—"

Protest, dearheart!

"That's a goddamned lie!" Normalyn stood up. "Mildred
Meadows made all that up! They were both decent men." And
Enid loved Mark Poe.

Applause at the passionate outburst came from the older
woman.

Lady Star smiled slyly at Normalyn.

Lips pressed tight, Normalyn sat down.

The petitioner for Nash McHugh was banished when he
offered to avoid controversy and petition for John Wayne.

Yes, some "fans" lay in wait to crucify the stars, pay them
back for loving them. Miss Bertha had said that to Normalyn.
She was seeing that here, how easily brutality posed as adulation as the Dead Movie Stars and the candidates raked over
the real tragedies of Lupe Velez, her many loves—cowboys,
stuntmen, hangers-on, one of whom made her pregnant, made
her choose to die . . . Montgomery Clift, seeking temporary
surcease in darkened sex-rooms, hiding his dying soul . . .
Linda Darnell, once as beautiful as a dark jewel, then aging,
alone, watching her old films on television when she was
consumed by fire . . . Johnny Weissmuller, hospitalized,
senile, tangled in the darkest jungle of his mind and still
howling like Tarzan . . . Karen Stone, buying sex, thinking
it was love, buying death . . . Tab Hunter, judged guilty
because he had not remained "a boy, a beautiful blond boy"
forever . . . Gene Tierney, seeking lost pieces of her fragile
beauty. . . .

But they survive, dearheart. They survive!

2

"And now!"—Lady Star had clearly prepared for this
moment—"for the first time in the history of the Dead Movie
Stars, we have allowed a petitioner for . . . Verna La Maye!"

Mesmerized awe hushed the room.

The petitioner was almost translucent. She wore a pale dress
of scarves embroidered with breaths of beads. She was barefoot, a delicate martyr. In a voice athrob with hope, she said
only, "I want *life!*"

Her unanimous elevation to pretender was greeted by cheers

from the assembled. "Proceed as Pretender of Verna La Maye!"
Lady Star exhaled.

The Pretender of Verna La Maye spoke in cadenced sighs,
now saddened, now on the brink of ecstasy, now soaring
beyond it and deep into despair: "I was born into the lap of
wealth. The family chauffeur kidnapped me. The truth came
out: *He* was my father, in love with me! My mother killed
herself. My grandmother banished me in revenge. With my
first film, I reached dizzying heights of stardom! Then! . . .
Mayhem, drugs, unspeakable orgies!" She breathed doom into
the hall: "And stalking murder."

Betty Grable defied the quickly woven trance: "Were you a
lesbian?" she tested slyly.

To the hushed audience, the pretender directed the great
star's famous words: "Lesbian? What is lesbian? I adore flesh!
I adore the sight of flesh, the odor of flesh, the touch of flesh!
I adore bodies! I know not *gender!*" Her own flesh shone in
silver rivulets under the drapes of her dress.

Applause led by Betty Grable, sustained by Hedy Lamarr!

"Yes!" Lady Star voted. With enthralled agreement from
the entire panel, the pretender was transformed into—

"—the Contender for Verna La Maye!" Lady Star exulted.
"Proceed with scenes!"

Envying, admiring sighs.

The Contender for Verna La Maye bowed her head. In the
dim penumbra of light, a menacing figure stood up.

"I walked naked in the moonlight, I laughed and thrilled
and lived!" The contender's hands flew up, reaching for invisible stars, creating them with grasping fingers. "Because I
knew that doom was stalking me."

"It was your *grandmother* who was stalking you." Tyrone
Power displayed his own knowledge of the famous tragedy.

"*She* killed you; then she killed herself," Errol Flynn
reminded.

The Contender for Verna La Maye shook her head. She
pointed a glittery finger at—

—the lurking figure! He stepped out of shadows—a youngman
wearing an elegant dress!

"I was in my bath." The contender approached terror. "In
my foyer, three men and three women waited, with arms full
of orchids, for me to choose whom I would possess—devour
hungrily—for that night, in my despair to live. At the same
moment, *he* entered . . . so silently."

The youngman removed the dress, stood now in men's
clothes.

"He took one of my silk stockings sent daily by Prince Fernand and—" She unclasped her hand, releasing a stocking so light it surrendered only slowly to the floor.

"He wrapped it about my neck!"

The youngman tightened the stocking about the girl's neck.

She collapsed. The youngman knelt over her. He kissed her in a long, tragic farewell. Dissolving into shadows, he left behind— . . . an aging book, a journal.

Within gasping silence, the contender rose solemnly. Her whisper echoed in the hall: "I was murdered by a man, a fan obsessed with my great beauty, longing to possess me entirely by taking my life. He killed my grandmother and made it appear like suicide; he stole her clothes and assured he would be seen as her pretending to hide."

"Ahhh," Lady Star sighed.

Billy Jack broke his own trance: "Verify your secret!"

The contender bent to the floor, retrieved the abandoned book. In beautiful jeweled hands, she held out to the panel the aging pages. "This is the lost diary of Helmut Franz, my killer. It was given to my mother, by her mother, who loved Franz and kept his secret until he died," the youngwoman spoke momentarily as herself. Then as Contender for Verna La Maye, she turned to exhibit the confessional journal to the congregation. She placed it on the floor, at her bare feet. She looped jeweled, glittering fingers.

"Glamour and tragedy linked forever in one moment of warped but encompassing love, and I was dead at twenty-three."

The Dead Movie Stars inundated her with a flood of "yeses," joined by many in the audience.

Inhaling for all to hear, Lady Star announced to the contender, "You are now . . . a Dead Movie Star." She waited for the enormity to be perceived within quivers of silence. "Welcome . . . Verna La Maye!"

Adulation! Resentment! Loud applause from the audience as Verna La Maye mounted the platform of power.

And so they had finally asked for evidence. But the book could have been any yellowing book, Normalyn noticed. And there was still—

"What about me!" The loud demand smashed the mood of fascination over the ascension of Verna La Maye. The words had been spoken by the youngman who had played the murderer in disguise.

"I vote no!" Verna La Maye snapped at him.

"Supporting players are not allowed consideration," Lady

Star informed the youngman. "You merely touched glamour, brought about tragedy; you should be grateful!"

"That's right," Verna La Maye agreed.

"Treacherous bitch!" the youngman said to the newly born Verna La Maye. "I'll tell your mother *everything!*"

"Go ahead!" challenged Verna La Maye. "She won't give a fuck. What's more you can screw her."

The youngman held the delicate stocking, an end in each fist. "I'll kill you for that, cunt! I'm gonna wrap this around your skinny neck and—" He twisted the stocking into a knot before Otto dragged him, resisting and shouting, out of the hall.

The girl on the panel looked frightened.

There was silence in the basement of the church.

Normalyn felt cold in the sweaty basement.

"Petitioner for Victor Mature!" Lady Star ended the interlude with a quickly dismissed petitioner, and two others.

"And now!" she intoned. "For the first time in the great history of the Dead Movie Stars we have allowed a petitioner for—" Her look held on Normalyn.

Did she really expect her to protest— . . . ? What? Normalyn felt tension without object.

"—for the star some would say was the most glamorous, the most tragic, the greatest movie star of all!" Lady Star paused . . . paused . . . paused. "Marilyn . . . Monroe."

Even the clammy air in the enclosed hall seemed to sigh.

3

"Petitioner!" Lady Star summoned.

Before the panel, the pretty youngwoman who had sat behind Normalyn did not look like the great star; but the star's outline was so powerful itself, so defining of the great creation, that the evoked presence quieted the gathering.

A signaling cough made Normalyn turn toward the older woman. The woman shook her head—No—at the petitioner. Then with a slightly raised hand she greeted Normalyn, and smiled.

The Petitioner for Marilyn Monroe froze in a pose before the panel.

Lady Star hurriedly announced that "because of impressive *advance* qualifications, darlings," the petitioner was being allowed to become a contender.

So easily—without being tested as pretender! A current of

resentment, surprise—and anticipation—zinged through the basement of the Thrice-Blessed Church.

Signaling shocking withdrawal of all preliminary support, Lady Star hissed at the blonde pretender, "What secret can *you* possibly tell us about the Great Monroe!"

In the breathy stammer of a hurt girl, the Contender for Marilyn Monroe said, "I h-h-had a daughter."

Twenty-Nine

"Beware, contender!" Lady Star's voice was ominous. "You will have to present evidence, evidence, evidence! Sources, sources, sources!" Her onslaught of warnings announced the evening's closest scrutiny. "*And*! You will have to name names!" she pummeled.

"But *you* t-t-told me—" the sudden contender stammered in bewilderment. Her hands trembled like dying butterflies.

"You are on your own . . . *darling*!" Lady Star decreed. Billy Jack and Veronica Lake nodded solemnly.

Shot down and left to flounder! Yet they had elevated her without examination, Normalyn evaluated. In days preceding auditions, they had praised the girl, perhaps provided guidance. At the same time that Normalyn felt sorry for the youngwoman abandoned in abrupt hostility, she was relieved that the contender's startling declaration had been pushed aside. Warm blood coursed through Normalyn's body, which had frozen when the contender declared her "secret." Still, the mere announcement had been so bold that the words echoed in the webby shadows of the basement of the Thrice-Blessed Church of the Redeemer.

"And, contender!" Lady Star piled dour warnings: "Be aware that there just might be someone who will challenge *anything* you claim!"

Who did she mean? She herself, Lady Star? Others of the "knowledgeable" Dead Movie Stars? The older woman—of course. Certainly Lady Star was not counting on *her*, Normalyn, to be the challenger.

319

"Proceed!" Lady Star barked at the contender.

"I-I-I was born out of w-w-wedlock," the contender was able, barely, to gasp.

"Now *that's* what I call a secret," Veronica Lake sneered.

"She, uh, got the, uh, s-s-stutter almost right," James Dean contributed.

The confused congregation suspected giggles were being invited. Some rowdy "ex-punkers" tested laughter.

Normalyn deduced quickly in order to prepare her reactions: By tossing the contender into the thickest area of interrogation, the Dead Movie Stars had also placed her closest to achieving the longed-for goal of Dead Movie Star. A gamble to heighten tension—and to push any protester—her?—to act impulsively, compete for "truth," assert *herself* as the real candidate!

Or as the star's daughter!

That thought hurled itself at Normalyn. If from these auditions there should emerge the bare suggestion that she might be the great star's daughter, that would guarantee the Dead Movie Stars serious validity as revealers of "glamorous" scandal. A startling revelation would bring them what they yearned for most—"*stardom!*" And it would end her hope to live her own life. Normalyn searched the basement for any "outside" presence, summoned secretly. No, the Dead Movie Stars could not risk such scrutiny at this point. Too much could go wrong within the loose rules of "auditions."

The contender went on in her frightened voice: "I was in and out of h-h-homes, never adopted."

The "guest," the older woman, moved her folding chair a row ahead.

"Who doesn't know that?" Billy Jack taunted.

Lady Star pretended to conceal an endless yawn. Her foot tapped an unnerving message of gathering impatience.

Now the blonde contender looked only like a schoolgirl with bleached hair, tacky heavy makeup, and an exaggerated beauty spot. Fresh, she had appeared good in the glow of the borrowed outline. "I worked in an airplane factory," she offered.

"Oh, *no!*" Betty Grable reacted in mock surprise. "Really?"

But what would have roused their suspicions that an association existed between herself and the movie star? Normalyn continued her hurried inner evaluation. She had conveyed only a vapory knowledge of some relationship between Enid and the star. Still, she was at the center of interest for at least some of the panel. Just watch how Lady Star—and Billy Jack and Veronica Lake—kept forcing her to acknowledge their stares. No. All they wanted was a reasonable contender for Marilyn Monroe, and she, Normalyn, had come to them bearing the sharp imprints of the star, she dismissed it all.

"I was raped when I w-w-was eight!" the contender was desperately grasping for shock.

"You're the only one who's just discovering *that!*" Errol Flynn sneered.

Normalyn tried to erase Ted from her mind now.

"I always wanted ch-ch-children," said the contender and followed her words with a yearning sigh.

"But!" Lady Star's accusing finger shot out at her. "You couldn't have any, *could you?* Because you had an operation, *didn't you?* And having children was impossible, *wasn't it?*"

"But I had *another* operation that made it possible again. Really." The contender's voice edged toward pleading.

The older woman in the dark dress cleared her throat for attention. "That's true."

This time Normalyn did not want to invite further contact between herself and the woman.

Lady Star allowed the moment its full impact. "So!" she said to the contender. "You *did* know that. Well, so did we, and so did our wonderful, *wonderful* guest. *We* were testing *you!*" she told the contender. Holding her orchid in place, she led a glissade of laughter. "As contender for the immortal Monroe, you must anticipate closest scrutiny."

Which had not been given to Verna La Maye, nor to John Derek when he had been briefly elevated to contender. Normalyn recognized more evidence of specialized manipulation of *this* contender.

"Everyone knows about the two operations," Rita Hayworth underscored.

"My grandmother tried to s-s-smother me when I was three," the contender tried valiantly.

Oh, who had borrowed that from whose life? Enid? The movie star? Normalyn's mind drifted to her own questions because her expectations of learning anything from the contender were fading.

The contender no longer attempted to pose in curves as she recited like a miserable student before a teacher determined to reprove: "I married a guy who went in the n-n-navy—"

Errol Flynn asked the contender, "Where the hell'dya get your scoops—the public library?"

The congregation, unleashed to heckle, applauded Errol Flynn's wit.

"We! Know! All! That!" Tyrone Power sneered at the contender.

Now James Dean slumped, Betty Grable coiled the same curl of hair over and over, Tyrone Power moistened his lashes with saliva, Verna La Maye explored her frail hands, Hedy Lamarr soothed one wayward hair, Rita Hayworth freshened her lips. Veronica Lake became utterly fascinated with the ceiling. Billy Jack added blood to the tombstone on his chest, with Rita Hayworth's lipstick. Lady Star propped her wearied head on her palms.

But they were not moving to banish the contender with a call for votes, the way they had with others all night. Because they had not achieved their goal with *her*, Normalyn deduced.

Even the sequins on her dress abdicated their glitter to beads of sweat on the contender's face as she withered, withered, proceeding doggedly: "Once, I tried to locate the man my m-m-mother said was my f-f-father. I telephoned him, and he denied it. He told me never to call him again."

A hot coldness enclosed Normalyn's body. *She* had called Stan Smith, whom *she* had suspected might be her father, and *he* had denied it, demanded she leave him alone. *She had relived that!*—coaxed by—

David Lange.

All was swept for Normalyn with deeper suspicion. Did she detect in this basement the invisible presence of David Lange?

Coincidence! she told herself forcefully. David had explained *everything*!

"Why are we letting her waste our time?" Hedy Lamarr demanded.

"Search me," offered Tyrone Power.

Rita Hayworth, Errol Flynn, and Betty Grable wondered, too.

In angry answer, Lady Star leaned over the table to glower at Normalyn. Veronica Lake and Billy Jack joined the stare.

Just cross your arms over your chest, dearheart, and stare them down! . . . Normalyn did both.

The contender stood frozen before the panel.

This contender obviously knew nothing. Normalyn would stay only to discover why they needed her and to learn who the older woman was.

Unnerved by the stasis, her orchid dangling dangerously over one ear, Lady Star screamed at the contender, "Well, go on, *darling*! Don't you know *anything*? Nothing? Nothing at all?"

"You are *so* wrong, Lady Star!"

Lady Star's orchid fainted on the table.

At the contender's bold words, scattered gasps emerged out of currents of excitement rushing through the congregated.

Facing Lady Star and the panel, the Contender for Marilyn Monroe curved her body, slowly, part by part. She rounded her shoulders, softly. She let fall, casually, one of the straps from her dress, which, suddenly enamored, hugged her body. With quick fingers she rearranged the blonde hair into soft tilts, courting sprinkled highlights. She reddened her parted lips bold-red. Out of nowhere, she brought forth a pair of dazzling earrings, slowly putting one on her right ear—a cluster of tiny stars! She tilted her head and attached another gathered burst of stars to the left ear. She touched a moist finger to the beauty mark on her cheek. Tension dissolved, nervousness fell as, before all eyes, she reasserted the magical outline of the great star as if she had been acting before . . .

. . . or as if she was just now beginning to! Normalyn wondered which.

The puzzled look on Lady Star's face confirmed her amazement—and found reflection in Billy Jack, Veronica Lake, the others.

Looking stern, serious, the older woman moved her seat closer to the clearing and the panel.

In a breathy voice, the Contender for Marilyn Monroe said, "What I just told you is the biography *everyone* knows—the evolution of an insecure girl." She addressed the audience: "but I *do* know . . . secrets."

The assemblage was in her hands.

"Do you want to know what really happened when I met the President of the United States . . . *and* his brother? Do you want to know about my last pregnancy? And the elaborate plan to allow me to have my child? Do you want to know what *really* happened in those fateful last days of my life?"

"Yes!" shouted Billy Jack—and all the Dead Movie Stars except Lady Star swayed in affirmation toward the contender.

Otto drew wooden shutters across the ground-level windows of the basement so that light would not seep in nor out.

Lady Star managed a twisted smile. She looked down at her orchid, held it, studied it, put it back firmly in her hair. "Proceed," she said to the contender.

The evening had veered into the unexpected. Normalyn felt

trapped in multiple realities, dreams, fantasies, interpretations, reflections on reflections—all banishing her life?

Almost imperceptibly, from the ranks of supporting players, four figures emerged to stand and wait in the shadows to make their entrances: Two youngmen; a youngwoman wearing a gray wig so that she could appear older; and another youngwoman, holding a cigarette lighter in her hand, revealed when, for a moment, it transformed vagrant light into a tiny sparkle of silver.

The Contender for Marilyn Monroe began:

"And now! In narrative and scenes! The Epic Tragedy of the Last Days in the Life of Marilyn Monroe! And! The Creation of a Legend!"

Thirty

Norma Jeane Mortenson was born at 9:30 A.M., June 1, 1926, at Los Angeles General Hospital. She was baptized Norma Jeane Baker, on December 6, 1926, by the flashy evangelist Aimée Semple McPherson. At the time of Norma Jeane's birth, her mother, Gladys Pearl Mortenson, had long been divorced from her first husband, Jack Baker, a gas station attendant, and separated from Edward Mortenson, a roaming baker, who one day had jumped on his motorcycle and fled, denying he had ever fathered a child. Gladys later introduced Norma Jeane to her "real father" by showing her a photograph of a somewhat rakish man, a salesman. "He was— " Those were the only words Gladys ever provided about the man she had probably loved. To Norma Jeane, he looked "just like Clark Gable." He, too, years later when she telephoned him, denied she was his daughter.

Norma Jeane's early years were spent near Los Angeles in the City of Hawthorne, then a scattering of flat stucco houses among vacant lots and wildflowers. It was not far from the ocean, which Norma Jeane called "the deep wet."

Because Gladys worked—as a studio film-cutter in Hollywood —she paid a trusted "foster family" five dollars a week to care for her daughter in Hawthorne. Still in her twenties, a pretty woman whose red hair fascinated Norma Jeane, Gladys had begun to feel an anguished restlessness because life had not even begun giving her what was her due: some stability, some happiness, much love—longings her daughter would inherit. Gladys had two commendable goals: to buy a pretty house for

325

herself and her daughter, and to marry a man who really loved her and would be a father to her child. Norma Jeane saw "the pretty lady with beautiful red hair" only on weekends. There was one exception, which Norma Jeane cherished forever, a time when she was sick and Gladys stayed with her "every single moment for three entire weeks until she was sure I was well." Thereafter Norma Jeane adored the red-haired lady who came to visit.

Gladys took the child to the beach for cherished picnics. Sheltering her fair skin from the sun, Gladys would nevertheless play on the sand with her daughter. Then, the mother would lie on the child's lap, looking up longingly into the sky while Norma Jeane stroked the wondrous red hair. Often, they went to the movies, which thrilled Norma Jeane, especially when they trekked into Hollywood to the Egyptian Theater: Norma Jeane would stand for minutes to admire its elaborate sunburst ceiling.

In 1933, Gladys achieved one of her goals: She bought a two-story house in Hollywood. It had a Georgian portico, and it was one of the handsomest homes along Highland Avenue. She bought a piano for Norma Jeane. To assure making her payments on the house, Gladys rented a portion of it to an English couple, who often looked after Norma Jeane when Gladys was out trying to accomplish her second goal.

On a drizzly day in January 1934, during an interlude of relentless lashing rain, Norma Jeane's life was altered forever. That was when she began to suspect that she had a terrible legacy, a legacy of madness—"the blackness, the darkness," she came to call it. There had been hints of it before that day, periods when Gladys would be so depressed she could utter not a single word, act as if she did not even see her daughter. Then she might become hysterically happy, once insisting on teaching Norma Jeane "how to sing like Ginger Rogers *and* Fred Astaire."

Years earlier there had been a violent indication of fears to come. Norma Jeane's grandmother, Della, who the child claimed had attempted to smother her at age one, a time of hallucinations and vague memories, had been carried away screaming to Norwalk State Hospital, her hands bloodied from aimless pounding on the wall. Della threw back her head—the sky was *so* strangely calm. Then she screamed.

Gladys watched that, holding Norma Jeane's hand so tightly—to keep the child from breaking away—that the young girl's fingers ached for days. Later, Norma Jeane would remember thinking then that Gladys was "passing something on" to her.

On that rainy day in January, Norma Jeane remembered her grandmother's screams. Gladys had just announced to the English couple that she felt "too ill, much too ill" to go to work at the studio. That was a rare occurrence. She could not define her illness. The rain, she said, was depressing her. She would hum a tune, then stop abruptly and look out the window, seeing desolate sheets of water wash the glass panes. When Norma Jeane left for school, bundled under an enormous orange raincoat, Gladys was reapplying her makeup, at first gaily, then angrily, over and over and over before a mirror—erasing it, starting again.

She began moving impatiently from room to room, opening doors, staring in. "What are you looking for, Gladys?" the English woman asked her. "A place to hide!" she answered. She huddled, trembling, under the staircase, the darkest place she could locate. Frightened, the couple called for an ambulance. When attendants arrived, Gladys battled them with raging ferocity. They strapped her to a stretcher. She shut her eyes tightly to banish the whole darkening world.

Norma Jeane arrived home to see her mother being taken away to Norwalk State Hospital, where Della had died of a heart attack after a violent seizure.

After that, Gladys was in and out of institutions, at times admitting herself. She alternately loved and ignored Norma Jeane—and refused to give her up to adoption. So, at age nine, Norma Jeane came to feel that she had become "someone else"—an "orphan"—because while Gladys moved in and out of the "blackness," the child drifted through orphanages and foster homes, treated not unkindly in some at times, in others abused. In one foster home she was raped. In all of those places, she felt "temporary": "Every day was a *new* eternity that could end suddenly and begin *another* one; I thought I was the only person in the world who felt this awful; so I didn't tell anyone because they wouldn't understand what I was talking about and they'd get mad at me."

Times of "stability" lessened, the times when Gladys was out of an institution and brought "lots of love, and took it away when she left soon after," leaving once for twelve years.

Along the way Norma Jeane learned to entertain by singing "Jesus Loves Me." "But I didn't believe it," she confided later. "I never believed Jesus loved me; I just liked the tune and it pleased everybody."

At age eleven she went to live with a friend of her mother's.

In school, she was outstanding in English. At sixteen, she married—the first of three marriages, three divorces. The following year she rehearsed the first of many suicide attempts.

An ordinary, blandly pretty girl with pleasant open features, Norma Jeane changed her name to Marilyn Monroe. Marilyn Monroe bleached Norma Jeane's hair blonde, then platinum blonde. She narrowed her nose, strengthened the chin through surgery, erasing the outlines of Norma Jeane's features. She turned the girl's nervous stutter into a sighed whisper by substituting a sexy breath where the stutter would be. She converted Norma Jeane's self-conscious walk into a sequence of sensual movements, punctuated by a careful pause, which allowed them finally to flow into a masterpiece of motion. The girl's lips had parted to cry, to attempt to protest, to smile anxiously; now they parted, just parted, crimson, the cry, the protest, the anxious smile shaping a wordless invitation on her beautiful lips.

Marilyn Monroe became a movie star.

One characteristic remained, the girl's look of bewilderment at constant loss and rejection, a startled violated innocence, which, melding with the practiced look of knowledgeability of the experienced woman she became, gave her the appearance of a wounded sexual angel.

*   *   *

Normalyn sat quietly, trying to think of nothing, nothing at all. But she could not push this away: Enid had at first given her the same birthday as Norma Jeane's—June 1.

With darting eyes, Lady Star pinned the Contender for Marilyn Monroe. The crooked smile on Lady Star's face remained in askew admiration. She had to consider what was occurring among the other Dead Movie Stars and among the audience—fascinated, bruised petitioners chafing in exile but still longing to return another time. A careless move might shift loyalties.

The Contender for Marilyn Monroe signaled with the tilt of one raised hand. Two youngmen moved into the clearing of light. One faced her. The other remained waiting a distance away.

The contender announced, "The last tragic days of my life began in 1960 when—"

*   *   *

—John, Robert, and their father, Joseph P. Kennedy, arrived in Los Angeles to attend the Democratic Convention that would nominate the next President of the United States.

The brothers stayed in separate suites at the Beverly Hills Hotel, layer upon layer of shiny windows. The old man borrowed a mansion from Marion Davies.

Soon after, John F. Kennedy stood movingly before jubilant crowds at the Los Angeles Coliseum and asked the country to fulfill its rich potential on "a new frontier . . . of unknown opportunities and perils." His call for "pioneers" into the new age stirred the hearts and minds of a thrilled generation. Instantly John F. Kennedy became a symbol of the noblest instincts in the country.

That night, at a party given by Peter Lawford in his Mediterranean villa to celebrate John's nomination, Senator John Kennedy drank a daiquiri, a superb one, concocted just for him—with the exact breath of lime, not lemon—by the head bartender rented from Romanoff's Restaurant for the occasion. The Senator was trying to separate himself for a few quiet moments to nurse his voice. Had he sounded convincing earlier in his acceptance speech? He meant what he said. He wanted the country to rebel against the injustices he saw entrenching poverty, exploitation, bigotry. He thought he had seen the grim face of such injustice—for a split second it flashed as judgment in the opulent villa—on a recent tour of coal-mine country. He had seen grim men with blackened dust-wrecked faces; and one of their women, all angular bones and coarsened flesh, exhorted him, *"Remember us!"* And he would, he swore, he would. He remembered her now, knowing that the nation had too long cultivated the ancient roots of injustice, ignoring the tender grapes of justice. "The big foxes that spoil the grapes—" That phrase had recurred in his mind. He had wanted to use it in his acceptance speech, but the metaphor did not fit into the imagery of a "new frontier." He wondered now whether that had been the reason he had hesitated or whether— . . . His father was greeting guests— John saw him, so sure—roaming the villa as if he owned it.

John Kennedy was aware of the irony, the paradox, of his father's wealth, his own, and his championing of the dispossessed. Oh, he enjoyed his wealth, what it could buy, like others who have known it all their lives; but unlike his father, John did not desire more, still more and more. All his life he had seen such men, dominated by greed. He was sure of this: He wanted to give some back! He never admitted this, but he felt that he and his brothers must do "social penance" for the excesses of their father's anxious capitalism.

In this palazzo once owned by Louis B. Mayer, John had been gravitating closer to an oval glass window in the large room. He didn't realize that until he was staring outside. The frontier of night, land's end, he thought. If he had been born poor, he felt sure he would have been a "radical," one who would have pointed out that *his* class of "rowdy new aristocrats" represented decay on the "new frontier." The "big foxes" encouraged the "little foxes." He hated the arrogant tyrants of the steel industry. Had he managed to convey his true longings for the country? America had a potential for greatness not evoked since Franklin Delano Roosevelt. John longed to follow in his steps and not his father's.

"—most eager to discuss the state of the country with you, Senator Kennedy," said Ken Lavet, a key figure in California politics. He was introducing a woman who looked, John thought, like a beautiful silver moth!

With the slightest curtsy—she had learned it when she was introduced to the Queen of England—Marilyn Monroe said, "I'm very pleased to meet you, Mr. President."

"I'm not President yet," John smiled.

"But you will be," she promised him.

During a period when he was recovering from an operation for his troublesome back problems, John had attempted to banish the heavy hospital atmosphere by decorating his room with a Howdy Doody doll, a fish tank—he watched intently as sturdy fish zigzagged to avoid tangles of seaweeds—and a life-size poster of Marilyn Monroe in shorts. He'd pinned the picture upside down.

Thinking of that silliness for a moment, he extended his smile. He had a charming, ambiguous smile, as if always holding two thoughts simultaneously—one serious, another amused. Perhaps a premonition of his imminent doom forced on him a certain premature detachment from day-to-day events.

Marilyn Monroe was telling him earnestly how thrilled she was by the possibilities of a new frontier for human rights when Joseph Kennedy clamped one hand on the movie star's shoulder and another on his son's.

"So! You've met. Of *course!*" The old man approved. He touched his glasses, to adjust his sight for greatest clarity on the lavish movie star.

His father! Marilyn Monroe thought. She still marveled how easily fathers existed for others.

Looking at the gorgeous woman, the old man had a fantasy that he and John and— "Marilyn Monroe, I assume!"

"And *you* are . . ." She dredged her mind for the most admiring words she could say to this powerful old man. *"The father!"*

Joseph's glasses fogged. He sighed wistfully, "You are a beautiful woman, Miss Monroe." Winking approbation at his son, he moved away, slightly saddened.

Now, some would claim that there was a crucial flaw in the truly socially concerned, truly committed Kennedy brothers, and that, along with wealth, their father had passed on to them that flaw—an urgent need to be sexually satisfied, over and over, by many beautiful women in quick succession. Among Joseph's conquests were the bedazzling Gloria Swanson and, in a brief interlude, Verna La Maye. Himself a "movie fan," John had courted Gene Tierney, Sonja Heine, Rhonda Fleming, and Angie Dickinson.

John drank another daiquiri. Marilyn sipped champagne. A buried beam of light in the glass fascinated her. "Like a hidden diamond," she said to John Kennedy. But when he looked, the reflection was gone.

John delighted in the curved body of "the beautiful silver moth," and Marilyn was charmed by his ambiguous smile.

Hours later, the Senator's bodyguards, a breed sworn to protect, to give up their lives—and be quiet—saw a dazzling woman being escorted into the Senator's suite by Ken Lavet. The woman wore a blue silk cape with a cowl shading her face, but her lips stood out like a split ruby. As she passed the stony men, Marilyn imagined she was Amber St. Clare, a favorite heroine, keeping an assignation with the King.

Then Marilyn Monroe and John Kennedy were alone in the hotel room.

*   *   *

In the basement of the Thrice-Blessed Church, the two youngmen with the contender spread on the clearing before the platform and the folded chairs an elegant quilted pad, with tiny fleurs-de-lis.

The sturdier of the two youngmen said to the contender:

*   *   *

"Miss Monroe."

"Mr. President."

This time the Senator did not correct her.

She spun about. "What a beautiful, *beautiful* room!" she gasped. Immediately she heard a disturbing echo of her giddy excitement. Where had it come from? She was not really impressed by this room. She had seen rooms *much* grander than this, even movie sets. Why had she reacted—felt!—like a dazzled child?

"I'm delighted you accepted my invitation to visit," said John Kennedy.

"I'm delighted you extended it," Marilyn Monroe said.

His hand about her waist was strong and sure.

He is going to make love to me! Marilyn Monroe announced to herself. Before lovemaking, and during it, she liked to verbalize to herself—and sometimes aloud to the added arousal of her partners—what was occurring, what would occur, what was being touched on her, what she was touching. That multiplied all sensations. Now she continued to herself, I am in the arms of the man who will be the President of the country! He is touching her breasts— *My* breasts, she adjusted. She has— *I* have my arms around him. . . .

She had a feeling that someone else had entered the room. Oh, not a spy. Not anyone actually. Just a presence, like an "unreal ghost."

Somewhat clumsily John attempted to remove her dress.

It split in a long jagged line. Sequins dropped to the carpet.

"I was sewn into this dress!" She laughed the matter away.

"Will I have to sew it back on before you leave?" He bit slightly at her flesh through the tear in the dress. More sequins sprinkled her feet.

"No," she told him, "when I leave, I'll just wrap myself in my silk cape—nothing under." Letting her tongue touch the lobe every few syllables, she whispered in his ear that sometimes she went out wearing *nothing* under her fur coat.

That aroused him more.

Tearing at the seams of the dress, she let it fall to her feet. She stood on stardust. Then she picked up tiny dots of glitter and pasted them with her saliva on her naked body. She raised a lazy arm over her head, she shook her hair loose so that it cascaded in waves only on one side—she assumed the famous nude calender pose.

That aroused him even more.

When he was naked—he was a little beefier than she had imagined, but she did not mind—his hands sculpted her breasts. Tiny glittering beads scattered. Laughing, she bent to put more sequins on her fingers, to paste them on her breasts for him to admire again.

He placed one hand on her smooth shoulder.

Her narrowed, dark-lashed blue eyes looked up at him. Now into her revery came this: *She* is looking up at the man who will rule from the country's greatest home, the man who can confirm the power of Marilyn Monroe, because he has everything, everything . . . father! . . . mother! . . . father—

. . . She felt like a child, not young, just a child, a needful child, desperate to be acknowledged. And for that she must please, be approved, be *wanted*!

He raised her up.

Now *she* is lying on satin sheets with him! She resumed her revery—and realized that for the first time in her fantasies she had been thinking *she, her*, not I, *me*.

He entered her.

She tossed her head back, her body jerked with his, her mind screamed: *Norma Jeane!*

The few sequins that had remained on her body clung to the hairs on his chest, a light film of sweat.

As he lay on the rumpled bed—his mind on to the political matters of tomorrow—she put on the torn dress meant to be worn only once, by *her*. Almost all of its sequins were gone. It occurred to her—an unwelcome thought—that she looked as if she had been raped. She covered herself with the flowing blue cape. She painted her lips, slashed moist red across them. In the mirror she saw an only vaguely familiar outline.

Before she raised the cowl to conceal herself again, she stood before him, so he would ask her to come back.

He smiled a vague smile. "You gave me a pretty present for my nomination." He meant that lightly, only lightly. He could be a cool man; he was not a cruel one.

"Th-th-thank you, Mr. President," Marilyn Monroe heard Norma Jeane whisper.

*   *   *

Be brave, dearheart, listen to what you must hear!

Normalyn tried to contain rampant feelings, rampant memories of Enid.

Oh, dearheart—. . .

Not even Miss Bertha could soothe her.

Inhaling sadly, the Contender for Marilyn Monroe scattered a few gold sequins over the quilted pad on which she had lain with the sturdy youngman before the panel of Dead Movie Stars. The youngman who had played the Senator in their elaborate audition rejoined the lanky one. The dark-haired youngwoman and the woman with the perfect gray wig still waited in the shadows.

In the basement, there was silenced awe.

"And how the hell do *you* know what went on in that bedroom, darling!" Lady Star yanked attention back to the reality of the darkened basement. The contender was emerging as a powerful figure. Lady Star must move swiftly, take a risk. At her words, the panel pulled back, only slightly, from the contender; so did some among the audience.

"There are secret tapes," the contender said firmly.

"They made tapes of *my* tragic romance, too—and sold them for thousands of dollars when scandal burst," a Lana Turner petitioner remembered bitterly.

Lady Star hushed her and concentrated again on the contender: "Who heard those tapes? Who told *you* about them?"

"Who told me?" the contender swung about to face the audience. "Who told me?" Spinning about, she walked right up to Lady Star. Hands boldly planted on the silver table, she addressed Lady Star, "Who *did* tell me . . . darling?"

Normalyn understood: Lady Star *had* to supply the name, a name; otherwise, her knowledgeability would be compromised at a crucial moment when empathy was swirling about the contender. Even Billy Jack nudged Lady Star to answer. And so Lady Star did. "Mildred Meadows, of course."

"But of course," said the contender. "Who else?"

Normalyn glanced quickly back. At the mention of Mildred's name, the older woman had raised her head in resolved anger. Then she spread away, carefully, any wrinkle that might have creased her dress.

The contender had tricked Lady Star into pronouncing an unassailable name, whether or not that was her true source. This contender had moved far beyond the prescribed function allowed her, Normalyn understood, and that function was to force *her* into this arena of warring secrets and memories. She was sure of it, but for moments only.

Confidently, the Contender for Marilyn Monroe said to Lady Star, to the eager panel, to the quiet congregation, "And when he did become President, just as I predicted, I continued to see him. In New York—"

Thirty-One

—President John F. Kennedy stayed at the Carlyle Hotel. There was a private entrance available for his glamorous conquests. Marilyn Monroe was one of several. Marilyn loved the intrigue of visiting him at the hotel, ushered in by a trusted aide. She often wore a black wig in disguise. Each time now at the peak moment, her fantasy would explode into this:

She is with the President of—!

This evening, she had applied her makeup and was putting on favorite earrings, pendants of clustered diamonds, tiny stars. In the few moments allowed after their liaisons, she made herself beautiful—so that he would want her to come back. No definite day was ever set for the encounter; she was invited, later, perhaps on impulse, sudden desire. She never knew whether *this* would be a last time. Now she touched one earring, to make it glimmer for him.

"Pretty," he said absently, because he had been thinking that in the morning he would have to confront the bastards of the steel industry who were forcing up prices. He would not let the sons of bitches screw the country. And more immediately, what the hell was he going to do about Lyndon, to keep him thinking he was busy?

"—the White House."

He heard only her last reference, although he was aware that she had been talking, and he had been smiling the way he did to convey attention when there was none. The tone in her voice made him inquire, "What?"

Standing, she let the strap of her dress fall from her shoulder so that one nipple was almost exposed. Now she touched the other earring, but the light had shifted and it did not

335

shimmer. She tried to sound casual: "I just said that I have always dreamed of going—wanted to go—to the White House." In her fantasies, often, when they were making love, she imagined they *were* there and she was "protected" by the majesty of the greatest home.

He laughed softly. "Well, Miss Monroe, there are tours—"

"I meant with *you!*" her words erupted in anger.

When he saw her hurt look, he apologized. "I'm sorry, Marilyn. Truly." He had not meant to wound her, no.

When she left him this time, he kissed her on the cheek.

He was not taking her seriously! She decided she would show him she was a woman of substance. And she was, much more than she was ever given credit for. She was quite intelligent—proud of her superior grades in English. What she lacked was an education, just that. She started reading many books, great books. She never finished any because she was so eager, perhaps, to be in touch with *everything*.

Back in Los Angeles, the day before she was to see the President again, she telephoned U.S.C.

"Who?" demanded the central operator.

"Marilyn Monroe," she repeated, "and I want to speak to an expert on political affairs."

"Well," said the operator, "I am the expert on crackpots."

So Marilyn called U.C.L.A. This time, having quickly learned, she asked to leave an "important message for the Chairman of the Political Sciences Department"—Professor Lucas Dambert. She left her number and identified herself only as "Monroe." When Professor Dambert called back, somewhat baffled, she disguised her voice: "Marilyn Monroe residence." The telephone was silent. "Please don't hang up!" she urged. She convinced him she *was* Marilyn Monroe and asked him to have dinner with her at the Westside Café, a small intimate restaurant near Santa Monica.

Professor Dambert called his wife to tell her he had a long faculty meeting he could not miss—a favorite colleague was being denied tenure. Only when he saw her did he fully discard the possibility that one of his students might be playing a practical joke on him.

He found her immediately knowledgeable, caring about liberal causes; she expressed her detestation of the House Committee on Un-American Activities for what it had done to good people like Lillian Hellman, Arthur Miller, Alberta Holland. She told him she was eager to hear his views on the "political exigencies of a truly new frontier." He was even more impressed. She took notes as he expressed his views, and he was flattered. She asked only smart questions, had an agile mind, was charming—and looked gorgeous, oh, gorgeous!

When their long dinner was over—in a second! he thought—she thanked him with a kiss on the cheek. He managed to move his face just in time so that her luscious lips almost brushed his. She said, "Now I can discuss"—she riffled through her notes—"the nuisances of liberal reaction."

His mouth flew open in horror for her. "Not nuisances!"

She laughed, a bright student who'd trapped her teacher. "I *know* it's nuances, Dr. Dambert. I was just teasing you. But you didn't trust me, Dr. Dambert." She tasted his important intellectual title on her glorious lips.

"I'll trust you *forever!*" he told her.

At home, she embellished her notes with original thoughts of her own. She would make John Kennedy ashamed of having hesitated even to consider bringing her as his guest to the White House—with others, of course, at a small dinner. She and Jackie would chat, equals. He would introduce her to his grand old mother. He would show her the room where Abraham Lincoln wrote the Gettysburg Address. Others would join them, pronouncing only bright conversation—in reaction to her remarks. He would show her where Mrs. Roosevelt sat quietly reading to a dozing Franklin Delano Roosevelt; and where Thomas Jefferson—

"—if it doesn't take into account the nuances of liberal reaction," she finished. They were in the quarters set aside for the President in Peter Lawford's villa by the ocean.

He hadn't heard her. Why had he committed himself to a breakfast with Lyndon and Connally? he was wondering.

Marilyn was looking at him expectantly, waiting for his reaction to her serious observation.

"Why, yes," he said. Then he drew her to him on the bed.

For days, she was depressed. There had been so much more she wanted to discuss with him. After all, she had been married to two very famous men, one a sports hero, the other an intellectual. And she was, after all, Marilyn Monroe—wasn't she?

More and more she became aware of the chasmic distance that separated John F. Kennedy's life from hers. He had a wondrous family—so close, constantly there for each other. There was his ever-smiling mother, in fashionable clothes just right for her, who knew, always, exactly what to say—Marilyn longed to meet her. And his father! Not only did Joseph

Kennedy know his children were his, but they could be with him whenever they wanted. . . . In her family there *had* been love, but it was so buried in other emotions, might manifest itself so strangely, that at times it had been difficult to locate it. Oh, yes, Della and Gladys—with her marvelous red hair—had been pretty, perhaps even beautiful, but finally their faces had been distorted by their battles with madness. . . . A father? The only knowledge she had of one was that three men had denied she was their daughter. . . . For *him*, there was Hyannisport, green lawns, houses so far apart you had to drive between them. She had memories of Hawthorne's desolate vacant lots, small stucco houses almost pasted sweatily together. The foster homes and orphanages she had been in were millions and millions of miles away from the White House.

Those times—when she was so powerfully aware of their two worlds—hurting memories, especially of Della beating with bloodied hands on a wall and of Gladys carried away strapped to a stretcher, pitched her into a quagmire of sorrow, down, down. She forced sleep all day with sleeping pills, another capsule each time she woke. The mood would lift, though never soon enough, but it *would* lift, with bruised hope. She could even feel a sweet sorrow for Della and Gladys—and then she would love them fiercely—sorrow that they had not escaped the trap of their sad lives, "sweet sorrow" because she knew they wanted *her* to escape.

Peter Lawford telephoned to invite her to a dinner for the brother of the President, the country's Attorney General, Robert F. Kennedy.

After she accepted the invitation, Marilyn telephoned Professor Dambert again. The professor quickly suggested dinner, but she pleaded for his "impressive office." He laughed, agreed. When he hung up, he let himself wonder: Was she going to ask him to run away with her? He would! He knew she admired intellectuals, and he admired beautiful, smart women. He knew of her depressions. Well, he would save her from them. They would live in Arizona—yes, outside of Phoenix, in the golden desert! She would come to share his fondness for Dickens, especially the less-known novels. It was natural that she would gravitate toward Dostoyevsky. He had read all about her soon after their first meeting—he had been in a grocery store and seen her electrifying face on the cover of a magazine and bought it immediately and read it. . . . She *would* prefer Dostoyevsky because the Russian was, after all, more . . . *passionate!*

Marilyn Monroe took a cab to the beautiful, sprawling campus in Westwood. Impulsively, she asked the cab driver to let her off at the gate near Sunset.

It was a cool day sprinkled with spring. She wore a scarf and dark glasses. Students milled about the campus of U.C.L.A., talking spiritedly. She had never been educated formally, and now, seeing these youngmen and women with their earnest books, she longed to be one of them, just as smart. She walked along the Rodin Garden. She paused by one of the statues. She touched its silvery black surface. Rodin had touched the very same place! When a group of students looked at her, she pulled her hand away. She did not think they recognized her as the famous star, the most famous in the world. No, she thought they were reprimanding her for touching *their* statue.

Hurrying away from them, she bumped into a youngman, athletic, good-looking. He said, "Oh, excuse me, ma'am." *Ma'am!* She pulled the scarf so he could tell who she was. But he had already walked on. She replaced the scarf so it shaded more of her face now. She felt isolated, lost.

Her spirits lifted in Dr. Dambert's office—it was lined with books. She went to his prized collection of Dickens novels! She confided, in a conspiratorial whisper, that *she* "loved" Dostoyevsky and longed—"some day"—to play Grushenka. "I'll never imagine anyone other than you in the part," he promised.

When he invited her to have a drink in the faculty lounge, she accepted because her nerves were still frayed. In the small subdued lounge, the exalted faculty members of U.C.L.A. pretended—with enormous ennui—not to recognize the movie star—or even Dr. Dambert—as the two sat at a small table.

A male student working as bartender was flirting with the girl who took orders from the intimate tables; the girl had a fresh, unadorned prettiness. *The young bartender didn't even glance at me*, Marilyn thought. *I'm not pretty like the girls he's used to.*

Marilyn touched her hair. Was it damaged from the bleach? She felt exaggerated. She put her sunglasses back on. When the girl asked her what she wanted, she ordered champagne. Professor Dambert told her he didn't believe they had "chilled it in the bar this early." She asked for a daiquiri, with lime.

"You look *so* beautiful." He had not even had to gather his courage to speak those words, he had just spoken them.

"Do I?" she asked him eagerly. "Do I? Really? *Really?*" she pleaded.

"Oh, yes," he said. So beautiful, he thought, that he wished he didn't have to blink, so he would not miss even one single glimpse of her.

Pretending she was his special bright student, she told Dr. Dambert—that's what she delighted in calling him, *Doctor* Dambert—that this time she needed to know "all about civil rights—problems, solutions, everything, Dr. Dambert!"

Or course, he had not really believed she would suggest their running away. Still, he admitted to feeling very real regret. He adjusted. "Well, I know *some* of the problems and *all* of the solutions." He was delighted to be with her for whatever reason; he felt like the luckiest boy in the world.

Again, she took eager notes, asking him to repeat or clarify a point she thought especially significant. She underlined a favorite observation. Professor Dambert watched every movement she made. Then their meeting was over.

"Just for you, Dr. Dambert." She kissed him on the mouth.

He waited until he was alone to touch his lips. He left his hand there as long as he could without feeling awkward. For minutes he had been with the most beautiful woman in the world.

As Marilyn Monroe moved through the campus, she did not look at the students. They made her feel old, unintelligent, ugly.

* * *

There was a brush of new activity in the basement where auditions for Dead Movie Stars were proceeding. Now the other youngman stood next to the Contender for Marilyn Monroe.

He resembled Ted, Normalyn thought, or only reminded her of him because he was—

* * *

—lanky, that was the word used most often to describe Robert Kennedy. And angular. He retained a coltish boyishness, emphasized by his unruly hair. He was the "shy" one in the family; John called him "the puritan." He was not reckless with women, unlike his brothers and father.

Peter Lawford—who loved sexual intrigue—and had, years earlier, pursued Marilyn, who called him a "kinky nuisance"— knew that she was still seeing John, though infrequently, sometimes at this beach villa. But he was not sure whether Robert knew of his brother's involvement with the movie star. It amused him to seat "the shy Kennedy" between Kim Novak and Marilyn Monroe.

Kim Novak, a survivor, had just bought a house in Carmel—to escape from Hollywood. Now she was telling everyone how beautiful it was to "watch the twisted trees against a graying sky, the mist flowing in so silently." One day, she promised, she would paint the quiet spectacle.

Everyone's attention except Kim's turned to Marilyn when she asked the Attorney General in a modulated voice, "Do you foresee a time in the history of civil rights when litigation shall not be needed to enforce what is, after all, nothing but *civility*?"

"Why—" Robert Kennedy was impressed. Her question indicated a refined sophistication. Then he noticed that she was reading from concealed notes on her lap. He smiled.

Realizing that he had seen her consult her notes—which *she* had phrased earlier—Marilyn was glad that Kim went on to describe "unbelievable crests of water that creep up to land's end in Carmel."

When dinner was over, the twenty-five or so guests milled about the grand oceanfront room, where Marilyn had met John after his nomination. The glass wall provided a spectacular view of the ocean. A strong breeze stirred the night. Robert Kennedy gravitated toward Marilyn, who was secretly waiting. She smiled at the lean Kennedy, thinking that although he, too, was smiling, he looked sad.

"You look sad even when you smile, Miss Monroe," Robert told *her*. That is what Rose Kennedy, the dowager mother, often observed in public about his eyes: "They look sad even when he smiles his best Irish."

"But do I look smart?" Marilyn asked the Attorney General. When she saw the frown that that created on his craggy yet youthful face, a frown of confusion perhaps, she instinctively revised her question: "But do I look *sexy*?"

"Yes!" He answered that question too quickly. He added seriously, "Miss Monroe, you are the most sexual woman in the world."

At that moment Marilyn thought he looked like an English Romantic poet who would die young, leaving only a few poems, the promise of many greater ones. Saddened by that thought, and because champagne was bubbling in her mind, she leaned her head just slightly on his shoulder. He touched it. It was as if they were alone in the room.

Robert's whole body responded to that contact. He loved sports because he marveled at the many individual movements that create one action—a chain of motion. Often he would concentrate on the components of that chain to the point that his movements would slow. When the family played touch football, John could tell when his brother was becoming "entranced with motion." If they were on opposite teams, John would take strategic advantage of it to score a touchdown. . . . Just now, Robert followed the sensation that spread from the first brush of Marilyn's head on his shoulder. He pulled away. "Everybody's looking!" he said.

"Why shouldn't they?" she laughed. "I'm Marilyn Monroe and you're Robert Kennedy."

His frown deepened. "You're talking too loudly. Stop trying to attract attention!"

Kim Novak was comparing the Santa Monica coastline with that of Carmel, "its soaring abutments like powerful wings, its—"

Peter Lawford told her to hush. Something amazing was occurring between John Kennedy's brother and Marilyn Monroe. He had counted on something, but *this!*

Marilyn confronted Robert's rude tone. "You know you desire me."

He turned from her and walked out of the room.

"Bast—" She only started the word.

In the suddenly placid night, Robert Kennedy was disturbed. He had felt a doubled desire—desire for this beautiful woman and desire for his brother's mistress.

*   *   *

Before the panel of Dead Movie Stars—as Lady Star draped one emphatically casual arm about her chair, to proclaim only mild interest while the rest of the founders sat enthralled—the lanky youngman moved back into the shadows, waiting to reappear.

Normalyn sat quite still as she saw the dark youngwoman in the shadows preparing to make her powerful entrance. The contender's next supporting player had just adjusted the veil on a dramatically slanted hat. She held a cigarette lighter in her palm. . . . Normalyn pulled her attention away. It jerked into the memory of Troja and Kirk. She separated them now in her mind, the way death had: Troja. And Kirk.

The youngman who had played the President lay on the soft padding sprinkled with fleurs-de-lis. Beside him, on a shimmery sheet, the contender stretched her body and rested her blonde head—

*   *   *

—on his arm. John Kennedy was slightly uncomfortable. Next to him Marilyn was dozing. In the morning he had to face Lyndon Johnson, a man he was coming to despise and admire equally. Among close intimates, John would imitate Johnson: "When Ahm Pray-see-dey-yent of the *U*-ni-ted States, Ah will call muhself Gentl'man Bird.". . . Now he edged his arm away. Marilyn woke, startled she had been allowed to stay this long. She saw John smiling his private smile, as if no one else in the world would be amused by what he was perceiving.

The door opened. A man walked in.

John's smile tilted. "Miss Monroe, I believe you've met my brother—"

* * *

"Robert Kennedy!" Billy Jack exclaimed. "*He* came in?"

The lanky youngman stood over the contender and the other youngman lying on the glistening sheet. As if profoundly startled, the Contender for—

* * *

—Marilyn Monroe looked at the President. Propped on pillows, he was still smiling, at Robert, at her, at himself.

"Miss Monroe," Robert Kennedy, too, addressed her formally. After silent seconds, he walked out.

"What—?" Marilyn only began her question because at that moment she did not know what it was.

She left without another word to John. She walked out. Street noises seemed to belong to another world. She knew she had entered the darkest time of her life. She stopped on a busy corner, to force herself to hear the city's sounds. They seemed to come from another world, as if hers had been separated. Of course, she knew what would happen now.

Thirty-Two

"What *did* happen!" Betty Grable demanded.

"Yeah, what, man?" James Dean was no longer slouching.

"Tell us immediately!" Hedy Lamarr ordered.

"Come on!" coaxed Errol Flynn.

"Now!" Rita Hayworth added her full authority.

Veronica Lake and Billy Jack glanced at each other, then at a thoughtful Tyrone Power. Billy Jack leaned away from Lady Star, and Veronica Lake shifted her chair an inch or so apart from her. Lady Star gauged those reactions of tilting allegiance and the audience's eagerness, and she was pensive, pensive.

The Contender for Marilyn Monroe put a finger to her lips: Wait! ... She directed her words first to Lady Star, then the panel, finally the audience: "Some say that in sharing their women, the Kennedy men came closer to each other. Once, after dinner at the White House, John Kennedy asked the Great Dietrich if she had had sex with his father and only then asserted his own desire for her."

"Wow!" Errol Flynn paid tribute to all three.

Lady Star seized this opportunity: "I believe the contender may be straying into antidotes—"

"That's for poison." Veronica Lake was bolder than usual.

"—into idle gossip"—with a lazy flutter, Lady Star's fingers mimed idleness—"and away from the purpose of her audition." At the last, she put warning into her voice, and her eyes thrust daggers at Veronica Lake.

As ripples of laughter approved Lady Star's delivery, the youngwoman lost a tiny fraction of her superb command; she scratched an eyelid.

Lady Star noted that. *"Continue with the auditions!"* she sprang at the contender. Now she knifed Normalyn with narrowed eyes.

Demanding that she counter with information of her own! That conclusion recurred more powerfully each time for Normalyn—and wavered less quickly. It was increasingly clear that this contender was now a strong possibility as a Dead Movie Star—and that was *not* Lady Star's intention.

The contender drew a sensual hand over her curvy hip. With authority she continued: "I saw the president less and less, and I saw his brother more and more. The first time I was with him, we lay—"

*   *   *

—naked. Marilyn Monroe and Robert Kennedy lay naked on the enormous bed with sheets that were the slightest shade of blue in a room bathed in golden light. For moments, lazily, their bodies had only slightly arched toward each other, just lain there, increasing their awareness of each other. Occasionally, when tall palmtrees parted outside in a soundless breeze, a slender moon peered into the room and brushed the edges of the room with silver.

In that light, Marilyn Monroe's body, one foot tucked under the bluish sheet, appeared goldly translucent. She held one arm behind her head, and that position extended one breast, which, even so, retained its astonishing, proud roundness. From her breasts, her flesh insinuated itself into the softest S, which disappeared into a puff of tawniness before extending into the full sweep of her legs. Under her raised arm, her hair was rumpled. A loosed wave dipped over one eye, a shade of blue unchanged by the burnished light.

Robert Kennedy leaned over her, only from the waist because he wanted to extend the gradual contact of his body with hers. Marilyn Monroe is naked—gloriously startlingly naked! Robert thought. No, he amended, she is wearing one earring, only one.

It glittered on her ear. Looking at his long, lightly furry runner's legs, Marilyn slid her hands along the bare wiry torso of this coltish man she had once seen in a film clip as he ran, all angles, to catch a football John had pitched at him on a lawn of impeccable greenness. She thought, I am with him, *she* is with *him*. Her scarlet lips parted, waiting for his.

He kissed her, thought he felt her lips bubble as he had imagined they would! He leaned back, to look at the lips he had just kissed so easily and could kiss again. They were crimson, moist, parted, Marilyn Monroe's!

There was a light film, a beginning nestling of moisture, on his chest. Marilyn touched it with a finger, to create drops that sprinkled liquid sequins on her breasts. Laughing—her *laughter* bubbled!—she reached up and tousled his sandy hair. He shook her hands away, biting playfully at her fingers, nails as glossy as her lips. Exultant, she tossed her head to one side, blowing at her hair, wisps of blondness. She thought, Soon he will enter me—will enter *her*!

The most sexual woman in the world! The fantasy of every man, of hundreds, of thousands, of millions of men—men dreaming about her at this very moment, and she is with me now, Robert thought. His hands touched her perfect breasts— they *were* perfect! His fingers paused on the tips of her nipples, to feel them react. He was remembering a photograph he had seen of her in a book. She had been naked from the waist up, holding two roses—enormous cloth roses—against her breasts. She had been half-smiling, half-pouting, teasing, forbidding. He pretended he was plucking the petals of those remembered roses with his teeth.

She winced slightly at the light bites, then quickly restored her smile, transforming herself into a girl, a kittenish young girl. She meowed. She extended the sound to a low growl. Then she softened it into a sensual purring. *She is with him*!

Only in rehearsal, he arched his body. She raised her hips. In the very second when he would have had to surrender to the voluptuous invitation, he thought, Not yet! He slid on her stomach and held her, flesh on flesh. Both laughed.

He remembered a blowup of her in shorts, a blowup once pinned in his brother's hospital room. He touched her waist, where those shorts had hugged her. He remembered—evoked— the photograph of her with her dress swirling lovingly over white panties. He touched her thighs where the delicate cloth would have touched. He remembered—evoked—the silvery sheath that had sliced a stark V between her breasts at his brother's birthday celebration. He traced that V now, at the exact moment looping his fingers away from the nipples, as if they were not yet exposed. Not yet.... He remembered— evoked—a photograph of her lying on saffron sheets, her hair the same color, the curve of one naked hip revealing the hint of a darker shade of gold—woman-girl, reclining on one elbow— ... He adjusted her elbow like that now. The image still did not shape, and so he closed his eyes—and thought of her covered with sequins on flesh moistened by desire.

She knew why he had closed his eyes. She held his face until he opened them again, on *her*. She tried to assume the exact expression the cameras celebrated in glowing, Technicolored photographs—dark-lidded eyes narrowed, glossy scarlet lips about to part, parting, parted. She reminded herself, I am with him, she is with him, *she* is—

Beautiful, he thought—and closed his eyes again, to see not just her, this woman lying with him, but to see *Marilyn Monroe*—myth, legend, his brother's mistress, the greatest movie star in the world, the most beautiful woman; closed his eyes in order to see *all* the reflections of her, the tantalizing kept youngwoman in that movie—he forgot the name—the woman wrapped in a towel and looking both innocent and delighted to have been surprised at her shower door, the woman slipping into almost invisible stockings, the woman peeling one long glove as if that were just a first promise of many, many, many more, the woman holding only a sheer scarf before her so that her breasts created a tantalizing smear in that movie in which—that photograph in which—the woman in— the woman—woman—

Urgently he tried to locate an image of her, lying, standing, dressed, undressed—his eyes remained closed—and he grasped the image of the woman posing for the calendar called "Golden Dreams"! Yes, her! Behind closed eyes, he saw the outline of her flesh against soft red velvet—the curved hips, the languorous arm, the crimson lips, one leg barely concealing—no, barely revealing— . . . Golden dreams, golden dreams, golden dreams! He stretched his body its full length, feeling the gathering release as she flung her body—*desperately!*—against his with a cry that muffled the name she almost spoke aloud: *Kennedy!*

He thrust once more, and he thought, This is—

*   *   *

"—a *lie*! An obvious lie!" Lady Star broke the heated revery of the supporting player who, as Robert Kennedy, had suddenly interrupted the Contender for Marilyn Monroe in the basement of the Thrice-Blessed Church of the Redeemer. He had gone on to deliver in a rush his heated fantasy of what had occurred between the movie star and the senator. Adjusting immediately to the unexpected, and to stave off a jarring effect on her own thoughtful presentation, the Contender for Marilyn Monroe had managed to interject into the outrageous account some tender and some solemn touches—and a Technicolored backdrop.

"How *dare* you!" Lady Star's anger at the insurgent supporting player grew. "You can't know what went on in that bedroom. You have no right! *How dare you!*"

"I just imagined it that way." The supporting player admitted the obvious.

Momentarily enthralled, rendered momentarily moony, the rest of the panel now became staunchly indignant at the supporting player as Lady Star's wrath mounted. Only Billy Jack protested: "Aw, lettim finish." His hand had been cuddling his warming groin.

During the sudden interruption, Normalyn had sat quietly, had stopped listening, awed anew by the living power of the movie star.

Like a stern judge, Lady Star directed the gathered: "You will disregard as totally unreliable *every*thing you have just heard from this—this—*supporting* player. Legends have *tragedy*. And *glamour!*" she pronounced. "They do not—do *not*—"

"What?" challenged Billy Jack.

"Legends don't *fuck!*" Lady Star made herself clear. "Now go *on!*" she commanded the contender.

Grasping dramatic authority, the contender silenced giggles instantly when she announced, "With Robert—"

*   *   *

—it became more than just an affair. He was tender with her, spoke softly. They laughed, he discussed Castro, Cuba, the bastard-Teamsters, the threat of the right wing, giant industries; his favorite season of the year—fall, "nature's rebellion against winter," he said; hers, of course, was early spring.

She saw him as often as possible. He came to her home. Once, in disguise—he wore a beard, she wore her beautiful black wig—they went—she dared him, he challenged her back—to Pirate's Cove, a nude beach near Zuma. There, unrecognized, the movie star and the Attorney General walked naked, hand in hand, along the sand of the sheltered recess formed by looming white cliffs.

She was in love.

She was sure he was in love with her. As a youngwoman, she had survived the ugliness in her life by forcing hope. If she could hope, she could live. . . . She came to believe that powerful hoping could nudge even fate. She was sure that Robert, unlike "stodgy old John," would take her as his guest to the White House, for a formal dinner. The press would record their excitement and pleasure. And soon after *that*—! She hoped even more powerfully.

To resolve everything, she invited him to a "special dinner"—
she would cook! With a small laugh at the extravagant
prospect—he never seemed totally committed to the flippancy
of laughter—Robert accepted.

On the day appointed, cooking seemed impossible. She wasn't
a good cook and she was nervous. Her spirits soared: She
would send out for food, put it in the oven to warm in
advance so that the house would be wafted by fabulous scents.
She would let him assume she had cooked, might even smudge
her face with something tasty. At a certain point, she would
sniff at the air and, running into the kitchen, she would say, "I
think dinner is ready. *Ummmm*—just smell!"

That way, too, she could spend more time to make herself
irresistible. Naked, the way she always made herself up when
she was alone, she reached for her best cosmetics. She stopped.
She looked closely into the mirror. What she saw fascinated
her. Someone else had been aging under the face she was
about to make up. She continued to stare. Her eyes looked
larger, alert—not sexily dreamy—as if, wide open, they wanted
now to see *everything*, face *everything*! She touched, in fascination, a maturing angularity on her face. She would let him see
her as *her*. She made herself up only lightly and wore a pretty
but not extravagant dress.

To test this new, exciting appearance, she stood quietly
before her male secretary—actually her companion, with her
since not long before, when she had experienced a near
breakdown that led to her self-commitment at Payne Whitney
Psychiatric Clinic.

He reacted in such surprise that she almost fled back to her
bedroom to restore the familiar face of Marilyn Monroe. But
he was already explaining his amazement: "You're so lovely
that way . . . really beautiful."

She kissed him in gratitude.

Alone now and feeling "*really* beautiful," she checked the
chilled champagne, the food in the oven. She heard a car; it
would be an ordinary car, with disguised license plates. She
went to the window because she loved to watch Robert walk,
his long determined strides. He would pause only a second.
An anticipatory smile would just barely begin to push away the
intense concentration of the long day.

Today he looked serious, stern.

He was. Before leaving Washington, he had learned from J.
Edgar Hoover of the existence of a scurrilous letter anony-
mously accusing the Kennedys of "sexual immorality." Hinting that there might be another, "more specific" letter, Hoover

had casually informed the Attorney General that, unlike others, *this* letter was being taken quite seriously at the F.B.I.— "for purposes of surveillance only, of course"—because there was "strong evidence" to confirm that the writer was "a man of power, with possible political connections." Hoover had pretended to hide his pleasure at this development. "I just figured that you and your folks should know that this is being said, Mr. Attorney General," he'd said in his cultivated tone of casualness and formality, a tone meant to camouflage his motives.

"Lies," Robert Kennedy had said to the stodgy old man. "Of course, Mr. Attorney General, what else?" He remembered Hoover's tiny eyes burrowing in on him.

At the door, Marilyn kissed Robert Kennedy on the lips, to ease away the knotted frown. It only deepened. He stared startled at her. She looked— Tired? Older than he had seen her?

The food was dry, left too long in the oven. She confessed she had not cooked it. On the table, one candle kept flickering until it went out; he did not relight it. Both poked in silence at their plates.

Even in this rationed light, she looked . . . different. Almost . . . ordinary. Robert cleared his throat and spoke words he had rehearsed after leaving Hoover: "Marilyn, I'm in California with my wife and my children this time." He had prepared more words, rejected now. He jumped ahead to the last ones: "I have to stop seeing you."

"You're not going to marry me!"

He reached out to touch her, as if to affirm her sudden odd reality to him. "You thought I would give up my political life, my family in order to—"

"—yes, to marry me, to take me to the White House, introduce me to your mother, have children and—" She had *hoped*, goddammit. She had hoped powerfully!

"I never gave you reason to believe that," he said soberly, sadly.

It was true, she knew it, he never had—*but she had hoped!*

He withdrew his hand from hers.

She grasped it back forcefully. "Touch *me!*" she demanded. She felt his tension, released his hand, which he eased away.

"But . . . you . . . love . . . me," she said, very slowly because she knew that otherwise she would stutter.

I desired a movie star, my brother's woman; she's someone else now, and not even my brother's any more, and she's asking me to marry her. . . . Without intention to do so, he imagined her at a state function, sewn into a tight dress, as he had first seen her, been aroused by her. He heard her breathy voice greeting dignitaries— They would leer at her, the women would turn away.... Now he felt deeply, deeply sorry for that vision of her.

"No," he answered her question finally, surprised he had spoken the single word so easily, because he did not want to hurt her, only to be honest.

She stood up. The champagne spilled.

To his astonishment, he saw that anger had returned the banished face, a flash of her vibrant beauty—and he desired her.

She hurled words at him: "What if I told you I'm pregnant!"

He thought of the vile look on Hoover's face. "You've seen other men." He tried to soften the words—impossible.

"Yes! Your damn brother!" she hurled at him.

He bolted up.

She pulled back her words. "I'm not pregnant," she lied. "I made that up."

He looked puzzled at the unfamiliar face. "I am truly sorry— truly—" And he was, trying to find words that would pain her least, but there was nothing.

Nothing.

Alone, she looked at the dried food, the spilled champagne. She stared at the vacant seat where he had been. She said aloud, "I thought you would marry me."

*   *   *

Dearheart, dearheart! Please don't shut your ears to me, please listen. The Kennedys were really good men and they tried to be even better—aimed at greatness. They were committed, and they roused fervent hope that justice might prevail among the dispossessed who had stopped hoping—and almost have again today, with truly amoral men again in high office. Why, when the Kennedys were murdered, black people and white, men, women, the young, old—all wept. Only tyrants applauded. That means something, dearheart. Oh, they made mistakes. And they had that deadly flaw inherited from their father, that damned old tyrant—the use of the women they needed only sexually. It was a grave flaw, a cruel flaw, a tragic flaw. Perhaps it kept them from being great men. Had they lived—not been slaughtered in their prime— they might have overcome it, become great men. But what they came to stand for—the country's potential for all that is good and which they believed in fervently—was greater than they were, and the symbol is what has to remain pure. Perhaps, someday, their children will—! Dearheart—?

Normalyn was not sure she wanted to hear what she thought Miss Bertha might exhort her to. She felt trapped in a vortex of confused emotions.

Suddenly, at its center was ... Ted!—and his subsequent conversion into the new, committed Ted. Yet she still bore wounds from what he had been part of, even though *he* had stopped the full assault. Without him there— That came to her for the first time. Without him there, the full violence would have happened with the other two men. . . . Had Ted's voice filtered into Miss Bertha's?

Normalyn heard a soft, protesting sigh. She did not have to turn to realize that it had been uttered by the older woman when, from the shadows, the youngwoman with the silvery gray wig walked—tiny, reedy, arrogant—to the edge of the clearing, ready to enter the performance. Beyond, the dark-haired youngwoman toyed nervously with the shiny cigarette lighter.

The contender raised her head hopefully. "I waited for Robert Kennedy to come back. I was sure—"

*   *   *

—he *would* come back, apologize, just come back, just *call*! Marilyn did not leave the house for days. Fearing wiretaps, she had learned to call Robert from public telephones, at his private number in Washington. Late one evening when the cruel telephone did not ring even once—she repeatedly lifted it and demanded, "Hello!" into its startled buzzing—she asked her male secretary to drive her to a telephone booth in the lot of a closed grocery store. The clang of each coin made her clasp the receiver more tightly.

She learned that Robert Kennedy had changed his private telephone number.

J. Edgar Hoover told Mildred about the accusatory letter concerning the Kennedys. Soon after, Mildred received another one, more implicating, involving Monroe in the scandal.

In her gray limousine, the great Mildred Meadows herself drove to Marilyn Monroe's house to give the star a chance to be saved, an opportunity to be extended one last time, in final deference to the symbol of beauty—and at a time when the star's personal life had put her career in disarray.

When there was no response to her ringing nor to her polite, though necessarily insistent knocking, Mildred positioned herself on the lawn—in dramatic, emphatic light—and delivered her message. In civilized but assertive tones, as required by the importance of the matter, she called into the house:

"Monroe! I intend to destroy you in my column!—"

* * *

"—and I will destroy the Kennedy brothers!" finished the youngwoman wearing the perfect gray wig.

Normalyn listened attentively to the ensuing narration of Mildred's raid on Marilyn Monroe's house—of her cunning extortion of the fact that Marilyn was pregnant, her discovery that Enid did not suspect by whom, and her powerful ultimatum. . . . This version certainly came, at least in major part, from Mildred, but it confirmed Mark Poe's, with only minor variations that placed Mildred constantly in lavishly favorable light.

"And then Enid became my ally!" the youngwoman in the gray sculpted wig announced triumphantly to the panel of Dead Movie Stars.

"That's not—" Normalyn stopped her protest when she saw Lady Star lean eagerly toward her.

Don't protest aloud, dearheart, Miss Bertha warned her, just in time. *Not yet. You know what Mark Poe told you. He was there, and he can be believed. Remember that, dearheart, remember!*

Lady Star leaned even closer, prodding, prodding.

But Normalyn was silent. She was recalling Mark Poe's description of what had occurred after the rage of confrontation between the two women—the reference to that third person who dominated them, Enid's accusing anger, and then the moments of caring, intense closeness when Enid soothed Marilyn with enormous love, determined the star's longing for this child, her passionate promise to assure that she would be able to have it. . . . Even then Enid could fluctuate between rage and protective love, Normalyn thought as she continued to discover—as if someone she had known as a ghost was now assuming flesh, the intense youngwoman of mystery, of "many lives"—to discover and admire her.

Of course, then, what the youngwoman in the gray wig had claimed, what Mildred herself had claimed about Enid's becoming her ally, was false. . . . *Was information being reiterated, for her?* That sudden thought, an extension of her recurring suspicion that she was being carefully guided toward a certain knowledge, pulled Normalyn back into the present, a disturbed present extending now to this: *Kirk is dead, really dead, and Troja is alone!*

Surrendering to Normalyn's pensive silence, Lady Star waved her hand at the auditioners. "Proceed."

In the clearing of ashen-yellow light, the dark-haired youngwoman wearing a veiled dark hat faced the woman in the silver wig. Standing to one side of them the Contender for Marilyn Monroe confided:

"Soon after—"

*   *   *

—the telephone at the stone gate that bordered Mildred Meadows's mansion was lifted. The butler told Mildred that "a Miss Enid Morgan, baroness," desired "urgently" to see her.

"Let her in at once!"

Mildred rushed to a window. She saw Enid walk away from her car—to accept the declaration of war? She saw Enid pause for a moment. She lifted the veil of her hat. She retouched her lips most carefully, perfecting their outline with a moistened finger. Mildred almost gasped. Her daughter, Tarah, had always prepared exactly that way before she faced Mildred for approval. Yes. And Tarah had been as naturally beautiful as this youngwoman. For a second, Mildred allowed herself to imagine that her daughter had returned. . . .

Minutes later, in the grand receiving room, Mildred sat on her throne and faced Enid Morgan.

"You're right, Mildred."

"But of *course* I am." The easy announcement of abdication did not disappoint Mildred. Drama has many levels, and anticlimax is not a desirable one. This was the only conclusion—a key line kept in abeyance—to the years of conflict between Mildred and Monroe. . . . Mildred offered Enid some of her best sherry. Enid asked for "iced tea" instead. Although Mildred was mildly charmed by the oddness of the request, she was at the same time a touch disappointed. She would have preferred that she answer, "Yes, just three sips, please"—the way Tarah always framed her exact request.

Moistened by the tea, Enid's lips gleamed. "There will be no child." She smiled over the crystal glass, which captured pins of light. "Just the way you want, Mildred."

Mildred did not feel compromised to clarify: "Oh, my dear, it isn't that I don't *want* her to have a child. It is simply that circumstances prohibit it. The brothers *will* be destroyed. It's a matter of whether she wants to accompany them into disaster."

"It's all very clear. Shall I state it back to you?"

Now Mildred was charmed. This beautiful youngwoman had

certainly been educated in some fine conservative school, like the one she had insisted Tarah attend.

Enid said, "You are allowing Marilyn Monroe to separate herself from destructive scandal. By using the full authority and power of your column you will dispel any rumors linking her to it. Your voice would never be questioned in those matters."

"Exactly!" Mildred leaned toward Enid: "And for the necessary time required, I will even withhold the letter exposing the Kennedys. Of course, afterwards—" She clasped her tiny hands in a gesture of triumph and destruction. "My dear, I simply want to guide Monroe away from those harmful leftists she has been attracted to."

"Yes—and into *your* gracious fold at last." Enid toasted with a tinkle of her iced tea. She continued her understanding of Mildred's generous motives: "A child born or announced would force the terrible association, whether true or not—beyond even *your* power to control."

"Beyond my *desire* to control." Mildred allowed no compromise to her power.

"Of course." Enid smiled, a bright, favorite prodigy.

"One can never count on natural miscarriage!" Mildred asserted harshly. She was thinking of her own daughter, of when Tarah had informed her of her pregnancy, years, years ago, sitting in that same chair Enid now was occupying and announcing her determination to have her illegitimate child, ruin her beauty, her life. Mildred could almost see her there now, just as beautiful as this youngwoman, her hair as dark, her skin as fair, her eyes— . . .

"May I have just a few sips of sherry?" Enid set aside her iced tea.

Mildred closed her eyes, to join two images separated by years, by death. "Just three sips?" she spoke aloud to herself.

"Yes, thank you. Please."

The summoned butler served the sherry into a goblet just slightly smaller than Mildred's. With only the tip of her lips, Enid tasted the sweetness.

Mildred watched every tiny motion, to link with every stirred memory. "*You* have never had a child, my dear?"

"Yes! I have!" Enid said quickly. "With—" She recovered. "—with a vengeance," she finished softly.

But clearly—and unlike her own daughter—this youngwoman had not allowed herself to be ruled by it; her life continued, superbly, glamorously.

"And *you*, Mildred, have you had the joy of a child?"

"A beloved, beautiful daughter—Tarah. She was killed in an accident, protecting her always disruptive child, who nevertheless died, too." She moved on quickly, quickly. "Since Monroe is to rely on me"—she tasted delicious words—"I must know everything, of course. All the details."

"Who could expect less of Mildred Meadows?" Enid's eyes fixed on her.

"My *dear*!" Mildred was flooded with delight.

"It will happen at the D'Arcy House," Enid went on to inform. "You will announce it as a miscarriage—occurring elsewhere, of course."

"Of course, as agreed." Mildred naturally knew of the D'Arcy House; designed by Frank Lloyd Wright for his notorious "friend" Dominique D'Arcy. Originally it was thought to be in the United States, but a careful mapping of the territory revealed that it was in Mexico. Still ostensibly a magnificent private home, it was now a secret hospital—its location making certain matters legal. There, prominent doctors and surgeons attended, in absolute quiet, to the needs of the famous, who were accepted through a network of important contacts that assured anonymity. What Mildred did not tell Enid was that she knew the D'Arcy House with much more intimacy. It was where Tarah had given birth, painful birth. Mildred had sat in the same room with her while the despised Dr. Janus—

Enough! Mildred ordered her thoughts to stop.

"Marilyn will be in disguise, of course," Enid continued casually.

Too casually. Mildred leaned back and to one side on her throne. "Oh?" She drenched the word in suspicion.

"A disguise you know extremely well," Enid assured. "You have a photograph of her in it."

"How do you know that?" Mildred allowed a note of warning in her voice, in case there was something to warn about.

"I read your column, religiously, Mildred. So does Marilyn."

"But of course you do!"

Enid crossed her heart. "And we read between the lines." She recited words from one of Mildred's recent columns: "Who was the blonde movie star in dark wig seen fleeing from—?" Enid laughed. "Marilyn remembered she was almost cornered against your parked limousine by your photographer."

Mildred's laughter almost bubbled. She recalled the photograph she had not used—kept. And she remembered the column. It was true that in it she planted secret messages, warnings, veiled instructions—to elicit prompt, telling, reactions from persons not named. She had had to wait, yes, but those coded messages, resisted until now, had prepared for the star's capitulation in this utterly charming way. "Of course she must be in disguise. It is essential," Mildred agreed and made the slightest toast, a mere tilt of her goblet, to the careful preparations.

Enid looked at Mildred over the refracted light of her goblet. "May I compliment you, Mildred?"

"Of course, my dear."

"I marvel at your stylish civility. I hope someday to match it. Less civilized people might accuse us of speaking too coolly about the death of an unborn child." Her laughter rippled. "May I have a bit more sherry?"

The pleasure of having the youngwoman appreciate the lack of vulgar emotionalism in practical matters was overwhelmed by that new request, which evoked another cherished memory, of lovely afternoons like this when she would pull all the drapes open in this room and she and Tarah would sit admiring the perfect garden. . . .

Mildred rose from her chair and drew all the drapes apart.

"What a lovely, lovely garden you have, Mildred," Enid complimented.

Mildred closed her eyes for moments to let nothing intrude on the suddenly recaptured past.

When Enid prepared to leave—she touched her hat, and the veil floated over her face—she promised, "Of course, I'll call you to inform you the exact date."

"*And* the time," Mildred extended.

"Of course," Enid agreed. "But you do know, Mildred, the enormous secrecy involved at the D'Arcy House. You will not be allowed; certainly you understand that."

"I understand, but you, my dear, must understand that I have ways of verifying . . . everything and absolutely." Mildred kept her warning mysterious.

"We counted on that, Mildred," Enid said, her tongue poised on her lips as if searching more sweetness. "No one could deceive you. It would be foolish to try."

"Very foolish," Mildred agreed in her most civilized tone of threat.

"And afterwards"—Enid smiled beautifully at Mildred— "afterwards, when you have your own verification—afterwards, Mildred, when you are convinced—Marilyn Monroe will apologize to you for not heeding your advice in the past. I'm sure she will long to thank you for saving her from a scandal not even she could survive—and from the dangerous birth of a child."

Mildred Meadows felt as if she had been holding her breath for years. Now she could exhale: *"Yes!"*

Thirty-Three

Smothered in waves of silent expectation aroused by the epic audition within the Thrice-Blessed Church was a reaction only Normalyn, attuned, was aware of: At the reference to Mildred's dead daughter, the older woman in the audience was not able to muffle a sob.

During this hiatus in the drama, as the expertly coached players relocated, Normalyn tried to collate important information from the contender's determined search through the entangled lives: Enid had admitted giving birth to a child, and there had followed a reference to "vengeance." That was a refrain now, asserting its reality, and Normalyn had come to disbelieve Stan's words about a boy. How better to deny the existence of a living daughter? . . .

The supporting player in the gray wig had moved much too quickly past the matter of Tarah's child-bearing at the D'Arcy House, with Mildred in chilling attendance. That would mean that the source of such information—Mildred, of course—had moved just as evasively, pulling back when she blurted an unwanted name—"the despised Dr. Janus."

Normalyn's feelings contained strong loyalty to Enid, even as evidence mounted that Enid had to some extent "joined" Mildred. There had to be more. . . . *There is more, dearheart!* . . . Normalyn reminded herself that she had learned from Mark Poe that the morning after Mildred's raid, Enid and Marilyn had gone out together. That was to seek Alberta Holland's counsel—on a spring day of jacaranda-snow when Miss Bertha offered them a cup of her chamomile tea— . . . Oh, she was inserting that information from *Miss Bertha's* rumina-

tions! Normalyn was thrilled to discover how well it fit—
and she knew that soon she would return to Long Beach. . . .
It would follow that Enid was armed with Alberta Holland's
advice when she proceeded to Mildred's mansion, only *seeming*
to join her. Yes. Normalyn welcomed that at times she and
Enid had acted similarly with the old woman, both asking for
iced tea. Or—this occurred to Normalyn—had that similarity
been inserted as yet another goad to her participation in these
auditions, to arouse her loyalty to the point that she would
protest with knowledge of her own? After all, Mildred admitted
coding her column with "secret messages" to elicit telling
responses from the objects of her scrutiny. Was Mildred sending
similar signals to her—guiding her to what she was expected
to explore?

Was the contender only a messenger!

The contender rushed ahead: "On the appointed day, at the
determined time, Mildred Meadows was at—"

* * *

—the D'Arcy House!

Mildred worked on two main levels of perception, instinc-
tive suspicion and commanded suspicion, the latter when there
seemed to be nothing to suspect. When Enid left after that
afternoon of sweet sherry, Mildred filtered through a sieve of
suspicion everything that had occurred.

She began with a given: Deceit must be assumed. By prohib-
iting her presence at the D'Arcy House, Enid had increased
Mildred's determination to be there. *Because they wanted her
there!* Enid's reference to the necessity of Monroe's being in
disguise had ample logic, of course; but she had been too
eager to remind Mildred of a certain photograph of Marilyn
in the same disguise. *To lead her to it!*

Mildred consulted her files of photographs of actors and
actresses fleeing the cameras of the photographers she employed; all were taken at times of intrigue, when stars did not
want to be photographed. She looked closely at several pictures of Monroe—"incognito in black wig," taken in response
to tips of her whereabouts. She studied several pictures under
a magnifying glass. She moved to a different light. With electrified excitement, she pulled out a photograph, another—
Could it be? Some of the pictures might . . . just . . . possibly . . . be . . . *of Enid pretending to be Monroe in a dark wig,*
Enid's own black hair *seeming* to conceal! Mildred had observed that the two women looked alike in a startling way,
alike opposites, as if in artifice Monroe had tried to match—

or outdo—Enid's natural beauty, to paint it, sculpt it on herself.

Mildred located the photograph taken when, from her parked limousine, she had watched the "disguised Monroe—fleeing" being photographed by one of the men the columnist employed. The star had backed up against the gray car, then turned to face into the window in shock. *Pretended shock!* To assure that she—*Enid!*—was seen in this "disguise" and assumed to be Marilyn Monroe!

Mildred riffled through more photographs of Monroe. *That* one might be of Enid in a blonde wig, posing as Monroe! They had interlocked two images into one—and succeeded even with her. Until now. Whatever their original purpose— foolish prankishness, a way to camouflage little intrigues common to all great stars—or preparation for more important subterfuges—whatever their initial purpose, now they clearly wanted her to carry with her into the heightened moments at the D'Arcy House that cleverly established single image. Enid, in the disguise they *thought* they had perfected, would be playing Monroe in an elaborately staged abortion. But why not Monroe herself in the pretense? Impossible to expose her delicate pregnancy to the risks of realistic charade.

It was so clear! They were trying to trap her—Mildred Meadows!—into the essential announcement of a miscarriage, to allow the secret pregnancy to proceed!

In all of this, Mildred now detected, like the wafting of a noxious odor, the dominating presence of Alberta Holland. Of course, the creature's trusted friend, that betrayer of her own class, would be in intimate attendance at the simulation. It pleased Mildred to sweep the Spanish exile into the scandal. Too bad that Enid had to be included. She had shown charming potential. With a certain rue, Mildred allowed herself to observe that Enid's presence brought even to Alberta Holland's clumsy intrigue a certain aura of style, like that in the melodramas of the time that Tarah had so enjoyed.

As agreed, Enid telephoned ahead to inform Mildred of the date and exact time when "the event fulfilling our mutual interests" would occur.

At the tall gates of the D'Arcy House were guards pretending to be caretakers. Mildred's limousine sailed past them. She had made arrangements to put the head guard temporarily in her employ, just as she knew Holland had counted on her doing.

Over the entrance of the house was an enormous stained-glass window duplicating in exact detail the corner in Algiers where Frank Lloyd Wright had met the notorious Dominque D'Arcy, who lived here in luxuriant squalor until her death. At the door two other attendants—predictable!—pretended to attempt to stop Mildred.

"Remove your ugly hands at once, do you know who I am?" Mildred was delighted to play in the subterfuge she would soon uncover. Past the retreating attendants, she entered the hall of the disguised hospital in this Mexican desert town. The corridor gleamed in watery streaks of colored sunlight created by the dyed panes of the windows. Mildred heard a familiar voice, agitated. It was Enid's, of course. So naive, my dear, she prepared to scold; you thought you could disguise even your voice?

But—

She saw Enid run out of one of the rooms ahead. Enid's face looked livid with horror as she passed Mildred and rushed out of the great house. Mildred stopped in the corridor. *All her conclusions were wrong!* She had been sure Enid would be in the room pretending to be Monroe—that's how certain they were that the two images they had interlocked would be powerful enough to deceive her during the tense and bloody seconds.

Mildred was deeply baffled. She reexamined the matter. Of course! At the last moment Enid had realized the impossibility of this deceit and had fled in panic. Mildred might consider that in extenuation later. *Now* she could proceed down the hushed hallway to the vacated room. A woman hurried to lock it. Yes, there would be new instructions to *really* keep her out because, instead of what they had intended her to see, there would be abandoned instruments for the simulated operation, a vacant bed, whatever else they had contrived for "authenticity."

Mildred slapped the key from the woman's hand. She thrust open the door and saw—

From the bleeding woman, the doctor had pulled— *The doctor was Dr. Janus!* No, he was Dr. Crouch. *And it was Tarah in bloody childbirth and Dr. Janus held out to Mildred the triumphant living child she had hoped would die and*— . . . No! *It was Tarah after the car crash—bleeding, still holding the hated, ugly child*—

Mildred leaned against the door, pulling herself out of past and present images, mixing. Only twice before did she remember having perspired: when she had sat with Tarah—*in this very room*—and in the hospital after the crash. Now, years later, she felt cold perspiration as Dr. Crouch—*not Janus this time*—held out to her . . . the mangled proof that the demanded abortion had, beyond a doubt, occurred. Mildred was certain who the pained woman was. *She saw an unmistakable face, the face of—* . . . Marilyn Monroe! Mildred's eyes yanked away to . . . sequins! . . . on the floor, among blood! Even to *this*, Monroe had worn glitter. No, what she saw were beads of gleaming perspiration.

Mildred closed the door. She considered . . . vomiting.

In her important Friday column, as agreed, Mildred Meadows conveyed to her millions of readers the "sad news" that Marilyn Monroe had, once again, miscarried after a "sweet attempt at reconciliation with the most loving of her husbands."

On Monday, there was a front-page announcement that Mildred Meadows was terminating her "vastly popular, internationally syndicated column."

* * *

In the church basement, the girl wearing the imperturbable gray wig moved solemnly into the shadows of self-imposed seclusion. Before the hypnotized audience, the Contender for Marilyn Monroe stood for silent moments of adulation.

Then no child had been born. That was Normalyn's first thought. Again, relief was followed by sadness for the great movie star.

But something essential was missing!

Normalyn reacted now against the account of Mildred's invasion of the D'Arcy House—and this version clearly came from Mildred. The telling had been much too carefully manipulated, too calculated in its fragmentary yet emphatic presentation, seeming to invite, with selective phrasing, conclusions only suggested by adhering to a rigorously tightened point of view. Mildred's firm belief that she had seen Marilyn Monroe in a real abortion had been declared from the controlled perspective of years later. . . . The motivation for Mildred's abrupt termination of her column had again been left glaringly unexplored. Only a real abortion could have disoriented the woman to the indicated extent at the D'Arcy House, and only a real abortion would have convinced her to announce "the miscarriage."

Yet not even to thwart the vast evil of Mildred Meadows would Miss Bertha have sacrificed a child in order to deceive. But would Alberta Holland? Now Miss Bertha's benign presence separated itself from Alberta Holland. No, it was Normalyn who was separating her, because she heard the persevering voice: *Dearheart, remember carefully all you've gathered* . . . Yes! Even today Mildred was questioning what she had seen at the secret hospital . . . The interlocked image of the two women—

Suddenly the memory of the distant shoreline swept over Normalyn. *Enid removed a black wig from the blonde woman.* She had only *remembered* her as being blonde from the first. *No, it was the other woman who—* . . . The memory jumbled before it melted and flowed away. Still, as distance extended between Normalyn and the origin of that memory, its prolonged clarity was convincing her of its reality.

"Then my life came crashing!" the Contender for Marilyn Monroe flung words into the spell: "Strange that today people forget the sadness with which I ended my life. I was broke, I had to borrow money, my production company had failed. There was talk I would be fired, sued by the studio. I couldn't sleep without pills. I thought I saw myself becoming old, discarded. I felt isolated, abandoned, alone—"

Sighs hinted the possibility of tears from the moved audience. Lady Star saw Billy Jack lean forward, taut with excitement, preparing to suggest unanimous approval of the contender. For a horrifying second Lady Star thought he might break into applause. She clamped her hand on his. Next to her, Veronica Lake was about to speak out approval—Lady Star *felt* it! She thrust her elbow against Veronica's. This could all lead to the first time Dead Movie Stardom was bestowed before an audition was officially over, that's how much dangerous power the contender was amassing.

"I locked the door of my bedroom. I swallowed a handful of sleeping pills . . . more . . ." the contender continued. She began to crumble onto the quilted padding on the floor.

Lady Star had not one moment to lose. She moved off the platform in a few determined strides and stood over the expiring contender. "Get off the goddamned floor this instant, *contender!*" she demanded.

Startled, the contender stood up.

Lady Star tried to pull the quilt from under the contender. "You're rushing your death scene much too fast!"

The contender stumbled on the rumpled quilt. "Huh?"

Lady Star heard angered mumbles in the audience—aimed at *her* and growing.

"What the hell!" Billy Jack stood up to protest. Veronica Lake planted a defiant hand on her hip. James Dean pushed up an angered collar on his red jacket. Lady Star had to smash the spell, but the situation demanded she proceed exactly, not too fast, allowing adjustment, then fast enough to let it all settle, then swiftly riding on momentum. She was careful to compliment the contender—the *popular* contender, she reminded herself: "You've told your story somewhat well, created some suspense, aroused our expectations. But—as others on the panel and the *attentive* in the audience must have recognized"—her cold look judged the impetuosity that had made them all so reckless—"you've left out quite a lot, *contender!*"

At Lady Star's words, Veronica Lake restored the waning wave over her eye, reorienting herself. Billy Jack sat down, slouched. Whispers sprouted among the panel. In the audience one biker turned to another and nodded—"Yeah!"—in grave agreement with Lady Star's evaluation.

The time was right! Lady Star bombarded: "Now answer this, contender. *Why* did Mildred stop writing her column? *Why* didn't she expose the promised scandal about the brothers? *How* does Dr. Crouch fit in? *And why was Enid running away in horror from the D'Arcy House?* But most important, *what about Marilyn's daughter? Why* have you left out what you claimed to be your secret scandal?"

"Because . . . uh . . ." Shifting her stance uncomfortably, the contender was silent.

Currents stirred, swayed, shifted. Hedy Lamarr observed, "She was too eager to get to the suicide."

"She *did* leave out a lot." Billy Jack pondered and reconsidered.

"That's the damn truth." Veronica Lake was testy.

"I always thought her hair was all wrong," Rita Hayworth offered.

"Give her a damn chance, you guys," said a tiny voice from the panel. It was Verna La Maye.

That was still enough to create factions! "Yeah, give her a damn, uh, chance," James Dean joined the new opposition, which just might include Tyrone Power and Errol Flynn. Betty Grable waited. "Yeahs" echoed among petitioners.

A picture of fair play, Lady Star opened beneficent arms. In syrupy tones, she addressed the contender: "You promised to tell us—*all of us*" she reminded the panel and the audience, "*everything* that happened. You simply haven't, darling, have you?"

Silence from the contender.

More silence.

"We're waiting," Lady Star reminded. "Perhaps it may help if I guide you. Now. You told us Mildred saw a real abortion. You told us Enid ran out of the D'Arcy House. You told us Marilyn had a daughter. What! Is! The! Truth!"

"I don't know!"

I'm Enid Morgan's daughter and I have no father! Normalyn supplied her own truth.

"You don't know!" Lady Star repeated the contender's startling admission. "You don't *know!*"

"The nerve of her!" Betty Grable denounced.

"She told us all that stuff like it was really happening," Tyrone Power accused.

"She made us believe we were really seeing it," Rita Hayworth complained.

"*Now* she says she doesn't know!" Errol Flynn condemned.

In her own small voice, the contender said, "I tried real hard to find out everything—from Mildred Meadows, Dr. Dambert, lots and lots of people. But the Crouches stopped speaking to me when the old woman said I wasn't right, and a guy at Nash McHugh's school stopped a girl from telling me about Mark Poe—and I couldn't locate Dr. Janus. And a batty old woman in Long Beach just babbled on before she chased me out—"

"Long Beach!"

Miss Bertha! Normalyn felt soothed by her memories of the old woman—who *had* given her information, even if in cautious code.

"And *you* told me some," the contender reminded Lady Star. "And I read lots of books," she continued, to authenticate her narrative. "But I couldn't find out *every*thing—who can? So I made some up."

"You *what?*" Those were the only two words Lady Star could utter. They were echoed variously by the stunned founders.

The contender flung herself on the mercy of the panel, the audience—and Lady Star: "But I *did* tell you a lot. You *know* I did!"

That was true, Normalyn knew, feeling sorry for the young contender who had explored so intimately the intertwined lives and been trapped by their riddles.

Lady Star stood her full length. "I move for the unanimous rejection of this . . . contender . . . pretender . . . *petitioner!*" she demoted. She walked up to each of the Dead Movie Stars: "Reject her!"

The panel, the audience, all were released from the deep spell; whistling, hoots rose from the congregation.

"Re-jected!" leered Billy Jack. "Re-jected!" Veronica Lake led the rest of the panel. Only Verna La Maye cast a timid affirmative vote—but was informed by Lady Star that new Dead Movie Stars would vote only at *following* auditions.

"The contender has been rejected unanimously!" Lady Star announced the verdict.

"B-b-but I was g-g-good," the youngwoman pleaded with

the panel and the fans. "You l-l-loved me, remember? *Why* did
you stop loving me?" She pleaded plaintively with them: "Will
you love me again when I'm g-g-gone?"

Boos of derision!

The youngwoman's supporting players fled the basement.

"Out!" Lady Star ordered the ex-contender.

Just like that! As dramatically as she had scaled the dizzying
heights of favor and stardom, the contender fell. The girl with
bleached blonde hair stumbled, crying, out of the basement of
the Thrice-Blessed Pentecostal Church of the Redeemer.

"Bye," called a forlorn Verna La Maye.

Lady Star stood before Normalyn and, with a look, cut her
in two pieces, then three, then four, five— Whirling about to
create a warning *Swoosh!* with her slit gown, she snagged her
dress on a nail protruding from one of the boards of the
platform. She snapped it free. *Rip!*

Back in her tall chair, she was aware of a new restiveness in
the basement. The evening could not end like this. It had to
have a soft focus, a touch of poignancy, the hint of further
revelations for a future interlude—oh, yes—and some quiet
mystery.

Inspired: "May we hear from our honored guest—Sandra!
Miss Sandra! Perhaps she will comment on the latter part of
the evening—some events she's familiar with? Miss Sandra,
please!"

The older woman, Sandra, shook her head. "No." Someone
encouraged her graciously by touching her elbow. Lady Star
goaded her with *please*s. Another hand was extended to her, to
encourage her to rise from her seat. Still hesitating—"No,
no"—she was ushered into the aisle, then the clearing. She
stood there uncomfortably. Then she looked at Normalyn. Now
she spoke with gentle authority, as if only to her:

"I was their best friend, Norma Jeane's and Enid's, in the
orphanage. They were so pretty, even then. I was always
homely; that's why I was put in the home. But that doesn't
matter now."

Normalyn answered the kind smile.

"Norma Jeane and Enid were so close I'm not surprised that
years later they acted at being each other, Marilyn in a dark
wig just like Enid's beautiful real hair, Enid in a blonde wig
just like Marilyn's own gorgeous hair—"

The memory was real! *On the shoreline Enid flung a blonde wig
into the black sea, and then the other woman—* . . . Normalyn sensed
the memory evaporating again, she tried to force it back. Yield
more! But it was gone.

"And I was there when they started playing the game years ago," Sandra had continued, with a touch of embarrassed pride. "It all began there, in the shadow of the angel's wing," she seemed to say only to Normalyn.

Normalyn closed her eyes and saw Enid's chipped angel—gone now, shattered.

As if in sudden bewilderment to find herself standing among them, Sandra said to the others, "Then it all turned uglier than that girl just told you. That vile, evil Mildred Meadows!" she said angrily. She moved away from the clearing. She paused before Normalyn and touched her hand. In control again, she said quietly to Normalyn, "You're so pretty, like your mother. When we received the jacaranda bouquet, we knew you were here. That's why I came." She whispered, only to Normalyn, "The Wing of the Angel." Softly.

Before Normalyn could say anything to her, ask anything, the older woman hurried out of the church basement.

Perfect! More than she had hoped for. Lady Star announced, "Auditions! Have! Ended!"

Otto removed the boards from the windows. Night had turned purple. Timeless hours—yes, decades—had been roamed through in this basement.

The audience left quietly. The Dead Movie Stars moved out amid whispers, all subdued as if everything that had occurred must be left in the shadows of this basement. Verna La Maye waited at the exit, as if terrified to leave with her new identity. Then she moved out.

Lady Star looked about for her orchid. It had fallen on the floor, dead. She picked it up, inspected it, forced the remains into her hair.

Alone on the front row, Normalyn faced her with arms determinedly crossed, reminding that she had contributed *nothing*!

Lady Star stared back at her. She touched her hand to her chin and leaned forward. After long moments, she said, "Well . . . darling . . . why *did* Enid run in horror out of the secret hospital?"

Normalyn shook her head.

Outside, the desolate young people, rejected again—makeup smeared, odd costumes disheveled in the creeping dawn—moved silently into the twilight of Hollywood.

Thirty-Four

It was the beginning of the day, the moments before dawn. Alone, Normalyn oriented herself outside the church. Which route would she take to avoid the blemishes of Hollywood Boulevard's battlefield of wanderers? With a silent sigh, she realized she had intended to go to Troja's and Kirk's. Only Troja's now. That was not her home any more. She considered going there anyway. No, she was too tired, depressed, confused, to risk possible rejection. She walked along silent streets lined with unfazed palmtrees.

Miles away in the evaporating night, a patch of the Hollywood Hills glowed with an eruption of fire. Gliding flames, like flashing neon, were destroying—so gracefully! Normalyn heard maddened screams of sirens in this terrifying, beautiful haunted city at the edge of the ocean—a city of flowers, lost identities, mysterious revelations.

Ahead, in a murky dusk, the château where she now "lived" looked sinister, gauzy, as if draped in cobwebs. She waited, watching, before she entered its twisting corridors. She did not want to encounter the shaggy Dead Movie Stars, not now, now that this strange long night had finally ended.

It hadn't!—she knew that when she was inside the château and incongruous beginning light was attempting to seep into the maze of hallways. Inside her room, mysteries, questions, at times only puzzling images—all she had kept in abeyance during the unfolding of the epic presented by the girl at auditions—inundated her: . . . *a real abortion in a hospital isolated in the desert . . . Enid running out in horror . . . the threatened scandal that had set everything into motion—poised over it all, never erupting . . . artificial jacarandas signaling to others her presence in the city— . . .*

Normalyn sat on her bed. She reined the rampage in her mind. She evaluated clearly. In her highly dramatic presentation, the girl who had crashed from contender had admitted "making up" some of her information. She had also told of being given information—obviously self-serving—by Lady Star. Much, shaded by omissions, had clearly come from Mildred Meadows, whether through direct contact with the contender or through Lady Star. That information had armed Normalyn with an arsenal of tinted knowledge. To be used how? Would Mildred attempt to extort answers from *her* later?

There *was* authenticity within the presentation: Enid's intimate presence, with her nervous silver lighter, affirmed that, as did close parallels with the chronicles of others—Mark Poe's, Miss Bertha's—and, yes, Enid's gasped utterances in her final days. . . . Sandra, the orphan, had also verbally confirmed a claim made at the auditions. Her silent acquiescence in familiar matters suggested agreement. Even the ex-contender's admission that she had "made up" certain parts might signal only the natural embellishments required in a complex narrative—the insertion of intimate points of view to clarify motivation.

Essential illumination had occurred! The shadows that populated the distant shoreline had been given sharper clarity, and she was certain the incident was real, not a dream. . . . She had relived an incident that belonged to Marilyn Monroe— the movie star had telephoned the man she thought was her father and he had rejected her, just as "Stanley Smith" had done only days ago to *her*. That fact restored all the suspicions David Lange had banished with easy explanations. He was the one figure who remained a constant question mark, unchanged. She would confront him again—*after* she located Sandra. *The reference to "the wing of the angel"?* . . . And she must locate Dr. and Mrs. Crouch, presences of enigmatic allegiance, whose names were entangled in coils in Enid's clipping. They had refused to speak to the ex-contender, determining she was "not the right one." Well, she, Normalyn would be! With Lady Star's assistance! Yes, because on that fateful dark night of separation from Troja and Kirk—*from Kirk forever!*—Lady Star had used them—and "the orphan"—as enticements for her to remain. Of course Normalyn knew the stakes for information would be higher now, but Lady Star still needed her for whatever purpose. Normalyn was ready to barter! She must do so now—not let full morning, about to erupt through her windows, bring false clarity to mysteries she must investigate.

She rushed to Lady Star's room before—she smiled at the thought—sunlight would turn the red-haired girl into dust.

The remains of the dead orchid tangled in her hair, Lady Star opened the door.

"I *will* audition!" Normalyn's words echoed in the château.

"But of course you will," Lady Star borrowed from Mildred Meadows. Her piping voice tried with unsuccessful huskiness to conquer her delight at the news: "We'll proceed to arrange auditions *very* soon. We have petitioners to spare." She waved a breezy hand out the window, where the hopeful might already have begun to gather, "and we have *scoops* of them left over from last night."

Normalyn tried to make her contingency casual: "Naturally I'll have to talk to the Crouches, and others." Whatever she and Lady Star suspected about the other's motives, both would proceed on the announced assumption—auditions. Normalyn prepared to barter. "If—"

But Lady Star had already said, "Done!"

Without another word, Normalyn walked away.

Daylight entered her room through tall undraped windows. She fell asleep, dreaming vividly about a house isolated in the Mexican desert, where wind blew soundlessly . . . and inside the echoless house, splotched with sunlight refracted through color-stained windows, a woman lay on a strapped bed, bleeding— . . .

Hours later—it was already dark in the room, because the sun shone on this wing of the château only early in the morning—Normalyn woke to the sound of voices in the hall. The Dead Movie Stars on their way to recruit for the new auditions? A folded white envelope was slipped under her door. She waited to retrieve it, not wanting to indicate that she was here.

She heard a voice—Billy Jack's? Tyrone Power's? "Have they, uh, found her?" It was James Dean's.

"Her mom's turned vicious. She kept yelling at us outside that she's going to call the cops!" That was definitely Rita Hayworth.

"Call them because we're glamorous?" sneered Betty Grable.

"Oh, let the old woman do what she wants, darlings!" Lady Star dismissed. "*We* don't know where she went after auditions, either."

"Maybe she made up with the dude who strangled her in her scene and went off with him." That was Billy Jack.

Normalyn waited until the voices diminished. She pulled the envelope into the room. On the right-hand side of a plain white piece of paper were inked flowing initials tangling like snakes: "L.S.," penned over and over in an effort to make the letters appear engraved.

Darling—
    Dr. & Mrs. Crouch expect you very soon—*today!!!*—about New Auditions as agreed!!! *Prepare!!!*
Yours trully—
L.S.

At the bottom of the note was a telephone number.

The peeling wall by the public telephone in the corridor was so scribbled over that it seemed now to convey only one huge unintelligible message. Normalyn was about to dial the number on Lady Star's note, then, instead, dialed Troja's number. "Hello!" Troja answered on the first ring. Normalyn was flooded with relief, then joy. Troja's voice demanded into the listening telephone: "Dammit, Normalyn, is that you?"

Normalyn hung up. How dare Troja assume it was her! How dare she speak to her in that tone again! Then her feelings devised another possibility: What she had thought was anger might have been eagerness for it to be her friend. For now Normalyn would leave that in promising ambiguity, especially because she felt relief that Troja's voice had not sounded slurred. . . . Oh, and she would have to call Mayor Hughes. The last time she had called, he had asked jovially, "Well, now, honey, have you *found* yourself yet?" She did not want to hear that now. She would call him later to inform him of her new address. Ask him to inform Ted?

She remained by the telephone booth, wondering whether she was suddenly afraid of calling to arrange to see that doctor and his wife out of the past, witnesses to terrible events. She thought of calling Mark Poe in Palm Springs again, to ask him— To ask him— But she knew he had told her everything that afternoon. Ask about Michael Farrell? Right now, she wished she could remember the book he said he had been reading that day so she could get it at the library. But she hadn't given him her number, so that was that.

Impulsively, she called Information. "Dambert, Lucas Dambert—in Westwood." There was an L. E. Dambert in Brentwood, the operator informed her. She dialed, doubting that she would reach Professor Dambert. A young, polite girl answered. Normalyn asked for Dr. Dambert. "Just a moment please," the girl said, and then announced, away from the mouthpiece, "It's for you, grandfather."

After seconds, a sturdy voice announced, "Lucas Dambert."

Easily, Normalyn said, "Dr. Dambert, please forgive me for disturbing you. My name is Normalyn Morgan. I'm doing research for a book on the life of Marilyn Monroe and—"

"You want to know what occurred between us!" the voice expressed immediate delight. "Why, the matter must be getting bruited about—another young lady interviewed me not long ago. Well, I don't mind talking about it." He was eager. "We were going to run away, Miss Monroe and I, to Phoenix, in Arizona, and we—"

A huge sigh interrupted his recollection. "Oh, young lady, I'm making that up. That happens only in my memory. What really occurred is that, once, she kissed me. Will you include that in your book? I always look in every new book about her, you know, and it's never there."

Normalyn promised that she would.

"Just say that, once, she kissed me on the lips," the old professor said, and then his voice faded: "So sad, that beautiful, intelligent woman killing herself. If only—"

Normalyn listened to his wishes that Marilyn might have turned to him that night. They would have had another intelligent conversation, and she wouldn't have— . . .

Normalyn thanked him, promised him again she would include him in her book. Yes, she thought, someday she might; she might just write a book some day. . . . The interview had made her sad, although she had gathered some evidence of the reliability of the youngwoman at auditions.

Suddenly, Normalyn needed to verify something else. She dialed Information again. No, there was no listing for Stanley Smith in Palm, California, nor anywhere in the area— Wait, there was a number but it was unlisted. . . . Normalyn hung up.

David Lange had told her Stan would not have asked where she had obtained his number because he was listed, not difficult to locate. All her questions David Lange had laid to rest so easily about Stan were even more strongly aroused, now that she knew that in calling him that one day she had reenacted an event in Marilyn Monroe's life. She found in her purse the telephone number she had called to reach Stan, the number David Lange had written for her. She dialed it. Stan answered! She listened to the despised voice, listened, listened longer as he demanded to know who was calling. "This is *Normalyn*," she said, and then she hung up.

Her fear about calling the doctor and his wife had been exorcised by her sudden call to Stan. She dialed the number Lady Star had left in the note under her door.

The woman who answered was instantly delighted. "Yes, Lady Star did call." She gave Normalyn careful, considerate directions on how to get to their house: "It's just blocks away from where you are, child." She added, "Dr. Crouch and I are *most* eager for your visit." They would expect her . . . within the hour?

After dinner at a nearby coffee shop, Normalyn made herself up to look the way she had the night she had gone with the Dead Movie Stars to the Silent Scream, the way Troja had first made her up. It surprised her how easy it was today. She moistened red lips, darkened long lashes. Her hair tumbled into place on its own. Again, she painted a beauty mark on the side opposite the one on the star's cheek.

Thirty-Five

"*You* look just like her! Doctor! I believe this may be the right young lady!" Too vain for needed glasses, the woman squinted at Normalyn. In her careful seventies, Mrs. Crouch was petite, with attentively coiffed silver-blue hair. She was dressed as if to go out to dine. Her clothes were out of date, but in fine condition.

The lovely home of Dr. and Mrs. Crouch nestled in one of several blocks-long strips that had survived the pillage of neglect in the declined neighborhoods off Hollywood Boulevard. Hidden vapory lights created sparklers of color where sprinklers watered the wide rolling lawn at night. A tall spiked fence enclosing the premises camouflaged as decoration; a sign with a red thunderbolt warned that the house was wired against intruders. Normalyn had been let into the grounds by an electronic buzz that released the gate for only seconds.

"Come in, child, *please*." The woman welcomed Normalyn with warm cordiality into a house where everything was attractive, everything was in place, everything was impeccable, and everything was outmoded, as if pulled intact from the past—*preserved*.

A man appeared, very tall, slender, elegant, the woman's age, smiling a genial welcome. He was dressed in an attractive suit that looked out of date but new, like everything else here. "Yes, I believe she may be the one we've been waiting for, Mrs. Crouch," Dr. Crouch approved.

Their words jumped into further meanings. Normalyn was again in a territory where everything ordinary might turn sinister. Yet the man and his wife were beaming at her like favorite grandparents receiving a beloved child.

They led her into their gracious living room.

"We courteously *had* to decline to speak to that other young lady after a short interview," Mrs. Crouch explained to Normalyn. The woman took short steps with precise grace; she made airy motions as if to further assure her smooth passage.

"She just wasn't right," said Dr. Crouch earnestly. "Lady Star should have seen that."

All three stood in the middle of the wood-beamed room.

"Dr. Crouch!" Mrs. Crouch was aghast. "You have not extended the courtesy of our home to—" She waited. "Your *name*, child!"

Let them know you're the 'right one,' dearheart!

"Normalyn Morgan."

"Normalyn Morgan." Dr. Crouch muttered the name.

His wife closed her eyes briefly. "And now you're here—"

"From Gibson, Texas, where I lived with Enid Morgan." Normalyn rushed the still-aching information: "She died . . . recently."

"Our deepest sympathy in your bereavement," Dr. Crouch responded.

"*Deepest.*" Mrs. Crouch bowed her head for a respectful moment.

Yet Normalyn noted a distinct apprehension in their voices, as if Enid's death meant that what had been kept concealed might now be exposed.

"Please forgive my bad manners." Dr. Crouch broke the silence. "Do sit down and kindly accept our hospitality."

"Thank you." Normalyn chose a plush chair.

"You're welcome," bowed Dr. Crouch.

"You'll have a whole sofa to yourself if you sit over *there*." Mrs. Crouch guided Normalyn.

When Normalyn was seated on the sofa, the man and his wife faced her on tall upholstered chairs as if to begin an interrogation.

Like the one Enid had recounted to Mark Poe! Normalyn felt both apprehensive and thrilled by the association.

Mrs. Crouch rang a bell. A sulking black woman in maid's uniform appeared with a silver Queen Anne service. Tiny cups, engraved, looked like buds of silver flowers.

"I had Mattie prepare cocoa with a stick of cinammon, just after you called," Mrs. Crouch announced with delight. She sniffed at the scent to make sure it was subtle.

Glaring at the old man and woman, the black woman left the set precariously perched on a coffee table and departed, making as much noise as possible. Adjusting the setting, Mrs.

Crouch served. She spread out puffs of pastry on a plate. With fastidious care, she placed Normalyn's steaming chocolate on the table next to the sofa where she had relocated her.

On that table was a single framed photograph of three handsome young actors and four pretty actresses, posed against a purity of white light. Marilyn Monroe's aggressive beauty shoved away all the others in the group; but another presence insinuated back, conquering attention—another beautiful woman, dark-haired and wearing a white gossamer dress. Hers was the only figure that bore no autograph under it.

"Child, is your chocolate . . . delicious?" Mrs. Crouch queried with the slightest suggestion of a frown; her smile sweetened in compensation.

"Oh, yes, it is," And it was.

"But is it just *right* . . . the cream, the cinnamon?" Mrs. Crouch's frown deepened.

Normalyn understood. "Oh, yes, thank you." The woman had been waiting for the ritual of fussy manners to be fulfilled.

"You're welcome," Mrs. Crouch accepted. *Now* she could sip her own chocolate.

Normalyn rejected a tinge of sympathy for this old man and old woman, who seemed to be waiting to be invited to dinner. Enid had called them "the genial executioners," this man and woman who reshaped lives to suit the studios.

Mrs. Crouch said over her silver Georgian cup, "Now then, you're here to learn about great tragedy, great glamour, great dead movie stars. And you have chosen one of the most extravagant, child." Mrs. Crouch seemed to approve.

Dr. Crouch leaned just slightly toward Normalyn and confided, "For auditions, you have to tell the panel *real* secrets."

"With *proof!*" said Mrs. Crouch.

Normalyn could not reconcile her sense of foreboding with the genial smiles of this man, this woman. And yet their penetrating looks were becoming . . . sinister. This might be a dangerous encounter. . . . In *this* home, with *this* smiling old man and woman?

Mrs. Crouch said brightly, "Details are always good for initial interest."

"*Cursum Perficio!*" Dr. Crouch intoned suddenly.

Mrs. Crouch laughed delicately in approval. "That's what the slogan said on the coat of arms on the tiles outside the last house Marilyn lived in, the only one she ever owned. It means, 'I am ending my journey.' "

"Now, why don't *you* say it so you'll remember?" Dr. Crouch guided Normalyn. "*Cursum Perficio*. 'I am ending—' "

"I am *beginning* my journey." Normalyn faced them.

Mrs. Crouch gave a fluttering look to Dr. Crouch. She held her cup to her lips as if to placate a sudden nervous twitch. "Oh, don't you just love the Dead Movie Stars, child, for wanting to restore glamour to Hollywood?"

"I wonder whether that's possible any more, or if it's all gone, forever—along with courtesy, manners, respect. *Their* Hollywood." Dr. Crouch indicated the photograph next to Normalyn.

"Please don't say it will never come back, Dr. Crouch— *please.*" Mrs. Crouch touched her head as if the thought might produce a headache. "Although it is true"—she acknowledged a saddened reality—"that those 'new' people don't need us— those . . . *independents!*" With a nod, she added her own look directing Normalyn's attention to the photograph.

The dark-haired woman in the photograph looked like— *was*—Enid . . . as she appeared in the picture on the dresser in Gibson. In the attentive silence, Normalyn knew they wanted a reaction from her to the photograph. She touched the picture, removing a grain of dust. She could not think of anything to nudge the stubborn silence; so she said, "Oh, thank you, Mrs. Crouch!"

"Why, you're most certainly *welcome*, child," Mrs. Crouch accepted with a flittering smile of satisfaction on her delicate lips.

Silence sealed again.

Tell them more, dearheart. They're testing you, just like I did, remember?—when we rehearsed.

"Who is the beautiful woman next to Marilyn Monroe?" Normalyn adjusted the advice.

"The only one who didn't become a star," Dr. Crouch judged sternly, pointedly evading the name. "Finally just disappeared."

Enid, so proud, remembered as the only one who hadn't become a star. . . . Normalyn felt a doubled sadness.

"*Certainly* you've done enough research to know who she is—perhaps in relation to Marilyn?" Mrs. Crouch held her cup halfway to her lips.

"She's Enid Morgan, the woman I told you about earlier. So beautiful, too." Normalyn added tribute to her identification. *Now turn it back on them, dearheart. . . .* "She had occasion to mention *you*." *That's it!*

"What did she—?" Mrs. Crouch reached nervously for a pastry.

"I believe you 'worked' on her life," Normalyn said.

"Heaven grant her peace," Dr. Crouch intoned; his voice veered. "But in life she could be rebellious."

"God love her, but she *did* have an . . . untidy life," Mrs. Crouch did not look up from her cocoa. "And perhaps a reckless spirit."

Normalyn wished they had been talking about her.

"We did our level best to clear up her life when she first came to us. *Level* best," Dr. Crouch emphasized to Normalyn, and he went on easily now to recall "the glamorous days, the days of the *real* Hollywood" when—

*   *   *

—a small elite corps of lawyers and advisers propped the giant apparatus of power at the studios. Among those were Benjamin and Mrs. Crouch. He was a graduate of Harvard, *magna cum laude*, a physician as well as a lawyer. She—then called Emily—was an honors graduate of Radcliffe. They became figures of refinement and intellect among movie moguls, for whom, with precision and courtesy, they would remake lives, rearrange any event that was necessary for the harmony of "the studios."

It was Dr. and Mrs. Crouch who supervised the creation of three wax figures of Jean Harlow, placed at designated times at her window for adoring fans to see—standing, sitting, looking out at them—so that they would believe her to be alive until her last film was released, a hit uncompromised by death.

At the request of the studios, the Crouches "chatted" with a young starlet named Enid Morgan. Dr. and Mrs. Crouch decided, in the confidential report to 20th Century-Fox, that "although beautiful," the youngwoman was "too bright, too excessively inventive, much too rebellious" to be a movie star. Additionally, she had claimed—"in a tone of serious levity"— to be constantly considering a "great revenge" on a vastly unsavory man, "whose life we will look into for any immediate complications." The starlet herself, they reported, had terminated the interview with "ambiguous gratitude," saying, "*Thank* you, *dear* Dr. and Mrs. Crouch," before adding her most inflammatory words: "I will never give up my life, however you may judge it."

*   *   *

"In kindness to the youngwoman," Mrs. Crouch added, "we suggested that she might be employed as a stand-in." Her fluttery smile did not disguise her tense stare on Normalyn.

"And you might say she did stand in—for Marilyn." Dr.

Crouch's smile seemed cut into his face now. "Did you know that, child?—that Enid Morgan stood in for Marilyn Monroe, whom she resembled—"

"—in a strange, haunted way," Mrs. Crouch interjected. She seemed to shiver at an association recalled suddenly.

On the distant shoreline the two women looked strangely alike— For a hypnotic moment, Normalyn felt pulled back into the ghostly memory—and away from it by Dr. Crouch's words:

"—and that once she stood in for her in a situation of grave danger?" he continued his question to Normalyn. "Did you know that? Did you?"

Say yes, dearheart!

"Yes!"

"And what else do you know?" The smile on Dr. Crouch's lips froze before it shattered.

Mrs. Crouch touched her own lips as if to pluck away the smile glued there. "Tell us, for God's sake."

They were pleading with her! "I know you were involved in what happened at the D'Arcy House when Enid ran out." She chose her words carefully.

Dr. Crouch inhaled a sigh, something very much like relief.

Mrs. Crouch's sigh hovered over his. Then her face changed back to the earlier collusion of smiles. "I believe, Dr. Crouch, that Normalyn is the right one."

"I have arrived at the same conclusion." Dr. Crouch restored his own quick smile. "Now we must give her all the information she will need soon."

Again that disquieting echo—Normalyn detected it—as if she would be expected to report to someone else what she heard here. And it was *not* to the Dead Movie Stars.

Dr. Crouch addressed Normalyn gravely: "It was an audacious plan! It was devised by Alberta Holland. Eventually she had to enlist me for it to work, and I, of course, demanded to know—"

Thirty-Six

—the full details of how it began.

The plan was concocted at first only to allow Marilyn Monroe hope that she might be able to have the child she wanted more than anything else in her life—and at the same time to stave off the threatened scandal such a child would enflame for the dynasty of the Kennedys. It pitted two archenemies, Alberta Holland and Mildred Meadows, against each other.

Enid Morgan had just returned from Texas, where she had gone, she said in her cryptic, cynical way, to have "the child of a son-of-a-bitch." Soon after, Mildred's rampage on Marilyn Monroe occurred. Enid knew they must turn to Alberta Holland. She admired the staunch counselor, and Marilyn "loved" her.

Sipping her fragrant tea, Alberta Holland listened to the reason for the visit of the two beautiful women. "Is the asserted involvement with the Kennedys—both of them—true?"

"Yes," Marilyn answered. She looked defiantly at Enid.

Alberta tempered her voice to soothe her words. "I'm sorry to agree that Mildred is right, in that a pregnancy discovered or a child born amid inflammatory accusations will implicate the brothers, one or both, and perhaps . . . destroy them." And with them would be crushed the inspired dream she championed, of a social Camelot, she thought but did not say.

"Nothing must harm Robert! Or *Mr.* President." Marilyn said the last with only a touch of resentment. "They mustn't even *know any*thing about *any* of this. And you both must promise me. Please promise me now!"

Alberta promised, touched. Her cigarette lighter dormant in her hands, Enid nodded her agreement.

381

Marilyn's voice diminished. "I still love Robert, and I want this child."

What Alberta had heard bruised her feelings about the Kennedys. She knew it is possible for men to be great leaders yet flawed in their private lives. Her second-favorite writer, Shakespeare—she preferred Proust—had dealt with just that. . . . So she did not judge. She had adored Marilyn Monroe from their first encounter—admired her intelligence, sensitivity, daring. Yet there was a distinct vulnerability about her that might cause her to misjudge intentions, perceive—*hope* for—commitment where none had been offered, perhaps not even implied. She knew, too, that if the Kennedys fell—with the symbolic power of a longed-for "new frontier"—the country would reel in reaction. Among others, Richard Nixon waited greedily. The good the Kennedys symbolized must be protected.

Alberta Holland had a reputation for being a profoundly, even blindly, earnest woman of dedication. According to her trusted friend, Teresa de Pilar, "the indomitable Alberta" had once claimed, "Smiling is frivolous when injustice is rampant." Still, she smiled fondly now at Marilyn. Borrowing a phrase the two women had used earlier, she promised, "You *will* have your child, perhaps in an interval of lavender spring which will occur just for you."

Then Alberta's mind tumbled furiously as she began to shape her plan: "Mildred must be tricked into using the offered item about a miscarriage, a reconciliation with a loving ex-husband." The brothers would survive the remains of the threatened scandal, she told them. Robbed of the enormous impact of Marilyn's name—and of the pregnancy—it would all become just gossip, accusations all men of power endure, rumors without evidence. "Rumors capable of arousing sympathy," she added, and hoped that that would be so. "The item in Mildred's column has to be false, but believed."

"That's very smart. Yes, that's what we have to do!" Marilyn was desperate to accept a firm solution.

Enid said with a wry smile. "Of course it is. But how are you going to make Mildred cooperate, Alberta?"

"By cunning, duplicity, lies—*her* terms." Through years of mutual detestation, she and Mildred had come to know each other intimately. They watched each other from a distance, read everything about each other.

Eager to be reassured, Marilyn let her attention wander away from the web of dangers, out the window, to peaceful breaths of lavender outside. She wished none of this were happening. She imagined that there would be the sudden eager honking of a car outside, and it would be Robert. She imagined their conversation. He would begin, "I love you—"

"Once the item appears"—Alberta's mind was sweeping over all her knowledge of the detested woman—"Mildred won't dare retract it. She'll separate herself from even defused scandal. To do otherwise would mean admitting that she—*Mildred Mead*-ows!"—she shredded the name—"has been duped, deceived, fooled"—she embraced each word—"*and* by Alberta Holland!" Again, she hoped she was right.

Even as Alberta's mind continued to toss with ideas, she studied the two women closely. They at first appeared to be opposites because of the difference in their hair coloring, their manner—Enid was dark-haired, cool, somewhat aloof; Marilyn was blonde, warm, openly affectionate. In that careful scrutiny, Alberta detected a natural beauty in Enid that Marilyn had copied—no, *created*, Alberta withdrew any implicit judgment in her assessment—created through masterful artifice that had now achieved its own reality, its *own* naturalness.

Enid must have understood the meaningful, careful attention to their appearance, because she offered this information: For years—"to confuse reporters for the hell of it and give Marilyn some privacy"—Enid had often appeared in public, not as Marilyn Monroe but as "Marilyn Monroe in disguise." One or the other of them would tip eager reporters: "Wearing a black wig, Marilyn will be at—, on—, dressed in—" When photographers sprang at her, Enid would shelter her face, just so, while making sure it was captured by the cameras. That image became so recognizable that several times her photograph appeared identified as "Marilyn Monroe spotted in her usual disguise." To lock the masquerade, during one daring and rare excursion together—

"*I* wore a black wig and was Enid, and Enid wore a blonde wig and was *me*; and *she* was asked for autographs while *I* was ignored." Marilyn joined in with the sudden delight of a schoolgirl.

Her eyes holding Alberta's tightening scrutiny, Enid went on to tell about her best performance as Marilyn, a time when she'd recognized Mildred Meadows spying from her limousine while her photographer pursued with clicking camera. "I deliberately backed up against her ugly car—a car I'll never forget," she added with a shudder of memory—and her look on Marilyn shared it. "I was so close that I saw her white face behind the dark pane."

Alberta knew how possible their subterfuge was. There was a unique "sameness" beyond appearance and similiar outline.

It must come out of an intense association, known only to them. An idea gained strength. Later, Alberta would wonder to what extent Enid had helped to guide it.

"So Mildred still has the picture," Alberta said to herself. During silenced moments, she freshened their tea. She brought out a few more of the plump little madeleine cakes she so enjoyed. As she sipped her tea and took a bite of her little cake, Alberta searched for an essential connection—it was already lurking!—from a distant time she had shared with Mildred, a connection to present circumstances. Now she roamed through that time:

Mildred had had a consuming closeness with her exquisitely beautiful daughter, Tarah. When Tarah became pregnant by an actor, a drifter, Mildred contacted him and suggested a meeting to explore "matters of mutual benefit." At her invitation, they met in her greenhouse—"where we will be assured of privacy"—at the exact time of day that Tarah tended to her rare orchids, a hobby Mildred encouraged. Separated from Tarah by lush vines, Mildred met with the actor, the drifter. She offered him a large amount of money to exit from her daughter's life. He eagerly accepted. Mildred turned to Tarah, who had heard every word just as Mildred had intended. "He didn't even barter for more," Mildred disdained. The drifter got nothing, not a cent. Tarah rejected him with a ferocity Mildred complimented at dinner that night—a celebratory dinner of lobster with the lightest butter sauce and an astonishing Dom Perignon.

Mildred stopped delighting in the evening when Tarah informed her that she intended to have her child. "You'll destroy your whole life, your reputation, your beauty!" Mildred appealed to logic.

Some time after, Mildred "eerily acquiesced" to the birth. Gaily, she informed Tarah that she had arranged for the child to be born "under the most careful circumstances, and, of course, at the D'Arcy House, under the care of that most trusted Dr. Janus." Afraid, Tarah turned to the one person beyond reach of her mother's arteries of power—Alberta Holland. Alberta agreed to contact Dr. Janus, to assure that all was right. Of course it was not. Mildred had been emphatic with Dr. Janus that a stillborn child would be "vastly appreciated and equally rewarded." Alberta "convinced" the doctor that if he did not reject the terrifying proposition, *she* would assure him prison.

With Mildred in chilling attendance in the amber-hued room at the D'Arcy House, Tarah gave birth to a live child. Dr.

Janus held it out to Mildred, who turned away in disgust. Five years later, driving away in a rage from Mildred's increasing rampages against the child's "ugliness," Tarah crashed in her car. Mildred blamed the death of Tarah on the child, insisting her daughter was always protecting "the ugly little creature," who, it was true, nestled in fear against her mother at every moment. . . . That violence in Mildred's past provided a strong undertow to her demands on Marilyn.

Alberta popped another madeleine into her mouth. Suddenly she knew how she would use that sad, ugly incident to protect Marilyn *and* her child. "We have to convince Mildred that she has *seen* the demanded abortion!"

Enid held her lighter tensely.

"I couldn't simulate—" Marilyn shivered with horror.

"Of course not," Alberta reassured her tenderly.

Now Alberta's plan formed—so daring, so audacious that it *would* work. In a few hours, at Mildred's mansion, as demanded, Enid would inform Mildred that Marilyn had—of course—acquiesced to her "logical demands." "Mildred believes in the irrefutable logic of evil," Alberta explained. Enid would provide the woman with all the information on how her insane demand would be carried out, identifying the place of execution—"the D'Arcy House, of course"; she would agree to verify the exact date and time later.

"You must keep saying 'of course' in order to plant suspicion," Alberta advised Enid. Enid would then inform Mildred that Marilyn must be in disguise—of course. "Then," Alberta instructed Enid, "you must add, very, very quickly, that the disguise will be one she's familiar with—say it as if to assuage her—a disguise one of her photographers captured on film while she oversaw from her limousine. When she—"

"I wish—" Marilyn sighed. Her own fantasy fought her. It had stopped as Robert was about to introduce her to his mother. Marilyn stood up. "I feel suddenly sad. You and Enid talk, please, and tell me all you said, later." She placed an appreciative hand on Alberta's shoulder. "I'd like to lie in the sun."

But there was no sun.

How alone she seemed, hoping for sun on an increasingly graying day, Alberta thought, placing her own hand over Marilyn's. For a moment she allowed herself to imagine that she had a daughter, that her daughter was Marilyn.

Marilyn called a cab. She would wait outside, she said, to allow them to continue talking. At the door she turned around, all curves and blonde beauty and outrageous sensuality, and breathed a puff of gratitude: "And *thank* you, thank you a whole lot, *really*," she told Alberta.

The gray day turned silver. Alberta imagined Marilyn Monroe standing outside studying the lavender blossoms that fascinated her. Yes, they were like her in that they, too, had a special beauty. But they lasted so briefly; Alberta did not welcome that thought.

Alberta directed her attention back to Enid—startled anew by Enid's cooler beauty. "Mildred will—" But she had lost her train of thought in the bedazzled moments.

Enid guided her back knowledgeably: "You want me to guide Mildred to the photograph by her limousine."

"Yes!" Then Alberta conveyed her evolving plan to Enid, "with embellishments to be supplied as required." It relied on stirring in Mildred a calculated series of associations and suspicions. From that time when the haunting youngwoman had sought her help, Alberta remembered being fascinated by Tarah's unique mannerisms, the perfection of manners demanded by Mildred in constant quiet war with a desire to rebel against such imposed rigidity. This resulted in quick but graceful movements, as if ceremony must be gotten out of the way: sudden attention to her makeup at odd moments; a soft lifting of the veil of her hat to reveal a new expression. She said "please" often, while her eyes flashed in rejection of pleading. She had asked Alberta whether she might have some sherry—"just three sips," she'd added automatically, then instantly rejected her own request, explaining that Mildred had come to expect those exact words from her, uttered first when she was only a girl and now cherished as part of a ritual, while they waited for dusk, to watch Mildred's garden change its shadings.

As Alberta spoke those memories of Tarah, Enid listened attentively, as if already rehearsing what Alberta was only now revealing.

"By suggesting those movements, using a few key words, you must arouse in Mildred her memory of the daughter she destroyed while claiming to love her." Alberta explained to Enid the horrible parallel between Mildred's unsuccessful demand on Tarah and the present one on Marilyn. They would use that to their own ends.

Alberta continued to explain: After Enid left the mansion of the hated woman, Mildred would suspect everything that had occurred between them. She always did, believing that one uncovered truth only by discovering lies. She would realize that Enid had *intended* to guide her to a certain photograph of

Marilyn Monroe, to verify the disguise to be employed at the D'Arcy House. She would discover what they wanted her to—that the photograph was of Enid pretending to be Monroe in a dark wig.

Alberta was certain of this: Mildred would then couple her discovery with Enid's admonishment that she, Mildred, would—of course—not be allowed into the guarded house. She would make the desired conclusion: They *wanted* her there, carrying in her mind the cleverly implanted image in the photograph, the same image she would see at the D'Arcy House in a grandly simulated abortion.

"She will be sure it will be me pretending to be Marilyn," Enid understood, "but it won't be."

"Exactly." When Mildred entered the D'Arcy House, Alberta continued with the excitement of a general about to vanquish another with impeccable strategy based on perfect knowledge of the enemy's own maneuvers, the systematic disorientation of Mildred, already prepared for, would immediately commence. The time would be set for a certain phase of twilight when visual perception is almost equivocal. From the elaborate windows of the D'Arcy House, refracted shards of light, colored by the stained glass, would slice at Mildred's eyes. Simultaneously, her confidence would grow as she encountered predictable obstacles—guards, attendants she would accept, thrilled, as part of the charade staged to deceive her. At the exact moment, Enid would run out of a certain room. Mildred's assumptions would crash. She would be forced into the only conclusion that would not prove her deductions wrong: At the last moment Enid had faced the impossibility of the contrived deceit and so had fled.

But—

When Mildred opened the room she would be triumphantly certain she would find vacated with only the instruments of the simulated operation remaining in judgment of foiled cunning, she would be pitched into a turmoil of memories by a graphic unexpected sight: In the same amber-hued room in which Tarah's child had been born, she would see a doctor she vaguely recognized, extending to her the mangled proof of the demanded abortion. In shattered moments of jarred perception, images of Tarah in childbirth, Tarah dying, Monroe in the demanded abortion once demanded of Tarah would tangle violently—Tarah, Monroe, Tarah, Monroe, Tarah— Rejecting the unmistakable pursuing face of memory, she would be forced to grasp defensively for that of present reality, convincing herself she had seen Marilyn Monroe.

Enid leaned away from the eerie confidence with which Alberta predicted the expertly manipulated confusion of images that would lead Mildred to the required conclusion.

"But Mildred will have seen *another* woman in the *simulated* abortion?" Enid spoke slowly, precisely, but she had not intended to form a question.

"What else?" Alberta said tersely.

With sustained care in her choice of words, Enid said, "It's all possible, Alberta. I agree that Mildred would be thrown into the terrible confusion your brilliant plan requires, but not by a simulated abortion." She held her eyes on Alberta's.

"Then we'll have to convince her that it *isn't* simulated." Alberta drank her tea.

Enid felt a cold apprehension, because when she spoke those last words, Alberta Holland, for the first time in their conversation, avoided her eyes.

Thirty-Seven

Years later, Normalyn felt that same chill of apprehension. Enid's fleeing from the secret hospital had been convincingly conveyed as occurring with real panic, beyond the dissimulation intended to confuse Mildred. Had Enid, too, discovered something *she* had not expected?

"How *did* Alberta convince Mildred the abortion wasn't simulated?" Normalyn forced herself not to flinch at her own question.

"An excellent woman was hired," Mrs. Crouch answered quickly. "We worked on the simulated flesh, the—" Her hands fluttered on her lap.

"What did she see, Dr. Crouch?" Because the old man's voice had gained vibrant life in roaming over the intrigue, Normalyn pushed her question to ride on the impetus of the narrative, to *force* a connecting answer.

"She saw the simulated abortion, what else?" Dr. Crouch snapped so quickly the smile was abandoned on his face.

"What did she *really* see?" Normalyn pursued.

Mrs. Crouch covered her ears. "I know nothing, nothing."

"We must tell the truth." Dr. Crouch seemed to be reminding himself of whatever personal summons they were responding to, had momentarily rejected.

"I knew nothing!" Mrs. Crouch pushed away any words of accusation.

"You pretended not to know!" Dr. Crouch scolded.

Normalyn ambushed these moments of alienated guilt: *"Tell me now!"*

"Mildred saw a real abortion of a woman hired by Stanley Smith." Dr. Crouch sat erectly in his chair.

And that's what Enid had discovered only then—a real abortion donated by Stan. "That's why Enid ran out in real panic," Normalyn said aloud.

"Alberta knew that only a real abortion performed before Mildred would throw her into the required confusions. And the woman *was* paid handsomely," Dr. Crouch added logic of his own.

Normalyn turned away in disgust.

Dr. Crouch extended his logic: "Of course the fact of the real abortion had to be kept secret from Enid and Marilyn—"

"—along with the fact that you and your wife were involved," Normalyn said with certainty, "because Enid hated both of you—she called you the genial executioners."

Muffling words of shock, Mrs. Crouch clasped her hands as if about to pray.

"Alberta *convinced* Enid our talents were essential," Dr. Crouch asserted proudly. "And she came to *respect* us, trust us."

Normalyn would keep that in abeyance. She had tested her power to demand information from them, a power she knew was borrowed from, enhanced by, another source. *Perhaps the lavender bouquets, dearheart!* . . . But Normalyn felt alienated from Miss Bertha. No, only from Alberta Holland. Yet she had discovered that the tea Miss Bertha had "imagined"—so sweetly remembered—*had* occurred.

"But listen!" The excited vibrancy returned to Dr. Crouch's voice. "Listen to why it had to be done as it was! Enid's encounter with Mildred worked splendidly!"

"Splendidly!" Mrs. Crouch congratulated.

"The deception at the D'Arcy House worked exactly as Alberta had known it would." Dr. Crouch leaned toward Normalyn. "Mildred informed her readers of the 'miscarriage.' And now— "

* * *

—still rationed, hope extended that the extravagant plan could work. Would tomorrow sustain it? Time extended. The letter threatening scandal seemed to have been defused. They lived tensely with the eerie fact of Mildred's terminated column— only stilled dramatically to announce its greatest scandal?

More hope emboldened the evolving plan: In secure hiding in the nurturing warmth of a secluded desert city, Marilyn Monroe was carefully tended by Teresa de Pilar during the careful period that must be overseen at every moment. Teresa enlisted an American doctor who had hidden with her—and loved her—in the Spanish hills of revolution. He was amply able to cope with any dangers to the pregnancy.

For the birth and care of the child, all necessary equipment was obtained by the doctor. Reasons for the star's absence from the studio and public view were provided—and verified as required—by the Crouches: suspension for the rebellious movie star; a series of mild illnesses that might become serious if unattended; self-imposed isolation to set her tense life in order. Marilyn made strategic telephone calls, asserting she was well, in hiding. She telephoned two of her ex-husbands. The Kennedys were allowed desired separation. "When lying, it is always advisable to use as much truth as possible so that the made-up parts convince," Mrs. Crouch stressed when they issued a report that the star was depressed over "a recent love affair."

At advantageous intervals—fleetingly, in order to emphasize the reported hiding of the star—Enid appeared as "Monroe in disguise." Reporters were tipped. Once, in the blonde wig—as Marilyn herself—she was spotted by screaming fans as she rushed into a waiting car. Daringly, Enid paused to give an autograph through the window.

It was all proceeding with uncanny ease. Dr. Crouch remarked on that to Mrs. Crouch. Of course he was thrilled by the success of the elaborate deception. Yet, some nights, its very lack of complications to overcome baffled him. There were *always* obstacles in complex intrigues—but none in this. One night, in bed, Dr. Crouch had an uneasy sense of obstacles *forbidden*. He sat up. In the dark, he could hear "a soundless ticking" he thought he recognized. He woke Mrs. Crouch to listen. She heard it, a clicking quietude.

Success emboldened, expectations firmed. Why shouldn't this plan work? Hadn't Dr. and Mrs. Crouch been able to cover up the murder of a *king* by— . . . Still, that very night, there was the listening silence, alert, sleeping.

Hope reigned. It *was* possible!

After the birth, Marilyn would be rushed home—with all due care—and reported "recovering from illness and exhaustion requiring quiet and rest." To add veracity, another woman—who would know nothing of what had transpired—would help care for the "ailing movie star," replacing Teresa, who would retreat slowly, as required. Taken to another location—an ordinary house already fully equipped to receive it—the child would be in the best of hands, the most deeply devoted and trusted—Enid's. The American doctor would join her immediately.

Alternatives were allowed as confidence grew. Enid told Alberta that she had connections in Texas. "A powerful, insular state," Alberta evaluated. Yes. And Enid could "blackmail rich political stepparents into total cooperation"—they had adopted her "illegally," she told Alberta, "by paying a lot—but not enough—for me." If necessary to protect the child's identity, she would retreat there for a period of safety, claiming the child as her own—in constant but guarded touch to assure Marilyn of the child's well-being.

"I gave birth there to a child of my own," Enid told Alberta, "away from the fray, in big, sulking Texas."

"Is your child still there?" Alberta ventured cautiously.

Clicking her lighter as if it were a revolver, Enid did not answer.

Late one night, the telephone rang at the home of Dr. and Mrs. Crouch. In predetermined signal, Enid left a number with Mrs. Crouch, for the doctor to contact her. Dr. Crouch called from a telephone booth. At another booth, Enid told Dr. Crouch to proceed with the next phase—reports of Marilyn's condition at home.

Enid said joyfully, "Marilyn's child was born—a girl! Marilyn is home now—very delicate, of course, but safe, and well. And the baby is in my care. She's fine—tiny, tiny, but fine, and *beautiful*." Enid inhaled in shared triumph: "And *strong*, with all of Norma Jeane's strength!"

* * *

Marilyn Monroe had a daughter. Normalyn accepted, and Enid had called her beautiful.

"Then immediately afterwards there descended over all of us a terrifying silence," Dr. Crouch whispered. Mrs. Crouch shivered as if the chilled quiet had invaded her.

Normalyn felt immersed in that distant silence.

Dr. Crouch spoke hushed words: "That tense quietude exploded when—"

* * *

—Enid telephoned Dr. Crouch. She was "stranded somewhere, not sure exactly where, on a highway, oh, in the area of—"

Signals of danger!

Dr. Crouch instructed her to inquire as to her precise location. To save time reaching her, he would drive out now and call her along the way, at the number to which she would return with the information. When he contacted her immediately after, public telephone to public telephone, she told him:

"We've all been deceived! The only reason the impossible plan worked is that from the beginning it's been overseen and encouraged—and made possible!—by a huge conglomerate of powerful interests with one purpose: to destroy the Kennedys. There was a vast conspiracy over our tiny plot that seemed so huge! *We were only a part of their plan, and we did exactly what we were manipulated to do!*"

The machinery of vast invisible power at work—*that* was what Dr. Crouch had detected in the dark of night.

"We thought we were stopping it all," Enid said now in soft amazement, "but we were giving them the means to destroy— with our own 'hidden' conspiracies." She had learned all that from the braggadocio Stan Smith—"he's in the secret employ of everyone!"—when—

—on this day of deadly revelations, he had called her answering service earlier and left a message: "Important. Personal. Urgent you call me." Enid responded only because of the untypical gravity. On the telephone, Stanley told her he had to see her because he had just "learned the damnedest thing" that concerned her and Monroe.

Enid waited tensely in her own apartment.

Stanley turned up with a bottle of Dom Perignon, to show he had "no hard feelings despite all that went wrong." He wanted to "balance everything now."

She could hardly restrain shouting out her detestation of him as he opened the wine, frowning because it had not popped. He poured the chilled champagne into two glasses he had brought with him, a touch of "elegance" he had learned from his friend, Johnny Stompanatto. He said casually, "The letter that got all of you started up in all this?—the anonymous letter about the 'immorality' of the Kennedys?" He sipped the champagne. "—that letter? When J. Edgar received it and it was linked to a Bel Air billionaire—" He waited for her to savor the wine.

She did, longing to fling it at him.

"—all Edgar knew was that he had a powerful unloaded weapon. You—Alberta, the Crouches, all of you—loaded it for him."

Enid could not yet grasp his full meaning, but the fragments were terrifying. She did not dare risk giving him information with a question. His raking looks on her, even now, revealed he was desiring her. She had to find out everything.

She held her champagne glass in both hands, close to her face so that the amber of her eyes challenged the amber of the wine; she smiled the "slashed smile" he admired on her.

He slid his fingers along her arm. She wanted to wrench away with loathing, for what he'd done to her before, how easily he thought all could be "forgotten." Instead, she poured more champagne into his glass, brought it to his lips, and then she sipped from the exact place, resisting, every moment, the longing to spit the wine at him.

"Of course. It all began when . . ." She pretended only to be pondering. She made her voice furry with sensuality, knowing that often Stan reacted more to the tone of a voice than the words he heard, even responded to, like now.

"Before any of you were involved," he said. "Hoover knew the letter wasn't enough. He gave it to Mildred, knowing how she hates the Kennedys, sure she'd know what to do with it—and she did." He looked at Enid in deep earnest, making sure that from her vantage his shoulders were at their widest. "Didn't you ever wonder how it all proceeded so damn smoothly, nothing going wrong—something that impossible—everything falling into place? I did, from the time Crouch asked me to get him the woman. He didn't tell me who she'd be replacing. You know, he heard of me through *you*; you must've expressed lots of admiration," he congratulated Enid.

"Oh, yes," she told him. No, she had not wondered how it was all moving without obstacles. She had been too eager to succeed to miss graver dangers. Marilyn had not wondered, nor Alberta, nor—

"All these powerful interests," Stanley went on with dramatic authority. "Edgar was just a part of it. . . . You're not drinking your champagne, Enid." He frowned harshly. He became suspicious when anyone was thoughtful.

"Oh, that's just because I love to hear you talk about important things that only *you* know," she purred at him.

"And I know plenty. Everything." He squared broad shoulders broadened even more by the suit made for him by Johnny's ex-tailor. "The C.I.A., Secret Service, factions in the F.B.I.—the whole fuckin' right wing, the huge industries, all those damn moralists out there, maybe even"—he said the next reverentially—"some Mafia, organized crime. That's who got behind your plan to make it work. They just waited for you to bring it all together." He paused to lower one dark eyebrow for impact. "You gave them all they needed to make the accusations in the letter true: Alberta's secret plot, the paid abortion of a real kid, Marilyn hiding the pregnancy, you going out pretending to be her to cover it all up, and now Marilyn having the kid." He ran his fingers along her shoulder. "Now it's about to end. Just odds and ends and then the scandal will bust open."

In a flash Enid saw it all—the flood of reporters, the blinding cameras—... COVER-UP INVOLVES PAID ABORTION ... MARILYN'S CHILD KEPT HIDDEN ... JOHN AND ROBERT KENNEDY— ... No! There would be no easy surrender.

Stanley assumed his gravest pose, square chin propped on firm fist. He leaned forward. "Now that it's about to explode, why the hell shouldn't you know first? After all you did for that bitch Monroe, who hates you—"

"You're wrong! She loves me as much as I love her—and we're bound together in a way that you—" Enid stopped. She could not afford with her rage to curb the bragging information she must have from him: why—exactly—he was here.

"Whatever." He shrugged his broad shoulders; he was already moving on to assert how he knew all these matters— because he was "deeply trusted" as a man who was "loyal, *completely* loyal."

Oh, yes, Enid knew, he was loyal to those who paid him for his petty crookery. His "loyalty" had been bought by so many that they and he forgot under whose silencing pay he was functioning at which moment. Now, in these moments during which she had to choke her rage, she was grateful he was such a puffed-up braggart that he did not realize that he would be swept with them on the tide of destruction they had been tricked into creating.

"You always pride yourself on how smart you are." Stanley could not keep judgment out of his voice. "So I figured if I told you now, you might find a way to separate yourself from it all. I'm here to help you, Enid." He leaned back to accept a surge of gratitude.

She raised her champagne glass to him, as if in a toast, but she held the glass by the stem because otherwise her hand would have crushed it.

"You're quite a woman, Enid." He ran his finger slowly across her chest. "No one else like you. You'll think of something, I bet."

"Of course I'll think of something," she said.

"By the way, where's Marilyn's kid?" He puffed up the expensive handkerchief in his jacket pocket.

He—they, the others he was working for *this* moment—knew everything except that! That was his purpose for being here. At least a main part of it. He was too stupid to dissimulate too much at the same time. He needed to find out that one essential detail—overlooked, while everything else was ready to churn destruction! Alberta had warned against "the one overlooked detail that so often annihilates the perfect plot"! Enid longed to laugh in Stan's face.

He waited for her answer, trying not to look anxious.

Enid bowed her head. She put down the glass of champagne. "You didn't know *that*, Stanley?" She looked up quickly. "You know everything except *that*?"

"Why, I—" Stanley was powerfully disoriented.

"You didn't know that Marilyn's child died?"

Thirty-Eight

That is what they must claim now, Enid told Dr. Crouch as she stood in the booth off the Santa Ana Freeway. Alberta Holland, to whom she had spoken first, agreed that that was the only possibility of jarring the machinery of destruction—Marilyn's child must be presumed to have died, already buried quietly. Someone must immediately inform Marilyn of the new subterfuge—and of the actual well-being of the child. Enid could not, nor could Alberta—because of close association, and because Marilyn's telephones were wired and the house under constant scrutiny. It must be someone who would not be suspected.

"It might work, it might not," Enid said, feeling the weariness of months of exploited intrigue. "All relies now on what happens in the next few hours."

Then she delivered to Dr. Crouch Alberta's firm message to him: "She told me to be sure to remind you"—Enid slowed her words for emphasis—"that she counts on *your* loyalty in order to ensure *hers* to *you*."

"Of course!" Dr. Crouch responded without pause.

After they hung up, having discussed one or two more details, Dr. Crouch waited by the telephone booth in Hollywood. In his time, he and Mrs. Crouch had devised what he had considered "enormous, ingenious plots" to destroy or save, as needed by the studios. But this! With its arteries of power, the omnipotent conglomerate cleared away all obstacles in their attempted deception, guiding them step by step to construct their own trap!

Dr. Crouch realized all this at the corner of Highland and Franklin avenues on a day bursting with sunlight. There were sweeps of flowers everywhere, all colors, all hues. Frowning down at a speck of dust marring his immaculate suit, Dr. Crouch knew they had all been pawns who had thought they were rulers—but he admired the superb cunning. A fly buzzed irritatingly around him. And yet, he realized with equal awe, even that seemingly flawless plan, which had ingeniously subsumed theirs, had missed attending to the most important component: the whereabouts of the child! Dr. Crouch swatted at the nettlesome fly. In disgust, he saw that he had squashed it, an ugly, tiny smear of dirtied blood on his palm.

*   *   *

Normalyn looked about this placid house containing disorder. She had seen still more of Enid, discovered more to admire—her courage, yes, and her quick cunning; less welcome, she was coming to know Stan Smith, adding her own detestation of him to Enid's. Later, she would identify Enid's act of vengeance on him, which she knew was central to the mystery she was exploring. . . . She tried now to adjust Mildred's sudden ambiguity within the vaster plan—a part of it from the beginning? Her accounts belied that assumption. There remained the matter of the terminated column. . . . For now, Normalyn retained this: A daughter had been born to Marilyn Monroe, a daughter in the care of Enid during crucial hours.

"Enid had emphasized there must be no further contact among us," Dr. Crouch had continued, assuming a precise tone; "so it astonished me when Marilyn telephoned us late at night."

"She should *not* have." Mrs. Crouch added her own exact admonition.

"Certainly *not!*" Dr. Crouch reasserted.

They were being too emphatic. Normalyn was alert; she would scrutinize their words carefully, carefully.

"On the telephone, Marilyn's voice," Dr. Crouch remembered, "was slurred—"

*   *   *

—pulled by physical jolts to her body, the pills she had taken to still pain. "My daughter—" she said.

"You know she's dead." Dr. Crouch was speaking the instructed words, asserting the lie to the hidden presences listening on the line. Naturally the star must have been informed of the subterfuge; why else would she be calling other than to assert it?

"Then it was all for nothing?" Marilyn asked Dr. Crouch.

"Yes." He had to speak definite words, and few.

Her voice was fragile, like a wounded girl's. "And Robert?"

He stopped her from further reference to the man she still loved. In the haze of pain and pills—and longing for the child she knew had to be kept safely from her now—she might slip, veer away from the necessary dissimulation. So Dr. Crouch said firmly—very firmly, to end the dangerous possibility of a misstep in crucial moments, "It was foolish of you to attempt all this—you, alone!" For added emphasis of the new subterfuge they must establish, he handed the telephone to Mrs. Crouch. "Yes," she added, "and you are going to bring destruction to everyone if you persist." They were—of course—speaking *only* to the invisible presences overhearing, adding—naturally—further authenticity to the child's death.

Dr. Crouch took the telephone again: "And there is no way you can stop it now." But clearly he knew there was new hope.

Marilyn's long sigh vanished into a voice full of resolve: "I know a way," she said.

* * *

"What was she going to attempt, the poor soul?" Dr. Crouch wondered now.

"We've pondered that so many nights—what she thought she could possibly do by then." Mrs. Crouch sustained a sigh. "We never found out because—" She put her hands to her lips. "Dr. Crouch, please, *you* say it."

"Because, instead, soon after"—Dr. Crouch's somber words slowed, his eyes closed—"in the early darkness of morning"—he opened his eyes in surprise—"Marilyn Monroe killed herself."

Normalyn felt deepened sorrow for the movie star—so beautiful, so famous, so alone at the last.

"Those were the last words she spoke to us." Dr. Crouch's voice had lost its force.

Normalyn did not believe their account of the telephone call—not *their* part of it. Telling it together, they had been much too selective in their rationed words, like someone not lying, exactly, because of fear of detection. Dr. Crouch had blurred details about how he was sure the movie star had been informed her child was alive, to be presumed dead. They had given much too much explication and necessity to cruel words. They had seemed grudgingly compelled to tell what they would have preferred to leave unspoken, battling with themselves as they told of events rushing toward doom.

"We did everything possible to salvage it all, everything for her good, child. Remember that! Remember!" Dr. Crouch exhorted Normalyn.

"*Only* for her, always, always, through all those arduous months of our sacrifice and fear, child," Mrs. Crouch affirmed.

Normalyn's suspicion firmed: Someone or something was coaxing them to tell her their ugly truths! She glanced at the photograph beside her, at the gorgeous blonde woman, the magnificent dark one. She would connect herself to their defiance!

And remember the artificial bouquets, dearheart, pretend you're sure they received one! Assuming strength, Miss Bertha's voice added resolution.

"I don't believe all you've told me about the telephone call," Normalyn challenged. "You weren't trying to help *her.*" She became surer. "It's clear that you were only trying to separate yourselves in any way from it all because you knew you were being overheard. That didn't work or you wouldn't be trying to explain it to me so carefully, distorting—"

"Young lady!" Dr. Crouch stood up.

"We will not be judged!" Mrs. Crouch stood with him.

Dr. Crouch shook his head as if to reorient himself to the demands of these moments. "Ask whatever you like." He stood staunchly. He held his wife's arm firmly, to demand her compliance.

"Nothing at all to hide! Ask!" Mrs. Crouch understood; then, as if her own harsh tone had baffled her, she added with a briefly resurrected smile, "Please, child."

They were allowing questions! Normalyn tested: "How the hell were you sure someone had reached the movie star to tell her of the new plan to pretend her daughter was dead?"

"Because Stanley Smith went!" Dr. Crouch answered.

"No, oh, no." Normalyn wanted to reject the hated presence.

"He was the only one trusted in both camps," Dr. Crouch defended. "When Marilyn called, we were *sure* Stanley had reached her."

"Were you really sure?" Normalyn demanded.

"Yes!" Dr. Crouch insisted, wiping his brow with an immaculately white handkerchief.

"Why are you sweating!" Normalyn asked harshly.

Mrs. Crouch protested with horror, "Dr. Crouch *never* perspires, young lady!"

Dr. Crouch mopped more perspiration.

"Were you *really* sure Stan reached her?" Normalyn pursued.

"So sure," Mrs. Crouch offered indignantly, "that we called her to verify—" She stopped her clumsy words.

"Mrs. Crouch!" Dr. Crouch admonished.

"*You* called *her*," Normalyn understood. "She *didn't* call you—that was a goddamned lie. When you found out there was danger, you called her to pretend you had just discovered what you were part of. *You* told her her child was dead—trying every stupid way you could to turn attention away from you—and she *believed* you." She remembered the pitiful words of hope in the letter in her purse: "—if she is alive!" . . . "And you told her she'd bring down those she wanted to protect. *You* called *her*!"

Dr. Crouch nodded somberly. "Yes."

"How the hell was Alberta able to coax *you* to join her—with all her goddamned principles?" Normalyn demanded.

Miss Bertha was curiously silent.

"Young lady, your *language*, please!" Mrs. Crouch reprimanded.

Dr. Crouch raised his chin. "Alberta needed us. And she had some knowledge of our youthful associations when we and she were members of the same—"

"Why should we be branded because of that subversive group so long ago?" Mrs. Crouch interrupted. "Why? Why, child, when we had found our rightful place with . . . the studios?"

Normalyn knew: "Alberta refused to name even you to that committee that sent her to prison. She kept your secret." Her respect resurged for the "indomitable Alberta."

"Yes, so she could use it when she needed it—"

"—and she did, in her plan that keeps us in grave danger!" Mrs. Crouch finished.

Were they in danger? Really? Now?

It was time to demand this: "Show me the bouquet of flowers I know you received—the ones Marilyn saw as herself, the ones to remind you of all you're responsible for!" And of loyalty, like Mark Poe's, Normalyn added to herself.

"We're not responsible for anything!" Mrs. Crouch's hands waved away the accusations, memories.

Normalyn stood up to face the man and his wife. "You thought as much about telling her her child was dead as you did about destroying lives for the goddamned studios!"

Mrs. Crouch gasped.

"Young lady, please!" Dr. Crouch reacted to blasphemy against the sacred studios.

"Show her the flowers, Dr. Crouch, *please*. Just stop her accusations!" Mrs. Crouch pleaded.

With a few long steps, Dr. Crouch left the room. He returned with a bouquet of artificial blossoms in his long, bony hands. There were no decayed blooms! But . . . there were fewer blossoms in this bouquet. Another message? Or was the sparsity an indication that rotting blossoms had been plucked out—by them? Yes! Normalyn was sure.

"Now *you* tell *us* who's sending *these!*" Mrs. Crouch seized the bouquet. She looked like an old, terrified bride.

"And why?" demanded Dr. Crouch. *"Are you Marilyn's daughter? Did she live? Are you her?"*

"I don't know!" Normalyn heard the confident power drain from her voice. "I don't know," she said more softly. She knew they had detected her sudden vulnerability.

"Who sent you to extort, then?" Mrs. Crouch took a quick step toward Normalyn.

"To blackmail!" Dr. Crouch took two steps forward.

"Who's doing all this?" Mrs. Crouch advanced.

Surely they weren't menacing her—not this old man and woman in their old-fashioned new clothes? Yet she detected a resurrected strength in their movements as they came at her. Normalyn edged away from the sofa, gliding her hand over the pane shielding the reflections of the two beautiful women.

The old man and the old woman flanked her—as if to close in on her!

Normalyn reached behind her for any object on the table, preparing to—

Wearily, Dr. Crouch located his chair and sank into it. Mrs. Crouch crumbled into hers.

As if they had exhausted all the energy they had dredged up to exhume troubled spirits, Normalyn thought, as she saw the pitiful old man and woman aging before her. No, they were *not* pitiful; they were the same evil man and woman who had ravaged lives so blithely, she reminded herself, who had protected Alberta's plan only because of fear of discovery of past associations—and who in the crucial last moments of her life had told Marilyn Monroe her child was dead.

"Oh, child," Dr. Crouch said, "we know nothing." The genial smile returned to his face.

"Why, it was all dramatic invention for the Dead Movie Stars." Mrs. Crouch smiled sweetly again. "Certainly you didn't believe any of it? Child, when you deal with Marilyn Monroe, you have to be extravagant in your own creation."

"The Dead Movie Stars," Dr. Crouch sighed, "bless them. They come around and listen to us; we dramatize now and then."

"There's so little left," Mrs. Crouch agreed.

Retreating, like Miss Bertha. Still afraid? Normalyn walked past them. She paused in the hall, under a starburst of a chandelier sprinkling diamond-pins about her; and as pointedly as she knew Enid had spoken these words years ago, she said to the old man and his wife, "*Thank* you, *dear* Dr. and Mrs. Crouch."

"Why, you're—" the tiny voice of Mrs. Crouch began to acknowledge automatically. Instead—fiercely—she flung the jacaranda blossoms to the floor.

"Murderers!" Normalyn thrust at them.

Thirty-Nine

She would never have a life, never! She had no one, no friends. She was in one of the largest cities in the world, lying in an uncomfortable bed trying unsuccessfully to fall asleep in a mangy furnished room in a crumbling châtaeu, still lingering in the past with phantoms.

After she had left the Crouches earlier, Normalyn had eaten a sumptuous meal at a restaurant crammed suddenly with tourists thrilled to have just sat in—live!—on "Wheel of Fortune." Forcing herself not to roam over discoveries and new mysteries, Normalyn had returned to her rented room, avoiding the Dead Movie Stars. She felt terribly alone . . . except for the closeness growing between her and the young Enid, a closeness aroused by Enid's drive, the daring with which she lived her life. At times Normalyn forgot—almost forgot—that that same woman had accused her cruelly, turning bitter—but, Normalyn reminded herself, continued always to express fierce love for her.

Surrendering to sleeplessness, she tried to read a book she had been thrilled to find in a paperback bookstore after leaving the restaurant—*My Life in Art* by Constantin Stanislavsky. She'd bought it because she remembered he was the author Michael Farrell had been reading in Palm Springs. But she was too restless to give the book the required attention. And something else kept pulling for scrutiny.

Evidence recurred that someone existed who could verify the truth of her birth, someone signaling to the reliability of witnesses with the message of the lavender bouquets. The Crouches were certain they were being extorted into giving information they would prefer to hide. In retrospect, it seemed to Normalyn that others might have felt "directed" in their recollections, as if at some point a judgment would occur! David Lange had told her there remained one person who could put together the gathered pieces of the puzzle "at the exact time." She was sure that person was not David. He was central to the mystery, but he was seeking answers. Enid's question mark constantly loomed over him.

2

In the morning, when the room was brightest, Normalyn decided with excitement, I'll go back to Long Beach today, to Miss Bertha! Yet she felt apprehension. The woman remembered by others as Alberta Holland had been so sure, so unswerving. Could she have become the subdued old woman in the Victorian house in Long Beach? Miss Bertha had told her to come back when she was "ready," Normalyn recalled. Now she *did* know much more. The wonderful old woman had been harsh in judging herself that afternoon with Jim in Long Beach. Because of the hired abortion? The necessary association with the deadly Crouches? Because she felt responsible when she, like the others, was devoured by the enormous unseen machine? She *had* to be the same woman.

"The wing of the angel." Normalyn pronounced aloud the phrase the older woman at auditions had left echoing in her mind. A connection to Enid's chipped angel—broken now? She *must* locate Sandra, attempt to find others. And then she would confront—yes, confront!—David Lange.

And she would move out of this dump, rent a clean apartment. That was one way to start her life. She tried to sustain wavering excitement.

Sounds outside the door! Normalyn walked there barefoot.

Buzz, buzz, buzz. ". . . the cover of *Rolling Stone*". . . . *Buzz, buzz.* . . .

Normalyn waited silently for the whispers to fade. There was an urgent knock at the door, startling her because her ear was pressed against it. She did not respond. The knocking insisted.

"Listen, inside, Lady Star wants to see you," said the voice of Veronica Lake. "I know you're in there."

Normalyn waited silently until she heard departing footsteps. Then she went to shower, dress. She was still surprised to see her reflection in the mirror. She was changing, had changed, even without the outline of the star's face.

She packed her things. Now she would go call the Mayor, hear a caring voice. And she *would* call Troja. When she opened the door, she saw Veronica Lake sitting on the floor. "Good morning, Ms. Lake." Normalyn tried to glide by coolly.

'Mornin',' said Billy Jack from the other side of the door. With his hand on her waist he guided her—firmly—along the corridor. Veronica Lake led her by the elbow to Lady Star's room. Normalyn refused to be alarmed. She put resolve into her movements, which were beginning to feel natural now, free.

"Darling!" Lady Star trilled as Normalyn was ushered assertively into the veiled light of the familiar room. Hedy Lamarr was there—and James Dean, Rita Hayworth, Tyrone Power— all sitting or lounging on the floor—and looking at her. Billy Jack leaned emphatically against the door. He had applied Day-Glo to the rose bursting out of the tombstone on his chest, so that it seemed to be bleeding.

The suggested menace that had occurred in the house of the Crouches had crept in here. Normalyn sat defiantly on the floor, on a large orange pillow. Tossed nearby was a copy of a large-size magazine: *Rolling Stone*. That's what they had been buzzing about outside her door.

Mounted on her chaise, a resurrected feather boa curling about her long neck, Lady Star announced to Normalyn, "We have to prepare for new auditions. Just. As. Agreed," she reminded. "I trust your meeting with the Crouches was a *grawhnd* success!"

Normalyn had no intention of "auditioning." Yet there remained central contacts she had relied on.

Lady Star explained: "We've called a special council, and we'll start as soon as those braggards arrive—"

"Laggards?" queried Veronica Lake.

Lady Star's voice deepened, her arms melted over the chaise. "As soon as those parties arrive," she alerted Normalyn, "we'll be discussing the addenda—"

Veronica Lake threw up her hands.

"—in order to get the word out immediately for auditions. *Tonight!*" She threw the word at Normalyn.

Tonight? Normalyn wanted to run out. But Billy Jack was guarding the door.

"We have a full galaxy," Lady Star informed. "We're allowing the petitioner for John Derek and Shaun Calhoun to try for Zachary Scott this time. He—somehow—managed—overnight—to convince Betty Grable *and* Errol Flynn to champion him."

"Yeah," sniffed Hedy Lamarr, "and I bet I know *how*."

Excitement once again punctured Lady Star's huskiness: "And just from outside we can recruit—" She snapped her fingers in rapid succession, indicating a vast number of petitioners they might choose from. "There's a Lana Turner, a Montgomery Clift, a Bette Davis, the usual Crawfords, *another* Valentino—"

"—and a *great* Johnny Weissmuller!" Tyrone Power enthused.

"And Sandra—" Normalyn counted on surprising Lady Star's mounting excitement for a truthful answer.

"You *never* can count on that crazy old thing; she—" Lady Star stopped herself. "But of *course* Sandra will be there," she guaranteed Normalyn. With a dagger of looks she kept Billy Jack from disagreeing—he had shaken his head.

"I'm not ready to audition," Normalyn said. She reached idly for the magazine on the floor. Eyes trailed her. Over its cover and attached with tape was a sketchy drawing of— . . . the Dead Movie Stars!—and prominent among them was a figure obviously intended to be that of Marilyn Monroe.

Normalyn calculated quickly: Whatever their loyalties to the Crouches and Mildred and whomever else, the Dead Movie Stars had their own goals, and fading into obscurity was not one of them. They had not been in "the media" for days now. And, Normalyn noticed, Lady Star's daily orchid had apparently not arrived today—testily, she kept touching a worn felt one in her hair. The buzzed reference to this magazine earlier and the hopeful sketch for a future cover indicated they were preparing to take a big plunge—and they were counting on her. Still, Normalyn was sure they were not ready to risk exposing to possible public derision any mishap that might occur during uncontrolled auditions.

"I need more time to prepare," she said.

"Auditions are *tonight!*" Lady Star was firm.

Normalyn got up. She would merely walk out.

Billy Jack leaned more firmly against the door. "Where the hell you think you're going?"

"Stay *put* . . . darling!" Lady Star emphasized.

The painted faces of the Dead Movie Stars looked at her.

Normalyn sat down. "Okay!" She searched for a strategy. "Auditions tonight. But I'll have to get myself ready!" She stood up again.

"We'll help you," Rita Hayworth offered.

Normalyn sat down.

Suddenly Errol Flynn and Betty Grable dashed into the room. "They *found* Verna La Maye!" Errol Flynn gasped. "It's on all the news—TV, radio! And they're all talking about *us*, and auditions!"

Lady Star . . . stood . . . up . . . very . . . slowly. "What . . . happened . . . to . . . her?"

"The guy who threatened to kill her—remember? At auditions? The supporting player? He was waiting for her outside the church that *same* night. He strangled her with her stocking!" Betty Grable said breathlessly.

"Just one thing, though," Errol Flynn told them. "They're calling her Mary Yarrow."

"You mean she's really dead? Really, really?" Hedy Lamarr seemed to be struggling to understand something ugly. *"Really?"* For a moment her hand at her lips seemed about to wipe away the purple paint.

"Really?" Rita Hayworth tested.

"You mean: *Really?"* Tyrone Power moistened his finger but didn't curl his eyelashes with it.

"Really . . . dead," Hedy Lamarr understood.

"Yes! Yes! Yes!" Betty Grable asserted. "It hit me right here at first—" She punched her stomach. "But, hey, that's life!"

"Oh, no!" Normalyn pronounced the words she had been repeating silently since Errol Flynn and Betty Grable flung the ugly news at them. She remembered the pretty youngwoman and the youngman who had threatened to kill her—meaning it! He had waited for her that very night, outside the darkened church basement.

Lady Star stood motionless on her mounted chaise.

Silence paused in the room filled with photographs of whitely lit movie stars against black backgrounds.

Hedy Lamarr walked out silently, quietly.

Billy Jack snapped the silence away with his fingers, his body involved in an excited dance with himself. "We gotta be ready with real hot secrets and lots of glamorous tragedy cause they'll really listen to us *now!*"

"And we won't need *you!"* Veronica Lake sneered at Normalyn. "Because now we'll get all the attention we want— *without you!"* She moistened the wave over her eye.

"The cameras'll be here any moment!" Tyrone Power realized.

"I'll have to freshen up, do my hair *up*, tan my legs," Betty Grable anticipated.

"I'll get my new red jacket!" James Dean did not stutter.

"We'll have a funeral at Forest Lawn." Billy Jack was inspired.

"Let's find that crazy who wanted to be the Lady in Black!" Veronica Lake encouraged.

For a moment, Lady Star seemed to be resurrected out of a pensive mood; "Yes, darlings, we'll—!"

Another Dead Movie Star, with a dramatic hat, stood at the door.

Lady Star said in shrill surprise, "Who the hell are *you*? Lena Horne? . . . You may *not* come in!"

Billy Jack tried to push the door back; the intruder pushed harder. Billy Jack fell sprawled on the floor. "I *am* in!" said the elegant figure at the door.

Troja!

"Normalyn! Are you in here?" Troja peered into the dusk of Lady Star's room.

Normalyn pushed back into shadows, to make Troja pay for a while for having shoved her out. But her voice said, "Yes! I'm here!" She stood up.

Troja walked in past aghast Dead Movie Stars. "Normalyn, what the hell you doin' hangin' around with this silly trash?"

"Trash don't get on the cover of uh, *Rolling Stone*," said James Dean.

"How did you find me?" Normalyn asked Troja, wanting it to have been difficult, very difficult.

"Easy!" said Troja. "You weren't at the Ambassador Hotel, and you'd told me about this creepy group—"

"The nerve of the bitch!" Betty Grable smoothed her tight sweater.

Billy Jack recovered from the shove. "Do you know the TV is coming from *all* the stations?" he informed Troja proudly.

"Whoever this *creature* is—" Lady Star began.

Troja yanked at her shoulder.

"Ouch!" squealed the little girl, pulling away.

With Normalyn standing next to her, Troja said to the Dead Movie Stars, "You're cruel little bastards, ridiculing pain. *Real* tragedy ain't glamorous, it just hurts, goes on hurting—here!" She hit her own chest. "Now get out of here!" she ordered.

"This is *my* room." Lady Star was indignant.

"Then *you* can stay, little girl," Troja allowed.

Normalyn laughed, with relief, release—and then stopped, remembering the murder of Mary Yarrow.

The Dead Movie Stars ran out to prepare for the television and newspaper cameras already on their way to the château built by William Randolph Hearst for Marion Davies.

"Real tragedy . . ." Normalyn directed her words at Lady Star. Troja held her suddenly cold hand.

"Yes." Lady Star touched her felt orchid. The earlier spurt of excitement had waned.

The Dead Movie Stars had celebrated tragedy and it had courted them back grotesquely. Normalyn felt sorrow for the lost girl at auditions, with only a frail identity of her own. Now Mary Yarrow was dead! These painted young people—beneath their postures and their odd clothes—what real sorrow of their own were they avoiding? Now they would get the massive publicity they had sought. But would they *want* this kind?

Lady Star was quiet, deliberating.

Normalyn had to ask: "Was that the only reason you needed me so urgently—because you thought I'd help you get on the cover of that magazine?" She pointed to the magazine on the floor. The sketched drawing pasted on the cover seemed desperate now.

"Why else?" Lady Star was clinging to her grand demeanor. "For some reason unclear to me, the photographer who saw you running out that first day thought you looked a lot like *her*." Her pointing finger tried to locate a photograph of Marilyn Monroe among the others cluttering the room. "He was *sure* we had a *good* chance, with a good Marilyn." She said that almost wistfully. Then her husky voice returned. "Why, what other reason did *you* think, darling? What?" Her eyes did not blink.

Was that the only reason? No, it had been an important part of it for the Dead Movie Stars; but there had been more, Normalyn was sure, much more that had to do with Mildred Meadows, the Crouches—

"But none of that matters now," Lady Star said as if to herself.

"Because you've been trapped by real life, little girl," Troja said.

"Real life!" Lady Star winced with deep dread.

Betty Grable yelled into the room as she hurried past the door, her hair a mountain of curls, "It's *all* going to happen just like we wanted!"

"I'm not so sure," Lady Star thought aloud. She fluffed out her red hair, just in case she was wrong. She leaned against her chaise. "No, I'm not so sure at all it will happen like we wanted." She let her body slide down, slowly, down to the floor. She sat there like a heavily painted doll. "This may be the death of the Dead Movie Stars," she said to Normalyn.

Normalyn nodded.

Troja looked at Lady Star in fascination. "You're really a sad little girl, aren't you?" she said.

"No!" Lady Star groped for her chaise. She raised herself on it. She stood to her full height. "You're wrong," she said to

Troja. "I am the *only* one left who knows what real glamour is!" Fatigue oppressed her at the impact the news might have on their survival. She lay back on the chaise, arranging herself like a laid-out corpse. In her deepest voice she said, "I am the last of Hollywood, the last of glamour, the last of the great beauties, the last of the great tragic Dead Movie Stars."

3

Outside, television crews were converging.

Normalyn and Troja drove away in the old Mustang, Normalyn's suitcases loaded hurriedly in back.

Normalyn was eager to tell Troja of the events of the past nights and days. She could not help feeling slightly proud to have been discovered in such a terrible place. Troja's suddenly distant look did not invite conversation.

They reached the familiar house. Normalyn rushed out, so eager to be back she did not notice at first Troja's hesitation to get out. Normalyn looked back and saw that Troja had closed her eyes, against the painful absence she was encountering again and again and again.

Kirk's section was cleared, the mattress replaced with a table, weedy flowers put in a drinking glass. Troja had made an unsuccessful attempt to clean the house—boxes were pushed against the walls. Normalyn tried not to stare at her, but she saw Troja's hands tremble, her eyes slice away from the dead television. Normalyn was encouraged that she had not seen Troja breathe the cocaine.

Studying her, Troja said, "You look beautiful, you really do."

"And you've been . . . okay?" Normalyn asked with concern.

"Got a good lead on a job," Troja said quickly. Her voice faltered. "I'm trying!"

She closed her eyes and spoke meted words: "I have to keep reminding myself, grasp it. Kirk couldn't make love to me because he was trying to think of me as someone else. But that last night he saw *me*. He was telling me he loved *me*—and proved it before he had to take himself away."

Yes, Normalyn understood, there were so many shapes of love.

In increasing silence, their movements now became very careful, courteous. Normalyn unpacked her clothes, folded them, unfolded them. Touching it, Troja called her attention to a small new glass angel on the table meant to replace Enid's.

But it didn't! Normalyn thought, and controlled the urge to remove it. It was garish, painted brightly, ugly. But it was Troja's way of indicating her regret for what had occurred. Normalyn looked away from it. "It's wonderful," she managed to say—and located Enid's makeup box beside it.

Troja understood. She removed the angel from the table, cupping it in her hands as if to hide that it had existed. She held her breath; she closed her eyes. "I'm sorry I was mean to you that day, hon, and I'm *real* happy you're back," she said. She embraced Normalyn tightly. Then she forced away the emotion: "Now tell me where you *been*?"

Normalyn told her some—only some—of the highlights of the last days.

"Why are you going through all this, hon?" Troja asked her carefully.

"Because I—" Normalyn started. "Because I may be—" She started again: "Because I'm beginning to think that I *am* . . . Marilyn's daughter." Immediately, she wanted to seize back those strange words, scream out, *Enid is my mother!*

4

Normalyn and Troja rode on the freeway to Long Beach. Normalyn was returning to see Miss Bertha. She would show her the letter and—

"So many sailors," Troja said. "They look so sad."

Miss Bertha would call Jim afterwards. He'd come over. Normalyn told Troja about Jim.

Troja liked him immediately—then remembered: "While you were gone, that Mayor of Texas called, and so did Ted Gonzales, from Arizona."

"From Texas," Normalyn corrected. Was she sorry she had missed his call?

"Him, yes, but he was calling from Arizona," Troja said. "That's why he couldn't leave a number. He's on his way to Los Angeles, hon."

Ted in Los Angeles! He existed for her in Gibson—and by the Rio Grande. Would he bring all that with him? Or would being here separate him from it, make him a *really* new Ted Gonzales? Normalyn was not sure whether she felt anticipation.

Sailors wandered the streets of Long Beach. To this beach town, Alberta Holland had fled finally, tired, away from the people destroying lives. From memory, Normalyn guided Troja to the Victorian house.

There it was! No . . . Normalyn did not see the disordered naturalness of Miss Bertha's garden. But that *was* the house. The garden was tidy, ordered.

Troja parked the car. "You sure this is it?" she asked into Normalyn's look of wonder.

"Yes," Normalyn said, but she wished she wasn't sure.

"I'll take a walk by the ocean, soothing, while you—"

Normalyn did not want Troja to be alone, and *she* didn't want to be alone now. "Please come with me."

Troja's hands were trembling ominously. "Okay." She fixed the dark sunglasses more securely to filter the world.

Normalyn ran to the door. She rang, knocked.

An older man came to the door. A woman called from within the house: "Just tell them we don't want anything."

The man looked at both women. His eyes tried to hide his approval. "Yes?"

"Miss Bertha." Normalyn could hardly pronounce the name. "She's my friend."

"You mean the lady who claimed she knew all the movie stars." The man smiled, not at all unkindly.

Troja touched Normalyn's hand.

"She *does* know them," Normalyn said. This house was already pulling away into a finished memory.

"I'm real sorry to tell you, young lady," the man said softly, "that your friend is dead."

Normalyn turned away from the unwanted word. Troja reared back, assaulted by it.

"We just rented the house." The man was eager to restore life, share his memories. "Used to live down the block, always liked it—and her. Maybe you know her friend?"

Jim. "A sailor," Normalyn said, wanting to cry.

"Yeah, him—and the old lady who came in to take care of everything."

"Who—?"

"A small woman," the man said. "Left soon after that. Very elegant. She wore white gloves, spoke with a Spanish accent. Why, she stopped by one day, I remember so well. She said she was used to death—her husband died in a car crash after surviving a whole revolution, imagine!—but she said death still shocked her. . . . She and the sailor took care of everything right away. It may help your sorrow," he offered Normalyn quickly, "if I tell you it was the sailor who found your friend dead, just like she had fallen asleep, in an old chair she favored, with one of her cats purring away on her lap. She was a good woman who deserved to die peacefully."

Forty

Miss Bertha was dead, her voice silenced! Insinuating itself into Normalyn's sorrow was the thought that gone with Miss Bertha was all she might have learned from her. But a new presence had entered the living past, an elegant Spanish woman who had come to Miss Bertha—"to take care of everything right away." There had been a figure like her in Alberta Holland's life.

In the car riding through the whiteness of Long Beach, Normalyn avoided looking at the sailors on the streets. Now Jim—she did not even know his last name—was locked with Miss Bertha in one memory to which nothing could be added.

"I'm sorry, hon," Troja said as she drove onto the freeway.

"She *did* know all those movie stars." Normalyn was surprised by what she had chosen to affirm. But *did* Miss Bertha really know them? The Spanish woman added some evidence.

Troja turned on the radio. The music that came out was the kind Kirk liked. Troja banished it—and the fevered voice of a cursing preacher. Frantic, she shifted past words, blasts of music. She reached for something in her purse. The trembling hand withdrew. "Goddamn, goddamn, god*damn!*"

Normalyn realized how fraily Troja's control was held; she had been seeking in her purse the destructive solace of the drug. . . . The soft music Normalyn located for her was replaced by the litany of the day's horrors, news spoken in a voice meant to predict fair skies. Normalyn listened only when she heard the familiar name:

"—Mary Yarrow in our special report on today's news," the

announcer introduced. "Police have arrested her former boy-
friend, Danny Palance, also eighteen, and charged him with
her murder. In a bizarre initiation, known as 'auditions,' Mary
Yarrow recently 'assumed' the identity of famed movie star
Verna La Maye. Like the star, Mary Yarrow was strangled.
She belonged to a cult group known as the Dead Movie Stars,
purportedly dedicated to the restoration of 'tragic glamour' to
Hollywood. The group was founded by Molly Ullman, whose
grandmother organized the first Marilyn Monroe fan club in
the world; William Jackson, a runaway from Oakapine, Ten-
nessee; and Rosa Mendoza, a Valley High School dropout.
Police lieutenant Otis Sleighton dismissed the group as "just
another shabby band of disturbed young people," but psychol-
ogist Howard Kissel, himself well known as a dis—"
  Normalyn snapped off the radio. Just another shabby band
. . . How would *they* hear that, she wondered? The same reporters who had courted the Dead Movie Stars would now
rake through the drabness of their real lives. Lady Star was a
pitiful girl—malicious, mean, but still pitiful like the others.
They were not responsible for the girl's death, but she was
dead. Her death, the death of Kirk, of Miss Bertha, all deepened Normalyn's awareness of sudden loss. She felt a renewed
urge to live.
  When they reached the house, Troja tossed her head slightly
back, a hint of the way she had exited the Hollywood Four
Star Club, Normalyn wanted to think. "Gotta keep moving,"
Troja said. "Always harder to start again than to go on."
  "Yes!" Normalyn agreed quickly.
  Inside the house, Normalyn immediately saw what had caused
Troja to rear in horror: her blonde wig discarded between
boxes on the floor. Troja went to it, picked it up, and flung it
into the shadows of the house.
  Not even Troja's urgency could summon Normalyn's attention now because as she saw the wig floating within dark
shadows, she recognized the missing association that had kept
her haunted memory blurred for years. Now she saw it all:
  On the shoreline in Galveston, in Texas, when Normalyn was three,
Enid led her to the dark edge of the Gulf—"to meet a woman who
yearns to see you." Click! Enid's lighter sparked. In flickering in-
stants, Enid vanished into the darkness out of which the blonde
woman emerged. Normalyn thought she knew her; she felt protected as
they sat for moments on the sand. "I came to tell you I love you; I
wasn't able to before," the woman said. She stroked Normalyn's head
resting on her lap. Then she said to Normalyn, "Wait here, I want to
show you something." She walked closer to the water and reclined on

*darkness, raising one hand over her breasts. "I'll just lie on the
darkness," Normalyn heard the woman say, "and finally it will be soft
at last and kind." A black wave advanced as if to engulf her.
Normalyn was about to run to her. The woman stood up and shouted,
"Don't come too close, the darkness mustn't touch you!" Click! Enid
removed the blonde wig she had been wearing and flung it into the
water. It floated away into darkness. "You're mine!" She clasped
Normalyn.*

With a sigh now, Normalyn knew it had been Enid, only
Enid, who had been with her on the distant shoreline.

2

The next day—Troja had left very early on a temporary job
as a "backup"—Normalyn dialed Stanley Smith's number in
Palm. He answered. "Who is this? Who? Who!" There was
fear in the repeated voice. "I'm Enid's daughter, Stan,"
Normalyn warned, and hung up.

Then she made herself up differently—from memory.

She took a cab to the bus depot. At a small magazine shop,
she bought a chrome cigarette lighter.

3

When Normalyn stepped off the bus in Palm, the day was
hot, sweaty, cloudless. In the small city, she saw scarce buildings, scattered houses, a few people—staring, hostile. All roads
branched off from a short main street dominated by a single
towering palm, which looked ancient, its lower fronds shredded, brown. An old man at the gas station that doubled as bus
stop told her she could walk to the address she showed him.

As she moved to her destination, she retained the memory
of what Enid had been—vibrant, charming—before becoming
embittered, attempting to soothe the past with liquor and
curses.

The two-story house Normalyn reached courted a further
separation in this isolated town. It touched the desert. Wooden
columns flanking dark steps created a stark symmetry against
the fierce white sky, where a desert bird glided so slowly that it
seemed suspended in unmoving heat.

Normalyn walked halfway to the steps and waited.

The front door opened. Still muscular, in his fifties, a man
stood there.

"Stanley Smith." Normalyn said.

"I've been waiting for you to show up," the man said.

Behind him, a woman appeared at the open door. Her silhouette was joined by a youngman's.

"Why did you wait for me?" Normalyn shouted at Stanley.

"To see you. To tell you to your face. I am not your father."

"I've never asked you. You've denied it twice."

"David Lange called me about you, told me."

Then he had prepared that interlude, lied to her. Normalyn pushed away the insistent presence of David Lange. *"I know you were hired to find a woman to abort!"*

The woman advanced out of the door. She was thin, Stanley's age, her hair flecked with gray.

An inexplicable sadness touched Normalyn's anger.

The slender handsome youngman emerged into the scorched day.

"What do you want from us?" Stanley said.

"The truth about your child and Enid's."

"Ask her in, father," the youngman said.

"No!" Stanley rejected. "She's here to judge, Ellen," he warned the woman.

"I don't want to come in!" Normalyn said. In the burning heat, she would assert her determination to know. "Tell me, Stanley!"

Ellen looked at her husband, questioning silently.

Words from another time bolted in rage from the man: "Our son died and Enid blamed me!"

"Because you rejected her when she was pregnant, ran away on your goddamn motorcycle!" Normalyn put into her voice the slight insinuation of a Texas drawl that had seeped into Enid's.

Stanley looked away from her.

Normalyn tasted her own perspiration. "Did you ever see your child, Stanley?" It was information she must have, but the sadness in her voice surprised her.

"No—because Enid went away to Texas, had him there."

"After *you* left her."

"But then I wanted my son back when she told me he'd been born," Stanley said softly. Under his thin shirt, the hair on his chest matted with sweat.

"Did you want Enid back?"

"Oh, sure. Of course. Her, too." He looked away from Normalyn, from his wife. "We were involved off and on for years." He couldn't keep the pride of conquest from his voice: "She thought I'd marry her finally."

Bastard! Normalyn said for Enid.

"I've told you everything!" Stanley turned away.

"No. There's much more. I've heard you at night when you're drunk," the man's son said.

"Jason! How dare you!" Ellen spoke for the first time.

"How? Because I'm inheriting your ghosts," Jason said to both of them.

He shared her sense of being bound to the past! Normalyn knew.

Beads of moisture glistened on Ellen's face. She inhaled. "Tell it, Stanley, for you, for me. For Jason. Finish it, finally—"

"Shut up!" Stanley stopped her.

"—or I will, what I know of it," Ellen finished.

Had Enid known Stanley had replaced her with an obedient version of her rebellious self? Normalyn understood her saddened fascination with this woman.

Stanley shook his head.

"Stanley hired me to abort our child," Ellen said to Normalyn. "That's part of what you've come to discover. Only Stanley can tell the rest."

Stanley had offered his own unborn child for pay! That's what Enid had discovered at the hospital. Within the stagnating heat, Normalyn felt nausea.

"Crouch needed a pregnant woman, we needed money!" Stanley thrust into the woman's confession. "And *you* agreed."

"Yes," Ellen whispered.

The white sun scorched the barren desert.

"We have to know everything now, Jason," Normalyn said to the youngman.

"Yes!" Jason said to his father.

"Tell her, Stanley," Ellen pleaded.

Stanley crossed his arms over his chest in locked silence.

Normalyn pushed her hair back. She opened her purse. She took out the cigarette lighter she had bought earlier. She positioned it so that it reflected silver in Stan's face. Then she clicked it, flameless.

"Always pursuing her goddamned 'justice'!" Stanley looked toward the horizon. "She'd play with that lighter of hers. Then the plotting started, in her eyes. They tilted, those eyes of hers," he remembered. "I could *see* her plotting—"

As Stanley spoke, Normalyn added to his blunt memories intimate details from her own knowledge of the woman she was constantly discovering.

"—saw it, so clearly, in her eyes," Stanley said, "the begin-

ning of her damned vengeance on me, that time she called me
to come to her house, told me she had a surprise—"

*　　*　　*

—but she didn't tell him what.

She lived in a second-floor duplex connected to the lawn by
a flight of steps overhung with bougainvillea. From her bedroom window, she could see rows of jacaranda trees in full
bloom. It was still spring, an exceptionally hot day, like summer.

So Enid cut from the garden two enormous white roses
laced with pale gold. They would have died in the fierce heat
outdoors. She placed them in a vase on the table where she
would tell Stanley her surprise.

Stanley Smith—some considered him handsome, in a flashy
way—brought champagne. He was in an exhilarated mood.
He had just finished a job for Mickey Cohn, a "gig" involving
political blackmail. He didn't tell Enid this because she always
refused to be "a part of that part" of him.

Stanley was pleased by the loud pop of the cork. He poured
the champagne. "Now, what are we celebrating?"

Tiny bubbles teased Enid's glowing lips. "I'm pregnant with
our child, Stan," she told him.

"You'll get rid of it." Stan savored the expensive champagne. "I'll give you the money."

Enid was aware of added heat, choking her. She had forced
herself to believe he would welcome her news. They had been
involved for years, and she had convinced herself he would
marry her, leave the ugly world he moved in.

"I intend to have this child."

"I'll make sure you don't. I have connections, you know," he
underscored in ugly determination.

"You're only a crook." She still smiled. She plucked a petal
from one of the roses she had picked. In ripe bloom from the
sudden heat, it disintegrated at her touch. She had spoken so
sweetly that she had thrown him into a quandary; he did not
react to the insult. She reached for her cigarette lighter on the
table where she kept her cherished figurine of an angel.

"You've seen other men, I bet," he told her.

"Only you—for very long." He had been the first.

"Of course." He accepted—*expected*—her fidelity. . . . Now
from his wallet he took out bills, large bills. He spread them
on the table so Enid would see how much he was lavishing on
her. "That'll take care of whatever is necessary." He added
more. When she still did not acknowledge his generosity, he
encouraged, "Go to the D'Arcy House, if you want the best

care. It'll keep things quiet, too," he added importantly. "Now *I'm* going to San Francisco, for a few days, on my motorcycle." He had never outgrown that—his motorcycle, the feeling that he was a young outlaw.

Enid clicked her silver lighter.

He looked at her. He saw the signs of beginning vengeance in her eyes. Perhaps he "saw" them only later, when he remembered the strange moments.

At the door, she placed something into his hand and closed his fingers over it. He was surprised to discover it was a cheap glass "necklace" he had given her years ago—a childish lark, five marbly blue beads knotted with an ordinary string. He was baffled she had kept it. "You know this is worthless," he reminded her.

"I know it now," she told him. Her smile intact, she said, "This child will cost you much more than money, Stan, I swear it."

He went to San Francisco, just left on his motorcycle, stayed away. Much later, she telephoned him at his office; he even had a secretary for his "gigs." She left word that she was at the Texas Grand Hotel, in Gibson. He assumed she had preferred distance and remoteness to the sheltered comfort of the D'Arcy House. He did not answer her call. She telephoned again. She told his secretary she was sure Stan would welcome what she had to tell him. When he answered, she told him, "You were right as usual. I understand what you want." The ended pregnancy, of course, Stan knew, although he had not even thought of it since that day.

Enid remained in Texas. Near the water of the Gulf, she took long walks, clicking her empty cigarette lighter at nothing, at indifferent black waves of water. That is what she told Stanley when she called him again from Texas. "And our child was born here, Stanley, a handsome boy full of life. Like you, Stanley, exactly like you."

She had let him believe she had got rid of the kid! By then he had another woman, a "Hollywood girl," Ellen Berrent. He was proud of the fact that when Alberta Holland had required some casual information from him once, she had remarked that Ellen reminded her of Mildred Meadows's beautiful daughter.

Enid's words kept echoing in Stanley's mind: ". . . a boy . . . exactly like you."

Stanley called Enid in Texas. They just talked. He telephoned again, twice in one day, again at night. "How is the kid?" "Oh, handsomer than this morning, stronger than yesterday; he's *you* again, Stan, so much *you*."

Stanley told Enid—firmly—that he wanted his boy.

Enid returned to Los Angeles. She registered at the Ambassador Hotel, in a room that overlooked the flowered lawn. She told Stanley she would see him there.

And give him back his child, Stan was sure.

She had never looked more beautiful. He told her that. "You just haven't been able to use your beauty. Like Marilyn. . . . Where's my kid?" He looked about the hotel room for his son. How old would he be? he tried to remember.

"Your son is dead," Enid told him. "I came back to tell you to your face. He was born despite you, but he didn't survive long—only long enough to reveal that he would have looked exactly like you. Every moment of the pregnancy, I was in danger of losing him, because of your threats. I knew you were capable of carrying them out. That affected the child finally, despite his early strength. The doctor confirmed it: *You* killed your son, Stanley." She flung at him the exact bills he had given her.

* * *

Heat whitened over the desert of Palm.

Normalyn felt the impact of Stan's betrayal of Enid—so proud, so vulnerable, so proud.

"And then *we* bought the death of our *own* child, too," Ellen accused Stanley.

Stan shielded his eyes from the stare of the sun.

"Enid didn't allow it—*I* did." Ellen judged herself.

"I made it up to you, I gave you a son," Stanley said.

Jason walked down the steps. He stood with Normalyn.

"And I married you!" Stanley reminded his wife.

"To silence me! And because I reminded you . . . of her, without her spirit," Ellen chastised herself. "You even told her that, on the telephone. I heard you, Stan—the day you called her, to see her again."

"Yeah!" He thrust this as evidence of commitment at Normalyn. "I tried to help Enid when I discovered they'd been trapped in Holland's plan. But she lied to me, told me Marilyn's daughter was dead, exposed *me* to danger—just as she knew would happen when I reported her lie as fact, and I did!"

Sweat stung Normalyn's eyes. "How do you know she lied?"

"Because Crouch tried to get me to go tell Marilyn her kid wasn't dead." Again pride seeped in: "Of course I refused.

I had my honor. I wasn't working for Crouch any more. Besides. I knew he was just trying to set me up, trying everything to save himself."

Then Crouch called Marilyn to tell her her daughter was dead! "Did Enid know you hadn't gone?"

"Yes! . . . when it was all over."

Normalyn had to learn everything quickly now—Stan had turned away. *Click!* She snapped the lighter.

Stanley whirled about.

"You said you wanted to see me, Stan. Why!"

"Because I've never been really sure what happened to my kid!" Stanley shouted back.

'Why!" Normalyn's lips were parched.

Stanley shook his head. "Enid always worked things out exactly, to get the response she wanted." He seemed now to speak to himself. "Sometimes I wonder if my kid *wasn't* born, and she made that all up to hurt me." He seemed to be studying Normalyn closely. "Maybe she had a girl, told me the kid was a boy to make sure I'd want him back." His look did not waver from Normalyn. "All of it could have been part of her revenge—never to allow me to be sure."

"If she had had a daughter, you wouldn't have wanted her?" Normalyn asked, immediately detesting her words. She did not *care* whether he would have wanted her or not!

Stanley looked away from her. He frowned. "Enid's dead now, with all her secrets."

"But someone else is keeping the intrigue alive!" Ellen said suddenly. "Whoever is sending those artificial flowers Monroe loved, reminding us again . . . of everything."

"Show me the flowers!" Normalyn demanded.

"I burned them. I hated their brown ugly blossoms!" Ellen said.

"Normalyn!"

She looked at Stan. He had spoken her name as if in sudden surprise.

"Normalyn," he repeated softly. "That's a pretty name, young lady." He held his breath, released it. "Maybe I am your fa— . . ."

"I wouldn't want you as my father!" Normalyn shouted.

At the same moment, Jason turned away from him.

Normalyn touched the youngman's hand, an acknowledgment of closeness.

Sweat drenched Stan's face, his body. Wearily, he brought from his pocket a glass necklace, dulled blue. "This is what Enid returned to me that day. It meant something to her. I looked for it after you called. Take it."

"Throw it to me, Stan," Normalyn ordered.

He did.

Jason's back remained to him. Ellen's hand reached out toward her son.

A sudden shadow, like a blade, severed the white landscape.

Normalyn allowed the necklace to fall to the ground. With one foot, she rubbed it in dirt. Then she picked it up, wiping the glass beads. "Now it's clean from your touch, Stan," she said.

Forty-One

A cool breeze sighed into Los Angeles as the Desert Valley
bus pulled into the Hollywood terminal.

In the cab riding back to the house, Normalyn sorted into
two sequences of possibilities what she had discovered in the
white desert city. In the first, to fulfill her sworn vengeance,
Enid lied to Stan, claiming a dead son when she had a living
daughter—her, Normalyn, left safely protected in secret Texas
when Enid returned to taunt Stanley with the contrived death.
Seeing a replication of her own dilemma in Marilyn Monroe's
dangerous pregnancy, she remained in Los Angeles through
the perilous time. She returned to Texas after Alberta's plot
smashed and both Marilyn—and the child—died.

In the second sequence—Normalyn evaluated as the cab
passed the Chinese Theater while dozens of tourists, always
there, inspected the prints of the great movie stars—Enid
returned to indict Stanley in the real death of the child she
had forced him to want. After the tumult of the last days of the
doomed movie star, Enid claimed Marilyn's daughter as her
own, at first in protection, eventually in total possession, to
replace her own dead child.

Certain events fitted either possibility: In a ritual of loyalty
performed on the Galveston shore, Enid, disguised as Marilyn
Monroe, shared her own daughter with the movie star—or
"returned" her to her rightful mother. Trapped in a coil of
the madness both women feared, a coil made taut by guilt that
she had not reached the movie star before the suicide, Enid
felt both love and resentment toward the child born out of
turmoil. At the end of her life—to share her own daughter
with the star completely and beyond death—or finally to rec-

424

tify the deception of years—she "returned" her to Marilyn Monroe by way of her letter.

Normalyn faced this as the cab moved out of a street of glorious flowers and silver-green trees and into the gaudy remains of Western Boulevard. In the first set of possibilities, the despised Stanley Smith would be her father. In the second, her father would be one of two blurred figures—John Kennedy or, more probably, Robert Kennedy.

When Normalyn got out of the cab before her house, she pushed everything out of her mind.

Except this—

Stan had spoken with genuine wonder of Enid's *exact* plotting to bring about her desired effect. Enid had left her own name on the birth certificate, to which she had added Marilyn Monroe's in the entry designating "Name of Mother." The annotated newsclipping provided information *and* a guide to discoveries. There were the odd initials, N.J.R.I.R.—and the two photographs left side by side on the table with the chipped angel. Did *all* provide *one* message Enid had left for her to find?

At dinner, Normalyn caught Troja studying her. Troja explained: "Sometimes you do look like Marilyn, hon—maybe like Norma Jeane—and then sometimes, like tonight, you look like someone else. And then, you know"—she smiled—"you look just like *you*."

"And you look beautiful again." Normalyn was disturbed by Troja's observation. Now she was surprised that Troja did not react to *her* words, as if that had begun not to matter to her. She would wait to tell Troja about her confrontation with Stanley Smith; Troja seemed suddenly preoccupied—and so was she, with fragments of mystery.

"The wing of the angel." Normalyn echoed aloud the phrase that had entered her mind, from the night of auditions. She answered Troja's look of surprise: "It's just another mystery."

"Not *everything* is a mystery, hon," Troja said. "The Wing of the Angel is a famous orphanage in Hollywood. It's real name is the Norton County Home, but everyone knows it as the Wing of the Angel because Marilyn spent a long time there and that's what she called it." Troja announced, casually, that—if Normalyn wanted to go there—she could drive her because her "important audition" of today had been postponed "for a few days." Then she slammed the table with both hands. "Not true! I did go today. But I panicked. I ran out!"

In the morning Troja announced her determination to attend the rescheduled call. She kept redoing her eyes—"all wrong!"— then her lips—"can't get them to look *right!*" Finally, hands trembling, she was ready. She did not ask, "How do I look?" before she left.

Normalyn walked to the Wing of the Angel Home. She was saddened that the jacaranda trees had lost their blooms, their limbs oddly barren among trees just beginning their full lives. No filigree of petals remained on the streets—except here and there, against a curb, a sweep of dusty lavender.

The administration building at the Norton County Home was two stories of brick, its windows framed white. Lawns were neatly mown. Lush shrubbery was trimmed in rectangles. Behind the building were two smaller ones, dormitories. The playground was enclosed by leafy trees. A statue remained from a time when the building was a private home and the ample grounds were a garden—a female angel looking down at her bare feet. One wing seemed about to rise, in tentative preparation; the other was pressed against her body.

That was the angel Enid tried to evoke with the figurine she had kept, Normalyn knew. And this is where "the game" had begun, where Enid Morgan had met Marilyn Monroe—"under the shadow of an angel's wing, an angel that had abandoned hope of flying again."

Quickly, Normalyn walked away from the home.

2

Her life had to begin!

From a telephone booth, she reached David Lange in his office. She told him she must see him right away. There were certain "urgent matters" she had to discuss. And *this* time she would, she told herself. He agreed to the time she set.

Back in her house—tired, longing for a cool shower—she almost didn't answer the telephone.

"Normalyn! I'm in Los Angeles!" said Ted Gonzales.

Warm anticipation was swept away by apprehension. She tried to conceal her confused emotions: "I'm glad you're here, really glad."

Ted explained excitedly why he was in Los Angeles. "I'm working for this lawyer who came to Gibson about the real terrible conditions of migrant workers in the fields. He thinks he can bring a suit against the growers there like he's doing now in California." He slowed his rushed explanation: "I've missed you a lot, Normalyn. I can't wait to see you. I'm in East

L.A. I borrowed a Jeep—I could be there in just a few minutes—. . ."

A shadow flung itself across her mind, across her body lying by the Rio Grande. "Not today . . . tomorrow . . . but please call me first." Her voice became frantic.

Forcing enthusiasm back, Ted promised to call tomorrow.

3

The door to David Lange's office was closed. To catch her breath, Normalyn paused at the ledge of a window in the corridor. She breathed deeply. One day she would be able to enjoy this beautiful city.

"You look radiant in that reflection." David Lange had been looking at her.

She stood up, destroying his vision of her.

Inside his office, he sat behind his ordered desk and against the commanding backdrop of photographs, the framed anarchy of the painting.

Suddenly Normalyn could not speak her accusation!—because what had seemed so clear as suspicion faded into fragmented conjectures as she faced David Lange. Accuse him of helping her in her journey? . . . She decided she would explore the components of her suspicions while she located the exact accusation.

"You didn't tell me you spoke to Stanley Smith before I called him, when he denied being my father."

David Lange reacted with the slightest indication of bafflement, a brief frown of confusion at the import of her statement. "I did speak to Stanley after I gave you his number—I simply verified it. And I told him you were in Los Angeles. When you mentioned your call to him, you were disturbed. Why disturb you more? Remember, Normalyn, we were trusting each other then, slowly. Certainly *you* didn't tell me everything, did you?" His smiled reminded her of mutual, close conspiracy. "Is any of that sinister, Normalyn?"

No. Instantly, it wasn't, not when exposed to his easy, disarming logic, the unangered voice. *That* was what she had to break finally, his instant control. Otherwise she would leave this office—again!—feeling thwarted, her doubts about his motives only briefly pacified before they reemerged. She reminded herself that he did not know of her further contact with Stan in Palm nor of her confrontation with the Crouches.

Immediately, she was sure he *did*—certainly with the Crouches. Through Lady Star? . . . If only she could find evidence that would firm her suspicions, her *exact* accusation!

"Stanley's telephone number isn't listed and you said it was—when I told you he hadn't even asked how I got it."

Even to her that sounded only desperate now. It was happening, it was happening again! He was only controlling her doubts, not answering them.

"I thought it was listed. But don't you think he'd assume I gave it to you—since I did mention you?" His eyes held her.

"The night after I left your office, you guided me to the Dead Movie Stars, what I would find there—"

"I *may* have suggested certain directions of discovery," he said.

Speak your accusation, dearheart, surprise him with it! It was Miss Bertha's voice! She could still hear it! But Normalyn realized now what she had known all along: It was her own voice; she had only been locating it. Yes, she *would* accuse, but first—. . . Slowly, Normalyn let her eyes scan the photographs on the wall behind David Lange. Swiftly she faced him. "What do you see, David, when you look at her every single day in your office?"

He reared back, his hands on his desk.

She waited, silently, challenging him to avoid her question.

He whispered delicate sounds so softly she could hear each breath. "What do I see? A perfect mask on which was painted weakness, strength, sorrow, joy. The conversion of vulgarity into elegance. The sensuality of a fallen angel, mocked. A creation that came to exist only in photographs, composed reflections. Marilyn Monroe's greatest art was the creation of herself out of a somewhat ordinarily pretty girl named Norma Jeane. It was great art, great artifice. She convinced the world that Marilyn Monroe was real. . . . Fascinating to see the transformation."

He looked at Normalyn, clearly startled, as if only now realizing he had spoken aloud. Silent, he touched the sphere on his desk.

The rounded crystal, it seemed to Normalyn, reduced the room into one central reflection possessed by him. *She would not be a part of what he controlled!* In the charged silence following his words, she experienced an instant clarity, and she spoke it aloud in amazement, her accusation found in his own words: "You've been attempting to re-create me as her!" She stood up. "But why me?" Glancing at the gorgeous movie star—*and the picture of the fleeing woman who might be Enid!*—Normalyn felt even more awkward and plain by comparison. Why me? He needed to believe she was Marilyn Monroe's daughter, that she was *that* close to her, "the ordinarily pretty girl named Norma Jeane" transformed into Marilyn Monroe.

Normalyn could shape her accusation now: "You've been guiding my life, David, shaping it to your wishes. You challenged me to live—by being like her. Be her! you said. And I think I tried, one eerie night. You told Stanley Smith I said he was my father, knowing he'd deny it—true or not, but exactly the way Marilyn Monroe was rejected by the man *she* thought was her father. You've maneuvered to keep me immersed in *her* life." He had never wanted her to find her *own* life; he had been pulling her away from it. "David," she said softly, "whether I'm her daughter or not, I'm *me*, not the reflection of her you've tried to make me into. I won't be part of your obsession!"

"Withhold your quick absurd conclusions!"

His voice was so harsh its power forced her to remain by the chair she had occupied.

"Learn this now, Normalyn! It can't wait longer!" He frowned at motes of dust captured within one reflected ray of light from the window. "I've told you there's only one person left who knows the full truth of Monroe's last days—Enid kept her secrets as mysterious as her life! We'll call that person—what? Our judge? Our accuser?" he asked wryly. "Ours, not yours, Normalyn." He spoke quickly: "Our accuser has made one condition for the truth all of us want for various reasons. The condition is that when we have ascertained that we have located the girl involved in the mystery, we confess to that girl—and through her to our accuser—our participation in the deceptions that surrounded the last days of Monroe's life. When I spoke to you first, you conveyed significant information. When I saw you, I knew you were our best candidate—from among all the women who contact me in response to every article I write."

The best candidate! All the confidence she had gained to make her accusation was being attacked, replaced by new fear. Again he was wresting all control from her.

"That's why you were tested, interrogated, informed! If you remained *only* our best candidate, you would have essential information about the events and the people involved, enough to convince our accuser. That's why you heard even harsh details. You were *given* that information—and you were challenged, guided even, to *feel* like her. Yes, I did that. You've been provided reflections of her to absorb. I did that, too, earlier. *That*—not your fanciful conjecture of my motives—is why you're here now!"

Normalyn tried to adjust to the violent reversal—and to this new harsh man thrusting cold words at her. To give those strange words reality, she spoke aloud: "You've been trying to convert me into an imposter who could get information for you."

"Choose the word you prefer." His voice remained peremptory. "Imposter, candidate." When he spoke again, the harsh tone broke. The concern, the caring that had made her return to him over and over came back into his voice: "Normalyn, Normalyn, that *had* to be stated bluntly. What I told you was so only at first. Now you've convinced us that you *are* that youngwoman and that you are, very probably, Marilyn Monroe's daughter." His voice lowered. "And his, Robert Kennedy's."

Later Normalyn would try to reconstruct her feelings in these jagged moments. Now she was aware only that all that had been said threatened to push her identity finally beyond her grasp, into chaotic darkness, the same darkness the two women had fought, had surrendered to. To clear her suddenly clouded vision, she looked out the window, at the bright cleansing sunlight of the present. Everything had reversed itself again, in his hands. She must grasp it back.

"From the start I told you, Normalyn, that there is one person who can gather the pieces of the fractured puzzle." David Lange paused. "That person is you."

And the person who could put it back together was the one he called their accuser. But who? Normalyn wondered.

"For years our accuser has awaited your arrival," David continued. "And so have we."

Then the lavender bouquets *were* summonses from someone alerted to her arrival? Miss Bertha! But now she was dead. Did the connection extend back to Texas, to Mayor Hughes? That question recurred, along with this certainty: He *had* guided her, along with Enid's letter. Who was the elusive figure in the girls' game played under the shadow of the angel she had seen earlier?—the undecided angel that had led her here today?

"And during those years of waiting," David went on in a tone of fascination, "our accuser has pursued, kept guilt alive with constant reminders. Call it psychological blackmail. Everyone involved has so much to hide. It hasn't been difficult to keep them terrified. Some have been exculpated. Others died—too soon for the grand summation of all the guilts! It's really quite Grecian in its overtones!" David seemed to exult in the prospect of judgment.

"Our accuser pursued some until the end—even that deadly clown Hoover. Peter Lawford, hounded into rambling denials, convinced now he knows nothing—his testimony is worthless. ... The Kennedys?" David stopped for long moments, and his eyes searched out the window and beyond the horizon. "No. Because Monroe loved them. At least one of them. And, after all—all along—*they* had been the real objects of the vast, brutal machinery of destruction."

There followed a long silence in the shadowless room of steadied twilight.

Now David Lange's voice was so soft it hardly broke the quiet interlude. "Ironic"—he seemed to speak to himself—"that only those who constructed that invisible machinery of destructive power are beyond anyone's reach."

Were *they* aware of her? Normalyn thought of the man at the Ambassador Hotel, the two men in the park, the men she had encountered that long hot night.

David broke the somber silence. "There are peripheral others." He laughed. "Oh, not Lady Star—she's been merely helpful. Poor Molly Ullman, so eager to barter for her own fame." He spoke with a certain pity. "She'll survive *her* scandal— and go on to be someone else, never herself."

During the subdued moments, Normalyn had found new confidence. After all, her purpose had not changed—break David's control, whatever he offered to provide now.

"What will you and the others gain from all the probing you've exposed me to?"

"Release from the aroused guilts," David said quickly, "the fear of exposure; or where, as in Mildred's case, there is no capacity for guilt, only release from ..." He paused. "... whatever it may be. There are other motives—always curiosity, perhaps even a desire for truth. Battered idealism trying to restore itself?" His hurt eyes fixed on her. "Certainly the fulfillment of a desire to solve the mystery that's haunted us: Did her daughter live? Is she you?"

"Your accuser will tell me in exchange for the required ... confessions?"

"Yes," David answered. He leaned toward her. "One more step, Normalyn, and you'll have your answer!"

Why did she feel saddened? Normalyn wondered.

Dearheart, ask him about his own— ...

No, she no longer needed to borrow another's voice. She had her own: "It's all being arranged through you, that's clear, and I assume you're in touch with the person you call your 'accuser.' But you haven't identified *your* participation in the events we've been talking about, David—why *you* should be accused—or exculpated, of course."

"You'll know everything, I promise, Normalyn." He leaned closer toward her. "But, first, I need to have *your* full commitment to the last step we're taking."

This is where it had led, she was sure. "How?"

His eyes prepared to seize her slightest reaction. "Perhaps there's a letter written at the very last by Monroe to Enid, perhaps something left by Enid— Our accuser may require certain verification from you."

Perhaps there's a letter! *Something* from Enid! He wasn't sure!

Her voice regained its control, certainty: "I'll let you know—very soon—about my further commitment, David. But before anything else"—she hardly paused —"show me the artificial flowers *you* received."

David Lange opened the door of a small cabinet near his desk. He brought out a bouquet of lavender blossoms. They were exquisitely wrought, each petal perfect, each flower in spring bloom, slender leaves enhancing the lavender purity of the full bouquet.

Not the slightest imperfection, no hint of decay!

From the same compartment, David pulled out another bouquet. This one was grayish brown. Dusty, desiccated pods cracked open to reveal more enclosed decay. He placed both bouquets, side by side, on his desk. Turning toward the rectangle of photographs of the beautiful movie star, he repeated the earlier question:

"What do *I* see there? ... Only what has always fascinated me: the reality of artifice."

Forty-Two

Facing Normalyn, David Lange remained standing behind his desk, on which the two artificial bouquets, one pure, the other rotted, lay in balance.

That was why he was the person orchestrating the gathering of witnesses, Normalyn thought, because he was either the most moral or the most corrupt, the most ambiguous, even to whomever he called their "accuser."

Reiterating her decision to inform him very soon about required commitment, Normalyn walked calmly out of David Lange's office, along the corridor, down the steps.

She *had* been given information—deliberately—by the people he had guided her to!

When she walked into the street—the sun still bright, evening shadows not yet extending—that revelation, whose impact had been buffered until now by the suddenness of its unraveling, threatened her reconstructed confidence.

Suddenly disoriented as to which direction to walk in, she stood at an intersection of Sunset Boulevard, amid a crush of colors pierced by chrome reflections from a huge record store displaying enormous blowups of posturing rock stars facing a quaint "old world" sidewalk cafe near a shiny gym next to a 1950s motel with orange and green plastic slabs.

She grasped for this: Beyond any possible control by David, beyond donated information, she had extracted from those involved much more than what they had intended to give her. She had maneuvered *immediate* fears and guilts—from Stanley and Ellen, under the white sun; from the Crouches, still trembling in a haunted past. Mildred Meadows remained the most rigid in her own cunning. But, Normalyn reminded

herself with pleasure, she had kept Lady Star in check. Even
with David Lange she had been able—for only a moment she
would explore—to penetrate his steely control. . . . On her
own, she had gathered evidence to detect flawed testimony;
from Mark Poe and Robert Kunitz—the purity of the bouquet
sent to them exculpated them, assured veracity; from Miss
Bertha—increasingly gaining definition as Alberta Holland.
All of that provided her weapons of her own. With the vague
smile she thought she remembered on his lips when leaving
him earlier, David Lange had confirmed that.

And there were others still to search out: Peter Lawford, the
actor whose testimony David Lange had dismissed as "worthless." No, not him—Enid's clipping also banished him. There
was Sandra and—

Now Normalyn was able to walk more calmly along the
pretty strip of Sunset Boulevard, along Technicolored cafes
and chic shops with arrogant mannequins stamped from the
same mold of beauty as the decorated people walking casually
on the glossy street. Luminous cars shot silvery rays back at
the sun as long shadows began to shade the city of palmtrees,
flowers, blurred identities. . . . A man with black sunglasses
slowed to look at her. Her suspicions stirred with disturbing
quickness: Was *he* one of the figures of scrutiny she thought
she was detecting, belying the stirrings of the still-restive conglomerate of power that had expropriated Alberta's plan?

2

"Normalyn!"
Within the chromy reflections on the street, Normalyn became aware that she was standing near the outdoor patio of an
attractive restaurant and that a youngman there had called
out her name. Other youngmen and women sat at pretty,
bright tables. Normalyn searched for a bus stop. Across the
street! She began to cross.

The youngman who had called to her leaped over the
wrought-iron railing separating the patio from the street. He
hurried toward her before she could rush away.

"Normalyn—it's me, Michael—Michael Farrell—from Mr.
Poe's school."

Too late to hide her pleasure at seeing him! He was
handsomer than she remembered, the dark leanness more so,
sensitive and strong.

"Will you sit with us?" he encouraged. "I'm with a couple

of friends from the school. Just for a while, come on." He tried to check her quick resistance.

She followed him into a patio overhung with delicately leafed ferns. Michael introduced his two friends—an earnest youngman and an attractive youngwoman. Normalyn was astonished to find herself sitting with them. Michael and his friends took brief turns telling her they were in the city as part of Mark Poe's course on structure. "We're going to the museums," said the girl. "And a play by Brecht," said the earnest youngman.

"And the Watts Towers!" Michael added. "Imagine! That man just wanted to make *anything* as long as it was beautiful, and look what he came up with—those great, beautiful towers shaped out of wire and cement and pieces of glass!" He looked in wonder about the restaurant as if to find its structure.

Then they all waited for Normalyn to say something.

To her they seemed suddenly to have been struck dumb—and so was she. She stumbled through her mind for something to say.

Modulating her tone, she asked the earnest youngman—because he seemed so aloofly sure of *every*thing, "What are you going to be when you—?" She stopped, aghast at what she had been about to say.

"When I grow up!" The youngman was shocked.

"I meant when you *leave* school."

"When I *finish*?"

"That's what I mean, dammit!" Normalyn was angry at herself.

'What are *you* going to be?" Michael tried to render her question ordinary.

"I'm going to write a novel," she decided at that moment.

"What kind of novel?" asked the attractive youngwoman.

Normalyn answered firmly, "A novel that will be partly like James Joyce's, partly like Emily Brontë's."

"That would really be something!" Michael approved. "A romance with a modern, new structure. Mark would love that—tradition *and* experimentation. God*damn*! I mean, to *create*— . . ."

Normalyn was caught in his excitement, yearned to express her own. But now that they were waiting for her to say more, she felt awkward—she just didn't *know* how to act with a group of people her age!

"I have to go now." She stood up, bumping into a waiter. "I'm sorry!" she yelled at him; the despised words echoed. She walked away hurriedly.

Michael followed her back to the sidewalk. "Will you have lunch with me?"

"It's *evening*," she reminded him. He didn't look insecure, and certainly didn't act it, but she could tell that he was, suddenly, and that calmed her—that he was bold *and* shy. And, she noticed, he had thick, long eyelashes.

"I meant dinner." Michael rushed to encourage: "Mark mentioned this great restaurant in Hollywood, the only *real* one left, the oldest. It's called Musso and Frank's. It was very popular with writers—Faulkner, Fitzgerald. I prefer Faulkner, do you?"

"Yes." She would make sure to read both. She added loyally, "And I like Dickens, Twain, Joyce. And Emily Brontë." She kept herself from telling him she could not finish the book he had been reading in Palm Springs.

"I like all those authors, too! Especially Brontë. What time for dinner?"

"I can't. I'm expected." That was the only excuse she could make up.

He was subdued. "Will you give me your number this time?"

"Yes," she said hurriedly so she wouldn't reconsider.

He handed her a readied pen, a piece of paper.

She wrote down the telephone number. She made an ambiguous seven that might be a nine.

"Is this a nine or a seven?"

"It's a seven," she said.

"I'll call you!"

She walked away, stopped, returned to where he still stood. "I made a mistake," she told him. "It's not a seven, it's a nine." She took the paper from his hands and retraced the number. Moving away, she waved, just waved, regretting that at the last moment, in fear, she had gone back to give him an incorrect number—regretting that doubly because she realized that, for a few minutes and despite her awkwardness, this contact had pulled her away from the entangled shadows of the past—and the question she had been shaping since leaving David Lange's office:

Was there such a person as the one David had described, who knew the truth? Or was this all another avenue of deception, to find out only what *she* knew—as the others had attempted to find out, too? At a precisely determined time, would the cold stare of publicity he had warned her against spring on her, released by him?

3

Troja was sitting on her bed, dressed in a glamorous pale orange dress. Normalyn sat next to her, perceiving a forced calmness. She accepted that her own life, which had earlier made *motions*, would have to stop now for Troja's. "You know he loved you a lot," Normalyn reminded.

"Yes, I do know that," Troja said firmly. "But that should have kept him alive!" She voiced the regret. "It would have," she said with certainty, "if other things hadn't been killing him. His youth was going, the damn drugs just blurred that for him for a while, killed him in another way. Some people gotta die at the exact time, or they'll go on dying each day."

"But how can you be sure it's the time to die?" Normalyn asked apprehensively, because she wondered whether Troja was talking about herself.

"Cause you just *feel* like dyin'."

"But you're facing things now," Normalyn reminded.

"Yeah, takin' one step after another." Troja's shanty tone kept the hurt in control. "I didn't do good yesterday; I know they won't call me back. Guess I lost my talent for impersonatin'."

Normalyn reacted in surprise. "You said you were working as a backup singer."

"Lied," Troja admitted. "Impersonating—but I don't know *who* to impersonate."

"You could be you," Normalyn said.

Troja touched her hair, arranging it with a sudden flair.

4

Night shadows gathered at the window, and a chilly mist penetrated Normalyn's room. But the cool breeze was scented with the aroma of flowers; so she left the window open. She held her arms close against herself, pressed against her body, huddled. She "saw" herself like that. No, that was— Who? What? She couldn't trace whom or what the position had evoked. She leaned back, altering it.

The memory of it—unshaped—lingered as a feeling of desolation through a restless night. She woke inundated by the developments of yesterday in David Lange's office—and by the awareness that Ted Gonzales would be calling today.

In her room, the door open, Troja was preparing herself for an interview when Normalyn went into the kitchen. "Myself," Troja was saying to the mirror. "Gotta be myself. Be myself. Myself."

Normalyn's pleasure ended quickly when she saw Troja hide something in her drawer. When Troja appeared in the kitchen, she seemed listless.

After Troja drove away in the Mustang—"backup singer" had been restored as a goal—Normalyn went into Troja's room. She opened the drawer. A needle, a packet of powder. . . . Saddened, Normalyn closed her arms against herself, the way she had the night before. She still could not locate the vague but strong association.

When the telephone rang, she rushed to it. It would be Ted!

She let it ring. When she left the house, it was ringing again. At the drugstore, she bought two books, by writers Michael had mentioned. She went to De Longpre Park. Stray bands of the young and the old were already there, some of the young in tattered decorations. It was a strange time, a time of lost identities, of looking for nothing . . . or not even looking anymore.

Normalyn knew where she would go now!

Only when she entered the long corridor of heavy trees leading to the Wing of the Angel Home did she wonder what she was going to do there. Ask— What? See— Whom? Normalyn waited, hearing the voices of children in the playground. Boys and girls, some as young as six, others near their teens, squealed, shouted, laughed, protested, cried. From here she could see only a portion of the angel. In bunched shadows, it looked frightened, huddled— . . . *That* was the position she had assumed yesterday, earlier today.

With deliberation, she walked along the tended shrubbery to the steps leading to the entrance of the administration building. Quickly, she opened the door.

A stocky girl—a student helper?—tended to some papers before her. Normalyn coughed to call attention to herself. The girl turned. She was a woman!

"Normalyn!" Sandra said. "I kept wondering when you'd finally come!"

5

Smiling and clasping her hand as if they were close friends reuniting, Sandra led Normalyn outside, into the playground. "I've done enough work for today," she remarked. A bell had rung, and the children were returning to the buildings.

Sandra sat on a shaded bench in the playground. She motioned Normalyn to sit next to her. Normalyn was glad they would not be facing the desolate angel.

"Playground hour is over now," Sandra explained. "It's resttime for the children." She sighed. "It's peaceful here. That's why I chose to stay. I've been here almost fifty years, Normalyn."

Fifty years! Normalyn would have said, I'm sorry, except that Sandra had said that without regret.

"Of course I'm not a ward any more." She smiled. "I help run the school for the director now." She said that with pride. "You know why I was placed here years ago?" she asked abruptly, as if to brush pain away. "Because I'm so homely."

"You're not, you—"

"Okay, then, I'm plain," Sandra settled the matter. "I'm happy the way I am, really. Everyone I know who was beautiful was *so* sad." She looked away, at memories. "Of course, I'm sure that's not so for *you,* Normalyn," she added hastily.

Although she was hearing it recurrently now, Normalyn still felt discomfort when told she was pretty; she was glad Sandra had gone on:

"Now that's *all* there is about me," she dismissed. She said to Normalyn, "When I saw you at auditions, I knew right away who you were. Of course, Lady Star had mentioned you'd be there—"

The stirred suspicion. Would she detect the influence of David Lange even here? Looking at the woman, her pleasant earnestness so apparent, Normalyn doubted it.

"I'm sorry I was so emotional that night when I ran out. But I knew you'd respond to my message and come looking for me." That pleased her, to be sought. She cleaned her glasses. "And you *did* come, and I know why, of course—to hear about Norma Jeane and Enid and the game they used to play until it wasn't a game any more."

"Yes." *Now,* that was why Normalyn was here.

Sandra's eyes explored the playground for long moments, as if seeking an exact entry into the past.

"It was so long ago she still called herself Norma Jeane. It was only later that—"

Forty-Three

—Norma Jeane became Marilyn Monroe.

But she arrived as Norma Jeane Mortenson, age nine, at the Norton County Home for Children in May, a misty month in Los Angeles, when the jacaranda trees are most luminescent. She was taken there by her latest guardian, Patricia Bradbury— Mrs. Edgar S. Bradbury. Norma Jeane's mother, Gladys, was once again in an institution. The Bradburys had had a serious discussion about what was "best" for the moody child: "For her own good," she would be returned to a home, another one. That did not surprise Norma Jeane. It had happened ten times before. The only question for the child had become how long she would remain with "new parents" before she was given back to the "the county." A year before she had been returned after less than a week. A favorite boarder in the home of her new "foster parents" had offered to teach her a "game." When Norma Jeane told her new parents about the molestation, she was slapped by the woman for "talking dirty about one of our best tenants." Norma Jeane began to stutter after that.

Norma Jeane had been a typically cute child. She became less pretty as a little girl; her straight blondish hair darkened; she was so skinny that she played a gangly boy in a school production. Quietly despondent, she would lie in bed *willing* her body to shape like those she saw in the movie-star magazines that Gladys read hungrily to escape her own drab existence.

Early in her life, Norma Jeane discovered that there must be a terrible wound somewhere inside her body. Only *she* had it. Sometimes she located it inside her stomach, sometimes in

440

her heart, a deep pit that was "empty" yet still hurt—a cold "painless" aching, she described it in her mind.

The only real happiness she experienced during that period was when Gladys—"the pretty lady with beautiful red hair"—sane again, would rent a house and bring Norma Jeane to live with her until the cloudy moods, "the blackness, the darkness," would return. That was the "blackness" that Norma Jeane increasingly remembered having "felt" as Gladys had clasped her hand so tightly when she saw her own mother carried away screaming to an institution.

That gray day in May, as Norma Jeane faced the new home, she felt cold even though she was perspiring. *That* was what deepened the "pit"—when she felt like an "orphan," a stranger among new strangers.

Waiting to receive Norma Jeane at the Norton County Home were Miss Kline, the director, and her associate, Mrs. Travers. Miss Kline was a tall, imposing woman. She had two deep creases over the bridge of her nose. She seemed stern without wanting to. When she smiled, she looked kind *and* annoyed. Often, she would attempt to smooth her furrowed brow. Mrs. Travers had an aging prettiness about her, as if she had become older in clothes that merely grew to accommodate her larger form.

"You won't be here for more than a month, I promise. We'll come back for you. This is for your own good. Think of it as a vacation," Mrs. Bradbury instructed Norma Jeane.

"Goodbye."

Norma Jeane had heard Edgar Bradbury instruct his wife this very morning, "Tell her we're coming back for her so she'll have something to look forward to."

Norma Jeane shut her eyes, hearing the quick clicking of Mrs. Bradbury's heels leaving her life. She imagined herself running away, searching block after block until she found Gladys, forced her out of the institution and into a pretty house they would share together. She'd yell at her mother, "Stop being insane, take care of me!"

"Don't shut your eyes," Mrs. Travers said to the new girl. "Look over there at the angel." She pointed to the statue, left over from a time when the home was a stately private house. "It's hurt, it's wounded. Look how it's holding her wings." Norma Jeane's tears spilled over.

"No." Miss Kline did not see the angel that way. "It's merely pausing, deciding."

At the time, the home housed fifty children, ages six through eleven. Some might have been older, their ages uncertain, perhaps as old as thirteen. Several were wards of the city, many were "semi-orphans," lacking only one parent, placed there "temporarily," eventually permanently. When they went to public school in their plain "uniforms," they were all "just orphans."

The first night in the dormitory—there were about twenty-five others girls there tending to their personal tasks—Norma Jeane could hardly breathe with new fear, new sadness. She tried to stop those burrowing feelings by declaring firmly. "I'm here because of a m-m-mistake. My father is a famous movie star who looks ex-ex-exactly like Clark Gable. My mother is a f-f-famous—" The memory of Glady's pained face stopped the lie. "I was left alone and I w-w-wandered out. Now everyone thinks I'm an orphan. My p-p-parents have hired detectives to find me and they will s-s-soon. A limousine is on i-i-its way."

The other girls laughed at her—except for the very young ones, including a homely seven-year-old brown-haired girl with thick glasses, Sandra. She stared at Norma Jeane in admiration of her fabulous story. She herself never talked about her young past: "I'm an orphan, period."

There was an indefinitely twelve-year-old boy—he looked older, had beginning muscles, strutted a lot—named Stanley Smith who bragged that his father was "a petty crook." He had heard him called that and assumed it meant he was important. He aspired to be that, too. "Then I'll have a son just like me, with no goddamn mother," he asserted, a proud lineage.

With the few cents given to the children as weekly allowance for chores performed about the home, Stanley would buy a wrapped candy—mostly sugar—called a "Guess What" because it contained a "surprise gift." Stanley learned how to feel the wrapping to detect the only one worth having, one that contained a paper with a star on it, which meant he could choose a gift from a box behind the counter. Stan always chose a "necklace"—five marbly beads on a knotted string. He would then sell it for up to five times his investment by swearing he had it on strictest confidence that one of them was "worth a loot." Grandly he awarded one to Norma Jeane, because she was the girl who by then received the most attention from the boys. He looked around to make sure they were looking at him. He said to Norma Jeane, "You're the prettiest damn orphan in the fuckin' home." He liked to talk that way, and with a crooked smile he would perfect as an adult.

At the time, Norma Jeane was not exactly "pretty." She had ordinary features, a nose slightly flat. But her body was giving startling hints of curves—and she "acted" pretty. For that reason, among the girls only Sandra liked her.

Briefly "sane," Gladys came to take Norma Jeane out on a Saturday outing. At a beauty shop she guided the woman to fix the girl's hair into beautiful waves, make her up "like a movie star." At home, she touched the girl's face, lovingly, outlining the redrawn features, asserting the prettiness of *this* face. "May I have your autograph, movie star?" Gladys asked her daughter. By evening, the frenzied look had taken over Glady's face—the traces of her beauty became etched over with scratchy lines when "the darkness" encroached.

At the home, Norma Jeane wandered into the recreation room. It was "mixer" time, boys and girls together. Norma Jeane's spirits crashed. She saw a new, pretty, dark-haired girl in the home. Sandra was talking to her. Stanley was lurking with his baby-shark's teeth. Norma Jeane touched her brown hair—it was already losing its wave. The makeup had faded. She felt terribly plain because the girl looked so confident, so unafraid. Norma Jeane wanted to be like that.

At night, Norma Jeane was startled to hear sobs coming from the girl's cot.

Sandra told Norma Jeane about the new girl: "Her name is Enid Morgan. And you're so alike I can't believe it. She told everyone that *she* doesn't belong here either. Her parents are rich, like yours. She's here by mistake, like you, and her famous mother and father have hired detectives to find her. A limousine will be picking her up, too, any day now. I'm sure we'll all three be close friends!"

Norma Jeane was skeptical about that—and annoyed, because what Sandra told her meant that the new girl knew *she* was lying, too.

When she saw the uncertain look on Norma Jeane's face, Sandra whispered, "*She* hurts a lot, too, Norma Jeane, like you do."

"I do *not* hurt. Whatever gave you *that* idea?" Norma Jeane denied.

Enid did hurt a lot. She was sure that only she felt sad every single moment of her life, even in her dreams. Her life to now had been a jagged journey from home to home. Because even at that young age she felt it might be possible to "figure life out," she had started what she called "a journal," entitled *Why?* It was really only scraps of paper on which she jotted down her thoughts—in between, inserting pictures of movie stars whom she—and her mother, who glided in and out of her life—admired. She made very few entries in the journal, because there was too much to question.

In the dormitory, a group of girls were discussing the number of homes they had been in, disguising hurt with bravado. "What about you?" one girl taunted Enid and Norma Jeane. "You've been in only one home, the rich one you accidentally wandered from?"

Enid answered quickly, "Yes, just one—but that one has a lot of them in it." She touched her stomach, her heart—

—locating the "pit," Norma Jeane knew suddenly.

Sandra continued to feel that Enid and Norma Jeane would become friends, even though a fierce competition developed between them. Sandra retained her loyalty to both.

The Number One Bed in the dormitory was a place of prestige, earned by "merit points" for excellence in home activities, crafts, drawing, playground performance, occupational skills. The real reasons for its desirability was its location, nearest the fire exit—fear of fire haunts unwanted children. The still night was often broken by screams out of a nightmare of consuming flames.

When Enid was placed three beds ahead of her, Norma Jeane began working earnestly, even in sewing class, which she detested. She earned enough merits to gain a place two beds ahead of Enid.

"You want to be Number One?" Those were Enid's first words to Norma Jeane.

"I *am* Number One." Norma Jeane spoke her first words to Enid.

Stanley watched with his crooked smile. Sandra thought, Well, at least they've talked to each other.

That weekend, when afternoon shadows tumbled on the playground, Norma Jeane knew Gladys would not come for her as she had promised. That meant she had gone away into the "blackness."

In the recreation room she saw Stanley with Enid. And Enid was wearing a glittery blue necklace exactly like the one he had given *her*!

Sandra gasped when she saw Norma Jeane dash toward Enid, who stood firm, waiting. Stanley removed himself. Whatever Norma Jeane had intended doing, it was interrupted by a monitor paging her into Miss Kline's office.

Miss Kline arranged her features into a smile, keeping a finger in the middle of her brow to smooth the frown. Sitting beside her, Mrs. Travers said to Norma Jeane, "Your mother called and said she had to go away; she asked us to let you make yourself up the way she did last week when she made you a 'movie star.' "

"It's an odd request, but we're granting it because your mother said it was important to you," Miss Kline said.

Norma Jeane was ecstatic! "Some rouge, please, and some powder. Please, some mascara," she kept requesting. Miss Kline would nod, and Mrs. Travers would bring forth yet another implement of magic from her makeup box.

Concentrating on exactly how she wanted to look, Norma Jeane made herself up in the light of the window.

Miss Kline looked startled by the transformation. Mrs. Travers smiled. "Very pretty."

Norma Jeane looked eagerly at Miss Kline: "Would you please touch my face—lightly so the makeup won't smear? That's what Gladys did when she saw me look so pretty."

Miss Kline removed the finger from her brow and took a step away from the girl. Then—with Miss Kline's smile encouraging her—she allowed herself to touch the girl's face, her features, tenderly. Trying not to show how deeply moved she was, she drew back her hand and said, "There. We've granted your mother's request. Now you must wash the makeup off."

Norma Jeane's hurt burst. For a moment, the "pit" had been soothed. "Oh, please! Just for a few minutes so they can see me. I'll even walk silly so nobody will take it seriously. I'll walk with a wiggle. P-p-please!" She took out of her pocket the necklace Stanley had given her. "For you, from me, forever." She gave it to Miss Kline.

Miss Kline's fingers embraced it.

Norma Jeane returned to the recreation room for the allowed rationed minutes. True to her promise, she did walk with a slight "wiggle"—a sexy one; she parted her lipsticked lips. "Hel-lo," she greeted everyone, putting a breath between the two syllables. She collected stunned stares and whistles from the boys. She was not even aware of "the empty pit."

"Who the hell are *you*, baby," Stan approved in his odd way.

"A movie star. A beautiful movie star." Norma Jeane almost hugged herself, and imagined Gladys applauding.

"It's just makeup," Enid said, not meanly. "Underneath it's still you, and it always will be."

"No," Norma Jeane rejected. That would mean that as she grew the "pit" would deepen. In substitute anger she said to

Stan, "I threw your necklace away in the garbage, where you found it." She looked at Enid's. "Just cheap glass."

It *was* cheap glass, Enid had known that all along. But it was also the first present anyone had ever given her. She touched the five blue beads of her necklace. Angrily she accused Norma Jeane, "You made yourself up to look like me."

"Goddamn if that ain't the fuckin' truth," Stanley blurted.

It was true, Sandra realized. Norma Jeane had made herself up to look the way Enid did naturally. Heavy, dark eyelashes, a full mouth, angular cheeks.

"I'm a natural beauty," Enid said to Norma Jeane. It was startling the way she said that. There was no boasting. It was the only reason so many foster parents chose her immediately. None came to love her enough to keep her. She was soon returned because she was "rebellious"—blamed because "it hadn't worked out."

The way she said what she just did meant she didn't think being beautiful was necessarily good, Sandra evaluated, and she thought about it all day.

Norma Jeane said, "We'll see who's beautiful!"

Norma Jeane won the bed of honor—for one night only. The following night, she was demoted to the last bed. Tossed on it was the necklace she had given Miss Kline. One of the girls had informed Miss Kline that Norma Jeane said it was found in the trash and that she hated it. Norma Jeane thought of explaining to Miss Kline what had happened. Instead, saddened by the whole thing, she threw the necklace away.

One late afternoon both Enid and Norma Jeane claimed the bench near the forlorn angel. Neither would budge even when the bell ended playground time. Sandra watched apprehensively.

A lost breeze rustled past the angel and stirred a jacaranda tree. Its frail blossoms fell in petals like—

"Lavender snow!"

Both girls said that at the same time. They looked startled at each other. Sandra rushed to them, took one hand of each, and linked them. "*Now* you have to make a wish because you said the same words at the same time." The two girls closed their eyes. Sandra wished, too—that *their* wishes would come true, that they would both become movie stars.

When Enid and Norma Jeane opened their eyes, Enid said, "We're both liars, Norma Jeane, we're both orphans. No one's looking for us, we're all alone."

Norma Jeane agreed sadly. "Sometimes I even feel I've got an empty pit inside me."

"Right here." Enid touched her stomach. Then her hand rested on her heart. "It feels cold—"

"—at the same time you're perspiring," Norma Jeane finished. She sighed. "That means you have an empty pit inside you, too." Of course, she had known it.

They told each other about their real lives—the powerful fragments of love from desperate mothers pursued by black desolation. Missing fathers, fears, rejections, violations.

Her heart breaking, Sandra listened. She could not keep in order which details belonged to whom because one would tell a part of her life, and a few seconds later the other would tell it as her own, as if they were constructing a single terrible existence they had both managed to survive.

That night, the two girls attempted to run away. Miss Kline found them at the edge of the playground, too terrified to cross the street.

Around the others, Enid and Norma Jeane still upheld their fabulous stories of "rich, famous parents." Then they extended their stories into the future, when they would both be "great movie stars," loved by their mothers and the whole world. Soon the two began telling the stories together, interchangeably, embellishing the other's detail.

Once, Norma Jeane slipped badly down the stairs—and bled. "If she needs a transfusion," Enid offered, "I'm sure we have the same blood." And it was true. An honor student always, Sandra was often given "special tasks." In the office, she had looked up their medical records. "I'm not sure anything that drastic will be needed for a nosebleed," Miss Kline said.

With only Sandra allowed to witness it, Norma Jeane and Enid started playing the game one afternoon after a hurried, giggled rehearsal. Sandra too, laughed with delight.

"I am not a lonesome orphan any more," Norma Jeane would say.

"Why?" Enid would ask.

"Because a lonesome orphan always feels unwanted and has a deep, ugly empty pit inside."

"Then what are you?"

"A movie star."

"Why?"

"Because a movie star is loved by everyone, including her mother. . . . And millions of fans." The last was Norma Jeane's addition, and she hugged herself with the thrill of it.

"How did you become a movie star?"

"I'm not sure." Norma Jeane couldn't remember suddenly. "How?"

Enid reminded her emphatically of the next line they had agreed to: "The *orphan* taught me to be strong."

Norma Jeane said it very quickly.

Then it became Enid's turn. "I am not a *lonesome* orphan," she emphasized.

"Why?" Norma Jeane would ask her. And the game proceeded.

That first day, the angel cast a long shadow, as if stretching the guarded wing. That's when Norma Jeane named the Norton County Home "The Wing of the Angel"—because "that makes it all seem better, like a movie with Jean Harlow." For Enid, Sandra suspected, the name evoked something else: As Enid passed the statue that day, she furtively touched the sheltered wing of the angel, gently.

Then Sandra began to detect that the game was changing.

On a moody day when Norma Jeane and Enid were eleven—an age when being adopted becomes almost impossible and when childhood is completed—the two girls played their game over and over while Sandra listened and watched with mounting alarm. At first the game would end in conspiratorial laughter as before, but the laughter soon began to diminish and they were playing it relentlessly, fiercely, without a pause.

It was Norma Jeane's turn to start: "I am not an orphan."

Enid stopped her: "You have to say, I am not a *lonesome* orphan."

"It's the same thing," Norma Jeane said testily.

"No, it isn't," Enid insisted. "It changes the whole game. What it means is that you *are* an orphan *and* you're strong. Let's start it again, clearer this time: I *am* a *strong* orphan," she prodded, tense.

Norma Jeane crossed her arms over her chest, which was becoming lush. "I'm not going to be an orphan any more—period. I'm going to be only a movie star," she said in a new voice. She started to walk away, a new walk she had been learning.

Enid stood up. "Norma Jeane!"

"I'm even going to change my name," the new voice said.

"You'll still be you," Enid said.

"I don't want to be me!"

"Norma Jeane!"

"Don't call me that!" Marilyn Monroe put her hands to her ears.

Enid forced them away. "Norma Jeane's been abandoned

again and again and again, remember?" Her voice was frantic, pleading. "You want to abandon her, too?"

"*Yes!*"

Sandra wanted to run away in fear when she heard Enid's words.

"All right! *Norma Jeane* will be the orphan," Enid said in a precise, clear voice, "half you, half me. *I* won't abandon her, and I won't let you abandon her, and if you try, she'll kill you."

Forty-Four

Early evening shadowed the playground.

And so "Norma Jeane" was the strong, elusive figure that commanded the game. . . . In discovering that, Normalyn saw yet another Enid, a tortured little girl hiding her fears behind proud pretensions—but always upholding the strength of her dark beginnings, finally sharing her secrets with Norma Jeane.

Throughout Sandra's recitation, Normalyn had withheld questions, not wanting to interrupt the delicate string of memories. Now she said, "You started calling Norma Jeane 'Marilyn Monroe,' and she didn't become that until much later."

"Did I? I guess that's because when I look back, I see that's when she became her, that time when they were playing the game over and over—and, you know, in truth she was Norma Jeane many more years than she was Marilyn Monroe."

Sandra was quiet for moments.

"Then they all went away except me. Norma Jeane's mother came for her again and later put her in another home; Enid was adopted by Texas millionaires she hated. And *then* Norma Jeane became Marilyn Monroe! Stanley, of course, became a petty crook. And Enid— We heard she kept seeing Stanley. I don't know why."

Because he gave her her very first present, Normalyn knew, establishing a bond as fragile as that, as powerful as that. "Enid is dead now," Normalyn told Sandra.

Sandra sighed. "I suppose I knew it, when I learned you were here, but it's just as sad to hear it." She looked about the playground, as if to locate where they had all once been, so real, removed now. "Rest in rest."

"What?" Normalyn felt at the edge of discovery.

"Rest in rest," Sandra repeated, tugged back into memory. "That's what Enid and Norma Jeane decided when we took a tour of the big cemetery on the hill, with all the swans and—" She paused, concealing a smile. "—and all those naked statues." She hurried on: "Mrs. Travers took us, because—"

*   *   *

—Miss Kline said she had too many ghosts in her life to go to a cemetery.

In the minibus provided by a charitable group for such occasions, about a dozen of the older children were driven up the roads of Forest Lawn, past swans that primped for them, past sensual statues that Stan kept whistling at, nudging Norma Jeane and Enid to notice. In a double column—Sandra managed to walk alongside Enid and Norma Jeane—they went to the Wee Kirk o' the Heather Chapel. Outside was a stone bench to sit on, make a wish. Norma Jeane and Enid held hands and wished aloud that they would become "adored movie stars." Stanley plopped between them and wished, "And make *me* a petty crook!"

Inside the chapel, Mrs. Travers told them to say a prayer for "unfortunate children," and they all bowed their heads, except Norma Jeane, who whispered that *they* were the unfortunate children. They didn't go to the great hall housing the panoramic painting of the crucifixion, because the performance had already started. Instead they went to the curio shop next to it. Enid bought a small figurine of an angel. She said it looked like the one at the home—"but I'll teach this one to fly." Norma Jeane laughed, the way she was beginning to, a breathy laughter.

Too late for Mrs. Travers to lead them away, they had come to the Court of David, with its enormous statue of a naked David looming in an alcove of sculpted greenery that opens into the Garden of the Mysteries of Life. Norma Jeane and Enid couldn't control their giggles at the sight of the nude statue. Sandra didn't have a chance to close her eyes. Stan said the man was "sure hung small." No one understood except Mrs. Travers, who gave a spirited "whoop!" they'd never heard before. Then she reprimanded Stan, gathered them all, and marched them to the Hall of Patriots.

Norma Jeane's voice was tense: "What does R.I.P. mean?"

Enid saw the designation on a stone. "It spells 'rip'!" Her voice instantly touched panic.

"It means 'Rest in Peace,'" Mrs. Travers explained.

"Rest in pieces!" Norma Jeane heard and repeated.

"Ripped in pieces!" Enid thought of the terrible hurt inside her and Norma Jeane. "That would mean that even after you die, you go on hurting," she rejected.

Mrs. Travers tried to soothe the girls. " 'Rest in Peace' is just a kind wish that you rest quietly after you donate your soul to God."

But the two girls were already running back in tears to the minibus. The other children started to cry when Stanley yelled meanly at them, "Rip, rip, rip—chop, chop!"—to hide his own fear.

Only Sandra didn't cry, because she knew all about ugly death.

Mrs. Travers ushered them all into the minibus. She joined them in their tears.

On the way back to the home, Norma Jeane said to Enid, "It should say, 'Rest in Rest.' " Enid agreed: "Rest in rest."

That same day—and only that one time—they ended their game forlornly with those words.

*   *   *

Rest in Peace. Rest in Rest. Norma Jeane, rest in rest. N.J.R.I.R. Rest in Peace, Norma Jeane. . . . That easily it had come, the answer to the initials Enid had written on her letter. That had been one of her last thoughts and she had left it as a new message to her, Normalyn, joining the two parts of the letter. Normalyn could not explore that further now because Sandra had just said excitedly:

"Then the limousine did come for them!" Instantly she was serious: "But not really." She looked beyond the grounds, "That ugly gray limousine with those darkened windows did come and—"

*   *   *

—the children saw it as it drove up. "The detectives found you, and your rich parents have sent the limousine for you!" one of the astonished girls said to Norma Jeane and Enid. Others joined the excitement: "The chauffeur's going to talk to Miss Kline!" "You'd better run and pack!" "Quick or they'll lose you again!"

Both Enid and Norma Jeane—puzzled—had to pretend the limousine had really come for them. Stiffly, they walked to their bed areas, the others following. The two girls folded their clothes, slowly, hoping the gray limousine would leave. Then they'd claim they hadn't been ready, prepare another story.

"Hurry, hurry!"

The two girls walked down the stairs together, with their few clothes bunched. Leaving Miss Kline's office, the haughty chauffeur walked past them on his way out.

"He didn't even *look* at you!" a girl laughed at the two girls. The excitement turned into mockery when they all realized the sumptuous limousine had come on other business. "You'd better run after it before it leaves," a girl taunted now, joined by another, then another.

In the mocking glare, Enid and Norma Jeane had to walk—slowly, slowly, but it still waited—right up to the long dark limousine.

A white face stared out of the smoky window at the two.

After extended seconds, the car drove away.

Silently, Enid and Norma Jeane had to "unpack" their clothes before the gleeful girls.

Sandra did not learn about those details until later, because when she saw the gray limousine, she ran and hid from it.

*   *   *

"Why did the limousine come here?" Normalyn asked Sandra. It had to have been Mildred's, when she had come on the unlikely "dutiful mission of charity expected of everyone in Hollywood"—as she had carefully described it to Normalyn.

"It was just an ugly mistake," Sandra declared firmly. "Norma Jeane never came back to visit us. She just said those terrible things about *all* the homes she'd been in. They weren't true of *this* one," she said loyally. "Miss Kline and Mrs. Travers always tried to care. It hurt Miss Kline when those awful tourists started coming to see 'one of those places where Marilyn Monroe was mistreated.' Even so, Miss Kline kept saying, 'Marilyn Monroe will come visit, wait and see.' The way she touched her fingers when she said that, I think she wished she'd come back with the blue glass necklace. . . . Only Enid came back, always when she was in the city. Each time she was more beautiful, with that hat and her silver lighter she clicked like she was commanding." Sandra tried to imitate the proud stance, gave up.

"Each time she came back—"

*   *   *

—Enid would spend a few moments by herself on the bench near the statue in the playground. Then she would face the placid angel. She squared her shoulders as if with renewed courage.

A certain time, she needed courage. She confided hurriedly to Miss Kline and Mrs. Travers—and of course Sandra—that she was going away "to have a child." She said that with defiance.

Sandra could not help assuming the child was Stan's—he was mean enough that she would have to go away to have it. They had all learned not to ask Enid questions. She would say all she intended, no more.

Miss Kline always managed to ask about Marilyn Monroe. "Oh, and by the way how is—"?

Enid told her joyfully that Marilyn seemed happy. "She's sure she'll fall in love again and marry, and she says this time it will be forever."

As Sandra walked her out, Enid told her, "Oh, we still play the game—when it becomes necessary to remember."

* * *

That was when Enid returned to Texas to have Stan's child, Normalyn connected. In sudden wonder, she realized that years ago, Enid had been *here*! Normalyn ran her hand along the bench, tenderly.

Sandra continued sadly. "When Enid came back again, the last time, we were all so sad because we learned that—"

* * *

—Marilyn Monroe was dead.

Enid had to speak to someone close before she fled—forever— "this city of pain and lost angels." Her hand kept touching her lips, to stifle sobs. Even behind the specked veil of her hat, her beautiful eyes looked steeped in sadness. At first Sandra thought that was the only reason she had asked the blinds to be drawn as they sat in Miss Kline's office. But soon Sandra began to suspect another reason as Enid stood recurrently, looking out, staring, as if someone might have followed her—or as if she were waiting for someone in secret. She rushed her words, which kept snagging on a gasp she attempted to control with a sigh: "I'm leaving right away, I wanted to leave from here." She looked out the window differently this time, at—

—the angel! Sandra was sure. Even in these terrible moments she would gain strength from it.

Enid spoke urgently now. "It was dangerous to return, but I had to go to her house when I learned she was dead." She seemed to see it all again, just as she had at—

* * *

—dawn!

The house was surrounded by reporters, doctors, photographers, policemen! Standing outside, Enid saw a stretcher being carried out of the star's home. The body of Marilyn Monroe was covered with a pale-blue blanket.

Enid felt torn in two. She screamed: *"Marilyn!"* Then she whispered: "Norma Jeane— . . ."

* * *

"Is it possible that so much life has stopped, just stopped, so soon?" In Miss Kline's office, Enid asked that aloud.

"She was so beautiful, so famous, so rich, so loved," Mrs. Travers said.

"So *hurt*," Sandra remembered.

"She wasn't rich. She had to borrow, she thought her career was over—the studio had fired her. She was sure she was losing her beauty, but she wasn't—she was more beautiful than ever." Enid roamed over reasons. "She'd lost her confidence —because the man she finally loved walked out on her when she was sure he'd marry her, that he would want their child as much as she did—"

"Marilyn was pregnant—?" Mrs. Travers began in surprise.

"Yes!" Enid covered her lips as if they had said more than she had intended.

"All that loss, all at the same time, and it was too much for her to bear, for anyone to bear." Miss Kline thought she understood. "And so she killed herself," she managed to whisper the terrible words.

As if something foreign had entered her body, making her rigid, her veins straining visibly, Enid stood suddenly. One hand pressed her throat as if to smother a scream of pain she would be screaming silently the rest of her life. "She *didn't* kill herself!" she gasped.

Forty-Five

Mrs. Travers pulled back from the startling words. Sandra thought urgently, Rest in rest, rest in rest—

"Then who—!" Miss Kline began in horror.

Agitated, Enid opened her purse. She looked at her silver lighter in surprise, as if it, too, had died. Then she held a letter and stared at it, as if to identify it. Slowly, gently, she returned it to her purse.

With such sudden tenderness! Sandra was sure it was a last letter from Marilyn Monroe.

Her back to the others, her gaze steady on the impassive angel outside, Enid seemed to speak to herself now, as if to find answers to her own questions, shape grief into words that—spoken aloud—*might* be understood. "The last time I saw her alive—when I went to her house to explain the final details of the plan that might make it possible for her child to be born in secret"—she pronounced private words the others did not understand, did not dare question—"Marilyn was concerned for me. It touched me when she asked me—"

*　　*　　*

"You'll do all this for me, put yourself in danger?"

"You'll be in danger, too," Enid reminded carefully.

"I know. But *you* don't have to be."

Enid said quietly, "We became a part of each other, remember?"

"In our game, yes," Marilyn knew. They had not played it since the day Mildred's raid had erupted into harsh recriminations between them.

"The game came true for you," Enid said. "You wanted to be only the movie star." She said that only to soothe.

"Because a movie star is loved by *everyone*." Marilyn's voice assumed a note of wistfulness that slipped into irony as she recited the key line from the game they'd first played under the shadow of the angel's hurt wing. Then she said with anger, "No one is ever 'only a movie star.' A movie star doesn't exist except as fantasy—it's just a creation for others, it's never real." She felt a wistful regret, the unreality of dreams.

"But you wanted to become your own fantasy. And you have," Enid reminded. "The whole world knows you, Marilyn Monroe."

They were sitting like subdued school girls on Marilyn's movie-star bed in her newly acquired Spanish-style home. Enid was aware of the sensitivity of these moments, the movie star's sadness that the man she had come to love must not even know she was having his child—and that sadness bruised the joy of anticipation of the new life. The two women knew, also, that they would not be able to see each other for long, even to talk, during the rest of the pregnancy and for a time afterwards. That added a special sad closeness to these moments.

"You could have been a star, too," Marilyn said. She had never understood why Enid had pulled away.

Enid shook her head. The dream for her had become tarnished when she knew her life would be redone.

"Was it because you loved Stan?" Marilyn would have given up her unreal life to become Mrs. Robert Kennedy.

Enid said harshly, "Whether I ever loved Stan or not, I don't even remember—*that's* how much I despise the bastard now."

Marilyn knew Enid had just recently returned—from somewhere—and that the reason concerned Stanley Smith. But Enid kept her own crises secret, like the rest of her life. "Where *do* you disappear to, Enid—when you go away?"

"To the shoreline, any shoreline." Enid smiled at the question unanswered for so many years, accepted in these delicate moments. "I love the dark ocean. I go to places where I can walk alone along the edge of the water. I click my cigarette lighter for attention—"

"But there's no one to hear it, just the dark." But Marilyn understood. She, too, loved the ocean at night, because it rendered darkness real, unlike the menacing "blackness" that was only perceived.

"That's why I carry it, as a signal to the darkness that I do
exist." Enid laughed, to temper the serious words.

Marilyn welcomed laughing now. "You've always been so
damn mysterious. It's as if I know you only when you're
present. When you're gone, you're just . . . questions. Do you
still write in that journal you kept for questions?" On the day
they had named the jacaranda dust "lavender snow," Enid had
shown her the few scattered pages she kept.

"I called it *Why?* I'm still wondering that."

Enid realized the glamorous movie star known throughout
the world was this saddened, confused isolated woman she
loved. And yet—Enid detected this gladly—there was about
her now a new saving radiance that came from her determination to have this child.

"And you also wonder what became of Norma Jeane?" Marilyn responded to the tight stare. "You said once you'd never
abandon her and you'd make sure I didn't either because if I
tried, I would—" Marilyn stopped. She had not meant to
remember that, nor to accuse.

"I always wonder about Norma Jeane," Enid said softly.

"But all of that was only a game we kept on playing,"
Marilyn said urgently. "We always laughed at the last."

"You *really* believe it was just a game?" Enid asked aloud.

Marilyn said, "Sometimes I'm not sure." She went to the
mirror over her dresser. She freshened her lipstick, adding
Vaseline to make her lips glow redder, as if makeup might
keep her from being pulled back too forcefully into the memory of dark days. "Enid," she said, and looked away, "when
you came for me in New York after I committed myself to the
psychiatric clinic, I didn't tell you everything. Now I have to
tell you what I left out, about all that happened after that
night of—"

*   *   *

—the waking dream.

When she found herself at the edge of the open window of
her high-story apartment, about to jump into the "warm blackness," she pulled back, startled.

The next day she discussed the "dream" with her psychiatrist, Dr. Irene Slasky, who believed compassion was most
effective when hidden. Marilyn remembered only then: "I
went to the window because I heard footsteps outside; then I
heard someone calling me."

"You know you were much too high to hear footsteps, even
a voice." Dr. Slasky was firm.

"Dammit, she was looking up at me, daring or coaxing me to jump—or telling me not to—I'm not sure now!" Marilyn had not realized any of that until this moment. "God damn it, doctor, I *saw* her!"

"Did you recognize her?"

"Y-y-yes."

Although Dr. Slasky concluded that Marilyn had experienced a "severe hallucinatory state" brought on by grogginess from pills, she encouraged her to commit herself to Payne Whitney Psychiatric Clinic—"just for a rest, observation."

The day Marilyn went there, the East River was icing. She stepped out of the cab and walked in her white fur coat toward the clinic. She saw in a window dulled by frost the outline of a woman. She recognized the reflection.

Inside the clinic, she was stripped of her clothes and her snowy coat. She tried to mold the drab hospital gown to her curves. Shocked to find herself locked into a bare room, she demanded, then pleaded to be let out. But no one responded, although throughout the long, terrifying night doctors, nurses, attendants made scratchy noises at her window, staring in, recognizing her.

She threw off her clothes before the spying eyes. "If you want to look at me, look at *me*! I'm Marilyn Monroe!" she shouted.

They rushed her screaming into a security ward, where she broke a chair against the barren walls, trying to smash this unbudging nightmare. Marilyn Monroe *couldn't* be in *here*, helpless, she told herself.

In exchange for her autograph, an orderly agreed to call her ex-husband in Florida. When he looked at the paper she'd signed, he shoved it back angrily. The name she had written wasn't hers!

Finally released by her ex-husband, she was smuggled through a freezing basement passage. Ahead, the East River froze in jagged shapes.

Dozens of newsmen and photographers sprang at her, advancing, crouching, kneeling, cornering her. Her hands touched cold walls, ice on ice. As she lashed out with her hands, she knew no one had heard Norma Jeane whisper:

"I am M-M-Marilyn M-M-Monroe."

* * *

Of course Enid had know all along what Marilyn had left out—barely suggested—when she'd first recounted those experiences: the assertive presence of Norma Jeane.

"So you see, Enid, Norma Jeane isn't gone," Marilyn tried to laugh now in her bedroom.

Enid was silent, thoughtful.

Marilyn Monroe said in surprise, "And sometimes I wake up startled, almost knowing I *am* Marilyn Monroe. I *almost* realize it's *me* on all those magazine covers, in newspapers, on the screen." She paused; her voice lowered. "Years ago, when *Photoplay* magazine gave me that award—"

Now there occurred an odd change in Marilyn's voice, Enid noticed. She had introduced the memory with a retrospective sadness, but as she spoke it further, her voice thrilled with pleasure as she remembered Joan Crawford's deliberately late arrival:

"Excitement poured away from *her*—"

*   *   *

—and gathered in a new wave at the entrance to the Crystal Room of the Beverly Hills Hotel.

Marilyn Monroe had just walked in!

In a gold lamé dress that dipped to her navel and opened at her breasts to expose half-crescents of dark pink flesh, Marilyn Monroe's body reshaped itself into even more curves as she floated in on a blaze of sensuality. She was lifted up on a wave of adulation, crests of gasps, applause, sighs. The "empty pit" the child had detected when she was only Norma Jeane was gone! It had been filled by the sweep of adoration spilling over, and she thought she felt alive for the first time. She was sure that at this moment Marilyn Monroe was being fully born!

But at that exact same moment—

*   *   *

"—I wanted to run, escape!" Marilyn confessed as she sat in her bedroom with Enid. She ran her finger along her lips, removing the Vaseline she had just applied, as if now that would pull her from the pursuing time. "When a photographer asked me to part my lips in a 'sexy pout,' I froze with terror because I was sure that if I did, I would hear a scream—my own!"

No—Norma Jeane's, Enid knew. But she did not say that during these delicate moments. "You just remember it differently now, that's all," Enid said, to calm the star's agitation.

Marilyn frowned. The spoken memory had just linked with another: "When I invited Robert to dinner, when I was sure he would ask me to marry him, I tried to look like *me, more*

than a movie star. He stared at me as if he didn't recognize
me." She could still see the look of bafflement, dying desire.
"There *were* times when I was sure Robert saw me, loved
me—" She placed her hands with delicate care on her stomach,
on the child forming inside her. "And yet, sometimes, when
they were desiring me—I was aware of this more with John
than with Robert—I felt they would be . . . embarrassed . . . to
be with Marilyn Monroe other than when we were having
sex—" she voiced her confusions. She said with anger, although she wasn't sure it was directed at Enid, "You said John
and Robert treated me like an orphan."

"A *weak* orphan. And that's not what Norma Jeane is." At
this crucial time, Marilyn had to understand that it was the
orphan who had struggled to survive, that their strength came
from that survival.

"Dammit, is that all there's been between us, Enid, just that
damn game? Is that all that ties us?"

And having seen each other completely vulnerable! *And* having become a part of each other! *And* having learned from
each other how to survive. . . . Enid tried not to show her
hurt. She remained silent.

"If so, then it's turned into a damn battle," Marilyn judged
Enid's silence. And yet— She thought of the years Enid had
come to her in crises, to remind her of their strength, defiance; and in a few hours she would go into seclusion and Enid
would replace her in public, putting herself in danger to allow
her to have her child, to cover the secret pregnancy. Gently,
she took Enid's hand in hers, to soften her words.

Enid held it back. "If it was a battle, then it was fought only
with love."

"Yes," Marilyn knew. Then she added quietly, "For Norma
Jeane."

* * *

"It was Norma Jeane who killed Marilyn Monroe!" Enid gasped,
the day she returned to the home, to the statue of the angel,
to talk to Miss Kline, Mrs. Travers, Sandra, when Marilyn
Monroe was dead. Enid's eyes were glazed with tears as she
looked at the three women, as if pleading not to be judged
harshly.

"Don't you see how clear it is? Norma Jeane wouldn't allow
herself to be mistreated like a weak orphan, and Marilyn kept
trying to abandon her. Even if I had been able to go to her
myself when it all shattered at the very last," she spoke to
herself, "eventually it would have happened. Because Norma

Jeane was strong. I saw to it!" Her voice was a whisper. "But
Marilyn Monroe was not."

"But Norma Jeane is dead, too," Miss Kline reminded.

"Yes," Enid whispered, so softly. She looked up, startled.

*   *   *

Was that the guilt Enid had battled all those years, her
support of Norma Jeane, her insistence on Norma Jeane's
strength? Normalyn wondered as she sat in the playground of
the Wing of the Angel Home, here where Norma Jeane and
Enid had first played their fatal game. In the years that had
followed, the years of Normalyn's life, Enid had reasserted
Norma Jeane's strength, and her own loyalty to Norma Jeane.
There had been the recurring times of anger vented at Marilyn Monroe. But, Normalyn remembered now, those were
always times of anguish, confusion, deepest questioning.

"And then," Sandra continued slowly as if hesitant to approach more sad memories, "that day, Enid stood up, and—"

*   *   *

—she said, "And now her daughter is—"

Alive? Dead? Sandra waited tensely to hear.

But Enid retreated from the words she had almost spoken.
She looked about the room as if hostile presences might
overhear.

There was the quiet sound of a car. Enid heard it immediately. She looked out the window. "It's here now! Everything
is prepared. It's up to me! . . . Now she'll be our child."

"Who? Whose child?" Mrs. Travers begged.

In the flooding grief of these moments, Sandra realized,
Enid had told them nothing about her own child. A boy? A
girl? Where now?

Enid was no longer addressing them: "She'll be our child,
and she'll survive. No matter what I have to do!" She raised a
clenched fist. "I swear it. *She'll* survive!"

*   *   *

"We never saw her again, and that's all she said," Sandra
told Normalyn.

The sun was withdrawing some of its warmth. A breeze rustled
the leaves of trees. They stirred like restless spirits.

"Whose daughter are you, Normalyn?"

Startled, Normalyn looked at Sandra. She had just asked the
very question whose answer she was seeking here.

"I thought you would tell me." Normalyn could not hide

her anger. "You said at auditions that I look like ... my mother."

"You do, whichever one she is."

Wearily, Normalyn closed her eyes. There had been many answers here, but not *the* answer.... "Are Miss Kline and Mrs. Travers still here?" There was something more she had to do.

"Only Miss Kline," Sandra said. "Mrs. Travers died a year ago."

Now Sandra ran the home. It was right. She would be kind. Normalyn felt glad.

"They lived up there." Sandra indicated the left wing of the second floor in the main building. "Now only Miss Kline does. Sometimes I coax her to come down to see the children. She's so old now, almost losing her sight—and sometimes she forgets. When she does manage to come down, she tries to look carefully at each child; sometimes she touches a face—the way she did Norma Jeane's, when she made herself up in her office."

"Will you give her this?"

Sandra gasped. "The necklace! Miss Kline wanted it back so badly."

It was Enid's, not Norma Jeane's, but Miss Kline would not know that. "Please tell her Marilyn really wanted her to have it," Normalyn said easily.

"Please, you give it to her, *you* tell her that. *Please*, Normalyn." Sandra was moving back toward the building, coaxing Normalyn to follow. "Please!"

As they walked up the steps, Normalyn imagined two pretty girls with their few belongings, pretending the gray limousine had come for them.

Sandra knocked softly and opened a door into a dim room. Against the light of the window, a tall, slender woman sat quietly in a chair next to a small table on which was—

A bouquet of flowers! Normalyn saw. But the dim light refused to identify more than their sketchy outline.

"Miss Kline, there's somebody here who wants to see you," Sandra said.

"Who, Sandra?" Miss Kline asked eagerly, readied expectations alerted. She leaned forward as if her eyes might still be able to detect a clear presence. Then she canceled her expectations with a sigh. "Is it one of the children?"

"A very special one."

Miss Kline raised her head. Then again resisting extravagant hope, she leaned against her chair. But she placed a finger on her brow, to smooth the crease there—although age had added wrinkles that had softened it permanently.

Sandra urged Normalyn forward.

"Is it—?" Miss Kline said.

"Yes!" Sandra said exuberantly.

Normalyn approached the tall woman. She stood close to her—and to the bouquet of flowers: perfect replications of unblemished jacarandas!

Miss Kline's trembling fingers barely touched Normalyn's face. "Why, it *is* Norma Jeane! I'd recognize your face always! . . . I told you she'd come back, Sandra!" She almost got up, but her body refused.

Normalyn noticed that the tired eyes were clouded over with an encroaching film of delicate gray. She said softly, "I came to give you something."

Miss Kline sighed. "The necklace."

Normalyn placed it in her hand.

Miss Kline's fingers embraced it. "Didn't I tell you and Mrs. Travers that she would come back, Sandra? And she has— even if I had to wait all these years. I told them, Norma Jeane—Marilyn Monroe— . . . I told them you would come back." Miss Kline touched her eyes, cherishing the tears of joy. "Now goodbye, Norma Jeane!" she called out.

Sandra motioned to Normalyn, and they walked out quietly.

2

Outside again, Sandra held Normalyn's arm. "It may not mean anything, but that last time Enid was here, she left with a man who came to pick her up. We looked out the window, and we saw him guiding her into the car. Such a courteous man—so distinguished! He carried an elegant cane and he had—"

"—the slightest limp," Normalyn finished.

"Yes!" Then impulsively, Sandra hugged Normalyn before she ran back into the home.

Normalyn remained in the playground. The restless breeze gathered more leaves, released them. They whirled about the pensive angel.

Mayor Wendell Hughes had come for Enid, here, years ago.

Forty-Six

In the orange dusk of Los Angeles, Normalyn walked away from the Wing of the Angel Home. Wendell Hughes had come from Texas to protect Enid as far back as then. How much had he known—ever—about the events of the exile he sheltered? Normalyn was grateful that the young, vulnerable woman she was discovering had found him as a protector as she began her slide into her hellish madness. . . . Had Stan finally realized that Enid's life had been tied to his only by a flimsy glass necklace—returned when he ordered her to lose her child? She would have to be that child, because, if not— the gradual insinuation had now become equal possibility—she *was* Marilyn's daughter.

Very soon she would return to David Lange. She would have to assert her commitment for the proffered answer, even if it meant revealing Enid's letter.

2

"I can't find *me!*" Troja said when Normalyn returned home after a particularly moody day of reading and walking. Troja's "audition" had been dismal. She had run out again.

Normalyn saw the devastated woman, pursued by memories. "Troja, if only—" She would have ignored the ringing of the telephone if Troja hadn't jerked back, instantly electrified, hands pushed against her ears.

"Answer the screaming!" she yelled.

It was Michael Farrell.

"It can't be," Normalyn said. "I gave you the wrong number."

"I know," he said. "The nine *was* a seven, the way you told me first. I figured it out."

She could not withhold her pleasure at hearing from him.

"I'm in Hollywood"—he tried to sound casual—"and I was wondering maybe I could come by for you and we'd have dinner." When she said nothing during his pause, he added, "There's something I have to tell you."

About Enid, from Mark Poe! Normalyn agreed to meet him, in two hours. Yes, for dinner. At Musso and Frank's, yes. Yes, she remembered that it was "the famous restaurant and the oldest in Hollywood." Yes, where writers used to go.

When she put down the telephone, Normalyn turned to see Troja tying an incongruously pink scarf about her arm. The hated needle and a packet of white powder waited beside her. Cautiously, Normalyn took the syringe, still wrapped, and the packet, unopened. Troja did not protest.

"You wanted me to stop you," Normalyn said softly, certain of her words—Troja hadn't even filled the needle yet, had tied her arm first. "Because you're not sure you want to do it." She took a deep breath: "I hope, with all my heart, that you decide you don't *ever* want to do it, that you want to live." Her voice about to falter, she added, "Please."

Troja did not answer.

Now Normalyn was not sure she would meet Michael. Troja might have been signaling her need of her. Yet she knew that she had to break a dependency that would make Troja weaker, invite rather than stop the slide down. And she had to keep their friendship from choking on resentment. Still, Normalyn hesitated to prepare to go out.

Troja understood. "Please go, hon; please have your date."

Her date! Normalyn felt excitement. "But you—"

"I promise I'll be okay. You're right. I didn't intend to do it—just imagining I did. Helps sometimes."

Normalyn hid the needle and the packet among her clothes.

3

In the wonderful old restaurant in the heart of Hollywood, Normalyn saw Michael Farrell immediately. He stood out from the others his age because he was so *easily* good-looking, unaware of it. Formally, they said hello and inquired how the other was. Then Normalyn asked about Mark Poe, wanting to urge the promised information. "Fine, just fine," Michael Farrell said.

When they were seated in one of the gracious wooden booths in the grand dining room with faded murals, there was a buzzing interest directed toward the entrance. A young familiar-looking actress had entered, pretending not to notice the attention—which suddenly turned covert—that she was drawing. Expertly trained to scan the room, her eyes paused on Normalyn and then swept away in pointed dismissal.

"You made her jealous," Michael said gladly. "Because even with all these other good-looking girls, *you* stand out."

Normalyn asked quickly; "What did you have to tell me?" She tried to avoid sounding too anxious.

"That I lied to you. I'd never read Emily Brontë—I just knew about her—"

That's what he *had* to tell her? Again, she had linked everything to the past.

He extended his confession. "And I've only read a short selection from Joyce. But I *have* read Dickens . . . one book. And Twain—*Huckleberry Finn.* . . . I love that goddamn book!"

Huckleberry Finn! Normalyn felt as if he had mentioned a close mutual friend. She considered whether now was the right time to tell him that she had lied, too, that *she* hadn't read the writers he had mentioned that earlier day. Now she had: *The Great Gatsby*—and Daisy infuriated her for hoping her daughter would be "a beautiful little fool"—and *The Sound and the Fury*, marveling at it, marveling.

"After we talked, though," Michael went on in a rush, "I did read *Wuthering Heights*, and I want to thank you for that. Goddamn!—the structure! Time's all broken up in flashbacks, but it *all* takes one shape, like one present *and* past." His enthusiasm seemed too much for only words. His eyes moved over the room, as if studying everything, and then they returned intensely to her, along with a wide smile. "It's already influenced me. See, I want to make documentaries—explore reality but use all the techniques of movie *fiction*. God*damn!*" The word encapsulated his awe. Again, embarrassment ganged up.

Silence.

Well, this time *she* would break it, Normalyn resolved. She was shy but she could be bold, like him.

"What I like most about Dickens are his characters," she said. "The way you get to know them so well it's almost like you can see them, right there before you, clearer than in a movie." She was surprised—and pleased—by the number of words she was able to speak so easily. "And in *Wuthering Heights*—" Catherine and Heathcliff, she remembered, and remembered when she had imagined herself walking along the moors, along the river with—

"Please go on," Michael coaxed her.

But she could not. Apprehension overwhelmed her suddenly, and she could think of nothing more to say. Nothing. Still, he waited for her. She was glad when they ordered, glad that the waiter had brought bread, glad when the food came—so she wouldn't have to talk, especially since Michael seemed to sense that something had gone wrong, was wanting to share, or accept, her sudden mood.

His enthusiasm resurged. Michael told Normalyn about the sketches he'd made during their field trip for Mark Poe's class. "Mostly of the Watts Towers. I went back. You want to see them, Normalyn? They're back at the motel. I'm staying there with the two friends you met. But I have a room of my own," he added hastily, because Normalyn knew that one of his friends was a woman and he didn't want her to think she was with him.

Normalyn turned away.

She thought he was asking her to go there to— Not that he couldn't want to *be* with her. But that hadn't been his intention, and she had turned afraid again, the way she had in Palm Springs.

"Would you prefer to see a movie?" he invited. *"Persona*'s playing at the Los Feliz Theater—"

She put down her silver. Even now, surrounded by people, she had felt fear stirring.

"I didn't mean anything right now when I—" he started.

"I'm afraid of you," she said aloud. She knew there was no reason to fear him. She carried the reason, within her.

"I wouldn't hurt you."

She hit the table, judging herself. "I'm just a damn coward."

"But you're here all alone in Los Angeles. Mark told Robert you're very brave. He's really glad I'm seeing you." He reached out to touch her.

She jerked back in terror.

He said, "Did someone do something ... terrible ... to you?"

"Yes!" Then it was *written* on her.

"Tell me," he said.

She heard her own words: "Three men, by the Rio Grande— ..." Only when she told him that one of them had finally stopped it before the actual rape, did she realize she had been speaking about Ted Gonzales, who had been on her mind— differently—since she had mentioned *Wuthering Heights*.

"I'm sorry." Michael said the only words he could find.

She stood up. "I shouldn't have come here."

"I'm glad you did, I'm glad you told me—" Michael paid as quickly as he was able to summon the waiter, because Normalyn had gathered her purse, preparing to leave. He followed her outside.

She had intended to walk home—until she saw lurking shadows along Hollywood Boulevard.

Michael drove her home in the car the three students took turns with. Even by the time they reached her house, he had not been able to find what he could say. Everything he thought of was inadequate.

As she got out of the car hurriedly, he thanked her "for a fine evening." Even before she reacted, he wanted to draw back his ineffectual words.

"It was *not* fine," she said. "It *could* have been. But I ruined it!"

"I'll see you again!" he said.

"Yes!" she agreed. She walked ahead, stopped, turned. "No. It would just be the same," she said. Her body ached with the tension of . . . just being with someone she liked. She ran toward the house.

"I *will* see you!" Michael yelled after her.

In the dark, Troja sat on the slanted porch. Normalyn sat beside her. Troja put her arm about her. "Can't go on being afraid of *all* men, hon," she said.

She had heard the exchange with Michael. Normalyn was touched by Troja's concern. Yet there were so many confusions, so raw right now, that she did not want to explore them.

After moments, Troja spoke about what she had been pondering in the darkness: "When you try to help someone who doesn't want to be helped, when you force someone to live who doesn't want to any more, or can't any more, then you pull them down in another way and get pulled down. No one becomes strong then."

"Yes," Normalyn agreed.

Troja said, "Sure, I would bring Kirk back if I could, even if it meant going on in that hurting way. But I *can't* bring him back. So I can say that, yes, I'm at peace in a way I never was when he lived." She said abruptly, "I'm glad you hid that needle and the shit, hon."

"I'll throw them away!" Normalyn said.

"Not just yet. Gotta know it's still there. For a while, that's all. Gotta slide away easy from it. Cause, hon, see, I shot up once—maybe twice. Then I didn't feel pain. I didn't *feel*."

"But that's just like dying," Normalyn said.

"Yes," Troja said.

Normalyn said carefully, slowly, "Maybe you should let yourself find someone else."

"Never!" Troja rejected quickly.

They remained outside a while longer—separated from the rest of the world, Normalyn thought, because only *they* knew what they were feeling in those moments.

4

Ted called to verify their getting together. Again, Normalyn hesitated. When silence extended, she filled it by agreeing that he could come over. She wouldn't have to go out with him, and Troja would be here. Yes, then, this evening.

Troja did return before Ted arrived, but so exhausted she mumbled a greeting and went into her room to rest.

Ted was at the door at the exact time. "Normalyn!"

"Ted—"

"Jesus Christ, are you beautiful!" He still wore the boots that made him even taller than he was, the slim Levi's, but not the cowboy hat. His hair was slightly longer. He looked even handsomer. He was carrying a giant cluster of pretty flowers—pink, blue, yellow, white.

"May I come in?"

"Oh, please."

"May I sit down?"

"Of course!"

He cleared a chair. Still holding the flowers, he sat facing Normalyn on a stool. Awkwardness clamped immediately into a silence so aggressive that when Ted finally spoke, Normalyn jumped.

"I can't wait to tell you," Ted plunged. "Remember the statue we hated so much in the memorial plaza?"

The Texas Hero. "Yes." Enid had hated it, too.

"A Fabens reporter did research on it, and the Unknown Texas Hero is a *Mexican general*!" Ted roared.

Normalyn burst into laughter with him, tension released.

"The reporter—she used to be the librarian until Clarinda had her fired for allowing 'dirty communist books' in the Gibson library—"

Miss Stowe! Normalyn welcomed her back.

"—the reporter found out that Gibson once belonged to the Mexicans, and *they* put up the statue honoring General

Buendía." Ted went on. "The Anglos in Gibson were furious when they found out, but the Mexicans from the college came in to celebrate in the plaza with some of the workers. *I* danced with them!"

Normalyn imagined him dancing with the pretty Mexican girls. It looked right.

"The Mayor's crazy wife wanted a committee to tear down the statue immediately. Remember how the Daughters of the Republic of Texas had their ceremonies there? But Mayor Hughes said"—Ted imitated the drawly voice—" 'What the hell, it's the same damn statue, i'n'it?' . . . He's a son-of-a-bitch, but there's something about him, a loyalty."

"Yes," Normalyn said. A deep loyalty.

"He sends his respects, and this—" Ted gave her an envelope, but he still held on to the flowers. "Papers to sell the house."

The starlet's room would be redone. Normalyn took the envelope. She did not want to open it yet.

Ted goaded her: "So much must have happened to you, I bet."

"Too much to tell right now," she avoided.

"Have you found what you came for?" he phrased carefully.

"Almost," she said. She thought of David Lange, of the promise of answers within the office of twilight.

Refusing to allow the threatening silence, Ted told her about the group of Los Angeles lawyers he was working with. "I'd be honored to have you meet my friends," he invited.

The Texas gentleman still. He had inherited all the exaggerated manners of the Texans he detested, Normalyn thought.

Troja coughed, announcing her entrance.

Ted stared in obvious admiration. Assuming his Texas cordiality, he stood quickly, bowed slightly. Normalyn introduced them.

The weariness etched on Troja's face was released for moments by the admiring reaction. Normalyn welcomed that. But had she felt a pang of jealousy? No!

"Aren't those for Normalyn?" Troja reminded casually as Ted stood with the flowers still clutched in both large hands.

Ted looked down in embarrassment. Recovering, he presented them to Normalyn. Troja offered her "the pretty vase" in her room.

Normalyn set the vase with the flowers on the counter. She served a delicious roast chicken she had cooked. Even Troja ate as if she were savoring it. They talked cursorily but easily. After dinner, coffee, Troja excused herself, clearly to allow them to be alone. Normalyn told Ted that Troja was her very best friend. "And a great performer." She raised her voice for Troja to hear that.

Before they would have to battle silence again, Ted told Normalyn, "I've missed you a lot." He leaned over cautiously. When she didn't pull back, he held her hand. She welcomed the warm sensation.

As she walked him to his new—borrowed—Jeep, he told her, proudly, that he had applied for law school in California. "I'm going to be here about a week this time, and then I'll go back briefly and come back. So I'll be here a lot," he told her happily. He lowered his head; he said softly, "I'm serious about you, Normalyn. I keep thinking about you."

I'm serious— . . . Normalyn was aware of a wondrous, baffling, fearful feeling. But she did not agree to see him tomorrow—he would call first.

When he drove away in his Jeep, Normalyn was sure she had seen an entirely new person. The "other Ted"—always to be hated—had been left behind in Gibson.

Forty-Seven

In her room, Normalyn opened the envelope from Mayor Hughes. Along with legal papers, there was a short letter. She heard his drawling voice pronounce the written words:

Dear, dear Normalyn, here are some papers for your signature—if this is what you wish. I've entrusted them to one of the "new breed." Remember, sweetheart, our lunch at the grand old Texas Grand Hotel?—presided over by dearest Enid, may she rest. Remember her kindly, always, as I hope you remember me. I pray you will find all you need to find so you can be free. My love to you, sweetheart. Wendell.

All you need to find so you can be free. . . . Normalyn thought she detected Enid's voice in those words.

2

Ted called, as agreed. She told him she was busy; "an appointment" was all she could think of as excuse. She felt too moody to see him, disturbed by questions about Mayor Hughes—if he *did* know more, why had he refused to tell her?—questions about David Lange, questions about everyone, everything! And she was disturbed by Ted's presence.

Troja had left early for a recording studio; another day's work as a backup singer. Normalyn checked to see that the needle, the powder were where she had hidden them. Now she passed the telephone. She paused.

In the days since she had seen David Lange—only two days had passed, an eternity—she kept finding new reasons for not calling him. Not yet. She must not seem eager to accept his proposal, his—or whoever else's—conditions for access to truth. There were other people she might locate. Beyond all that, she had resolved that when she faced him again, she must be strong and confident, and she—

A knock at the door. Ted?

Michael Farrell!

She was glad to see him. Each time, although only a few days intervened, he looked handsomer, more mature.

He said quickly, "The other night you told me you didn't want to see me—but you said that after you said you *did* want to. I think you always say first what you really want. We're on our way back to school. I just stopped to give you this." He handed her a small package.

"Thank you," she managed to say, startled.

He walked away as if the boldness had expired. In the car, his friends waved at her. She waved back, watching the car move away from her, regretting that . . . and watched it turn around. Return. Park!

Michael got out again. He walked up to her. "Normalyn," he said, "you've got to face that it doesn't have to be ugly, being close—that you don't have to be afraid. But only *you* can do it, and only if you want to." He waited.

She did not answer. She stood at the door until he had driven away. Then she opened the package he had brought her. A book. *Poems* by Emily Brontë. There was a marker indicating one page in the slim volume. She read the poem.

> No coward soul is mine,
> No trembler in the world's storm-troubled sphere;
> I see Heaven's glories shine,
> And faith shines equal, arming me from fear.

3

Even as her life now gave hints—which she evaluated and exulted in several times a day but which could fade so quickly— even as her life gave hints of shaping, beginning to shape, even then she felt, in moments that came unexpectedly, like a pursuing presence, the powerful pull of the mystery of her past. Then the memory of David Lange would invade with all *his* mystery, his promised answer. She would hear his words of exhortation, even the sound of them—soft inflections, whispered commands. . . . More and more, she was coming to believe that to resolve the mystery entirely, she had to discover the exact purpose of the dual letter Enid had left her.

These considerations would almost fade, never entirely and only sometimes like now, when she had finally decided to go with Ted to meet his friends, the people he worked with.

Buildings floated in a watery sky as they moved onto the freeway in Ted's borrowed Jeep. Laughing, he was telling her that he'd discovered he wasn't even *half*-Anglo: "All these years, my mother's been hiding that *she's* half-Mexican—it's why she and my dad had problems. Now that's helped me clear my head even more—like about that I couldn't make it with—I mean, relate to—Mexican girls. Well, when we danced around the statue of General Buendía, there was one, real pretty, and—" He stopped quickly. "All I'm saying is that your being Anglo doesn't have anything to do with the fact that"—he inhaled—"that I really love you, Normalyn."

Those curious words, so ordinary, really, and yet she felt a clutching in her heart, as if *it* had held its breath. To be seen as herself *and* to be loved!

He veered off at Boyle Heights, into a section of Los Angeles known as "East L.A." Almost everyone here is Mexican; some occupy handsome homes in purified hills. Many more live in small stucco houses, others in torn apartment buildings or blocked units, disguised by flowers all about, every color.

Ted parked the Jeep in back of a small, square building. On one side of it was a giant mural of resplendent Aztec princes in ceremonial plumage. In the background, pale friars and Spanish conquistadores waited to invade.

Normalyn and Ted entered a busy clutter of desks, chairs, typewriters. There were about ten men and women, who greeted Ted warmly. He called back in camaraderie. Black and red strike placards decorated the walls.

A youngwoman looked up from behind her desk. She was a very pretty Mexican girl with huge brown eyes, luscious black hair, silky brown skin, a firm, sexy body. Ted introduced Normalyn to the others. Normalyn maneuvered toward the youngwoman.

"You're Normalyn," the youngwoman said. She had a lovely smile. "I'm Gloria Martinez."

Ted had talked about her to this girl. Normalyn extended her hand.

Gloria took it warmly. "Ted told me you're pretty," she said, "but you're beautiful."

"*You're* beautiful," Normalyn shifted away from those words.

"This is our director." Ted pulled at a tall, sturdy Mexican man with a giant moustache. He bowed courteously to Normalyn. Then he told Ted about recent developments enhancing their chances of bringing a suit in Texas against growers. Normalyn saw Ted's excitement; he slapped his hands happily. Gloria offered her own views. Ted listened attentively, agreeing, laughing happily, turning serious.

Normalyn wandered to a small cubicle she was sure was Ted's: a desk, a chair, two blowups, one of John F. Kennedy, the other of Robert Kennedy. She turned away from the disturbing presences.

Ted saw her do that. "You hear so much now about how they might have been in their private lives," Ted phrased carefully. "But what they *represent* remains good," he said staunchly. "It has to."

Normalyn thought of the beautiful, hurt movie star, dazzled by their power, not able to grasp her own. At one time, Ted had seen *her*, Normalyn, as a symbol to be conquered. Had his heroes seen Marilyn Monroe only as a symbol, too?

One of the men called to Ted. Normalyn moved back to Gloria Martinez.

"He loves you very much," Gloria said to her.

Normalyn did not answer, because she was sure that Gloria was herself at least beginning to love Ted.

"You're lucky," Gloria said, adding quickly, "and, of course, so is he. He's an exceptional man." She laughed. "Even here, some of the older men can be so damn condescending to the women. But not Ted. He's entirely free of all that." She blushed, aware of her words. "The reason I'm saying this to you is that I'm sure you helped to make him the fine man he is." She smiled. "Although he can still look like a boy."

4

Very early the next day, Normalyn drove out of the city with Ted. They traveled for miles, and then off the freeway. Ahead were green, fertile fields. Ted stopped the Jeep. She got out with him. He pointed to Mexican men and women—and some children—stooped over, gathering rich crops. Beyond, desolate shacks spotted green land. "Conditions you wouldn't believe possible today, and we have a chance to change it." He snapped his fingers happily, eagerly.

We. He looked so proud in his affiliation. He intertwined his fingers through hers. A soft warm breeze glided across the fields. Ted held Normalyn's hair against her face, to look at her, closely, clearly, at the beautiful youngwoman she had fully become. Slowly, he held her closer. He kissed her, just barely pressing her lips.

Normalyn thought with sudden, frantic urgency, This is the only way to expel the terror, to conquer it with *him*. His rage was gone, and he had thwarted the violence even then. With the same man, she would conquer those ugly beginnings.

5

A few minutes later, in a motel they agreed on in a small city just beyond the fields, Ted touched Normalyn's shoulders, tenderly. His hands moved softly over the opening of her blouse, and down, along her skirt.

Normalyn froze.

His touch became even gentler.

She tried to release her fear.

He kissed her, and—

Violent darkness swept into the room! She was enveloped in it. She saw hands tearing at her clothes, heard a windstorm howling, and—

She pulled away from his touch. She pummeled him fiercely with clenched fists. *"Goddamn you!"* she screamed. *"You tried to rape me, and now I'm too scared to let anyone close!"* With fury gathered for years, she lashed at him again and again—until he held her hands tightly, kissing them urgently.

"Normalyn, Normalyn! It's me!" he pleaded.

"I know, and it always will be!" she yelled at him. "And I'll never forgive what you tried to do to me—even if you stopped it!" She leaned back, against a wall, and she turned her head and cried.

6

The scent of evening flowers saturated the city as Ted drove Normalyn home. He parked. "Something as ugly as what happened that afternoon never goes away, and I can't ever forget it either," he said, facing it.

"But you can with someone else." Normalyn was thinking of him and Gloria, who would see only the man he was now. But when she heard her own words, she wondered whether they contained a meaning for her, too.

"I hurt you and I hurt myself because I've lost you," Ted said. "Please, please believe that I am truly sorry, with all my heart, for what I did to you." He looked down at the scar on his hand, and rubbed it quickly as if to erase it.

Normalyn touched it. She saw tears in his eyes. "I do believe you," she said.

That night—sad but at peace—Normalyn read the Emily Brontë poems Michael had given her. Then, on the blank pages, she began to write a story, or a book, whatever it might become:

In spring, when she was eighteen years old and living in Texas, Jeane Morgan discovered that she did not know who she was. It wasn't that she didn't know who her parents were—she did. It was that without knowing it, she had become afraid of life. There were reasons.

7

In the morning she found Troja at the breakfast counter. Normalyn was immediately aware of tension.

"Couldn't sleep. Dreamt, tossed all night," Troja said. "Where's that fuckin' shit you took from me?" she demanded.

"You don't want it," Normalyn said firmly.

"Who the hell you think you are to tell me what I want?"

Normalyn felt anger about to crack. She closed her eyes. "I threw it away."

Troja stood up. "Fuck if you did. You hid it! I want that shit back, girl!"

Anger snapped. "*You* listen!" Normalyn shouted.

Troja's head snapped back.

"I came back when you went looking for me—because you're my friend and I love you and you're in pain. But you're taking advantage of that again. You still think *I* don't feel!"

"Just give me the goddamned shit!"

Normalyn went into her room, located the syringe, the powder. She had to do this. She set both on the floor near her own door. "Troja!" she yelled. "You said there's a point when if someone wants to destroy themselves, you can't stop them. So I'm putting your precious 'shit' right here on the floor where you'll have to stoop even lower to get it. And when you're doing that, remember this: That's *exactly* what Kirk tried—*with his life!*—to keep from happening to you!"

She waited tensely for Troja to move. If she did, would she

try to stop her? She *had* to gamble. If she relented now, her desperate words would lose their power, their *possible* power. Normalyn remained leaning against the door.

"Please break the goddamn needle; throw the damn shit away!" Troja said without turning.

In the bathroom, Normalyn opened the packet. The powder glistened beautifully! She flushed it into the toilet. She crushed the hypodermic needle against the trash can. It made the frailest sound!

"The goddamned dying's got to end," Troja said.

Yes! Normalyn felt stronger than ever. She had challenged Troja to live—and she had won! And yesterday with Ted she had purged rage! She was strong enough to confront David Lange—and whomever he would lead her to—and whatever would be revealed! Because *she* was dying every moment she did not live her life. *The goddamned dying's got to end!*

Forty-Eight

This time it was David Lange who called her. "It's imperative that I see you today in my office. There will be someone
else who is eager to speak to you."

She would agree—she was ready to see him—but she had
immediately to clear the field of encounter: "How did you get
this telephone number?"

"From Mildred—from your address when her chauffeur
drove you home," David did not hesitate to answer, signaling
that connections would now be unmasked, there would be no
more subterfuge. All would be revealed, including his own
participation—Normalyn was certain of that at this moment,
and suspected that his "confession" might be the most chilling
of all.

"I'll be there, David," she said in a firm voice that asserted
that she was not coming as a petitioner for truth.

The "someone else" would be the person David had offered
to put her in contact with. This new urgency had to mean that
David—and that other person—had withdrawn any precondi-
tions. She agreed to the soonest hour. She did not need even
to consider the staggering implications of what was about to
happen, what would be revealed.

Normalyn found a positive augury in this: This morning
there had been no tension between her and Troja at breakfast.
Already made up for a new interview, Troja had said, "I slept
real good for the first time since—" She stopped, a dangerous
moment. Normalyn's eyes encouraged her to speak the avoided
words. "—since Kirk died," Troja had finished.

2

A dark limousine with smoked windows was parked in the no-parking zone before David Lange's office. Beside it, a uniformed chauffeur waited. Normalyn recognized him—and the limousine that floated like a shadow of doom through the recollections of so many.

Normalyn ran up the steps and into David's office.

"My *dear*!" the frosty voice of Mildred Meadows admonished. "You mustn't rush, you'll wreck your lovely dress."

David had tricked her into believing there would be someone else here, the person who—! No, he hadn't designated whom. *She* had assumed. She would not be ambushed by the unexpected. "Why, it's the dear baroness." With a jabbing tone, Normalyn masked whatever surprise she might have registered.

Behind his desk, David Lange only smiled his greeting at Normalyn. She nodded. In this unexpected meeting, who would be adversaries, who allies?

Dressed in dark gray elegance, Mildred Meadows sat to one side of David. Her back was to the light, which had been muted further, the blinds slanted. Away from her mansion, she seemed plucked out of her time, hiding from the sun in shadows created for her.

Normalyn sat facing the diagonals of light.

David explained quickly: "I encouraged Mildred to come here to clarify some matters. An interim step has become necessary."

Or another tactic of deceit because *she* had not responded? Normalyn wondered, but she did not really suspect that.

Mildred waved away David's introduction. She said to Normalyn, "David insists I must tell you certain things I considered irrelevant during our charming chat. He is sure that the person he so loftily calls our 'judge,' our 'accuser'—whom I prefer to call a 'witness'—will demand to know them, in this rather quaint way of confronting us for our supposed 'culpability' in the events occurring during the last days of Monroe's life. I am here to supply omitted truths." She looked at David. "But there may be surprises."

"I warn you." David's alert was quick, serious. "I'll recognize lies."

"Oh? Somewhat like those trained hounds devoted only to one pursuit?" Mildred spoke as if she were paying a compliment.

"The truth? From Mildred Meadows?" Normalyn added her own warning.

Mildred did not wince. "For lies to be clever, truth has to be known. I am an expert on truth." She made a sound like laughter. "David, when one is with you, words like 'truth' and 'culpability' simply dash out of one's mouth." With a thrust of her hand—one finger displayed a perfect pearl—she mocked the banished words. She dismissed the power of the summons: "My motives are uncomplicated. In exchange for participation, our witness will tell us what we are all dying to know"—she affected a shiver of suspense—"what really happened in those last days."

She pondered in mock earnestness: "But surely our witness won't summon us all together like suspects in a mystery story! You're the only one who knows where that font of truth resides, David. I suppose it's somewhere ghastly like . . ." She pretended to give it great thought. ". . . like Phoenix, Arizona," she masticated the name, forcing a tremble at the prospect. She eyed David craftily. "I seem to remember that postmark on the package that brought me those ugly artificial flowers. . . . Oh, and *why*, David, have *you* been appointed by the witness to be the collector of truths?"

"It's your time to answer, Mildred, not to question. But I do seem to remember that the package I received was not from that city." David thwarted her conclusion.

Mildred seemed to know—or was pretending to know—the identity of the witness; yet she had battled—if lightly—for access to that person, but David had not granted it, Normalyn recognized.

"I see," Mildred Meadows understood. "*You* want to hold the master key, David. Always to be in control." She said to Normalyn, "Have you found him to be so, my dear—always in control?" Then she rejected it all flippantly: "C.B. filmed in Arizona once, in their desert, one of those Biblical things he became fond of."

Mildred was in icy control. She was interjecting levity into the situation that had forced her here, attributing all to "curiosity." Normalyn knew there had to be more, an enormous coercion—by David or the other person?—to bring her out of the sheltered world of her mansion. And yet, Normalyn evaluated, Mildred cared only about her column—ended—and her daughter—dead.

"To sweeten our memories, dear David, perhaps a bit of sherry?" The iciness in Mildred's voice did not thaw for the request.

"You'll have to settle for bourbon."

"One makes sacrifices."

David went to the small cabinet near his desk. He unlocked its lower section. He brought out a glass and a bottle and poured the liquor for Mildred.

"David believes in locking away temptation," she told Normalyn, and then brought the liquor to her lips. "David, how could you have lived on *this* so long?"

Normalyn saw David's eyes pull away from the deadly bottle. "It no longer tempts me."

"Of course not." Mildred toasted Normalyn with her glass.

Normalyn toasted her back with an empty hand, thumb up, for Mildred to interpret.

"What exactly am I supposed to tell her, David?" Mildred affected bewilderment.

"How you were duped," David aimed lethal words.

Mildred shrugged them away. "I'm here in a spirit of cooperation, I insist. David says I was duped." The voice did not trip. "I assume he means by Alberta Holland." Indignation hardly brushed the cool voice.

"And—" David extended.

"And"—Mildred glided over the words—"by the patriots I trusted."

"Tell how all that was possible, with your vast experience in the art of duplicity," David ordered calmly.

Normalyn understood: Whatever other reasons there were for Mildred's presence, David was extorting her humiliation.

But Mildred was rejecting that intention with the ease of her delivery: "Alberta Holland managed to convey some clever truths, knowing I would assume that they were clumsy lies— and I did." Her words only slowed. "Beyond that, Alberta and I only thought we were confronting each other, through Marilyn Monroe's pregnancy. In fact we were all—shall we say?— 'manipulated' by what that pontificating old babbler, Dr. Crouch, called, with his typically dour solemnity, 'an invisible conglomerate of power.' Somewhat less melodramatically, I prefer to call it the 'overplan.' " Mildred smiled a twisted smile at Normalyn. "You seem tense, my dear."

"But I am not," Normalyn asserted.

"Good. Let me put you at further ease by expelling certain inevitable suspicions so they will not clutter my narrative with extraneous considerations! The Kennedys were *not* involved in the overplot. Nor in Holland's plan. Certainly not in *mine*! They were not involved at all! They merely made everything possible with their clumsy womanizing. It would have been

Greek tragedy except that it was all careless, shoddy, vulgar—
unpleasant. With the uncanniness of the moth she really was, it
was inevitable that Monroe would wander into their tawdry
flaming light."

"Your mind is wandering, Mildred." There was an edge to
David's voice. "Has it begun to do that? Shall I reorient you
from time to time as to your train of thought?"

"My mind does not wander," Mildred asserted. "I remember *everything*," she seemed to warn.

She faced Normalyn. "You know of the letter accusing the
Kennedys of rampant immorality. And you know of a second
letter addressed to me, linking Monroe to both brothers."
Mildred sipped slowly from the bourbon.

"Tell it all!" David prodded.

"Whyever not?" Mildred spoke lethal words with delicate
contempt. "In my column, as agreed, I reported the 'sad
miscarriage' of Marilyn Monroe, because I believed that it *was*
she at the D'Arcy House. I learned differently at dinner, in
my home, when"—she seemed to retreat from the name—
"when J. Edgar—"

                    *   *   *

—Hoover said, "I am able to tell you only now, Mildred,
that the letter accusing the Kennedys of immorality is a fraud."

In the stilled great dining room, the candles did not breathe.
"A fraud?" Mildred inspected the word. She pushed away her
stroganoff, in a sauce so light it was ecru.

Edgar poured more paprika over his goulash on the grandly
set table. "Yeah. It was written by a crackpot—he lives out on
Alvarado Street, writes unsigned letters to everyone. Smart,
though, writes with authority. He gave us the idea from what
was just another crank letter." He looked at Mildred with the
mischievous grin his mother had adored.

"Another . . . crank . . . letter." Mildred pulled her eyes
away from his plate; he had made the goulash look like drying
blood. "You led me to believe it was written by a respected
ex-ambassador living in Bel Air, that he would identify himself, and that the contents of the letter were true." Certainly
those words were not being spoken by Mildred Meadows. Still,
she had heard her voice form them.

Edgar's jowls framed the delight of a nasty child who has
tricked a crafty adult. "Yes, we did. We knew you'd do what
was necessary with such a letter. It wasn't the *fact* of the
Kennedys' womanizing that would bring them down—we knew
the President was involved with many women—it was the

evidence of much more than that. You turned a crank letter into a powerful weapon, Mildred. With your inspired threats at the Monroe woman, you pushed them to act, and they did. They and you together gave us a woman *paid* to abort, pretending to be Monroe, a petty crook enlisting her, a famous movie star dangerously hiding her pregnancy, another woman going out disguised as her—all presided over by a notorious left-winger!"

Mildred's memory was suddenly as fresh as on that day. At the D'Arcy House she had seen a real abortion, but not Monroe's. They had cunningly exploded each planted expectation— and connected her to the disorienting memory of Tarah—

Edgar bubbled with delight. "You see, Mildred, we knew your abilities and capabilities."

This marionette! This caricature of Mussolini! This mincing bulldog she tolerated only because he gave her information— *he* was telling *her*— Mildred had never spoken more precisely: "Why not enlist me openly? My patriotism is unassailable."

"You're best when you think *you're* in command, Mildred. Look what you came up with! It was inspired when you made the Monroe woman believe she was named."

But she had been. Mildred studied Edgar. Then he knew *only* about the first letter—not the second, addressed to her, the one linking Monroe, the one she had acted on!

Edgar tucked his napkin in anticipation of the green-jellied pie now being served for him. "You've said yourself that you create truth in your column, Mildred. You created Monroe's 'miscarriage.' It sure convinced the Kennedys. And it emboldened the *commie* woman and the others to proceed with the 'secret' pregnancy. Naturally, we've helped Holland's plan whenever there was difficulty, at every stage—we have a liaison among them, a petty crook. Of course, Alberta's faction knows nothing about our making their plan possible."

All, all known! Allowed! If she were not involved, she would be utterly thrilled by the duplicity, Mildred thought. Even now, she could not restrain her fascination. "The birth will continue without interference?"

"We count on it. We will do *everything* to assure it! We'll secure the best circumstances to—"

"You keep saying 'we.' " That was annoying her.

Edgar's chest puffed up like a strutting pigeon's. "The Kennedys have made many powerful people angry with their 'progressive' ways—me, certain members of my F.B.I., the C.I.A., the Secret Service, chairmen of huge industries— Let's just say patriots of the Republic conceived the overplot to

undo them with scandal. Naturally, the patriots appointed
me—"

"—their puppet!"

Edgar used his harshest voice: "Do you know how many
presidents have tried to get rid of me? Do you know how
many succeeded?"

"Damn you *and* your presidents! *I* am Mildred Meadows!"

"We *chose* you to be a part of it!" Now Edgar employed the
tone he used to award medals to proud, deserving men. "You
should feel privileged."

"Privileged!"

"At the exact time, you will be allowed—"

"Allowed!"

"—to reveal the whole scandal." Edgar expanded with pride,
emotion. His belt bit into his stomach. He tried to release it a
notch without calling attention. "*You* will connect all the intrigue to the Kennedys. I'd like to see Mr. President and Mr.
Attorney General when they find out. They don't suspect a
damn thing! Both had already decided to stop seeing the
woman because she was becoming troublesome."

Monroe. Marilyn Monroe. Marilyn Monroe, "troublesome."
Mildred saw the great star's shimmering beauty as if Monroe had stepped before her at that very moment. Troublesome? That creation of beauty?

Edgar exhaled in his mightiest tone, "It will be *you*, Mildred
Meadows, who announces the collapse of the dynasty of the
Kennedys."

"I will not." Mildred did not even exclaim.

Edgar glowered, a look he reserved for times of deepest
gravity. The look imitated that of a burly boy—so well remembered, proud, erect, muscular, commanding—who had taunted
him when he was a child; a boy who haunted his fantasies and
nightmares. "It will proceed without you, then. Nothing can
stop what you set into motion. Nothing! Consider—"

"I will have no part of it." Mildred stood up calmly. "I will
end my column," she decided.

Edgar gasped. "Mildred, you have *integrity*!"

"Nonsense!" Mildred's tiny fist hit the enormous table with
such force it trembled. "I simply refuse to extend a deception
that included me—a deception clearly inspired by the very
techniques that *I* invented!"

*   *   *

In David Lange's office, Mildred Meadows leaned into her
chair, converting it into a throne of exile.

In that light, she looked to Normalyn like a hawk, alert, preparing its slow circling.

Now Mildred leaned toward David. "I have satisfied your reasons for my coming here, stated *and* unstated—and whoever else's. There is yet another: My own." She fired words: "Who wrote that second letter linking Monroe?" She said to Normalyn, "The writer had to be someone who knew of the first letter, who knew it excited me with possibilities but did not *inspire* me like the addition of Monroe's name to the accusations of scandal!"

Normalyn asserted, "She had only contempt for you. And so did Enid. You wanted to control them—and you couldn't."

"Whatever!" Mildred dismissed that for now; the circling hawk was too intent on narrowing its own search: "The writer of the second letter had to be someone who—so suddenly—felt betrayed by the 'heroic' brothers, someone who finally came to believe—and care about—the accusations of immorality." The hawk swooped. "A prized journalist who really *believed*, an idealist who really *hoped*, a moralist who really *trusted*." She emphasized words as if they were curses. She said conspiratorially to Normalyn; "David worked for me briefly when he was quite young. He simply needed any job; his idealism was not yet honed. I tried to enlist him again by showing him the *first* letter, knowing he would be a powerful ally because no one is more vengeful than a betrayed idealist. *And the subject here is vengeance!* But David disbelieved the letter, staunchly denied its accusations. He idolized the brothers. He was writing a book about them—"

"*The First of the New Heroes.*" David pronounced the title quietly.

Mildred told Normalyn; "And then suddenly David was convinced that the accusations against the Kennedys were true. He came to me and offered to contribute, to my revelations and at the proper time, all his 'journalistic authenticity'—you'll recognize his words, my dear, by their tone." The hawk landed by its prey: "What convinced you to join me?" Mildred asked David. "Was it when I showed you the letter naming Monroe?"

"I never saw that letter. You told me of it," David said.

"Oh, but I did show it to you. And the snapshots of *them* contained in the letter—pictures so lurid, disgusting—"

David touched the sphere of crystal on his desk. In this light it was unmarred even by a single reflection.

Mildred nailed her eyes on him, studying his movement of purification. The hawk bared its talons. "It *was* the snapshots

that convinced you—taken in secret by the writer of the letter,
the way such things are done, stealthily, in hiding, to capture
every single vile—"

"I saw no such photographs!"

"But you did! And with them, tapes that recorded every
moan, every salacious—"

David yanked his hand away from the unblemished sphere
as if it had scorched him. *"There were no photographs, there were
no tapes!"*

"How do you know? How!" The hawk clawed: "Because you
wrote that letter, David! In your arcane language, it is *you* who
is guiltiest, because without that letter I would not have proceeded as I did, and it was only you who knew that. Oh, yes,
you're right; there were no photographs, no tapes."

David answered Normalyn's stare: "I would have told you
about that letter."

Normalyn looked away from him.

"We'll never know that, David, because I *made* you tell us
what I've long suspected. Now *we* know." Mildred said to
Normalyn, "I told you, my dear, that he keeps temptation
locked, but it is so easily unlocked when one knows the key.
And that doesn't require much to find. After all, he has it
displayed in the center of his wall."

In the calculated silence, Normalyn looked at David, so still
now against the colored coils and slashes contained within the
silver frame.

Mildred Meadows said to Normalyn, "You should be grateful to me, my dear. First, I armed you with messages that you
cleverly perceived when I sent them to you through that
foolish child at those wretched things called auditions con-
ducted by that skinny girl. Now I have exposed David for
you."

Normalyn said, "If you had had your way, Mildred, I wouldn't
have been born."

"If you are Monroe's daughter!" Mildred rasped.

Her own words spoken earlier startled her only now.
Normalyn stared at the despised woman. She wanted to hurt
her, yes, and deeply. But how? "Such enormous evil from
such tiny motives," she said.

Mildred seemed only amused. "Evil? A quaint word, a bit
archaic." She touched her lips with her tongue. "But still
tasty." She sat back, extending moments. "Whatever you call
it, evil or duplicity, it all lay dormant"—she measured her
whispered words—"until you came searching and roused it all.
Then those ugly decaying flowers came from *her.* To David

first—*why?* How appropriate that our witness—our 'accusing judge,' as David prefers—should be a Spanish exile who betrayed her own aristocratic class! Teresa de Pilar!" She flung the revealed name at Normalyn with a look that ricocheted defiantly onto David Lange.

Of course. The woman who flowed like a soft shadow through the narratives she had heard, who had overseen the birth and the time after—and who married the doctor in attendance, now dead; the woman who claimed the remains of Miss Bertha, who was Alberta Holland. The person who had kept judgment alive had a name now: Teresa de Pilar. . . . Normalyn waited for David's confirmation.

He remained silent.

"Has David, my dear, offered *you* the specialness of stardom?" Mildred's sudden startling words attacked. "He could, you know. The daughter of Monroe and one of the Kennedys—whichever one it might have been. Imagine! Oh, my dear, is that what you really want? Have you been using your considerable cunning on David? Or has he on you?" Mildred moved to rip all allegiances.

"I want my own life," Normalyn said. "He knows that." *Did he!*

"But does *he* have other plans, for you, my dear? Watch him carefully!" Mildred hissed.

"I determined long ago what she truly wants, Mildred," David told the old woman, looking at Normalyn to emphasize that understanding. "Your cunning was not clever, not worthy of you. You're flailing like a wounded bird."

Mildred shrugged her shoulders, as if to test for any possible bruise. None.

Normalyn wanted desperately to wound her. Her aim had to be deadly, for Enid, Marilyn, herself. She had to locate the exact weapon: "Why are you really here, Mildred? What brought *you* out of your shadows?"

Mildred answered quickly: "What I announced at the beginning. Curiosity, my dear."

"Fear," David corrected. "And now that you've said everything you were *required* to, Mildred, I can tell you that it was a needless fear. For years you've been terrified that scandal will ensnare you the way you ensnared with it. But your world is gone. There wouldn't even be a tiny scandal, not a word in any newspaper if it were known that you put your grandchild in a home simply because she was—"

"Ugly." Mildred spat the word. "And she killed—"

"Sandra didn't kill Tarah. She only survived the accident

that did. You claimed the child died, too, so you could hide her in a home."

Sandra. The ominous limousine. Normalyn thought of the kind woman in the Wing of the Angel Home—and her sense of Mildred's evil deepened.

"You don't realize that you're not important to anyone anymore, Mildred," David said. "All you have left to do now is to die—quietly."

Normalyn saw that the woman's cold smile was unscathed.

"Not at all," Mildred said. "I can still live on the triumph of my conquest of *your* precious integrity." She prepared to rise. "Forgive me, David, if I don't linger for your full confession. Conscience gives me a slight headache. . . . You will, of course, let me know what our 'witness' reveals?"

She said to Normalyn: "When I thought it had been discovered that that . . . girl . . . was in that home, I offered to take her for a drive. That was the afternoon I saw Enid and Norma Jeane. The two pretty girls pretended my limousine had come for *them*. I wished it had. Or for you, my dear. You're just as pretty, you know—quite, quite pretty. Perhaps you may even become beautiful. I suppose Enid tried to keep you from knowing it. You hide yourself when it's even suggested. Yes, Enid would keep it from you. She came to blame beauty for their unhappiness. But beauty, my dear, is special—like nothing else." She smoothed her finger over the pearl on her ring. "The chafing of an oyster produced this. Is *this* worth that constant pain?" She held out her hand. Even in the dull light of the room, the pearl was superb, as if it existed only in admiration. "Yes! Worth it all!" Her eyes swept over the photographs on the wall.

Normalyn found the words she had been waiting for: "Mildred, of all the people who detest you—"

Mildred's contemptuous smile remained stamped.

"—of all the people who have ever hated you—"

The smile held, intact.

"—Tarah—"

The lips trembled.

"—hated you the most," Normalyn finished.

Mildred's face crumbled in fury. *"How dare you!"* She stood up. Her hands quavered. Something like pain replaced the icy smile. Her body shook. She leaned for support against the chair.

Normalyn and David stared at her.

Frowning, Mildred seemed to see herself suddenly in a

posture foreign to her. She looked down at her clenched fists as if she did not recognize them as her own. Finger by finger she released their tight clasp. She touched the straining veins on her neck, her temples, soothing them. Delicately, she smoothed her brow with the pearled finger. She leaned away from the chair. Again, she stood erect, composed. "And so you forced me to react to your lie," she said to Normalyn.

"To the truth," David said. "You still confuse one with the other."

Wrenching every particle of strength from the anarchy of power that defined her life, Mildred Meadows moved to the small cabinet beside David's desk. She stood there. "I'm trying to think of a superb exit line," she said. "Let's see. It's a bit difficult, because what could match the drama we've roamed through? But let me think. . . ." From the cabinet, she brought out a glass. She poured liquor into it. Drops spattered the immaculate surface of wood as she placed the glass before David, destroying the symmetry of his desk. "Have you ever wondered whether the same forces that *you* aided with your letter struck again—*twice!*—once in Dallas, once in Los Angeles?"

Mildred pushed the glass toward him. "Drink it, David! Your precious conscience will need it again!"

Forty-Nine

David Lange pulled the blinds open, expelling the lingering shadow of Mildred Meadows. Behind his desk, he faced Normalyn.

Her strength had survived. With new fascination Normalyn studied the photographs surrounding the silver-bordered anarchy on his wall. She inhaled. "What did she do to you, David, to bring about all the revenge?"

"Monroe?" He pronounced the name as if it itself were a question.

Normalyn felt again the great power of Marilyn Monroe, a power the movie star herself had not fully recognized.

David Lange rose and stood by the window, as if locating an exact point in the distance. He spoke very quietly—words might shatter fragile memories:

"The night I met Robert Kennedy, I saw her in person for the first time, that night—"

* * *

—in Santa Monica, at the villa of Peter Lawford, the actor who had married the sister of the President of the United States.

David Lange was introduced to the President's younger brother, a lean, intense man. David was already becoming convinced that Robert would become the great leader the country waited for, greater than his brother. As Attorney General, he had already initiated the most dedicated assault on organized crime and political corruption in the country's history.

"David Lange?" Robert Kennedy repeated when they were introduced. "You worked to elect my brother. I know he thanked you, but let me thank you again." He shook David's hand, holding it for a moment to extend his appreciation. "And," he smiled, "you're the writer who *deserves* the Pulitzer Prize!"

David was younger than the Attorney General. His prestige as an honored journalist allowed him to travel among the great. He knew that politicians are primed about the activities of guests so that they seem to be responding personally to everyone. But there was an unabashed earnestness about Robert Kennedy as he went on to discuss one of the main points in David Lange's recent book—that the Bill of Rights *mandates* a social responsibility of the government.

As they spoke, David was more inspired by the man's enthusiasm—yes, *enthusiasm!*—for justice. That enthusiasm created an energy in the very air. Robert Kennedy spoke as if he truly believed justice was possible in our time. Occasionally, though, he would smile a bemused smile; this would occur at odd moments. David became certain that smile was an acknowledgement of the realistic idealist's sense of irony that justice should have to be fought for, not demanded. Yes, Robert Kennedy would lead the country beyond the new frontier his brother was staking—into a visionary era. Even now, there were certain—

Marilyn Monroe walked in.

Everyone turned. Her presence had issued a silent command. She let slide from her bare shoulders an emerald cape, which a butler was not able to catch before it fell in folds at her feet. She wore a cream-tinted dress, so sheer it seemed smeared on her body. Sequins of gold ice splashed it. Her lips were a shade of red that defined red. Long, darkened eyelashes enclosed the blue of her eyes, the eyes of an innocent but sensual child. Against a backdrop of candles being lit that very moment in preparation for dinner, her outline seemed to have been drawn by an adoring artist in one masterful flow of curves. She was the most beautiful woman in the world, David Lange knew.

Lawford had arranged for Robert Kennedy to be flanked at dinner by Marilyn Monroe and Kim Novak, herself a thrilling woman, "discovered" after Harry Cohn, having allowed Marilyn's contract to lapse, demanded that Columbia Studios' talent department *create* "another Monroe." Despite that, Kim Novak had a more subtle beauty of her own.

David Lange sat two seats away from Marilyn Monroe.

While Kim Novak talked passionately about her new ranch in Carmel, "its hypnotizing horizon, mesmerizing mists at dusk," Marilyn asked the Attorney General sophisticated questions about civil rights. David had not anticipated such a refined intellect. Surprised by the range of her knowledgeability, Robert Kennedy answered seriously. At the same time, he was clearly charmed. David wondered when Robert would discover what he himself just had, that Marilyn Monroe was reading from hidden notes. Robert Kennedy only smiled when he saw that. Marilyn Monroe was unfazed by the discovery. "I wrote them myself," she convinced everyone. "I like to organize my thoughts." She faced the Attorney General of the United States. "Don't *you*, Mr. Kennedy, when you go into court?"

"Of course, Miss Monroe," he agreed soberly.

After dinner, guests mingled, about twenty-five or so. Robert and Marilyn drifted apart from the others.

At the time there were rumors that Marilyn drank too much—and she had clearly enjoyed the splendid champagne served tonight; that she was frequently "out of control"; that pills she took for sleeping deepened darkening moods; that she was at times abusive, then regretful. Her late-night calls to the few people she considered friends were frantic, demanding. David Lange knew—Mildred Meadows had shown him a copy—that a scurrilous letter in the hands of J. Edgar Hoover accused the Kennedy brothers of "sexual immorality" with many women. David disbelieved all that, completely. He had denounced it to Mildred as "lies that are spoken about all great men."

That night, Marilyn Monroe was like a flirtatious girl, David saw, and, yes, that only added a certain youthful insouciance to her startling presence. She was clearly intrigued by the bright, coltish Attorney General. Why not? And why should *he* be expected to resist the charm of so beautiful a woman? After all, it was all public, all uncomplicated, all natural.

David's eyes remained on them as they stood at one end of the dazzling room, by an enormous free-form sculpture of cut crystal—its reflections speckled Marilyn Monroe's dress with split gems of light. Robert's carefree laughter matched Monroe's. Then her head brushed his shoulder, as if she might rest it there. Yanked out of a spell, Robert pulled back. His laughter stopped.

At the same time all conversation around them halted. The girlish laughter was isolated in the silenced room. David heard fragments of words: Robert's—*"are watching!"*; Monroe's—*"know you desire—"* Robert Kennedy stared in horror at the guests looking at them. He said something to the movie star. Her laughter was throttled. She turned her head as if his words had struck her. Robert walked out of the room. The beautiful woman stood abandoned within her glitter and beauty, entrapped by stares.

"Bast—!" She did not finish the enraged word, hurled at the man stalking away from her. She took a step toward him, to follow. The dress frosted over with beads parted, revealing a bare strip of her legs. A bodyguard blocked her path. She looked like a scolded child. She backed away from the forbidding man. Then she ran out of the house, through a side exit.

To separate himself from the breathless conjecture that would certainly follow among the guests—he did not want even to wonder what had occurred—David went out onto the balcony. Illumined by dark light, the night was silver. A layer of clouds concealed the moon. The ocean was calm but the sound of distant waves was growing. David looked down, away. He saw Marilyn Monroe running toward the beach!

He felt a moment of terror. He had heard that she had attempted suicide several times. He jumped the short distance from the balcony, not taking the time to go down the stairs. He hurried, following her along the beach, stumbling on the sand.

He stopped.

Ahead, Marilyn Monroe was looking at the ocean. She stood very still and stared into darkness. She seemed like an apparition, a silver presence created by the night's reflections. In that dim light she shone as if rejecting the darkness about her. The moon—he had been wrong, there *was* a moon that night—floated in and out of clouds as if fascinated by her.

David Lange watched, watched her.

She removed her shoes. She tore at the slit at the bottom of her dress so she could walk without difficulty on the moist sand. He saw a spray of glittering dust sprinkle the sand.

David Lange gazed at the silver outline against tossing clouds of night, restless dark water.

Marilyn Monroe turned!

She was laughing! Joyfully! She beckoned: "Come on!" she called in that eager voice that could convey the greatest excitement, the greatest need.

David Lange hesitated. She had clearly mistaken him for the angered man who had walked away from her, although he himself was shorter, somewhat heavier. She kept motioning him closer as he approached—slowly, to make sure, cautiously, that she was calling to him.

"Come on, hurry, come on!" she said. She laughed happily. "We'll take a walk along the beach."

He looked at her. So close. So close to him. When they had been introduced earlier, she had nodded politely, said a few words. Now—

"Take off your shoes, like *me!*" she said in delight.

Embarrassed, he did, not knowing what to do with them, holding them.

She linked her arm through his. She shivered. He began to take off his coat, to give it to her.

"No," she said, "don't do that, because then I won't have an excuse to do this." She leaned against him, nestling her head on his shoulders.

His hand rose and almost touched her. He had not yet said a word. They walked through tatters of ocean mist, through pockets of dark light. Crests of water rolled almost to their feet.

Again, he began to remove his coat, to offer it to her.

Again, she refused.

He could feel her body—shivering coldly, trembling warmly —as it pressed against his.

For erratic moments the water became turbulent. Now a wave rose, tumbled, frothing white at its crest. They felt a spray of water. Marilyn welcomed it, her hands up, out, exultant. The wet dress turned translucent.

Marilyn trembled, again, pressed closer to David Lange. "Save me!" she whispered.

*　　*　　*

David Lange transferred his gaze from the past and into this office, to Normalyn. He had brought the memory intact into this room. "She ran back to the house," he said. "I followed her, and there—"

*　　*　　*

—where the Mediterranean villa rose in tiers of lights, Marilyn Monroe waited, barefoot, her dress torn, her luminous flesh almost revealed in wet patches.

"You *promise?*" she said.

"What?" he asked, wanting to hear it again, to hear her voice, to hear words spoken to him by her.

"Have you forgotten what I asked you? Will you promise to save me?"

"I haven't forgotten," David Lange said.

"Will you come tomorrow to my house?" she asked him.

Only later would he know the magic moments were real. He memorized and quickly wrote—and then looked at it and looked at it and looked at it—the address she gave him, the time agreed.

*   *   *

"Eight o'clock." In his office, David Lange remembered the hour that had continued to make his memory real that night after she returned to the villa and he left. "And I was there, at her house. She came to the door, eagerly. When she saw me—"

*   *   *

—Marilyn Monroe said, "Who the hell are you? What do you want?" She was about to close the door.

"Last night," David formed words. He touched the paper on which he had written the time, the address—assuring reality. "Last night, on the beach, we walked together and you said—You told me—" He withheld the cherished words. The beautiful tender face of the previous night was smiling in a different way now. The lips curved slightly. In disbelief. Or in contempt?

"I've never seen you in my life," she said to David Lange.

*   *   *

David Lange turned to face Normalyn. "I accepted an assignment I had turned down, in Europe. When I returned months later, I drove again to her house. Another car had just parked nearby. I recognized Robert Kennedy as he walked into her house. That night I wrote the unsigned letter to Mildred. Shortly after, she read me the essential 'new explosive document' in her possession, linking Monroe. I agreed that at the proper time I would donate all the authenticity I possessed to her revelations of immorality."

Out of those moments on the beach, the destruction had begun, Normalyn understood.

"And then I pulled away from it all, knowing what I had done, knowing there was nothing I could do to stop it, longing to, yet able now only to watch it in horror."

The most culpable, the least culpable. That was the significance of the dual jacaranda bouquets. And that was why it was he who was the "collector of truths." Because his conscience, unlike that of the others, was still alive, still chafing, still questioning. That was the deep sadness she had detected from the very first in his eyes, and in his voice, in its bruised firmness. She did not have to ask him that. She was as certain as if he had confessed it. And yet— . . . He would have sought absolution through deceit! He had attempted to convert her into the "most likely candidate," whatever other motives were involved—into one who would extract from his accuser the needed truth—and who would release him, like the others, from that person's constant judgment and reminders, even if not, finally, from his own continuing self-judgment. Again and still, that fluctuating duality in him!

"Is the person you call your accuser Teresa de Pilar?" Normalyn asked.

"I'm not at liberty to disclose that identification," David answered quickly. "Mildred assumed it to be; Mildred *still* believes she has a reliable network of private information."

"You promised me that at the right time you would tell me everything about your own involvement. All that I'm 'required' to know." Normalyn used his words.

"I have." David gazed out the window, where he had sought his distant, bitter memory, still alive. "About myself, my own involvement. Anything further will come from the person in question."

Yes, it would be Teresa de Pilar, Normalyn was sure. He did not want yet to surrender access beyond himself.

"If there's more, Normalyn, ask it!"

Seeking her judgment? But she chose to ask the question that had long baffled her, the others: "What stopped the scandal?" There had been none, no revelations, none. Even Mildred had been warned that nothing could thwart the machinery set into deadly motion, the machinery Dr. Crouch had heard "ticking" ineluctably. Yet, she remembered, the movie star had told him on the telephone, "I know a way."

David looked at Normalyn. He frowned. "Why, Marilyn Monroe, of course."

"But how?" She thought she understood—

"By the ultimate step in her own creation of Marilyn Monroe—her suicide," David said slowly. "Whatever else occurred that night, she must have evaluated all that had happened, not only in those last days but in her life, even what would occur in her future—"

*　　*　　*

—pursued by debts . . . sustained by pills . . . age attacking her beauty . . . her career in limbo . . . the crushed love affair

... the tumult of the secret days ... and now the impending exposure of those she loved. ...

And so she locked her bedroom door.

She swallowed deadly pills. She made one more telephone call. She lay in bed. Her body began its drift toward sleep. It reached the very edge of death!

It poised there, deciding.

And in that synapse between living and dying, she chose: She reached for one more pill. Her movements were airy, weightless, she made graceful motions with her hand. She swallowed the pill. Then she curved her body on its side, one hand resting on her breasts, assuming the same pose as that in the darkly shining photograph she loved, beckoning ... seductively ... to darkness itself. She welcomed it now, the darkness she had fought throughout her life—welcomed it at last. It wasn't cold anymore, no longer frightening. It soothed and warmed!

She knew exactly what would happen now:

She would float, was floating on this new, soft blackness into sleep, deep sleep, deeper sleep, deepest ... and she would flow, was flowing now into death—

And out!

—into the undying glow of ... *Legend!*

*   *   *

Exultant! In gleaming dress. Parted scarlet lips inviting, Marilyn Monroe stood forever alive!

That is how Normalyn saw her in the photograph her eyes sought on David Lange's wall, the photograph in which, it seemed now, Marilyn Monroe was born.

David spoke in fascination: "With her death, she completed the creation of Marilyn Monroe. She allowed the legend to live. The day her suicide was known, the whole world paid attention. Love and sympathy rushed to embrace the legend, the way they had stopped embracing the woman. In life she had become vulnerable, easily used for the purposes of deadly scandal. By killing herself, leaving her motives forever in ambiguity, she stopped the scandal—and added the grandeur of enduring mystery to her legend. The legend of Marilyn Monroe vanquished the powers poised to destroy the Kennedys through her. Now those forces didn't dare release the carefully crafted scandal. Risk connection to her death? Be blamed as murderers, exploiters of tragedy? Lose their protective invisibility in the glare of culpability?" David meted out the words as if they must be spoken with care, so enormous was their meaning: "They had counted on everything except the power of a legend."

But only when she finally believed her daughter was dead did she commit suicide, Normalyn had to believe. Or perhaps she thought the destruction would have sucked in *all* those she loved, including her daughter—if still alive.

David Lange said, "The legend survives, always loved."

The way Norma Jeane never was. Normalyn wanted to believe that at the last the abandoned "orphan" *had* known that she would attain what eluded her in life.

Almost inaudibly David echoed Mildred's last damning words to him: "*Did* all that destructive power, geared to crush with scandal and thwarted by her death, did it flail more surely, twice, to murder the Kennedy brothers?"

In a sudden move, David overturned the glass left on his desk by Mildred. The liquor spilled in enraged shapes. Startled, he looked at his open hands as if to make sure he had released all the unwanted passion he had confessed to.

The most culpable, the least culpable. . . . Normalyn had just heard in his words his enduring horror.

David rushed peremptory words: "I've told you all this because our accuser will want to know it. You have all the information necessary up to now."

He was trying to erase the moments of crushing emotion. Normalyn saw again the man she had first seen. No. He had lost his power to control her. She might finally come to pity him.

Quickly David touched the telephone. "I can proceed immediately to arrange for you to see the person who can unlock the mystery of your birth. Are you ready to take that final step, Normalyn?"

She nodded.

David said quickly, "Our accuser claims that a letter written by Monroe to Enid was given to Enid when she attempted to return once more to Monroe's house after she learned of her suicide. Do you have that letter?"

"Yes."

Fifty

Teresa de Pilar studied Normalyn, then closed her eyes as if to separate the youngwoman before her from the image her mind had conjured for so many years. The woman's eyes—startling, green—focused again on Normalyn. "Normalyn." She held the name reflectively, then extended her hand, which was, thin, translucent—and steady—toward the youngwoman.

Standing before Teresa de Pilar in this spare elegant house outside of Phoenix, Arizona, Normalyn took the extended hand. "*Señora* de Pilar—" That was all she could think to say to the woman who could solve the mystery of her origin.

Would she? Doubt ripped across Normalyn's mind as it had so many times since David Lange had arranged this meeting.

Teresa de Pilar was in her sixties, and the years lay lightly on her. Her features seemed to have been chiseled by a meticulous sculptor. She had brilliant graying hair, like Enid's—before Enid had stopped caring. Small, thin, she was dressed in flowing black, as if in mourning for the past events she had kept alive to be judged.

In the bright Arizona light, she didn't look sad, she looked radiant to Normalyn, who wondered whether the black she wore was more commemoration than mourning—not black but lustrous gray, darkly silver as desert light shifted slightly.

The hand holding hers was so firm that Normalyn accepted immediately that this seemingly fragile woman would be able to control with quiet strength. Even her smile conveyed resolution. Yes, it would be to her that Alberta Holland would have entrusted overseeing the care of Marilyn Monroe during the days of the secret birth—to this aristocrat who even as a girl had proved her courage in a bloody revolution. Normalyn

501

had learned from David that Teresa de Pilar had retreated to
the edge of Phoenix after the death of her husband, the
American doctor, now dead, who had fought beside her in the
Spanish hills and who years later was trusted to bring forth
Marilyn's child.

Outside an adorned window that extended the length of a
full wall, the Phoenix sky was as blue as a Texas summer day's.
Giant white clouds roamed the horizon. Even within the warm
day, a breeze had found this airy house. Normalyn was
pleased to notice that just outside was a single palmtree, lush
with green fronds.

The woman indicated a chair for Normalyn to sit in. It
resembled one in Enid's house, remembered suddenly from
early years—"a falcon chair," Enid had called it, velvety brown
leather on a cradle of chrome, not incongruous in her eclecti-
cally furnished house. On cold Gibson nights Enid would sit
there—Normalyn located another hoarded memory—while she,
a child, placed her head sleepily on her lap and watched in
dreamy fascination the shapes of blue flames.

Teresa de Pilar sat on a beige couch. Normalyn thought
instantly of Troja—because one of Troja's favorite dresses was
of that hue. Normalyn realized why she was picking out these
associations. She was trying to find auguries of harmony in
this crucial meeting—and so to banish stabbing suspicion. *Had
David Lange guided her to yet another figure within his range of
control?* . . . No, she resisted. This woman was an *ally*. She was
sure of it when she saw that Teresa de Pilar had prepared a
pitcher of iced tea, with lime wedges, exactly as Enid loved
it—with a sprig of decorative mint.

On a table beside the woman, a reminder of why they were
together, stood an exquisite bouquet of jacarandas like the one
Miss Bertha had kept under the lithograph of Marilyn
Monroe—the sensual silver body floating on darkness . . . into
darkness. About the room, the house, was an array of other
artificial flowers, all colors, shapes. On shelves, tables, on the
floor, were single blossoms, budding vines. Bits of silky mate-
rial specked a drawing board; tiny pieces of cloth scattered on
the floor, like petals. There was about the house a cultivated
dissonance that reminded Normalyn of—

Miss Bertha's wild garden!

She welcomed that connection, which pushed farther away
doubts about this woman to whom David Lange had granted
her access immediately after seeing Enid's letter. He had read
it—and returned it in unsurprised silence. Then he proceeded

by telephone to arrange this meeting for the following day—
something kept so long in secret allowed so quickly!

"Your flowers are beautiful, *Señora* de Pilar," Normalyn
said, to fill the moments of the woman's scrutiny.

"I've often puzzled that others who make artificial flowers
imitate only those that last." The firm voice was touched by a
Spanish accent. "Of course, they have their resplendent beauty.
I prefer to duplicate only flowers that bloom briefly in nature—
to make them permanent in artifice." She touched a blossom
of haunting, exquisite beauty, a pastel rainbow: "A guadalupe—a
favorite. And look! These yellow carnets bloom only in the
hills of *my* Spain." Her mind brushed memories of exile.
"When Roberto was alive, we—" She still called her husband
by his Spanish name. She smiled at the private memory aroused,
and then moved away from the one that followed, of loss. She
pointed to more creations: "Those berras bloom in the desert
during three days only. They glow fiercely, then die." She
touched another flower, delicately—even in artifice it might
be damaged: "A merla, it appears in coldest winter." A pale
yellow star erupted to display another, white, which opened
to reveal flamy red petals. Then the woman's hand glided
toward the mists of lavender near her: "Of course, the
jacaranda—"

They were about to enter the territory Normalyn had come
to explore. *Would there be hidden mines even in this peaceful house?*
Normalyn tested slowly but boldly: "I saw a bouquet like
that one, in Long Beach, in the home of Miss Bertha. I'm not
sure that was *always* her name." She sipped the sweet, limy
tea.

The delicate features of Teresa de Pilar clouded. "We're
here to speak openly—*only*! Of course the woman you met in
Long Beach was Alberta Holland!"

Mysteries would be solved! Normalyn welcomed Teresa de
Pilar's seconds of displeasure, banished now by a charming
smile. The woman had dismissed any need for cunning! That
meant she could ask questions. "But why didn't Miss Bertha
tell me she was Alberta Holland?" She could not keep away a
sense of betrayal.

"You came to her too soon," Teresa de Pilar said. "She had
to be careful. There had been attempted deceptions, impos-
tures." The green eyes waited to capture the slightest telling
flinch from Normalyn. When there was none, Teresa de Pilar
continued: "Remember, too, that Alberta longed to end her
days away from the glare she had lived in—we announced her
death in Switzerland so she might return to privacy. Before

she committed herself, she had to be sure you were the youngwoman we've waited for since Enid disappeared."

"That's why she asked me to come back when I was ready." Normalyn was glad to release Miss Bertha from accusation. "And Mayor Hughes *did* lead me to her," she calculated aloud, still not sure how much he knew, but certain his guidance of her to Long Beach had been a part of Enid's exacting instructions.

"Yes, he guided you to her—that Wendell Hughes! That despot!" Teresa de Pilar snapped.

Normalyn set down her tea abruptly. She would not accept only that assessment of the graceful old man.

"A *benign* despot," Teresa de Pilar amended to Normalyn's disapproval. "He was very kind to you, and to Enid—perhaps even noble." Her voice was swept by indignation again: "But in the area of social justice—" She shook her head.

Normalyn shifted the focus away from the old man she had come to love, more a father than anyone else she knew! . . . She allowed herself this question: "When you returned to Miss Bertha . . . when she was dead . . . did Jim—?"

"The handsome young sailor," Teresa de Pilar understood. "He loved Alberta like the mother he'd never known, and she loved him like the son she'd always wanted. Yes, he spoke about you, with much affection." Teresa de Pilar averted Normalyn's eyes by attending to the tea, some pastries.

That meant Jim had remembered her with bitterness—but that had been created by her confusions. Normalyn would explain that later to this woman.

"And Miss Bertha—?" Normalyn could hardly form the question.

But Teresa understood: "She loved you from the moment she saw you—even during the moments when she mistrusted. She loved you very much."

Normalyn felt embraced by Miss Bertha's love.

"There was still another reason why Alberta didn't tell you who she was," Teresa de Pilar explained. "There was much you had to discover on your own, for yourself, by yourself."

And she had! She had discovered Enid, the woman who had come to full life only *after* her death. Normalyn felt closer to her now, understanding her—she exulted in the thought—much more than others would ever know mothers or fathers whose identities went unquestioned. Too, she had come to know Marilyn Monroe in intimate moments—and even to feel like her that one long night—and she had come to feel like Enid, too, when she faced Stanley in the desert. She also knew—with complete certainty—that when she had finally confronted Ted, she had learned from both women, from *their* pain. They had given her strength. "I understand, *Señora* de Pilar," Normalyn could say now, and to the memory of Miss Bertha.

"I love your young courtesy, Normalyn—so rare in our days. But now you may call me Teresa. . . . How old are you, Normalyn?"

"Eighteen." Now the testing would begin. Again, Normalyn resisted suspicions of a sudden ambush. "Enid kept changing my birth date," she volunteered.

"To camouflage a dangerous birth."

That of Enid's child? Or Marilyn's? Teresa had clarified while sustaining ambiguity. In either event, the birth date of June 1 was made up, commemorating Norma Jeane's, Normalyn was now sure.

Teresa de Pilar closed her eyes. "The only time Enid really spoke to Alberta—both were so private, proud, afraid of hurt— Enid said that at eighteen she finally felt free, as herself, and that Norma Jeane began the actual creation of Marilyn Monroe at eighteen, when she first modeled for a magazine."

Normalyn set down her iced tea. Enid had told Mark Poe that, about the age of her freedom. Normalyn felt a slight shiver. She backed away from a possible discovery, about Enid's suicide. . . . "Did Miss Bertha tell you I was here; is that when you started sending out the flowers, Teresa?" The name sounded right.

"Yes. When we discussed it, and she became sure—*almost* sure"—again Teresa's eyes held Normalyn's for any significant reaction—"that you were the girl we waited for. And you read my signals well, Normalyn, the decay in some blossoms."

She looked out the window, a white sheet of desert light. "Marilyn Monroe was fascinated by the beautiful jacaranda— she saw them as herself. She told your Miss Bertha that they didn't last because they *couldn't* last. Alberta said all she was sure of: 'But they're unforgettable.' That's when she asked me to make a bouquet of them for the great star. . . . Marilyn Monroe," Teresa de Pilar uttered the magical name. "*That* artificial flower became much more beautiful than her antecedent; and she became confused as to which she really was."

She meant Norma Jeane. "You made some flowers for Enid, too," Normalyn reminded.

"While I cared for Marilyn in the days of her pregnancy."

Normalyn saw Enid's hands reaching out to touch the bou-

quet of jacarandas next to the chipped angel. This room in
Phoenix suddenly glowed in amber light, like Enid's.

Gathering her strength, Teresa rested on the tangerine-
colored couch; it had only appeared beige earlier, when it was
swept by early sun. What memory was stirring? . . . A memory
of Kirk! Troja had given him a tangerine shirt he loved, which
revealed every muscle he had created, Normalyn remembered.

With her eyes closed as if to separate Normalyn from these
words, Teresa de Pilar said; "*They've* called it blackmail, those
jackals! Let them! For years I've kept their guilts alive—I and
Alberta—until"—the voice softened—"until Alberta grew . . .
tired, confused by so many memories of struggle," she glided
over Miss Bertha's disorientations. "And so it was left to me
only. What the jackals, so fearful of exposure, did not realize—
what only that reporter knows—"

She was hurrying past David Lange! Normalyn felt a hint of
alarm at what that omission might signal, a possible alliance
that would cloud—

"—what they did not realize was that my 'blackmail' had lost
its *real* power, that it was now given power only by *them*, their
belief that they were still important. But the world had passed
them by. Alberta knew it—because it had passed her by, without her regretting it; she invited the soothing obscurity. But
the others! Why, even if I truly cared to expose them, the
world would merely ask, 'Who *were* they?' " She sat up erectly.
"Did they confess everything they had to, Normalyn?"

Normalyn detected indomitability in the strong voice. "I'm
sure of it," she answered. She hated to roam through the ugly
confrontations, but she was sure now that was what she was
here to tell—David had *not* lied! And so she told Teresa de
Pilar about Mildred Meadows facing that she had been deceived; about her terrible hiding of Sandra, her own grand-
daughter; about how she, Normalyn, had managed finally to
crack the steely composure.

"Mildred *admitted* her fascist 'patriots' duped her?" Teresa
leaned forward with delight. "She admitted Alberta *used* her?
You made her quiver by telling her the truth of what she had
done to her own daughter?"

"Yes!" Normalyn could not hide the triumph in her voice.
She went on to tell Teresa about Dr. and Mrs. Crouch—his
deadly call to Marilyn Monroe in attempting to extricate himself and his wife from guilty association; his claiming the child
was dead—

Teresa de Pilar shut her eyes tightly as if to reject their
presence even in her mind.

"But they're still terrified—especially by *your* blossoms. Still cowardly, always hiding, afraid and threatened every moment of their lives," Normalyn extended.

"They deserve their hell," Teresa said.

Normalyn told her about the day of white heat in the desert, about Ellen—sadly—"condemning herself for what she had allowed—"

"But she agreed," Teresa reminded quickly.

Because *that* judgment might touch Alberta? Normalyn allowed silence to ask. Then she told about the judgment Jason had added, discovering the horror he had only sensed before. "I *know* he'll become stronger from it," she assured. Now she was glad to tell Teresa about Mark Poe: "He truly loved Enid and she went on loving him."

"It was inevitable you would turn to him," Teresa said. "And so I sent him the perfect bouquet. A good man—and his friend, too. So abused by that evil woman, and by the evil times, but so courageous and triumphant."

"And David Lange—" Normalyn spoke the name abruptly, and this time she watched to see whether Teresa's eyes would avert hers.

"David Lange." Teresa pronounced the name with gravity. "Who else to contact first and to enlist but the man who had once had a conscience?"

Without flinching, she had confirmed what Normalyn had already inferred. "He did love her," Normalyn surprised herself by saying after she told of his treasured moments of closeness to the movie star on the beach. Normalyn remembered then the sorrowing, possessed eyes, the bleeding within the commanding voice. "It still torments him—but *he* wrote that letter!" She pulled away from sadness for him.

"*Does* it torment him?" Teresa de Pilar insisted. "He may be the most evil because he *recognizes* evil. He has a pursuit of his own. *Perhaps* he will redeem himself. Withhold your total trust of him," she warned.

Normalyn knew she did not have to—because he had no more power over her. He had become too vulnerable in his confession.

"Tell me more, Normalyn."

Still testing her? Normalyn would disarm any lingering mistrust with irrefutable candor: "Before they finally believed me, they intended to use me as their 'best candidate' to deceive *you*—and so, Teresa, they only ended up by giving me even more information than they had intended to!" Normalyn laughed, expecting that Teresa would, too, with new delight.

Instead, the woman said seriously, "I would see through any such foolish attempt—and I would withhold *everything*! Now tell me more, Normalyn."

Normalyn attempted to conquer panic. She had misjudged. Instead of ensuring confidence, she had aroused doubts. Teresa had waited for these moments so long that she needed to extend them. . . . Normalyn saw Teresa's eyes studying her anew, tracing her features against the memory of others. Quickly, Normalyn told her about Mrs. Travers, Miss Kline. About Sandra.

"I knew she would find you, and so I sent them the bouquet." Teresa spoke more slowly, cautiously. "Please tell me more, Normalyn."

Normalyn felt tense, hot; even the tea seemed warm. "Lady Star—" she began, uncertain how much she must convey.

"They used her cleverly, but she's cunning, too," Teresa dismissed. "Tell me more, please."

Normalyn knew she would soon begin to sound frantic. *Teresa must not withdraw from her!* But what exactly did she want to hear now? Normalyn told her about her own isolated life in Gibson, and—she heard herself speaking it—about the ugliness by the river, her confusions finally resolved about Ted.

"You were right to end it!" Teresa said emphatically. And she coaxed for more information.

Normalyn rushed on now to tell her *everything*, because she had to convince her or— . . . She told her about Enid, the constant memories of Norma Jeane clashing with others of Marilyn Monroe; told about the time Enid "became" Marilyn on the shoreline—expressing multiplied love—and about the uncanniness of certain incidents in one life recurring exactly in the other—

"They were so close they forgot what belonged to whom. It became *one* background—theirs."

No, it was Norma Jeane's, but Normalyn did not correct. Now, as the unrelenting gaze of the woman's green eyes held her, Normalyn poured out even matters that had nothing to do with her purpose for being here. And yet, despite her growing alarm, she felt relief to speak all this aloud! . . . About Troja!

"A perfect creation!" Teresa de Pilar admired. "So exotic." She pointed to an orchid that was a shade of deep, deep gold brushed with scarlet at the edges. "The rarest orchid—like your friend."

Then Normalyn told her, sadly, about Kirk.

"One of those who have to die young," Teresa accepted. On

her lap her fingers moved carefully as if fashioning another flower, and her gaze seemed to release its questioning. "Tell me more, Normalyn."

Still more! What did she want to hear? Why didn't she ask? Normalyn floundered. She told her . . . About Michael Farrell!—what he had told her about her being the only one who could free herself from the terrible fear—and that she believed it now, that she could—would! Then she tried to explain a warming feeling: "I think that Michael feels about Mark Poe like a father and Mark looks at him like a son—I'm sure of it; and Enid loved Mark— . . ." Her words slowed. "I think that I . . . like . . . Michael Farrell . . . very much. I think—" She felt suddenly shy, but the woman's beautiful, radiant smile allowed her to finish: "I think that with him I can stop being afraid of . . . being close." She marveled that she had spoken that aloud, and not only to ensure Teresa's trust by sharing intimate confidences—and she could tell that that was working by the way the old woman listened so caringly—but because she *wanted* to speak about all this.

"When that youngman calls again—because you know of course that he will—will you say 'yes' to seeing him," Teresa's smiling voice inquired as she refreshed Normalyn's tea and her own, "without contradicting it?"

"I think so." Normalyn wished she could have said that with more certainty. Oh, *would* she be able to say "yes" immediately?

Teresa de Pilar said firmly, "Of course he will have to understand—won't he, Normalyn?—that you *must* have a life of your own."

"Yes!" Normalyn was astonished by this woman's understanding. Then, why, even now, was she still demanding—

"Tell me more, Normalyn."

"Goddammit, I've told you *everything*!"

Teresa leaned toward Normalyn. "Do you ever wonder . . . about your father?"

"I don't *want* a father!" Normalyn said quickly.

"But what you learn today," Teresa de Pilar spoke even more softly, "must reveal that."

Normalyn realized that she had not told Teresa about Stanley Smith! *That* was what she had been waiting to hear. Quickly, Normalyn told her about the man "driven by deserved guilts, constant nightmares." She said, "Of all of them I hate that bastard the most."

Teresa touched the perfect jacarandas. Eternal moments passed. "Now please show me the letter."

Normalyn sighed in relief, release. She brought from out of

her purse, where they had remained throughout her journey
from Texas to Los Angeles to here, the letter and the other
papers.

With steady fingers, the woman took them. She looked first
at the dual birth certificates—and she only smiled. Then she
looked at the photograph of "Monroe in disguise." "You know
that this is Enid," Teresa said, "of course."

"Yes." And she knew, too, that it was Enid on David's wall,
in the blowup of the figure pursued by photographers. Placed
there to test her? Normalyn wondered, and then was certain
of that, too.

Teresa read aloud Enid's note about "lavender snow." "A
memento of precious moments she wanted to share with you,
Normalyn," Teresa evaluated. "So much beauty, so much
hurt—in both women." Now she looked at the marked
newsclipping. "Of course, Enid would leave this as guide!
Her planning was complex, Normalyn, only until one understood it—and then it was *exact*."

And soon, very soon—Normalyn was sure of it now—she
would understand exactly why Enid had shaped the mystery
as she had.

Teresa de Pilar studied the letter carefully, the note from
Marilyn Monroe, the postscript from Enid—the doubled as-
sertion of love. "Enid added what I knew she would add."
Teresa returned the letter and the papers gently to Normalyn.

Normalyn felt cold, cold, waiting—

Teresa said somberly, "What happens to you with the information I will give you, only you can decide. If you ask me not
to, I will not reveal to them what I tell you—what they long to
learn, the answer to the mystery they helped to create. They
have lived with lies, let them continue being haunted by
mystery—*and* my accusations! I will continue to pursue their
guilts! I owe them nothing, nor do you. What I will speak is
for you to hear, to do with what *you* will."

Then she recited words as if they had always been on her
mind: "When Marilyn was returned to her home after the
birth, it was essential that I depart as soon as the transition to
a hired housekeeper was accomplished. Marilyn received one
call—I know now it was the deadly call from that evil man.
When I went to her bedroom before I left, she gave me a
letter to give to Enid: 'Make sure please!' she said. I promised.
I placed the telephone on her bed—she indicated she wanted
it there. Then I kissed her goodbye." Teresa de Pilar's words
slowed as if to keep fate at a distance. "Near dawn, Alberta
called me at my home. Marilyn Monroe was dead." Her words

slowed, stopped. She continued: "I learned only then of the new developments about to crush us all. I *had* to return to Marilyn's house—to prove that what I had heard was not true. There, I saw Enid running toward the body being carried out. I held her as she screamed. Then I gave her the letter you now hold." Teresa's hands trembled slightly. "It was then, between sobs, that Enid told me what I would confirm."

Normalyn waited a million seconds of panic.

Teresa de Pilar held Normalyn's hands in both of hers, warming them. "Normalyn, you must know by now that you are Marilyn's daughter and that your father is Robert Kennedy."

No!

Normalyn thought of Enid, who had raised her, remembered in a flood of recollection the early years of kindness, love, birthday celebrations, songs—the moments on the shoreline when—as both women—she had asserted her love so urgently. And she thought she could cherish now even the years of anger, madness, because always—yes, always!—there had been bursts of love. Normalyn closed her eyes. She said aloud—firmly, "Normalyn, you are *Enid's* daughter and your father is—"

*   *   *

As Normalyn stood on Sunset Boulevard—only moments after leaving David Lange's office—the sound of her own voice thrust her out of the imaginary encounter she had just shaped with someone named Teresa de Pilar in Phoenix. The imaginary meeting had begun to form in her mind as soon as she'd stepped into the street brushed by evening shadows.

After she had acknowledged having the letter he knew of, she had told David she would have to go get it—said that even as she touched it in her purse. She needed to be away from him in order to— ... What? ... He had designated an exact time for her return with the letter to his office. "Three hours— I'll wait *only* till then," he emphasized. "And if not—" His eyes had looked darker than she had ever seen them.

As dusk had faded into early night on the glossy street, Normalyn had allowed herself to imagine it all—the woman who would come with kind answers into her life, the house furnished from cherished associations— ...

Now as she hurried along the street, she knew her elaborate imagined meeting had had firm purposes. Within it, she had fitted essential pieces in the puzzle, had found logical motivations. She had glimpsed a reason, a strange, haunting reason, for the timing of Enid's suicide within her careful plotting:

to free her, Normalyn, when *she*, Enid, had felt free, at age eighteen. . . . She had located surviving doubts about David Lange. For the real meeting he was this very moment preparing for her, she had rehearsed what to say, what not to say. She had anticipated critical moments of apprehension she must overcome—yes—and explored her own feelings about . . . so much. . . . And she had tested what she might finally hear.

She passed the restaurant where she had seen Michael and his friends. She wished they were there now, would invite her to sit with them—and she would, easily. They would talk, easily, about serious things—about books, about movies—writing books, making movies. And they would be able to laugh, too, so easily.

Instead, her life was *still* in abeyance—but poised to resolve itself in three hours.

Who was the person David Lange would lead her to? Why in three hours?

Normalyn crossed the street to catch the approaching bus, to go home, to talk to Troja about what had occurred, to sort it all out. Oh, please let Troja be all right!

On the bench at the bus stop was a picture of Marilyn Monroe—triumphant with life!

Fifty-One

In the bus, Normalyn felt the weight of David Lange's confession—the love that had contorted into vengeance, obsession, guilt, leaving a wake of turbulence he now sought to end. And he did, he did, Normalyn told herself. His tense composure when she'd left him, the darkening eyes—had they been misted over as if with undecided tears?—she remembered these belatedly, because after leaving, her mind had reached needfully for the palliative imaginary meeting.

When she got off the bus, Normalyn ran to her house. Would Troja be—?

Troja had made herself up fully again! In a lustrous blue dress, she looked like the Troja Normalyn had first known. Beautiful, glamorous, vibrant. *Herself.*

Trying unsuccessfully to conceal her excitement, Troja announced quickly, "I'm performing this weekend, at a new club. Just two performances, that's all—kind of a try-out before an audience. It *could* extend." Terror flickered within the excitement. "A number of my own—"

"As *you?*" Normalyn wanted to hear that.

"As me," Troja said pensively.

Normalyn hugged her in congratulation.

When the telephone rang, Normalyn was jerked back into an awareness of what she had to do—return to David Lange—*and an awareness of what would then follow*— ... She felt her blood pulse in instant panic. "Hello!" she shouted into the telephone.

"It's Michael—Michael Farrell. Is that you, Normalyn? Should I call another time?"

"No!" she said quickly. "Now's just fine." This *was* the right

513

time to hear from him, a welcome reminder of life possible away from unburied mysteries. It was exactly the right time.

"I can come into Los Angeles next weekend." Michael's voice was firm. "Would you like us to get together then? There's a play—*Six Characters in Search of*—"

"Yes," she accepted before he finished.

There was a pause. "God*damn!*" Michael said. "You haven't changed your mind. This is the first time."

He'd been expecting to have to overcome her usual vacillation—but she had felt none. Normalyn was glad to laugh—to distance David Lange and his world. "That's because I'm sure that I want to see you," she let herself say. . . . But before that would happen, she had to return to the dusky office.

"I'll pick you up at your house."

"I can take a bus." Normalyn wanted to extend mutuality.

"I'd like to pick you up."

He was precluding her not turning up. "Okay, yes," she agreed—and just as easily to herself, too. Setting this date ahead assured that her life would begin no matter what she learned in the interim. "And I'd like to see the Watts Towers!" she told Michael.

"God*damn!*" He was elated. "Wait till you *see* them!"

Oh, if only the expectation of being with him was all she was facing, Normalyn thought when she hung up. But she was confronted with a deadline for information buried in the past. She glanced at her watch, not letting herself notice the time.

Troja observed casually, "Got two boyfriends now, hon, Ted and—" She reached for Normalyn's arm, inviting her to sit next to her at the kitchen counter.

"Ted's gone," Normalyn said. She told Troja that he was one of the three men who had tried to rape her—but then had stopped the attack.

"You did right to let him go," Troja said angrily. Her hand clasped Normalyn's. "Ain't life sad and bafflin' sometimes, hon?"

"Most of the time," Normalyn said. "But it doesn't have to be *always*," she added hastily.

"I haven't made it easier for you," Troja admitted.

Normalyn did not disagree. Without wanting to, she had begun recording each passing minute.

"Haven't even listened to you, and lots of things been happening in *your* life. Selfish," Troja judged herself. "That's how Kirk used to do to me sometimes. Like everything was happening to *him*, even when there wasn't anything left, except remembering." She continued cautiously; "Strange thing to-day. When I went on a studio audition, a grip working there—he wasn't like Kirk; no one in the world can be that special, ever—this grip looked at me, you know, smiling. Now that's not rare." She automatically touched her curves. "But this was: I smiled back, first time since Kirk died. Not all that much, but—"

Normalyn welcomed the smile that indicated how "much" that really was.

"There I went again—like it's *only* me." Troja offered strict-est attention: "I'm listening, hon—want to hear *everything* about you!"

Normalyn heard in her mind the *snap* of each second. She covered her watch with her hand, in order not to look at it. She smiled at Troja—all she could think to do to keep Troja from suspecting—

"Something's wrong, hon. What is it?"

No longer attempting to disguise tension, Normalyn told Troja all she could cram into these enclosing moments: what she had learned from Sandra, about Enid and Marilyn Monroe and Norma Jeane, the warring identities: "Just like in their game, Enid kept holding on to Norma Jeane, and Marilyn wanted to leave her behind, with all her unhappiness—"

"Far, *far* behind, but you can't, she couldn't," Troja understood.

Had Enid seen the cruel paradox that she, too, was finally conquered by the same despair, the same darkness? Did that account for some of the enraged confusions of the last years? Normalyn wondered. . . . Rushing—not wanting to estimate that more than an hour *had* to have elapsed, almost two hours—Normalyn told Troja about the events in David Lange's office just earlier, the promised unraveling of knots "very soon." She did not tell her of the narrowing time. "And then I can find out—"

"If you're Marilyn's daughter." Troja pronounced the enor-mous possibility and stared closely at Normalyn.

Normalyn had glimpsed that possibility in her fantasy earlier—and veered away from it. Now she voiced a strange sensation: "It's so hard to think that someone like *her*"—she pointed to Troja's books of photographs of the greatest movie star in the world—"could possibly be—" She couldn't finish. She started again: "That someone I never *really* saw could be— . . . It's like being born eighteen years old!" Enid's words—suddenly her own—resonated.

Troja got up, went to her books.

Normalyn glanced at her watch, again not allowing herself to register the hour, but she was aware that another minute was passing . . . another. . . . She wanted to stretch time! Earlier, David had surprised her with Mildred's presence. Would he again, with the person he called their "accuser"? Was that the reason for the designated three hours?

Troja had returned with one of her favorite books—Bert Stern's *The Last Sitting.* "She's all here, hon. This is how you can 'see' her—who she was—and is, always." She flipped through the photographs.

Normalyn felt moved, saddened, awed by the unreally beautiful woman—beautiful and haunted, as if hurt had created her beauty. In the photographs there recurred a mixture of fear and exultation, then only fear, then only exultation. Even when she was most sexual, she could look lost. . . . *If she had lived, what kind of mother would she have been?* . . . Normalyn stopped Troja's hand from turning a page. She looked for one she had glimpsed earlier. No—she rejected one of the star with her head bowed, surrendered. This one! She studied the photograph of the woman, looking her age, thirty-five—looking beautiful, dressed in black, one hand pressed pensively to her lips—deciding— . . . No, that was not the photograph Normalyn wanted to locate either—but this might be: In almost the same pose, the move star seemed to be touching the beginning of a smile, cherishing it. Normalyn's hand smoothed the photograph.

"Hon, look!" Troja had turned some pages. "It's *you!*" It was a photograph of the star looking like a very young woman, her hands at her side delighting in the fullness of her skirt, her eyes wide, expectant, her lips— . . . About to smile? Withdraw their smile?

"Do I look sad, too?" Normalyn asked.

"Sometimes, yes," Troja answered softly. "But also like this." And there she was, Marilyn Monroe, astonished by how much one moment of life could contain. "And so pretty, and *so* stubborn," Troja added slyly.

"Determined," Normalyn corrected, studying the picture.

The last pages of the book revealed photographs the movie star had rejected, drawing X's and slashes through them. Reproduced now and enlarged with the pictures, those marks looked like smears of her blood. . . . Normalyn turned away from those, to another picture she had glimpsed: In it, out of all the vulnerability, the movie star had seemed, for golden instants, to realize suddenly that *she* was Marilyn Monroe, her head thrown back, triumphant in her creation!

Now Normalyn found the one she had really been looking for: a full closeup in which the movie star's face—serious, beautiful—was partially shaded by a slanted hat under which her eyes looked away from the camera, into herself, understanding and accepting her completed life. . . . That is how Normalyn saw the photograph in which Marilyn Monroe looked like Enid, just like Enid. She placed her hand over the photograph and held it there. After moments she closed the book.

Troja waited for Normalyn to order her reactions before she said, "Hon, there's a line Marilyn says in her last movie, when she knows a hurting part of her life is over, a new part beginning: 'If a child could be brave from the beginning— . . .' What she means—what it means to me—is that no one can be born brave because you got to learn to be brave. Know how? By protesting what hurts. That *makes* you be brave. There's lots of beginnings, hon, lots of endings, too—and not just being born, nor just dying. Every new beginning is brave, hon. You and me know that. Maybe a new beginning needs even more courage than the last one. Know why? Cause hope's been shoved around more. I just bet Marilyn knew all that. At the last, she just didn't *want* to begin any more, for whatever reasons—just needed a final ending, a rest—like Kirk. That takes another kind of courage. Gotta honor that, too," she said to herself, and added admiringly, "and they sure as hell had *their* share of brave beginnings!"

"Troja—"

The telephone jangled!

Normalyn answered. She heard David Lange's tightly calm voice: "Normalyn, you have exactly one more hour to be here. I've alerted the person I'll put you in touch with, who is ready to see you." His voice became a private whisper: "It can't wait any more." Then he said firmly, "One more hour, exactly, Normalyn, and I swear you'll be in touch with the person who will confirm everything."

Confirm? Then he already knew? . . . "Yes," Normalyn told him, then her finger pressed down on the telephone's connection. David Lange's voice resounded mournfully in her mind. Had it been slurred? He had asserted his promise to take her into the heart of the mystery. *It can't wait any more.* . . . Was he trying to solve another mystery, his own?

Normalyn told Troja about the narrowing time for discovery. "One hour. Less now."

"I'll drive you!" Troja instantly had the car keys in her hand.

Normalyn made no motion to leave. She opened her purse. She took out Enid's letter.

"Got to find out!" Troja coaxed.

"I'm not sure—" Normalyn listened attentively to her own words.

"You got just enough time left!" Troja urged.

"I haven't!" Normalyn's body bolted. "I don't have any more time—no more time to live with other people's ghosts and pain—"

Troja offered desperately: "I'll go with you, stay with you if you want me to. If you don't go—!" She left the words for Normalyn to finish.

Normalyn stared down at the letter that had dominated her life since the morning of Enid's funeral in Gibson. It looked different—as if it had changed, or as if she were seeing it clearly for the first time. . . . N.J.R.I.R. That was how two unwanted children in a home had tried one moody, meaningful time to end a sad game, to end their own sadness.

Rest in peace, Norma Jeane!

That was Enid's last message—that she allow "Norma Jeane," finally, to rest. Whatever the two women had intended "Norma Jeane" to be at first—a fulfilled wish of escape from their unhappiness—she had been shaped out of their violent pasts, determined by others. Their "game" had turned fatal—for both of them. Enid was freeing her from the legacy of a stark, troubled past—theirs, "Norma Jeane's," the composite of their blurred identities. What she had learned from the two women would give her the courage to reject their shared "darkness," inherit their strength.

Troja's voice attempted control: "Half an hour left—less!"

Normalyn understood: With expressions of love from both of them, Enid had left the letter to let her choose who she would be—beyond them, and at age eighteen, the age of choices. She had only *thought* her life was in abeyance. It had started when she decided to leave Gibson. That's how Enid had freed her—by guiding her into a journey within which she would discover them, the two women—and herself.

"You can still get there—just barely!" Troja pleaded.

Troja's warning shook Normalyn out of clashing thoughts, rearranging themselves.

"Call him, tell him you're on your way. You *have* to know, hon!" Troja insisted.

Yes! Normalyn ran to the telephone. She dialed one number, another, a third— She stopped.

"Hon, you're so pale! Hon, you all right?"

Normalyn closed her eyes. She had perceived darkness and then she had seen it enclosing a faceless woman lying on a dark shoreline. It was Enid! No, it was Marilyn Monroe! Enid! Marilyn! . . . Then she knew: She had seen . . . *herself on that black shoreline.*

Normalyn opened her eyes. She banished the image. She pushed herself out of the roiling darkness. With all the strength she had gathered, she *chose* to move out of the blackness.

"Oh, hon, hon, you still got time. Call him!" Troja waited at the door.

Normalyn clutched all the papers Enid had left her. She walked to the small kitchen. She turned on a burner of the stove.

"No!" Troja understood.

Normalyn moved the letter toward the burner.

"Be sure—" Troja warned.

Normalyn held the letter over the fire.

The telephone!

"Don't answer it!" Normalyn shouted at Troja. At the same time, she pulled back the letter. It fell to the floor with the other papers.

Troja had already picked up the telephone. She was holding it out, away from her ear. They both heard David Lange's voice:

"Normalyn!"

Normalyn grasped the telephone. She heard David's words screamed at her with anger and regret and pain: "Normalyn! I've known all along that you *are* her daughter—that's why I could have turned you into her—*and then I would have saved you as I promised long ago!"* There was a long, terrifying moment of deepening silence.

Then Normalyn heard the horrible sound of a gunshot exploding in her ear.

She dropped the telephone.

She rushed back to where the letter and the papers had scattered. She gathered them. She held the letter over the burner.

"As long as you have the letter, you can still find out!" Troja shouted at her.

As long as I have the letter! Normalyn saw the flames touch it. Its edges curled inward without protest, a circle of fire slowly enclosed it until the letter was only a smear of ashes. Out of those ashes two voices would remain, for her only, in her memory, and in peace—both professing their love.

In a moment, Normalyn would feel the horror of David

Lange's act, his last attempt at— What? Purgation? Revenge extended to her as Marilyn's daughter? . . . Normalyn moved away from the ashes of the letter and the other burned papers. She had saved the note on which Enid had recorded the moment of joy when the two girls had first become friends, and she had kept one birth certificate—the one Enid had left, designating an "unknown" father and identifying *both* women as her mother.

Feeling Troja's hand on her shoulder, Normalyn closed her eyes. *This* darkness contained only the sounds of traffic, of nearby voices, someone's distant joyful laughter—*and she was aware of a summer breeze sighing into the house*—sounds she heard, startled, as if for the first time in her life.

Fifty-Two

Los Angeles Tribune   May 29, 1980

TWICE PULITZER AUTHOR
DAVID LANGE FOUND DEAD

LOS ANGELES—David Lange, well-known author, one-time syndicated columnist, and twice winner of the Pulitzer Prize in nonfiction, was found dead in his office last night. Death occurred from a self-administered gunshot wound, according to Coroner Tom Curela, who ruled the cause of death to be suicide. Lange was 50.

His body was discovered by Teresa de Pilar, 64, who called police. Miss de Pilar told reporters that she had an appointment that night with Lange. The meeting, which did not take place, "involved Marilyn Monroe's daughter," Miss de Pilar said. She identified herself as a "very distant acquaintance" of Lange and as a long-time associate of Alberta Holland, once a powerful figure in Hollywood politics. (See box story.)

At the time of his death, Lange was awaiting the fall publication of his fourth book, *Last of the Heroes*. According to Grove Press Publisher Barney Rosset, the book is "a bold examination of the real and symbolic accomplishments of John and Robert Kennedy."

Lange's first book, *The Moral Imperative of Justice*, won him his first Pulitzer Prize when he was 29. It has sold over 2 million copies, in over 20 languages. The following year, he became the first writer to win two consecutive Pulitzer Prizes when he was again honored, this time for *The Un-Americans*, an indictment of Senator Joseph McCarthy and the House Committee on Un-American Activities. His book *Images: Hollywood as Politics* is an investigation into the impact of films on American social attitudes.

Lange began his newspaper career in 1954 as a reporter for the *Wisconsin Tribune*. In Los Angeles, he was briefly affiliated with gossip columnist Mildred Meadows, whom he later repudiated. He attributed the association to "youth and sheer folly." Lange's twice-weekly syndicated column, "Lange Reports," was honored with the W. H. Berridge Award for Distinguished Journalism.

A campaign adviser in John F. Kennedy's successful bid for the presidency, and one of Robert F. Kennedy's earliest champions, Lange announced in November of 1963 his separation from the journalism that brought him fame and fortune. In the last of his syndicated columns, he attributed his separation to "personal considerations." "For now I am retreating into the shadows," he wrote.

In more recent years, Lange became a frequent figure on television and radio talk shows. He aroused criticism by announcing his "increasingly strong belief" that through an "elaborate deception," actress Marilyn Monroe had given birth, in secret, to a daughter "fathered by a man in very high office." Becoming associated primarily with that subject, Lange became controversial, and his appearance on talk shows became less frequent.

In 1975, Lange acquired an interest in the widely circulated tabloid *The Star Informer*. That allowed him to continue his exploration into the last days of Marilyn Monroe's life. In an irregular column and in featured stories in *The Star Informer*, Lange pursued the subject, finally announcing his determination to prove that Marilyn Monroe had a daughter, "who is very probably still alive and living in anonymity." He extended his claims in recent years, asserting that the father of the movie star's daughter would be revealed to be either John F. Kennedy or, "more probably, Robert F. Kennedy." He made frequent references to "the child of two legends."

The Star Informer co-publisher, Bernard Safonsky, lauded Lange as "a great writer who perhaps became too preoccupied with one single story." Safonsky added, "Who knows that he wasn't right?"

Lange was born in New Haven, Wisconsin. He is survived by a sister, Mrs. Helena Blair, of New Haven. A private nondenominational memorial and burial are planned for Lange in his hometown, according to Mrs. Blair.

Book Review editor Charles Nelson described Lange as "an impeccable writer of keen intelligence and highest principles."

Fifty-Three

Los Angeles Tribune

David Lange Suicide

May 29, 1980

POSTSCRIPT TO MARILYN LEGEND
FROM 'A WITNESS'

By Irene Mallick

LOS ANGELES—The suicide of famed journalist David Lange
was discovered Thursday night by Teresa de Pilar, 64. (See
accompanying news story.) Miss de Pilar is remembered by
observers of "Old Hollywood" as a figure who was privy to
Hollywood "secrets" because of her association with Alberta
Holland, once known as a "counselor" to movie stars.

The Tribune solicited an interview with Miss de Pilar, who
refused until she was informed that her report to the police
had been made public. Miss de Pilar agreed to "only a brief
and dignified interview."

The reporter met Miss de Pilar at the hotel where she was
staying. She presently resides in Phoenix, Arizona. A slight
woman who still speaks with the accent of her native Spain,
Miss de Pilar, during the entire interview, continued to fashion artificial flowers—"my beloved hobby"—while she talked.

According to Miss de Pilar, she was to keep an appointment
with David Lange "to meet a young woman who had been
identified as the daughter of Marilyn Monroe" and, presuma-
bly, of Robert Kennedy. Miss de Pilar was to be shown by the

young woman in question a letter "written by Marilyn Monroe on the eve of her death" and given to Miss de Pilar to deliver to the movie star's "life-long, intimate friend." Without that letter, Miss de Pilar claimed, no definite authentication would be possible.

When the young woman did not turn up, Miss de Pilar says she "assumed certain wishes" and left. It was on her way out that she heard the gunshot that took David Lange's life. Miss de Pilar stated without further clarification, "David Lange was a complex man pursued by the past."

Asked why she finally was discussing matters kept secret for years, Miss de Pilar clarified, "Because it gives me the perfect opportunity to inform the young woman in question of certain matters I was not able to convey, and it allows me to assure her that I will accept her wishes not to reveal herself. She has done everything that she had to do."

Miss de Pilar claimed she had returned to Los Angeles because of "these matters which are now ended with the sad suicide" and also to tend, earlier, to details concerning the death of her long-time friend, Alberta Holland. However, it is well known that Holland died in 1962 in Switzerland. Holland was sentenced to a year in prison for contempt when she refused to provide to the House Committee on Un-American Activities names of "fellow travelers" during the so-called Hollywood "witch hunts."

Miss de Pilar said that eventually she would return to "my beloved Spain, to die in peace, knowing that I've done everything I had to do."

Informed of Miss de Pilar's statements, Bernard Safonsky, copublisher with Lange of *The Star Informer* tabloid, said, "David Lange was always interviewing people who claimed knowledge about Marilyn Monroe's 'secret last days.' It's possible that he finally found his answers."

Part Four
The Angel

One

The small cemetery is almost hidden in the midst of one of the busiest sections of Los Angeles. Perhaps two blocks square, it reclines away from noisy streets, tall buildings, a parking lot, a movie-theater complex.

Its grounds are always green. Although most of the monuments in the memorial park are plain marble blocks, here and there a more elaborate one rises assertively. A gravel driveway loops about the grounds, past a green-vined chapel. At the far end of the cemetery is the Mausoleum of Memories. There, wall crypts shelter the remains of the dead.

Normalyn saw it immediately. Troja stood with her before the simple vault.

> MARILYN MONROE
> 1926 – 1962

Troja wore a subdued gray dress, subdued makeup. Once again she was the imposing woman Normalyn had first met, even grander now because, just earlier, she had told Normalyn her age. She was twenty-three. A full life had been crowded into her few years.

Normalyn wore a pretty lemony dress. She did not want to mourn. She had been to Enid's grave in Gibson less than two months ago. Now she had come to end that journey in another cemetery.

Normalyn had decided to visit the memorial park that morning, soon after Troja had mutely shown her the news story
about David Lange's death.

"So sad," Normalyn said quietly. She would always feel
sorrow for that driven man.

"Then you are her daughter," Troja formed the words that
had kept astonishing her silently.

Yes, Normalyn accepted—but she added to herself; I'm *their*
daughter, hers *and* Enid's. She knew she would love Enid
more than ever now, the woman who had raised her, loved
her. Enid's anger had been resentment at war with love, she
understood. She hadn't lied to Stanley about the death of their
child, a terrible aching void she had to fill—and she had answered the movie star's plea that her daughter be protected.
Enid's letter was true. Yet it had left Normalyn mysteries to
solve that would give her strength, allow her to find her own
life. Enid, too, would *always* be her mother.

It had been a morning of sadness wafted by a curious sense
of exhilaration uniting Normalyn and Troja closely. There
was the lingering awareness of the violent suicide—and other
memories stirred—but at the last David Lange had turned
against his own obsession, chosen his own serenity. Troja's
engagement at the new club had been extended definitely
only for another weekend because she was still being "considered"
along with another singer. But she was becoming used to
"being herself." For Normalyn, the excitement of again seeing
Michael was brushed with apprehension, but she was *sure* she
wanted to see him, and would see him.

Within that limbo of feelings, Normalyn had decided she
would visit the memorial park. Troja quickly agreed to go with
her.

At an outdoor flower shop on the way, Normalyn bought
three white roses, a breath of gold at the edges.

As they entered the cemetery, she was aware of a monument in the near distance, on the soft green grass, a monument on which a statue— . . .

She turned away from it, avoiding it.

Now before the vault of Marilyn Monroe, Normalyn placed
a rose in an urn beside it. For Enid. She placed another. "For
you," she told Troja.

Troja closed her eyes for a moment.

Placing the third rose in the urn—from herself—Normalyn
said aloud, "Rest in peace, mother." Then she and Troja
walked away from the plain plaque, the flowers.

It was a warm, hazy day. The sun spread thinly over a sky

hinting of blue. The cemetery looked peaceful, all the lives it contained at rest. The two women walked along the road to the gate.

Again Normalyn avoided the stone figure mounted on a distant grave.

"Now your new life begins," Troja said.

"And your new one already has," Normalyn said.

"Yes," Troja asserted. She held out her hand. "See? It's steady."

It *was* steady, Normalyn saw. Almost, almost, almost steady.

There was in the air the scent of fresh grass, abandoning spring, bringing summer. Normalyn felt elated! Then that feeling linked, unwelcome, with another. She stopped on the gravel road. Troja waited with her.

"Troja—"

"Hon?"

"I'm afraid," Normalyn said.

Troja sighed. "Of course you are, hon, cause everybody is when— . . . cause living is— . . . cause—" She stopped forced words. "Because you know you have to be brave, hon—that's why you're afraid." She faced Normalyn in recognition of fear and courage. "And you *will* be brave. Know why? Because you *have* to be."

"Yes," Normalyn said, and she allowed her eyes to roam over the calm green lawn of burial in search of the stone figure she had avoided earlier—because it had reminded her of the abandoned angel in the playground of the home, its wings clasped. Now she faced the figure mounted on a white stone.

It was the statue of another angel.

Within shifting shadows of sun-lit trees, its wings seemed to Normalyn to be just about to open to begin its daring flight.